# The Rebel

# The Rebel

## May McGoldrick

A SIGNET BOOK

SIGNET
Published by New American Library, a division of
Penguin Putnam Inc., 375 Hudson Street,
New York, New York 10014, U.S.A.
Penguin Books Ltd, 80 Strand,
London WC2R 0RL, England
Penguin Books Australia Ltd, Ringwood,
Victoria, Australia
Penguin Books Canada Ltd, 10 Alcorn Avenue,
Toronto, Ontario, Canada M4V 3B2
Penguin Books (N.Z.) Ltd, 182–190 Wairau Road,
Auckland 10, New Zealand

Penguin Books Ltd, Registered Offices:
Harmondsworth, Middlesex, England

First published by Signet, an imprint of New American Library,
a division of Penguin Putnam Inc.

ISBN: 0-7394-2664-8

PUBLISHER'S NOTE
This is a work of fiction. Names, characters, places, and incidents either
are the product of the author's imagination or are used fictitiously,
and any resemblance to actual persons, living or dead, business
establishments, events, or locales is entirely coincidental.

*For Carol Palermo*
*Friend, Motivator, Scheduler, and Promoter*
*Extraordinaire*

# Chapter 1

## London
## December 1770

The snow lay like white icing over the stately plane trees and the walkways of Berkeley Square. Dinner guests, bundled in fine woolen cloaks and mantles of fur, scarcely spared the picturesque scene a look, though, as they hurried from the warmth of Lord and Lady Stanmore's doorway to their waiting carriages. Across the square, a wind swept up from the river, raising crystalline wisps from the barren tree branches, and flakes of snow curled and glistened in the light that poured from the windows of the magnificent town house. Soon, all but one of the carriages had rolled away into the darkness of the city, the sounds of horses and drivers and wheels on paving stones muffled by the fallen snow.

Inside the brightly lit foyer of the house, Sir Nicholas Spencer accepted his gloves and overcoat from a doorman and turned to bid a final farewell to his host and hostess.

"Spending Christmas *alone!*" Rebecca chided gently. "Please, Nicholas, you *must* come with us to Solgrave for the holiday."

"And intrude on your first Christmas together?" Nicholas shook his head with a smile. "This first holiday is for you—for your family. I wouldn't impose on that for the world."

Rebecca left her husband's side and reached for Nicholas's hand. "You are not intruding. My heavens, that's what friends are for. When I think of all the years that James and I were alone in Philadelphia! If it weren't for the hospitality of our friends—especially at the holidays—how lonely we would have been!"

Nicholas brought the young woman's hand to his lips. "Your kindness is touching, Rebecca, and you know how hopeless I am about denying you anything. But I've spent more than my fair share of holidays with that beast you call your husband. Besides, I understand you have some rather joyous news that you'll be wanting to share with young James . . ."

The prettiest of blushes colored Lady Stanmore's cheeks, and she glanced back at her husband.

"I am slightly better at keeping state secrets, my love." Stanmore reached out and took her tightly into his embrace.

Nicholas stood and watched as his friends slipped into a world that included only the two of them. The bond that linked their hearts and their souls was so pronounced, so obvious . . . and Nicholas frowned at the unwanted ambivalence pulling at his own heart. As happy as he was for them, he could feel something else squirming about inside of him.

He looked away, forcing the frown from his face. Only a fool, he told himself, would be envious of a life that he has been avoiding like the plague.

He already had his overcoat on and was pulling on his gloves when the two became aware of him again. Nicholas couldn't help but notice the protective touch of Stanmore's hand on Rebecca's waist, the intimate entwining of her fingers with his.

"Come anyway." Stanmore spoke this time. "Come after Christmas, if you must wait. You know my family likes to have you with us . . . though God only knows why. Seriously, though, I know James will be anxious to tell you about his term at Eton, and Mrs. Trent will love to fuss over you."

Nicholas nodded. "I'll do that. That is, if my mother and sister don't follow through with their threat of coming across from Brussels for a visit. From the tone of my mother's most recent letter, the brat Frances has become too much for her to handle alone. The latest threat is to leave her in England so that she can finish her schooling here."

"Well, that is very exciting news," Rebecca chimed in.

"Not for me." Nicholas shook his head and took his wide-brimmed hat of soft felt from the doorman. "I know nothing about how to deal with sixteen-year-old children who talk incessantly, without the least semblance of reason . . . and still think themselves mature beyond measure."

"There is a season for everything," Stanmore countered as he and his wife followed Nicholas toward the door. "It is all part of the great scheme of life. Marriage. Children. Moving the focus of our attention from ourselves to those we love. As Garrick said so eloquently at Drury Lane the other night, 'Now is the winter of our discontent made glorious summer.' "

Any other time and Nicholas might have made some lighthearted retort about humpbacked, wife-murdering kings; but as he looked at Rebecca and Stanmore, the words knotted in his throat. Somehow, even the words "happy and carefree bachelor" seemed difficult to conjure at the moment.

Nicholas leaned down and placed a kiss on Rebecca's cheek. "Merry Christmas."

Outside, the snow was coming down harder, the wind picking up in earnest. Nicholas pressed his hat onto his head and gave a final wave to his friends from the street. As the door closed against the weather, though, he found himself still standing and staring—considering for a moment the events that had brought such happiness to that house. He finally roused himself and turned to his groom.

"Go on home, Jack, and get warm. I believe I'll walk from here."

A gust of wind whipped at the capes of Nicholas's overcoat, and the groom moved on as he was ordered.

The baronet turned up the collar of his overcoat and walked past the fashionable houses lining the square. The handsome windows were still lit in many, in spite of the lateness of the evening. It was the season for entertaining. A solitary leaf danced along the snow-covered street, pressed forward by a gust before being caught in a carriage track. The chill wind burned the skin of his exposed face, reminding him of the warm fire in the Stanmores' library. The image of his friends in the foyer kept pressing into Nicholas's thoughts.

The improvement in Stanmore was so marked. For all the years since his first wife had left him without a word—taking their son James with her and disappearing—he had been a tormented man. And now, since he'd found the lad and had married Rebecca, Stanmore was so obviously happy. "Fulfilled" was perhaps the best word. The change was stunning . . . miraculous.

It was not long before Nicholas's house on Leicester Square came into view, but he was far too restless to settle in for the night. The snow was beginning to let up, so he turned his steps toward St. James's Park.

Since coming back from the colonies more than ten years ago, Nicholas Spencer had worked diligently to keep his life as uncomplicated as possible. He had wanted no ties. He had endeavored to inflict no pain. During his years as a soldier, he'd seen enough suffering in those wounded and killed, and enough anguish in those families that were left to endure the loss, to cure him of ever desiring any kind of attachment. Life was too fleeting, too fragile.

Somewhere over the years, he'd also found that women were more than willing to put themselves in his path for their mutual amusement and enjoyment. Live while we can. Carpe diem. No harm in it for anyone.

Wealth only meant having enough for good clothes, good horses, a little meaningless gambling, and a bit of concealed philanthropy. It mattered little to him that the most polite reaches of society scoffed at his roguish lifestyle. He knew that they perceived him as a gambler and a womanizer, as a sportsman who had chosen to shrug off the responsibilities of his position in society.

And Nicholas Spencer did not dispute this reputation. He was proud of it. He'd earned it. He'd worked hard to establish it. He had never wanted to be answerable to anyone.

So when, he thought, had he become so discontented?

He strolled through an open gate onto the tree-lined walks of St. James's Park. The usual prostitutes and gal-

a step back. With a slight nod, he turned and
nt was on the street.

s to the harshness of the winter night or the
las Spencer walked the streets. The injustice
death was so wrong. And more innocents—
d dying—surrounded him. And what he had
about it was clearly not enough.

here and there. A house to offer meals and
off the street. All well and good, but where
hildren go from there? How had his insignifi-
charity in any way changed their lives? What
ne to keep them from ending up drunk or
dead on the streets?

d to be something more that he could do. A
e country where they could grow up healthy.
here they could learn to fend for themselves.
d something like a permanent home.

, he found himself back at Berkeley Square,
at the darkened windows of his friends' home.
ight and winter could not hamper the glow
radiating from inside.

was getting old and he was terrified of it.
ion hurt less than he'd imagined. But he'd
g the emptiness and coldness of his life for
t now coming to terms with his ailment was
le relief.

of the innocent face of the dead child came
yes. His life had become a waste and there
h more that he could do. He would need to
changes, though. A new life for himself. A
where he could truly influence the fate of
uls.

a thing required a wife, and where on earth
nd her?

lants who frequented the park—even this late—
appeared to have searched out warmer haunts, out of
the wind and the weather. He left the paved walk of the
mall, moving into the open field, his boots crunching on
the dry snow.

Indeed, he was as independent as an eagle, but something unexplainable was happening to him. Why, for ex-
ample, had he felt driven to spend so much time over
the past six months with Rebecca and Stanmore? Of
course he cared for them deeply, but spending time in
their company often did nothing to lift his spirits. On
the contrary, it only served to point out how empty and
insignificant his own life was in comparison with theirs.

Fight it as he may, it seemed a desire for belonging,
for permanency, had been edging into Nicholas's heart.
It was an odd sensation, new to him, though he knew it
was a condition as old as time. Nonetheless, he didn't
want to believe it. He was happy with who he was.

Or so he thought . . .

"Spare a ha'penny, sir? Jist a ha'penny fer my sister
an' me?"

Out of the dark shadows of a grove of trees, he saw
the boy's scrawny bare arms extended in his direction.
Nicholas paused to look at him.

"A ha'penny, sir?" Walking on feet wrapped in dirty
rags, the waifish figure came cautiously nearer. The top
of his head barely reached Nicholas's waist. Even in the
darkness, the boy was pale as death, and the baronet
could hear his teeth chattering from the cold.

Nicholas glanced past the thin shoulders of the child
toward the bundle of bare legs and arms curled into a
ball and lying motionless beneath the tree. Hanks of
long dark hair covered the other child's face.

"Is that your sister?"

The boy tugged at Nicholas's sleeve. "A ha'penny,
sir . . ."

He teetered slightly, and the baronet put out a hand
to him. As Nicholas took hold of the boy's arm to support him, he was immediately dismayed by the thin ragged shirt that covered the bony frame. He took his
gloves and his hat off and handed them to the boy.

"A ha'penny, sir?"

It wasn't until Nicholas had taken off his overcoat and was draping it around the boy that he smelt the spirits emanating from the child.

"If you and your sister follow me to a safe house I know, I'll see to it that there are hot food and warm clothes . . . and half a *shilling* in it for you."

Dwarfed by the size of the clothes, the boy stared at him blankly and said nothing.

"No harm will come to you or your sister, lad. You have my word on it."

Nicholas turned his attention to the girl on the ground. She was much smaller than the boy and, as he pushed back the dark tangle of hair, the baronet was stunned by the angelic look of innocence in the sleeping face. Like the brother, she was dressed in nothing more than thin rags that barely covered her. He touched her face. It was deathly cold.

Nicholas immediately gathered the child in his arms, stood up, and turned to the brother. The boy was gone.

The frail bundle of bones and skin in his arm concerned him more, however, so he started across the park in the direction of the house on Angel Court, off King Street. There, he knew, a couple of good souls would look after this child while he searched out the brother.

The loss of his coat and hat was not what concerned him. The boy was welcome to them. What bothered Nicholas was the money he would find in the pockets. There was enough there to keep a man drunk for a fortnight. For a child who would use it for pouring spirits and beer down his throat, there was enough money there to kill him.

The girl weighed no more than a kitten, and Nicholas frowned fiercely at the smell of alcohol that her body reeked of as well. The excessive drinking of both rich and poor was still one of the curses of England. While the rich could afford to take care of themselves and their families, though, the misery of the poor was passed early on to their children.

A face appeared at the window when Nicholas knocked at the house on Angel Court. At the sound of his voice, the door quickly opened. The old woman's

face, bright with recog
when she saw the bundle

"I found her in the p
think she is unconscious
surely hasn't helped her

The old woman hurrie
right, leading him into a
spread a warm glow ove
A few children peeked
wide-eyed with curiosity.

"Which one, Sadie?"

The old woman pushe
empty bed, and Nichola
clean blanket.

"Go fetch Martha for
on the nearest cot.

As the child hurried o
back, watching the olde
they moved over the gir

He was no expert on
this young one couldn't
curled hands lay on the
from beneath her rag
drawn to the dark hair f
the face. Long eyelashe
pale beneath the dirt.

Looking at her, Nicho
ning. The city was a di
own. Perhaps he could
grave when she was a li
more wouldn't mind it,
idea. After all, they had
become a new lad enti
would thrive in the cou
school in Knebworth. Sh

Sadie's sharp glance i
went nearer, and the we

"The poor thing has
He stared at the wom
A sudden need to deny
he restrained the uttera

He too
in a mon

Oblivi
time, Nic
of such
helpless
been doi

A shel
a safe be
did these
cant acts
had he d
abused o

There
house in
A school
They nee

Sudden
staring up
Even the
of warmth

Nichola
The admi
been batt
so long, tl
an incredi

An ima
before his
*was* so mu
make a fe
real home
these lost

But such
would he

# Chapter 2

## Waterford, Ireland
## August 1771

Through the stony fields the roaring fire moved, leaping ahead and coiling before jumping forward again, a monstrous living creature greedily devouring all before it. Smoke and ash swirled above, blotting out stars that had filled the night sky not an hour before and replacing them with sparks and cinders that climbed and glowed and quickly died away.

Legions of men armed with clubs swept down into the vale, torching the fields as they approached. The thatched roofs of the first of the clustered hovels flared up, and dozens of panicking men, women, and children ran in confusion into the night. There was no way of fighting such an onslaught. There seemed to be no escape.

From beneath a hide that served as a doorway of one of the hovels, a squalling baby crawled out into the madness.

In the rocky fields around them, crops that had been painstakingly sown and nurtured with toil and sweat flared up as the inferno spread. Barley, potato, cabbage, wheat—gone in moments while the consuming flames licked the smoke-blackened sky.

A screaming mother, dragged away by others, looked back in desperation at the fiery mass that was once her cottage. Carried along by the swarm of cottagers, she was led toward the only place that was not ablaze, the marshy bog to the north of the huts. Beyond the fetid muck and swamp grass lay the safety of higher ground.

A solitary rider tore through the night and met the group as they emerged, their dark shapes silhouetted by the inferno.

The ride overland had been hard, and there had not been time to raise help. The attack here had come without warning, without legal proceedings, without justice, and the same was happening all over Ireland. The rider looked out at the burning village. Tomorrow, these same brutes would be pulling down the walls. In a week, they would be digging ditches to enclose the fields. Next spring, there would be sheep and cattle grazing here, and these tenants would be wandering the byways of a tragically changing countryside.

The desperate cries of a mother rang out across the hills as she ran to the mounted newcomer.

A moment later, the rider was skirting the edges of the marsh, spurring the steed toward the burning hovels. At the center of the cottages, the infant sat in the dirt with her hands raised to the sky, oblivious to the cinders raining around her.

Seeing the child, the rider drove the horse through the hellhole like one possessed. A hut collapsed with a loud crash, silencing the infant's cries for only a moment. The rider dismounted as the marauders approached through the smoke and flames. Gathering the child up, the rescuer climbed back on the restless steed and raced away into the darkness.

On the hill, the mother ran forward to meet them, her face stained with tears and soot, her throat choked with emotion as she received her screaming babe into her arms.

"Bless ye, Egan!"

# Chapter 3

~~~

## Cork, Ireland
## One month later

The patchwork of tidy, newly harvested fields north of Cork City had long since given way to a wilder, rockier countryside, and the woman looked out the carriage window with an artist's eye. This land was so different from the relentlessly flat plains around her own native Brussels.

It was certainly no less green than the lowlands of the coastline to the south. Indeed, the darker hues of numerous pines served to set off the silvery greens of the birch trees. Now tinged with autumn yellows, the birches huddled in groves on the rugged hillsides rising abruptly from the valley floor. Looking at the azure sky above, marred by long scrapes of gray, she thought with satisfaction that they had suffered hardly any rain at all since crossing over from the bustling English port of Bristol.

The carriage, wending its way along a surprisingly good road, had been following the bends of the river at a leisurely pace. Occasionally passing a small cluster of cottages—some more rustic than others—Alexandra Spencer had also seen a number of handsome manor houses with fields of pastureland spreading out around them. The scattered forests were beginning to grow thicker now, and she turned her attention back to her two traveling companions with a contented smile.

Her daughter was speaking with all the exuberance

one might expect of a girl of sixteen, and Lady Spencer broke in when she paused to take a breath.

"Really, Frances! Hanging from a castle wall . . . upside down . . . and kissing a stone just to win some dubious gift of eloquence? What nonsense you spout, young woman!"

"But it is true, Mother. They believe the stone is part of the Stone of Scone at Westminster. Not just one but three of the sailors on the ship were telling me about the magic in kissing Blarney Castle's stone."

"Well, I for one have no desire to kiss anything that might have been sat upon by any king . . . English or otherwise."

"Mother!" Frances replied with shocked delight.

"But more at issue . . . what were you doing talking to sailors? How many times do I have to tell you that a young woman should never engage in—?"

"But Nicholas was with me." The younger woman moved to the seat across in the carriage and looped a hand through her brother's arm. "There was a prizefight in the hold. I simply followed Nick down to watch the sport."

"Nicholas Edward . . . !" she started to scold, but changed her mind as her son's sharp gaze moved from the passing countryside to her face.

Running a hand over the fabric of her skirts, Alexandra Spencer searched for the most appropriate way of expressing her disapproval. A difference of eighteen years in the ages of her two children had certainly been harmless when they were younger, but as Frances was now a blossoming young woman, Alexandra needed to find a way of instructing Nicholas on his brotherly responsibilities.

She gazed at her son as his attention drifted back to the window. When Frances had been an infant, Nicholas had been studying at Oxford. A few years later, when Fanny had started attending school, Nicholas had been fighting his way across the Plains of Abraham during the taking of Quebec. And shortly after that, when her husband had passed away, Nicholas had inherited his father's title and estate. It was then that Alexandra had decided it was time to return to her own ancestral home across the channel where she could stay clear of her son's affairs. Of course, she'd hoped he would use the time to start a life . . . and a family . . . of his own.

Well, that hadn't happened yet, and Alexandra was afraid that she had spent too many years away from Nicholas to be able to exert any kind of control over him now—any overt control anyway.

Frances started again, not sounding deterred in the least. "They tell me that one can also lie on one's back now and lean out to do it with a pair of strong arms gripping one's legs." She paused with a frown. "I don't think I should care to rely on anyone else doing that for me but you, Nick."

"I don't believe the world can stand any more eloquence in you, Fanny," Nicholas replied passively. "You are far too perfect just as you are."

The young woman giggled with delight. "You really should save these pretty words for your darling Clara, you know, and not waste them on your sister."

"*Darling* Clara?" Nicholas Spencer asked with emphasis.

Frances darted a hesitant glance at her mother. After receiving an encouraging nod, she turned to her brother again.

"Well, we *are* headed to Woodfield House, are we not? You *have* accepted the invitation of Sir Thomas Purefoy, Clara's father, to stay a fortnight on their estate in this ravishing country, have you not?"

"Frances, I *do* wish you wouldn't use the word 'ravishing' . . ." Lady Spencer put in.

". . . And you *did* escort that extremely attractive young woman to no less than *three* social functions this past spring in London, did you not? Shall I go on?"

"Don't pressure me, Fanny. I can feel the noose tightening without any help from you or our esteemed mother." He ran a finger inside the high collar of his crisp white shirt. He looked meaningfully from the younger woman to the older. "We are making this trip for the benefit of the two of you, not for me. In spite of some contrary opinion, it is important in a young woman's education that she be introduced to members of society outside of the circle of spoiled brats you've been associating with so exclusively at school."

"Liar!" Frances slapped him on his arm.

Nicholas shrugged. "Very well. Have it your way, then. We're here for me . . . because of my love of horses. Sir Thomas is reputed to have one of the finest stables . . ."

"That is so incredibly unmannerly, Nick," Frances scolded, a practiced pout breaking across her young and beautiful face. She withdrew her hand and slid to the farthest end of the seat. "I must tell you that in lying the way you do, you are ruining the very fine image I cherish of my only brother. There is no help for it . . . I shall not speak with you for the rest of this holiday."

Seeing Nicholas's obvious satisfaction with the state of affairs, Alexandra reached out and touched her son's knee. "Pray resolve this right now. If she is not talking to you, then it means she will be complaining endlessly to me. So if you cannot make up with the little vixen, I would just as soon have you let me out at the next coach stop, where I shall find my way back to London without the two of you."

For a longer span of time than his mother liked, Nicholas appeared to be considering the second threat. He finally turned to his sister, and his tone told Lady Spencer that all joking had been put aside.

"I have been very careful not to create any misunderstandings with regard to Clara and my intentions toward her. The girl is nearly half my age."

"She is *not* half your age!" Fanny corrected, sliding over to her brother's side. "Clara Purefoy turned eighteen this past winter. You are thirty-four. At no time since you've known her have you been twice her age."

"By 'sblood, what does one *do* with a child of eighteen?"

Lady Spencer arched a brow. "From the steady stream of rumors reaching me in Brussels, I might have been led to believe that you are quite proficient in managing women of all ages." Alexandra patted her frowning son on the knee. "Your uneasiness, my dear, stems from the thought of marriage and commitment. Clara's age is only an excuse, and you shall quell your fears quickly."

"Truly, Nick . . ." Frances chirped from his side. "She is everything that you could possibly want in a wife."

"And as an only child, Clara brings with her a great fortune."

"Not that you need it," his sister cut in.

"But considering your lifestyle, my dear, it never hurts to have a little more." Lady Spencer gazed out the window, not wanting to pressure him too much at one time. "A matter which I find highly endearing, though, is how smitten with you the whole family appears to be."

"But Mother, everyone knows how advantageous it is when a daughter marries someone with a title. After all, even a baronet with a reputation as bad as Nick's is—"

"It isn't that!" Alexandra waved off her daughter impatiently. "It is your brother's warm personality that has charmed them. His education. His exemplary military service. His respectability—"

"Before the age of twenty."

Lady Spencer directed a severe glare at her daughter. "Frances Marie, you will mind your tongue." The older woman smoothed out the imaginary wrinkles in her skirts again and turned her full attention to her son, who was once again enthralled by the passing scenery. "Where was I?"

"You had just expressed your wish for me to stop this carriage," Nicholas suggested darkly. "So that you *both* can find your way back to London."

The old bishop and his secretary watched in terror as several of the white-shirted rebels whipped the flanks of the horses and sent the driverless carriage down the road. The bishop's half-dozen attendants, who'd been forced from their places when the carriage was stopped, ran off down the country road after the horses.

"You cannot get away with this, you filthy ruffians." The bishop's voice shook with anger. "Your masks and your devilish linen shirts shan't do you a bit of good when they put ropes about your necks and send you off to the Lord's judgment. 'Vengeance is mine, sayeth the Lord.'"

Five men on horseback looked on as twenty on foot encircled the two clerics. The silence of the group was unnerving. Before the bishop could speak again, his secretary—a portly younger man with flushed cheeks—saw one small opening in the ring of attackers. Seizing the opportunity, he dropped the satchel he'd been clutching to his chest and ran. A thick leather binder filled with papers and a very healthy-looking purse of coins spilled out onto the road. No one bothered to stop the terrified secretary.

"I know every one of you behind those masks," the bishop bluffed. "I know your kin and I know the filthy hovels you each live in."

A number of the assailants moved forward menacingly, forcing the old cleric back against a tree at the edge of the road.

"You touch me, you dogs, and I'll call down God's wrath on all of you. I am the servant of righteousness, and you are the spawn of devils. You are . . ." He gasped as a rope looped around his middle from behind, yanking him hard against the tree.

"This is for forcing the payment of the tithe on the tenants north of Kinsale who lost their crops to the tempest last month."

The bishop looked fearfully at the masked man to his right who had spoken the words. Last spring, he'd heard of a *papist* priest who had been left tied to a tree near Kildare. The bugger had gone for two days without any food or water before someone had found him and let him go. There had been another incident involving a curate near Caher Castle not three weeks ago. He didn't care to think of that one. Of course, neither of the clerics had been killed—only badly mistreated and frightened half to death.

Two men grabbed the bishop's hands and tied a rope around his wrists.

"This is for refusing to baptize bairns in Ulster simply because the kin couldn't afford your higher fees."

"That was not I! I have no say what goes on up . . ." The bishop's protest trailed off weakly as his bravado turned to fear. Another member of the group approached with a rope and dropped it deftly over his head. "No! I beg you . . . !"

The clergyman's mind immediately conjured images from the meeting he'd had with the magistrate, Sir Robert Musgrave, not three days earlier. He'd been promised that all priests would be protected against such attacks by the Whiteboys. As a concession, he'd offered to support the landowners around Youghal who were forcing their farm tenants out to make way for pasturing, and in the end, his own safety had been guaranteed. Guaranteed! Where was that bloody magistrate *now*?

"Do you wish to say a final prayer, Your Excellency? Do you wish to ask forgiveness of the Lord for staining His good name? Perhaps for your shameful acts of greed?"

The clergyman's eyes focused on the rope dangling from his neck. The clerics abused before had been simple parish priests. He was a *bishop*. He couldn't help but wonder if these people would actually kill him to send their message loud and clear across the land.

The words that began spilling out were indeed prayers. Prayers asking forgiveness for exactly the things he was being accused of.

As the carriage suddenly slowed, Nicholas put his head out and looked beyond the horses. He'd heard that travelers occasionally encountered highwaymen on the roads—here as at home—but this was the strangest-looking outlaw he'd ever seen.

Beyond a fork just ahead, where one road bent sharply to the right, a fat clergyman was puffing toward them, his arms waving madly in the air, his piteous cries nearly incoherent from his lack of breath.

Nicholas shouted to the driver and stepped out as the carriage rolled to a stop.

"Whiteboys . . . bishop . . . killing . . . there . . . there . . . !" The man appeared nearly out of his mind with terror, grabbing on to him for support. "Save me . . . help . . . bishop . . . !"

Nicholas detached the man from his arm, handing him over to his valet, who'd been riding behind on his master's horse. He motioned to Frances to remain in the carriage as she opened the door to step out. He glanced in the direction from which the clergyman had come.

The wooded slope running up to the west was dark and densely forested. There was nothing to be seen from here.

" 'Twould be safest, sir, for the ladies if we was to keep moving," the driver offered from his perch on the carriage. "Locals call 'em Shanavests. That'd be Irish for Whiteboys. They're a troublesome bunch . . . if ye be asking me."

The cleric, who was slumped against the carriage and trying to catch his breath, suddenly straightened. "But . . . but you cannot simply . . . simply leave him . . . They'll kill him."

"Maybe," the driver agreed. "But these boys'd be armed to the teeth, sir. Rebels through and through, to be sure, and they always travel in fair-sized numbers. 'Twould be dangerous . . . for the ladies, of course . . . not to be going."

"How many?" Nicholas addressed the priest.

"Five on horse . . . I'd say about two dozen on foot . . . I don't know if I saw all of them or not."

Nicholas took the reins of his horse from the valet.

"Can I come with you, Nick?" Frances called excitedly.

He turned in time to see his mother pull the carriage door shut with a bang, squashing Fanny's attempt to step out. As Nicholas directed the driver to go straight to Woodfield House, the valet took a place on the back of the carriage.

He turned to the cleric. "You . . . inside."

Mumbling words of undying gratitude, the bishop's secretary yanked open the carriage door and jumped inside with more nimbleness than his size warranted.

"The new magistrate, Sir Robert Musgrave, has a bounty set on the heads of these boys," the driver said in confidential tones to Nicholas. "Word is, he's planning to hang every Shanavest he catches in the old Butter Market in Cork. Now, if ye be asking me, that's the wrong approach, what with most of the popish farm folk loving those rebels as their own. But I'm just a whip man . . . so what do I know?"

Lady Spencer poked her head out of the window before the carriage pulled away. "You *can* walk away from a fight, Nicholas. I am concerned for you. There are too many of them . . . and this is a strange land."

"No need to be concerned, Mother. I only intend to get near enough to keep a close watch."

"Then why not wait until the following wagon arrives? With the servants to help you . . ."

"I'll be fine." He motioned for the driver to move on. "Just keep a firm hold on that sister of mine."

Nicholas waited until the carriage disappeared around the bend of the road before climbing on his horse. Drawing his sword, he spurred the animal down the road.

The edge of the knife's blade formed a thin white line in the ruddy wrinkled skin of the man's throat.

The terrified bishop had offered everything he could think of in exchange for his life—from having bags of coin delivered wherever they wished . . . to waiving every church fee in the diocese for an entire year. Baptisms, marriages, funerals . . . everything.

They had accomplished what they had come to do, so the leader of the group motioned for the men to withdraw. The quivering cleric remained tied to the tree, his eyes tightly closed, his mouth now moving involuntarily as he mumbled prayers and promises with no particular rhyme or reason. The man's fine clothes were stained with muck. A few scratches on the face were all that he'd suffered outwardly.

"The next time you think of making any deals with the magistrate, just remember this day," a young giant of a man whispered menacingly in the bishop's ear as he sheathed his knife. "We can always find you."

The leader watched the same member of the Shanavests jab a fist into the cleric's side before walking away. The ropes restrained the man from bending over in pain, but the grimace on the old face showed his distress.

The bag of coins was emptied. The loot taken from the bishop's carriage earlier was piled into sacks and carried off. The group dispersed as quietly and unexpectedly as they had come. In a moment, only the masked leader remained, sitting on a handsome horse.

\*     \*     \*

With his mount tied to the branch of a birch down the road, Nicholas watched from the safety of a grove of pines. It was some time before the bishop lifted his head and looked up at the solitary figure.

"Please don't kill me!" the man pleaded as horse and rider approached in measured steps. Nicholas's fingers immediately tightened around the hilt of his sword, and he moved silently forward. The rebel leader had a single pistol tucked into his belt, but Nicholas knew he might be able to take the man by surprise, before he had a chance to draw and fire.

"I admit my guilt! I offer you every worldly possession I have . . . I . . ." The man's face drained of all color as the rider quickly drew a knife from his belt. "I . . . I . . ."

Nicholas ran forward, but stopped just before reaching the road when he saw the rebel lean down and cut the ropes binding the bishop's hands.

"Teach mercy and compassion to your people, priest. They are virtues that are wanting."

The voice was hoarse and low, and yet something in the tone caused Nicholas to pause. He immediately drew behind a tree again and sheathed his sword as the rider wheeled his horse in his direction. He listened to the sound of hooves starting up the road toward him.

As soon as the head of the horse passed the tree where he was hidden, Nicholas moved forward quickly, taking hold of the rider's shirt and yanking him from the horse. They both tumbled to the ground, the rebel's pistol bouncing into the brush at the side of the road.

Rolling away, the rebel leader picked up a rock, but Nicholas was faster. As the other man hurled it at his head, the Englishman raised a hand and deflected the gray slate away from his skull. Ready to face him again, he was disappointed to see his foe turn and run toward the woods. Without a second thought, Nicholas took off after him.

The man was small but extremely quick and agile, and he moved speedily through the thick undergrowth. Nicholas's long legs, though, enabled him to overtake the rebel not very far from the road. As he was about to tackle him from behind, the outlaw swung around, kick-

ing viciously at his groin. Nicholas sidestepped the blow,
and the kick struck him on the hip as he closed on the
man.

Falling forward, Nicholas connected with a right hook
a moment before leveling the rebel with his body.
Sprawled on top of the masked man, he pushed immediately to a sitting position, trapping the slight body beneath him and drawing back his fist to deliver another
blow. He froze.

The rebel's hat lay in the dirt, and the scarf that had
masked the outlaw had been tugged down. To Nicholas's
utter amazement, a woman's face glared up at him. No
wonder it had been so easy to pull her from the horse.
Her size. Her weight.

By 'sblood, Nicholas thought, staring at her. A woman!

Ringlets of black hair had escaped their confines,
framing a most attractive face. Black eyes, dark as night,
shot darts of hatred at him. The side of her mouth was
already swelling from the blow. Without thinking, he
reached down to touch the bloody lip, but she slapped
his hand away, spitting out a string of words in Gaelic.
From his time spent ringside at dozens of boxing
matches that featured Irish fighters, he understood the
woman was not extending any complimentary greeting.

"I . . . ? You definitely leave me speechless."

Nicholas raised an eyebrow at the next prolonged
curse she hurled at him.

"I should watch what I say if I were you, my little
hellcat." He reached inside his coat pocket and took out
a handkerchief. "I am willing to forgive you for the
names you call *me* . . . but my father? mother? wife *and*
horse? That is really going *too* far."

The blood from her mouth had trickled across her
cheek. When he reached down to wipe at it, though,
she started thrashing beneath him. Nicholas immediately
captured her hands, trapping them with one of his own
above her head.

"By 'sblood, I am *not* going to hurt you."

As he reached down again to dab at the blood with
the cloth, her dark eyes turned on him. It may as well
have been an eternity that he gazed into them, for time

stopped. The woman was stunning in her beauty, and he saw fires banked in those eyes the likes of which he'd never seen before.

He was still pressing her body into the leaves and ferns with his weight. He could not help but admire the rise and fall of her breasts beneath the white smock. His eyes lingered on the wild pulse beneath the skin of her throat. His gaze took in the dark ringlets in total disarray around her face and stopped at the full sensual bottom lip. The bruising he'd inflicted filled him with a pang of remorse, but then those magical eyes drew him back.

The moment she ceased to struggle against his hold, he was bewitched.

"Who are you?" he asked huskily, gently pressing the handkerchief against her lip. He fought the sudden urge to lower his mouth to her face, to her throat, to stretch his body fully on top of hers and find out if she was afflicted by the same physical desire that had taken hold of him. The attraction was so strong that Nicholas forced himself to release her. He stood up abruptly, struggling to clear his mind of such thoughts. Frowning fiercely, he extended a hand to her, but she didn't take it. Reaching down, he grabbed her by the arm and pulled her roughly to her feet. He didn't release her.

"If I were you, I would start explaining now . . . before the magistrate's men arrive." She said nothing, her dark eyes flashing defiantly. "Do the Whiteboys make a habit of having their women fight for them?"

He was trying so hard to shake off the spell she'd cast that he didn't see her reach for the knife at her waist. She slashed at his arm deeply enough to cause him to yank his hand away in shock and pain. The moment that Nicholas took to look down at the cut was all the time that she needed. Before he could act, she was off and running.

By the time he had reached the edge of the trees, the woman had regained her horse. Quick as a summer breeze, horse and rider disappeared along the road. Nicholas looked down at the pistol lying at his feet and picked it up. He tucked it into his belt. He went back into the woods and fetched her hat as well.

Blood was staining his coat sleeve, and he shrugged

out of the garment. The cut on his forearm was minor, and he used the handkerchief still clutched in his hand to bind it before putting his coat back on. He stared after her.

"A woman," he muttered, walking back down the road to where the cleric was removing the ropes.

"You took him down. Did you see him? Did you get a good look at his face?"

The man stared at the hat that Nicholas was holding.

"The magistrate is offering a great reward for him, you know. *Especially* him!"

"Who is he?"

"The blackguard is one of their leaders. Of all of them, he has the largest price on his head. He goes by the name Egan . . . though 'tis undoubtedly an assumed name!"

"Undoubtedly," Nicholas answered vaguely, looking down at the hat.

# Chapter 4

"I definitely did not see *any* man's face well enough to describe him."

Sir Thomas Purefoy frowned and resumed his agitated pacing across the brightly lit Blue Parlor of the Woodfield House. Outside the mullioned windows, the green hills of the Irish landscape rolled downward to a sparkling river.

Nicholas's mother and his sister, Frances, were sitting comfortably on a sofa before the hearth, sipping tea and looking on unconcernedly, while Lady Purefoy and Clara fluttered around their injured guest like butterflies around a flame. Fey, the middle-aged Irish housekeeper, was just finishing up wrapping the wound on his forearm in clean linen. The thick fabric of the jacket and the shirt had served to minimize the depth of the cut, and Nicholas found all this attention a bit overdone. But he remained silent and allowed the red-haired woman to finish.

Sir Thomas came to an abrupt stop before him again. "But you are certain the attacker—the one you came face-to-face with—was the rebel leader. You're *certain* it was Egan."

"Not in the slightest. I had no previous knowledge of the group or its members. I am only repeating what Bishop Russell said afterward."

"He *would* know, by thunder," Sir Thomas muttered before starting his pacing again.

As Fey packed her things into a basket, Nicholas thanked her and rose to his feet.

"If you will forgive me," he said, bowing to Lady Purefoy, "I believe I shall go and change out of these travel clothes."

"Oh! Of course, Sir Nicholas." The blue-eyed, round-faced gentlewoman curtsied pleasantly. Immediately, though, she reached for her daughter's hand. "How foolish of me to be so inattentive. Clara, my dear, why don't you show our guest upstairs to his room. Perhaps as you go, you can also give him a brief history of Woodfield House. It is really quite an interesting history, Sir Nicholas."

The young woman, blushing prettily as ringlets of gold danced around her young face, started to lead the way.

Nicholas made a point of ignoring the mischievous look Fanny was directing his way as he followed Clara from the parlor.

Only a few hours' ride from Cork City, Woodfield House was an impressive ivy-covered stone structure dramatically situated on a high, southern-facing hill. The present manor house had been here for more than a hundred years, Clara informed him, built over what had been the ruins of an earlier house or castle.

"There are four stories in the building . . ." The young woman's soft voice echoed in the halls as they passed along. ". . . though only two of them are used by the family. The ground floor contains the kitchens and the brewery, storage rooms, and a servants' hall. The rooms on the top level are also occupied by the servants. This floor has a number of parlors, my father's study, a fine library, and a hall that we sometimes use for entertaining . . . receptions and things."

Nicholas placed a hand on Clara's elbow as they arrived at the bottom of the stairs. The deepening blush in her cheek, the demure lowering of her gaze, reminded him of the reason why he'd been so fascinated with her since they'd first been introduced in London. Beautiful and unpretentious, she possessed virtues he'd always found attractive in women.

This was the first time they'd been left alone since he'd arrived. Nicholas paused, correcting himself. This was the first time they'd been left alone since meeting in London. Sir Thomas and his wife were becoming too sure of his intentions . . . and that wasn't a particularly comfortable feeling.

His gaze fell on her lips, and he considered whether he should take the liberty of sampling the young woman's other charms. Perhaps—he found himself thinking—if he were to become more attentive on that front, he wouldn't continue to dwell so morosely on the years dividing them.

And then there was another matter entirely that he needed to forget. The face of the woman he'd met on the road—this "Egan"—was an image he couldn't seem to shake from his mind.

The corridor and stairs were deserted, and Nicholas reached out and took hold of Clara's chin, raising it until he was looking into her blue eyes.

"I've heard enough about Woodfield House for the moment. Now I want to hear about you. I wonder if you have missed me at all since we last met."

"I . . . well . . . I have . . . missed you . . . Sir Nicholas."

He saw the tip of her pink tongue unconsciously wet her lips, and Nicholas knew this was his chance to proceed. But a sharp ache from the cut in his arm cleared his mind of the thought. He released her chin and glanced up at the steep stairs.

"I have been looking forward to this visit, too," he said pleasantly, starting up the stairs.

If she was disappointed, he had no way of knowing, for as they proceeded she kept her eyes on the family pictures that adorned the wall.

"What can you tell me about this group of rebels the bishop called the Whiteboys?"

"I hardly . . . well . . . not much. Nothing more than . . . than gossip, anyway."

Her stammer drew his gaze. Her face revealed no emotion, but Nicholas's observant eyes noted the restless fingers fraying the end of the ribbons she wore at her waist.

"While we were trying to catch up to his carriage and servants, I spent a little time in Bishop Russell's company, yet the man had a great deal to say about them. He was quite eloquent in his description of their violent

for much more than money. And even though she and Nicholas had spent many of their recent years apart, she was fairly certain he would need a wife who did not lack confidence.

A shadow filled the doorway, and Alexandra's gaze was drawn to the figure entering the parlor.

The woman was dressed completely in black.

The newcomer wore a fine black gown. The tips of black shoes showed beneath. Black gloves, edged with Italian lace, were met at the wrist by the long sleeves of the dress. Her hair, pulled tightly back, matched the color of the garments, and large dark eyes provided a stunning highlight to a perfect ivory complexion.

Perfect, of course, except for the nasty bruise on the side of her swollen mouth.

No one else appeared to have noticed her arrival but Sir Thomas, and Alexandra arched an eyebrow at the look of open hostility that she saw pass between father and daughter as they stood glaring for a moment at each other.

A chair scraped against the floor in the far end of the room, and the newcomer's gaze shifted in that direction. A look of shock immediately etched itself upon the young woman's face, and Alexandra saw her reach out a gloved hand to steady herself.

Across the room, Nicholas was standing by the table . . . looking as if he'd just seen a ghost.

"Come in, Jane," Lady Purefoy said hesitantly. "Sir Nicholas . . . Lady Spencer . . . Miss Frances. I would like to present my older daughter."

# Chapter 5

Jane only hoped that she looked less surprised than he did at this moment.

She stood straight and tried to gauge what the Englishman would do. If he revealed their earlier encounter, she was a doomed woman. Of course, she could deny everything—but she doubted that either her father or Sir Robert, the new magistrate, would take her word over an English baronet's.

The silence hung like a shroud over the room. Jane averted her eyes, unsure how much more of this she could endure. Then the middle-aged woman who had been standing and looking at one of the paintings approached her.

"Miss Jane . . . or rather, I should say Miss Purefoy, as you are the elder daughter."

Jane stared in surprise at the extended hand of their guest. The Englishwoman appeared to be about the same age as her own mother, but the sharp blue eyes spoke of inner strength that far exceeded Lady Purefoy's.

"Calling me Jane will suffice, m'lady," she replied quietly, taking the hand and dropping a small curtsy. "I have been well beyond such formalities for some time."

"Then you shall call me Alexandra." The woman didn't release Jane's hand immediately, drawing her into the room before taking her by the arm. "You don't know how delighted we are to have finally met you. Your family has been very secretive about you, my dear.

I cannot help but feel quite privileged to have been given a chance to meet Sir Thomas and Lady Purefoy's hidden treasure."

Treasure? Jane would have laughed if her mouth did not hurt when she smiled. She glanced at her father and saw him turn toward the hearth as he raised a tumbler of brandy to his lips.

"This is my daughter, Frances. A more incorrigible young woman you shall never meet."

Slightly taller than her mother and wearing her dark blond curls fashionably styled, Frances was a younger image of Lady Spencer. She also showed a nature that was equally congenial, leaving the card table and approaching the two of them.

"My, but that is a *handsome* cut on your lip, Miss Purefoy . . . if you don't mind my saying so."

"Good heavens, Frances!" the mother remonstrated.

"Honestly, it calls to mind a few that I have seen Nicholas sporting after one of his boxing matches."

"Fanny!"

"Please do not chastise her on my account, m'lady," Jane said to Lady Spencer before turning to greet the bright-faced young woman. "I'm certain that Miss Spencer's comment is exactly correct . . . though I must own that I myself try not to make a habit of boxing."

"Do tell how you got it! Don't take me wrong. I *do* believe it is quite handsome."

Lady Spencer let go of Jane's arm and stepped toward her daughter. "Frances Marie Spencer, you are a most garrulous, undisciplined magpie. I *must* apologize for this creature standing before you. I am certain she must have been changed at birth for my own true ch—"

"I'd be happy to relate the origin of my little bruise . . . though I'm afraid my tale is somewhat mundane." Jane met the friendly blue eyes of the young woman. She hesitantly touched her sore lip and felt another set of eyes closely studying her face. "Just a bit of bad luck, you see. I bent over to pick something up and struck my face on the edge of a dressing table in my bedchamber earlier today. I am generally known to be more careful than that."

Frances opened her mouth to say something else, but a sharp tug on her arm by Lady Spencer curtailed her next question.

Jane shifted her gaze first to the face of her sister. Clara looked pale enough to faint, and Jane saw her sister glance quickly at the Englishman's bandaged arm.

"Sir Nicholas," she managed to get out, turning to the other visitor. "It is an honor having you here at Woodfield House."

She hoped her voice would not betray her. He was still staring at her in a wholly discomforting fashion, and her uneasiness only escalated into the realm of panic when he crossed the room to her. It took great restraint on her part not to take a step back. For nine years she had been actively involved with the Shanavests. Why, after all that time, did her sister's intended husband have to be the first foe to succeed in glimpsing her identity?

"Miss Purefoy." He bowed politely, and when he looked up at her, Jane found herself suddenly arrested by the same intensity emanating from the depths of that gaze as she'd seen before. Allowing this man to look into one's eyes was tantamount to opening the window to one's soul. A feeling of extreme vulnerability washed through her, but Jane could not bring herself to look away.

"You are not the only one injured today, Miss Purefoy." Frances Spencer's words cut through the silence, and she was grateful for the distraction.

"Jane," she said quietly to the younger woman. "Please call me Jane."

"Jane, you should have Nicholas tell you about the great fight he had with the leader of the bandits today. He walked away with a rather dashing wound himself." Frances paused thoughtfully, casting a proud glance at her brother. "Knowing the shrewdness with which Nick fights, I have no doubt the blackguard received far worse in the exchange."

"No doubt," Jane murmured, relieved to see her mother step forward to urge everyone toward the dining room.

Jane retreated into the background and managed to touch Clara's arm in passing.

"I am sorry," she whispered, to which the younger sister nodded with a gentle smile.

Of all the people in this room, her sister Clara was the only one whom Jane cared a rush about. From the day that her own life had become so inextricably entwined with the secret resistance group, her sister had become and had remained the only ally Jane had in the family. Clara was the only person she had ever dared to trust. There were many dangerous and reckless acts Jane Purefoy had committed in her life, but she had always made certain that none of them would ever bring danger or heartache to Clara's door. Until now.

As her mother took Lady Spencer's arm and Sir Thomas escorted the vivacious young Frances into dinner, Jane drifted toward the window . . . as always, forgotten. She didn't mind it, though, as she watched the tall Englishman offer his arm to Clara.

In her mind, he was hardly the kind of nobleman her father would have chosen to bring a good name and restore honor to their family. With his broken nose and his unpowdered blond hair tied back with a ribbon, the blue-eyed giant looked more like a rake and a highwayman than a respectable member of London's *ton*. Handsome in a rugged sort of way, Sir Nicholas Spencer obviously harbored a rebellious quality beneath his refined manners . . . otherwise he would have charged her immediately with crimes against the king.

Looking at him now, she wondered what reason might lie behind the man's silence. More important, she wondered how long that silence would last.

They were the last pair leaving the room.

Nicholas paused by the door and glanced over his shoulder at Jane Purefoy, who appeared forgotten and lost in her own world.

"Will your sister not be joining us for dinner?" His question was addressed to Clara, who was barely allowing her fingers to touch the sleeve of his jacket.

"I . . . I believe she is."

He turned to face the older sister. "Miss Purefoy. Would you give me the honor of accompanying both of Sir Thomas's beautiful daughters in to dinner?"

An instant flash of distaste ran across her fair features, and Nicholas wondered for a moment if he and his offer or the mention of Sir Thomas's name were the cause of it. All the same, though, the dark-appareled woman approached and accepted the offer of his arm. Her hand lay lightly on the bandaged cut hidden beneath his jacket sleeve.

Nicholas couldn't recall when in recent years he'd been so instantly intrigued by a woman. After all, what a curious situation he'd suddenly found himself in. Sir Thomas Purefoy, an ex-magistrate of the king—a man who had been raised to knighthood in the Order of the Thistle after fighting with distinction beside the Duke of Cumberland himself at the battle of Culloden—was harboring under his own roof a noted rebel renegade who just happened to be his daughter. Of course, Nicholas thought, he hadn't ever had a woman cut him with a knife, either.

And this wasn't even half of it. Bishop Russell had told Nicholas all about Sir Thomas's heavy hand when it came to crushing out the Whiteboys' rebellious ways. Apparently the new magistrate, Sir Robert Musgrave, had quite a distance to travel to match Purefoy's severity with the Shanavests and other factions like them.

Life could *not* get more entertaining than this.

He directed a quick glance at the woman who held his right sleeve and was rewarded by the intelligent flash of dark eyes in return. The question was etched in her face, demanding an answer. She no doubt wanted to know what his game was and what he wanted. Nicholas looked straight ahead as they approached the dining table. Well, he had no intention of satisfying her curiosity. At least not while the game was so young.

Dinner itself was a pageant well worth the price of admission. Fanny and Alexandra did most of the talking, while Clara and Lady Purefoy quietly played their roles as the perfect hostesses. Sir Thomas, on the other hand, was clearly a man highly accustomed to his position as lord of the manor. In between drinking large quantities of wine and finding some fault with everything that was served, he managed to talk endlessly about his greatest passion, the breeding of horses.

Normally this was a subject that Nicholas would have found extremely diverting. At present, however, he was far more interested in the family's treatment of Jane Purefoy. Not once during dinner was a single comment directed toward her. For the family, she did not seem to exist, it appeared. The scent of scandal lingered in the air.

"You shall have the pleasure of meeting our dear Reverend Adams after dinner," Lady Purefoy offered quietly, in response to a question by Alexandra about Woodfield House's neighbors. "He is quite a diligent young man, traveling every day through the country-side—"

"He is not coming. He sent his excuses yesterday."

At the abruptness of her husband's words, Catherine's voice took on a placating tone. "You are, of course, correct, Sir Thomas. But he sent a second letter this morning, saying that he shall make a point of stopping here on his way back to Ballyclough. Parson Adams said we could expect him sometime after dinner."

"And when were you planning on telling me all of this?"

"I . . . well, I didn't think it was a—"

"I had a driver take a letter to him this afternoon. Bloody hell! If I knew that he was coming, I would not have wasted the man's time. Once again, you have succeeded in making me look like an ass. By the devil . . . !"

"My apologies, Sir Thomas. I . . . I was in error . . ."

The older woman's stammering discomfort spread a thick layer of embarrassment over the table. All conversation ceased. Even Fanny seemed at a loss for words.

"You see what I am forced to endure, Sir Nicholas?" The older man shook his head and reached for his glass. "Thoughtless, empty-headed women. Do you believe this deficiency is inherent in the species, sir, or is it that I have been cursed with a bad lot?"

Nicholas could see the Englishman was making an attempt at humor to cover his show of temper, but Nicholas was not amused.

"It has been my observation, sir, that thoughtlessness and empty-headedness are no more innate a feature in women than in men. However, considering how delightfully congenial these ladies have been in not reminding us of our own glaringly male deficiencies, perhaps we should not be too hard on them for such a small lack of communication."

"Oh, well . . ." The man made a great show of clearing his throat and reaching for more wine. "We shall just see if you continue to sing such a merry tune, Sir Nicholas, after you've spent some time in these chits' company. I tell you, they are a troublesome bunch, by thunder. You shall come around, sir. You certainly shall."

As another course was served, Nicholas's gaze fell on the profile of Clara, who was seated beside him. The young woman's complexion had turned a shade paler, and she appeared preoccupied with the intricate weave of the tablecloth beneath her plate. One glance at Jane, who was seated to the left of her mother—across from him—and Nicholas knew the pulse of Purefoy women beat the strongest in the older sister. Her face was flushed red, her temper barely contained. Lady Purefoy laid her hand casually on top of Jane's, and the older sister fisted her hand before tucking it beneath the table.

"Miss Purefoy," he asked, "what kinds of activities occupy *your* time out here in this beautiful countryside?"

"I . . . I am . . ." Clara started to answer, but she stopped abruptly, realizing that Nicholas's question was directed at Jane and not at her.

The older sister appeared as surprised to be addressed. As she searched for an answer, Nicholas enjoyed the opportunity of staring openly at her.

Despite the severe hairstyle and the "handsome" bruise by her mouth, there was a vibrancy in her face that shone through brightly. Considering her manner of dress and the injury she'd sustained, Jane's beauty was far different from the kind aspired to by London's fashionable set. But looking past the superficial ornamentation, he saw a vitality there—a natural beauty and spirit—that was impossible to ignore.

"I believe that there is very little difference in the way an Englishwoman is expected to spend her days in Ireland than in England."

"It has been my observation that what is expected of women and what they actually do is not always the same."

"You seem to be quite the observer of human nature, Sir Nicholas," Jane commented.

"You would be amazed at the things one observes when one takes the time to look."

A soft blush crept up her cheeks. "Well, I cannot know anything of that, sir, but I do know that when it comes to satisfying the curiosity of observers, it is a woman's duty to blend what is expected and what must be done. If she is careful enough in her actions, all that one will notice is . . . compliance."

"Do you mean that one should say one thing and do another, Jane?" Fanny asked excitedly.

"I should hope not, Miss Frances," Jane said gently. "Repeated back to me, my own words have a horrifying ring to them. What I am trying to say is that even within the rigid constraints of societal decorum—constraints that are imposed on women practically from birth—there are freedoms that can be exercised, good deeds that can be accomplished. Though silence is imposed upon us—"

Sir Thomas's loud call for one of the servants to bring in more wine made the older daughter pause momentarily.

". . . we have voices, and we can be heard. Being a woman should never be equated with helplessness. We—"

"*Now* do you see what I mean, sir?" The former magistrate glared at his older daughter.

"Jane likes to draw," Lady Purefoy hurriedly interrupted. "She has assembled quite a portfolio of her work."

"Do you?" Alexandra asked with enthusiasm. "May I see them? I have an interest in art, myself."

Lady Purefoy cast a nervous glance in her husband's direction. "Though I am afraid none of them are completely finished. Is that not correct, Jane? Perhaps . . . sometime in the future . . . we shall have some of her work sent to you. Clara, on the other hand, has an excellent hand for needlework, Sir Nicholas. She's done a fine rendering of Woodfield House. After dinner, I shall show you and Miss Spencer . . ."

Nicholas lost interest in the discussion and stopped listening. Once again, the family had effectively shut the older daughter out of the conversation. Jane's face was a picture of tautly controlled anger. He turned his gaze from Lady Purefoy to her husband. Nicholas was beginning to resent the blatant pushing of Clara in his direction. Sir Thomas had all the subtlety of a horse trader. Though he had once been interested, the Purefoys' behavior with regard to both daughters was quickly putting him off.

The host placed his empty glass firmly on the table.

"Now we shall have some time for ourselves, Sir Nicholas." He looked meaningfully at his wife, and she immediately rose to her feet. "You and I shall remain here for a cigar and some brandy I have just received from my man in Cork City. We have a few details to work out that we may put behind us tonight. I'm sure you have a few questions you'd like to put to me regarding the settling of affairs."

The other women followed Lady Purefoy's lead and rose from the table.

"We shall retire to the Blue Parlor, Sir Thomas, and leave you men to your discussions."

Nicholas had no recollection of having yet offered for Clara's hand in marriage, and the confident tone of the knight regarding any possible marital discussions only managed to annoy him further. He had never been one to tolerate being pushed.

"I believe I will excuse myself from accepting your invitation tonight, Sir Thomas." He stood up as soon as the women had left the room. "The ride up from Cork City, combined with this injury, will not make me very agreeable company. Perhaps some other time we shall have an opportunity to discuss *whatever* it is you had in mind."

Nicholas knew from the look on Purefoy's face that the older man was again surprised, though he shouldn't have been. Sir Thomas had been well aware of his reputation as a bachelor and as a rake when they were introduced in London. Despite it all, though, Nicholas's position and his wealth had obviously made the gamble of inviting him to Woodfield House a chance worth taking.

"Very well, sir." The man stood up.

In the hallway outside the dining room, Nicholas spied Jane Purefoy speaking quietly to a very attentive and sober-faced stranger he had not seen before. They stood far too close, their heads bent together in a confidential gesture. The jagged blade of jealousy that Nicholas felt running through him at that moment was as unexpected as it was palpable.

"Reverend Mr. Adams," Sir Thomas called out loudly, drawing the newcomer's attention. "You've arrived earlier than expected."

"Indeed I have, sir."

Jane murmured something in parting to the parson and, with a quick look at Nicholas, disappeared toward the stairs leading to the upper floors. It took a great effort by him not to go up after her.

The minister turned to the two men. "I hope I'm not intruding on your company, Sir Thomas."

"Not at all, sir. Not at all. We were just telling Sir Nicholas about you."

As the introductions were made, Nicholas studied the cleric. The man had lean, regular features. His gray eyes were keen, and his face expressed a seriousness appropriate to his calling. His boots and his clothes, though spattered with mud from his travels, were well made. He had the look of a man who would have proved an able soldier, had that been his calling. The intimate appearance of the little tête-à-tête they'd broken up made Nicholas wonder if the dark-haired young minister might be the object of Jane Purefoy's affection. The pang of disappointment that he felt at that very distinct possibility was sudden and sharp.

To the surprise of the ladies, the three men joined them in the Blue Parlor and, as Lady Purefoy made the rest of the introductions, Nicholas moved to the younger daughter's side.

"I can see that we will not have the pleasure of your sister's company tonight. I saw her retire upstairs."

"Like you, sir," Clara replied after an almost imperceptible hesitation, "my sister has had a tiring day. She asked me to make her excuses to you."

"To me?"

"Of course, Sir Nicholas. She would not wish you to take offense."

"None taken. She is not unwell, though, I hope."

"No. I believe Jane is quite well."

"The bruise on her face appears serious. Has anyone looked after it, do you know?"

"I am certain that Fey has," Clara offered politely.

Nicholas watched the parson conversing comfortably with Alexandra. "Reverend Adams is a close friend of your family?"

"Indeed he is, sir."

"Is he married? Does he have a family of his own?"

"No, he doesn't." With a strained smile, Clara moved a step away from Nicholas, effectively stopping any further questions he might have.

Nicholas casually studied the young woman. With a pretty smile painted on a pleasant face, she stood quietly, not participating in any discussion, but still playing the part of the proper hostess. He found himself suddenly bored beyond measure.

"If you will forgive me, Miss Clara, I believe I, too, shall retire," he said.

She made no objection and expressed no opinion. Nicholas bowed to her politely and made his excuses to the host and hostess as well.

The parson, though, was quick to make a comment. "Sir Nicholas, I was sorry to hear of the attack on you this morning. I hope, however, that you will not judge Ireland as nothing more than a land of barbarians. The trouble you encountered was, after all, an isolated incident. There is a great deal of good that we have to offer here."

"I am quite certain that is true, Parson, though I am hardly one to judge. The little incident this morning was no different than anything one might run into while traveling from London into the surrounding countryside. Besides, it was a trifling thing for us. It was Bishop Russell who was subjected to the greatest fright."

"Tell me, how much truth is there to the rumor I heard in the village this afternoon that you unmasked one of the leaders of these rebellious Whiteboys?"

"No truth whatsoever," Nicholas replied, glancing impatiently toward the door. "We scuffled, that's all."

"But surely you must have some inkling of the man's size. His build or his complexion. Something that could aid in the new magistrate's efforts to arrest the blackguard."

"I can offer nothing," he insisted, no longer trying to keep the impatience out of his voice. "The 'blackguard,' as you call him, could have been anyone. I doubt very much that I would recognize him if I saw him again."

"But you unhorsed him . . ."

"The man I unhorsed could have been *anyone*, for all that I can recall. He could have been *you*, sir."

"I hardly think so, Sir Nicholas," their host replied with a gruff laugh. "What would a respectable Episcopal churchman be doing fighting for a handful of discontented papist peasants?"

"My point exactly," Nicholas offered dryly. "I know nothing at all of the matter. Now, if you will excuse me . . ."

"Indeed, my duties are quite taken up in my living at the parsonage in a little town called Ballyclough, not an hour's ride to the north. In fact, sir, you should see it. It is beautiful country." Henry Adams turned and directed his next words to Lady Spencer. "I would love to have you all come out and visit us sometime soon. Perhaps even tomorrow."

"I fear I shall have to decline, Parson. After such a long day of travel . . ." Lady Spencer shook her head and looked meaningfully at her daughter. "Thank you, but no. Frances and I would never allow ourselves to impose. You would find us dull company, indeed, after our journey. But Nicholas, on the other hand, you will find to be generally ready for whatever challenge is offered to him."

"Aye, a fine idea," Lady Purefoy put in cheerfully. "Clara, dear, why don't you ride over with Sir Nicholas in the morning . . . if he wishes to go. There are a great many things you can point out to him. I'll have the cook prepare a basket for you. You can take your time and stop somewhere for a picnic if the weather permits."

Henry Adams turned to Nicholas. "It would be my great pleasure to have the opportunity of visiting more with you, sir. I promise that you'll not find the day a total waste. And perhaps, Lady Purefoy, you might be able to convince Jane to accompany them."

"Yes, indeed, Parson," Lady Purefoy replied, obviously taken aback by the suggestion. "I shall certainly ask if Jane would care to ride along."

"*I* would also be delighted if Miss Purefoy agrees to go along," Nicholas said, turning to meet the parson's sharp gaze. "I was disappointed to not have the opportunity of becoming more acquainted with her this night."

A deep silence flooded the room. But Nicholas didn't give a damn about the suitability of his claim and continued to size up Henry Adams's reaction. The man's expression appeared impartial.

"Then . . . I shall . . . insist that Jane go . . . along." Lady Purefoy's flushed face reflected her confusion.

Pleased with the results, Nicholas bowed to their hosts and paused by Parson Adams on his way out. "We shall meet again at Ballyclough tomorrow."

The household was still alive with the activities of the night when he left the room. But his mind was totally preoccupied with the decisions that had to be made.

Nicholas refused to be a deuced deceiver if he could help it. Despite his wild reputation regarding women, he found it totally improper to be pursuing these two sisters at the same time. But was this what he was doing? Had his curiosity about Jane already settled into an attraction strong enough to convince him to disregard the younger sister?

As he made his way up the stairs, he tried to examine his feelings toward Clara. She'd appeared to be so charming in London. He'd imagined she would make a proper wife, now that the time had finally come for him to settle down and make a home in the country. But all of that was before he'd seen her here among her own family. She appeared too young—too naïve—too indecisive. The girl lacked will and spirit.

Before he'd reached the top, though, Nicholas admitted the truth to himself. It was meeting Egan . . . or rather, Jane, that was causing him to see so many flaws in Clara.

He heard a door quietly open and close as he neared the top of the stairs. Pausing in the shadows of the landing, he saw the dark figure of a woman glide away from his door. He'd told his valet and his manservant that they were not needed anymore tonight, so his room was unoccupied and unattended. He watched as Jane Purefoy disappeared through the last door on the left.

His curiosity aroused, Nicholas stepped out of the shadows and went to his room. Inside, his belongings were as he remembered his valet leaving them. He checked his pistol and sword. They were untouched as well. His gaze lit on the bedside table where he'd placed the pistol and hat left behind by the fleeing Egan.

Both, of course, were gone.

# Chapter 6

On a steep hill facing south, a half-dozen stone huts huddled together against the approaching storm. Small dark windows stared like vacant eyes into the night. Beyond the top of the hill, in a small gorge carved out of the rugged terrain, the solitary wreck of a barn that had long ago been a center of farm life crouched in shadow, its large thatched roof partially collapsed and sagging.

A cloaked figure walking quickly from a grove of scrub pine and birch looked up as a flash of distant lightning accompanied the first drops of rain. It was almost a relief to feel them, for the September air was far warmer than it should have been.

Of the larger group that had gathered inside the dilapidated barn earlier in the evening, only six men and two women remained. They had heard the whinny of a horse, and they sat in silence until a low whistle from the watcher signaled them of Egan's approach. A moment later, everyone stared, their eyes showing their concern and alarm at the bruised face of the woman who came into the light.

She paused just inside the door and met the circle of familiar gazes.

"It is nothing to gape at." She cast aside her cloak and approached the small fire. The silence and the stares continued. "I'm sorry to be late. I'm certain you were saying something, Liam."

She nodded toward the leader and crouched before the fire, where Ronan made room. She kept the bruised side of her face in the shadows and tried to ignore the close scrutiny of the man sitting beside her.

The leader cleared his throat. "Everyone has agreed, Egan, that some of the coin from today's raid should be sent to Seamus's widow and the children. Finding . . ."

Ronan reached over and turned Egan's face around so they all could see the damage. Liam fell silent again.

"I'll cut his throat for this, Egan," Ronan threatened menacingly. "I swear to God I will."

"I know you could shave a sleeping mouse, but don't be a fool," Egan snapped. "You can see it is only a bruise."

Concern was etched on everyone's face. She brushed off Ronan's hand and nodded her head toward the older of the two women.

"Jenny has often enough sewn up many a lad so badly mauled that she could barely pull the flesh together. Look at Patrick here." She touched the man sitting on her left on the arm. "On his best days his face looks hardly less bruised than mine. This is nothing, I tell you."

"He cut your lip open," the hot-tempered young man started again. "He has to—"

"Enough!" Egan stood up abruptly, waving an impatient hand in disgust. "I've been fighting my own battles since you weren't even a wee glint in your father's eyes, boy. I don't need to be taken care of by any *runt* like you."

A low chuckle from Liam broke the ensuing silence. A moment later, everyone else joined in.

Well over six feet tall, with muscles hardened by work quarrying limestone and a temper renowned from Cork to Kerry, Ronan finally joined in as well. They all knew that only Egan could get away with calling him "runt." Anyone else would have been needing new teeth to eat their next meal.

"You were speaking of sending some coins to Seamus's widow," Egan said, not daring to sit down again. She leaned her back against a dark beam. "I can take it to her myself, as I'm to go with my sister and this Englishman to Ballyclough in the morning. While they are visiting with Parson Adams, I'll ride over."

"Warn her to mind how she spends the money," Jenny warned. "With three wee ones at her skirts and a husband dead little more than a fortnight, she has no need to be drawing the suspicion of the magistrate or his men just now."

"I'll speak with her," Egan assured them.

The talk turned to the markets in Cork where some of the local farmers were having trouble getting fair value for their crops. As they spoke, Egan considered yet again the English governance of Ireland and the grinding poverty and injustice that these people lived with because of it. Over the years, she had seen the blood and the pain that resistance cost, but she was not willing to give up entirely the small fights and victories. She knew that this group of fighters, the Shanavests of Cork, had their counterparts in every county and town in Ireland. But deep within, Egan also knew that their daily attempts would ultimately change nothing. It wasn't every day they could get their hands on a bishop. The great landlords were Englishmen, and those with real power were untouchable by those fighting at this level.

On the other hand, here in Ireland there were far too many dead—like Seamus—and too many widows and children left behind to go hungry.

By the time their meeting broke up, the storm was lashing the countryside. Sheets of rain, driven by gusting winds, swept across the sodden fields, while intermittent lightning illuminated the scene. The few who lived in the huts on the hillside trudged off, while others waited for a break in the rain. Ronan fetched Egan's horse from the grove of trees and led the animal back to the ruined barn. Despite the fierceness of the storm, the steed appeared undisturbed by any of it.

Jenny put a hand on Egan's arm as she was donning her cloak. "Everyone was sick with worry at the word of this Englishman seeing your face this morning."

Egan patted the older woman's hand reassuringly. "Some folk worry for nothing. The rogue took my hat, but saw nothing." She thought about the pistol that he had taken—now safely hidden in her bedchamber again—but said nothing of it. "I sat with him tonight at dinner and not a word was said."

"If he suspects, but hasn't said a word yet, it could mean a trap is being laid." Liam's deep voice sounded behind them. Both women turned. "He may already have spoken to Musgrave. They could have followed ye tonight. Maybe they are thinking of laying a net for all of us."

"Say the word, and I'm telling ye I'll cut his throat."

Ronan's low growl raised the gooseflesh on Egan's back. The young man's red hair was soaked by the rain, and the fury of the weather behind him was a perfect reflection of his mood. She saw the exchange of looks between the two men and felt her blood run cold.

"No," she forced out.

Liam's eyes narrowed.

"No," she repeated, taking a step toward Ronan, still holding her horse's bridle. "We are *not* killers of the innocent."

"He's one of them."

"But he hasn't done anything wrong." She turned sharply to Liam. "The Shanavests believe in honor. We fight for justice."

"And justice calls for revenge at times," the older man replied. "If this Englishman is a threat to us, we must do whatever it takes to protect ourselves and those we fight for."

"But he is *not* a threat," she exclaimed a little too passionately and a little too quickly. The three stared at her. "He is here to marry my sister. He is only interested in his future bride and some horses . . . all of which he will take back to England when he goes. From the way he spoke this evening, he cares not a rush for what goes on in this country."

"He saw your face."

"I say he didn't!" she barked at Liam. "He punched me. The hat fell off. I stabbed him in the arm, and before he could look up I was gone. I tell you there is no way he would have made the connection . . . or even have known that Egan was a woman."

"He has the hat . . ."

"I took it back," she said. "Fey is having the man's travel clothes washed. He'll think she took the hat by mistake. I'll have another put back in his bedchamber."

"But he saw the bruise on your face tonight. How—"

Jenny raised a hand and silenced Liam's question. "We *will* trust each other." The woman looked long and hard into the faces of the two men. Her advancing age, the years she'd given to this cause, and the kin she'd lost to it gave her a voice of authority that neither man cared to challenge. "Egan has been fighting for us longer than ye, Ronan, and nearly as long as ye have, Liam. If she believes that 'tis safe to leave this Englishman be, then I say we accept her word for it."

The awkward pause that followed was a test of fortitude for Egan herself. She had been involved with the activities of this group for most of her adult life. As the years passed, however, and as younger, more hot-blooded rebels like Ronan joined in the fight, there wasn't a day that Egan didn't feel her place—never mind her authority—being questioned. She was an English-born Protestant raised in the household of her father, a man who served until recently as the king's magistrate. For those who did not know her history, it naturally took time to learn to trust her.

And now that trust was being tested yet again. With good reason.

Liam spoke finally. "If we kill one of them in cold blood, Musgrave will use the excuse to massacre more Cork folk, young and old, and call it the king's justice." He turned to Egan as she climbed her horse. "Keep an eye on him, though. We'll do what must be done if ye sense your Englishman is about to stir the pot."

She nodded, and as the two men moved back into the darkness of the barn, Jenny's thin fingers reached up and clasped hers for an instant. The woman's green eyes were gentle when they met her own.

"Ye always have been like a daughter to me, my joy, and I know in my heart that ye'll always be. Let's just hope that your sister is grateful to ye for the chances ye take now on her behalf."

Egan squeezed the woman's hand but said nothing.

She had no desire to hear Jenny explain herself further. Some words were better not said openly. She left the barn alone.

The rain pelted both horse and rider as she descended the slippery hill and broke into a gallop along the hedgerows. On the flat, she leaned forward, giving the mare her head as they made their way home.

Though the old woman's concerns were very real, for the first time in her life, Jane actually agreed with something that her father was attempting to do. Clara needed a husband.

She needed a respectable home and a future far away from the turmoil that continued to rip at the entrails of this country. For too long, the blood and pain and anguish that had caused such a chasm in Ireland had affected her family as well, festering and contaminating all.

Clara, however, was young, beautiful, and pliable enough to forget everything here. There was still time for her to start a grand new life for herself in England.

The younger sister had come to Jane's room tonight after everyone had retired, but not to question her about the incident that had occurred in the afternoon. She'd come to inform her of the plans to visit Ballyclough tomorrow. She'd asked her to go along, and Jane had reluctantly accepted.

And as Jane now shielded her face against the stinging rain, she only hoped that her family would complete this marriage negotiation soon. She didn't care to look upon Spencer's face for even a moment longer than necessary. Her first meeting with him was a memory she wished to bury forever.

The stone arch over the recessed doorway that led out into the gardens afforded Nicholas a dry place to stand and smoke his cigar. The teeming rain ran in rivulets down along the stone-paved paths into the garden. One of the dogs that wandered about the estate lay curled in a ball near his feet. Beyond the gardens, he could see the dark hulk of the ancient stable with its two long arms of horse stalls reaching out to the stone wall that completed the paddock enclosure. A newer, more modern horse barn loomed beyond. When the lightning flashed, the slate of the roof looked silvery in the rain.

Despite the excuses he'd used to escape earlier, sleep continued to elude Nicholas long after the inhabitants of Woodfield House had settled in for the night. The sound of the storm and the lash of the rain against his windows had finally driven him from his bed. Restless and dissatisfied with the world, Nicholas stood in the darkness and smoked and watched the falling rain.

A brilliant array of lightning flashes in the distance drew his eye, and he silently counted the delay as he had always done since childhood. Leaning against the stone and mortar of the arched entry, he waited until the thunder reached him, one peal building on the last, impressive in its untamed power. Then, unbidden—even as the air reverberated from the thunder—from somewhere in the back of his mind the image of Jane Purefoy's face formed itself. Ringlets of black hair dancing in the wind. Black eyes, dark as the night, daring him to follow her into the storm.

Nicholas threw the cigar into the dirt and crushed it with his boot, angry for allowing himself to be so easily bewitched. He'd never allowed himself to become consumed with any woman before, and he wasn't starting now.

As he turned to go back into the house, another bolt of lightning lit the fields beyond the stables, and he stopped, fairly certain he had glimpsed a solitary rider skimming across the valley floor.

"Bewitched" was the right word. After all, everyone knew Ireland was the land of ghosts and faerie folk. Of pagan priests and haunted hillocks and storm-riding banshees who carried with them the promise of sudden death.

He stared out into the darkness until another flash illuminated the scene. There it was again—a hooded, dark-caped phantom—and it was covering ground. The rain-slick sides of the black horse gleamed as it tore across the valley. As the blackness enveloped the field again, Nicholas could see in his mind's eye the windswept cape flying behind as this ghostly apparition rode hard out of the heart of the storm.

He waited, listening for the approach of the horse, but the thunder rolling in across the fields and the teeming rain obliterated any further sign. When another bolt of lightning finally lit up the sky, the dark green fields were empty.

He remained still for a long moment, waiting for any telltale sign of what he might have really seen. There was nothing in the pastureland beneath the gardens and the stables, but in a few moments, the sound of a horse drew his attention to one of the stable wings. As he peered through the darkness, he thought he saw a horse being led into the paddock. As if prodded into action, the shaggy gray dog stood up, sniffed the air for a moment, and then trotted off unconcernedly in the direction of the stables.

Nicholas stood for a moment more. There was no sound from the dog. His curiosity finally getting the best of him, he moved out into the rain. By the time he passed by the walled formal gardens that separated the house from the stables, his shirt was soaked through and the rain was dripping from his chin. He approached the stable cautiously, keeping to the shadows.

Looking over the stone wall at the line of stalls opening onto the paddock, he also listened for any sign of the midnight rider.

The rain was pouring off the roof into puddles, but through it he thought he could make out the sound of a horse's hooves shuffling. The soft murmur of a woman's voice. He strained to hear. The words had the quality of one speaking comfortingly to an animal. Nicholas hoisted himself over the wall and moved along the stall doors. The top half of one door was partially open.

*"Oidhe maithe agut, mo bourine."*

Jane. Whatever it was she said, the words had been whispered in Gaelic, and Nicholas would have wagered that they carried a far gentler meaning than the curses she'd hurled at him this morning. He smiled in the darkness and waited, not wanting to surprise her in the stall. She was quick with a knife, and Nicholas didn't trust his own actions if he were to corner her again. He waited a moment more, expecting her to come through the stall door into the paddock, but there was no other sound.

Finally, he pulled open the top half of the door, clearing his throat as he did.

The smell of the horse and wet leather greeted him, and he could hear the mare shift in the darkness inside, but there was no other sound. A blanket covered the back of the steed.

Speaking in a low voice to the animal, he entered. He caressed the beast's damp mane and glanced over its high back to another door that led into the stables. Pushing past, he made his way through the stall to an alley lit only by small windows. Frowning, he turned and stroked the horse's forelock.

Even in the darkness of the narrow space, he could see that everything was in order—all was where it belonged. Except for the wet face of the horse and the dripping saddle on the door leading to the stables, it was as if Jane Purefoy had never ridden in from a violent storm only moments earlier. The routine was practiced and perfect.

"So fast and so smart," he whispered to the mare before backing out of the stall the way he'd entered.

Retracing his steps toward the house, he moved through the rain with more speed than he'd employed when heading down. He wanted a moment with her. Alone. As he strode quickly up the hill, he realized that he was looking for a reason to put himself again in her path.

The door where he'd been standing before was partially open, as he'd left it. Taking the stairs three at a time, he hurried upward through the house. Whatever secret passageway or hidden stairs she had taken to this floor and her bedchamber, Nicholas was determined to head her off.

He arrived at Jane's chamber too late. A line of candlelight showed beneath the door. Impulsively, he raised a hand to knock, but as he did, the light was extinguished.

Nicholas lowered his hand. His fist relaxed. A smile broke across his face, and he shook his head as he started down the hallway and toward his own room.

He could wait. And tomorrow was certain to be an interesting day.

*        *        *

The bed remained untouched, though the candles had been put out hours ago. A middle-aged man, looking far older than his years, sat on a well-worn, upholstered chair by the window, keeping his solitary vigil. It had been a long night, hang it. Far longer than usual.

The storm outside was easing a little when he heard an ancient hinge creak at the bottom of the secret passageway. As she so often did, she was using the passage that led from the wall between his and the next bedchamber down into the cellars of the original castle and out to the old stables.

Instantly alert, he waited until he had heard the only sounds that brought him comfort these days. He listened closely to Jane coming up the narrow and dusty stairs, to the panel in her room opening and closing, to the click of the latch behind her.

Relieved, Sir Thomas Purefoy flexed his aching joints, pushed his weary body out of the chair, and padded silently across the floor to his bed.

Nine years had passed, but he knew nine hundred more might come and go before she would forgive him.

Jane was so much like him. She never forgot, and she never forgave. But he was still her father. She would never know how much he had already suffered from her rejection of him.

Lying awake, as he had so many endless nights before, Thomas Purefoy stared up into the blackness of the bed canopy above him and tried to recall the days when a black-haired girl had run happily in the green meadows around Woodfield House.

# Chapter 7

Her body ached. Her bones creaked from the impact of Spencer's hard body landing on hers. But this wasn't the worst of it. It was morning.

Mornings were not a favorite part of Jane's day—especially not *early* mornings. The housekeeper Fey was accustomed to her failings, though, and despite all of Jane's complaining, the servant simply remained, gently pushing the young woman along until she was up and washed. Supervising with the air of a benign despot, Fey watched with satisfaction as a maid helped her mistress into a black riding dress and black boots.

Looking sleepily into the looking glass, Jane winced at the color of the bruise on her face. Though the swelling on her lip and the side of her mouth had subsided considerably overnight, the sixteen shades of green and yellow seemed to be overtaking the purples and the pinks in the race to dominate. She touched the tender bruise and cursed her negligence for the hundredth time in allowing the Englishman to best her the way he had.

She could only hope the cut on his arm ached like hell.

Another glance at her reflection and she knew there could be no going out in daylight looking like a week-old carcass. Despite her customary nonchalance regarding how she dressed or looked, Jane simply couldn't imagine parading a face so hideously discolored in public. It was one thing to shock her father when he'd demanded that she meet their guests in the parlor, but today was a different matter entirely. And bringing attention to herself was something that Jane Purefoy habitually avoided like the plague.

With a weak smile at Fey, she hobbled out into the hallway and slipped into Clara's bedchamber without knocking. Perhaps her sister would have a solution to her problem. Clara was already up and dressed and greeted her with the usual morning cheerfulness that was so much a part of the younger woman's nature.

Jane thought this might be a perfect time to kill the little cherub, if she only had the energy.

"I can put some powder on your face," Clara suggested, "and tame down the wilder shades of the bruising." She followed Jane to the side of the bed. "But it will still show. And people will be asking questions. And please Jane, for heaven's sake, don't use the same excuse as you did last night."

"I thought it was quite clever."

"Come now. Striking your face on the edge of the dressing table is an excuse far too lame to try to run over any distance."

"You're starting to talk like Father." Jane eyed the smooth bedclothes of the tidily made bed. "I think it is a very good story. Such an accident could happen to anyone."

"Indeed, to anyone who is trying to fib. I don't believe anyone could do this amount of damage only to one's mouth and not the rest of her face . . . or to her brow . . . or . . ."

"I cannot comprehend such analytical reasoning at such an early hour." Jane pulled back the bedclothes and climbed into the bed with her boots and dress on, pulling the coverlet to her chin. "Go without me, shrew, and let me sleep."

"No! We cannot go without you," Clara protested, trying to wrestle the covers off her older sister. "I cannot be left alone with him on such a long ride. Even with a groom to attend us, it would not be . . ."

"Of course you can go. Everyone concerned knows that our dear mother has already seen to it that the finishing touches have been put on your wedding dress. I shouldn't be surprised if the wedding notices didn't go out last evening."

"Don't be horrid. You *must* come!" Clara continued to tug on the blanket that the older sister held tightly to her chest. "Please, Jane. Do this for me. It is not proper for me to be alone with Sir Nicholas, and you know it."

"Proper be dashed. He is here to marry you, and that's all there is to it."

"Jane!" she whined.

The older sister shook her head and held on tightly. "There is nothing that you two can do now that you shan't be doing in a very short while . . . after you are married. What difference should a fortnight make?"

Clara continued pulling. "Please come with us."

"I need sleep." Jane rolled over and pressed her head into the pillows, tucking the blanket around her. "I need rest—peace and quiet. Let me be."

"But I need you. I do not *want* to be left alone with him."

Jane let go of the blanket, and Clara fell back hard on her buttocks onto the floor.

"Why not?" Half rising on the bed, Jane looked down over the edge at her sister.

"That hurt. You intentionally made me fall."

"Why don't you want to be left alone with him?"

"Help me get up." Clara stretched her hands up to her sister.

Jane climbed out of bed, but instead of helping the younger woman, she crossed her arms and towered over her. "Is Father forcing you to marry this man against your will?"

"Don't be silly. He is not forcing me to do anything."

"But you *are* trying, once again, to be the perfect daughter, are you not? You are going along with this whole thing, not because of your own feelings toward the Englishman—as you led me to believe after your return from London—but because you think this would be best for the family. Sacrificing yourself for the . . ."

"I am not doing any such thing." Clara pushed herself to her feet and faced her sister. "You are putting words in my mouth."

Jane studied the younger woman. "Then *do* you like him?"

"Of course I do. How could one not? He is a handsome man, well-to-do; he is a baronet and well-connected in London society. He is every girl's dream. He is the *perfect* catch."

"Then do you *love* him?"

Clara's cheeks immediately flushed, and she turned abruptly and walked toward the mirror. It took a long moment before she answered. "If you want me to tell you that I love him as you loved Conor, the answer is no."

Jane frowned, feeling the old and familiar tightness in her chest as she met her sister's gaze in the mirror.

"I know of no woman who could love a man the way you have loved Conor. I shall probably never come anywhere near having what you have had—your joy when he was still alive, or the suffering you have endured since he was killed. Honestly, Jane, I know of no one else who is as capable of loving a man as you are."

A painful lump in her throat kept Jane from responding. She fought back tears threatening to spill.

"But in my case, you are making a great deal more of things than you should." Clara turned and faced her sister. "The reason why I don't want to be left alone with Sir Nicholas is that he is so much older, so much more experienced. Naturally, I still feel quite shy in his company. I believe, in time, I will learn to trust myself and not be so intimidated by his good looks or his charm."

Jane studied the nervous smile on her sister's face and tried to remember if she'd ever felt this way. She thought of all those times she had run off to meet secretly with Conor by the standing stones on the moor near Knocknakilla. That year, she had turned fifteen and Conor sixteen, but shyness had never been a problem with either of them. But how could it have been? The two had known each other for all of their lives . . . she, the daughter of the magistrate; he, the son of a poor cottager. Just as Jane's mind started to drift off toward those memories of the past, Clara's voice jolted her back to the present.

"You can wear the black hat with the dark veil that Mother wore to the funeral of Parson Adams's mother last winter. That should cover the bruise and more."

Clara reached for Jane's hand and started pulling her toward the door. "Fey tells me that Sir Nicholas has been ready for some time. We should hurry, I suppose. We don't want him to form a poor opinion of us now, do we?"

"Not at all," Jane muttered under her breath as she was dragged from the room. "As his future sister-in-law, I am absolutely desperate with fear that he should form anything but the highest opinion of me."

For the hundredth time, at least, Nicholas watched Jane try to straighten the silly-looking hat perched on top of her head. Thwarting her at every turn, the autumn breeze continued to push the thing this way and that, tugging at the strands of dark hair she must have tucked with such care beneath. The long pins had loosened, though, and the waves of hair threatened to escape, and only the dark veil covering her face kept the foolish thing anchored.

The older sister had not appeared at breakfast with the rest of the family. And even afterward, Nicholas had seen no sign of her until he and Clara had walked to their horses waiting in the paddock. She was waiting for them there amid bustling grooms and stable boys. Arrayed in black, she sat astride her ebony mare, a sight to behold. No sidesaddle delicacy for this one. Jane Purefoy was a "goer" in every way.

Except, of course, for that ridiculous hat.

The breeze stiffened as they rode north across open fields. Though the sun shone brightly overhead, to the northwest clouds lay like a tattered shawl over the round-shouldered peaks of ancient gray mountains. In his mind's eye, he could see so clearly the vision of Jane last night, riding the same animal, carried along on wind and the storm. He'd fervently wished to catch up to her and talk to her before she returned to her room. He'd assumed she'd want to speak to him, too. Nicholas had discovered her secret, but how much he was to reveal—and to whom—had to be a gnawing question. And Jane Purefoy didn't strike him as a very patient person.

The wind continued to buffet them. From his vantage point, riding half a dozen lengths behind Jane, Nicholas could see that she had finally pushed up the dark netting over the narrow brim of the hat.

On impulse, Nicholas spurred his steed forward, suddenly desirous of a glimpse of her face. Upon hearing him approach, though, Jane nudged her mare, keeping the safe distance between them that she'd maintained since leaving Woodfield House. For an insane moment he considered laying his riding crop onto the flanks of his mount and daring her to race with him. But the thought of Clara straggling along behind checked him in time.

He reined in, suppressing a frown as he waited for the younger sister to reach him. Unlike Jane, she sat fashionably sidesaddle and appeared a little flustered. Coming up beside him, she reached up to adjust the delicate feathered hat that she was wearing.

"I'm so sorry. I see I should have chosen a livelier horse this morning." She patted her brow with the back of her gloved hand and tucked some of the golden curls under the hat. "I am not as horrid a rider as you must think. It is just my choice of . . ."

"Not at all. You ride well," he complimented, pulling on the reins of his steed so it would fall in step with hers. He could see that Jane had slowed down ahead and was pulling the veil back over her face. "It is for me to apologize for not keeping to your pace."

"No, sir," she said softly. "No apologies are warranted, I assure you."

Nicholas's attention again was drawn to the tantalizing image of the expert rider ahead and the cruel game that she was playing. She was once again staying just ahead of them. Close enough to torment, but not close enough to be touched.

"I've been wondering, Miss Clara," he said, nodding his head in Jane's direction, "why it is that your sister refuses to ride with us?"

"She . . . I assume . . . I should think she doesn't want to intrude."

"Intrude on what?" His words were tinged with mockery, and he cleared his throat to correct his tone. "What I intended to say is that there could be no intrusion, and this would be a far more comfortable ride if we could travel together. I had very little time to converse with your sister last night, and frankly I fail to see why the three of us shouldn't spend an hour enjoying each other's company."

"I should very much like you to become better acquainted with my sister," Clara responded, and Nicholas watched Jane again reach up and adjust the abominable hat.

"Would it help if we both were to approach and tell her that she would not be *intruding* upon our conversation?"

"I fear that my sister has a mind of her own." The blue eyes turned to him. "I hope you believe me when I say that it wasn't my idea for Jane to be riding so far ahead."

"I do believe you. But if you would allow me to pry a little into your family's affairs, I have a question I'd like to ask you." Nicholas continued after receiving a cautious nod from Clara. "I've been quite perplexed since meeting Miss Jane yesterday. Could you tell me why it was that your sister did not accompany your family to London this past spring?"

"Certainly. That was Jane's choice. She has made a habit of never traveling with the rest of us."

"Why, then, did your family never mention that there was an older daughter?" Nicholas directed a piercing look at her. "Was it Jane's decision, as well, not to be acknowledged by either parent or sister? Tell me, Clara, was your sister dropped by gypsies in her infancy at your parents' door?"

"Hardly, sir!" Clara's gaze fell on the reins looped tightly around her gloved hands. "Jane is my only sister, and very dear to me . . . to all of us."

"And yet you have no answer for the secrecy surrounding her existence? Though I am not particularly opposed to a little mystery . . . or scandal, either . . . I must say that there is a hint of both in the air at Woodfield House. But perhaps I should take this up with Sir Thomas."

"I . . . I . . . well, as you see fit, sir. But I can tell you honestly that my sister never had any desire to be presented in society, as I have been presented. She had no balls thrown in her honor. There were no callers courting her. Jane never had any intention of choosing a husband from London's *ton*." She hesitated. "My parents, however, had different plans for me. It is no secret, and there is no shame in admitting to you that my parents took me to London for the purpose of arranging a proper marriage."

And given the right title and qualifications and wealth, Nicholas thought, anyone wearing breeches would have sufficed. Once again the business of marriage reared its mercenary head, and Nicholas found himself repulsed by the idea. To him, the entire process wasn't much different than the owner of a likely mare going to a country fair and choosing a stud. All that was left was to haggle over the price . . . and Sir Thomas was, no doubt, well prepared for that.

As they rode on in silence, thoughts of the marriage of his friend Stanmore to Rebecca Neville last year sprang to his mind. Before leaving for Ireland, he'd made a short trip to Solgrave to meet the new member of their family. Samuel Frederick Wakefield was born at the end of July. With the older boy, James, home for the summer and doting on the new baby, Nicholas could not recall ever knowing a family as content and happy as the Stanmores.

Starting up yet another of the rolling green hills that seemed to go on forever, Nicholas couldn't help but wonder if Rebecca and Stanmore knew how lucky they were that they had so completely avoided the ordeal of bartering for a spouse. Yes, he was certain that they did indeed know.

But, he thought with a pang of guilt, when all was said and done, how different was his own approach to finding a wife than the approach used by the Purefoys? Not very, when one came right down to it.

Up ahead, at the top of the hill, Jane was withdrawing a pin to adjust the hat when a strong gust suddenly tore the thing off her head and sent it—veil and all—swooping past them like some tattered and malevolent raven. In an instant, Nicholas had wheeled his horse and, drawing his sword, leaned down and pinned the thing to the ground. Raising the hat like a trophy on the point of his sword, he did his best to look embarrassed as he turned back to the two women. Gingerly he pulled the hat from the weapon and sheathed his sword as he rode back to the sisters, who were staring at him wide-eyed.

Jane's face, however, was all Nicholas had eyes for as he approached. With her hair now loose around her shoulders and dancing in the wind, her dark eyes were watching his every movement as he approached. Once again, he saw the woman he'd knocked down the day before. As he drew nearer, his gaze took in all of her— from the tips of her black boots to the proud chin and bruised mouth. He could not stop himself from staring at her sensual lips and wondering about their taste.

"Well, sir . . ." Jane said as he reached them. She seemed flushed and breathless, as if she'd been guessing at the direction of his thoughts. "It appears . . . it appears you've not only run it to ground; you've dealt it a death blow!"

"I fear that I have." He inserted a gloved finger where his sword had cut the beaver skin. "And I insist on buying a replacement at the first opportunity."

"No need," Jane responded. "I can wear it as is. When we get back to Woodfield House, I am certain Fey can mend it . . . well, somehow."

She extended a hand for the hat, and Nicholas nudged his horse nearer. But just as Jane's hand was about to close on the brim, he released it. As if shot from his hand, the thing flew off again, carried away on another gust of wind.

Jane watched the hat take flight. Instead of going after it, Nicholas enjoyed the close study of her pretty face. "I see you shall *have* to allow me to find a replacement, now."

"It was actually our mother's," Clara said softly from behind before pulling her horse abreast. "I assure you that she shan't miss it."

Jane watched the hat tumbling across the moor for a moment before turning her attention back to her sister. "Well, as fate would have it, I fear I cannot escort you to Ballyclough, after all. But if you could make my excuses to the Reverend Mr. Adams and Mrs. Br—?"

"No, Jane. You promised to come."

"I know I did. But under the circumstances of my . . . appearance . . ."

"The parson already saw the bruise on your face last night."

"But Mrs. Brown has not."

"It doesn't show so much in the light." Clara leaned over and touched the other woman's arm. "You look fine, Jane. Tell her, Sir Nicholas, that she looks fine."

"I would say that Miss Purefoy looks far better than fine," he offered quietly as his gaze caressed her face. "I should be greatly disappointed if she were to rob us of her charming company on such a pleasant day."

A soft blush actually crept into her cheeks, and Nicholas was happy to know that she was not totally immune to his words.

"Come, Jane. Please? Parson Adams has been after you for some time now to come to Ballyclough, and we are almost there."

A look of frustration crossed the older sister's fair features, and she glanced again in the direction that her hat had flown off. It was still visible far off in the distance, the veil caught on a bramble while the hat itself dangled in the mud of what appeared to be a water-filled ditch.

*"Jane!"* Clara's insistent and pleading tone made it clear that she didn't want to be left alone with him, and this suited Nicholas perfectly.

"I shall escort you to the edge of the village, but no farther. There I shall leave you and ride over to visit a friend near Buttevant. If you insist, though, I shall return in time to have a very short visit with Parson Adams before returning to Woodfield House with you."

Clara was obviously relieved, and the three again turned their horses northward. Before Jane could move ahead of them again, though, Nicholas immediately directed the conversation toward her.

"I must say, Miss Jane, that I am quite surprised that your family would approve of you riding off on your own—to that Buttevant place—without an escort. No fears of the Whiteboys?"

"None, Sir Nicholas." She kept her gaze straight ahead. "They have never been known to remain in the same area after an incident such as the one yesterday. Are *you* concerned, sir?"

"Not at all."

"And how is your arm today?"

"Much better. And your face?"

"I am *very* well, thank you."

Nicholas suppressed a smile, and the three rode along in silence for a moment.

"Those were capital storms last night. Either of you have any difficulty sleeping?"

"Sleep is just about the only thing that Jane holds precious in life," Clara offered. "In fact, part of my sister's crankiness this morning has to do with being awakened too early in the day."

"I sympathize with her completely," he replied casually. "As a creature of the night myself, I had difficulty sleeping last night. So I ended up going outside and watching the storm from the safety of the archway facing the stables. It is amazing how enchanting the night can be when one spends some time in it."

Jane cast a questioning glance at him, and Nicholas held her gaze. Her eyes darkened, sparkling like sapphires, and he reveled in the knowledge that he had again captured her attention.

Clara's voice broke in. "There is the village. Small but quite charming, don't you think, Sir Nicholas?"

Ahead of them, nestled in a valley and surrounded by a patchwork of brown, harvested fields and green pastureland dotted with a few cows and more sheep, lay the cluster of cottages. Up against an ancient castle at one end of the village, the squat gray tower of a chapel could be seen.

"The castle was built by the Desmonds centuries ago," Clara said, following the direction of Nicholas's gaze. "The Purdens live there now, but we don't associate with them. And there is also a limestone quarry at that end . . ."

"I shall be on my way, then." Jane reined in her horse and turned it toward a road heading east. "I shall see you again sometime this afternoon."

Nicholas tried to think of some objection, some excuse

that would keep her with them. "It is too bad we cannot accompany you on your visit to Buttevant. I should very much like to see more of this countryside."

Jane's look told him there was no chance in hell that she would be taking him along.

"That is a fine idea, Sir Nicholas. Why don't you go with Jane to Buttevant?" Clara's remark brought the others' heads around sharply. "It is fine horse country, you know. Why, the valleys along the River Awbeg are famous throughout Ireland. Even the Irish here are riders from childhood. My father often sings the praises of the fine animals he's seen and purchased from the folk who raise them along the river."

"But I am not visiting any horse traders, Clara." Jane's words were spoken through clenched teeth. Her dark eyes flashed.

"I know that, but it would be much safer," Clara assured her pleasantly. "And while you are visiting your friend, I'm certain Sir Nicholas wouldn't mind waiting in the village and enjoying the beautiful scenery. There is even a ruined abbey there, rumored to be as old as any church in Dublin. It's quite lovely, really."

"You don't say," Nicholas responded with interest.

"Excuse us for a moment, will you?" Jane pushed her horse toward her sister. Her whispered words were intended only for Clara, but Nicholas could not help overhearing them.

"*Why* are you doing this?"

"You know why."

"I give you my word that I'll be back. I *shall* go alone!"

Clara shook her head, and Nicholas could see the color rising in the face of the older sister.

"I believe Sir Nicholas is correct about the possibility of the Shanavests still lingering in the area," Clara said out loud, turning to him. "Would you do my sister the honor of accompanying her to her friend's place and then back here, sir?"

He looked from one sister's happy face to the other's tense one. "Are you quite sure Parson Adams would be agreeable to this change in plans?"

"Absolutely."

"But what about you? I shouldn't care to see you slighted."

"Not at all, sir." Clara gave him her brightest smile ever. "I suggested it, did I not? Actually, I am looking forward to spending some time in the parson's company. And with you keeping Jane safe from roving bandits, sir, I shall have the peace of mind that both of you will return shortly. I'll see to it that Mrs. Brown has tea waiting for you."

"If that is your wish . . . ?"

"Then it is settled." Clara smiled and touched her riding whip to her mare's flank. "We shall see you soon."

"What about *me?*" Jane protested, watching her sister descend the hill. A small flock of sheep separated as the younger woman approached them. "No one asked me if I am willing to take *him* along . . ."

Nicholas nudged his horse between Jane and her departing sister. "I'm very sorry, Miss Purefoy, but it appears you are stuck with me for the remainder of the morning. Now, will you try to recall some of your English charm and hospitality and at least pretend to tolerate me?"

"I think not, sir!" She glanced meaningfully at his arm. "You couldn't handle me at your best yesterday. But if you are not careful, today may prove infinitely worse for you."

# Chapter 8

"Miss Clara, how lovely to have you here." Mrs. Brown met the guest by the door of the parsonage. "The parson was hoping that you wouldn't mind waiting in the parlor and entertaining your company until he gets back. He was called away unexpectedly and he feared he might be a wee bit late in getting back. But wait, miss, where *is* your company?"

The housekeeper peered out at Clara's solitary horse tied by the gate in front of the parsonage.

Sunlight glinted in the puddles still standing in the rutted road that led through the village. Though the wispy smoke from a dozen cooking fires colored the breezes over the thatched roofs, the village was nearly deserted. Only a few ancient chickens, a goat in a stone enclosure across the way, and a workman carrying a load of sticks on his back at the far end of the hamlet hinted of other inhabitants.

"My sister needed to visit a friend in Buttevant, so I sent our guest Sir Nicholas with her. I wanted to be sure Jane would get back here in time to visit."

"Good for you," Mrs. Brown said encouragingly. She closed the door and led the way down a narrow passage toward the parlor. "We do not see enough of Miss Jane's bright face these days. There's not a day that goes by that someone in the village is not inquiring after her health or asking when her next visit will be. She is greatly missed here, I assure you, and I know for a certainty the parson has been concerned about her absence from Ballyclough."

"Has he?" Clara was surprised by the sharpness of her own tone.

"Indeed. Thinking on it daily, I should say." The housekeeper nodded emphatically and opened the door to the parlor.

The curtains had already been pulled open, and the shutters folded back. Sunshine slanted through the open windows, lighting the spare but comfortable furnishings of the room. A homey, cozy scent of peat and pipe tobacco hung in the air. As she breathed in the smells, a feeling of well-being spread through her, warming her, making her forget the disquiet the housekeeper's words had caused. She loved this house.

Mrs. Brown lowered herself into her chair by the small peat fire and rang a small silver bell that she took from the pocket of her apron. Clara sat down in the settle across from her.

"I hope you don't mind my saying so, Miss Clara, but it would have done your sister a world of good if she'd gone off to England with the rest of you this past spring."

A young servant poked her head into the room, and Mrs. Brown ordered a pot of fresh tea to be brought in.

"Aye. As I was saying to Parson Adams this very morning, if Miss Jane were to find an English husband . . . a good one as you have found . . . why, the child might just shake off the sadness she's been carrying all these years. Aye, what she needs is a good one like yours."

"Really, Mrs. Brown, I haven't found myself a husband, English or otherwise. Sir Nicholas is my father's guest, and he has yet to ask for my hand in marriage. To be honest, I don't care for people going around and presuming things that may not come to pass."

"You are quite right, my dear," Mrs. Brown said, picking up her needlework from a basket beside the chair. "We shouldn't be counting our chickens . . . and all that. But I shouldn't worry. You are so lovely."

"This is the baronet's first visit to Ireland. He might not care for what he sees." Trying to hide her impatience, Clara stood up and went to the window. In the pretty garden beside the house, one of the year's last rosebuds bobbed its head in the breeze. "If I may ask, Mrs. Brown, has Parson Adams expressed a position regarding my sister?"

"Indeed he has. The parson told me, in no uncertain terms, that he does not believe that one English-born nobleman in a hundred—your gentleman excepted—is good enough for your sister."

"Is that so?"

Mrs. Brown continued without looking up. "He thinks most of them are too shallow. And to give him credit, the parson was educated among them, so he should know well enough. And not to bring up a difficult subject, my dear, but he believes once a would-be suitor learns of Jane's younger years, the average English gentleman would cry foul and leave the poor thing standing at the altar. But I say, find a decent one and tell him nothing. She's a fine woman for any man, if you ask me."

"Well, I believe Jane has no intention of accepting suitors." Clara reached up and pulled off her hat. "My belief is that she is perfectly happy at Woodfield House and will remain there for the rest of her life." She put the hat down on the wide windowsill and rejoined the housekeeper by the fire.

"I'm happy to hear that you feel that way, child, but the parson doesn't agree with you. He is a very observant man, and he has been watching Jane closely for some time."

"Really, Mrs. Brown?"

"Aye, and if he says your sister is unhappy at Woodfield House, I believe him."

Clara held her tongue as the young servant entered the room with a tray containing a teapot with cups and several small cakes. Mrs. Brown took the tray from her and placed it on the table beside her. Just as she was preparing to pour the tea, however, the parson could be heard coming in through the back of the house.

"Here he is now." Mrs. Brown finished pouring the tea and pushed herself immediately to her feet. "I'll go and tell him that you are here. Oh my heavens, I also need to tell the cook to wait luncheon until Miss Jane and your Englishman get here."

Clara watched the round figure of the older woman scurry out of the room. She, too, stood up as a wave of unhappiness regarding everything she'd just been told gripped her stomach. She walked to the window, removed her gloves, and placed them next to the hat. She wished for a mirror, but she knew there was none. Absently, she reached up and tried to arrange the curls.

"There is no need for that. Your fiancé is not here yet, Miss Clara."

The young woman jumped and turned quickly to the door. Henry Adams stood on the threshold, filling the doorway. She saw the gray eyes studying her critically, and she felt the heat rise into her face.

"Mrs. Brown tells me that you sent your English baronet off with Jane to Buttevant." He removed his gloves as he entered the room. "You know you are risking your sister's wrath when you start meddling in her activities."

Clara moved to the small table. "May I pour you some tea?"

He nodded. The breeze had ruffled his short black hair, and his probing gaze only added to her unease. "So how did you manage it? Or, a better question, *why* send them off together?"

The cup rattled slightly against the saucer as Clara extended it toward him. "I was hoping for a few moments alone with you . . . so that we could talk."

"What do we have to talk about?" he said coolly.

"About . . . about us."

Their fingers brushed as he accepted the cup from her. "We have nothing more to say to each other—in private, that is."

Her heart sank, and she fought down the tight knot clawing its way up into her throat. "Please give me a chance to explain."

"You have explained, Clara—clearly and utterly. You did so six months ago. I've moved on, and there is no point in revisiting that unpleasantness."

When she lifted her head, his handsome image was blurred, and she blinked back her tears. "I never knew you could be so cruel."

"I? Cruel? Please!" He placed the teacup on the shelf above the hearth and frowned at her. "Shortness of memory has never been one of your failings. But having said that, I must leave you. I find it totally inappropriate to be dallying here with a nearly married woman." He bowed curtly. "I believe I left my . . . my *Daily Meditations* in the chapel. You can have Mrs. Brown send for me when your fiancé and your sister return."

Clara stared for an instant at his broad back as he turned away. Panic seized her, and she ran toward the door, blocking his path. "I beg of you, Henry."

He halted a step away. "Clara, you are making a fool of yourself."

"So what if I am?" She blindly reached for the door behind her and closed it, leaning her weight against it.

"You mustn't jeopardize your reputation this way."

"Reputation means nothing to me now." Fresh tears rolled down her cheeks. "I cannot let you go. Not until you hear me."

"Clara, open the door." He took a step closer, and she could see the sparks of temper burning in his gray eyes.

"I love you, Henry." The words tumbled out. "Please, you must forgive me for what is past . . . for the way I behaved before. Those were empty words I spoke six months ago. I know I offended you . . . hurt you. I was a fool."

"Clara, it is too late for this. You have a suitor who has come all the way from England for the sole purpose . . ."

"I don't care." She threw herself against him, wrapping her arms around him. He stood rigidly as she held him, but she couldn't stop now. She pressed her face against the coarse cloth of his jacket. "Six months ago you asked me to become your wife. You told me that you loved me . . . that you wanted me at your side forever. Please, Henry, ask me again."

"No."

"Please just ask me, and I will be yours."

"I was not good enough for you then"—his fingers grasped her shoulders firmly, and he pushed her back until he was looking into her face—"and nothing has changed. I could never measure up to your expectations for a husband. I am still a second son—a poor clergyman who is happy to labor here, away from the pleasures of society. Six months ago, I was a fool to think I could compete with the advantages you were about to receive in London. Fancy dresses, receptions, and balls awaited you. Wealth and fame awaited you. 'I must marry someone with a title,' you said."

"Please, Henry," she sobbed. "But you know that wasn't for myself. I was doing it all for my parents. After Jane—after what she had done to disgrace their name—I had to do something to mend the past."

"Jane! Always blaming Jane!" He spat out the words. "I wish you would put aside this pretence of selflessness, Clara. Others might believe you and be fooled, but not I."

His words jolted her, tearing the air from her lungs.

"No," she gasped. "It's true. I was doing it for them . . . and I thought I could go through with it."

"And now?" He towered over her.

"I cannot. Now that Sir Nicholas is here—now that I see that he may truly offer for me—I cannot go through with it. I care nothing for this Englishman. I never will. You are the one who has my heart. You are the only one whom I think of. You are the one I want to spend my life with." She reached up with trembling fingers and touched his lips. "He is too experienced. Too worldly for someone like me. Everything about him intimidates me. But you, Henry . . . my gentle Henry . . ."

She stood on her toes and pressed her lips against his. Softly, tentatively, innocently, she placed small kisses on his firm chin, his clenched cheek, and again on his lips. She kissed him with the same innocence that he had kissed her six months earlier when he'd proposed to her.

"So what is to happen now?" His hand fisted roughly in her hair, and she cried out as he pulled her head back until he was looking into her face. "So what if I yield to your wishes? I only make a fool out of myself before you again. So what if you send away this suitor that frightens you with his . . . with his manliness? I'll tell you. Tomorrow your restless and greedy nature will again assert itself, and another will appear to take this one's place."

"No!"

"Yes! For you know that there are no new wardrobes

of dresses every season for the wife of a country cleric. There are no journeys abroad. No London parties. No dozen or so dashing rogues chasing you about the drawing rooms of Bath. You would be bored to death, Clara. You would curse me for eternity for leading you into the dull drudgery of a clergyman's life."

She shook her head. "I shall be true to my promise. I shall never regret our life together." Tears continued to soak her cheeks. "The love we share will be enough. I ask for nothing more."

"And what of your parents? Of the honor that you presumably wanted to restore to your family name?"

"I . . . I cannot think of any of that now. Not when there is a chance of losing you forever."

"You are so beautiful," he whispered bitterly, his gaze scouring every inch of her face. "So young and naïve and beautiful."

Before Clara could object, Henry's lips crushed down on hers. But this was no kiss of innocence, but an unleashing of repressed desire. His strong fingers delved deeper into her hair and his mouth devoured her lips, forcing her mouth open, his tongue surging inside. She gave a stifled gasp and felt her body mold against him. The sudden awareness of her limbs made her long for something more. Her hands reached up around his neck.

Then, without warning, he abruptly ended the kiss and pushed her away.

"I understand you better now than I ever did before. Like a child, you only want what you cannot have."

She shook her head and tried to move back into his arms, but he kept her away.

"Well, your 'gentle Henry' is gone," he said mockingly. "He was just a fool who treated you like a rare and delicate flower, but found himself stung by those fair petals." He pushed her farther away, his voice hardening. "You chose your way six months ago. Marry your Englishman and finish what you have begun. I wish you all the worldly treasures you were born and brought up to possess, but leave me be."

In an instant, he was gone.

Clara stared in shock for a long moment at the closed door, and then turned to the wall. Standing alone, she wept bitter tears of anguish for the one true love she had so stupidly thrown away.

Her mount was indeed a fine one, and well accustomed to the soft turf and uneven terrain of the Irish countryside. And Jane was the rider to handle her.

For a quarter of an hour, the woman led him on a merry chase. Up hill and down. With her black hair streaming wildly behind her, she leaped streams and ditches and hedgerows with stunning ease and grace.

The pace she set made it impossible for Nicholas to talk to this fiend of a horsewoman. If the ground leveled out into a smooth green meadow, she was sure to cut away to some higher passage where the sharp edges of white rock protruded from the hillside, endangering both horse and rider.

Emerging from a broad, fast-running stream that left him half a field behind her, Nicholas shook his head at her spirit. He had to give her credit. Jane Purefoy had successfully used every racing ploy known to slow him down and create distance between them. She might have been forced to take him along, but that didn't mean that she had to endure his company. At the top of the next hill, Nicholas saw Jane rein in her steed, and he quickly closed the distance between them.

Her cheeks were flushed with health, and she turned slightly in the saddle, black eyes flashing, her chest heaving from the exertion of the ride.

Nicholas didn't think he'd ever seen a more magnificent sight.

She looked away as he rode up to her. The Awbeg came into view. There, along the steep green banks of meandering river, he saw the buildings and broken walls of an abbey and the neat little village just to the north.

"You should be able to find the main thoroughfare through Buttevant with no difficulty," she said, uttering her first words since leaving Clara at Ballyclough.

"What are those two towers?" Nicholas pointed in the direction of the village. He was searching for a way to detain her.

"The ruins of Lombard's Castle."

He noticed the activity beyond it. "And what is being built beyond the town?"

"A barracks to house troops."

"I see." He raised a curious brow. "Well, that should discourage rebellion, I should think."

"With that thought, Sir Nicholas, I take my leave of you."

"I thought you planned to visit a friend here yourself."

"I do, but she doesn't live in the village proper. She lives close by, though." Jane gestured in the vague direction of the abbey. "But the village has an inn and a number of shops and a couple of very fine stables to while away your time. I shall come after you when I've finished my business."

She started along the ridge by the river, but stopped and turned sharply to him when he started to follow.

"That way." She pointed toward the village. "You go that way. That will take you where you want to go."

"Would you at least tell me who it is that you are visiting? Just in case I become lost and in need of your assistance?"

"Come, Sir Nicholas, it is impossible for you to lose your way. Now please be off. Clara and Reverend Adams are expecting us back by noon."

For a moment, he considered being completely disagreeable and trailing after her, but decided against it. With a nod at her, Nicholas nudged his horse down the incline, all the while keeping an eye on Jane as she rode off along the crest of the hill.

He was a man well acquainted with women of all social classes and types. It had long been a leisure activity of his to attempt to understand the many feminine moods and needs. For the most part, women liked him and sought out his company. He'd generally expected the same response here.

Obviously Jane Purefoy was not to be classed with other women.

Nicholas reined in and watched her disappear beyond the crest of the hill. Somehow he had to make her understand that he was not a threat to her or her seditious pursuits. At the same time, he wanted to let her know that he no longer had any interest in courting the younger sister.

He spurred his horse toward the village, knowing that explanation and extrication could be complicated matters at the best of times.

And these were hardly the best of times.

The path from the rectory to the chapel was empty of the town's inhabitants, and Henry Adams was glad of it.

His passion had taken control of his reason, and he was already regretting his behavior. He had given way too quickly to his anger. His own personal pride, stung long ago, had possessed his soul far too easily.

The sun was shining down on his bare head, but he didn't notice it at all, focused as he was on his own failings. How could a man of the cloth, he thought harshly, possess a character so fallible and weak?

As he reached the heavy iron-banded door of the chapel, he hesitated, turning instead to the pathway that led across the small stream and up the hill toward the graveyard by the road to Mallow. He would not step into the house of God with the heat of passion still raging in his mind and body.

Clara's soft mouth had been so willing. The press of her firm body offered the fantasy of many tempestuous dreams. But her words plagued him. They were words that he longed to believe, but knew not how to trust.

Henry's passion for the younger Purefoy sister had taken hold of him a year ago, but the fever of it still raged in his blood.

Although he had known the family for years, it was Jane whom he'd known best from their youth. The two of them were about the same age. The two of them had shared so much of the same outrage over the ill treatment that Ireland endured. When they were younger, they had both even spoken out—with that indignation found so often in the naïve—against the English Penal Laws that afflicted the peasantry and the landowners and the merchants alike. Indeed, despite the gossip surrounding Jane when they were younger, their own friendship had remained true throughout their adolescence and his years at the university. To this day, he knew that she considered him a trusted friend, and he considered her the same.

One thing he had not confided in her, though, was his feelings for her sister.

Henry sat on the low stone wall surrounding the crowded graves of peasants, tanners, and quarrymen. Here lay the history of this village, he thought, enclosed by a square of rough gray stone. Our time here is so short. We're born to toil . . . and toil we do. We suffer and then we die. But somewhere between the years of blood and tears, we hope for moments of love.

He looked back across the stony brook at the village and at his rectory. Last summer, the flowers were blooming in his little garden and the fields around Ballyclough green and alive when Henry saw, for the first time, that light in Clara's eyes. No longer a child, she had somehow, without his noticing, grown into a beautiful young woman. There had been other things, as well, that Henry had become aware of then. Her quiet dignity. Her determination to keep peace between the members of her tumultuous family. He also noticed the way that she tried to hide her inclination to hang on every word he said and on his every movement.

It had been easy to fall in love with Clara. It had been even easier to allow himself to dream of someday asking for her hand in marriage. And dream he did. For though he was well born, he was still a country clergyman and she a knighted magistrate's daughter. Nonetheless, whatever her parents might have wanted for her, when he set out to court her privately, she'd been more than willing to receive his attentions.

The rosebuds were full and ready to open when Henry Adams held his heart in his outstretched hands and approached Clara with his offer of marriage. He'd wanted her consent first before broaching the subject with Sir Thomas. His greatest mistake had been in taking that consent for granted.

Anger at the memory drove him to his feet, and Henry walked across the road and into a field that had lain fallow this year. Upon these lands, he knew, cattle and sheep and goats had once grazed freely, their hides

supplying the tanners of Ballyclough with the materials
of their trade. Now fertile farms surrounded him, the
profits of the tenants' labors going into the pockets of
the great landowners. The planted lands of the English
were far superior to the marshy patches of bog land that
the Irish were allowed beyond the next line of hills. And
it was the same worship of Mammon that was ruining
this country that made Clara refuse him.

Frustrated beyond words, Henry stopped in the middle of the field. He was just not good enough. It simply
came down to that. There was no way she could consent
to a marriage that didn't improve her family's name—
or wealth—or position—or whatever. Clara had been
bred to reject him that day. She'd been raised to take
that fertile ground . . . and he could offer her only a life
in the marshes.

Though he'd been hurt, he had never mentioned any
of this to Jane—not out of pride, but because he knew
this would be another blow to her. In a family that
thrived because of the privilege and superiority that
went with being English, Jane had always fought against
it, and he knew she believed she'd had some positive
influence on her younger sister. How disappointed Jane
would be to learn Clara's true feelings. How many sleepless nights had it taken him to come to grips with it!

Henry Adams shook his head. Well, that was behind
him now.

He turned his back on the green fields and started
toward the decrepit ruins of the tanners' cottages crowd-
ing the stream at the lower end of the village. He knew
where to go.

Darby O'Connell, with a stubbornness inherited from
his father, had remained in Ballyclough, determined to
eke out an existence in the tanning trade that his grandfather and his grandfather's grandfather had practiced
before him. But his hard life became harder when his
wife delivered a dead baby two weeks ago.

She had not once gotten back onto her feet after
that—not once stopped losing blood. For nearly a week
now the woman had been delirious with fever, and yesterday the husband went for the priest in Mallow. While
Darby was on the road, Henry had looked in on her. A

woman from a nearby cottage was doing what she could to keep the dying woman comfortable. During Henry's visit, the three little O'Connells had simply looked up at him with blank expressions from the dirt floor beside their mother's pallet. He could see at a glance that the poor woman's time was at hand, and he knew that Darby would surely go mad when his wife passed away. He didn't want to think what would happen to the children.

The tanner's cottage came into view, and Henry thought for a moment how different this thatched hut was from the grand buildings of Woodfield House.

No, he needed to clear his mind of the words and promises Clara had spoken to him today. She was far too acquiescent to ever withstand the social and family pressures that would surely pour over her if he were fool enough to broach the subject of marriage with Sir Thomas.

Sir Nicholas Spencer had arrived to take his prize, and there was no competing with him. Title and money spoke loudly . . . and Henry had neither. She had been the wise one and he the fool six months ago. Well, he was wiser now, and it was best for all to keep it that way.

Darby's youngest, barefoot and only just covered by his rags, was sitting against the stone wall of the cottage when Henry came across the stream. As the parson watched, the child dropped a dirty piece of uncooked potato that he'd been clutching in a filthy hand into the mud. The young boy's face was stained with tears and dirt, and as he got on all fours and crawled after his lost possession, a small dog darted up and gobbled down the bit of food, running off again as quickly as he came. The child immediately began to wail, but stopped suddenly as he noticed Henry's approach.

The teary eyes and dirt-smeared face turned to the parson with recognition, and the boy raised his thin arms into the air to be picked up. Henry leaned down and lifted the child without a moment's hesitation and headed toward the cottage door.

As the boy nestled a tired head against his shoulder, Henry knew that he could waste no more time in snug

parlors, courting young women who had never wanted
for anything in their lives.

No, he thought as he ducked his head and stepped
into the dark cottage, this was where he belonged.

of canvases, it didn't hurt Mrs. Cawardine to have Sir Joshua Reynolds himself as a friend and mentor.

But Alexandra found it entirely pleasant to think of Jane Purefoy, here amid the rustic greenery of Ireland, rebelling against such backward notions.

Pulling off the cloth covering them, she looked quickly at the first two paintings. They were landscape scenes and well executed with a unique style that would have made even the great Gainsborough take note. Alexandra's thoughts of style and structure, of the use of light and color, dissipated into thin air, though, when she uncovered the third landscape. As the older woman gazed at the work, Jane's intention began to dawn on her.

She went back and looked hard at each picture again. They were all done from the same perspective, looking down from an elevation into a rural valley. There was no doubt in Alexandra's mind that they were painted by the same artist and depicted the same location. But the three paintings did not reflect the same scene.

She brought the canvases out into the window's light and stood them next to each other, against the easel and stool. As she studied them more closely, she found herself fascinated by the deft touches that accentuated the passage of seasons in the paintings. The young woman's talent was obvious. Through her use of light, Jane drew the eye to a different object or person in each painting, but she had also created an entirely new perspective on the same scene with only a few adroit brush strokes.

Alexandra crouched before the first one that she had looked at—the painting most recently done—and studied the summer pastoral scene. Cattle grazed in pastureland enclosed by ditches and low hedges. Picturesque ruins of something—perhaps an abandoned abbey that had once stood in the dell—could be partly seen through the tall summer grass.

She looked at the next, a painting that depicted the valley in spring and contained a few men working along the edge of the field. She looked back at the summer painting and then back again. The men were digging the ditches to enclose the pastureland. A man on horseback, his back to the painter, was pointing at something and directing the laborers.

Alexandra moved on to study the third canvas, a winter landscape. An impenetrable mist spread through the lower reaches of the valley, its thick fingers of fog spreading claw-like across a blackened field. The overall effect of the scene was a disturbing one, and Alexandra shivered involuntarily as she stood back for a better look.

The painting contained numerous details that were cleverly hidden in the edges of the mist with mere touches of the artist's brush. The ruins that appeared so picturesque in the summer scene now pushed through the vapor—ghostly and ominous. Alexandra peered intently at the broken stone walls. What were they? She found herself wanting to reach out and brush away the mist with her fingers, as if to discover the secret beneath it. Mist or smoke? She thought for a moment that the stones might even be charred ruins of a building . . . of more than one building.

She looked over at the other two canvases that were still standing against eaves.

Excited, Alexandra crossed over and turned one around. A shocked gasp escaped her lips when her gaze fell on the painting. Leaning it against the worktable, she backed up and sat heavily on the wooden chair.

A great fire consumed the valley. Violently alive with a shocking splatter of color, there were faces and upraised hands, all helpless against the raging inferno. Fear and anger silently screamed out at the viewer. With the subtle touch of oil to canvas, the anguished faces of lost souls became part of the flames that reached upward into the black, midnight sky.

Alexandra felt hot tears well up, a painful knot threatening to choke her. The painting showed an entire village being put to the torch. She stared at the images of people running out into the night and others caught in the raging holocaust. Depicted in the distance, groups of men looking more devilish than human could be seen torching the fields and hunting down the innocents.

It was a nightmarish view of evil incarnate, and Alexandra Spencer believed no one had done it more effectively since the passing of the Flemish genius Hieronymus Bosch.

She looked back again at other paintings. And now she was able to see through the mist. Now she understood that the ruins were the untended gravestones of a terrible tragedy.

The sadness of it all lay heavily on Alexandra's heart. She glanced in the direction of the last canvas still sitting in the shadows. Forcing herself to her feet, she trudged to the painting and turned it to the light.

A cluster of huts. Not quite a village. Neat, well-tended cottages with thatched roofs and kitchen gardens and two old peasant women talking by a well. Children running happily along a sparkling brook. Men and women just beginning the harvest of the fields surrounding the cottages, with older children binding sheaves of golden grain. The painting bespoke the joy of hard-won prosperity, of family, of the pride of heritage.

The sense of serenity that this canvas instilled in Alexandra was fleeting. As soon as she placed this one beside the others, she was struck full force with the power of the sequence. In taking in these scenes, she *felt* rather than simply viewed the destruction of a farming community and its people.

She pressed her fist to her lips to quiet a sob. She'd never been affected by any work of art more than these paintings at this moment. She'd never even glimpsed the ugly reality of what was happening to the people of this land until this instant. It was the kind of work that Hogarth had done in his series of satiric depictions of London . . . but this young woman had taken the work into the ethereal realms of high art.

Jane Purefoy's ability to capture the essence of a people's suffering was a marvelous gift. And her work told of someone who'd experienced this suffering—more than simply the perceptions of an artist who had witnessed a persecution firsthand. But how could she have?

The sound of the door opening at the bottom of the stairs jerked Alexandra out of her chair. As Lady Purefoy called up to her, she quickly replaced the canvases against the eaves and threw a cloth over them. Wiping her hand over her face to compose herself, she turned to see the woman's head appear at the top of the narrow steps.

"Lady Spencer, what on earth are you doing up here?"

Alexandra looked casually at the other woman. "Enjoying myself."

"Here?" She glanced disdainfully around the attic space, but didn't climb the last couple of steps. One might have thought it was a pit of vipers. "I wouldn't even house the servants here. And what is that horrid odor?"

"It is the scent of greatness, Lady Purefoy. Don't you recognize it?"

The mistress of Woodfield House looked sharply at her guest.

"But I couldn't agree with you more heartily about this area. This is a far too wonderful room to be used only for sleeping quarters. For an artist, this attic offers a splendid retreat. And I simply love the way Jane has organized the space. Is it not absolutely grand?"

"Well, I shall defer to your judgment, of course . . ." She cast a doubtful look around.

"And your daughter's paintings!" Alexandra made a sweeping motion over the rows of canvases lining the walls. "There is amazing talent exhibited here! Though I have only seen a few things, her work rivals the greats of our time."

"Jane?" Lady Purefoy replied skeptically.

"Indeed! Who schooled her in the fine arts? I am *most* curious to know what kind of professional training she received. I cannot tell you how impressed I am by all of this."

"Professional?" The woman looked at her guest in bewilderment. "I am sure I don't know what you mean. Jane's education was no different than Clara's."

"Even more impressive. Pray show me where in Woodfield House you have hung her masterpieces. They are surely of a quality that they might adorn any gallery in England."

"Well . . . I . . . We . . . I do not believe we have gotten around to hanging any of Jane's paintings." She stopped, obviously at a loss. "But if you would join me downstairs in the parlor, I can show you some of Clara's needlework that I had framed this past summer. She is quite competent in her own right, I want you to know. I myself find it most soothing to look upon her work."

Now it was Alexandra's turn to stare in disbelief at the waiting woman. Soothing! That is what things had been reduced to. Clara was soothing and Jane was not. How disappointing, she thought, knowing deep in her heart that *soothing* was something that would never do for her son.

Kathleen stared incredulously at the bag of coins in her hand.

Seamus's widow and the woman known as Egan were standing outside the tiny cottage, a growing breeze riffling the young mother's tattered skirts. The rebel leader closed Kathleen's hand around the bag as the eldest child ran into the yard, the other two children trailing behind.

"Let no one see it. Spend it only a little at a time and never on the same market day," Egan whispered. "Now that I know how much you are doing without, I shall bring some clothes for the wee ones and some food for you and the old woman. If I cannot come myself, I'll send someone."

The thatched cottage that Kathleen and her three children had taken shelter in was half the size of Jane's bedroom at Woodfield House. Hardly large enough for the woman and her brood, the hut was being shared with an older widow named Bridget, whom disease had made blind in both eyes this past summer. The arrangement worked well for both women at present, but both knew better than to get too attached to it. No ground or shelter was secure. As poor tenant farmers, they knew they lived at the mercy of their landlords' next whim. The brutal taking of land by the Royal Dragoons for their new barracks just north of Buttevant only added to the increasing number of homeless families.

Kathleen had fled her own burning cottage in the middle of the night, holding under her arm a Bible she could hardly read and pushing her three young ones ahead of her. Ignoring his wife's pleas, Seamus had stayed behind to face the attackers.

Here, as in so many places across Ireland, complete

villages of tenant farmers were being cleared. Once the
landowner's crops were taken in, the remaining fields
were set ablaze and the cottages pulled down. Land that
had been held as common land for generations was now
being enclosed. Grassland that had been taken by force
and planted by the colonizing English two centuries earlier was now being turned back into pastureland. Cattle
now grazed where tenants had been struggling to survive
by dint of their hard work and sweat.

Seamus was killed that night, and Kathleen had not
yet been given a chance to grieve. The stark reality of
poverty that was facing her and her children was a fate
far worse than the brutal but sudden death her husband
had met.

Now, standing in the sun with the breeze pulling at
her skirts, she looked down at Egan's offering of coins. It
was clearly too much to comprehend. Though the money
represented the desperate woman's first ray of hope
since the tragedy, she could not cry.

"God bless ye, Egan. God bless your Shanavests."
The woman's gaze lifted from the treasure in her hand.
"I . . . I didn't know how I'd be taking care of us."

"This is no replacement for your loss. You take care
of yours . . . and Bridget . . . but mind that you keep
mum. And don't attract attention by spending it too fast.
I'll come back with more when I can."

As Egan turned to go, Kathleen pulled the shawl from
around her own shoulders and extended it in her
direction.

"For ye, Egan," she whispered shyly. "Ye might be
needing this to hide the bruising on yer face."

The coarse wool shawl had more holes in it than a
beggar's breeches, but the thoughtfulness of the gift
touched Jane deeply. She accepted the offering and
poured her emotions into the embrace she gave the
woman.

"I shall wear it." And she did, draping it over her
shoulders and knotting it in front.

The three children escorted Egan to her waiting horse
and even ran after her until she reached the crest of the
next hill. Beyond it, she tried not to stare at the growing
patchwork of ditch-enclosed fields and remember the

lives that had been displaced. Nevertheless, Jane's mood was black as scorched soil by the time she arrived at the bridge leading to Buttevant. She considered for a moment leaving Spencer to his own devices and heading north toward Churchtown, where she'd heard from Kathleen that some of the other families had fled. But she had nothing to offer those families now, and Clara's ploy of sending the Englishman along could not be disregarded without consequences. She had no option but to escort the rogue back.

At one end of the narrow stone bridge across the Awbeg, she waited while a cart pulled by an ancient donkey finished its slow trek across the bridge. A little old man, looking like some gnarled leprechaun, sat on the cart smoking a clay pipe. As she waited, she adjusted the knot of the wrap at her throat and tried to decide on how she could arrange it to hide her chin and mouth, if need be. She gave up finally. The blasted bruise was just too pronounced. She wished now that she hadn't lost her mother's hat.

As the donkey and cart were almost over the bridge, Jane spotted the tall, lean frame of Sir Nicholas leading his horse behind. There was someone else following the cart as well.

Despite her well-founded bias against him, at this moment she had to admire the air of confidence that surrounded the Englishman. Here was a man who was well aware of his advantages in life. But where the other aristocrats wallowed in them, Spencer appeared quite unencumbered. The man maintained no air of hostility to hide his fears of the lower classes. He seemed to feel no need for cloaking himself in displays of haughty indifference. She had seen the way he'd treated the grooms at Woodfield House this morning. She'd also been aware of him on their ride earlier, looking about with keen interest at the landscape and at the people. He had sharp powers of observation—that was obvious—and it was a quality that was sadly lacking in others of his class. Most, Jane thought, preferred to live insulated lives, moving about with blinders on.

He was one who would bear watching.

The cart neared the river's edge, and Jane knew the

moment when Sir Nicholas turned his gaze upon her. Their eyes met for only an instant, and as an already familiar warmth washed through her, she immediately looked away.

This was a future brother-in-law, she sharply reminded herself, totally appalled by the sensations racing through her body. The image in her mind of Clara standing beside Spencer calmed her immediately.

As the loaded cart went over the last bump and cleared the bridge, the old carter raised his battered hat to her, but said nothing. Nodding in return, Jane pushed her horse forward to meet their guest, and noticed with whom Sir Nicholas was walking. Her fingers immediately tightened around the reins. Every nerve in her body became taut, and she fought the desire to ride away.

"Top of the morning, Miss Jane. I cannot believe my good fortune today."

She made no pretence of returning the exuberance of Sir Robert Musgrave's greeting. Instead, she turned her attention to Spencer, trying to imagine how well these two men might be acquainted. She considered once again the possible reason for his silence at Woodfield House about her secret. She frowned, realizing that she simply didn't want to believe that he'd just been biding his time until he could meet with the magistrate. Spencer's expression revealed nothing.

"I must apologize for keeping you waiting, Miss Jane," Nicholas said as the two men finally reached her. "I was intercepted by the magistrate here. It appears that he was planning a visit to Woodfield House for the purpose of interviewing me. I tried to finish our business and save him the ride over."

"Good morning, Sir Robert," she said tersely. "No company of dragoons to accompany you this morning?"

"Not on so fine a morning as this," the man answered, his gaze lingering on the bruise by her mouth. "But to be completely honest, Sir Nicholas, I did have a second reason for calling at Woodfield House . . . and here she is before me."

From the very moment of the magistrate's arrival this past spring, Jane had found herself at odds with the man. The ordeal had begun at a fair in Mallow where, after their initial introduction, Musgrave had been almost belligerent in attempting to make himself her escort. Jane's refusals of him had fallen on deaf ears, unfortunately. And when she finally put her foot down—rejecting his continuing advances in no uncertain terms—others had overheard, and word of it had circulated quickly.

Of course, all of this had occurred before the new magistrate had learned of the scandals of Jane's past.

And that had made the insult cut much deeper.

Jane refused to flinch beneath the man's predatory stare. "What business have you with me, sir?"

"I think you know, Miss Jane."

"I fear that you are mistaken, Sir Robert."

"But you see, I have decided to improve my last offer . . . substantially."

Jane restrained her temper. Having seen Queen Mab in passing at the Buttevant Horse Fair this past July—and having observed Jane's attachment to the horse—the magistrate had suddenly developed a keen desire to acquire the animal. Since then he had been pressing to purchase the horse, claiming he wanted Mab to breed with his own prize stallions. Feeling Jane's resistance to sell, Sir Robert had made an offer to Sir Thomas for the purchase of the mare.

Naturally, Jane had been irate. Though it was her horse, there was no telling what her father might do. Sir Thomas, however, had apparently not been particularly inclined to satisfy the whim of the new magistrate—a man he had openly called a fop before the family—for he had bluntly declined the offer.

"I have learned my lesson, Miss Jane. I now know that it is wiser to talk of purchasing your fine mare with you—the person who obviously has the final say."

Sir Robert's words smacked more of condescension than humility. Even as she considered this, she watched the confident smile steal across his face as he let his gaze travel the length of her before coming to rest again on her bruised mouth.

"I would have been far more comfortable discussing with Sir Thomas such decidedly earthy activities as mounting, coupling, and breeding . . ."

"I shall take you at your word on that, Sir Robert."

His eyes narrowed at her insinuation, but she didn't care. She was tired of the sexual innuendo that the magistrate insisted on weaving lately into his conversations with her. Always—at the edges of his words, in the inflection of his voice, in the look in his eye—she found his sly intimations.

"But before we get to that, miss, I am most curious to know how you came by such a nasty bruise to your lovely face. Indeed, your lips are . . ."

"Accidents happen, sir. This bruise is none of your concern. But if you have any thoughts of making another offer for my horse, the answer is the same. She is *not* for sale."

He nudged his horse a step forward, until his boots brushed against her own. Mab stood firm, and Jane, too, refused to be intimidated. She patted the horse's neck.

"But you haven't even heard the new offer."

"The answer is the same." She drawled each word as if she were speaking to a small child. "And I beg that you not make this the source of any further unpleasantness."

"I let it rest for now. But about the bruise . . ."

"And now, sir, if you will forgive us, Reverend Adams is expecting us."

She wheeled Mab away from the magistrate and found herself looking into the stern face of Spencer. The murderous glare that the man was directing toward Musgrave somehow pleased her.

"I fear that I cannot allow you to go just yet. Accidents *are* my concern," Musgrave called out, turning his horse, as well. "Especially when they happen to a charming damosel that I have sworn to protect."

"Sir, I am no *damosel*, and I have *never* needed your protection."

"Say what you will." The man's dark eyes narrowed—his gaze focusing more on her mouth. "But it is my responsibility to tame all rebelliousness in Cork . . . and that might arguably include solving the mystery of how and why someone like you should sustain such violence to her face."

Clara had been right. The excuse she'd used the day before would only make matters worse and draw the magistrate's suspicions. But her mind was empty of any other explanations.

"I am responsible for the condition of her face."

Jane whirled about to look at Spencer.

Musgrave's attention focused on the visitor. "Is that so, Sir Nicholas?"

"The kind lady is simply trying to protect my reputation, I fear. A clumsy accident in the stables yesterday, and one for which I must bear total blame."

"I don't think that Sir Robert . . ." she started, uncertain of what was to come or what she could say.

"The magistrate"—the Englishman cut her off—"strikes me as an understanding man. Indeed, he knows that accidents *do* happen. The fact is, sir, I pushed open the upper half of one of the stable doors, not knowing Miss Purefoy was approaching on the other side. It was a grievous mistake, but she has been *very* gracious in not embarrassing me before her family."

"Do you mean to tell me that *you*—?"

"I mean exactly what I have told you."

Spencer turned to Jane, who was having some difficulty hiding her surprise. The tingling warmth that spread through her as his blue eyes met hers briefly did nothing to help, either.

The magistrate yanked at his mount's bridle. "It would appear, sir, that you had an *exceedingly* busy day yesterday. Single-handedly rescuing a clergyman from a horde of outlaws, unhorsing their leader, and then this extensive damage . . . I just wonder what are the chances of . . ." The words trailed off, but the suggestion hung in the air.

With deliberate slowness, Spencer removed one of his gloves. "From the tone of your words, sir, it would appear that you have some difficulty accepting statements that are conveyed to you. I *hope* I am mistaken."

The magistrate's stare locked with that of the baronet for a long, tense moment.

"My deepest apologies to you and to Miss Purefoy," Musgrave said finally, bowing with cool courtesy. "One's duty to the Crown can make one jump at shadows sometimes, I'm afraid. My best to your family, Miss Jane."

# Chapter 10

"Thank you."

The words were just whispers in the wind, but Nicholas heard them nonetheless.

As they topped the next hill, leaving the river valley—and the magistrate—behind them, he glanced over at Jane but did not respond. His anger still gnawed at him, but he was pleased to have her finally riding with him, rather than leading him all over the countryside in another merry game of fox and hounds.

"Is he always so insolent?"

"Each time I meet him, it seems to get worse." It was obvious that she was still feeling the effects of the exchange. "But I understand that many of the English gentry find him quite accommodating."

"So he is impudent only when he chooses to be."

"And when he has considered the social rank of the person he is dealing with." She gave him a pleased look. "I believe you intimidated him."

Nicholas didn't say it, but he wished he'd done more.

He had felt Sir Robert's eyes on their backs as they rode away from Buttevant. Not that he particularly gave a damn. By 'sblood, he'd come damned close to challenging the unprincipled dog for his treatment of her.

"I admire your restraint," he said. The simply spoken compliment earned him a warm smile. "Despite your agitation, you never lost your temper." Or cursed in Gaelic, he silently finished.

"It might sound like cowardice, but it is not. I prefer

not to draw any undue attention to myself . . . especially from someone like him."

She didn't have to explain more, for Nicholas understood her. Her practiced self-restraint was due to her covert activities with the Shanavests.

She moved in front of him through a narrow passage at the crest of a hill. Talking with Jane was already settling his frame of mind. He hoped that he had the same effect on her.

"I should have insisted on coming along on your visit to your friend."

She half turned in the saddle. "I don't believe she is one whom you might generally find in your circle of acquaintances."

"I shan't correct you on what you do not know. But I will say that anything would have been preferable to hanging about Buttevant and consorting with some bloody government official."

"Better you than I, sir."

He smiled and noticed for the first time the ragged wrap she had around her shoulders. "I see you have found a scarf to replace your long-lost hat."

She touched the wool on her shoulder as he came alongside her. "Very observant. It is a gift, and it came from a woman who, I know, valued it highly. Aside from her children, it may have been her most prized possession."

He watched the way she touched the wool again as if it were made of the finest silk. The simple gesture revealed another layer of this woman whom he was finding most fascinating.

They rode along for a few moments, both lost in their own thoughts. Nicholas broke the silence.

"Despite the little unpleasantness at the bridge, this has been a most enjoyable day. I owe you my sincere thanks for your insistence on having me come along."

When she turned her gaze on him again, Nicholas was amazed at the jolt of awareness that ran through him.

She stared at him for another lengthy moment and then a bubble of laughter escaped her. Delighted by the transformation in her, he joined in. When she laughed,

Jane Purefoy threw off the sadness that hung over her like a cloud. Something else took its place. Something free and full of life. She was attractive to the point of being truly stunning.

"*Insistence* that you come along?" She shook her head. "Sir Nicholas, you speak as if you heard not a word that passed between my sister and me."

"I admit to hearing nothing of what was a private conversation. But you *must* have been agreeable, otherwise I'm sure I would not be riding with you at this moment."

She shook her head good-naturedly. "Sir, you know quite well that I was not given a choice. But now that you mention it, I believe you must have been in on this entire scheme."

"Cut me as you please, Miss Purefoy, but do not wrongfully accuse me." He added as an afterthought, "But tell me, isn't this much more pleasant than our little disagreement in the woods yesterday?"

A flicker of shared knowledge passed between them. Nicholas couldn't help but notice the gentle blush that crept into her face.

"We are late," she finally replied quietly, spurring her horse into a canter.

He fell in beside her and looked at his timepiece. "We have plenty of time. The sun is not yet high, and my watch tells me we have more than enough time to keep our appointment with the good Parson Adams. Do you have some other reason to rush?"

"Sir, you came out today to spend the day with my sister. I have already taken you from her needlessly. It is my responsibility to return you to her as expeditiously as possible."

"Allow me to correct this misunderstanding." He watched her carefully to gauge her reaction. "I came out today with the hope of spending time in *your* company. I have been looking to find an opportunity when we could speak."

Her face immediately sobered. "It was an unfortunate thing that we had to run into each other yesterday as we did. There must be many questions . . . concerns that you have." She gradually slowed her mare to a walk. "I assure you that Clara takes no part in anything inappropriate. She is a perfectly well-bred daughter and subject of the Crown. She is totally innocent of my . . . well, my interests . . . and always has been."

"I don't care to speak about Clara."

"And you should not allow that scene yesterday to affect your marriage plans," Jane insisted. "You should not blame her for what I do . . . or hold my family responsible for *my* actions. Believe me, for years I have lived with the certain knowledge that if my parents ever found me out, they would be the first to hand me over to the magistrate and his executioner."

There was a sadness in her tone, and Nicholas wished he could dispute her words. But based on the little that he'd seen himself of Sir Thomas and his wife, he didn't doubt her in the slightest.

"And now . . . suddenly . . . I find I am at the mercy of a stranger," she added a moment later.

Nicholas knew he should assure her that he had not revealed her secret to anyone and he had no plans of doing it in the future, either. Whatever motivated her to act as she did was her own concern. He didn't give a damn, personally, about the possibility of scandal. And in spite of Bishop Russell's unrelenting condemnation yesterday, Nicholas himself had seen her cut the ropes binding the hands of the clergyman. But he wasn't ready to admit anything that would set her mind at ease. He wasn't ready to have her totally disregard him.

"All I can assure you so far is that my answers to those who have questioned me about yesterday have been—" he searched for the right word—"imprecise."

"And why *is* that?" Her eyes were sharp as she awaited his answer.

"Because I have seen how we Englishmen tend to treat those whom we conquer and colonize." Unconsciously he tightened his grip on the reins. "I make it my business not to judge others based on so little information. I make it a habit not to intervene unless there is a sound reason."

"Although he didn't deserve it, I set that bishop free yesterday. So what was your reason for pulling me off my horse?"

"I was desperate for an introduction. I apologize. I *am* trying to improve my methods of meeting people."

Her laughter this time was full and lingered in his ear like the prettiest of songs. He gazed at her, wondering if she had any idea about her power to charm. Her dark and enchanting eyes turned on him, and he felt the undeniable pull in his gut.

"Then I can assume that you said nothing about our earlier *meeting* to the magistrate?"

"You are perfectly safe in making that assumption."

"How about revealing anything in the future meetings with the man?"

"You are quite persistent," he remarked, enjoying this undivided attention. "As things stand now, Sir Robert and I seem to have developed an immediate aversion toward each other. Unless something changes, I doubt we would have future discussions on the topic, either."

Mischief danced in her eyes as she pressed him further. "Of course, this vague assurance is only good until I stab you in the arm again."

"You shall not have that opportunity very soon, Miss Jane." He gave her a meaningful glance. "I don't believe next time I shall allow you off your back so quickly."

This time the blush was deeper—the awareness between them potent. Nicholas realized the edginess was starting to take charge by the way her hands tightened around the reins of the horse. He was quick to change the subject, as he had no wish to shorten their time together.

"In any case, I assure you that I would not be choosing Musgrave as a confidant. If any questions or misunderstandings arise, my inclination would be to seek explanations and answers from *you*."

She studied him more closely, and Nicholas found himself hoping that she would approve of what she saw.

"You are far more open-minded than I expected—and far more candid. Clearly, we do great wrong in judging a person purely on his station in life."

"You are too hard on yourself."

"I think not," she said matter-of-factly. "Though I can think of no other Englishman I have ever met who would not have seen it as his duty to expose me—an outlaw *and* a woman—if not to the magistrate, then certainly to my father."

"I can see that you do not think too highly of my brethren."

"I fear you are correct in that observation." She gave him a half smile. "But of course, there are always exceptions. Parson Adams is a man who places decency and compassion above greed and class and colonial domination."

Even the mention of the minister's name managed to irk Nicholas. He was enjoying the feeling of ease that was developing with this woman, and the thought of a possible competitor rankled somewhat.

"And may I ask if you have formed any firm plans regarding your marriage to the good Parson Adams?"

The look of incredulity she directed at him was as pleasurable as it was unexpected.

"What in heaven's name should cause you to say something like that? Marriage? Henry Adams and I? That is simply preposterous!"

"Is it?"

"Absolutely. We are no more than old and trusted friends."

"A relationship that most couples can only hope to achieve . . . in the *best* of marriages."

She shook her head adamantly. "I fear you haven't been around a sufficient length of time to understand what things are like here, sir."

"Perhaps you'd be kind enough to enlighten me."

Jane took her time to answer, and he watched with some interest the internal battle that was all too openly reflected in her fair face.

"He . . . Reverend Adams is a respected clergyman. And I . . . well, I have a reputation that I managed to ruin in my youth. And my transgression was such that, no matter how many decades go by, no one shall ever forget." Her cheeks were flushed when she faced him fully, but her eyes were clear and steady. "It is just as well, though, that this topic has come up. And it is best that you should hear the truth from me, for sooner or later you are bound to hear it from someone else. And, frankly, I don't want any embellished version of *my* life to ruin my sister's future happiness."

"So this is 'what things are like' here? You and the good parson are kept apart by gossip and—what I assume to be—some ancient transgression against what are probably vague and outdated standards of respectability?"

"No."

"What did you do, Miss Jane? Participate in this . . . this steeple-chasing race I was just hearing about from the innkeeper in Buttevant? You must have given the bishop's horse and rider a sound thrashing before they found you out. Is that it?"

"Joke if you will, sir, but that is not it, at all. Nothing of the sort keeps Parson Adams and me apart." She gave a firm shake to her head, and more tendrils of her silky hair danced around her face. "As far as my past . . . and reputation . . . the truth and the charges against me are much more severe than what you just mentioned. Let me just put it this way . . . I am *not* considered in any way marriageable by genteel society."

Nicholas could only guess an elopement would be the cause of such ruckus. There was so much that he wanted to know about Jane. But he had to wait until she was ready to confide in him.

"But as I mentioned before, rumors and accusations are *not* what keeps us apart. Henry Adams and I are simply friends."

"Friends?"

"Indeed. We are friends and nothing more. *Nothing* more! Have you never had a woman as a friend? A relationship that is simply built on trust and mutual respect? A friendship that is pure and elevated . . . one that might be considered platonic?"

Nicholas put on a great show of thinking about the question. Inside, though, he was delighted to hear that he wasn't competing with the clergyman for her attentions.

*Competing for her attentions.*

The admission made him glance at her again. He found her still waiting for an answer.

"Once or twice, I believe I have come close to establishing a friendship such as the kind you describe. But each time it occurred, my *friend* soon became dissatisfied with the boundaries of that relationship. I beg your pardon, but it has been my experience that women always seem to want more."

"Once or twice?" She shook her head disapprovingly. "It has been my experience that generalizations based on limited knowledge are rarely correct and never productive in finding the truth, sir."

"My apologies." He bowed politely. "Women whom *I* have known happen to seek more."

*"Englishwomen."* She uttered the word as if it were poison on her tongue.

"I find it curious that you do not classify yourself as an Englishwoman, but I see you don't think much of *them*, either."

"I cannot believe you *really* want to hear my opinion on this topic."

"But I do."

There wasn't much silent debate now.

"Many Englishwomen that I have met have simply submitted to traditions that have been impressed upon them. As a result, they have allowed themselves to become blinded by the shallow niceties of being admired for their pleasing looks or for the fashionable cut of their garments or for their silent obedience. And in the process, the things that are important—spirit, independence, intelligence—are viewed by the world, and by many women as well, as highly unfeminine and even *unnatural*."

"I take it that you find this to be false and limiting to women."

"And to society! Dr. Samuel Johnson, a man who is perhaps the leading light of English letters today, is reported to have said, 'A woman preaching is like a dog walking on its hind legs. It is not done well, but one is surprised to find it done at all.' How very narrow this kind of low humor is when one considers such women as Margaret More Roper and the Duchess of Pembroke and Lady Mary Wroth, to name but a few!"

"Indeed," he replied. "Women of great wit and character."

"And yet," she pressed on, "many Englishwomen—perhaps even most—are willing to overlook how low they are ranked in the world. They are trained to lead their lives in obedience and blissful ignorance, and they bury their spirit and their will and their deepest passions before they even cross life's threshold into womanhood. They allow themselves to be robbed of the essence of what it is to be a human being."

Jane's cheeks were flushed, her eyes bright with passionate conviction. And Nicholas knew in that moment that he'd never met a woman as exciting and intelligent as this one. The fact that she was Egan, a rebel leader, made perfect sense, for it would be impossible not to follow her if she carried this same passion into the cause she fought for.

As they approached the end of a field, she nudged her horse to the edge of the tall grass, keeping their horses side by side.

"I didn't mean to sound so complaining . . . so critical. Certainly your own family is so different from what I just described."

"Indeed, my mother and sister can easily be considered 'different.' " He smiled. "But there may be something in what you say."

"No." She bent her head under a low branch as they passed into a grove of trees. The leaves brushed against her hair. "I *must* apologize. After how civil you've been to me, and how pleasant Lady Spencer and your sister were to all of us last night, it is utterly wrong of me to commit the same error I have just accused you of making. No generalizing. There are many exceptions to the kind of women I was speaking of. There are so many exceptions to everything in life."

"And I'm thankful for it, as there is nothing more tiring than the mundane . . . a charge that could never be lodged against you."

Their gazes locked again when she turned to him, and it was impossible to ignore the awareness of desire that flowed between them. She immediately looked away, but Nicholas's gaze lingered on the few autumn leaves that had entangled themselves in her hair. She was part of nature—part of this land. None of the discontent he felt in the company of Clara existed in these moments with Jane. He was perfectly at ease with her.

He was disappointed to find the village of Ballyclough beneath them when they crested the next hill. Jane reached up and removed the wrap from her shoulder. Handling it carefully, she folded it and held it in her lap. She caught him watching her.

"For Clara's sake, I cannot look too tattered in public. She would be horrified to think you saw me wearing this."

"I'll keep your secret."

She smiled self-consciously. "I find I am in debt to you for keeping so many of them."

They were on the edge of the village, but Nicholas was not ready for their time together to end. A muddy dog trotted out from the first of the village cottages, sniffing at Jane's boot.

"What we were speaking of before . . . of friendships between men and women. You really believe such a thing is feasible?"

"Absolutely. There are many men that I consider friends. A difference in gender has never stopped me from treating another person as an equal. As a woman, however, I can only hope to be treated the same."

Jane answered the wave of an older woman who straightened up from digging in a small kitchen garden beside a cottage.

"And do you think *we* might be friends?"

She turned to him, obviously surprised. "I . . . I cannot see why not. As a future brother and sister, it will certainly be beneficial for all if we were—"

"I have changed my mind. I shall not be asking Clara to become my wife."

Jane yanked at the reins of her horse, halting Mab suddenly. He, too, stopped.

"Why?" she asked. "You told me that you would not let what you know of me—"

"My decision has nothing to do with you," Nicholas lied, knowing full well it had everything to do with her. "Even before my family and I left London, I was not fully persuaded on the notion of marrying. If I had been committed to marrying your sister, I would have at least sent along my lawyers beforehand."

"But my parents. Clara believed . . ."

He let his agitation show. "I misled no one. I served as your sister's escort on a few occasions this past spring, but hardly placed any claims upon her. There were no promises made—no assumptions made—no talks ensuing. And when your parents made the invitation to visit Woodfield House, they understood that I had made no marital overtures."

"But you just told me that you have *changed* your mind. Change indicates that there was a—"

"I was attempting to be completely honest with you. I have always assumed one friend can be honest with another. And since I have never discussed marriage or proposed, Clara should never know the difference."

She leaned toward him, grasping the bridle of his horse. Her eyes showed the temper burning within. "Then, as a *friend*, pray explain to me what caused your change of heart."

"She is not the one . . . and for many reasons. The difference in our ages. Her naïveté and my experience. Her hesitant approach to life and my recklessness." He didn't release Jane's gaze, nor let her speak when she opened her mouth. "It is true that this past year I have been seriously contemplating marriage. I have arrived at a stage in life when it is necessary to have a wife and an heir to fulfill my family obligations. And I . . . I also wish to pursue some other plans that have been ripening in my mind for the past few years. I realize now that I had an impractical, almost hypothetical view of marriage. I had not considered thoroughly enough the qualities of the woman I should be marrying."

"Come, Sir Nicholas. The truth is, now that you've learned about *me*, you find my sister 'impractical.' And you can afford to be more judicious in your choice."

"I told you this has nothing to do with *you*."

"But it does," she spat back at him. "If she was good enough a week ago . . . a month ago . . . last spring. Then she should be now."

"But she wasn't . . ." The look of hurt in Jane's face was immediate.

"May I be so bold as to interrupt?"

Both of them turned simultaneously. There were nearly a dozen people staring from a respectful distance around them. Reverend Adams stood nearby as well, looking up at the two riders expectantly. Nicholas hadn't realized that Jane was still holding the bridle of his horse until she abruptly let go.

"Of course," Nicholas responded belatedly to the clergyman. He realized that they were within walking distance of the parsonage, so he climbed down from his horse. "We were finished with our discussion."

"I hardly think so," Jane corrected, dismounting as well before Nicholas could offer to help her down. "But we shall continue where we left off at a more appropriate time and place."

The comment was addressed to him—her direct look challenging him to contradict her. Nicholas bowed politely. If this meant that Jane was willing to spend more time in his company—even to try to sway his decision about marriage and Clara—then he would be a fool to object. In fact, he was quite pleased with the turn of events and of the prospect of what was to come. His mood darkened, though, when he saw the country parson reach up and remove those loose leaves from Jane's hair.

The touch seemed too intimate, too casual, he thought. And the minister's attentions toward her caused Nicholas to question again if there could not be more between them than she was admitting.

"Are you coming?" she turned and asked after Adams had led her a few steps in the direction of the rectory.

"I am." Nicholas started up the hill after them. "I have no intention of being left behind."

# Chapter 11

"*M*other!"

At the sudden outcry from behind her, Alexandra Spencer jumped and then pressed a hand to her chest. She hadn't heard the door to her daughter's room open. She hadn't been aware of any other noise but the creaking she'd heard inside these walls. She could have sworn something was behind this stretch of painted plaster.

"Did I frighten you?" Frances closed the door of her room behind her.

"Of course not!"

"Then what are you doing listening to the wall?"

"I wasn't listening to the wall, Fanny."

The young woman came closer and peered at the solid wall of the hallway and back again at Alexandra's face. "Then what are you doing standing here? Mother, it was not my imagination that you were pressing your ear against this wall."

"It certainly *was* your imagination." She took a handkerchief out of her sleeve and patted the beads of sweat that had formed on her forehead and upper lip.

"Did you hear a noise?" Apparently unconvinced, Frances mimicked what she had seen her mother doing and pressed an ear to the cold plaster. "Maybe this place is haunted. Or do you think there are secret passages running behind these walls? I love that in the novels, don't you? From what I have learned so far about the history of this place, there was a castle that was previously built on this hill. Now wouldn't it be exciting if . . . ?"

"No, it would *not* be." Lady Spencer placed a hand on the small of her daughter's back and, pressing lightly, started her down the corridor. "Whatever you thought I was doing, it was only your imagination running away with you. My room is extremely warm this afternoon, and I was simply enjoying some of the coolness of this corridor before going downstairs to dinner."

Frances gave an impish grin. "Do you know there are patches of red that climb right up the skin of your neck whenever you try to fib?"

"Frances Marie, this is no way for a young woman to be speaking to her mother." Alexandra paused at the end of the hall and before starting down the stairs. "But on a totally different matter, what were you doing in your room? I thought I heard your and Nicholas's voices coming from the corridor only a few minutes ago. Why are you not with him . . . pestering him . . . doing your sisterly duty?"

"He dismissed me." Fanny pouted in the direction of his door. "He wouldn't say a word about his day. He's horrible. He wouldn't answer a *single* question. And he became quite agitated—snappish even—when I asked him if he'd had the opportunity to propose to Clara yet. He'd better marry soon, Mother. He's becoming positively curmudgeonly."

"You know, dear, I think it might be best if you were to leave that topic alone for now."

"But why?" The young woman crossed her arms over her chest. "Did we not come all the way to Ireland so that Nicholas could propose? It would be so much more pleasant to get to know Clara in the fashion of a sister-to-be than continue in this required hostess-and-guest relationship. We are so close in age, and there is so much we could plan and do together if everyone stopped tiptoeing around the subject. We . . ."

Both of their heads turned as Nicholas emerged from his door. From his shining dark boots to the short, fitted black jacket to the buff-colored buckskin breeches, he was the very image of the country gentleman on his way to dinner. Alexandra noticed, though, the tenseness that had settled around his lips. The look he was directing at Fanny was impatient, if not downright dangerous.

"Am I interrupting something?"

"Why, yes!" The young woman was quick to answer. "You are interrupting my complaints to Mother about . . ."

"Why not be on your way downstairs, young lady." Alexandra turned a sharp look on her daughter.

"But Mother, I think this is a perfectly good opportunity for . . ."

"Downstairs, Frances Marie." This time the mother's tone left no doubt that she meant to be obeyed. "Tell Sir Thomas and Lady Purefoy that Nicholas and I will be down shortly."

Rankled but dutiful, the young woman gathered her skirts in two fists and disappeared down the stairs.

"Thank you." Nicholas closed his door and offered his arm to Alexandra. "I love her dearly, but I have lately acquired so much appreciation for what you have been saving me from these past few years."

"Fanny is a good girl. And she is not always so impatient." She placed a hand in the crook of her son's arm but refused to go downstairs yet. "Is there anything that you want to talk to me about?"

He glanced at her cautiously.

"You know, Nicholas . . . I could be of assistance to you." She paused, gentled her voice even more and looked up into blue eyes that could not hide his distress. "I am still your mother, and there is no reason why you should shoulder all of this pressure alone. I can, with great subtlety, bring up a topic. I can drop a hint regarding your state of mind. Whatever you wish. I can even distract them, if that is what you desire. I want you to know most of all, however, that you have every right to take your time before committing to anything permanent."

His other hand came up and pressed Alexandra's affectionately against his arm.

She looked about the empty hallway and lowered her voice. "I know I should have had this talk with you before we even arrived here. But now is as good a time

as any, I suppose." She paused, gathering her thoughts.
"We both know that in our society there are certain
requirements—*formalities* is perhaps a better word—that
must be observed before men and women enter into a
marriage partnership. Yes, indeed, partnership is the correct way of stating it, for it has become very much a
business relationship. Therefore, a business contract is
required of all parties."

"What is your point, Mother?"

"I am getting to it, Nicholas. Knowing you as I do . . .
understanding you better than you think . . . I believe
you need more than a business partner. You need a
woman who can match you in will and in wit. You do
not need some ornament who will expect to be put on
a pedestal as a wife."

"You are *very* observant."

"And so are you." She patted his arm. "A quality
inherited fully from my side of the family."

He gave her a gentle bow of the head and smiled.

"I hope you will not consider my comments as meddle-
some, but I have been greatly disturbed by the thought
that perhaps my presence here might press you into making a hasty decision . . ." She let the words drift in the air.
This was the most she'd allowed herself to become openly
involved in Nicholas's life in many, many years.

"As well, you should be the first one who is told." He
placed a hand on the darkly gleaming wood of the banister. "She is *not* for me. I shall not make an offer for
Clara's hand."

Alexandra stifled a great sigh of relief. She tried to
withhold any sign of jubilation and keep her expression impassive.

"And I am not for her, either. I shall make my intentions known to Sir Thomas tonight, for I do not wish
for any misunderstandings or hard feelings to develop.
We shall try to avoid any unpleasantness." He glanced
down the shadowy stairs before turning his attention
back to her. "In fact, if Sir Thomas and Lady Purefoy
have no objection, I wish to remain at Woodfield House
for the fortnight we had originally planned."

"Splendid!" she managed to squeak, too pleased to
say any more.

As they started down the stairs to join their hosts for dinner, Alexandra considered telling Nicholas about her little discovery in the attic that morning. Though he'd never pursued painting himself, she knew he was as much of a connoisseur of the arts as she was. She was certain that he, too, would be much taken by Jane's paintings. She would like to be there to see his face as the power of her message conveyed itself to him. But she refrained from singing the praises of the older sister. Nicholas would have to discover her all on his own.

And staying at Woodfield House for the full fortnight could present the most provocative opportunities.

"And how did you find the new magistrate, Sir Nicholas?"

Clara idly pushed the pheasant about on her plate as they all waited in silence for the baronet to answer her father's question. She dared not peek up at him, though, for she was beginning to suspect that Sir Nicholas had not heard the question at all. Indeed, for most of dinner he'd seemed considerably distracted. His interest appeared to dwell thoughtfully on Jane's empty place across the table.

Earlier, when her sister and the visitor had arrived at the rectory in Ballyclough with Henry, Clara had immediately sensed the tension between the two. The air in the small dining room felt charged, like a summer night before a thunderstorm. Indeed, there had been few words exchanged between the two during the modest luncheon. Thinking about the time there at the rectory, Clara felt the cold lump form again in her stomach. Henry had never once looked at her during the meal.

Then, on the ride back to Woodfield House, Jane had again chosen to ride far ahead of Clara and Sir Nicholas. No one had said anything beyond the necessary courtesies, either on the road or upon reaching Woodfield House.

All of this, however, did little to distract her from her own pain.

Her father pointedly cleared his throat, drawing their brooding guest's attention. "I was hoping to get your opinion on—"

"The new magistrate."

Clara was relieved to hear the baronet finally speak. "Yes."

"I was considering my response, Sir Thomas."

"Measuring it, you mean." Her father let out a burst of laughter, and Clara felt her mood lighten. "You didn't like him, by thunder. I'm sure Musgrave would be distraught to hear that."

Sir Nicholas directed a sharp look toward the head of the table. "I had no idea the magistrate would care about my opinion one way or the other. Perhaps I should have shared it with him before we parted ways this morning."

"Then you do not deny it." Obviously pleased, Sir Thomas shook his head and downed a great swallow of wine. "Please allow me, sir, to pass on your reaction to the man. I would very much enjoy ruining Sir Robert's day with such news."

"You really would waste your energies on such a pointless exercise? Surely there must be more stimulating things for one to do in this country."

The comment, delivered in a slightly mocking tone by Sir Nicholas, caused a ripple of amusement to emanate from all the women at the table. Clara, though, quickly stifled her own mirth as she saw a dark cloud descend immediately over her father's mood.

He cleared his throat in that all too familiar manner that indicated his displeasure. She stared at him, thinking desperately for a way to ease the renewed tension.

"I wonder, though," Sir Nicholas added soberly, "if your enjoyment in 'ruining Sir Robert's mood' might stem from the fact that he has succeeded you in a task that you excelled at for so many years. I believe it is not uncommon to be somewhat critical of the person who has taken on one's own position and responsibilities."

After a long uncomfortable pause, the older man's head nodded once in agreement as he gestured to a servant for more wine. "Indeed, sir. Very observant. And no harm in it, either."

Clara fought back her surprise at the exchange. She had never heard anyone speak to her father quite so bluntly. But Sir Thomas's calm and equally candid response nearly bowled her over. Her father emptied another glass of wine before continuing.

"I was the king's magistrate in this region for more than twenty years. When I took the post here, the violence against the gentry was more vicious than anything you might have heard in the stories of the Sussex smugglers' war of the forties. But I handled them, sir. With a strong hand, I made the people here know that civil authority would be respected and obeyed. Those who would not respect the king's law, however, would learn to fear it. Because of my work, sir, the landlords finally found it possible to take charge of their own lands and control their tenants."

Sir Thomas's hand shook as he lifted his glass again. "And later . . . when the investment in pasture became more profitable than tillage, when some of the landlords decided to lease the land to graziers instead of to tenant farmers, I was the one who challenged the rebels . . . the Whiteboys . . . or Shanavests . . . or whatever bloody hell they call themselves."

Clara's stomach clenched in a knot. Her mother's face had gone deathly white. Totally unconcerned, Sir Thomas drank down another glass of wine and continued.

"The Whiteboys only exist because they dare to defy common decency and threaten their own kind. The wretches force others of their class to take an oath under threat of violence. And that, sir, is illegal. Nine years ago, we caught five of their leaders not far from Waterford. I was one of the judges who ordered the ruffians hanged. By hanging those five, I was sending a message to everyone that the administration of oaths in such a way would be treated as the capital offence it was. In a single stroke, I curtailed their aggression dramatically." He pointed a finger at Nicholas. "And this is the root of the problem with Musgrave. I keep telling him that instead of wasting so much of his time socializing with the landed gentry . . . people who for the most part find him intolerable anyway . . . and instead of going around the district harassing the papist tenants on insignificant matters like the nonpayment of rents, he should be going after these rebel leaders. He needs to be concentrating his efforts on scum like this Egan that you ran into yesterday . . . or these two others they call Liam and Patrick, a pair of blackguards as bad as the first. And then there is another rogue who goes by the name of Finn. That one doesn't show his face very often, but we know he has his fingers in the activities of at least three of the neighboring counties. Until the day these black-guards' heads are hung on a post in Cork City, Musgrave will garner no respect from the gentry. Thus far he has done nothing to instill fear into the hearts of these rebels."

"I saw a rather large barracks being erected in Buttevant."

"By thunder, talk about a pointless exercise!" Sir Thomas banged his glass on the table. "Those dragoons will do nothing but stir up these rebels. We need strong *civil* authority in Ireland, not military occupation."

Stealing a glance out of the corner of her eye, Clara could see that Sir Nicholas was staring at the brocade on the silk tablecloth. His face was a mask, but she sensed that he *knew* about Jane. She had not openly questioned her sister about what had taken place yesterday, but when Clara considered the cut on his arm, the blow to her face, the silent message that clearly passed between them when they first met, she was certain. Sir Nicholas *had* to know that Jane and Egan were one and the same.

"I have even made some recommendations to Mus-grave on how he could proceed to set a trap for them."

"A trap . . . ?"

Lady Purefoy practically jumped to her feet. "I . . . I . . . believe it would be best if we women retired to the parlor. This kind of talk is far too shocking, Sir Thomas, and you shall be frightening our guests out of their wits." She looked across the table. "Will you favor us with your company tonight, Sir Nicholas? Or are you staying behind with my husband this evening?"

Clara knew it was not like her mother to take charge such as this, but as her father drained his wineglass yet again, she was grateful for the interruption.

"If you will forgive me this evening, m'lady"—the bar-onet stood and bowed politely as the rest of the women rose as well—"I should like to stay behind and speak with Sir Thomas. There are a few topics pressing that I believe we need to discuss."

Catherine Purefoy practically beamed. "Absolutely, Sir Nicholas. And please take your time. We shall be waiting in the parlor for you both."

Clara felt as if a cold stone had lodged itself in her stomach. She dragged herself toward the door, watching her parents exchange a look of satisfaction. The momentary air of harmony that hung between them, though, was a stark reminder of the sacrifice that she had decided six months ago to make—the sacrifice she'd confessed this very morning that she hadn't the heart to go through with.

But with Henry's rejection today, Clara was now lost, set adrift, destined to be swept along on life's currents.

This marriage was to be an emotionless contract between families. Very well. She would suffer through it and reap the good it would bring her parents. She *was* selfless—in spite of Henry's condemnation—and she would prove it.

Egan held back her immediate objections to the idea and—as she always did—tried to consider what good it might bring to the people most affected by the English king's brutality.

"Ye all know that this is not the first time they've extended an invitation to us," Liam said. "But this gathering in Kildare of the Shanavest leaders will be the largest ever held. And by having representatives from all over the south, they know they can plan a campaign of unrest that will be felt all the way to London. Many feel it is time to send that message of unity to every magistrate and high sheriff in Ireland."

"It could be a trap." Jenny, the eldest in the group, frowned at the circle of faces before turning back to Liam and Egan.

Liam shrugged. "It could be. But we all live every day with a noose about our necks."

The leader paused, and Egan watched him focus on the discussion of those who had gathered inside the ruined abbey. She knew as well as he did that this decision could not be made without a consensus of those who were here. What they decided would affect the future of all.

Liam shot a look at Egan, but she continued to keep her silence. In the past, she had always spoken against uniting their own efforts with the work of the Shanavests of Carlow, Queen's County, or Kildare. Word traveled quickly in the countryside, and what she had mostly heard of those groups in recent years had to do with their increasing tendency toward violence. Where her own small band would only go so far to scare a land-owner or cleric or to sometimes steal back what had been taken from tenants, these others were known to burn houses, maim cattle, and even commit murder if they saw the need.

While both Liam and Egan tried hard to focus their efforts on helping the displaced, many of the Whiteboys from Dingle to Dundalk seemed only bent on revenge. For now, though, attending this gathering in Kildare seemed to offer benefits too great to ignore.

" 'Tis a good two days to get there . . . and the same to get back," Patrick said, voicing the concern that a few had already expressed quietly. "Most of us cannot just go off and leave our families and our farms. I've still got a harvest to finish . . . and I'm a wee bit surprised that the meeting is to be held now."

"That's the very point of having it now." Liam crouched and picked up an old straw. "Wait until after the harvests are all done, and the English will be watch-ing for us."

Liam's gaze met Egan's. He was looking for her sup-port. She nodded.

"Is Finn going?" Jenny asked next.

"He cannot . . . and well he should not," Liam replied, studying the shredded bit of straw in his hand. Throwing it to the ground, he stood up and faced the rest. "Finn serves as our eyes and ears. We cannot afford to do without him for so long. Besides, outside of Cork, Wa-terford, or Tipperary, most of our brothers and sisters say he is something we've dreamed up."

"Ye don't have to go that far to hear that." Everyone laughed and turned to look at Ronan, who was standing against a ruined wall, his muscular arms crossed over his massive chest.

"Liam and I should go," Egan said to settle the matter before anyone could get distracted. "And while we are gone, Patrick can keep an eye on the runt here. Everyone else should go on with the harvest as if nothing were amiss."

Egan looked around at the group. She knew them all. Jenny. Liam. Ronan. Patrick. All of them. All of them had lived their entire lives in this little corner of Ireland, and they knew each other like family—celebrating and supporting each other through baptisms and weddings and funerals.

All seemed willing to go along with the suggestion. Jenny, though, was the one who brought up the problem Egan still had to resolve.

"We will all lend a hand and be sure Liam's absence will not mean trouble for his family. His landlord shan't miss him. But ye, Egan . . . to my thinking, ye shall be needing to do some fancy stepping to be away unnoticed for so long."

"That's my specialty." She nodded reassuringly to the group. "Fancy stepping."

"Aye, we have faith in ye, Egan." Patrick asked, "So when must ye be going?"

"Ten days," Liam answered. " 'Tis the latest we can go, if we want to get there in time."

# Chapter 12

None of this made any sense. None of it!

The young maidservant held the robe as Catherine Purefoy pushed her arms into it. Her nerves just couldn't take this. She hadn't retired more than half an hour earlier, and now her husband wished her in the dining room?

What a night! Sir Nicholas's comment at dinner had surprised her. Anticipation had then nearly killed her as she'd waited for the men to emerge from the dining room. Minutes had rolled into hours and there had been no news. Hope had finally given way to disappointment, though, and it became clear that she could not wait up any longer for them. Decency dictated that she should go to bed, so she had . . . though reluctantly.

How curious that Lady Spencer did not appear to share in the excitement at all. What a strange woman! And daughter, too! Soon after the women had retired to the parlor after dinner, the young Miss Spencer had simply gone to her room with a book under her arm. Lady Spencer had gone up to bed soon after the daughter without a worry in the world, it seemed. Well, Catherine thought with satisfaction, Lady Spencer would have her time when Frances was ready for the marriage market.

"Are you certain that he did not wish for Miss Clara, as well?" Catherine asked again.

"Aye, quite certain, m'lady," the servant replied.

"And Sir Thomas *said* he wanted me to come alone?"

"Well, m'lady . . . not exactly in those words. The squire just asked for you."

The older woman looked down in search of her slippers. The serving girl immediately produced them. Nothing made sense. *Nothing*, she repeated to herself.

She and Clara had kept their vigil for a while longer, but it wasn't long before Clara had been begging to retire to her room. Catherine remembered thinking that this was a night for celebration, but the dispirited look on her daughter's face had soon put an end to her own happiness.

"And did you say Sir Thomas is still in the dining room?" She pushed her feet into the slippers.

"Aye, m'lady. Waiting to speak with you."

Catherine started for the door, but then thought of what she must look like in her robe and slippers and nightcap. She turned abruptly to the maid. "Is Sir Nicholas still with him?"

"Nay, m'lady. The gentleman left the dining room a while ago." She thought for a moment. "And there was no one in the parlor when we were cleaning up, either. Fey thought he'd retired for the night, as well . . . though I didn't see him, myself, ma'am."

He'd left a while ago, Catherine repeated to herself, hurrying downstairs. The house was quiet. The servants had apparently retired. She hardly knew what to expect, but she knocked quietly on the dining room door before entering.

Her husband was still sitting in his usual chair. A single candle flickered brightly in the center of the table. A half-empty decanter of port and a glass sat before him. He didn't acknowledge her when she came in and closed the door. The passage leading to the kitchen wing was dark and deserted. They were alone.

"You wished to speak to me."

He swirled the dark-colored liquid in his glass and drank it down before looking up.

"Though I should not be surprised, you have failed again, Catherine."

His voice was harsh—the attack wounding her dearly. She stood attentively at the opposite end of the table from her husband, her fingers clutching at the high back of the chair.

"I was under the impression that you had brought this silly chit up right. You assured me that this one would not disgrace me, that this one would know what to say . . . or do . . . or how to act to fetch herself a proper husband."

She shook her head. He was attacking the only bright thing that had come of this marriage. "She does, sir. Clara's manners are impeccable. Her charm—"

"Not enough, by thunder." He slammed a hand on the table, making her jump. She saw his hand shake as he poured more port from the decanter. "She lacks finesse. She acts like a simpleton. Young . . . naïve . . . innocent. The chit appears to the world to have no mind of her own." His words were slurring, and she watched him push the glass away, ignoring it when the liquid sloshed over the rim, staining the tablecloth.

"How else would you have her act?" Catherine could not comprehend him at all. "She is the perfect young woman. Accomplished in the feminine arts. Moral. Deferential. Quiet."

"Well, these things are apparently out of fashion." He leaned back against the chair, glaring at her. "And I do not blame him for not wanting her. I have yet to hear her express an opinion . . . on any subject. The chit has never taken a stand on anything. Defended anything. I never hear her speak without being spoken to first. She is just a pretty face. She has no soul. No substance. No presence. She's a bloody ghost."

Catherine felt hot tears rush to her eyes at this unfair and critical view of their daughter. She knew she could defend her. She could easily remind her husband that Clara was the opposite of *everything* that he hated in Jane. That it was he himself who had required that she be brought up to be exactly as he described.

She fought to be calm, wracking her brain for the real reason that Sir Nicholas had not proposed as they'd expected. There must be another reason, she thought. Well, she was not going to shoulder the responsibility for this. No, indeed.

"There will be other suitors," she said assuredly. "Clara is a noted beauty, and has a fortune to offer, as well. Others who are not as critical or *fashionable* will find no flaws in our child."

"This is it." He leaned forward. "Clara is *not* a child. I do not particularly care to be entertaining other suitors. I want *this* man. He is not like the other fops we saw hanging in the doorway of every party in London. His title and wealth be damned, I tell you. Even without them, I would gladly welcome this one into my family. He is a real man."

Catherine stared, shocked by her husband's words.

"I tell you, he gave me a reprimand after you all left . . . the likes of which I have not seen since the Duke of Cumberland relieved General Hawley of his command in Scotland." Sir Thomas rose to his feet, placing a hand on the table to steady himself. "Hang it, this one is not afraid of me in the least. The valiant rogue looked me right in my eye and said, 'You are wrong.' *'You are wrong,'* he tells me!"

Sir Thomas's shout echoed in the room, and Catherine glanced hesitantly behind her, glad she'd closed the door.

"The . . . *talk* . . . he wanted to have with me this night had little to do with Clara at all." He eyed her critically from across the room. "He had the gall to reprimand me . . . rebuke me . . . for the way I allow *Jane* to be treated."

"Jane?"

"Jane. He does not care at all for how I allow her to be treated by *Musgrave*. By thunder, he went on for a quarter of an hour about the insolence with which the new magistrate addresses her. He complained how *we*"—he pointed a finger at her and then back at himself—"fail to include her properly as a member of this family. He talked unceasingly about Jane. Defending her. Do you hear me? Not Clara . . . he has no interest there. But only defends *Jane* and her bloody impertinence." He laughed shortly and then drew a breath. "Oh, yes. He did say that your prize filly is far too young for him. He cannot possibly consider taking her as a wife."

"What are we to do?" she asked nervously as Sir

Thomas started around the table toward her. "We can't change her age . . . how can we convince him otherwise?"

As he reached her, she could see the look in her husband's eye. She'd seen it more than she cared to admit. He placed a hand on her shoulder, and she tried to hide her distaste.

"Our guest will be staying the fortnight as originally planned. So it is now *your* job, madam, to see to it that while he is here, he . . . he recognizes Clara's other charms."

She swallowed hard as his gaze descended to her bosom.

"I can . . . I can plan a party . . . a ball," she said as he began to move his hands over the silk brocade of her robe. "Girls are always seen in a far better light in such settings. I . . . I shall plan it for this coming week."

"You do whatever you must," he said vaguely, turning her toward the table.

At his urging, Catherine leaned forward onto her elbows. He lifted the layers of her robe and nightgown to her waist. She felt him position himself behind her and stared at the burning candle as he fumbled with his breeches.

"I shall send the invitations out tomorrow and . . ." She winced slightly and braced herself as he took hold of her hips and entered her. "I shall have Fey bring in half a dozen more workers from the farms to help with the serving." Her husband's tempo was increasing, and she felt the heat rising into her face. "I . . . I shall have her . . . have her get more help for . . . for the kitchen, too. And yes, a new . . . a new dress for Clara. Something more sophisticated and . . . and revealing." She was glad to hear his final grunt of release. She frowned and waited as he backed away from her.

"Sir Nicholas was smitten with her in London," Catherine said firmly. "He shall be smitten with her again."

She pushed herself off the table, smoothed the nightgown and robe back over her hips, and turned around. Her husband was already at the door, ready to leave.

"You are ignoring the most critical thing," he said darkly. "Jane."

"Jane?" she repeated simply. "You do not believe he is seriously interested in Jane, do you?"

He shrugged. "Have one of your maids reveal the truth about her past to Lady Spencer or her daughter. That should effectively put an end to any spell Jane might have cast over him."

"But do you . . . do you really think it is wise to let them know? I mean, Jane's past is a shameful reflection on all of us."

"Do it," he ordered. "They will find out sooner or later, in any case. At least this way we can be sure he is chasing the right girl."

Catherine Purefoy watched her husband turn his back and open the door. As he disappeared into the gloom of the corridor, she decided that, for once, she couldn't agree with him more.

Nicholas breathed in the cool night air as he strolled in the direction of the stables. It was difficult to stay calm, but he needed to be patient and keep his wits about him. His talk with Sir Thomas had cleared his conscience and his path. He was free now to be himself and to pursue Jane.

She was a mystery, though. High-strung, impetuous, yet completely lacking in vanity or self-absorption, she was unlike any woman he had ever met. And she was avoiding him.

After inquiring about her when they'd first come down for dinner, he'd been told by Clara that her sister was too tired from the activities of the day. She was resting in her room but might possibly join everyone later.

Dinner had come and gone, but there had been no sign of Jane. Not that any of her family had seemed to care about, or question, or miss her presence among them. No one at the table had been as aware of her absence, or as disturbed by it, as he.

After his blunt and candid chat with his host, Nicholas had thrown caution to the wind. Going up to her bedroom, he had knocked. No answer—no light visible beneath the door. He'd even tried the handle, but it was locked. In spite of it all, though, he had known that she was not inside . . . and he was equally sure that her horse would also be missing from her stall.

A solitary groom stood smoking a pipe and leaning against a post by the entrance to the paddock when Nicholas stepped around the stone wall. Curled up at his feet, two dogs looked like piles of fur, and they lifted their heads with only casual interest as he approached. On the far side of the paddock, a lantern swung gently on its hook beside the main door to the stable. Even in the darkness, Nicholas immediately recognized Paul, the stable master and trainer in charge of Sir Thomas's ongoing breeding venture.

When they had come back this afternoon from their ride to Ballyclough, Nicholas had spent a good hour talking to the man about the training of hunters. Breeding horses was not only a gentlemanly pursuit in Ireland, apparently, it was also a profitable one.

"Beautiful night, wouldn't you say, Paul?"

"Aye, that it is, sir." The older man straightened up and took the pipe out of his mouth. "We shan't have too many more of these before the cold settles in."

"I don't mind the cold. That was a wild storm, though, last night. It seemed to fairly race out of the hills." Nicholas stopped beside the burly man and glanced down into the shadowy fields where he'd seen Jane. He could still envision the black cape flying behind her. "It must have bothered the horses some, I should think."

"Most of them were fine, but there is always one or two more high-strung than the others." He put the pipe back in the corner of his mouth. "But I keep my eye open. Always about, I am. So I look in on those that need it. Talk to them. The smell of pipe smoke comforts the horses, too."

The two stood in silence for a moment. "I checked on yer mount last night. He was a brave young gentleman throughout. Picked him up in Cork City, ye said?"

Nicholas nodded. *Always about.* Behind wisps of clouds, a moon was starting to rise in the east. He cast a sidelong glance at the man. Jane no doubt came through here regularly and at all hours of the day and night, so it would just figure that she would need an ally here. "How does Miss Jane's horse fare? She is a pretty stepper over rough ground."

"Aye, that she is. And Queen Mab fears nothing." The man's bearded face wrinkled into a smile. "And Miss Jane knew it the first moment she looked on the poor wee thing as a foal. Now, the rest of us could see plain as day that the filly was lame and unlikely to amount to much of a horse, but not Miss Jane."

"Lame, you say. You couldn't tell to look at her now."

"To be sure, sir."

"Did she name her?"

"Aye. She called her Mab after the queen of faeries. I can tell ye, sir, the good lass spent enough time caring for her and training her and spoiling her till even the mare believed she was Mab herself. 'Tis been four years, now, and I can tell ye that horse *knows* she's a queen." He finished with a chuckle.

Nicholas glanced at the wing containing the row of stalls where he knew Mab was kept. The shadows of the night lay heavily across the line of doors. He wondered if the horse was there now.

"On our ride over to visit Parson Adams, I was watching Miss Jane. She is quite a skilled rider. One might even say she is a bit of a daredevil . . . particularly when she knows someone might be watching."

"Every gray hair I have in this head is there because of Miss Jane, I can tell ye." Paul gave him a knowing nod and a grin. "Ye should see them, sir. There are times when I look down this hill and I see the two of them, horse and rider, moving together like a single creation. Across those fields they go, so fast that ye expect 'em to sprout wings and take to the heavens. Aye, sir, there are times I scratch my head and wonder if what my eyes are seeing is real or only my imagination."

Nicholas had a similar image branded in his mind. One of the dogs stood up and stretched, putting her muzzle in Nicholas's hand and getting a scratch behind the ears for her trouble. He considered his growing fascination. Jane Purefoy was a contradiction to every woman he'd ever known. He knew beyond doubt that the approach he generally used with others would be totally insufficient with her. This was a woman who lived life fully every day. She would accept nothing less than the real Nicholas Spencer.

"But I do not think I'm speaking out of turn to tell ye not everyone approves of the way herself and that horse roam these hills."

Nicholas understood the "everyone" to be her family. He nodded, and they fell silent again for a few moments.

"I heard the new magistrate today leaning on her to sell the mare to him. Your mistress became somewhat riled."

"The devil take the man!" Paul took the pipe out of his mouth and spat on the ground. "Sir Robert will be stoking the fires of hell long before Miss Jane agrees to sell Queen Mab to the likes of him . . . and the cur knows it!"

Watching the groom come alive, Nicholas saw that the man was much more spry than he pretended to be, fiercer than he allowed to be known, and more protective of Jane than Nicholas had initially guessed. Paul stepped impatiently away from the wall.

"For all the years I've worked for this family, I've ne'er known Miss Jane to be asking for one single thing. From the time she was a wee sprite, running barefoot and getting in everyone's way, the lass has not once asked for a bleeding thing. Other first-born lasses get spoilt to their bones, but not herself. I can tell ye, sir, the first time that girl e'er wanted anything for herself was the day she set her sweet eyes on that foal."

Paul drew a leather pouch from the pocket of his battered coat and began packing his pipe again. His eyes seemed almost to gleam, reflecting the rising moon.

"And by the time Mab came into being, 'twas not easy to do any asking of her father." He paused and looked up at the house. "Not after all the muddied water standing between them in recent years. But the lass swallowed her pride and asked."

"And asking for a lame filly was a difficult thing?"

"Aye, sir. More than ye know. But Sir Thomas was planning to put the animal down anyway, so he gave the foal up to Miss Jane." He stuck the pipe back into his mouth. "Four years, she's had her now. For the past four years, Queen Mab has been Miss Jane's horse . . .

the only thing she's ever laid claim to at Woodfield House. And that bleeding magistrate had better turn his covetous eyes toward someone else's property, I'm thinking."

Nicholas felt his own anger rising inside him. "Their exchange had better be the end of it, for Sir Robert heard her response . . . and I can tell you Miss Jane's refusal was clear and direct."

"The magistrate's head is filled with cobwebs, I'm afraid, sir. He hears what he likes."

"Then I may just knock a few of those cobwebs loose. If he ignores Miss Jane's refusal, he shall do so at his peril."

The gruff possessiveness in his comment drew Paul's curiosity immediately, for Nicholas saw the shining eyes turn on him. He didn't know why he'd spoken his thoughts aloud, but it was too late to worry about it now. Hell, he thought, he'd felt protective enough of Jane to give her own father a good tongue-lashing. What did it matter if anyone else at Woodfield House guessed where his interest lay?

Paul continued to study him quietly.

"It's getting late." Nicholas glanced toward the stables. "I think I shall check on my 'brave gentleman' before retiring."

The stable master wished him a pleasant good night, but Nicholas noticed that he kept his vigil in the paddock until he was certain the guest had accomplished his task and was headed back toward the house.

Reaching the stone archway by the main house, Nicholas turned and looked back at the stables. As he watched, Paul finally crossed the paddock and put out the light in the lantern.

The shadowed Woodfield House loomed into view beyond the crest of the hill, and Jane decided how she was going to conceal her journey to Kildare.

Her old tutor, Mrs. Barry, was living with her married daughter in Dublin. Perfect. She'd been invited many a time to visit with the retired teacher. The fact that the older woman would not know anything about the visit was irrelevant. All that mattered was that her parents should be told that she was starting out for Dublin. What happened to keep her from reaching there was something she could work out later.

She thought about the last time Mrs. Barry made a point of inviting her for a visit and an extended stay. Last Easter. Yes, perfect.

Jane had always been a favorite of the Englishwoman. Widowed not long after her husband had brought her and their daughter from the north, Mrs. Barry had been Jane's first teacher and undoubtedly the most patient. She'd been the one to recognize a child's restlessness with traditional subjects, and thought to encourage the young Jane to move beyond sketching and to experiment with paints.

Naturally, there were more than a few Protestant families in search of well-grounded instruction for their girls, so Jane had not been the tutor's only pupil. Despite her popularity, though, Mrs. Barry hadn't stayed around too long when her only daughter had married into a good Dublin family. Jane knew that the woman had been happily overseeing her grandchildren ever since.

Relieved to have a plan, Jane spurred her mount up the hilly fields toward the familiar black shape of the stables. As she drew closer, however, she was surprised to see the glow of Paul's pipe in the shadow of an oak a few yards from the paddock gate. Slowing Mab to a walk, she guided the animal where he stood.

"Is something wrong?"

"Nay, lass. Nothing at all." He put the pipe between his teeth and reached for the horse's bridle as Jane dismounted.

"Why did you wait up?" she asked, walking beside him as they moved toward the paddock.

"Old habit."

Something was bothering him, she thought, as he glanced back at the deserted countryside.

"Ye did not see anyone out and about now, did ye?"

"Not a soul." How many years had he been waiting up for her? She thought of all those early years, and how she would find him sick with worry at the bottom of the hill. Waiting. Scolding. Caring. For too many years than she could count, he'd been more of a father to her

than Sir Thomas. She glanced up at the cap that he wore
low on his head, at the sparkling eyes that continued to
scan the fields she'd crossed only moments ago.

"What's wrong, Paul?" she asked softly.

"I heard about that mealy-mouthed cur Musgrave giving ye a hard time today. That was plenty to get me
going."

"You talked to the Englishman."

"That I did, lass . . . and more than once."

How curious that Spencer refused to limit his time to
socializing only with the gentry. Even at Ballyclough
she'd silently observed him befriending Mrs. Brown and
Henry's cook and even two of the villagers who had just
happened to come by on some business with Reverend
Adams.

They reached the paddock. He pushed open the gate.
"And that's what has me out here thinking, miss."

"Come now, Paul. Out with it."

"Very well. 'Tis just this. I'm thinking everybody's got
it wrong."

Jane turned away, closing the paddock gate behind
them. "Everybody's got *what* wrong?" she asked over
her shoulder.

"He doesn't want Miss Clara, lass. He's set his cap on
ye, sure as I'm standing here."

"Really, Paul! Of all the notions!" Her denial echoed
faintly as the stable master pulled open the door to
Mab's stall. She followed. "You don't have to do that.
I can take care of her."

"I know, my joy. But I don't mind spoiling ye a wee
bit . . . every now and then."

"Thank you."

"Be on yer way to the house now."

She stared after them as they disappeared inside. Jane
shook her head and turned away, not quite understanding what was going on with her old friend.

The house lay dark and quiet on the hill. The moon
lit a bright path through the garden. Though she would
not chance to go that way, Jane also decided against
going through the dank underground passage that had
been in existence since a castle had stood on this hill.

The night was too beautiful, and there was too much

rattling in her mind that she needed to clear. She decided on taking the walk-path, knowing that if the door beneath the great stone arch was barred for the night, she could go in through the kitchen wing. With a sigh, she started for the paddock gate.

"And Miss Jane . . ."

Paul's whisper stopped her. He was peering out from Mab's stall.

"There's far more to that one than meets the eye, I'm thinking."

# Chapter 13

Following the path, she climbed the hill toward the sleeping hulk of a house . . . just as he'd hoped she would. As she approached, Nicholas felt his senses sharpen perceptibly at the sight of her. With her came the smell of wind and the tingling promise of darkness. She moved like a cat, her lithe body gliding effortlessly through the night.

By 'sblood, Nicholas thought, he couldn't remember the last time a woman had stirred in him such anticipation.

"A far more pleasant night for riding, I should think."

Startled, Jane whirled and peered into the shadows of the garden entry. Nicholas was almost disappointed when she didn't reach for the dagger he knew she would be carrying. He would have enjoyed getting close enough to have to handle her and the knife.

"What are you doing here?" Her dark eyes flashed like two jewels in the moonlight. "I shouldn't have thought you were one who hides in dark corners and spies on people."

"I'm not . . . usually." He continued to lean a shoulder against the rough stone of the garden wall. His gaze took in the loose-fitting dark breeches, the high boots, the black smock. "I was only enjoying the beautiful view."

She was dressed as a man, and yet Nicholas could not for a moment fathom how anyone who looked at her could be fooled. His eyes lingered on the dark ringlets framing a complexion that rivaled the moon's glow. How could any observer fail to see that she was *all* woman?

Jane cast a glance over her shoulder at the house looming behind her. "If a beautiful view is what you are after, then you are facing the wrong direction."

"I don't believe I am."

The true meaning behind his seemingly matter-of-fact statement was slow to hit her. She was not accustomed to receiving such compliments. He slowly pushed away from the wall and moved through the moonlight toward her. Her objection to his compliment withered on her tongue as a strange, tingling sensation began to spread quickly through her limbs. He had discarded his jacket. Her gaze moved uncontrollably to the open collar of his shirt and the sleeves rolled up to display muscular arms.

"It is very late. I should be going in." But her feet, for some reason, seemed to have taken root.

"Please stay."

If he had made an attempt to use his physical charm in persuading her, she would have escaped easily. But the simple request only managed to unnerve her more. She searched for safe words to say as he came to a stop before her, but could think of nothing.

"Clara!" she blurted out. "Yes, Clara is an early riser. You should go in, too. She will certainly be looking forward to having breakfast with you."

"Well, I intend to sleep until noon tomorrow."

Anger flared within her. "I do wish you would stop treating her so poorly." She couldn't bring herself to look up into his face—not when he was standing so close. "She doesn't deserve to be treated that way."

"She appears to be perfectly happy with the way she is being treated . . . as are your parents and everyone else at Woodfield House. You, Jane, are the only one who complains."

This time, her rising temper forced her to look up, and she was immediately amazed by how tall he was—and how intensely he was studying every flaw in her face. Paul's words came back to her. "But Clara . . ."

"Surrender that cause, Jane. I simply do not care to talk about Clara."

His arm brushed against hers, shocking her with the heat that emanated from the spot. She took an immediate step back. "I . . . I need to go in."

"Stay . . . just for a few minutes." A strong hand reached out and took hold of her wrist. His thumb gently caressed her skin.

"Why?"

"It is a beautiful night. I've been desperate for a tour of the gardens."

"I shall go and awaken Clara for that. She is far more knowledgeable—"

"I lied."

"What?"

"I lied. I do not want a tour. But I recall seeing a stone bench by the wall at the lower end of the garden. I would very much like to sit on that bench and talk."

She tried to ignore the gentle pressure of his fingers— the warmth. "Since you do not wish to talk about my sister, then we have nothing to say to each other."

"But we do." He tugged gently and drew her gaze. "I have questions that I would not want to ask of anyone but you."

She arched a brow. "About Clara?"

He laughed—a deep, hearty laugh that made her smile in spite of herself. "By 'sblood, madam, you are persistent."

"Thank you for the compliment."

"But it was not a compliment," he growled good-naturedly, tugging again on her wrist and unbalancing her slightly. "Trust me, when I give you a compliment, you'll know. Come and sit with me for a few minutes. You might just earn one yet."

Jane pulled her wrist free, and hesitated a moment. There was no denying it. She wanted to go with him. At the same time, she didn't dare even to think why she wanted to. She nodded and tried to make light of the whole situation.

"You are greatly lacking in the power of persuasion." She saw him open his mouth to argue and waved him off, continuing. "*Nonetheless*, I suppose I have let you beg enough. I've decided, therefore, to humor you a little, sir. I shall walk to the garden wall and back."

Another rumble of laughter from the baronet brought a smile to Jane's lips. As far as the rules of propriety were concerned, she knew it was completely improper to be walking at midnight with a gentleman through a dark garden. But then again, she rationalized, she had no reputation to protect. And regarding any potentially dishonorable intentions on his part, she knew she was quite capable of protecting herself. She was a rebel leader, and he knew it. She was not some naïve, starry-eyed virgin hoping to be kissed by some rogue under a trellis of late-blooming roses.

These thoughts set Jane's body and mind more at ease—at least momentarily—as they walked beneath the stone arch. Immediately, though, the fragrant scents of the garden beds surrounded them, and she felt her pulse begin to race again at the sight of the seductive shadows cast by the light of the moon. She felt her sense of security beginning to dissolve, and forced herself to push away such foolish thoughts. She simply needed to treat him in the same way that she treated every other man she knew . . . with blunt honesty and indifference.

"The early hours we keep in the country must be a torment to someone like you."

"The hours *we* keep are perfectly satisfactory. To be candid, I shouldn't care to have anybody else about right now."

Jane found him watching her, and she shook her head. "I was speaking in general terms when I said 'we.' But you might as well put aside your cleverly disguised discourse and charming ways, Sir Nicholas. They have no effect on me."

His arm brushed against hers again, this time intentionally, she thought. "Are you certain I have no effect on you, at all?"

She shook her head and smiled at him. Stepping to the edge of the path, she put some space between them. "I am not one of your London society maidens. I am incapable of being dared or taunted or tempted. Now kindly tell me what it was that you wished to ask me."

The look he gave her told her that he didn't believe her bravado for a moment. But he was clearly enough of a gentleman not to press her. "The topic is a matter of some seriousness."

"I'm glad. I should hate to think of forfeiting needed sleep for anything less."

His hands were now clasped behind his back, his expression grave, as the two of them continued down the
path.

"Since our arrival in your part of the world," he continued, "I have had the good fortune of coming face-to-
face with a band of well-known rebels and their leader. I
also have been questioned about and endured interminable
lectures regarding this very same group. Unfortunately,
many of those doing the questioning and lecturing I find
to be scarcely objective in their presentation of the
truth."

Jane frowned in the darkness. She'd been expecting
the questions. It would only be natural that he should
want to know the reason for her involvement with the
Whiteboys. As a member of the English gentry, Spencer
would no doubt see it as his absolute duty to ask these
things. And after the answers would come the advice
that a gentleman *must* provide to insignificant, unintelli-
gent, vulnerable females. She could almost hear him
already.

Jane had to give him credit, though. At least he'd
been able to delay his meddling for nearly two days.

"So much of what we read and hear in England is
based on gross generalization. I know that to be true,
for I recall the discussions I heard with regard to the
American colonies after I returned from there. What
was said often had little to do with the truth or with
accuracy. We speak of strife and division here, but ignore the poverty and exploitation that cause it. We discuss the threatened involvement of Spaniards and
French against England. We confer the titles of 'hero'
and 'villain' on the basis of whether a person is English
or not. We only see what it is in our interest to see."

They reached the bottom of the garden, but Jane
found herself too captivated by his words to turn back.
The two walked beneath a long, trellised arbor of grape-
vines. Without thinking, she pulled a bunch of the ripe
fruit from the vine.

"I saw this kind of ignorance when I fought many
years ago against the French on the Plains of Abraham
in the taking of Quebec, and later in the campaigns
against the Cherokee. I was even carried along by it to

some extent. But this time I want to do better. I do not
want to make the same mistake. I want to understand
the truth." She heard him take a deep breath and let it
out slowly. "For the past two nights I have—with your
father's permission—spent some time in his library looking through papers he has collected regarding this area's
culture and history. But I should not need to tell you
that these accounts have been written mostly by Englishmen, and lack any attempt at objectivity and
accuracy."

They stopped at a stone bench beneath the trellis, and
he placed his boot on it. Leaning on a knee, he turned
to her. "So, what I am asking is whether there is someone at Woodfield House . . . or someone who lives in
the vicinity . . . who is knowledgeable *and* objective
enough to give me a clear understanding of what is happening here."

This hadn't been what she was expecting. She'd been
so continually faced for so many years with the flaws of
an English system—and the flaws of the aristocracy—
that she could not help but wonder about this man's
motives. He was not at all like his brethren.

"I must ask you, sir, if this desire for 'understanding'
can be traced to our little skirmish yesterday and to your
silence about the identity of the rebel. Perhaps you are
concerned about your decision not to give me away."

"No." His denial was emphatic. "And I give you my
word that as far as the rest of the world will ever know,
you and I never met until last night . . . in your parents' parlor."

She paused. "Tell me, then. Why do you care?"

"I told you. I have been questioned about it, lectured
about it by people like Sir Thomas, and this morning
by Musgrave. I like to know the facts before I form
an opinion."

"Facts." She leaned a shoulder against the trellis and
met his challenging look. "Facts are all just a matter of
perception." She held up the fruit in her hand. "What
do you see here?"

"Grapes. Nourishment. The raw materials for wine,
I suppose."

"What I see is the substance that holds the seeds of

future growth. The individual grape seed has little hope of growing into a vine. But if I were to bury this entire bunch, in the spring we would find a number of vines sprouting up from the soil. Facts can be interpreted in different ways."

Nicholas pulled a grape from the bunch in her hand and popped it into his mouth. "And sometimes a grape is but a grape." He smiled. "But I accept your point."

"Why do you *need* to form an opinion about us?" She shot him a challenging look. "You are here today, but you will be gone with my sister tomorrow. Why—"

"I shall not be leaving with Clara tomorrow . . . nor anytime thereafter. And stop muddying the discussion."

"Very well." She shrugged. "But my point is that you are here today, but you shall be gone tomorrow. My understanding is that in Quebec, you were sent to fight. It was impossible not to get involved. Here, you are visiting with your family. Why not simply enjoy the beauty of the countryside? Entertain yourself with all this area has to offer? In substance, you will leave here as the same person that you were when you arrived. There is no need for you to know any more about us."

His gaze narrowed. He leaned toward her. "Why are you so set against me learning about your cause?"

Jane shrugged and walked away a step. She looked up at the blanket of stars overhead and tried to keep her tone light. "I am trying to do you a favor . . . save your holiday . . . eliminate undue concerns."

"I did not ask for your charity, but your knowledge."

She felt him move close beside her. She tried to hide the unexpected shiver that coursed through her when their arms brushed.

"Of all the people you have met since arriving, why are you asking me?"

"Because, despite your birth and parentage, you have chosen the more difficult path. And . . . you are the only famous rebel leader that I have had the privilege of becoming acquainted with." Even in the darkness she could feel the weight of his gaze on her face. "It was quite impressive to hear Sir Thomas use Egan's name in the same breath as the others who are such a thorn in the side of the Crown."

"And you thought, 'How sad that he is so blind.' "

"Hardly! I was oddly grateful for his ignorance. There is something impressive . . . and yet disconcerting . . . in the irony that an Englishwoman is a leader in such a movement." There was no mockery in his tone, only quiet admiration. "When you first became involved in all of this, did you ever think that one day you might be considered a hero to those you fight for?"

"Or think that one day I would be hanged as a traitor?" Jane looked down, digging the dirt with the tip of one boot. She was not accustomed to being complimented. "The paths we travel are not always the same ones we started on . . . or would have continued on . . . if we were given the choice."

"Do you regret your involvement?"

"I am content to be the person that I have become. I am resigned to the role I seem destined to play. But I would sacrifice all . . . sacrifice myself . . . if I could change just a few of the tragedies of the past or even one tragedy to come."

Jane dropped the bunch of grapes into the dirt beside the path. A breeze, scented with late-blooming flowers and cool on her face, stirred memories long buried, images of faces long dead.

"I became Egan to close off the pain . . . to forget . . ." A sudden tightness squeezed at Jane's throat. She would never have become Egan if those five young men had not been hanged so unjustly. She would never have lashed out at the viciousness of this country's ruling class if she had not seen her lover's corpse rotting upon the gallows.

If Conor had lived, the extent of Jane's involvement would most likely have consisted of pining for him during his absence. She was no hero. The man she'd loved and his four unfortunate friends were heroes. She was just a survivor.

When Jane felt Nicholas's fingers brush away a tear that she had unknowingly shed, she turned and their gazes locked. She had an uncomfortable, hollow feeling that too much had been revealed.

"Will you someday tell me about your past?"

"My past is an open book . . . up to where the change

was wrought in me. Ask anyone and they will surely tell
you all about it."

Too much emotion lay too close to the surface, and
Jane recognized her vulnerability at this moment. Her
feelings were too raw. The scabs of old wounds were
opening up. Jane drew a deep breath, summoned her
strength, and turned toward the house.

"Someone like Henry Adams should be able to tell
you whatever it is you wish to learn about this country's past."

"How foolish of me to not have guessed. He is a man
who seems to be all too familiar with everything and
everyone around here."

She was too wrapped up in her own thoughts and
ignored the disapproval in his tone.

"Though my life is my own, Sir Nicholas, I know that
there are expectations that go along with being a guest.
Perhaps we should retire to our respective places.
Good night."

She knew the formality of her words sounded forced,
but she had to get away.

Jane moved quickly along the garden path, praying
that he would not follow. As she walked, she made herself breathe normally and forced herself to be calm.

She couldn't explain the melancholy she found herself
suddenly afflicted with. With just a few words, spoken
there in that same spot in the garden, the years had
melted away and long-buried memories had burned up
from within, destroying her insides on their way to the
surface. Now she could feel the fiery ache once again in
her flesh and in her very skin.

But this was not what she had worked so hard to become. She had never expected time to heal, but to teach
her. And she had learned over the years how to survive.
She'd struggled and finally succeeded in keeping herself
above the molten flood tides of remembrance. But this
night, with this man, she had once again become vulnerable and fragile.

Wiping away a sheen of tears, she looked ahead. The
sky was clear, the house black and intimidating. The
breeze was coming from the east, from Waterford. And
Jane remembered.

Nine years ago, she had walked down this same path to meet a man she'd loved. It was the eve of her birthday. She was turning seventeen, and Conor had met her under that same trellis at midnight. A kiss. It was to be a farewell kiss, but neither had known it. They'd only whispered of the future.

How could they know that he would be arrested the next day and executed before a fortnight had passed? How could they know?

"Jane," Spencer called after her.

A painful cry broke free with the next breath, and she quickened her steps.

"Jane!"

As the tears streamed down her face, she hurried through the garden gate, hoping to escape into the house. But his strong hands caught her just as she reached the landing, spinning her around to face him.

"Jane, what's wrong?"

No words would escape her lips. The tears, though, she fought to control. The past was behind . . . why did it still haunt her?

She struggled against the pain, forcing it back, and in a moment or two managed to look up into his face.

"If what I said upset you . . . I . . . I had no idea that your friend meant so much." His fingers squeezed her shoulders. "It was none of my bloody business to—"

"What friend?" Sobriety came instantly as she realized how disconcerted he seemed. She wiped at the wetness of her face with the back of one hand.

"Reverend Adams. I have no right to be critical of him. It is just that you say he is only a friend, but I find myself . . . hell, I find myself competing with the man for your attention at every turn."

"Competing for my attention?" She found herself actually smiling up at him through her tears. "Why? Why would someone like *you* . . . want to compete for *my* attention?"

"You can mock me . . . or continue this stubborn ignorance of my interest in you"—his thumb gently brushed away the wetness under her eyes—"but I ask you to forgive me for the way I spoke of your friend."

The baronet's face was deadly earnest, but Jane was

too consumed by his words and his touch to notice. The need to take comfort from another human being, to feel the unfamiliar warmth of a man's touch almost over- whelmed her with its power. She stared at the glimpse of skin beneath the open collar of his shirt, at the solid pillar of his throat, at his broad and muscular chest. In an instant, she felt a different kind of heat stirring in her middle. A soft glow seemed to flow into every limb, softening the aching there and replacing it with another.

She abruptly tore her gaze away. What was wrong with her? She was clearly losing control of herself. She needed to regain command of her unraveling emotions.

"It is I who . . . who should be sorry," she managed to get out. "This . . . how I acted . . . was totally inappro- priate. My tears have nothing to do with Henry . . . or with whatever it was you said."

He didn't appear convinced. While still holding her shoulders tightly, he looked more closely into her face. "Then why are you so upset?"

The whispered question went straight to her heart, taking her to yet another level of awareness. The caress of his breath against her skin felt so right.

"Ghosts." She searched and found her voice. "From time to time, I have ghosts that haunt me."

"So your tears have nothing to do with Henry Adams?"

"Nothing at all."

Jane shook her head and felt the warmth continue to spread through her as his face relaxed. She had not al- lowed herself to dwell on his striking good looks until this instant. She had not allowed herself to admit that she was wishing that the distance between their bodies might disappear.

Jane immediately tried to make herself push him away, but she couldn't. Nicholas lifted his hand from her shoulder and tenderly touched the bruise by her mouth.

"Now that we are getting around to apologies, I should tell you I am very sorry for this."

Jane had every intention of making some light remark, but the next breath was caught in her chest as she felt his fingers trace the lines of her lips.

"You are so beautiful, Jane. You are so alive . . . and beautiful."

She had to deny this. She had to walk away. But his touch had let loose a flood of sensations, and she found herself fighting just to stay afloat.

"I . . . I don't think this . . . is a good idea."

"You are quite right." The words were drawled as if he meant it. Suddenly, though, she was wrapped tightly in his arms, and his lips were crushing hers.

She forgot to breathe. She could find no reason to complain. All she was conscious of was the consuming fire that was racing through her.

Her hands seemed to move of their own accord, pulling at his shirt, feeling the muscular lines of his back. He groaned his approval. Powerful arms gathered her closer to his body, pressing her to him until there was nothing left between two hearts pounding wildly as one.

Passion had been something she had experienced long ago, but buried away. She'd believed no man could ever conjure in her the need she had once tasted and even become consumed by. But now, wrapped in Nicholas's steely grip, she found herself burning.

As he kissed her, she opened for him, driving them both an inch closer to an edge of oblivion. She felt his tongue searching, tasting. As he pressed her back against the stone arch, his body followed, scorching every inch of her with his heat.

"Jane." He tore his mouth from her lips and pressed it to her throat. His hands glided down over her body—touching, possessing—and all she could do was clutch his hair and drag his mouth back to hers for another searing kiss. "I knew it would be like this between us."

His mouth moved to her ear—teasing, biting, suckling.

. . . *be like this between us . . . between us . . .* The words reverberated in her mind. *Us . . .*

It was almost as if she were floating outside of her own body. As if in a dream, Jane looked down at herself. Nicholas's mouth was tracing a path down her neck while his hands were on her back, sliding over the curve of her buttocks, pressing her to him.

*Us . . .*

And then, as something clicked in her brain, she was back in her body, conscious and nearly panicked. The moan in her throat became a cry, and the hands that couldn't bring him close enough suddenly pushed to get free.

He stopped instantly and took an immediate step back. "Jane . . ."

Jane still had difficulty catching her breath, but she made sure to speak the words that were screaming within her. "There is no *us*, Nicholas. There can never be an *us*!"

She raised a hand to silence him as he opened his mouth to speak.

"And please . . . please . . ." she begged him as she edged toward the door. "Forget what happened tonight. We both made a mistake. And it can never . . . *will* never . . . happen again."

Jane ran inside, not knowing how she would ever be able to forgive herself for nearly seducing her sister's future husband. Never again, she swore silently, climbing two steps at a time to her workroom beneath the roof. Never again would she allow herself to be alone with Nicholas Spencer.

Not for a second.

From the window of his darkened bedchamber, Sir Thomas watched the baronet walk back into the night. Even from this distance, he sensed the man's frustration as he ran a hand through his hair.

"She is far more of a handful than you thought her to be," he murmured.

As he always did, Sir Thomas had been waiting for Jane's return. Standing by his chair, he'd happened to see her come up the pathway, only to be approached by the visitor. And then he'd watched the two of them walk down into the gardens.

The sight of the two of them had given him a moment's pause, but he had quickly shaken off the thought. There was no chance of anything developing between them. Jane wouldn't allow it. Perhaps he should have advised the young man about it during their private talk after dinner.

He'd been correct—as always. It hadn't been long before he'd seen Jane practically run back toward the house with Spencer hot on her heels. And now he was looking at the frustration of a man rejected.

It was more than the scandal of her past that would keep the baronet and Jane apart. It was more than his own order to hang that presumptuous papist boy nine years ago that kept the wedge solidly between himself and Jane.

There was, indeed, much more.

At first, when he'd become aware of her coming in and going out at all hours, he'd been fool enough to think there was another man involved. Soon after, he'd started studying her paintings and watching her carefully. It had not taken him long to realize that his own daughter had taken up the cause of her dead lover. Jane was now supporting the Shanavests.

Sir Thomas moved away from the window and sank heavily onto the edge of the bed. It was to protect her that he had remained magistrate for so long, hoping that she would tire of the foolishness of the movement. He himself would not move against the rebels again while Jane was involved with them, but she was the reason he continued to harp at Musgrave to take stronger actions now to capture and hang the local leaders. The old man knew that with the ringleaders gone, there would be little fight left in the rest.

Only then, Thomas knew, he'd have a chance of removing the wedge. Only then, he prayed, he might have his daughter back.

# Chapter 14

⟡

The small workroom Catherine Purefoy used as the center for running her household was abuzz when Jane poked her head in the next morning. There were four servants already standing in a line before her mother and taking a variety of directions from their somewhat hysterical leader. Meanwhile, Clara stood by the single window of the room, staring sullenly out, and totally unaffected by the madness in the room.

A sharp needle of guilt immediately pricked Jane as she saw the gloominess in her sister's face, but just as she'd done a thousand times during the sleepless night, she shut the door firmly on the image of Nicholas and herself standing together beneath the stone arch. Bitterly, she pushed the image deep in the bottomless well of mistakes she had made.

Just as Jane was considering if she should give this lunacy an hour or two to settle down, her mother's victims began to disperse. Two upstairs maids practically tripped over each other in their haste to escape. One of the kitchen servants stormed out muttering a profane curse in Gaelic. Fey, to her great misfortune, was the solitary victim left behind. The mistress's voice rose in excitement as she fired a dozen directions pertaining to a dozen different tasks at the red-haired woman. It was upsetting for Jane to see that even the housekeeper's usually calm demeanor was affected by her mother's ongoing harangue.

As Lady Purefoy paused to take a breath, Jane seized the opportunity and stepped in.

"I need a moment of your time, Mother."

"It shall have to wait, Jane. Not now."

"But it cannot wait." She walked in and sat comfortably in one of the two available chairs. She was relieved to see Clara give her a side glance and a smile before returning her attention to whatever she was so consumed with outside.

Her mother gave her an exasperated glare. "Well then, what is it, Jane? Be quick about it."

"I am planning to visit old Mrs. Barry . . . in Dublin. I shall be taking a coach from Cork and will leave in about nine days."

"And how long will you be gone?"

"A fortnight, perhaps a few days more."

"Very well. I shall tell Sir Thomas about it." Lady Purefoy turned back to the housekeeper.

All as Jane had expected. With very few exceptions, she had not spoken directly with her father for years. Everything he needed to know could be communicated through her mother. And now that she knew of the trip, there really wasn't any reason for Jane to remain. Curiosity, though, held her in her seat.

"Oh, yes. The seamstress we used before our trip to London," Lady Purefoy said, recalling her instructions to Fey. "I want Paul to send a groom with you to Cork City and bring the woman back. Now, I told you what to buy as far as fabrics and colors. Make sure whichever groom Paul chooses to send, he must understand he is not to hurry you."

"I'll not be rushed, m'lady."

"But I want you back immediately. No dallying in the city, mind you. There's much to be done, Fey. *Much* to be done!"

"Preparing for a party, Mother?" Jane asked good-naturedly, trying to gain a moment's respite for the housekeeper.

"A ball," Lady Purefoy corrected immediately. "The grandest we've ever had at Woodfield House."

Catherine leaped out of her chair and scurried behind a writing table, scowling at a neat stack of papers.

"I thought you were planning to help me with these invitations . . . Clara?" She stared at her young daughter's troubled profile for a moment. "You have to start these now so we can have them delivered *today*."

Jane watched her sister, obedient as always, leave her place and sit behind the desk. She was the angel of the household, trained to dutifully follow their parents' orders.

"Is this the engagement party . . . er, ball that has . . . that everyone has been waiting for?" Despite what he'd said to her, Nicholas Spencer was here to marry Clara and everyone knew it. Everyone had accepted it. She had no right . . . no reason . . . to feel this hot iron that had suddenly pierced her chest.

An uncomfortable silence descended over the room. Her mother and Fey were both staring at her. Clara, though, was continuing to scratch the pen across the paper without pausing.

"Miss Jane has just come down," Fey gently reminded Lady Purefoy. "She does not know yet."

"If you were not sleeping half the day away, as you do, then you would know what is happening around here." Jane's mother turned her back and moved the wax and seal closer to Clara on the desk. She picked up a list and started to complain about all that needed to be done.

"Well, does anyone care to tell me what is going on here?"

Clara put down her pen and spoke. "There is no offer of marriage. Sir Nicholas told Father last night that he does not wish to marry me."

"There is no need to state it as if it were final," Catherine protested immediately. She moved behind her daughter, placing her hands protectively on her shoulders and glaring at Jane. The younger sister simply returned to writing the invitations. "He is obviously not ready to make a decision, but his intentions are very clear. He and his family are planning to stay for another fortnight . . . as originally planned."

"So you are giving a party . . . pardon me, a ball?"

"Why not?" Lady Purefoy took an invitation that Clara had finished and carefully folded it. "A young woman's advantages are best displayed on such occasions. There is nothing like good food and drink and dancing to open a baronet's eyes to what he will be missing. I predict he'll be asking for our Clara's hand the day after the ball." She nodded to Fey. "You can go now. And do not forget what I told you about the dallying."

Fey hesitated before leaving. "Now should we not be planning for a dress to be made for Miss Jane, as well, m'lady? If she has no plan of leaving for nine days and the ball is in six . . ." Fey gave Jane a gentle smile. "Do you not think, miss, that 'tis high time you gave up wearing black? 'Tis been—"

"Be on your way, Fey," Lady Purefoy cut in sharply. "Jane is too old to reap any benefit from any of this. And besides, you know as well as I that she does not care for this sort of thing. She never has. Do you, Jane? In fact, what is the difference between nine days . . . six days . . . or two days? Why not plan to leave for Mrs. Barry's right away? You shall be much happier there, anyway, while all this activity is taking place here. I shall tell Sir Thomas to allow you to go immediately."

"No, Mother," Jane protested. She rose to her feet as Fey disappeared out the door. Lady Purefoy had stung her. In spite of the difficult state of affairs at Woodfield House, it was still rare to hear her mother openly assert that Jane wasn't wanted. But that was enough to make her stay. "I shall be leaving in nine days as I told you."

Catherine looked mildly annoyed when Jane stopped at the door and turned to face her. "And Mother, for Clara's sake, please think before you talk. I do not believe you even know how hurtful you can be sometimes."

Jane glanced at Clara, who looked up from beneath hooded eyes only for an instant before silently and diligently going back to work on the invitations.

Patches of thin forests snaked through the worn hills. A solitary trail wove in and out of the wood and disappeared over the crest of the next rise. Alexandra Spencer lifted the charcoal off the paper as a patch of gray cloud moved across the sun. She turned her attention to the east and studied the contrast of shadow and light as the cloud slipped over in the sweeping panorama of foothills, forests, and pastures.

Looking at Jane's work the day before had stimulated that old, familiar thirst in her again. Alexandra needed to draw and paint. She needed to create.

She also needed to talk to Jane and congratulate the young woman on her work. She doubted that Jane got much encouragement, living with the dull rustics who were supposedly her parents. Alexandra couldn't help but wonder if the older sister hadn't been a foundling, after all.

The sun reemerged, but as Lady Spencer readied the charcoal over the paper again, another shadow moved over her. This one belonged to her own daughter, who now stood directly beside the garden bench, effectively blocking her light. The artist's complaint, though, was silenced when she looked up into Frances's tearful face.

"Oh, Fanny. And what is wrong now? Is Nicholas not back yet from his ride with Sir Thomas and the trainer?" She pressed a comforting hand to her daughter's and pulled her down beside her on the stone bench. She had heard Nicholas and Frances exchange a few words this morning at breakfast. She wasn't about to side with anyone over a petty dispute, but all the same she'd thought her son's temper had been shorter than usual. In fact, he'd been quite impatient even to hear what Frances's request was. "He was right about not wanting to take you along. They are looking at horses—talking business—riding through pastures and walking through stables. Why, they're probably knee-deep in manure as we speak. Now, what enjoyment would a young woman like you get out of something so appalling?"

"I am not angry with Nicholas." Frances wiped away the wetness on her face. But fresh tears were soon coursing down her pale cheeks again.

"Then why are you so upset, my dear?" Alexandra put aside her artwork and took out a handkerchief. She handed it to her daughter. "There is no reason to be bored. Lady Purefoy tells me that they are planning a great party for the end of this week. I am certain she could use some help if you were to offer."

The young woman shook her head. "I am not bored, Mother. And I was . . . I was planning to be of some help . . . but when I heard the story . . ." She hiccuped. "Oh, Mother . . . it is *so* sad . . . so sad . . . poor Jane."

Before Alexandra could say a word, Frances had laid her head on her mother's chest and was sobbing wretchedly.

"What happened to Jane? Is she unwell? Did she have an accident?"

It took a few moments before Frances finally began to explain.

"No, she is well now . . . I mean on the surface . . . this happened some time ago . . . but still . . ."

A dull ache had begun to eat away at Lady Spencer. In the short time they had been at Woodfield House, she was already beginning to care for Jane, and all this puzzling talk was too worrying.

"Frances Marie. You start explaining to me what . . ."

"I found out why . . . why the family treats her so . . . so poorly." The young woman straightened on the bench and used the handkerchief to blow her nose. "They . . . are ashamed of her . . . I think."

Instant objections arose in Alexandra, but she bit them back as Fanny turned her watery gaze on her.

"It is true, Mother. These people never told us about Jane . . . until we arrived. And . . . and . . ." She waved an impatient hand toward the house. "They care nothing for her. Last night . . . no one asked where she was. Did you notice? And this morning . . . did anyone inquire after her even once?"

There was a great deal about the Purefoy household that Alexandra didn't understand. "Each family has its own little eccentricities. Just because we have not seen much of Jane, that certainly does not mean—"

"But it does!" Frances clutched her mother's hands. "It does if they believe her reputation is ruined and they consider her a disgrace."

Alexandra kept silent. She knew her daughter. She knew that as distraught as Frances was, everything she must have heard would spill out.

"The problem is that I think Jane is a tragic victim. Mother, I had to question *two* people before I had all of it." Frances's blue eyes narrowed and her voice lowered as she glanced back at the house. "And that's another thing. I think they planned this whole thing out. I mean, letting us know about Jane's past."

"Really, Frances . . ."

"Honestly! Thinking me a simpleton or something, they sent a maid in to tidy my bedchamber. And while she was there, she just *happened* to tell me all the gossip about the older daughter. I hardly think it a coincidence, Mother. I believe, after they saw how Nicholas last night was not happy with Jane's absence, they wanted to make sure that we all think the worst of her." She looked into her mother's eyes. "I might be only sixteen, but I have been brought up to know what is what. As soon as that girl started prattling on about how *horrible* it was for the family when Miss Jane eloped nine years ago with a poor, good-for-nothing papist, I knew something was wrong. Naturally, she went on to tell me that—despite the disgrace—generous Sir Thomas and Lady Purefoy were quick to take her back."

Although Alexandra didn't have all the details, she was still pleased with her daughter for viewing the tittle-tattle with skepticism.

"I knew they weren't going to tell me everything. So after the maid was finished in my room, I went in search of Fey."

"The housekeeper?"

Frances nodded, wiping the last traces of wetness off her face. "It is obvious that she cares for Jane. So I thought the best chance of hearing the truth would be from her."

"And was Fey willing to talk to you about this?"

"She was, after I told her what I'd heard." The young woman lowered her voice again. "Jane's reputation *was* ruined nine years ago. But the thing that the first woman failed to say was that she never got so far as actually running away. She couldn't. Because the boy she'd been in love with for some years was arrested and ordered to be hanged in the same week. Oh, Mother . . . Sir Thomas ordered the boy's hanging . . . and Jane . . . and Jane had to watch him die."

There were fresh tears that the young woman dabbed at.

"That's why she wears black. After all these years . . . she still mourns the young man she loved. That is . . . so sad . . . so sad!"

Alexandra gathered Frances in her arms and let the young woman weep. Such a story, even with the tragedy of the father ordering the death of this young man, was perfectly believable. A reputation lost was a lifetime sentence for a woman. But she didn't want to remind her daughter of any of this now, for what was customary was not necessarily right . . . or fair.

She recalled the paintings she'd seen in the attic room. The power in them bespoke someone who knew suffering. And now Alexandra understood. What greater anguish could a young woman bear than to be sentenced to a lifetime living under the same roof as your beloved's executioner? Especially when that person was your own father!

"I think we . . . we should tell Nicholas about this." Frances once again pulled out of the mother's arms and blew her nose. "I can already tell that . . . that he is interested in Jane . . . but he cannot . . . it would never work."

"We shall tell him nothing, my dear." Alexandra lifted the young woman's chin and looked into her surprised face. "Your brother shall learn what he needs to know on his own. He will then make his own decisions. We shall be here whenever he needs us. But Nicholas can decide on his future without our interference."

# Chapter 15

A t first, Nicholas didn't know what it was that awakened him. It was still dark outside, and there were
no predawn noises coming in the window he'd left open
overnight. He listened closer and thought he could hear
the soft whisper of voices in the corridor.

He was out of bed and had his door opened a crack
in the next instant. The passageway was dark with the
exception of a flicker of light coming from down the
hall. He recognized the housekeeper's soft voice. He
opened the door a bit more and saw Fey standing before
Jane's door—speaking hurriedly.

He could hear only snatches of what was being said.
". . . Seamus's widow . . . wee ones . . . Buttevant . . ."

By the time he had retired last night, he had been
impatient enough to kick down every locked door and
search out every secret passageway in Woodfield House.
She had successfully avoided him for two entire days.
Most of the day on Saturday, he'd spent with Sir Thomas
and Paul. The former magistrate was very proud of
showing off his stables and what progress had been made
since retiring from service to the Crown. When they'd
gotten back to the manor house, though, Jane had continued to be absent throughout the afternoon, not even
appearing for dinner. Nicholas had worn a path between
the house and the stables, but her horse was missing.
Later, he'd found Mab settled for the night, though he
had still not seen Jane. And on Sunday, the only other
person who'd asked about her had been Parson Adams,

who'd come back with them after the church service to stay for dinner.

The clergyman's curiosity had only fueled Nicholas's impatience.

". . . Musgrave . . ."

He frowned at the whisper of the name. The door to Jane's room closed. As Fey's footsteps started down the hall, Nicholas shut his own door quietly. He hurriedly dressed. Though he didn't know the nature of Fey's early-morning visit, the few words had managed to fill him with distress. He was almost certain that Jane would be leaving soon.

The corridor was again immersed in darkness when Nicholas left his room. Taking a moment and letting his eyes adjust to the dark, he glanced in the direction of Jane's closed door. He knew better than to assume that she would be leaving this way, so instead he started down the stairs. He would intercept her at the stables.

Soft tinges of dawn were lightening the sky above the eastern hills when Nicholas arrived at the stables. Going first to Mab's stall, he found the horse saddled and ready, though there was no one tending her. He moved quietly to where his own horse was kept and began readying it.

Saturday, when he'd been out with Sir Thomas and Paul, the trainer had continuously sung Jane's praises whenever the father was out of earshot. If Nicholas had been fairly certain before of the older man's devotion to Egan, now he entertained no doubts.

And this morning he'd discovered Fey passing on a message to her. Nicholas wondered how many others at Woodfield House were supporters of Egan, despite the passionate hatred the former magistrate harbored for the rebel.

He had just finished saddling his horse when he heard the sound of a horse in the paddock. A moment later, he heard her riding off. Hurrying, he was coaxing his steed out of the stall when Paul's tall frame appeared in the open doorway.

"Sir Nicholas," the man said with a hushed surprise.

"I am going with her, Paul." He started to mount

up, but stopped when the stable master put a hand on his arm.

"Going with who, sir? Everyone is still asleep at the house, to my knowledge."

"I'm going with Jane." Nicholas kept his voice low and turned to face the man. "I don't plan to get in her way. And I won't interfere unless she needs me."

The trainer reached for the horse's bridle. "Nay, sir. I've no doubt Miss Jane is sleeping like the angel that she is. Why—"

"She is going to Buttevant, on business that has to do with the new magistrate." Though Nicholas knew he could overpower Paul if he had to, he was hoping for the man's cooperation and trust. But the stable master had roughly five seconds. "Whatever the trouble is, it could be a trap set by Musgrave."

The man stared at Nicholas.

"I've known who she is from the first day. I've witnessed what she does. She knows her secret is safe with me." He lowered his voice further and brought up the arm that had been knifed by Jane. "I have great respect for her abilities, and I know she is quite capable of defending herself. But I saw Musgrave in Buttevant three days ago, and I believe he is planning something."

Paul's hand dropped from the horse's bridle. "What'll ye do?"

"Just be there," Nicholas answered confidently. "Just by being with Jane, I may be able to distract Musgrave's attention from her."

Paul's grim expression of hesitation gave way to a trace of relief. "If ye ride hard up the valley north and then follow east along the stream, ye should catch up with her."

Nicholas climbed onto his horse. "Make some excuse for me if anyone asks."

"Aye, sir. I've become an expert liar, when it comes down to it," Paul assured him. "But I need to warn ye. Once ye catch up with Miss Jane, there is no saying she'll be taking any comfort in yer company."

"I once thought myself an expert in charming women, but your mistress tells me that my powers of persuasion are wanting when it comes to her."

"Then how are you going to convince her to have ye along?"

"Beg," Nicholas said conspiratorially, putting the spurs to his horse.

Jane rode through the night, her dress and cape flying behind her. She'd considered whether it would be best for her to ride out as Egan or as herself. Until she could be sure of what needed to be done, she had decided it would be best for her to act as herself. Later, if need be, she would get her fellow Shanavests involved.

The message had come from Buttevant. A mother's plea to look after her three children. Kathleen, Seamus's widow, had been dragged by the dragoons to the barracks gates.

The boy who had brought the message to Woodfield House had also told of the soldiers showing up yesterday afternoon at the decrepit cottage and tearing Kathleen from the desperate hands of her screaming children. The little ones had been left behind to fend for themselves in the company of the blind old woman who shared the same roof. The charge lodged against the mother was unknown, but as Jane cut across a shallow stream and onto the Buttevant road, she fretted that it might have had something to do with the bag of coins she'd given the woman three days ago. She spurred Mab along the road, thankful for the first slivers of dawn spreading across the eastern sky and lighting her way.

Jane had another reason for not getting her fellow rebels involved immediately. She knew there was no way they could challenge Musgrave and a barrack full of dragoons without considerable bloodshed. And she was smart enough to know that this may have been exactly what the magistrate was hoping for when he arranged for the arrest of the poor woman.

The first realization that she was *not* the only traveler heading north this early in the day came almost a half hour after she'd left home. On the crest of a hill—as was always her habit—she looked back and spotted the horse and rider racing across the countryside after her.

At first, because of the distance and the dim light of dawn, she didn't recognize him. But as she hesitated a few moments longer, Jane realized that the man pushing the gray stallion at breakneck speed could only be Nicholas Spencer.

Jane's immediate spark of delight quickly turned to annoyance. Forcing the smile from her face, she allowed the anger to well up within her. No one followed her. For all the years she'd been leaving Woodfield House— at all hours of day or night—no one had ever come chasing after her. Until this man.

She had enough confidence to know she could lose him en route if she set her mind to it. But instead she let her temper rise and wheeled Mab around to face the meddling rogue and challenge his presumptuous behavior.

Waiting for him was tough, but Jane endured it by imagining the most wicked punishments she could inflict on him. She even considered riding down into the grove of trees in the next valley and springing on him by surprise. But time was short, Kathleen's children needed her, and she could not allow herself to be distracted, no matter how sweet the reward.

"Good day to you, Jane."

The upbeat greeting as he drew near fueled the fire even more. The smile on his handsome face had a contagious edge to it, so she gave him her fiercest frown.

"You need to be corrected on two counts, sir," she said as horse and rider came to a stop beside her. "I do not consider this hour to be officially day, and I much prefer we retain formal manners of address, Sir Nicholas."

"My apologies, Miss Purefoy."

He didn't appear sorry to her. And she tried to overlook how downright appealing he was with a day's growth of whiskers and blond hair loose and wind-tossed about his shoulders. He was the very image of the rogue, rather than the noble gentleman everyone assumed him to be.

"Sir Nicholas, would you please explain to me, and briefly, what you are doing here?"

"Riding, miss. I happen to enjoy the exercise."

"You might save your wit, sir, for the drawing room. Would you please explain why you are following me?"

"I—"

"And tell me why I shouldn't be suspicious of your motives."

"Well, I—"

"For you have told me repeatedly that you have no intention of exposing me, sir. And yet I find you . . . well, trailing after me."

"Now—"

"And I should tell you I consider lying a dreadful thing . . . in situations such as this." She could see the amused expression etched around his blue eyes. "And this is not the time to think of one of your witty comments."

"Jane—"

"I refuse to be treated as some half-witted, rusticated ass, sir," she blurted out, leaning menacingly in his direction. "The least you can do is to try to think of an answer."

He smiled. "If—"

"But if you cannot, I strongly suggest that you turn your horse around this instant and start back . . ."

He reached over so quickly that Jane was stunned when his large hand slipped around the nape of her neck and his lips crashed down on hers. Everything became still for an insane moment. The urge to fight was suspended in air. And as his other hand drew her still nearer, the temper instantly turned to heat. Her hands clutched desperately at the lapel of his jacket. She was further shocked by the unfamiliar sound of satisfaction that she realized had come from her own throat when he deepened the kiss.

"Now, that's better," Nicholas said in a voice like velvet as he broke off the kiss. His fingers lingered a moment longer, and he traced her lips. "I hope I have not bruised you again. You have the most delicate skin. If anyone were to come upon us, they would know for certain that you have been properly kissed."

A fog hung over Jane for the longest moment. Then clarity suddenly returned, and she straightened in her saddle. How vulnerable she was to his charms, she thought with alarm.

"I promise that these bruises will fade much sooner."

He ran a hand over his unshaven face while his blue eyes reflected his smile. "But I will be better prepared the next time."

She wanted to slap the grin off his face, but she thought the punishment too trivial. She had to think of something more painful. To keep her hand off the small dagger at her belt, she lifted the reins, making them look like a noose.

"I had no intention of following you at a distance," he started, watching her hands. "My intention was to accompany you to Buttevant. But you ride with such skill and speed . . ."

"How did you know where I was headed?"

His gaze returned to her face. "I—"

"You *have* been spying on me."

"I—"

"There is no other way that you would know."

As he reached for her again, she made Mab sidestep out of his reach. "Do not dare to kiss me again."

"Oh, I thought you wanted . . . Well, will you give me the opportunity to explain, then?"

Jane opened her mouth, but immediately closed it as the truth dawned on her. She couldn't deny it. Deep within, she wanted to be kissed by him. She coaxed Mab another step back to let her own passions cool.

"Very well, Sir Nicholas. This is your opportunity. Explain."

Nicholas nudged his steed toward Mab until the riders' boots brushed. She felt their knees touch.

"Quite by accident, I overheard snatches of a conversation in the corridor earlier. My intentions were not to spy, but to find an opportunity to spend time with you." He leaned forward on the horse—and let his gaze caress every part of her face. "It has been bloody hell, Jane. You have been running away from me since our talk in the garden."

Jane didn't want to acknowledge the warmth that his words produced instantly in her. She didn't want to admit how much of the past few days she'd spent thinking of him—remembering everything he'd said and then the kiss they'd shared. Her fingers trembled as she pretended to adjust the tie of the cloak. She prayed that, in the dim dawn light, he wouldn't see the blush rising into her cheeks.

"I did warn you, sir . . . pleaded even . . . that we never discuss that night in the garden again. I've already put it out of my mind. I ask the same of you."

He looked stung, but only for a moment. "I do not believe you have forgotten what happened. Our kiss a few moments ago was proof . . ."

"Please. I am having great difficulty understanding my own behavior. I beg of you." She shook her head. "I have important things to do, and I must be on my way."

There was a lengthy silence. "As you wish . . . but I am letting this subject rest only for this morning."

The battle had to be fought in many stages. His concession was a good start. Jane gentled her tone and tried to focus on the more immediate concern on hand. "I have already lost too much time. And I am not taking a ride for exercise or making a social visit this morning. I would greatly appreciate it if you would respect my wishes and stop following me."

"You are not dressed as Egan, so I assume you are not leaving for any secret meeting."

"Nonetheless, sir, this is a private matter and none of your concern."

"Whatever the trouble is, you are going to Buttevant . . . and you might have to deal with Musgrave."

"I resent people who assume that I am incapable. This is not the first time I am making this trip . . . nor is it the first time I have been faced with this type of matter."

"You are quite capable. I admire you for it." His tone was so confident that she couldn't stop herself from looking searchingly into his face. All previous signs of amusement were gone. "I am asking this favor of you for my own peace of mind. I was tremendously irritated when I met the magistrate the last time. Perhaps if I were honest, I would admit that the source of my irritation lay in the fact that each of us was vying, in his own way, for your attention."

"I do not think—"

"Please allow me to finish." He pushed his horse nearer again, and this time Jane didn't retreat. "I outmaneuvered Musgrave in that incident, but I believe the man is contemptible enough to try to hurt you . . . if only to teach me a lesson."

"Sir Robert doesn't need an excuse to be hurtful. And I believe the matters leading to the distressing news reaching me today are totally independent of your meeting with the magistrate."

"Please, Jane," he pressed. "Will you do this for me? Allow me to come along. Only this once."

She should have raised a thousand objections, but said nothing. She felt torn between what she wanted and what she felt she should do. In the end, she couldn't bring herself to refuse him.

"If I . . . if I let you come along, you should understand that you are going only as an observer and nothing more."

"I understand."

"I am planning no meeting with Musgrave. In fact, based on what you've told me, I prefer that you *do* remain with me instead of separating at Buttevant."

"Nothing would please me more."

His quick and obviously heartfelt agreement caused a new flutter of excitement to form in Jane's stomach.

"But in coming," she continued, "you must give me your word that there will be no more talk of . . . of anything that happened between us . . . either in the woods or when we met in the . . . garden."

There was no immediate response. Then he gave her a perceptible nod.

"I agree."

She should have been happy, but deep down she mourned his concession. She turned Mab's head back down the road.

"I can certainly manage this punishment . . ."

Jane glanced over her shoulder and saw that Spencer appeared to be talking to himself . . . or to his horse. She turned her attention back to the road ahead.

"But, of course . . . talk I can do without . . . She didn't say I needed to forfeit anything else."

Jane hid the smile that tugged at her lips. She should have known that he was too much of a rogue to make real concessions without putting up a fight.

# Chapter 16

In a shadowy corner of the single-room cottage, a young girl crouched beside her older brother, who continued to sleep fitfully, despite all the noise in the place. The streaks of dirt staining her innocent face indicated tears that had only recently been wiped dry. The child's eyes had turned fearful as soon as Nicholas entered.

He was told by Jane not to speak a word to any Irish whom they might pass. She'd also asked him to remain outside. Nicholas could not let her go in by herself, though, and had stayed directly behind her when she'd passed through the warped wood planking that served as a door. Once inside, however, he had stayed true to her other request and said not a word.

"I do not know where she'd be getting herself those coins," the old blind woman explained, stirring a pot that hung over a small peat fire. The liquid in the pot looked to be nothing more than a thin broth. "Kathleen came back from the village and right away sent Bowie here out to bring word to young Mick to take to ye. She knew trouble was to come and come it did."

The youngest child continued to wail steadily and miserably, but shied away when Jane tried to reach for him.

"She wanted to send word to Egan. Would ye be Egan?"

This was the third time the blind woman had asked this same question. Nicholas wondered if someone else had walked in here and claimed to be Egan, the woman would be revealing as much.

"I am Egan, Bridget," Jane replied softly. "You must remember my voice. I was here not three days ago."

The widow's expression revealed nothing that said she remembered. Meanwhile, Nicholas thought, the lines of age and pain on her face told of one who'd suffered greatly over the years—one who had finally found a way to forget.

"I heard her say it. She wanted a message to be sent to Egan." She lowered her voice despite the loud squalling of the child. "I heard her talking to herself of the coin you gave her, too. She ran to the patch of garden in the back . . . She was still there when the soldiers came."

The baby continued to wail. The young girl in the corner crept cautiously across the dirt floor and picked up her sibling in her arms. The child instantly laid his head on her shoulder and the crying relaxed into a gentle sob. Nicholas thought that she was not much bigger or older than her brother, but the little girl had aged emotionally far beyond her years.

"Did they say anything when they took her? Did they come inside and hurt the children?" Jane moved to the corner and crouched beside the sleeping boy. Nicholas saw her shoulders become rigid as soon as she touched his face.

"They took her in the garden. Only one came in, turned over the table, and left," Bridget said quietly.

"How long has Bowie been sleeping, Maire?" Jane asked of the sister, trying to keep her tone calm. Her hands ran down the boy's neck and pressed against his chest while she waited for an answer.

The young girl didn't seem to have heard the question. She continued to rock the baby in her arms and keep a wary gaze on Nicholas.

"Maire," Jane called softly, but there was still no answer.

She turned her gaze from the sleeping boy to the frightened expression on the girl's face.

"Can you crouch down?" she asked softly of Nicholas. "I believe your size . . . and your clothing might be the distraction here."

He felt like a fool not to have realized that himself.

He immediately removed his jacket and dropped it on the floor beside Jane's cloak. Rolling his sleeves up, he moved to the boy and crouched down beside her. He realized that Jane had intentionally not called him by name.

"That was quite thoughtless of me," he whispered. He could see that Jane had opened the front of the boy's shirt. There were dark bruises on the ribs.

"Who'd be with ye?" Bridget whispered, fear evident in her voice. Frail hands searched the air frantically. "Where are the children? Maire, where is Daniel? Wake up Bowie right away, Maire. Wake him up."

The young girl pressed her young brother tighter against her frail chest and moved farther out of the widow's reach.

"There is nothing to fear, Bridget," Jane assured her. "This man with me is a friend. Like me, he is only here to help."

"Ye must not be Egan," Bridget said accusingly. She tried to push herself up to her feet, but fell back. "She came alone. Ye brought a man with you. Nay . . . Egan would ne'er do that."

Nicholas placed a hand on Bowie's brow. The boy was burning with fever. This close he could also hear the wheezing sound from his chest.

"He is only seven, but has suffered more than someone who is seventy," Jane said quietly. "And there is more wrong with him than the fever. I think he might have broken some bones in his chest."

Jane moved hurriedly to the blind woman as she managed to push herself to her feet. Her hands continued to reach out around her, and she nearly tripped over the steaming pot.

"Bridget, it is I." Jane grasped the thin hands in her own. "Feel this . . . this is the same shawl Kathleen gave me only three days ago." She pressed the woman's hand against the wool and then eased her hold on her, allowing her to feel it on her own.

Nicholas had seen the tattered shawl when Jane had discarded her cloak. His gaze was drawn now to Maire's pale face. The little girl's face had brightened, and she looked alert for the first time. The child moved hesi-

tantly toward Jane. Even little Daniel stopped crying and
lifted his head to stare into his sister's face.

"Bowie is ill, Bridget." Jane spoke as the blind woman
reached up and lightly touched Jane's face.

Nicholas had no faith in Bridget's state of mind. If
this woman were questioned by Musgrave and his men,
who could say that she wouldn't describe Egan to them.
It was bad enough that she knew Egan was a woman.

"I want to take Bowie away . . . to where I can have
a doctor see to him."

"Nay." Bridget shook her head once. "Kathleen is
coming back for them."

"I know she is. But Bowie is sick with fever now. He
needs help right away. We have to get him help before
his mother returns."

At the word "fever," Bridget took a tottery step back.

From the other corner of the small room, Maire crept
even closer, fresh tears sprouting in her eyes. Nicholas
wasn't certain if Jane was aware of the transformation
in the girl since she'd recognized the mother's wrap. He
looked for a way to tell her and then he saw Jane's hand
stretch out toward the girl.

"I want to take the three of them with me. The children should be kept together."

Nicholas's heart warmed when he saw Maire put her
small hand in Jane's. His gaze was uncontrollably drawn
to the woman who continually managed to amaze him.

"Nay, miss. I don't want Kathleen be thinking that
I . . . that I pushed her wee ones out onto the road."

"She will never think such a thought," Jane assured
her. "She knew these three would be too much for you.
That was why she sent for me."

Before Bridget could think of an objection, Jane
touched the blind woman's arm. "I'll arrange for word
to get to Kathleen about the children. I shall make certain she knows where to find them when the authorities
release her."

This time when Jane reached for the baby, he moved
willingly into her arms, though his gaze remained on his
sister's face. For her part, Maire pressed herself into the
folds of the black skirts.

Bridget mumbled some words about saints and faerie folk and went back to the cooking pot.

Nicholas took charge of the feverish older boy. As he wrapped his coat around the limp body and lifted him gently, the bitter image of the young girl he'd found in St. James's Park on that night just before Christmas came back to him. Bowie was almost as light and as oblivious as she was. Both of them were dressed in nothing but rags. They each seemed like children abandoned to their suffering, though this boy's situation was very different. A weak cough sounded in Bowie's chest, and Nicholas forced himself to shake off the feeling of doom that was afflicting him. There was still time.

*Let there still be time for this one*, he prayed.

The bright sunshine outside offered a startling contrast to the gloom inside. The brush of the early fall breeze against Bowie's face made him cough again and bury his face deeper into Nicholas's chest.

The baronet started briskly toward his horse, but he paused for a moment to brand into his memory the gladdening sight before him.

Jane had already climbed onto the back of Queen Mab, and the two children were seated before her. She was speaking softly to Maire and at the same time holding Daniel's hand and encouraging the little one to caress the horse's soft mane. There was softness— affection—love in the actions. It occurred to Nicholas that this might be the most beautiful sight he'd ever been blessed to see.

Jane's gaze turned in his direction, and he saw her anxious look at Bowie. She then looked up to Nicholas's face and, as their gazes locked, he saw in her the woman he'd been searching for.

Silence hung like a pall over the Morning Room. Seated with her two female guests at a small table by the fire, Lady Purefoy sipped her tea and eyed the French-style pastries tastefully arranged on a small platter. Clara sulked in a chair by the window, ignoring the small plate and saucer of tea on the table beside her. The words of greeting this morning had been brief and perfunctory, and the appetite of the Spencer women scarcely matched their hostess's.

Lady Purefoy motioned to one of the servants to pour more tea for Alexandra, and glanced over at her daughter, hoping to get her attention. Clara gazed out the window, ignoring her mother.

Catherine, frustrated with the girl's aloofness, bit into a pastry that she could do without. It had been the same for the past two days—Clara moping about openly before their company. Not once had the young woman followed her directions to ask Sir Nicholas to go out for a walk—or to give him a tour of the gardens—or even to read to him from one of the books she always kept her nose buried in. Why, Clara had not once tried to initiate a conversation.

Giving a ball had been a grand idea, but Catherine knew that one night would hardly be enough to settle her daughter's future. She chose another piece of pastry, but before putting it into her mouth, another idea dawned on her.

"Have you ladies heard of our legendary Blarney Castle?"

Their guest turned to her daughter, seemingly waiting for her to answer. But Frances's surliness had increased daily since they'd arrived. She and Clara made a perfect pair, Catherine thought.

"Yes, we have," Lady Spencer finally replied. "On our drive here from Cork City, Frances was telling us all about the gift of eloquence that is rumored to be connected with kissing some stone in the castle wall."

"Yes . . . indeed. That is exactly the case," Catherine said excitedly. "I was just thinking . . . when Sir Nicholas comes down this morning, perhaps we can convince him that he should take my Clara and Miss Spencer to Blarney Castle. I don't know a young person who would not find it thrilling to . . ."

"I would prefer to stay in today," Frances said quietly. As her mother opened her mouth, Lady Purefoy noticed the sharp look that the sixteen-year-old directed her elder. "I've a headache."

"Clara, I'm certain, would love to go, anyway. Would you not, my dear?" Catherine pressed.

Her daughter's lack of enthusiasm, though unspoken, was very clearly etched in the troubled and pleading blue eyes.

"Then it is settled." Catherine turned to Lady Spencer and gave her a reassuring nod. "This is what these young people need these days. Someone to push them out the door and make them enjoy themselves. Now, when I was younger, we didn't need our mothers to tell us how to court a young man."

The housekeeper entered the room at that moment, surveying the tea and pastries.

"Fey, I was just about to send for you," Lady Purefoy called out jubilantly. "Lady Spencer and I had a wonderful idea that Sir Nicholas and Clara should go out for a picnic today to Blarney Castle. Kindly tell the cook to prepare a basket for them. Oh, and tell Paul it would be best if he were to prepare my open carriage." She smiled at Alexandra's dubious face. "I know your son is fond of horses, and I assure you my Clara is a most talented rider. Call me old-fashioned if you will, but I think a young man and young woman can enjoy their conversations so much more in a carriage rather than on horseback."

She saw the housekeeper still in the room, obviously looking for an opportunity to speak.

"What is it, Fey?" she said curtly.

"Sir Nicholas has already gone out, m'lady."

"Out? Is he out with Sir Thomas?"

"I've no reason to think so. I heard Sir Thomas asking for him when he was taking his own breakfast. When Paul came up, I heard him say that Sir Nicholas had gone out for a ride some time ago."

"Alone?" Catherine turned curiously to her guest, who was delicately sipping her tea. "Do you know where he is gone, Lady Spencer? Or when he is coming back?"

"More years ago than I wish to count, ma'am, I stopped worrying about Nicholas's whereabouts."

"But it is such a beautiful day." Catherine rose to her feet impatiently and walked to the window, glancing outside. "I simply *hate* to see it go to waste. Don't you agree?"

"I do." Something in her guest's voice made Lady

Purefoy turn in time to see the other woman smiling enigmatically over the rim of her cup. "But perhaps Nicholas is not wasting it, after all."

The two women looked with mutual concern at the ailing child lying on the bed between them.

"Where did these bruises come from, miss?"

"On our way here, little Maire told me that Bowie came back just as the soldiers were taking their mother away yesterday. The little fighter picked up a stick and tried to stop them."

Jane squeezed the excess water out of a towel into the washbasin and gently continued bathing the boy's face. Mrs. Brown clucked compassionately and tried to remove his tattered shirts as gently as she could.

"Maire said he was kicked a few times."

Mrs. Brown's ruddy face became even redder as her temper rose. "Sons of devils, they are. Striking down wee ones!"

Jane swallowed her own anger, but promised herself that there would be retaliation for this. Some of the Shanavests, like Ronan and even levelheaded Patrick, had repeatedly suggested that there should be an ambush against the dragoons at the Buttevant barracks for the violence that they were committing more and more freely against the Irish. But Jane had always spoken against it. She did not want to give Musgrave a reason to start searching out the Shanavests. It wasn't any fear of the magistrate's successes that bothered her, but the certain knowledge that many who were innocent would be hurt by the fighting that would surely ensue.

Innocents like Bowie.

"Has Parson Adams sent for the doctor yet?" Jane touched the boy's fevered skin again.

"He went after Dr. Forrest himself. He didn't want the man tarrying because it was only some Irish widow's child that needed tending. Ah, no . . . will you look at that?" Mrs. Brown pointed to more bruises along Bowie's side.

"Will he come, though?"

"The parson will make sure he does," the housekeeper replied with certainty.

"The boy's sister also said that Bowie had been sick for a few days before the soldiers came. Coughing and shivering." Jane watched the other woman's capable hands gently open their patient's mouth and feed him a few drops of water. "The sickness . . . and then the upset of the mother being taken away . . . and then the beating. Far too much for one as young as this."

The young boy's throat worked painfully, but he seemed to swallow the liquid.

"Aye," the older woman said, straightening her back. "If you don't mind, Miss Jane, would you go and look in on the wee ones? Cook was trying to feed them, but the lass . . ."

"Maire."

Mrs. Brown nodded. "I don't think she'll take a bite unless you comfort her yourself. She is a worrier, I can tell."

The housekeeper raised Bowie's head on some pillows and pulled a clean sheet over the boy's chest.

Jane reluctantly stood up. She knew Mrs. Brown was far more capable than she was in seeing to the needs of this sick child. But she also knew how fragile Maire, in particular, was.

"Is Sir Nicholas still downstairs, or did he go with Parson Adams?"

"Neither." The housekeeper looked up in surprise. "I don't know where he disappeared to. He carried the lad up here and put him on the bed, and then went down those stairs and out the door."

Not surprising, Jane thought. This was surely much more than he'd bargained for. Much more than he'd been ready to commit to.

But she had no time to think of any of this now. She cast a final glance at the child's still form and quietly slipped out of the room.

This was what she was meant to do with her life. And she wouldn't let herself take a step off this path, no matter what the temptation.

She told herself she should be glad Spencer had come to his senses.

# Chapter 17

Praying that she wouldn't be seen, Clara tucked the worn copy of *The Castle of Otranto* under the blanket she carried over her arm, and scurried past the small grove of fruit trees where she'd accidentally come upon Lady Spencer busily sketching.

More than anything else, she just wanted a few moments of relief. A few moments alone. One more careless word by her mother, one more vulgar mention of how she could more effectively flaunt herself in front of Sir Nicholas, and Clara knew she would surely go mad.

Out of the corner of her eye, she saw Lady Spencer put down her sketch board, stand up, and stretch. Looking away, Clara moved deeper into the meadow. Though their guests—both mother and daughter—were nice enough people, she simply couldn't bear to be engaged in conversation right now.

After breakfast, Lady Purefoy had insisted on having a long chat with her daughter in her workroom. The *chat* had consisted of a long lecture on how disappointed both her parents were with the way Clara had been conducting herself with their esteemed company. And the scolding had ended with direct instructions about just how Clara should behave in order to win the distinguished gentleman's attention, affection, and proposal of marriage.

Clara felt sick at the recollection of some of the things her mother had said. How different now from the instructions she'd received en route to London! She shook her head, realizing how shockingly ruined she would be if she attempted to put into practice most of what her mother had told her. She might as well walk to Cork City and join the streetwalkers along the waterfront.

And to think that Catherine was quick to object to Clara reading mere books like the one under her arm! And here, when it came to real life . . . !

She soon arrived at a favorite spot—a corner of the meadow, close to the paddock but protected by a hedge behind her. Here, with the valley spreading out beneath her, the sun was warm and she could hear the goings-on in the paddock and stable without being seen herself.

Spreading her blanket, she sat down and opened the book on her lap. As she paged through it, Clara recalled the exciting part where she'd left the story last. *Isabella had just vanished from the monastery.*

As she searched for the place, she paused for a moment, thinking of the seed of an idea that had occurred to her while she was enduring her mother's lecture.

Henry had been invited to the party given this Friday, and Clara knew that he would be here. Now, her mother had made certain that absolutely no one outside of the immediate family and Fey had been told of Sir Nicholas's rejection.

How interesting it would be if Henry were somehow to be told . . . perhaps through a letter. Henry had loved her once. The thought that he might conceivably see it his duty to console her regarding the loss made her tingle with anticipation. And how absolutely delightful it would be to use some of her mother's suggested methods—not to try to trap the worldly Sir Nicholas—but to seduce the infinitely more kindhearted Henry Adams.

The very thought sent an excited shiver down Clara's arms. Without having read a single word, she closed the book and rose impatiently to her feet.

This was it. She had the way. She'd had a taste of his passion three days ago. He still loved her, despite his hard words. He would succumb if she pursued. And he was far too honorable not to marry her if they were . . . to somehow . . . find themselves in a compromising situation. All she had to do was send him the letter to start her plan in motion.

Almost giddy now, she was gathering up her blanket

when she heard a horse come up the road. The rider called out to someone in the paddock, and Clara immediately recognized the man's heavy brogue. The voice belonged to a groom who worked for Henry. She would send her letter to Parson Adams with him. Surely, she thought, this is Providence itself at work.

She stepped through the hedge and walked toward the paddock gate. She would make the letter very short. Perhaps, she wouldn't even explain anything, but say it was critical that Henry meet with her somewhere . . . in private.

Yes. In person and in private. Face-to-face, she had the greatest chance of success.

Clara intentionally slowed her steps. She couldn't look too eager. The man had dismounted and was talking with one of the Woodfield House stable boys.

"Roger," she called.

Henry's groom immediately turned and, recognizing Clara, doffed his cap.

"Why, Miss Clara! A fine good day to ye. I was just coming up to the house to deliver a letter from the parson."

"Perhaps I can take it . . . since I am here . . . and I am going that way."

The other groom nodded politely to her and walked away with Roger's horse. The messenger took a letter out of his pocket and offered it to Clara.

"Thank ye, miss."

"Is it for my father?"

"Nay, miss . . . I mean aye, miss. Now that I think of it, Parson Adams didn't say which one of your parents to deliver it to. I just thought to give it to Fey, though I believe there is a name on the outside, is there not, miss?"

Clara looked at it. "Indeed, there is."

"Does it say Lady Purefoy, miss?"

"I didn't know you can read, Roger." Clara tucked it into her pocket. "That's exactly what it says."

"Reading is something I've ne'er had time for, miss. But I thought, 'tis about Miss Jane, so it must be meant for your mother."

"I shall take it up to her directly."

"Thank ye, miss."

"Would you mind waiting a few moments before you return, Roger? My mother might wish to send a message back. Also . . . I have a letter that I would like you to take to Ballyclough for me."

"As ye wish, Miss Clara." He nodded politely again. "I need to be seeing to the parson's horse, anyway. The old devil threw a shoe at the bottom of the hill, just now."

Clara started up the hill, but instead of thinking about what she was to write, her attention focused on the message in her pocket. Roger had said that the news was about Jane. For too many days now, Jane had been flitting in and out of Woodfield House. For the past two days, Clara had not even thought to worry about her when she hadn't shown up for meals. She knew, though, that their parents hadn't bothered to notice any of Jane's comings and goings, either.

As soon as she left the paddock, she crossed over and took the path through the gardens. When she was safely out of sight, Clara took the envelope out and stared at Henry's seal. Lady Purefoy always asked her to read and respond to correspondence anyway. So her curiosity of what was inside—her worry about Jane, Clara corrected herself—pushed her to break the seal.

Leaning against a tree, the young woman let her gaze wander over Henry's graceful handwriting before the actual words began to register.

Jane was in Ballyclough today. Henry was letting Lady Purefoy and Sir Thomas know that their daughter was visiting some of the families in the parish. And since she was also determined to spend some time at the bedside of an ailing child in the village, the parson's recommendation was for her to stay at the parsonage overnight rather than risk traveling home late at night.

It took a moment for the words to sink in. When they did, though, a jealousy she had never before experienced clawed sharply at Clara's entrails. Tears hot and sudden stung her eyes.

Henry no longer cared for her. He was smitten with

Jane, and Clara should have known. She crumpled the
letter and stuffed it in her pocket before running for
the house.

She should have seen it, she thought bitterly. For all
these years, Clara had secretly admired him, watched
him, had been in love with him, but his attention had
always been on Jane.

Clara blindly climbed the stairs to her room.

She had rejected his offer six months ago, not only
because of her parents' plans, but partly because of that
continuous measuring with Jane. The day before his proposal, Henry had spent the entire afternoon with Jane.
The week before that—and a dozen times since—it had
been Jane's opinion that he'd come seeking at Woodfield
House. Time and time again, he would ask after Jane's
health . . . or her art. Indeed, he was the only one who
Jane would invite to her workroom in the attic.

Clara seethed to think how much time the two of them
spent up there together. Alone. Now she knew the *real*
reason Jane had not made any fuss about not going to
London.

She banged open the door to her bedchamber and
slammed it shut behind her. The tears had stopped
somewhere along the way, and a cold fury had taken
their place.

"How blind!? How blind could I have been?"

She started pacing the large room. Even Mrs. Brown
had hinted at Henry's concerns and interests last week,
but Clara—too blind to recognize the obvious—had
thrown herself at him.

And he'd rejected her. He had *rejected* her, not because of the reasons he'd listed, but because he wanted
her ruined sister.

Hurt . . . anger . . . revenge . . . Emotions so long
suppressed churned within her. She felt ready to burst
when a persistent knocking finally drew her attention.
She stormed to the door and yanked it open.

The young servant took a step back when she saw the
wrath blazing in Clara's face.

"What?"

"Beggin' yer pardon, miss. Someone saw ye coming

up to the house. Yer mother wants to know what the message was about—"

"Take her this." Clara tore the crumpled letter from her pocket and threw it at the girl. She was ready to slam the door shut again, when the girl put out a hand plaintively.

"Pardon, miss. She was asking if ye have something to go to . . . to Parson Adams, as his man is waiting."

"No! Nothing." Clara's hand gripped the edge of the door. "But there is something you can do for me."

The servant nodded worriedly and waited.

"Find out if the baronet is back. If he is, then have the cook prepare a picnic basket and ask Paul to get an open carriage ready. He and I are going for a ride."

"And if he is not?" she asked nervously.

"Then come and get me as soon as he is."

Clara continued to hold the door even after the serving girl disappeared down the hall. Her parents were right—her mother especially. She was too fine a creature for a place so coarse as Ireland. She was too beautiful and well-bred not to be able to make an advantageous match for herself.

Nicholas Spencer hadn't asked for her hand in marriage, that was true. But it was only because, since leaving London, she had worked on hiding her charms, her pleasing attitude, her intelligence, and her wit.

Now that she was resolved that he would do for a husband, the handsome baronet didn't have a chance. They would be married in a fortnight.

Her mother was always right, she thought with bitter clarity.

Slumber was finally taking the children into her soft golden arms. Daniel's eyes drifted shut for a long moment, and then immediately opened wide. He clearly didn't want to miss any of the story. Maire's two small hands were clutching one of Jane's, and the young girl's green eyes became huge when Jane reached a particularly exciting moment in the tale.

Despite the significance of the news he had to share, Henry Adams couldn't bring himself to intrude on this serene scene. The two children shared the bed. Jane sat beside them, telling an Irish tale in Gaelic. He watched her reach over and caress the little one's hair.

A new awareness washed over Henry, taking him by surprise, as his gaze was drawn to Jane's face. He didn't remember ever being so taken by her beauty. She seemed to shine from within. A softness, a maternal side of her that he'd never known, made his heart ache and recall how cruel her own society had been to her.

This was her right—to be a woman, a mother. She had loved once and had suffered greatly in losing her lover. But people never forgot. They never looked at the person beyond the gossip and scandal.

She ended the story happily, with peace and harmony prevailing for the good folk who triumphed over evil. Daniel's eyes were already closed, but Maire's pale face was smiling. Henry watched Jane lean over the child and brush a kiss over her brow. The young girl's hands were reluctant, but finally released her hand as Jane stood up.

Jane blew out the candle on the table near the bed. When she straightened up from the children, she noticed him for the first time. "How long have you been here?"

She smiled and Henry felt another tug of warmth in his heart. She had been his friend for so long.

"Long enough to be lulled and even enchanted by the magic of your tongue."

"After all these years, I cannot believe you have never learned to speak Gaelic, Henry," she whispered, giving a final glance over her shoulder before following him out of the room.

"How do you know I don't speak it?"

She gave him a suspicious look. "Because I have never heard you."

In the narrow passage, she partially closed the door to the children's room.

"You'd be amazed what you might learn about me if you came around more often." He took her hand and lifted it to his lips. "Why is it that you always smell so good?"

She paused and this time gave him an odd stare. "What are you about tonight, Henry Adams?"

He laughed and, letting go of her hand, placed an

arm affectionately around her shoulder. Together, they started down the corridor. "You always see through me, do you not, Miss Purefoy?"

"I should . . . considering all the years I've known you." She stopped at the closed door of Bowie's room. "How is he?"

"Still running a fever. But he was awake when I looked in on him."

Excited about this change, she had her hand on the door latch when Henry stopped her.

"Be prepared for a surprise."

His expression revealed nothing, but Jane remembered his relaxed attitude standing in the other doorway.

"This can only be good." She pushed the door open and immediately gasped with delight. "Kathleen! You are here!"

Bowie was awake and was holding his mother's hand tightly. Still, the young woman came to her feet and smiled tearfully at Jane. "I just arrived . . . a scant minute or so ago."

Jane walked in and hugged her fiercely.

"Thank you E . . . Miss Jane," the young mother whispered and cried quietly. "I knew you'd be coming after them. I knew you would never fail us."

Behind them, Mrs. Brown entered the room with a tray carrying a bowl of soup and a loaf of bread. Jane finally let go of the young woman.

"Maire might be still awake next door, Kathleen. Daniel is with her."

Bowie reached for his mother, and Kathleen sat down again beside her feverish but happy son.

"Aye, miss. I'll go to them in a minute."

Too happy for words, Jane turned around and saw Henry leaving the room. She followed and caught up to him at the top of the stairs. When he heard her footsteps and turned around, Jane—overwhelmed by the magnitude of his efforts—threw her arms around him.

"Thank you, Henry. You are a good man. Thank you for managing this."

The arms that had wrapped around her in return gently caressed her back. "I wish I deserved your sentiments. But 'twas not I who brought Kathleen back, but Clara's fiancé . . . Sir Nicholas."

Jane's head immediately jerked off his shoulder. Her
arms released him, and she looked up to his solemn face.
"But I thought he left . . ."

"He left for Buttevant this morning. He told me he
intended to find Musgrave. He mentioned something
about some donation of coins he'd made with your help
to some of the needy families in the area. He told me
he was going to ask the magistrate about the reason for
Kathleen's arrest. If it had anything to do with that
money, he was determined to demand her release."

"You didn't tell me any of this!"

"I didn't think he had much chance of succeeding."
He turned to descend the stairs.

She tugged at his sleeve to stop him. "What do you
have against him, Henry?"

"Why ask such a question?" he said evasively, his face
devoid of emotion.

"It is obvious that you two do not like each other.
Why is that?"

"If you insist on knowing, I can name a number of
reasons why I find him objectionable for Clara, but you
will have to ask *him* the reason for his surly behavior
toward me."

Jane blamed herself for Spencer's attitude. She should
not have praised one before the other. She might as well
have given a bone to one fighting dog while the other
stood watching.

"Where is he now?"

"I believe he was returning to Woodfield House."

"You didn't invite him to stay for something to eat?
Or asked him if he wished to see me?"

He shrugged. "No! I thought he would be anxious to
return to your sister."

"Oh, Henry! Sometimes you can be so thickheaded."
She slipped past him on the stairs, and he followed her
down. "How long ago did he leave?"

"I didn't slam the door in his face, Jane. And he didn't
ask to see you, in any case."

Jane gave him a sharp look. "*When* did he leave?"

"Not very long ago. But you are not going after him
now, are you?"

"I am going back to Woodfield House," Jane stated

when they reached the front entrance hall. She threw her cloak around her shoulders.

"How about Kathleen and her children?"

"Tell them I'll be back tomorrow."

"But I sent a message to your mother, telling her that you would be staying here tonight."

"She won't know the difference," Jane assured him, giving him a light kiss on the cheek. "Good night, Henry."

Lighting a wick from a candle in the front entryway, she walked out toward the stable where her horse had been settled for the night. Working quickly, she saddled Mab, blew out the tiny flame, and led her out.

Nicholas had done this for *her*, she thought as she tossed the reins up over the horse's head. He had gone back to the barracks at Buttevant . . . and most likely saved the young mother's life in doing so. She couldn't wait to find him and thank him.

Jane was about to mount up when she saw Henry's long frame leaning against a tree next to the parsonage, watching her silently. And this was another man that had to hear her appreciation. With a guilty smile, she walked back toward him.

"I am sorry . . . I had no right to be so critical."

"You are forgiven." He spoke solemnly, but she detected the trace of a smile tugging at the corner of his mouth.

"And I never thanked you for what you are doing for Kathleen and her children. I take so much for granted in you, Henry, and—"

"Just go, Jane," he said with a knowing nod. "Go and catch up to him."

# Chapter 18

"Perhaps we should get Sir Thomas to send out a search party for him. Your son has been gone *all* day!"

Alexandra patted Lady Purefoy's arm. "I am quite certain that is completely unnecessary. Knowing my son, he is probably developing a fond friendship at this very moment with a number of your neighbors at some village inn. As we speak, they are probably drinking and rolling up their sleeves and trying to outdo the next with war stories. And in a few hours, they will be wagering on a brawl taking place outside . . . that is, if Nicholas is not one of the combatants."

The horrified expression on their hostess's face was precious, but soon the woman let out an uneasy laugh.

"I am not always prepared for your quick wit, Lady Spencer. So many times I just cannot separate truth from jest."

Alexandra arched a questioning eyebrow. "Do you think I was speaking in jest?"

She was pleased to see the cloud of confusion settle heavily on the other woman's face. Casually, but before she was asked again about Nicholas's whereabouts, Alexandra walked to where Fanny and Lady Purefoy's daughter were engaged in a card game of some kind. Clara's stylish and revealing dress tonight was far different from anything she'd worn before. But there was something else different about the young woman tonight. Alexandra used her artist's eye to try to discover what it might be.

Clara certainly appeared as quiet as ever. But the air

of dreaminess that had pervaded her manner seemed to have evaporated. She appeared alert—even intelligent.

Alexandra sat in a chair near them. "So what do *you* think of a wellborn Englishman who becomes deathly bored with spending too much time with the people of his own rank?"

"I find him charming. Where could I meet such a man?"

"Frances!" Alexandra scolded lightly. "I was speaking to Clara."

"But Mother, you need to be clearer in your description. I, for one, would be curious to know if this noble gentleman happens to be young and incredibly handsome and desperately in search of the love of his life." Frances's blue eyes danced with mischief when they met her mother's. "After all, I am not too young. Sixteen is the perfect age to start the search for—"

"*This* discussion doesn't concern you, young woman." Alexandra spoke the words quietly and sweetly, but she made sure that daggers laced her tone.

"Oh! Now I understand. You were referring to *Nicholas.*"

Lady Spencer glared at her daughter as the young woman hid a smile. Knowing any further reproach would be completely useless with the little troublemaker, she turned toward Clara.

"And what is your opinion?"

She was greatly surprised to see this young woman was trying to stifle a smile, as well, hiding her face behind the cards.

"Well, Miss Clara, this is a side to you we haven't seen."

Clara lowered her cards and looked Alexandra in the eye.

"My apologies, Lady Spencer. But I find your daughter's gift of honesty and candor delightful."

"What a curious way to describe a curse."

As the two of them giggled like conspirators who had just snitched the church wine, Alexandra considered with some amazement the transformation that had taken place in the relationship between the two of them, as well.

"The incorrigible and the corrupted," she said breez-ily, walking away with an arch smile.

In her heart, though, a heavy weight was settling. It was difficult to admit, but she had been much happier *not* liking Clara. Whom this young woman was trying to imitate, or had suddenly become again, was a woman who had a much greater chance of success. She was no doubt once again the woman Nicholas had, at some point, considered marrying.

Walking to the window, Alexandra stared out into the darkness and thought of Jane. She had made a decision not to interfere. She'd thought it would be best to allow Fortune's wheel to turn as it will. But now she wasn't sure if that was such a good idea. With Clara obviously setting her mind to compete for Nicholas's attention, the older sister didn't have a chance to succeed. And though Jane had not shown any hint of even being interested in Nicholas, Alexandra had been watching her own son. He was wrestling with feelings that were leaving him unset-tled. For every meal the older Purefoy sister had been absent, Nicholas's attitude had worsened tenfold. He was not one to allow himself to become so affected by a woman—unless there was something more between them than anybody knew.

Sir Thomas's brooding figure appeared in the door-way, and he cast a look around the parlor before settling a frowning glance on his wife. "Sir Nicholas is not back yet, I take it."

Catherine Purefoy laid down her needlework and rushed to her husband. "I've had Cook wait dinner, but it is getting late and"—she lowered her voice—"Lady Spencer believes we shouldn't wait at all."

The man gave a curt nod. "Have a tray sent to me in the library."

Alexandra watched her host's rude behavior with dis-gust as he walked abruptly away. A glance at Clara showed the young woman's cheerful demeanor return as soon as the conversation between her parents had ended. But Jane. Where was Jane?

Armed with new purpose, Lady Spencer knew that she had to help the older sister. Fortune's wheel sometimes did not turn quickly enough, she decided. It was up to her to meddle.

The rising moon cast long stretches of shadows and made the mountains in the distance appear to loom large over the land.

Nicholas tried to restrain his anger and frustration and instead focus on the moonlit countryside. So much of the land was already familiar. The Blackwater River lined by rolling farms and pastures. Farther south, the higher moorland cut by deep valleys of marsh and woodland. The sight and the names of mountains and pagan stones and villages nestled into the hills were becoming inscribed in his memory. Boggeragh, Banteer, Drommahane, Nad. Tonight though, wherever he looked, Jane's face was all he saw.

He wanted her. This fierce yearning for a particular woman was a new sensation. It was one he'd never experienced before. And frankly, he found it as maddening as it was magical.

He wanted to spend endless hours with her. He wanted to see her. He wanted to touch her. He wanted to lose himself in her taste and softness. He wanted to see her smile and watch her turn to him as she had done this morning when they'd left Kathleen's cottage.

But he couldn't have her. By 'sblood, he'd be damned if he would compete for her affection if she were already in love with another man. Nicholas refused to play the part of any second. He wanted her body, heart, and soul all for himself. He wasn't about to share her with anyone.

Jane had said that there was nothing between Henry Adams and herself, but he believed she wasn't being honest with herself. It had been to the parson's house that she had wanted to take the three children. It had been the parson's help that she'd sought.

There was trust, friendship . . . and something much more, he suspected, between them.

A sound coming from somewhere to his left caused Nicholas to rein in his horse and peer into the darkness. He was the only one abroad as far as he could see. He could see no one on foot. No light shone from any cottage or villages nearby. He put his hand on the hilt of his sword and tested the convenience of the knife in his boot.

Confident that he could handle whatever trouble might be lurking in the moon's shadows, he turned his gaze on the appearance of a horse and rider coming over the crest of a hill to the east. They were still quite a few yards away, but the drumming of his heart in his chest—more than the strength of his vision—told him who the rider was.

The moon was over her shoulder. Woman and horse presented a magnificent sight, and Nicholas found himself swallowing hard. With her loose dark hair dancing in the wind and her graceful body moving in harmony with the animal, she was surely an apparition from his dreams. As she drew near, she slowed Mab to a walk. With each step, Nicholas's tongue knotted tighter in his head, and his heart hammered louder in his chest. Her beautiful eyes, shining in the darkness of night, studied him, appraised him—and a different kind of tightness formed in his gut when she reined Mab to a halt right beside him.

"You give an incredibly good chase, Sir Nicholas."

"You have the eyes of a cat." His voice was hoarse and low. "Have you been following me, Miss Jane?"

Her gaze studied his face with a longing that scorched him—then it fell on his mouth. Nicholas's hands tightened around the horse's reins, but he didn't move.

"I have."

"What do you want from me?"

She leaned toward him, her hand reaching behind his neck. Drawing him to her, she stretched herself upward until their lips met. Her mouth was soft and her tongue playful as she teased and tasted him. Nicholas savored the pleasure of the kiss, but his restraint was short-lived. Starved for her taste and her touch, his arms reached for her as their mouths engaged in a duel of passion. But just as he was about to pull her from her horse and onto his lap, she ended the kiss. Mab took a couple of steps back.

He eyed her across the short span between them. "This is a dangerous game you are playing."

"I know." She sounded breathless and it took great effort on Nicholas's part not to reach for her again.

"What was the kiss for?"

"To thank you . . . for what you did for Kathleen . . . and for her children."

Gratitude? That was no kiss of gratitude. Suddenly, he wanted her to admit that the kiss was more about her desire . . . passion . . . about the way she felt about him.

"Were you equally grateful to Reverend Adams? He helped . . . he is helping that family, as well."

"Do I hear a hint of suspicion, even *jealousy*, in your tone?" She smiled.

"I am just a simple person asking a simple question."

"There is nothing simple about you, Sir Nicholas Spencer." Her softly spoken words caressed and soothed. "You have amazed me and surprised me and charmed me from the first moment that we met."

"Was that before or after I knocked you down?"

"Very amusing."

"Do you mean you didn't kiss Parson Adams?"

She laughed, and Nicholas found his mood improving. "No . . . I did not. Not the way I kissed *you*, in any case."

Before he could ask the question about how was it exactly that she had kissed the minister, Jane reined Mab around and pointed at the hills to the south and west.

"If you are in no great hurry to get back to Woodfield House, then I can properly thank you by showing you one of the most interesting sights in Munster. And before you ask"—she smiled at him—"I've never taken Parson Adams to the stones at Knocknakilla."

"I should not have dreamed of asking." Nicholas brought his horse alongside hers as they started off. "And, to be frank with you, Jane, if you are not at Woodfield House, I haven't any particular care *ever* to go back."

Even in the darkness of the night he could see the way the words affected her. She looked at him and, for a moment, he thought she was about to reach her hand out to him. An owl hooted somewhere in the distance, though, breaking the spell. She smiled and turned her gaze to the western hills.

"Try to keep up, Spencer," she said, spurring Mab on. " 'Tis a good ride we have ahead of us, and I do need to return you to my family at some reasonable hour."

While their horses grazed on the windswept moor, they walked together toward the ancient circle of stones. The stillness of the night, so perfect and complete, could not have been more at odds with the turmoil going on within her.

The agitation Jane was feeling had nothing to do with the man walking beside her. It had everything to do, rather, with coming back to this place.

There had been certain things that had remained sacred to her during the past nine years. She continued to wear black. She had never allowed herself to become emotionally or physically attracted to another man. She had foregone passion. And she had never come back here.

There were other things that had remained constant, too, for a rebel's life is often cut short. She never allowed herself to plan or dream of a future. She never wished for things that she could never have. Love, family, children—none of them had any place in Egan's life.

And yet, being here now, surrounded by night and the magic of the land . . .

For the first time in so many years, Jane felt the growing ache of what might have been.

She placed a hand on one of the stones and found it warm. Within it, she sensed the pulse of life.

"Is it not beautiful?" She filled her lungs and, looking up at the blanket of stars, turned her back to the breeze that came up at that moment.

"Stunning."

Jane turned her head and found Nicholas looking only at her.

"*You* are stunning," he repeated, coming closer. With each step Jane's heart pounded faster. Every limb in her body tingled with awareness as his gaze swept over her.

He stopped only a breath away. His large hand covered hers on top of the stone. An unfamiliar rhythm of need began to pound within her. It was as terrifying as it was exciting.

Jane tried to focus on the beauty of the land and not on the man. The moon had risen high in the sky. Not far from the circle of stones, a deserted cottage stood half-hidden in the high meadow grass. In spite of the brilliance of the moon, a million stars lit up the velvet cloth of heaven.

"I had forgotten how this place made me believe I could touch the sky . . . become part of the wind." She met his gaze. "Too many years I have been away from here."

"Wearing black—staying away from here—playing the hermit—being frightened of any attachments. They are all related, are they not?"

"I am not frightened of attachments," she immediately protested, not entirely certain that she was ready to pour out her heart . . . and her past.

"But you are, Jane." Nicholas's fingers brushed the windblown hair away from her face. His warm touch lingered on her skin. "You are frightened of me. I am not talking about my physical size, or if I can handle you or not when you are pointing a knife at me. And I am not referring to whatever knowledge I might have of your secret activities, either." He gave her a knowing smile. "You are afraid of the man, of our mutual attraction, and what is happening between us."

"There is nothing between us." She tried to pull away from the stone, but the pressure of his hand held her in place. She still wasn't ready to give up the fight. "If you believe that because I kissed you, I am attracted to you . . . I told you that was an expression of gratitude . . . I was moved by what you did . . . and . . ."

"You appear flustered, Jane." He brushed his mouth against hers, and pulled back before she could either push him away or melt against him. "You want to ignore 'us.' But you do not know what to do with everything you are feeling here." He pressed a finger at her heart. "And here." He gently touched her temple. "I could gladly show you where else you are confused, but I would not take such liberties until you readily admit you are as attracted to me as I am to you."

"This is foolishness." She turned her face away, not wanting him to know how accurate his words were.

"Why did you bring me here?" Nicholas cupped her chin and turned her face to him. "There is something here that you want to show me . . . or perhaps tell me."

"I only brought you here for the excellent view."

"At night?" he asked softly.

She asked the same question of herself. The impulsiveness of riding after him, and then kissing him, and then wanting to share . . . this particular place. What had she been thinking? These pagan stones at Knocknakilla held a special place in her life. They had belonged for so many years only to two young people in love.

Looking up at him, she wondered with a moment's panic if it was just because of this man that she was willing to open this door to her past. How could so much change so quickly?

"I have seen you in action, Jane. You have no fear in risking your life for these people—for your beliefs. And yet, right now you are afraid."

Of course she was afraid. She knew the pain a wound to the heart inflicts. She knew the rending ache that comes in the night, tearing at you until you pray you will die before the dawn comes. She knew what it was like to lie curled in the corner of a room and watch the evening light fade, and have no more tears to cry.

Yes, she was afraid. She was afraid of how he would act—how he would feel—if he knew the whole truth.

But she was also afraid that she cared for Nicholas Spencer much more than she could ever put into words.

The stars seemed to disappear in the sky. Everything around them became still. The birds. The breezes. Nature itself appeared to be waiting for Jane to speak.

"It is inevitable that you should hear scandalous rumors of my past while you are staying at Woodfield House." She spoke quickly before losing her courage. "I myself have hinted more than a few times of my ruined reputation. I brought you here because . . . because I thought instead of rumor, you deserve to hear the truth . . . from me." She took a deep breath and met his gaze. "Once you hear what I am all about, then we can rethink this business about your . . . your attraction to me."

He entwined his fingers with hers on top of the stone. "Tell me this thing that is so horrible about your past."

It would have been much easier to talk of her past if she were not faced with the reality of the present. Nicholas Spencer was all around her.

"Right here, in this very place, I gave my maidenhead to a man I loved." She hoped to shock him with the bluntness of the truth. "We played together as children, fell in love quite by accident, and—on many nights just like this—stood where we are standing and planned our future together."

Jane looked around her and saw all the images of long ago imprinted on the grass and stone.

"Conor was everything to me. He was my past, my present, my future. He was my life and my dreams. He was my hero and my hope. He offered the sanctuary I had never found within my own family." She looked up into Nicholas's face. "I have no regret for what I did, and I feel no shame in talking about him . . . to you or anyone . . . ever."

"Nor should you." His touch stayed—his eyes dark and shining and never once wavering from hers.

"But he was a poor farmer. A commoner. A Catholic. Even worse, Conor was a Shanavest who had a heart generous enough to love me despite the sins of my father and my country against his people." She didn't want the tears to come. By God, she didn't! But they burned her eyes, and she turned away from him, this time pulling her hand free.

The wind began to pick up again. Jane pulled the cloak tighter around her shoulders and walked to the center of the circle of stones.

"Unlike my own people," she said bitterly, "who spend their entire lives judging others by narrow, hypocritical standards and acting in ways that breed hatred, Conor treated me as a living, breathing person . . . and not as some straw figure representing his English oppressors. He refused to judge me based on the past. He

refused to be intimidated by our differences in station—
or my so-called education. We would all be judged as
equals in God's eyes, he would say."

She looked up at the stars through a sheen of tears.
The hurt still cut so deep. The memories, though hazy,
continued to stab at her heart.

"Where is he now? Where did he go?"

"He was hanged." The salty taste of tears reached
Jane's lips. She tried to take a deep breath to steady her
voice. "Conor was hanged on the orders of my own father. He was killed not because of any horrible crime.
He was always the most peace-loving of the Shanavests.
The magistrate"—she stabbed at the tears—"my
father . . . issued his death warrant because of his
involvement with . . . *me*."

The tears choked the words in her throat. Jane let out
a broken breath and tried to fight the sob rising in her
chest. She walked out of the circle and stared at the
valley beyond. In her mind's eye, she could see Conor's
dead body swaying heavily. In the wind, she could almost hear her own cries echoing through the town.

Nicholas's arms reached around her and captured her
hands, and Jane welcomed his strength when he drew
her gently back against his chest.

"This is a hard world, Jane." His chin brushed against
her hair. "And I am sorry for the injustice we bring
to it."

She leaned against him. Nicholas's strength gave her
courage to find her voice again.

"We were to elope the next day. But somehow—
through one of the servants, I think—my father found
out about our plan. I was locked in . . . but I managed
to send Conor a message. Still, though, he showed up . . .
hoping, I suppose, that I'd be able to get away." She
closed her eyes to lessen the pain, but it could not be
shut out. It was inside of her. "Four other Shanavests—
Conor's friends all—were arrested that night, as well,
not far from Waterford. None of them, though, had any
idea how quick their end would come."

Jane tried to pull a hand free to wipe her face, but
Nicholas turned her gently in his arms and carefully
brushed her tears away himself.

"They . . . my family . . . were planning to keep me locked up. They wanted to hide what I had done . . . what Conor and I were going to do. As far as they were concerned, no one outside of the household would ever know about their daughter's shame. But they couldn't hold me. I ran away." She stared at the lapel of Nicholas's jacket, but all she saw were five bodies dangling in the wind. "When I found him . . . them . . . I made sure everyone knew. I was mad, I suppose. I forced my way through and cut those bodies down. I knelt on that gallows and cursed my father and the others who were responsible. I told the crowds that gathered that Conor was my lover. I . . . I even claimed that I was carrying his child."

"Were you?"

"I thought I was. I prayed that day that I was. But it was just not to be."

Nicholas lifted her chin. The brush of his callused thumb against her skin caused her to shiver involuntarily. In her mind's eye she saw another man, barely more than a boy—a work-roughened thumb brushing away her tears. How many times had she cried in Conor's arms, fearing for their future?

"The only vengeance I could wreak that day . . . on my father . . . on my family . . . was in ruining their name. I never thought for an instant that their peers would sympathize with them over the incomprehensible wickedness of a daughter. Indeed, the world . . . and my father . . . would cut me out of the light. From that day on, I would become the daughter who they never had."

He simply pulled her tightly against his chest and held her. Jane let her sorrow pour out, her tears falling on his jacket. She didn't know how long they stood there. No words passed between them, but with an occasional brush of his lips against her hair, the press of his hands on her back, a change began to occur within her.

For too long she had lived for vengeance she could not exact. Deep inside, she knew that killing one man—her father—would never bring back those five men or ease her pain. But joining the Whiteboy movement had helped.

Sometime later, Jane realized she had stopped crying.

As if just awakened herself from a deep sleep, she found her gaze focusing on the dark shapes of the standing stones. There were five.

Five stones standing for longer than anyone knew. Five stones carried here and erected for some mysterious purpose by people long gone. Five of them standing against the elements. Standing against wind and rain. Against sun and ice. Five of them.

Perhaps, she thought, the descendants of those people still lived here. Still worked this land and claimed it as their own. Despite the invasions of marauding Vikings and Romans and Englishmen, these people—these stones—still stood defiantly on the moor. Five that would stand forever.

Jane breathed in the clean smell of the fresh night air. She looked at the stones and felt the endless hours of loneliness and anguish quietly slip away. She would no longer allow herself to be crushed by grief.

"I see tragedy and sorrow in your past—but no shame," Nicholas whispered. His fingers threaded gently into her hair, and he pulled her head back until she was looking up into his face. "I admire your courage. I admire the woman you have become despite the adversity in your life."

There was understanding and compassion in his face . . . but fire, as well. Something within Jane thrilled to find that, despite hearing the truth of her past, he still wanted her.

"The present and the future belong to those who seize it, Jane. Seize it with me."

"Genteel society shuns me. It will be scandalous for you to have anything to do with me."

"Genteel society can go to hell," he growled. "I know the hypocrisy of the world. And I know what is good and decent when I see it, too."

His mouth descended, brushing over hers, before coaxing her lips apart. Jane's hands moved up his chest as he kissed her thoroughly. Realizing she was falling too deep and too fast, her fingers fisted on the lapels of his jacket, and she tore her mouth away.

"Wait! There is Clara . . . We cannot."

"I have said this before, Jane. There is *nothing* between Clara and me, and there never will be. I have already spoken to your father." Nicholas's large hands framed her face, and he looked steadily into her eyes. "How must I say it for you to understand? Who else should I tell? What will it take to convince you that *you* are the one who fascinates me. *You* are the one I am pursuing."

Jane rose up on her toes and kissed him again. This time, she tried to convey all of her frustration—all of the longing that tore at her—into the heated press of lips, the chafe and dance of tongues. Nicholas's reaction was immediate. His arms wrapped around her, his mouth as greedy as her own as he gave as much as he took. Jane clung to him, trying to keep her balance and retain a shred of sanity.

Too many years had passed. It had been so long that she'd forgotten what it was like to lose herself in a haze of passion. But as Nicholas's hands caressed and molded the cloak and dress against her body, and as every inch of Jane's body came alive with a sensual awareness, images of young love no longer danced before her eyes, but the hard, hot reality of this man and her own admission of what all of this meant.

There could no longer be any denial. Nicholas already had become much more to Jane than she would have thought possible. Still, though, she had gone this route once before and had suffered. And what was worse, this time around she saw the journey would be even rougher and more painful.

She pushed at his chest, and he immediately let her go. Jane took a step back, but couldn't bring herself to look into his face.

"We . . . we should go . . . 'Tis late. They shall be worrying about you." She took a few steps toward their horses, but turned around when she realized Nicholas was not coming.

He hadn't moved. He stood there among the stones, the moon behind him, his face in shadow, watching her. Her own heart was hammering in her chest, her tingling body crying out for his touch. It took all of her strength not to run back to him.

"Nicholas, I . . . I am planning to go back to Ballyclough

tomorrow. I will be going from there and making other visits, too. If you . . . if you wish to come with me . . .''

"I do.''

She tried not to be distracted by the relief washing through her.

"Then . . . I shall let you know tomorrow morning.''

"I'll be waiting.''

Patrick placed a firm hand on Ronan's arm, stopping him from moving out of the ruined cottage.

"Nay, ye have no business going out there. Let's get back to the horses.''

"I've business enough.''

"Ye'll not lay a hand on her.''

"I've nothing against Egan. That filthy English bastard is another thing entirely.''

"He's done nothing to rile ye.'' Patrick watched the two begin to mount their horses.

"The dog has made a pact with Musgrave, hasn't he?''

"We don't know if he has or if he hasn't. We only know that he went into the barracks at Buttevant alone and came out with Seamus's widow. We don't know what went on there, but I'm thinking we have as much reason to be thankful as we do to suspect him. Maybe more. We don't know what that magistrate will do for someone like him.''

The two men, keeping an eye on the barracks since news of Kathleen's arrest, had followed Spencer and the widow to Ballyclough, and from there they'd kept a discreet watch on him . . . until Egan had caught up to the man halfway to Woodfield House.

"I still want to break the bastard's neck.''

Ronan's menacing tone made Patrick put a hand on the fighter's muscular arm. "Ye want to break his neck, sure, but is it because he was kissing Egan, maybe?''

"The man is taking advantage of her,'' Ronan growled.

"Ye seem to be forgetting that she's the one that came after him,'' Patrick retorted. "When are ye going to get it in yer thick head that Egan is a grown woman? She doesn't need the likes of ye to be pining and drooling after her like some lovesick whelp.''

"What do you mean, the likes of *me*?'' The young

man turned fiercely toward his companion. "The likes of *him* is what she's been running away from all these years. She . . . she's fond of me. She's just waiting for me to do the asking . . . and she'll be taking me in the place of Conor . . . bless him."

Patrick shook his head disbelievingly. "I'm thinking when she calls you 'runt,' she must be talking about the size of your brain."

"Ye may be my mate, Paddy, but ye are about to feel my knuckles on yer head."

Patrick met Ronan's glare without flinching. Age and experience gave him an upper hand that he knew Ronan would not test.

"Ye can do yer worst with me anytime, Ronan, but get it in yer thick head right now that ye'll never do for her. Ye'll never be a Conor. And ye have a better chance of becoming Lord Lieutenant of Ireland than ye do of making her take ye as her man. I've known Egan since she was a wee spit of a lass, and I'm telling ye *she* is one that'll be doing her own choosing."

Patrick looked over his shoulder and found Egan and the Englishman had disappeared. Thank the saints.

"I say Liam should know about all of this."

The older man returned Ronan's hostile glare. "And Liam will. But remember, not a word about this kissing business, or I'll tell Egan myself about your stupid notions of becoming her man."

Ronan waved off the threat and started out of the cottage with Patrick on his heels.

"And God help you then, runt."

# Chapter 19

⟨⟨⟨⟨⟨⟨⟨⟩⟩⟩⟩⟩⟩⟩

The moment he heard the light tap on the door, Nicholas yanked open the latch and grabbed Jane's arm. Her gasp of surprise was silenced the next instant when he closed the door again and pressed her back against it. The next moment his mouth was ravenously devouring hers.

It was some time before he drew back and let both of them catch their breath.

"I . . . I do not recall . . . ever being so delighted with a morning greeting." She smiled up at him.

"That's because I had all night to plan it."

"You have quite a way with words, Sir Nicholas."

His body was still pressing hers against the door. The mold of her soft curves against his hard edges was perfect. "I didn't care much for your insistence on arriving at Woodfield House at different times last night. I had no chance to kiss you good n—to say good night."

Jane's dark eyes danced with mischief, and her arms tightened around his waist. "Are you telling me that the want of a single kiss last night is responsible for your greeting this morning?"

"Very well. It wasn't only the kiss . . . but everything about you that is responsible."

His mouth descended. This time with patience, he coaxed and parted her lips again, his tongue darting inside to sample and tease and unleash her passion. Jane's body arched against his. Her hands rubbed the shirt's fabric against his back, and her hips answered the slight but seductive movement of his own.

Nicholas dragged his mouth to her ear and bit the lobe. "All night I dreamed that I was making love to you."

His hand pressed against her breast through the dress, and he felt the peak of the nipple harden as his thumb brushed over it. Jane laid her head back against the door and closed her eyes, and he tasted the skin of her neck.

"You were here. We locked the door." His hand moved down the front of the dress. "I slowly peeled away each layer of your clothing until my mouth tasted and feasted on every inch of your sweet flesh."

A low moan escaped her lips when Nicholas's hand cupped her mound through the layers of cloth.

"We made love on that bed . . . and then on the floor . . . and once there on the chair, with you mounted upon me . . . and once more against this door."

Her face was flushed. Her eyes, incredibly dark and large, opened and stared at him when he pulled up the heavy fabric of her skirts and pressed his fingers against her moist folds.

"What do you say to that, Jane?" He brushed his lips against hers while his fingers stroked her below. "What do you think of my dream?"

He didn't wait for an answer and slipped his tongue between the parted lips. He felt the moan of pleasure as his fingers copied the motion of his tongue.

The time for questions or answers was past now, and he pleasured in her body's responses as his gentle ministration of her flesh set her on fire. Slowly, expertly, he manipulated the center of pleasure and sweet torment, lifting her ever higher, reveling in her cries of release as she finally came apart in his arms.

Fighting to ignore his own raw need, Nicholas cherished the feel of her in his arms. He loved the softness and the strength—the struggle and the surrender—the beauty and the intelligence. He held her tight while the waves of release continued to ripple through her, and kissed her tenderly.

The sound of two women's voices in the corridor outside his door jerked Nicholas back to reality. Jane descended like a stone from her place of bliss, and he couldn't help but smile at her efforts to focus on the

present. He dropped her skirts and pushed her behind
him as the knock came. Nicholas chuckled inwardly,
thinking it was a good thing he hadn't dragged her directly to his bed for he hadn't even latched the door.
With a reassuring look at Jane, he opened it a little.

The surprised faces of two young servants greeted
him.

"Oh, sir . . . begging yer pardon, sir. We saw yer valet
and . . . we . . ."

"We thought . . . ye were already . . . down . . . taking
your breakfast . . . downstairs . . ."

"We were making up the bedchambers and . . .
and . . ."

"Come back in half an hour," he told them. "Then
you can do with the room what you will."

Both curtsied hurriedly and disappeared down the
hallway. Nicholas waited a moment and then cast a
quick glance up and down the now empty corridor before closing the door.

"I . . . I cannot tell you how shocked I am . . . by my
own behavior," Jane whispered from the wall. A
trembling hand pushed loose tendrils of hair behind an
ear. "Acting the way I did . . . falling so wantonly into
your arms . . . allowing you to . . ."

"Yes, such a moment can leave you shockingly satisfied." Nicholas pulled her away from the wall and into
his arms. "If it were not for those two coming back, I
would show you the meaning of wantonness."

He brushed his lips against hers, and he felt her body
melt again into his embrace.

"Tell me, my love. Where are you taking me?"

It took her a moment to focus on his words, but he
watched her eyes clear as she placed her hands on his
chest.

"As it turns out, only to Ballyclough to check on
Kathleen and her children, and back again."

"Nothing after that? No bishops to rob? No kingdoms
to overthrow?"

"On the days that I spend at Woodfield House . . . of
which there are many . . . I use the afternoons for
painting."

"And where do you paint?"

"In my work area, in the attics."

"Will you take me there?"

Jane fixed a wry look on him. "Are you always so demanding?"

"Only when I can get away with it."

"Why do I have this feeling that there is a great deal that you get away with?"

She smiled up at him, and Nicholas held her tightly, cherishing the wild beat of their hearts.

"I will take you there, sometime. But we do have more important duties to attend to first."

Nicholas couldn't bring himself to let this moment go. "Tell me, are you going to force me to wait for five minutes after you have left before I can face the household? I will not be required to go to breakfast by way of Cork City, will I?"

"As a matter of fact, I am going to insist that you go and have breakfast with my family without me." She did manage to break free of him. "Apparently, my mother was complaining incessantly yesterday about not seeing you. You can meet me at the stables when you are finished."

He caught her arm as she reached for the door. "I will only go down into that den of lions if you come with me."

"Are you serious?" she scolded over her shoulder before peeking out into the corridor. "Do you want the pyramids to crumble? The oceans to run dry? No, sir. If I join them, they will think the Second Coming is surely at hand."

"Jane, I will *not* go down if you will not join me. We can leave for Ballyclough now."

"But we cannot just go," she insisted, her expression growing serious. "In spite of anything you say . . . about your plans not to marry Clara . . . they have high expectations of you down there, and it is—"

"Then come with me."

"Heavens, you are stubborn, sir."

"Come, Jane. We shall go down separately and behave as perfect strangers."

As she stared at the door, considering momentarily, Nicholas had to stop himself from bending down and placing a kiss on her long and graceful neck.

"I just want to look across the room and see your beautiful face before me."

"Well, that is too much to ask." She sent him a cross look.

"What? Sitting across the room from me?"

"Nay! Making my face beautiful."

He laughed and placed that kiss on her neck to show her exactly how beautiful he already thought she was. Jane sighed contentedly but then placed a hand on his chest.

"Very well. But I shall make my entrance before you. And not one look . . . nor touch, either . . . "

"I give you my word." He stole another kiss before she quietly slipped out of the room.

Nicholas buttoned up his shirt, tied his cravat, and reached for his jacket. Glancing once in the mirror, he was amazed at the starry-eyed face staring back at him. He'd seen other men wearing this look, he realized.

Men in love.

"What do you mean, she's disappeared?" Sir Robert Musgrave planted his hands on the desk and pushed himself to his feet. "Yesterday you told me the woman is old and blind. How far can a blind old woman go?"

"We have turned the cottage inside out."

The captain of the dragoons was sitting bolt upright in his chair. He was an idiot, of course, Musgrave thought, but he was also the youngest brother of the earl of Kildare's wife.

"I had my men scour the countryside around the place. I even had them drag out a few of the farmers in the area and question them about her. Naturally, no one knows anything of her whereabouts. She was there last night, Sir Robert, but she is gone this morning."

Musgrave strode angrily to the window. He should have followed his intuition and had the older woman brought in yesterday, right after the baronet had left with the other one. All that slop Spencer had fed him about wanting to help the poor still sat ill in his craw.

He'd had Kathleen arrested because she was the widow of the miserable cur who'd been killed last month. He knew how the Whiteboys worked—and he knew they took care of their women and children. So he'd had his spies keeping an eye on the widow. And just as he'd expected, the woman had shown up with money to spend in the market.

"Spencer be damned!" Musgrave muttered to himself. There must have been someone else . . . someone from that damnable gang of thugs . . . who had been in touch with her. He was determined to find out who.

Kathleen, though, had been as stubborn as a mule in answering any of his questions. But he'd thought time was his ally. A few days in the hole with his lonely dragoons to keep her company, and the woman would be singing like a lark.

How he was beginning to hate Sir Nicholas Spencer! The arrogant bastard had shown up, threatening him with the serious displeasure of the lord lieutenant, who just *happened* to be a dear family friend of the blackguard.

As he'd lain abed last night, the situation had run through his head over and over. He knew he had released the widow too hastily, but one couldn't be too careful with the influence of *dear family friends*. But something else kept nagging at him. So many times in his mind's eye, he had kept seeing the tattered shawl Jane had been wearing around her neck the day before. She always dressed in black—but never in rags. But why would she even have such a thing in her possession, unless it were a gift from some papist woman? It must have come from the widow. Sir Nicholas had not mentioned it, but who else but Kathleen would have given it to her? And why did Kathleen give it to Jane, rather than to Sir Nicholas himself, unless she was extremely grateful for something other than a few coins?

He turned on Wallis, who was studying his thumbs closely.

"Did you learn anything else, Captain?"

"Aye, Sir Robert. We did confirm that Sir Nicholas and Miss Purefoy were the ones who took the widow's children yesterday."

The magistrate turned sharply to his captain. "And where did they take them?"

"We . . . er, we have not ascertained that as yet, sir."

"Are you telling me that you did not have someone follow Spencer and the widow yesterday? I am certain he would have taken the woman to where her children are."

A dark shade of red crept up the officer's thick neck. "I beg your pardon, Sir Robert, it never occurred to me that you . . ."

"Must I do *all* of your thinking for you, Captain Wallis?" Musgrave clamped his hands with disgust behind his back and walked toward the embarrassed officer. "Is it absolutely necessary for me to give you minute-by-minute orders? Your leadership, Captain, is a reflection not just on you, but on me as well. And it is a reflection on your family, sir. Do I make myself clear?"

"My apologies, sir," the man said quickly. "I assumed . . . mistakenly, it appears . . . that you were satisfied with your meeting with the baronet and . . . and I clearly erred in not having them followed. But I was quite wrong, Sir Robert. I shall never make such an assumption again."

Musgrave's pique called for more haranguing of his subordinate, but his common sense reminded him that there was always more to be considered than just the immediate situation.

"There is another matter—a related matter—that I want you to attend to, Captain."

"Indeed, Sir Robert," the officer replied, standing up. "I shall not fail you."

"I'm sure," Musgrave said, nodding solemnly. "This matter is of the utmost importance, and I want you to be certain your men do not miss anything. And I want *you* to conduct the questioning personally."

The dragoon captain waited attentively.

"Yes . . . questioning. I want everyone who has *ever* come in contact with the rebel Egan to be brought here and questioned. By everyone, I mean your own dragoons, as well, who might have caught a glimpse of him. I mean the area clergy. The landlords and their tenants. Even Sir Thomas's guest."

"What about the bishop, Sir Robert?"

"I shall handle the bishop . . . but I want you to talk to that fat clerk of his." Musgrave stared down his subordinate. "The questioning, this time, will be different. Instead of what happened and how many and all those other useless things we usually try to find out, I want your full attention to be given to this Egan. I want his description. His build. The color of his hair. The color of his eyes. His weight and height. I want to know everything we can learn about him. I also want to know details about the horse he rides. Is it always the same one or does he ride a number of different steeds? Does he ever travel on foot? What language does he speak normally? Does he speak English with an accent? Do you understand what I am after, Captain?"

"Perfectly, Sir Robert. You want to learn the identity of the cur."

"I want that blackguard's head, Captain."

"Aye, sir."

"Then get your men moving. I want results . . . and I want them now."

To Jane's great disappointment, all the members of her family were still at breakfast when she walked into the Morning Room. She uttered a quiet greeting to Lady Spencer and Frances, ignored Sir Thomas's suspicious glare, and sat in a chair by her surprised mother.

"What a delightful surprise to see you this morning, Jane," the young Miss Spencer blurted out excitedly. "We were just told by Lady Purefoy that you were visiting some people in Ballyclough, and no one knew when you would return."

"I see. Well, I decided I would return last night . . . late." Jane nodded gratefully to the young serving girl who poured her some tea. "There was no way for anyone to know."

"And how was good Parson Adams?" Lady Spencer asked interestedly.

"Very well, I think. Both Mrs. Brown and Parson Adams send their regards." She hid her face behind the cup and let her gaze drift to Clara, who was sitting by the visitors. A distinctly petulant thinning of her sister's lips made Jane wonder what had Clara so riled this morning.

"I hope you do not mind my persistence, Jane," Lady Spencer continued, "but I was hoping to steal a little of your time for the selfish reason of the two of us just chatting about . . ."

"Clara *loves* to chat," Lady Purefoy interrupted.

"Indeed, Lady Purefoy," the guest replied breezily. "However, I find that Jane and I have quite a few interests in common, and I was hoping to spend some time in *her* company."

Their guest's emphasis on the word "her" immediately silenced Catherine. But Jane actually felt sorry for her mother momentarily. If she only knew how much damage she inflicted on Clara's chances each time she pushed her forward so brazenly.

"Thank you, Lady Spencer. I . . . I should love to spend some time with you," she responded quietly. "But I promised to return to Ballyclough this morning to check on a sick friend. Perhaps . . . perhaps this afternoon when I get back."

"As you wish, dear. I . . ."

The appearance of Nicholas in the doorway threw the entire room into chaos. Lady Purefoy immediately sprang to her feet, ordering the servants back to the kitchen for hot platters of everything. Clara, too, was on her feet. Frances made some teasing remarks about her older brother sleeping the morning away, and if it weren't for Lady Spencer's interference, the young woman would have relayed a story about her brother that was obviously not too flattering. Sir Thomas even made some casual remark about Nicholas's solitary excursion yesterday being a sure sign that he must be feeling quite at home in Ireland.

Her sister's reaction, however, was the most disturbing one for Jane. Unlike the first night, this morning Clara's attention was focused completely on Spencer. And her mood of a minute earlier had altered considerably.

Jane watched her sister bring him a cup and saucer, taking the tea from the servant and pouring it herself before sitting down near him. Amazed, she looked on as Clara made some private comment that brought a smile to his lips. When her sister reached out, however, and touched his sleeve, laughing in a charming way at his vague answer about what he'd had for dinner last night, Jane sat back, stunned.

Clara was interested.

The resentment that cut sharply through Jane appalled her. She refused the offer of food by one of the servants and tried to hide her flushed face behind a cup of tea while lively conversations ensued around her. As she regained control of her feelings of anger, though, she wondered with horror if perhaps she had guessed wrong about Clara's true interest. The realization that she herself might be having an illicit affair with her sister's future husband only compounded her dismay.

Watching them, Jane knew that she could live with shame, but she didn't think she could endure the ripping pain in her heart that jealousy was causing at this moment.

"You have been here less than a week," Sir Thomas asserted, "and you are already better acquainted with the countryside than most who have been here for years."

"Only with the inns, sir," Nicholas said in a humorous tone. "I believe that to know the land, you need to get to know its inhabitants. Now, what better place to meet them than where they gather to eat, drink, and . . . the rest of it."

"But that is one of the reasons that we are having the ball on Friday, Sir Nicholas," Lady Purefoy offered enthusiastically. "This will be a perfect opportunity for you to meet everyone who is anyone."

"But they will hardly be the ones who are one with this land, madam."

Jane didn't have to look up to know that Nicholas's gaze was on her with every sentence that he uttered.

"Why should I leave London if my interests lay only with the gentry?"

"Well said," Clara spoke softly from her chair. Jane looked up and found her sister's admiring gaze on Nicholas's face. "But as important as it is for someone like you to get a feel for the people and their lives, it is critical that you also get a proper view of the land. There are some very fine views that surround Woodfield House. And now that I know the depth of your interest, I am assigning myself to be your guide. We can take a carriage or we can ride, whichever you prefer. And—starting this morning—I guarantee that you shall be totally enchanted by everything that I show you."

"You are very kind, Miss Clara, but I regret that I must refuse your offer."

Nicholas's words stunned those listening into a shocked silence. Jane felt her own hand trembling as she put down her saucer of tea and hid her hands on her lap.

"I fear I have a previous engagement for today. But perhaps some other time."

"When?" Lady Purefoy chimed in immediately. "When? Outings such as this should certainly be planned in advance."

"If you will excuse me," Jane murmured as she rose to her feet. "As I mentioned before, I am expected at Ballyclough this morning."

Avoiding the looks of everyone in the room, she started for the door. She didn't wait. She didn't even pause. Positive that the lump in her throat would surely choke her, she rushed from the house and ran blindly toward the stable.

# Chapter 20

His excuses about the day slipping by sounded about as hollow as an ale cask after May Day. His responses to the queries about his "previous engagement" were vague and brusque. Nicholas had only one thing in his mind, though, and that was going after Jane. And he didn't give a damn about what everyone thought of his hurried exit.

If it was too obvious that he was going after her, then so be it.

"Where is Miss Jane, Paul?" Nicholas asked, catching sight of the trainer in the paddock. One of the grooms was just leading Queen Mab out into the pasture in the back. Her black coat was gleaming in the sunlight. "I was to ride with her to Ballyclough this morning. Has she left?"

The stable master shook his head and nodded toward a building beyond the stables. "Ye'll find herself in the carriage house, sir. Miss Jane has a load of clothes and blankets and things that Fey packed for the widow and her wee ones. Ye might go right through the stable there."

As Nicholas started past the man, Paul laid a hand on his arm.

"A word of warning, sir. 'Twas no happy lass what passed through here a few moments ago. So don't ye be telling her I sent you that way, for she told me in no uncertain terms that she wishes to go on to Ballyclough alone today. No groom for the carriage . . . and no Sir Nicholas, either."

"I shan't get you in trouble with her, Paul," Nicholas assured him before striding quickly in that direction.

With high ceilings and partitioned stalls for ten carriages of various types, the carriage house was obviously a new addition to the stables of Woodfield House. One carriage was missing, and Nicholas found it on the drive beside the building. The two-horse phaeton, modern and handsome with its oversized wheels and shock-absorbing springs, was already loaded and ready for Jane.

One of the stable boys stood holding the horses' heads.

"The kitchens, sir," he replied to Nicholas's question of Miss Purefoy's whereabouts.

Starting quickly toward the house, he found her coming out of the kitchen door with a large basket of food in her hands. He had the advantage of studying her for the moment before she saw him, so he saw the red-rimmed eyes and the sadness that showed so clearly in the set of her shoulders. He immediately moved to her and reached for the basket.

"Can I help you with this?"

She seemed startled for an instant before jerking the basket away. "I can handle it myself. Thank you."

Her tone wasn't sharp or angry, just tired and defeated. He fell in beside her. "Would you like me to ride my horse and pretend I am heading south? I could catch up to you on the road to Ballyclough later."

"I wish to go alone today."

"But you told me—"

"A change of plans. Sorry . . ."

Frowning, Nicholas cast a side glance at her. There were unshed tears shining in her dark eyes. He brushed the back of his hand gently against hers. She recoiled from his touch and stepped aside.

"What's wrong?" he asked quietly.

"Nothing is wrong." She shook her head and turned her face away.

With the exception of the lad waiting by the carriage, no one else could be seen around the carriage house. The fellow took the basket from Jane and placed it securely on the seat. She asked him to lead the vehicle to the drive beyond the paddock, and Nicholas placed a hand on her arm as the carriage rolled away. "Can we talk?"

"I fear I haven't the time right now."

"This won't take long."

"I said I haven't the time." She tried to shake off his touch, but he only tightened his hold. Temper flashed in her eyes. *"Let me go."*

"Not until you give me a moment of your time."

"I shall see you in hell before I allow you or anyone else to bully me."

He'd have been ready if she pulled her dagger on him again, but he wasn't prepared for the solid punch that she delivered to his midriff. Hiding his momentary inability to breathe, he flashed a broad smile at Jane, who was flexing her fist in obvious discomfort.

"Is that the best you can do?"

"It is not."

He saw the next barrage coming. As her temper exploded, a flurry of kicks and punches erupted. Knowing his best chance of avoiding injury was to attack, Nicholas moved quickly forward, managing to pin her arms to her sides and lift her off the ground. He moved briskly into the carriage house.

"You let me go, you . . . you boor . . . you blackguard." Writhing like a snake, she fought him every step. "I am going to cut you into a thousand pieces. I'm going to gut you like a hare and feed your heart to my dogs."

"This is such an improvement over the first time we met, Jane." Nicholas smiled, holding her tightly against one of the stalls to minimize the damage she could be inflicting on him. "But perhaps not, considering I could only understand about half of the curses you were hurling at me in Gaelic that day."

"No one gets away with what you—"

His mouth captured hers, and he felt the vibrations of her next complaint fade to a murmur as he deepened the kiss. Her halfhearted struggles against him lasted only a moment longer, and Nicholas tried to control his own body's urge to make love to her here . . . now. The moment she melted against him, he felt his surging desires flare up, nearly overwhelming him. Images flashed through his mind of her soft flesh this morning, moist and alive, welcoming him. He pressed into her, relishing the feel of her mouth and body eager to receive him.

His body held hers tightly against the wall, his hands feeling beneath the cloak. Her breasts were firm through the dress, and her hands were pulling at him with growing ardor, drawing him close. And then she stopped.

The salty taste of her tears mixed with the kiss, and he tore his mouth away. Through the haze of his passion, he saw her closed eyes and the crystal droplets rolling down her cheeks.

"Jane," he whispered against her lips. "Jane, talk to me. What happened before I came to the Morning Room?"

She turned her face away, but he took hold of her chin and drew it back. She opened her eyes, and he found himself drowning in the sadness he could see there.

"You should have . . . accepted Clara's offer . . ." she managed to get out. "You should be . . . be spending time . . . with her and not . . . not with me."

He paused for a moment, stunned by his own blindness. Of course she would be upset at the constant thrusting of her sister upon him. But nothing had changed.

"There is nothing between Clara and me, Jane. *Nothing.*"

"She invited you and—"

"Must I accept every invitation extended to me? Do *you* acquiesce to every request for your time?"

She shook her head. "But this is different. You see . . . I . . . I let myself become . . . become interested . . . because I thought Clara was not."

"Did I never have any say in this?" He tried to keep his tone light. "I have told you before. I never pursued her. My interest has only been in *you* since arriving here."

" 'Tis not that. My own reaction is what appalls me now." Fresh tears escaped. "No matter . . . whom you might have been interested in . . . I would never have allowed myself . . . to become . . . entangled with you if I knew my sister had the slightest interest . . . or hope.

It was . . . is wrong of me . . . to be near you . . . to spend time with you . . . to become tempted."

Thousands of arguments formed in Nicholas's head, though expressions such as "*Who cares* if Clara is interested!" were burning on his tongue. He felt his frustration and anger growing. The younger sister had everything that she could possibly wish for in life—parents who doted on her, wealth enough to guarantee an excellent marriage, beauty, and a well-hidden intellect that wouldn't intimidate many potential husbands among the gentility. Nicholas wanted to shake Jane and wake her up. Her concern for her sister was needless. Instead, she needed to look inside and see what *she* wanted from life. But Nicholas already knew this kind of talk would only push her farther away from him.

He looked deeply into her eyes. "I have been involved with enough women to know that Clara's apparent interest this morning was all a show. There is no substance in this sudden attraction to me."

As Jane shook her head and turned her face away, he again captured her chin and forced her to look up at him. "Can you not see she was acting for the benefit of your parents? She is trying to be a good daughter and show them . . . especially your father, I think . . . that she is doing her part to win me over. I know what the purpose of this ball is this Friday night. I'm not blind to the expense and trouble they are going through. And it is all for the sole purpose of getting my head spinning enough to change my mind and ask for Clara's hand in marriage."

"She seems to want it now, too."

"She does *not*," he corrected harshly. "If no one else were about this morning, she would never have even stayed behind to keep me company. In so many words, she has already told me that I am too old for her. She appears intimidated by me. Frightened, even, at times. What kind of marriage would this be?"

"A genteel English marriage?"

Angry, he pushed himself away from her. "I am *not* willing to waste my life with the likes of Clara. I know of dozens upon dozens like her in England. Why should

I have her when I have already met someone else who suits me so much better? Someone who has a heart and a soul that I already hold dear." He took a few steps away, but then whirled around. "True, a few months ago I stood in the snow in London and thought that almost anyone with a pleasing look and reasonable fortune would do . . . but no longer do I think in so limited a way. No, Jane. I will not accept just anyone . . . and I refuse to be manipulated by your parents."

Nicholas stormed toward the door of the carriage house. By 'sblood, he loved the damn woman! But admitting it . . . but saying those words to her . . . would accomplish nothing until she could shed her blinders and begin to see *him*.

"I would . . ." The brush of her fingers against his brought him to an abrupt halt by the doorway. Her voice was soft and tentative. "I would very much like you . . . to come with me this morning."

"Do we ride separately or together?"

He saw the struggle play out on her face as she looked out the door. When her gaze came back to his face, her eyes were decided.

"Together."

It was midmorning before Alexandra caught Fey alone, lacking the troop of servants who were always swarming around her. The visitor immediately seized the opportunity and walked into the Blue Parlor, closing the door partially behind her. The housekeeper glanced up from her inspection of the fireplace.

"Lady Spencer, may I help ye with anything?"

"Yes, you may." Alexandra smiled encouragingly and moved closer to the redheaded woman so their voices would not be inadvertently overheard by someone passing in the hallway. "Was it my imagination, Fey, or has Lady Purefoy arranged for a dressmaker to be staying at Woodfield House this week?"

"Indeed she has, m'lady. The woman has been brought in from Cork City. She is a very capable seamstress, too, I must say."

Alexandra moved closer. "How attentive of Lady

Purefoy always to be thinking of her daughters. I assume she is here to make ball dresses for Clara and Jane?"

"Only Miss Clara," Fey put in shortly, turning to brush an invisible speck of dust from a clock on the mantle.

"But why not Jane, as well? I can see that she favors the color black, but surely for something as grand as what is planned, Lady Purefoy would want her elder daughter to be dressed in the height of fashion."

"I do not believe Miss Jane has a place in the mistress's plans for the evening."

"Her plans or her hopes?"

Alexandra's whispered question drew the housekeeper's intelligent gaze. A moment of silence preceded the woman's answer. " 'Tis not my place to suppose I could know the mistress's thinking. 'Tis not my job to meddle, either, m'lady. However, if there is something I can do for ye . . . ?"

Lady Spencer idly picked up a book lying on a table by Clara's customary seat. *Sternwood's Sermons.* Dreadful, she thought, laying it back down. She could understand Fey's answer perfectly. She could also sense the frustration just beneath the surface of her words. She looked up to see Fey waiting with an expression of subdued hope on her face.

"Indeed there is, Fey. You must have a good idea of how much work Lady Purefoy has given this woman— this dressmaker—for this week. Now, do you think if I wished to have something made . . . say, a dress . . . could the woman manage it?"

"Would this be for . . . someone we both know, m'lady?"

"It would, indeed."

"I should have to ask her, m'lady," Fey replied excitedly. "But I think she could do it. But there is a matter of fabric and accessories that would need to be attended to . . ."

"I believe my daughter, Frances, and I will be making a quick trip to Cork City this afternoon to shop for exactly those same things." Alexandra moved closer to the housekeeper again and lowered her voice. "Now, do you

think this dressmaker might be clever enough if I were
to work with her . . . and tell her exactly what it is that
I am looking for?"

"Aye, ma'am. I think she might."

"Of course, this dress I have in mind would not be
able to be tried on for size until it is done."

"I've a lass working in the kitchens who might suit ye
for size, m'lady."

"Excellent. And of course, I'll make it worthwhile for
the dressmaker . . . beyond whatever Lady Purefoy is
paying her."

"She is a working woman. I believe she will do as ye
tell her."

"Very well." Alexandra beamed, turning to go. "You
have a talk with her, and I shall return this evening with
all she shall need."

"Is there something, m'lady . . . ?" Fey's question
stopped her. "Is there anything more you might be needing from me?"

"In fact, there is." She gauged the woman's expression
for a long moment. "I was hoping you would keep this
little discussion just between us."

Fey nodded, the trace of a smile on the housekeeper's
lips. "If you insist, m'lady."

"Perfect." Lady Spencer smiled broadly and started
for the door. There was nothing like a little surprise to
brighten up a grand ball, and she was determined to
make this surprise—and this ball—the brightest and the
grandest these people had ever seen.

Kathleen waited until Mrs. Brown, following a serving
girl carrying an empty tray, had left the room before she
clasped one of Jane's hands to her lips.

"God bless ye, miss," she whispered, sinking to her
knees. "Lord knows, I cannot think of any words good
enough to use in thanking ye."

Jane pulled the young woman to her feet. She led her
to the two chairs by the window and sat the widow beside her. "You deserve far more, Kathleen, after the
hardship you have all been through." She glanced at
Bowie, pale and weak. There was reason enough to be
happy. His fever had broken, and he now looked down

at his siblings playing on the floor beside the bed. "And
I am hoping things will improve a little from here on.
Parson Adams told me this morning that he has offered
you a cottage that is vacant in the village here."

"Aye, that he has." Fresh tears rolled down the mother's cheeks. " 'Twill be a blessing to have a roof over
our head again. And with everything ye brought us this
morning, we'll be living grander than when my Seamus
was with us."

"I am sorry, Kathleen. I know nothing will replace
him. But the way you all had to run from your own
place, I thought you might be needing these things."

The young woman nodded and wiped at her tears.
"Ye have a generous heart, Egan." Her voice was
hushed. "And a brave one."

Jane held on to Kathleen's fingers.

"Ye know, long before I met ye, I would hear these
wild tales of Egan. The little fire, the elders called ye."
She gave her a teary smile. "Egan could fly over the
mountains, they'd say. Egan could walk through fire . . .
ye could vanish in the bright of noonday. But Egan always arrived in time when a mother cried out in the
dead of night." She blushed slightly. "To be truthful, I
never paid much heed to what was being said, for I know
the way of us Irish. We need wondrous tales to help us
get through the suffering of our daily lives."

"But those *were* tales. You were right not to believe
them." Jane patted the woman's hands gently and
looked at them. The palms were hard and callused, with
dirt so deeply engrained in them that St. Peter would
surely know her for a worker when she arrived at heav-
en's gates. "Kathleen, the folk around here have always
made much more of me than I deserve. I am just a
woman . . . like you."

The widow shook her head. "But that's it, don't you
know? Ye're *not* like the rest of us. And knowing now
who ye really be . . . knowing the sacrifice ye've
made . . . the love you carry here"—she touched her
heart—"for poor folk like us . . . makes me believe in
ye more than all the legends and stories of angels and
saints. Ye be *our* joy, Egan. Our own angel sent by the
Lord himself to watch over us."

Jane fought back the tears burning her eyes. "I . . . I am not worthy . . . of all that you say, Kathleen. I was not chosen . . . or sent . . . by the Lord. I am just a simple woman. That's all."

The young mother again cupped Jane's hand in her own. "This is a land of believers, Egan. And no matter how unworthy ye might think ye be, I believe in ye. We believe in ye."

Jane wished she had the strength to argue with her. She wished she had the courage to be everything that these people wanted her to be.

"But 'tis not what ye do for us in the future that matters so much, as what ye've done already," Kathleen started again. "Ye've given us courage . . . a hero to call our own. And we must protect ye, as well. And this is the reason I'm telling all this now . . ." She lowered her voice. "They are after ye, Egan. The magistrate and his dragoons are becoming more brutal in questioning everyone about you. But we cannot let them discover ye."

"They shan't discover me." Even to her own ears, her tone lacked conviction. She needed time to think—to refocus on her purpose.

"Do not put yerself at risk, miss. If they take ye, we'll all feel the lash here, inside," she said softly, pressing Jane's hand to her heart.

"I will not let them take me."

"I'm glad of it, miss. For mark me, 'twould be better for Egan to disappear unbeaten than to see her hanging from the gibbet in Cork City." Kathleen's eyes shone with her belief. "Our memories keep us strong, but to lose her to these brutes would surely break our backs."

Though Nicholas walked the width and length of the village of Ballyclough, he saw nothing of what he passed. Finding himself sitting on a low stone wall encircling a graveyard situated on a hill overlooking the village, he shook off his haze and looked at the small, crumbling castle and the chapel near it. Following the brook with his eyes, he considered the humble cottages at the lower end. Abandoned wooden vats and stretching racks in various conditions of disrepair indicated that the village

had obviously thrived at one time on the tanning indus-
try. But no longer.

Things change, he thought.

He pulled up a tuft of green from his feet. Green
three-leaved plants that looked much like tiny clovers
were interwoven with the grass. Looking at the roots, he
wondered if one could separate the two plants, once
joined like this, and have them both survive. He was
beginning to have his doubts.

The attraction between Jane and him was undeniable.
Nicholas had already admitted to himself that he was in
love with her. Once the awareness had set in, the admission was not difficult.

But so many complications lay in their path.

She was an active member of this Whiteboys movement. By the devil, she was one of their leaders.

Nicholas didn't give a damn about the reputation
she'd destroyed years ago, but it obviously made a difference to her, and so would affect any future decision
she made about the two of them.

Plus, she was worried about Clara's future.

And as much as she tried to put on an air of indifference, Jane was deeply hurt by her parents' rejection of
her.

There might have been even more issues that he could
think of if he set his mind to it. Jane's earlier rejection
of him and the silence that had settled between them en
route here this morning had indicated her own difficulties. But Nicholas was not one to be so easily deterred.
He loved her, and he was determined to resolve every
problem.

But he needed her help.

Pressing the tuft of green back into the earth, he stood
and followed the path back toward the village and the
parsonage.

A young servant led Nicholas to the parsonage's parlor. As he removed his hat and gloves, Henry Adams
appeared in the doorway.

Ah, yes! And then there was the matter of the good
parson.

"Did you have a pleasant walk, Sir Nicholas?"

"Yes, I did."

"I am afraid Miss Jane has not concluded her visit this morning," the parson announced, remaining in the doorway. "I realize you shared a carriage coming down. If you wish to get back to Woodfield House, I can arrange for one of my grooms to ready a horse for you."

Nicholas bristled. "I am in no hurry to get back, Parson, but I thank you for your concern."

"But I was under the impression that you are spending the afternoon with Miss Clara."

"Were you?" Nicholas moved to the center of the room. "Do you know something, Reverend Adams, that I do not?"

"Perhaps I do." With his hands clasped behind him, Henry entered the parlor, a disapproving glare painted clearly on his features as he studied Nicholas. Adams was easily as tall and broad as the baronet, and the room suddenly became much smaller. "Perhaps I find your behavior . . . odd. Spending the mornings in the company of one sister and the afternoons in the company of the other. I find it improper, sir, to see you charming these two young women at the same time. I wonder if you are considering the implications . . . and the possible consequences for one of them?"

"You are treading a dangerous path, sir," Nicholas growled.

"Am I?" The minister took another step toward him.

Regardless of the man's profession, Nicholas realized he was about to call the man out. He didn't like his insinuations. He didn't like his tone. And frankly, he was beginning to dislike the man's looks.

But for Jane's sake, he reined in his temper for the moment. "And I wonder if you are asking these questions in your capacity as these young women's *spiritual* advisor."

"Now it is you who is treading dangerously."

"Am I?" Nicholas crossed his arms and turned only slightly, measuring the man. "I don't know if it is any of your business, but I spoke with Sir Thomas the day after my arrival to correct any confusion regarding my supposed interest in Miss Clara. There is not going to be a proposal. There have never been any marriage plans, and I have no wish to marry the younger daughter. And, having clarified that point with the parents, I do *not* spend any time in her company."

"And how does Clara feel about that? About being led on, I mean?"

The man's accusing question pricked the visitor's restraint. His glare menacing, Nicholas took a step toward the parson. "Miss Clara was never led on by me, and I am warning you now that I am finding your insinuations an intolerable affront to my honor."

"If your intentions have been as honorable as you claim, sir, then there is nothing to be offended by. Which, in turn, brings me to your intentions regarding Jane." They stood an arm's length apart, Adams's fierce glare matching Nicholas's. "I have known and valued her for too many years to allow a stranger to walk in today and leave tomorrow, and cause her pain. I refuse to allow . . ."

"What is between Jane and me is none of your concern, and I . . ."

"I am making it my concern—"

"Am I interrupting something?"

Jane's softly spoken question from the doorway stopped the two men. But like two bulls ready for combat, neither moved nor averted his killing stare until she repeated her question.

Henry Adams was the first one to turn and face her. A look of tenderness passed between the two, and something in Nicholas's belly curdled when the parson took her hand and raised it to his lips.

"And here is Jane. Interrupting? Nay, I was practicing my . . . my hospitality."

Her brilliant smile as she brushed a kiss against his cheek was another blow to Nicholas's midriff. He was roughly five seconds away from breaking the good parson's jaw, and he found himself taking a step toward the two.

"Are you ready, Sir Nicholas?" She turned her magical gaze on him, and he felt the room warm around him. "To avoid giving our host any temptation to poison you . . . with his hospitality . . . I am refusing Parson Adams's insistence on our staying to dine with him."

Adams hadn't asked them to stay, and Nicholas wished he could smile at her attempt to lighten the tension between the two men. But his jaws were clamped too tightly shut to move.

"Indeed, I think we will be leaving immediately," she said, blessing Adams with another smile as she looped her arm through Nicholas's. "I'm quite sure this house can handle only so many guests at one time."

# Chapter 21

For the hundredth time, Jane glanced over at Nicholas's brooding face and contemplated her best approach. The man clearly needed to bleed off some of his anger. What she'd seen in the parlor of the parsonage had been no illusion. Whether they would have resorted to fists or swords or pistols, Nicholas and Henry had clearly been ready to do battle. And considering her involvement and friendship with each of these two men, Jane was deeply disturbed to think *she* might have been the reason for their obvious hostility.

"Are you trying to give me a taste of my own medicine?"

She might as well have asked the question of the blue jay that darted from the hedge as they passed. Nicholas continued to glare straight ahead as he drove the horse and carriage. He gave no indication that he'd even heard what she'd asked, other than flicking the reins at the pair.

"I know I was not very talkative on our drive to Ballyclough. But I needed time to think and consider everything . . . between us. I needed to think through all that you told me before we left." A bump in the road jounced Jane against Spencer's side. She moved away only a little. "I have come to accept that nothing between you and me can be simple. Our pasts, our lives, even the people whom we care for seem to be doing their best to wedge themselves between us."

She stared at the familiar countryside. "Though it might appear reckless to someone looking from the outside—this life I have chosen for myself among the Whiteboys and the locals—it fills some need in me. It is a deep-seated need . . . for justice . . . and for adventure, I suppose. There is security in what you come to be comfortable with . . . even this. Despite the danger, I consider the ground I walk upon solid . . . and good."

He cast a sharp glance her way. "Are you telling me that you do not want what is happening between us?"

She looped her arm through his and looked into his eyes. "It would be much simpler if I could say that I do not want it, but I cannot say that." A layer of darkness lifted from his expression. She brushed her cheek against the wool of his jacket when his gaze shifted back to the road. "I wish I knew how long this thing might last between us, but I have no such gift for seeing into the future. The way I feel about you, though . . . the way you've thrown my emotions and my life into such total disarray . . . I cannot simply turn my back to it."

She moved closer to him, trying to take strength from his presence. "Most people search all their lives and never find even once what I have been fortunate enough to come across twice in my life. I am willing to take the chance."

"How about Adams?"

He hadn't even looked at her to ask the question, and Jane understood his frustration. After all, she, too, had been plagued with the same uncertainty this morning . . . about Clara.

"He is a dear and trusted friend. Nothing more."

"Perhaps to your thinking. But there is a great deal more at his end."

Jane searched for the right words to explain what it was that made the friendship she shared with Henry so different and special. "We've known each other all of our lives. We've been as close as a brother and sister who are about the same age can be. We've shared the same interests and beliefs. And for many years, since Conor's death, Henry has taken it on himself to fill the emptiness that my parents' treatment of me has created in my life. He is always there if I need him. And he is as protective of me as you would be of Frances."

"I would not face someone who was waiting for Frances the way he faced me today."

"I believe you would," Jane challenged. "Put yourself in his position. What exactly does he know of you? He believes, as we all did, that you came to Ireland to marry Clara. Now he finds that you are spending many hours in my company."

"I explained that to him today. But there was no change in his hostility."

"That is because Henry is a man of reason and logic. He knows the scandal of my past. He knows that such a past allows no possibility of a future in your society. Therefore, he concludes you and I have no chance of finding a future together . . . not an honorable one, at any rate." As he opened his mouth to speak, she shook her head and continued. "He is also aware of how I feel about you . . . how much I care for you . . . and this disturbs him. He is determined to intervene, for he does not wish to see me hurt again. You cannot tell me that you would not do the same for Frances . . . or for any friend who might have suffered in their lives. I believe you would intervene if you thought that ill-conceived choices were about to be made."

Jane stared at his rugged, handsome profile. He looked away and murmured a name under his breath. She drew his chin back to her.

"Would you care to repeat that?" she said, brushing a kiss against his cheek.

"Stanmore." He spoke more clearly this time, giving her a grudging half smile. "He is my oldest friend. And I did poke my nose in his private life last year when I had my doubts about the woman he was set to marry."

"I see. And what happened?"

"The woman turned out to be innocent of all suspicions. They've since married. And now, I'm happy to say, Rebecca and I are the greatest of friends."

Jane wrapped her arms around him and hugged him fiercely. "You see . . . given time, you and Henry could end up friends, too."

"I doubt it."

"Oh, you foul-tempered, bull-headed . . ." She gave

up on the words, drew his face down to her, and put all her frustrations and passion into a kiss.

As she kissed him, Jane felt the carriage come to an abrupt halt, and she found herself pulled onto Nicholas's lap. His mouth slanted over hers with a kiss deep and hot enough to set her entire body on fire.

"I . . . I want you," she whispered raggedly when his mouth left hers.

His lips touched and teased the fevered skin of her throat, and his hands were already beneath the cloak, caressing her breasts.

"I want to make love to you, Jane."

She thought for a moment that the meadow they were crossing would serve them as well as any bed, and then an idea dawned on her.

"How long can you be patient?" she asked with a smile, scrambling off his lap and taking up the reins of the carriage herself.

"Where are you taking me?"

"You shall find out."

"Very well. Then you be sure to pay complete attention to your driving, for I shall be otherwise engaged."

As the phaeton raced across the countryside at breakneck speed, Nicholas's mouth and hands continued their teasing play. Jane thrilled to the feel of his attentions until the pressure in her body was so overwhelming that she thought she would lose her mind if they didn't arrive at their destination soon.

The ruined stone castle, deserted by people and time, sat high on a ledge looking over the Blackwater River. Jane—as Egan—had many times taken shelter there against the weather.

"I thought we'd never get here," Nicholas said, reluctantly withdrawing his attentions as the edifice came into view. "Where are we?"

"Just a little place I keep in the country," she joked, urging the horses up a slope toward the castle wall. "They call it Cuchulainn's Seat."

Nicholas gazed up at the impressive rise of the walls and then at the rolling valley. The two ducked their heads as she maneuvered the carriage through the narrow, ancient gate and brought the horses to a halt.

"Are you coming?" she asked, stepping down from the carriage and taking the basket of food Mrs. Brown had sent along with her. She backed toward the door of a square tower that formed most of the western wall.

The intensity of Nicholas's blue gaze on her made Jane shiver with anticipation. She saw him take a blanket from the seat and start across the courtyard after her. It was dark in the spiral stairs leading up to the upper story of rooms that had surely been inhabited at one time by the lord of this castle and his family. Near the top, she stumbled once, nearly losing the basket of food, but Nicholas was beside her in an instant. As he set her back on her feet, he claimed a kiss for his efforts.

She led him to the only room on the upper floor that still had a part of a roof and three standing walls. The wall facing the valley, though, had long ago crumbled to the riverbank.

"This is one of Egan's secret hiding places," she said quietly, watching the room fill with Nicholas's presence as he walked in. "You mention it to anyone, and there will be a price to pay."

His silence only made her skin burn hotter. When he dropped the blanket to the ground and approached her, she realized that this was to be nothing like the experience she'd shared so many years ago with Conor. That was simply the discovery of passion's fires by two innocent youths. What she was facing now was a man. And Nicholas Spencer was a man who'd spent his life in the company of worldly women. She was certain there was little he did not know about the ways of love. Fears and insecurities cast a shadow across her mood, but he was quick to hold her close.

"Stay with me," he growled against her lips as his hands undid the tie of her cloak. The garment pooled at her feet. He turned her in his arms and had her lean against a wall while his hands started undoing the buttons on the back of her dress.

"I am frightened," she whispered, pressing her forehead against the cold stone.

"I am, too."

She felt the air, so cool on her skin, as he spread the back of the dress.

"I want so badly for this . . . to be right. For me to be able to show you . . . how much I love you."

Stunned by his words, Jane turned in his arms, only to be overwhelmed by the depth of emotion she found in his blue eyes.

"Nicholas . . ." The words caught in her throat. Tears burned her eyes.

"It is true. I love you, Jane." He kissed her deeply, thoroughly, while his hands peeled the dress to her waist. The feel of his large hands holding her breasts through the thinness of the chemise made her arch her back for more. Her breathing stopped altogether when he slipped the straps of the chemise, as well, down her arms. When he drew back, she saw his eyes darken as he gazed at her breasts before returning to her face.

"You are so beautiful."

She gasped out loud as his mouth lowered and he took her flesh into his mouth. There was no longer a doubt, but only need in her soul. She felt herself melt, become moist. Her arms wrapped around him. Her body was ready, eager to accept him. Drawing her down onto the blanket, he pushed her clothing down over her hips, helping her to extricate her legs.

He quickly shed his own clothing, and a moment later the walls rang with her cry of ecstasy at the joining of their bodies. She felt the sky wrap around them, lifting them both up on a cloud of infinite blue.

*I love you.*

His whisper echoed in her mind again and again, but Jane tried to blot it out, trying for once to lose herself in this one miraculous moment.

All rational thoughts soon fled and only the throbbing pulse of the love dance was left. Even time hung suspended, counted only by the beat of their bodies pounding together as two souls rose up to that joyous moment of release.

Later, as she lay in his arms, Jane thought again of the declaration she could not make. No matter what she was feeling, "love" was a word she could not say.

Love, she thought, dashing a tear away, was something their world would never allow.

\*    \*    \*

Patrick found his man in Cork City's old Butter Market. The young fellow, organizing the goods on his cart before the ride back to Woodfield House, spied him and dropped a crate of tea onto the cobbled ground.

Under the pretence of helping him lift the crate back onto the cart, Patrick whispered the message that had to be delivered to Egan before nightfall. ". . . to meet at the same time and place as the last. Liam says Egan should come early. Finn is to be there. Be sure to tell her."

Casually rising to his feet, Patrick picked up his youngest son. The lad had lagged behind a little to stare at a brilliantly painted gypsy wagon. He lifted the boy onto his shoulders, pleased that the message had been delivered without any trouble.

As father and son started off toward the river, though, Patrick failed to notice the two dragoons watching carefully even as they followed at a safe distance behind.

Clara shifted a little, forcing herself to sit straighter in the chair. The sharp end of one of the French stays was digging mercilessly into her flesh. It had taken two maids, working under her mother's supervision, to squeeze her into the undergarment. Surely, some cruel woman-hater must have devised the insidious thing.

Frustrated, she glanced down at her breasts propped up like pillows by the stays. Her nipples were barely concealed by the dreadfully low neckline of the dress. She was certain that if she were to reach forward even a little, or allow anything to tug even faintly at the dress, she would be spilling out of her gown like springwater over the dam.

And for what? she thought, the warmth rising in her cheeks. The baronet had not spared her a glance.

Clara wasn't blind. Since sitting down to dinner, Nicholas's attention had been focused on Jane. Jane and her high-collared black dress, so conservative that it didn't reveal even an inch of skin. Jane, who had managed to show up for the second time today to a meal. Jane, who actually participated in the conversations at table and even seemed not to take offence at anything their parents said. Jane, who actually smiled at an attempt at humor on the part of Sir Thomas.

Clara found herself disliking this Jane a great deal.

"Lady Spencer, you have been very mysterious today, spiriting your daughter to Cork City and back."

Clara shifted again, trying to ignore the pressure on her ribs. This was the second time her mother had asked this question tonight.

"Not at all," their guest replied cheerfully. "I just thought it would be good for Frances to see what your shops had to offer. Of course, we couldn't help picking up a little of this and a little of that while we were there. Fanny picked out a lovely bonnet."

"Well, if you would like to go again, I should love to accompany you. I know of the dearest little milliner's shop, not far from the new Butter Exchange."

"That would be lovely."

"But how about you, Sir Nicholas?" Lady Purefoy turned her attention to the baronet. "Tell us which little corner of our countryside you were exploring today."

"I went to Ballyclough with Miss Jane."

His blunt response drew every eye in the dining room. Lady Spencer and Frances exchanged a quick look. Sir Thomas, his glass halfway to his lips, grunted and downed the wine before sitting back in his chair. Catherine gaped for a moment before recovering herself. Clara thought that it might be the first time in her life that her mother had been struck speechless. The color had risen in Jane's face, and her gaze was now fixed on her plate.

Clara began to seethe, and she shot darts with her eyes at her sister. For most of the day, she'd been brooding on the fact that Jane was going more and more to Ballyclough. She didn't like it, not one bit.

Henry had never wanted Clara herself to come and visit him every day. Henry had never asked *her* to join him on his visits to the parishioners. Henry never shared his thoughts or his plans with her. Clearly, it just came down to this—Henry was infatuated with Jane.

And so was Sir Nicholas.

Obviously having a tarnished reputation was what a woman needed to attract attention these days.

Her own malicious thoughts shocked and hurt the young woman, and her chin sank to her chest.

But the bitterness continued to eat away at her. The thoughtlessness of her sister to want to take away *both* men was appalling . . . unfathomable. For all her talk of having loved only *one* man in her life—of her devotion to Conor, of the grief she still carried—all of it was nothing more than a lie. Jane was just looking for sympathy. And attention. And obviously, Clara thought, she had succeeded.

"I . . . suppose . . . we should leave the men . . . to their port and their cigars," Lady Purefoy finally managed to get out. She rose to her feet, and everyone else followed suit.

Clara's eyes remained on Jane. There were silent messages passing between the baronet and her older sister. Even as an observer, she could feel the heat in the air between them. When Jane left the room ahead of the rest of the women, Clara saw the scarcely concealed desire in the man's eyes.

She was quick to follow her sister out. She was riled and resentful enough to say something while the women crossed to the Blue Parlor. But as she made her way along, Clara saw Jane disappear up the stairs.

Her brutish Shanavests must be calling, the young woman thought. Going into the parlor with their guests, Clara began planning her talk with her sister. It was time someone advised Jane about the futility of her attempts.

It was time someone told Jane that she didn't have a chance . . . with either of these men.

Though Sir Thomas had wanted to toast everyone in London society individually, Nicholas had excused himself before the second bottle of port appeared.

She hadn't said anything to him, but Nicholas knew that she'd be gone. A trip to the stables had confirmed it. Queen Mab was not in her stall.

Strolling back up the hill toward the house, Nicholas could think of nothing more tiring than joining everyone in the parlor. It seemed he could think of nothing else but Jane. Hell, he didn't *care* to think of anything else but Jane.

Visions of their lovemaking this afternoon played again and again before his eyes. The haunted look in Jane's eyes when he'd confessed his love was an image he would never be able to scratch from his memory.

Nicholas glanced up at the dark lines of the house and tried to guess where her workroom might be. He wanted to be surrounded by nothing but her.

"I thought I might find you out here." His mother's voice drifted out of the shadows of the arched entryway. "I am disappointed, though, to find you alone."

"No more than I." He'd made a pact with himself today. There would be no denying of his feelings for Jane . . . publicly or privately. "What are *you* doing out here, m'lady?"

"I tire of drinking wine with our hostess, I'm afraid. And though Clara is ostensibly playing at cards with your sister, she looks like she might cut someone's head off."

Lady Spencer took a couple of steps into the night and looked up at the star-filled sky. "So, with Jane shunning our company and Sir Thomas retiring to his study a few minutes ago, I decided that whatever excitement Woodfield offers, it must be out here."

"And pray, what were you planning to do if Jane and I were out here alone?" he asked, amused as always by his mother's way of thinking. "Not planning to spy on us, I should hope."

"Heavens no! Only keep watch on your behalf." She smiled tenderly. "I know you do not need my approval. But still, I want you to know that I think very highly of Jane. She is a very special young woman."

"I know," he agreed quietly.

She walked past him and stopped by the edge of the garden—her eyes scanning the dark valley beyond. "Perfection does not exist, Nick. Beauty is only a passing illusion. Happiness is not a beginning or an end, but a lifetime of commitment. It is a journey." She turned to him. "To love is to give."

This was not the first time Nicholas had heard these

same words. They represented the principles he'd been raised to believe in, to live by. He'd heard them many times in his youth, though he wondered where it was that he'd begun to feel unworthy of happiness. Somewhere on the Plains of Abraham, he supposed.

"I haven't forgotten."

"That's good." She nodded, satisfied. "You'll need to remember them. Jane deserves it."

Nicholas said nothing as his mother walked back toward him.

"However, seeing that you obviously have nothing to do this evening, would you care to see the greatest treasures Woodfield House holds?" At his wry smile, she shook her head and patted him on the arm. "No, you can find your own way to Jane's bedchamber, my dear. I am speaking of her workroom. The studio where she paints."

"Your vast knowledge and wisdom continue to amaze me, m'lady." He offered her his arm.

# Chapter 22

"I spoke with Finn earlier today, Egan," Liam said as the two waited for the others to arrive. "He said that John Stack's and Denis Cahill's tenant farms were paid a visit this morning by the dragoons. And this afternoon, they were over to Kilcorney, putting their noses in at the Connell place, at Jock Dineen's, and at Ned Ryan's, as well. They were questioning everyone about ye."

She tried to make light of her friend's worry. "Unless they're dividing and passing out bits of heaven, I do not think these folks will say anything different about me than they did the last time . . . or any of the times before."

The farmers Liam had mentioned would cut off their right arms before informing on her. The families mentioned all knew perfectly well who Egan was. Each of them had aided the Shanavests or, at one time or another, provided shelter for displaced families over the years.

"But Finn thinks this is only the start," Liam warned. "There are many others out there who shan't be as loyal . . . or as brave . . . or as smart to know what to say or not to say. He's worried about ye."

"About me? In all this time, the man has made a point of not making himself known to me!"

"Aye . . . well, I cannot answer for him on that. But, sure as I'm standing here, the man is concerned. He even had us move the blind woman, Bridget, to Charleville last night because ye had talked to her. And don't ye know, this morning at dawn there were dragoons searching all over Buttevant for her."

"You and I have been involved with this fight too long to become frightened so easily," Egan said confidently. "This is not the first time they have searched through the straw for us."

Liam shook his head. "There has always been safety in numbers, and in knowing that when they come after us, we can spread in a dozen different directions and give them the slip. But this time, they appear to be after ye alone, my joy, and none of us like it."

Egan glanced at the group that was now gathering. She looked past Ronan's deep frown across the fire and searched the faces in the crowd until she found Patrick. Her friend's gentle and loyal face was a reminder that she needed to push aside her own disregard and really listen to what she was being told. These people *did* care for her, and she for them.

"What does Finn recommend?"

"He wants ye to stay in the shadows for a while. With a wee period of calm and easy going . . . with no sign of Egan . . . he thinks the searching and the questioning will soon die down."

"How about the gathering at Kildare?"

"Finn thinks we should decide on someone else to go for ye." Liam studied the gathered crowd. " 'Twill be good if we can tell the people about the change in plans tonight."

Very well, she thought. So she would not go on the trip. As everything stood now—and especially after today—she was afraid that she would be distracted by her feelings for Nicholas. Her friends needed better representation from their group than what Egan could offer now.

"So who do ye think should go for ye?" Liam pressed the question again.

"Patrick," Egan answered. "He would be perfect for it."

At the sight of the empty stall, Sir Thomas's hopes dropped like stones into a chamber pot. At the same time, frustration fueled his temper.

All along tonight, he'd assumed Jane was with the baronet. Seeing both of them disappear after dinner, he'd thought—nay, he'd hoped—that the two would be sneaking off together to some dark and private corner of the night.

He had not been mistaken. Subtle as they were, the signs and gestures had been all too apparent. Spencer was smitten with Jane . . . much to the blackguard's credit. And, by thunder, if the scoundrel was man enough to go after her even after learning of her scandalous past, then, hang it, who was he to get in the way? Aye, something good might turn up after all. Despite his roguish reputation, the baronet looked to him to be the type to act honorably when it came to Jane. He had the look in his eyes. This had all the makings of a love match—if such a thing existed in this world of hard hearts and itching palms. But Sir Thomas had known straight away that Spencer was cut from a different cloth.

He glanced again around the empty stall.

Damn Jane for trying to ruin it!

Sir Thomas stormed out of the stables and up the hill toward the house. The cursed Whiteboys needed to be set back on their heels soon. They needed to see their leaders dancing in the Cork breeze. They needed a goodly taste of fear. Scare the buggers off, and Jane might just be discouraged enough to give up the cause while there was hope of something with Spencer.

Enough was enough, hang it. He had left Musgrave to do his job too long. Sir Thomas needed to get involved once again and show the dandy how an old dog goes for the throat.

The flickering light of a dozen candles brought to life the images on the canvases. Nicholas stood back and stared at the paintings he'd uncovered and stood up in every available space.

After bringing him up into the attic studio, Alexandra had gone without a word, leaving Nicholas alone to peer through this window into Jane's mind. To view on his own a young woman's burning talent. To sense the life that had produced such work.

He had pored over her paintings with the fervor of a

treasure seeker who had just found the long-hidden riches of Croesus himself. And as he went from canvas to canvas, he'd felt an unexpected rush of emotion that had forced him simply to sit and gaze from time to time. He had been touched, impressed, and his eyes had opened to the battles and the grief that had played such an important part in her life.

But the most disturbing revelation had been the magnitude of Jane's love for Conor. For a woman to forgo *so much* of her life, to become so consumed with a cause that she wasn't born to, bespoke great devotion to this man. It was daunting to think that she would ever be able to love another . . . that he would ever be able to win her.

But hell, he thought fiercely, the taking of Quebec had not come easily, either. And this was far, far more important.

He strode to her worktable and opened a leather case of sketches there. A charcoal drawing of himself was on top of a number of other sketches. He gazed at it carefully. It was quickly drawn, but unmistakable in its intent and its power. It was a depiction of him looking at someone he was holding captive beneath him.

It was a representation of the first day they'd met. She'd captured the mixture of surprise and heat in his face. The rest of the picture, however, confused Nicholas until it occurred to him that it was the work of her imagination. In the sketch, he was wearing a loose flowing shirt, unbuttoned and showing the muscles of his chest beneath. His hair was loose and wild around his face. His hand was reaching out of the sketch, reaching toward the artist.

What he was looking at was an erotic evocation of what might have been . . . of what was yet to come! She had been drawn to him from the beginning.

The creak of the door opening at the bottom of the stairs jolted Nicholas into the present. He peered down the steps and saw Jane looking up at him.

"So you found this place," she whispered. Her face was hidden by shadows, and he did not know immediately if she was pleased or angry.

Nicholas watched her come through the door and

latch it. Desire rushed through him as he watched her slowly ascend the steps. She was wearing the black breeches and shirt—her white smock had been discarded—and the image from the sketch came to life in his mind.

"I took the garden path back from the stables . . . but when you were not outside, I thought you might already be . . . asleep." Nicholas saw her eyes take in the jacket and cravat he had tossed aside. Her gaze lingered on his rolled-up sleeves and bare arms.

"Our time together this afternoon was too brief." He extended a hand to her, and she took it. He drew her up onto the top step and into his arms. "I must warn you that you have created an insatiable appetite in me for what I sampled today."

Her lips opened under his and Nicholas tasted the sweetness and smiled even as he kissed her.

"And I thought I was the only one who was suffering," she murmured.

Her fingers worked the buttons of his shirt. The feel of her cold hands touching his warm skin sent another surge of desire through him.

Nicholas led her to the middle of the attic studio. She frowned slightly as her gaze took in the paintings he'd uncovered and displayed around the room. The look of uncertainty in her eyes pulled at his heart.

"There are so few who know that I use this place as my studio . . . and even fewer who have seen any of my work. I am not . . . traditional in what I do. Perhaps, what I lack in . . ."

"I would account myself only a fairly knowledgeable critic of the fine arts, but I have seen enough of the acclaimed works to say your work places you easily among the greatest of those artists painting today."

"These are . . ." Jane shook her head and spoke softly. "You mock me."

"Hardly." He cupped her face and looked steadily into her eyes. "I want to make love to you, Jane. Here . . . with these works of genius . . . with these windows to your past around us."

He kissed her until she was leaning into his touch and

her hands began to move down over his chest. He caught her wrist as it reached his waist.

"We should not rush through this. Not this time."

Jane's eyes rounded as he pulled the narrow cot to the middle of the room. Around them flickering candles and glistening paintings provided both light and color, and he drew her down onto the cot. Once again, his mouth feasted on hers. She shivered with anticipation and leaned back on her arms as he started unfastening her shirt. With a deliberateness that he hoped would not prove his own undoing, he caressed each inch of exposed skin . . . until he reached the top of her chemise. There he found not only the linen undergarment, but also a specially made inner shirt, one doubled in thickness and tight to bind and conceal her breasts. He smiled at the dozen tiny hooks that appeared as he finished opening the outer shirt.

"Do you remember the first day we met in the woods?" he asked softly.

"Yes," she replied.

Laying her down on the cot, he carefully undid hook after hook. When the task was done and the inner shirt lay open, he looked at the buttons of the chemise.

"Just to torment me," he murmured. "Well, two can play . . ."

As he unfastened each button, he pressed his lips to the newly revealed expanse of skin, causing her to draw in her breath sharply and grip the sides of the cot as he reached the soft curves of her belly. He lifted his head and slipped the shirts and the straps of the chemise over her shoulders. Sliding his hands lightly over the smooth lines of her collarbone, he drew a line with his index finger down into the valley between her breasts. Freed of the constraining clothing, the perfect ivory flesh and the hard, extended tips rose and fell. She arched her back as he cupped one breast and ran his thumb across her nipple.

"So beautiful . . . and ready to be tasted."

One of Jane's hands slipped over his hip and touched the burgeoning manhood trapped in his breeches. He slid down along her body, moving himself beyond the reach of her hand.

"No, my sweet. You cannot move, and you are mine to torment." He gave her a look of mock warning before lowering his mouth to her waiting breast. She moaned and he felt her fingers thread their way into his hair when he started to tease and suckle.

This afternoon they had not had time for discovering each other's bodies. Their lovemaking had been passionate, powerful, and direct. It had not been a time for seduction and exploration. But Nicholas was determined to give her just that now.

He let his mouth trail to the other breast where he feasted until her breaths became ragged. He slid still lower, and his lips kissed their way down her soft, smooth stomach. His fingers were deliberately slow as they undid her breeches and began pushing them over her hips.

"Nicholas . . ."

Jane's hands reached for him as he moved down on the cot and removed her boots and stockings and peeled the breeches from her legs.

"Come to me," she whispered hoarsely. "I need you now."

"Yes . . . and I need you."

Her naked limbs were a glimpse of eternal beauty glowing before his eyes. They were unmatched in art. Not Michelangelo or Botticelli or Titian—or any of the modern masters, either—had ever captured the curve of this foot where it bowed gently from toe to heel. He lifted it and placed his lips there. He slipped his fingers over the tapered lines of the ankle to the softly muscled calf and the perfect machinery of this knee. He kissed the dimpled skin and smiled at the little panting sounds of her breathing. With her foot now resting in his lap, his hands caressed with the lightest touch the firm flesh of her thigh until they reached the apex of their journey, that tantalizing triangle of hair and the moist folds beneath.

He saw her breathing heavily, her breasts rising and falling with no discernible regularity. But her dark eyes were watching every move he made.

"Nicholas . . . I never . . . I . . . ."

This was the response he'd been waiting for, so he pressed his mouth to her moist flesh. He heard her moan as he entered and stroked her with fingers and lips and tongue, suckling the very center of her womanhood until he knew she had entered a paradise of bliss.

When she cried out softly, clutching at the cot as her body arched and shuddered, he knew that no artistic joy could ever rival the natural joys that lovers share.

Slowly he relented in his ministrations as her waves of ecstasy subsided—for the moment.

"Nicholas," she whispered, reaching for him.

He sat up just out of her reach and discarded his shirt. "Not yet, my love."

Her eyes were smoky pools of ebony as she watched him stand and remove the rest of his clothes. When he tossed his breeches aside, her gaze narrowed as it fell upon his erect manhood.

A soft blush colored her cheeks and spread down her neck and breasts. "Is it possible that you . . . and I . . ."

"Let me show you the possibilities."

Moving back between her legs, he pressed her down against the cot and kissed her as the head of his staff entered the slick folds. She drew a sharp breath as he drove into her, and he silenced her cries with his mouth.

Passion that he'd never known overwhelmed him when her tight sheath closed around him. When her hands clutched at his buttocks, he felt her drawing him even deeper, demanding that he drive into her again and again, filling her sweet depths with his own pulsating flesh. Together they found the rhythm of the dance, and together they rose to what he was sure must be the very heights of Elysium.

When her release came, it came with the sweet abandon of the innocent, triggering a matching explosion in his head and in his loins. He muffled his cries against her throat as he continued to drive into her, pouring his seed into her body. As he came, she wrapped her legs around his hips and kept him locked in her arms and in her body.

A long time passed before either could speak or even catch their ragged breaths.

"How long can we stay up here without being discovered?" he managed to ask finally. He lifted his head and looked into her beautiful flushed face.

"A long, long time. Months probably. No one ever comes up here, but me."

"Good." With their bodies still joined, he felt himself hardening again inside of her. He rolled Jane on the cot, until she was on top. He took hold of her buttocks and drew her tightly against him, eliciting a surprised gasp. He gazed at her full breasts pressed against him—the cascading ringlets of hair framing her smiling face. He was once again fully erect.

"You want to make love again?"

"Actually, I was hoping for a tour of this magnificent gallery of art. But, of course, I shall need little enticements between the works, to keep my attention and sustain my self-esteem. I am very limited in my talents, you know."

"I fear I cannot agree on that score at the moment," she said, raising an eyebrow and then smiling. "But what kind of enticement did you have in mind, sir?"

He let his gaze travel around the large space. "Let me see . . . after we have finished with this cot, we would need to make love with you on my lap in that chair. And perhaps once against the wall . . . and once again with you facing the wall. We definitely need to try the strength of your worktable. And then that beam certainly has an interesting angle to it, I should say . . ."

Laughing, she pounded her fist lightly on his chest. "You are not planning to take advantage of a poor artist now, are you?"

"Of course I am." He pulled her knees until she was upright and straddling him. Lifting her bottom, he lowered her again, driving deep inside of her. "Indeed, I am planning to make love to you many times, in many ways, until you beg me to stop. And then I shall set a condition for stopping . . . temporarily . . . and you shall be forced to agree."

"What . . . what is the condition?" she asked vaguely, rotating her hips slowly on top of him.

"That you marry me, Jane."

*       *       *

The dawn had barely broken in the eastern sky when Jane cast a last wistful eye over her work area and started down the steps. She had sent Nicholas away about an hour ago, after convincing him that she would definitely make an appearance downstairs in a couple of hours.

It had taken longer than she'd expected to put her attic workplace back in order, she thought, fighting back a smile.

*Marry me, Jane. Marry me, Jane.*

Her smile disappeared. Like some liturgical chant, Nicholas's words kept repeating over and over in her head. She had avoided answering him, but she could not prevent the warming power of it over her heart and her mind. Even to dream of spending the rest of her life with him was far beyond anything she'd ever allowed herself to hope.

She loved him. She knew that. And indeed, she had found the most passionate and fulfilling moments of her life in his arms. This, she had thought, would be the extent of it. It was all she could have hoped for. A moment and a memory.

But to *marry* him . . .

Jane still had a smile on her face when she opened the door of her bedchamber and stepped into the half-darkness of the room.

"Late night for you. Or should I say 'early morning'?"

Startled, Jane turned around and found Clara sitting on her bed. The young woman's back was against the headboard, her face hidden in the shadows. Her slippered feet were stretched out on the undisturbed bedclothes.

"Early would be correct," Jane answered brightly. She had an impulse to run over and hug her sister, but fought it. This foolish giddiness was a sensation so new, but she didn't want to frighten anyone. "Good morning, Clara. Why are you up so early?"

Without waiting for an answer, she laid out underclothes and a dress. The water in the basin was cold, but she didn't care. She dipped a washcloth in it, and started to undress.

"I have been up all night."

"Are you feeling unwell?" Jane asked over her shoulder, thankful for the darkness of the room for it occurred to her that her fair skin might show the marks of Nicholas's attentions.

"You might say that."

"Then why are you here? You should have stayed in bed. I shall go and ask Fey to bring up . . . "

"*Nothing* that Fey could bring up would make me feel better." Clara's feet swung over the bed and made contact with the floor.

Jane heard the touch of sadness and temper in Clara's voice, and she paused in her washing and wrapped herself in a linen wrap.

"What is wrong?" she asked softly, moving toward the younger woman.

"*You* are what is wrong."

Jane came to an abrupt stop. "I . . . ?"

"Yes . . . you and your thoughtlessness." Clara stood up. "You and your lack of consideration for anyone else in this family."

Jane bristled at the charge. "What is Sir Thomas accusing me of now?"

"This is not about Father." Clara moved out of the shadows. The tearstains and swollen eyelids were a shock to Jane. "And this is not about Mother. This is about me, Jane—your only sister—the one in this family that you have always claimed you cared for."

Jane opened her mouth to ask more questions, but immediately shut it as a sickening feeling gripped her middle.

"What do you have against me?" Fresh tears rolled down Clara's cheeks as she came within a step. "Why is it that you . . . are so set against . . . seeing me happy?"

"I . . . I do not . . ."

"It is jealousy, is it not?" Clara attacked before Jane had a chance to find her words. "You have managed to ruin your own life. Now you cannot accept the fact that I might have a chance . . . a chance to get away from the disgrace you brought upon our family. You are jealous of me ever being happy."

"That is not true."

"You are lying," the younger woman snapped. "Why

else would you intentionally keep him away from me? Sir Nicholas came to Ireland for *me!* He wanted *me!* But you could not stop yourself from hurting me. You had to take the happiness that should have been *mine.*"

"*You* were the one who pushed him away." Jane was able to find her voice as the arguments roiled inside her. "You . . . you were the one who forced me to come with you . . . and then pushed him at me."

"So it was right for you to take advantage of my shyness? You could not let him be . . . or give me time to . . . to find myself. To become accustomed to him. It was right for you to take him away to Ballyclough yesterday . . . and the day before that? Do not deny any of it, Jane. I am no fool. I know he was with you that day, as well."

The thought ripping through Jane's mind at that instant was that Clara didn't know about last night. She had no way of knowing the two of them had been making love all night only two floors above where they now stood.

"What do you hope to accomplish by any of this, Jane?" The younger sister seethed. "Do you believe you are good enough to become his wife? Are you so selfish that you will not hesitate to bring shame to another family's honor? And what about your dear Shanavests? How will you manage to keep him while you are riding about the countryside until dawn . . . like this . . . with groups of ruffians and marauders and *traitors*?"

Tears sprang to Jane's eyes. She sat heavily on the edge of a chair. She tried to swallow the painful knot in her throat and speak.

"But there was no marriage proposal. I . . . I was told that he . . . did not ask . . . for . . ."

"He did not ask . . . *yet!*" Clara snapped. "But given the time, he would . . . he still will . . . if you *let* him be."

Jane turned her face away as tears slid down her cheeks. She felt Clara's hand on her knee as the younger woman crouched beside her.

"I have never asked anything of you, Jane, but I ask you this. Please do not ruin this chance for me." Her voice was no more than a soft whisper. "If you ever loved me as a sister . . . if you care even a little for me . . . then please give me a chance to win his affection." Clara clutched Jane's hand. "I need this chance. I need him to take me away from this place . . . from this godforsaken land. I promise to make him happy, Jane. I will be as good for him as he is for me."

Jane turned around and looked into her sister's face through a sheen of tears. "I cannot tell him whom to marry . . . or whom to love. That is not the kind of man he is."

"Then go away, Jane. Leave Woodfield House and stay with one of the dozens of friends you have around here. Let *me* convince him." Clara squeezed Jane's hand hard. "Please."

# Chapter 23

The doors of the study were closed and locked. On direct orders from Sir Thomas, the arrival of their visitor was not announced to the mistress of the house or to anyone else. This meeting was highly private.

The message delivered to Sir Robert Musgrave not long after dawn had explained Sir Thomas's genuine interest and willingness to help in whatever way he could to arrest the leaders of the local rebel faction. In addition, the former magistrate had hinted at methods and even informants that he was willing to share in order to guarantee success.

By midmorning Musgrave was at Woodfield House, and whatever differences of opinion the two men had harbored before meant nothing now. They were both keen on achieving the same results.

Sir Thomas listened intently to the new developments in Buttevant. And he was careful not to show any signs of surprise when the magistrate informed him that Jane and Sir Nicholas were the ones who had relocated the papist widow's children. He was also told about the baronet coming back after the mother.

"An act of charity, I have no doubt," Sir Thomas explained with a dismissive wave. "But tell me . . . this woman . . . where is she now?"

"My understanding is that she was taken to the village of Ballyclough."

"Ballyclough?" the older man growled. "How do you know that?"

"It appears Dr. Forrest was sent for by Parson Adams

to see to an ailing Irish boy. The doctor has indicated that the mother . . . this woman Kathleen . . . now does indeed reside in the parsonage."

"And you truly believe this woman can identify Egan?"

"I do, sir," the magistrate asserted. "The issue of who exactly gave the money to the woman is insignificant compared with the fact that the two *must* have met. Otherwise the Shanavests would not go to the trouble of removing the other woman . . . the blind widow . . . from the cottage."

"Very astute, sir. But you have been unsuccessful in gaining Kathleen's cooperation before. What changes now?"

"I plan to be more . . . persuasive. We shall arrange for her children to be brought in as well when we arrest her." A grim smirk thinned the man's lips. "I have heard she has a small daughter. If need be, we shall give the little chit over to one of our jailers and let the mother watch. The woman will be telling us more than what we need to know."

"I insist that you leave the children out of it," Sir Thomas snapped, rising to his feet. Wrestling with his temper, he turned and walked to the window. "You err in arresting the mother while she is staying at the parsonage, as well. Henry Adams will not take kindly to having people dragged out from beneath his own roof, and we do not want our own people rising against us."

"As magistrate, sir, I have the right to—"

"Keep peace!" the older man roared. "Your job is to maintain at least the appearance of peace and justice in the king's name. You let that woman go once. You cannot take her out of the care of Reverend Adams without having a damned good reason."

"She is my strongest connection with Egan right now."

"That does not say much for your efforts, does it, Sir Robert?"

Musgrave was red in the face when he bolted to his feet. "If your purpose in inviting me here today was to insult me, sir, then—"

"Blast your thin skin, Sir Robert, and get hold of yourself."

"I say . . . !"

"Focus, man! Put aside all this wasted effort that will surely come to naught." Sir Thomas clasped his hands behind his back and walked toward Musgrave. "To catch these foxes, we must make bigger plans. My suggestion is this . . ." He stopped, frowning at the man. "But perhaps you are not interested in succeeding."

"Of course I wish to succeed!" Musgrave sputtered.

"Then this is our plan. Carry out a punitive raid on one of the larger villages. You have the authority to do so. But before the attack, make certain . . . in a discreet way . . . that word of the raid leaks out. Meanwhile, have your men keep watch. Lay a trap. The Shanavests *will* show up."

"But there is no guarantee that any of their leaders will be there."

"There is no guarantee that you won't be buggered in your sleep tonight by the man in the moon, either!" Sir Thomas glared disapprovingly at the magistrate. "I will tell you the secret to succeeding here. You must plan carefully and then execute those plans quickly. Today is Wednesday. Plan the raid for tomorrow night. The word should get out no sooner than tomorrow at noon and only after some of your own people have been placed in strategic places in and around the village. This will not give the Whiteboys much time to react. One of their leaders . . . if not more . . . *will* show up to assist with the villagers."

"As far as these people that you say I should place in the village." Musgrave tugged on an ear. "I have no one whom I could put there . . . without raising suspicions."

"That is why I wanted us to plan this together." Sir Thomas smiled. "I can be of help."

The night air was heavy with the feel of an upcoming storm. The two men standing in the paddock were the only ones outside.

"I was in the forge with the smith when she left. I didn't even see the lass go." The trainer leaned a wide shoulder against a post and made a great show of poking at the tobacco in his pipe.

Nicholas was receiving the same answers from Paul

that he'd heard from everyone else. He was being thwarted everywhere he'd turned with his questions. Each person seemed to have been prepared. Each said the same thing. They didn't know where Jane had gone.

Nicholas wasn't convinced, though, and the way they all spoke to him triggered a feeling of anxiety in him that he could not shake off.

When he'd seen no sign of her by midmorning, he'd stormed down to the stables and found Queen Mab gone. Deciding that she must be at Ballyclough, he had saddled his horse and raced across the Irish countryside after her. Though Parson Adams was not at home, the housekeeper had assured him that Miss Jane had not come visiting the parsonage that morning. But, of course, he was welcome to stay and speak with Reverend Adams when he returned. Nicholas had not bothered, and had rushed back to Woodfield House instead, thinking she might be back.

In any other family or household, he would have had some success in questioning the parents as to their daughter's whereabouts. But Lady Purefoy's breezy response, "I long ago gave up keeping account of Jane's coming and going," had been a dark reminder of how *little* she was cared for by this family. Sir Thomas appeared to have even less interest than his wife, and questioning Clara had only managed to sharpen his ongoing suspicion that something had gone terribly wrong. Rather than answering him, the young woman had simply extended her previous invitation of acting as his guide, if Jane was unavailable. When he had declined, she'd done her best to try to engage him in a conversation regarding horses and racing.

He had struggled, but somehow managed not to be rude.

And Paul was being equally unhelpful. " 'Tis hardly amiss, sir, for herself to be off like this for a day or so."

Nicholas forced away the dark thoughts in his mind and watched the wreath of smoke around Paul's head. He tried to remind himself that it was completely within reason that she may have received a message after he'd left her this morning. But the anxiety wouldn't ease up . . . for he was certain she would have left him some word. "How long does her family wait before they grow curious about where she is?"

The arching of the stable master's bristled eyebrow gave Nicholas his answer.

"How long before *you* become concerned?"

Paul turned his attention to his pipe again, giving Nicholas his answer to that as well. The man knew where Jane was, and he wasn't concerned.

"I've spent the better part of that lassie's life worrying about her," he said evasively.

"At least tell me that she is in no danger," Nicholas pressed doggedly.

"I wisht that I could, sir. But the truth of the matter is, Sir Nicholas, ye might just resign yerself to what ye be feeling today. Miss Jane is not like any other lass. For a long while now, she's answered to no man—nor woman, neither. She's been given her own head for so long that I don't think she even remembers the feel of the bit between her teeth or the lash about the flanks, either. She's fierce in her independence, and that's all there is to it. So if ye be set to care for her, ye might also set yerself that you'll be having no peace of mind this side of the grave. 'Tis good for ye to be facing this now."

Paul's gaze was thoughtful when it met Nicholas's.

"Now, sir . . . if ye be looking for something . . . someone safe, then ye should be looking up that hill, for it appears as Miss Clara's giving up waiting on ye."

Nicholas glanced in the direction of the house, annoyed at the sight of Clara, candle in hand, making her way down the hill. As he turned back to Paul, he found the man already halfway to the stable door, doffing his cap to the young woman as he went.

"I should have known that your love of horses would draw you here. My guess is you could probably spend endless hours with my father's trainer. He is quite knowledgeable on the topic." Clara smiled brightly as she reached him. "But after everything I have heard of your own involvement and interest, Sir Nicholas, you cannot possibly be lacking anything."

He found the false adoring tone repellent, but he kept his views to himself. "Were you looking for someone down here, Miss Clara? If it was Paul with whom you wished to speak, I can still call him before he gets away."

"No. I had no wish to speak to Paul." She ran her free hand up and down her bare arm. "I should have brought a wrap. The night is far colder than I thought."

But then again, he thought grimly, a wrap would have defeated the purpose behind the fashionably revealing dresses Clara was beginning to wear. Be fair, he chided himself. All his frustration over Jane's absence was getting the best of him. He knew he had to get away.

"If you will excuse me, miss, I was just on my way back to the house."

He did not wait for a response from her before starting toward the paddock gate.

"Do you mind if I walk with you?" she asked a bit breathlessly, catching up to him. "We haven't had much time alone together since you've arrived, and I have been missing . . ."

"Do not do this, Clara," Nicholas barked, stopping abruptly and turning to face her. "I find this to be a very deceitful game . . . and entirely unworthy of you."

"But what do you mean?"

"Do not pretend that there is something romantic between us—or that there ever could be." Her eyes were large and innocent-looking, and they glistened in the lamplight. But Nicholas felt no pity. "I have no doubt that your father has already passed on the gist of our conversation. And regardless of what your mother may be planning, I am *not* interested in you, Clara, and I cannot express my feelings more clearly than that."

Her chin trembled, but she held her head high. "But that is now, sir. If you gave us a chance . . ."

"No." Impatient, he took a step away, but then turned around again, facing her. "I know you are young, but you must try to understand that giving 'a chance' to two people as different as we are will not change things. I do not want you for my wife. And in spite of whatever foolishness is going through your head at this moment, I know that you don't want me, either. But this does not mean that my rejection should be the end of it all for you. You are a beautiful and intelligent young woman.

You have great promise. And you should be doing your own choosing, rather than allowing yourself to be guided by the whims of your parents."

Tears stood out in her blue eyes, and Nicholas gentled his voice.

"There are many men out there, far more deserving than I. In time, you will meet someone who will be your perfect match. Until then, do not throw away your pride by settling for someone whom you can never love."

"There are many kinds of love, Sir Nicholas."

"There is only one kind of love fit for a husband and wife," he responded roughly. "And I, for one, intend to have it."

Clara turned away, and Nicholas frowned at his harsh tone.

"You deserve better, Clara," he said as gently as he could. "Do not settle for anything less than the right man."

Without another word, Nicholas strode up the path. When he reached the house, he turned to look at her. She had blown out the light in her lamp, and he could just make out the hooped expanse of her skirts' light material where she stood motionless in the dark.

What he could not see were the uncontrollable sobs that were wracking her body as she wept.

Two full days had passed, and Jane still was not back.

Alexandra sat on the bed and ran her fingers over the delicate cloth of the gown that Fey had carried into her room only minutes earlier. The workmanship was excellent. The design was exactly as she'd desired. But what good would this garment be if the one it had been made for was nowhere to be found?

Ah, but where could she be?

Tomorrow night was the ball, and still no one seemed to care where the older Purefoy sister had gone . . . or when she was to return. And if that were not distressing enough, Alexandra had been faced with having to find excuses for Nicholas's empty chair at dinner.

Oh, she knew he was at Woodfield House . . . when he wasn't out combing the countryside. He, too, was looking for Jane. She was sure of it. His features had been set in an expressionless mask, showing nothing of what she knew he must be feeling inside. His words gave away even less.

In recent years, when she'd thought about Nicholas settling down and marrying, she'd never considered the situation might also entail any of this pain that he was going through now. Women, in general, had been plentiful in Nicholas's life. Foolishly, she'd assumed that taking the next step would be as simple as picking one from the flock of eligible heiresses. She had been so wrong.

Alexandra left her bedroom and went directly to Jane's attic studio. When she'd run into Nicholas before dinner, she had seen him going in that direction.

The quiet of the upper floors pressed on her ears like January cold. Every servant in the household was apparently downstairs, bustling about under the sharp eye of Lady Purefoy as the house was prepared for tomorrow night's ball.

She knocked on the door before opening it. Nicholas appeared at the top of the stairs, his face hopeful for a moment before seeing who it was. He was wearing no jacket or tie. His sleeves were rolled up to his elbows and the white shirt lacked the crispness with which he always presented himself.

"May I come up?" she asked softly.

"I assume she has not returned."

She shook her head and climbed the stairs. Alexandra wished she could be the bearer of good news, but other than just wanting to be here with him, she was at a loss as to how she could help.

At the top of the stairs, she paused, not trying to hide her awe at the display of Jane's work. Unlike the first time that she'd been here, when everything had been hidden beneath covers, nearly every painting was now arranged for viewing, and the space was ablaze with the light of dozens of candles. If she overlooked the rough and inadequate finish of the room, she could easily imagine that she was in one of the finest galleries in Europe.

"So much talent," she murmured. "I am so glad she has decided at least to display her work up here."

Nicholas had moved to the opposite end of the room

and did not respond, if he heard her. She watched him uncovering another canvas and looking carefully at it, before placing it against a wall with others that were similar in color and theme. Alexandra realized he was the one who'd taken it on himself to uncover her incredible gift. She picked up a candle from one of the tables.

"She is so prolific a painter." She admired the sheer amount of work. There was much here that she hadn't seen on that first day. "I never had a chance to speak to Jane about coming here and looking at more of her work. I hope she doesn't mind . . ."

The words died in Alexandra's throat as she heard a low curse. Nicholas was crouched down before a canvas he'd just uncovered. She wanted to go to him and see for herself what had affected him so. She held back, though, silent as death while her son sat for what seemed like eternity.

Alexandra remembered her own reaction to the canvases Jane had painted of the seasons' passage and the destruction of an Irish village. Finally, she could wait no longer and broke the silence.

"If someone were to convince Jane . . . to tell her about the genius so apparent in her work. If someone were to convey to her the powerful sense of reality she depicts in every painting. The balance, the structure, the coloring, the use of light and shadow. All of these things. Perhaps these paintings could provide a new beginning for her somewhere beyond the walls of Woodfield House."

He remained engrossed in the work.

"This family does not deserve her. They have no appreciation for the person and the artist she is." She whispered her feelings. "These paintings must be shown at the Royal Academy in London. Or, if not, then on the Continent."

Alexandra didn't know how far the relationship between Nicholas and Jane had progressed. Though she was sure the beginnings were there, she had no way of knowing their level of commitment to each other. Understanding her own son's independent and rebellious nature, she could not pressure him or ask his intentions, but at the same time she decided to explain the plans that had gradually been developing in her mind for most of this week.

"I should like to invite Jane to come back to England with us. From there, if she wants, she can come back with me to Brussels." There was no reaction to her words, and Alexandra slowly approached Nicholas. "I think she should be introduced into the top artistic circles at Court. I am certain that Sir Joshua Reynolds, your neighbor in Leicester Square, would love to take her under his wing. He is a powerful force at the Royal Academy. He is also tremendously jealous of other portraitists, of course, but I have great confidence in her work and know that he and others will see her genius. After a lifetime of receiving no encouragement here, she could use some genuine praise . . ."

A gasp escaped her as she glanced over Nicholas's shoulder at the canvas in his hand. Her candle flickered, and she dashed a tear from her face.

The small canvas portrayed five bodies hanging from gibbets in a town square. The background of faces in the crowd and the buildings framing the scene were only muted brushstrokes—an effect that highlighted the shocking reality of those who'd been executed. Their condition cried out from the canvas. It was obvious this was a work that had been completed much earlier than anything else that Alexandra had seen, but still Jane had managed to capture the tragic emotion of the scene with power and style.

"I have asked her to marry me."

Nicholas's voice drew her gaze to his solemn profile.

"I believe she was frightened by the offer—and perhaps by my persistence. I should have given her time to become accustomed to the idea before pressuring her. Now I have driven her away." His fingers touched the three-quarter view of the man's body hanging in the foreground. "He has been dead for nine years, and she is still in love with him."

"Devoted to him," Alexandra gently corrected. "And she will always have a sense of loss when she thinks of him. But I am certain she thinks of him less now than she did then. And that does not mean she is incapable of loving again."

He rose to his feet, and she saw the doubt clouding his features.

"We must remember that life has not been kind to her," she continued. "She has been alone—held responsible for a scandalous act from such an early age. Regardless of how she feels for you, she undoubtedly sees so many obstacles that stand between the two of you."

"Damn her reputation and everyone else here."

"You can afford to ignore society's view of your life and future. You are a man, first of all, and you have intentionally worked at establishing a reputation for recklessness. As far as the *ton* is concerned, once you do settle, they will recall your roguish ways only as youthful wildness. But Jane knows nothing of how your society works. All she knows is that you were reputable enough to be considered the ideal husband for her sister, but now you are interested in her." She followed him when he moved away. "If she were any other woman, she would have jumped at your offer. Clara would have jumped at it. But not Jane."

"She might at least tell me how she feels . . . then I will know what is to be done."

"But she is." She placed a hand on Nicholas's arm. "Nick, you have all the blind stubbornness of your sex. Can you not see? In her own way, she *is* showing you her love by running away. She doesn't want to ruin your reputation by linking you with her . . ."

"Ha!" he laughed bitterly. "I have thought about what she should have to bear because of *me!*"

"But don't you see? She values you more than she does her own future and happiness." Her hand made a sweeping motion over the paintings in the room. "Look at this place—at all of this work. These paintings are a window to this woman's soul. The compassion with which she paints these canvases is the heart of the woman herself. And yet what does she do with this talent? She hides it in an attic. She covers it with cloth. She brings no attention to herself or her gifts." She met her son's burning gaze. "You have a great challenge ahead of you, Nick, but you are the man to handle it."

"How?"

His question tugged at her heart. It had been a long while since he'd asked her advice on anything.

"You must be here for her. You cannot give up. You must try to understand the motives behind each of her actions . . . the same way that you try to understand the message behind each of these paintings." She placed the candle on the worktable. "It will all work out. You two were made for each other. Just make her see it. Prove it to her."

As Alexandra descended the stairs and made her way back to her room, she knew the biggest challenge still lay with her. If these two were to have any chance of finding a future, she had to locate Jane now and bring her back.

The village, peacefully perched on a curl of the Black-water River, erupted not an hour after sunset in an explosion of activity. They were coming.

The western sky still glowed with the last shreds of orange and red when a half-dozen masked Whiteboys came silently out of the darkness on foot, led by a single rider dressed all in black—but for the white smock of the Shanavests. The news swept through the village like the wind, and each cottage sprang to life as the inhabitants roused themselves.

*The entire village was to feel the blade of the King's justice for their history of helping the Shanavests. Indeed, the dragoons were coming.*

Disbelief quickly faded as panic chilled their souls. The villagers knew what their fate would be if they didn't escape. They'd heard of the barbarism that had been inflicted on other towns larger than their own. The horrors were nearly unspeakable.

Now was not the time for packing the treasures of a lifetime. Now was not the time to tarry at all. They were coming, and the shock of the news quickly gave way to action.

The poorer villagers—those with less to part with— were the first to start down the river road to the place where the bog land offered the best protection. They could all hide there for weeks, if need be, deep in the marshes that flooded each spring with the rising of the river. If the dragoons decided to leave their horses at the edges of the murky swamps and follow, then the villagers would push beyond, leaving the bogs in the dead of a moonless night, climbing into the hills, and making their way to the south.

But where would they go then? they wondered as they gathered their children and the few belongings that they could carry. Where?

The torches of a hundred mounted men lit up the road on the far side of the river. As the leader of the Shanavests ushered the last and more resistant of the fugitives along, the raiders closed to within a league or two of the deserted village. Looking back, the mounted Shanavests saw the advance riders reach the village bridge, and it was only a moment later that the screams began to cut through the night.

"Old Rohane's cottage," someone from the group gasped.

"I went to their door, but there was no one inside," another man explained.

"They are not with us," a voice from the dark called out.

"My wee Kevin is with them, too," a woman cried.

Egan touched another member of the Shanavests on the shoulder. "Move them on. I'll go back for those missing."

Without paying any heed to the man's immediate objection, Egan spurred Mab back toward the village. The main body of dragoons was still minutes away, and the screams that now were recognizable to be those of a woman were continuing. They seemed to be coming from the livery stable sitting on the riverbank by the bridge itself. Drawing her pistol from her belt, Egan dismounted in the shadows and ran toward the building.

When she pulled open the heavy door, the acrid smell of smoke greeted her. Panicky livestock pressed to escape through the same opening. Egan pushed her way through them and stepped into the smoky darkness.

The first cold flash of fear clawed at her when she realized the cries of the woman actually were retreating from her. She felt her way quickly across the stable floor and saw two people slip out the door leading to the smith's forge. She reached the door in seconds, only to find it already barred from the outside.

She could no longer hear a cry for help, and a sickening chill crept up her spine. She sensed the presence of others in the stable. It was a trap.

Egan whirled around and saw soldiers coming out of every corner of the darkened stable. Pistols and swords glinted dully in the dim light. She could hear more outside, and she knew that the dragoons across the river would be here in a moment. Once they surrounded the building completely . . .

Someone doused a burning blanket in a corner near the door that she had used to enter. Another one shouted to others outside.

"We have him. We have Egan."

She pressed her back against the barred door and looked frantically about for any means of escape. Someone with a torch came in at the door to her left.

Pointing her pistol at one and then another of the steadily closing circle, she realized her only route of escape lay in shooting one and then trying to run through the dozen drawn weapons. Not a very good plan, she thought, considering that there were probably quite a few more waiting outside.

Egan drew her dagger with the other hand. She would kill first before they took her down. She took a step toward the approaching group.

"The magistrate's order," someone shouted, coming in the far end of the stable with another lantern. "Take him alive. He must be taken alive."

The distraction was all Egan needed, and she leaped into action. As she charged the two men farthest to her left, she spotted a rope hanging from the high rafters and leading to a loft. Perhaps if she could just get from there to . . . to where?

Screaming Gaelic curses as she attacked, she delivered a sharp kick to the first one's groin, whirling and slashing at the hand of the man holding the torch. He cried out in anger and shock, but the torch fell to the ground, and Egan leaped past him as the dry straw immediately crackled and caught fire beneath her feet.

Tucking the pistol into her belt, she jumped at the rope and climbed a couple of feet. The shouts were echoing around her and she felt a soldier's hand grab her boot. Before he could drag her down, she managed to draw her pistol and fire. The man screamed and fell back as the bullet struck his foot. Someone else already had a grip on her neck, but she swung the pistol hard, striking him across the face and knocking him into several soldiers behind him.

The flames were spreading fast around their feet now, and the soldiers were in total disarray. Seizing her chance, Egan climbed the rope as quickly as she could, expecting a bullet to end her escape at any moment. Her mask and hat were dangling down her back, but she didn't pause or look back. Instead, she pulled herself hand over hand until she could clamber into the loft.

The smoke was thick and she could hear the shouts of the dragoons. Working her way through the mounds of hay, she found a shuttered window that she kicked open. In a moment she was out on the sloping thatch of the roof.

Egan climbed quickly, trying not to think of what would happen if a section of the roof gave way. The smoke was billowing up through gaps in the thatch. She stood up and glanced at the mayhem surrounding the stable below. Dragoons—afoot and on horse—were running here and there, clearly in disorder because the village was empty.

Or because Egan had eluded them . . . so far.

She knew it would not be long before the soldiers made their way to the loft and then to the roof.

Somewhere below, she heard the neigh of Queen Mab. Scurrying to the end of the roof, she peered over and saw her horse rising on her back legs and pawing furiously at the air and at the soldiers who were trying to capture her.

Flames appeared through the smoke, licking the dry thatch and sending sparks crackling into the air. Egan climbed to the peak. There was a lower slate-roofed building across a narrow alley, but she also saw three dragoons already waiting by that building.

"Jump, Egan! Jump!"

She recognized Patrick's shout, and a thrill of hope lifted her spirits. Crossing a patch of open ground at the edge of the village, a dozen Shanavests on horseback raced toward her.

The encroaching flames were beginning to light up the roof like an inferno, and she realized she had no choice but to jump across. Backing up, Egan ran a couple of steps and leaped for the slate roof of the next building. She landed hard on her ankle, but this was no time to be delicate. As she was scrambling to the edge, she heard an exchange of pistol fire. Peering over the side of the building, she saw the mounted Shanavests swarming the soldiers and Mab. While a dozen of them fought fiercely with the dragoons, two of them pulled her horse away.

She jumped again without hesitation, again feeling her ankle when she hit the ground. The pain burned through, nearly overwhelming her, but she limped to the horse and pulled herself onto Mab's back.

There were whistles and shouts. Surrounded by the masked group, Egan and the rest withdrew as speedily as they'd arrived, galloping across the fields away from the village. After passing through the first line of hedges, though, they wordlessly split into groups of twos and threes and headed off in different directions.

Egan found herself in the company of two masked Shanavests, Patrick and another on a horse she didn't recognize. She frowned at the man's back. He was a stranger, but one adept at the use of a sword . . . that she knew. Though he spoke in Gaelic, his accent was unfamiliar. There was, however, something distinctly familiar about his voice.

What perplexed her most, though, was that he was giving orders.

"After crossing the river, Patrick, I want you to take her east. I'll draw anyone coming after us to the north. You have a place to hide your horses."

"Aye, the same places we're always hiding them."

"Finn!" she whispered. She tried to get a better look, peering through the dark. The large, tricornered hat and the mask thwarted her efforts.

"Are you Finn?" she asked finally.

"Ye see, Egan, our Finn is not a ghost of Liam's making, after all," Patrick answered, riding to her right.

Before she could ask another question, they splashed into the shallows of the river and then continued to ford it. There was no sign of any followers. Her ankle was throbbing badly.

She stared at him again. For several years, she had known of Finn. Liam had used his name often in conveying key information to their group. He appeared to have many contacts in the English regiments as well as the volunteer militias. He had at times even seemed to know things that had to come from someone close to Ireland's Lord Lieutenant himself. In spite of his participation in the fighting tonight, she had never known him to step out of his usual role.

Indeed, she had never met him—or seen him—until now.

"Act as if nothing has happened," Finn told her as they prepared to separate on the far shore. "Resume your other life. Pretend you know nothing of tonight. They are bent on capturing you, and you must not allow them to succeed."

He turned and she watched him disappear quickly into the darkness. Patrick urged her to move, and she proceeded. But Egan's mind was racing with Finn's words.

*Resume your other life . . . Resume your other life . . .*

What other life? She no longer had any other life. Just as the hard slate roof of the stable had hurt her ankle, Clara's words had destroyed the already unsteady footing she was feeling at Woodfield House.

Though the pain shooting up her leg from her ankle hurt tremendously, the ache in her heart was hurting far worse.

Between the two wounds, Jane knew she had nothing to stand on.

# Chapter 24

The housekeeper saw the curious glances of the cooks and servants and grooms—some working, some taking their breakfast—when she entered the servants' hall with the persistent guest on her heels. She simply had to put a stop to this. She turned and left the room with the woman still dogging her.

In the narrow corridor, still dark in the morning light, she whirled around. "Ye just cannot follow me about like this, m'lady. Certainly not on a morning such as this . . . with so much left to do before the rest of the house is up. I told ye once, and I'll tell ye a hundred times, if I must, but I cannot help ye find Miss Jane."

"But you *know* where she is," Alexandra persisted. "And by God, I am not giving up until you tell me where she is . . . or at least have someone take me to her. It is absolutely urgent that I should bring her back here for the ball this evening."

"But clearly she doesn't care to come back, m'lady. She wouldn't give a beggar's boot for any of this fanciness. I'm telling ye, mum, she doesn't care to hear their sniggering behind her back."

"This will be different, Fey." Alexandra lowered her voice and looked into the other woman's face. "I shall make the whole lot of them eat their words. We did not go to all our trouble to have them laugh at her. After tonight, your gentry will think twice before they ridicule her."

"A fine dress is nary enough, m'lady." Sadness shone in the gentle woman's eyes. "She has been hurt too much before. I do not think she wants to face such things again."

"But she must! She must come out of hiding and face them." She placed a hand on Fey's arm. "Do you think she is truly happy where she is, or how she is treated by . . . well, by certain people close to her? Does she not deserve better than what she is getting?"

"What I think and what will happen are hardly the same, m'lady."

"But they *can* be . . . with our interference," Lady Spencer quickly interjected. "I know them. They are like parrots . . . waiting for one to say something so they can all repeat it. And that is what will work to our advantage. That is what Jane needs. Someone to begin talking about her in a way that points out the noble qualities in her."

Fey stared at the floor, unconvinced.

"There is something else I am planning to do as well, but I need Jane's permission to do it."

Fey's eyebrows arched with interest.

"Without revealing very much to Lady Purefoy, I have received her permission to remake one of the parlors to a theme of my choosing." Alexandra lowered her voice. "I wish to make it into a gallery, but I need Jane's permission to use her paintings."

"Her paintings, m'lady?"

"Indeed. I wish to bring some of the canvases down from that attic work area of hers and display them about the room."

"But she . . . Miss Jane never . . . never shows her work to anyone." Fey wrung her apron in her hands.

"But Jane has tremendous talent. Unless they are complete boors, all of them will be impressed by her paintings far more than by anything else we can do." Lady Spencer nodded with conviction. "I am speaking the absolute truth, Fey, when I tell you Jane's work is equal to some of the greatest masterpieces of our time."

"But some of what . . . she paints . . ." The house-keeper frowned and shook her head. "I am no expert, mum, but some of it is a wee bit revealing of her . . . her private life."

"That is exactly why I need her . . . why you must

help me find her. Only Jane can decide what to show and what not." Alexandra took hold of the servant's hand. "If my praise of her as a person has no weight with these people, I know her talent will turn the tide. This is a perfect opportunity for Jane to come out before her peers. There could never be another chance like this anytime soon." She gentled her tone and met the woman's thoughtful gaze. "If nothing else, please take me to her so I can explain these things to her. The decision will be hers—but she has to be told, while there is still a little time left."

After a moment, a look of resolve replaced the indecision in the housekeeper's face. "No one else can be going with ye."

Alexandra nodded.

"And ye shall need to wait until midday, when I can find someone to spare for a few hours."

"Just tell me when, and I'll be ready."

With a book tucked under her arm, Clara once again took refuge in the gardens. The entire household continued to be in an uproar over the ordeal tonight, and the young woman had even found the privacy of her bedroom invaded by the dressmakers and seamstresses and servants who were ready to bathe her and do her hair and whatever else Lady Purefoy had ordered them to do.

And she was ashamed of all of it.

Clara couldn't forgive herself for the lunacy—for assuming that she was capable of seducing Sir Nicholas and getting him to change his earlier decision about asking for her hand. The cutting remarks he had delivered to her two nights ago had been as mortifying as they were sobering. Instead of learning from Henry's rejection earlier and trying to make a change in her life, more so than ever before she was trying to be her parents' puppet.

Clara moved deeper through the garden and thought of the injustice she had done to her older sister. Jane had gone away without a word to her of where she was going and how long she was staying away. Her older sister had done just as she had asked her to. And for what?

Henry was right. She was selfish. It was Jane who behaved selflessly . . . and deserved better.

Tears were running down her face by the time Clara neared her favorite spot by the paddock. As she approached the hedge, the voices of two men engaged in a tense conversation on the other side cut into her misery.

"I do not understand this at all, Captain," her father was saying in an angry but hushed tone. "I have been generous enough to offer him a plan for capturing these leaders of the Whiteboys. It is not too much, I should think, to expect Musgrave to be frank about what happened last night."

"As I said before, sir, he sends his regards and says he intends to give you a full report tonight." The other man's voice was apologetic. "I have been ordered to say nothing more."

"But I am entertaining tonight." Sir Thomas seethed. "My wife has a blasted ball planned that I must attend. Come, Captain . . . you served me well when I was magistrate. What did he find or whom did he arrest that requires such secrecy?"

"I fear, Sir Thomas, that the present magistrate must make his own explanations, sir."

"Out with it, Wallis. You were there. What happened?"

Clara cringed at her father's menacing tone now. She could only imagine the man facing Sir Thomas must be even more affected by his growing fury.

"I . . ."

"The devil take you. Did we succeed or not, man?"

There was a long pause.

"This . . . this must remain just between us, Thomas."

"As you wish," the older man growled impatientl

"I only tell you this out of respect for our ef' together."

"Indeed, Captain. We made a good team, you ar

"Last night, we made no arrests, but we were a unmask the rebel Egan. That is all I can say. Ou bles are far from being over, but the magistrate plans to explain to you tonight—is confident tha' close to capturing the . . . the rebel."

Clara's hand was tightly clamped over her mouth as all
she'd just heard continued to whirl in her mind. *They'd
unmasked Egan.*

"I see." Sir Thomas's voice was far more subdued
when he spoke again. "So, other than coming here and
keeping anything of import from me, why do you want
to search my stables? Does Sir Robert think I am hiding
rebels in the hayloft?"

"The magistrate wishes to know if any horses were
missing from the stables of any of the landowners last
night. We are looking, in particular, for a large black
horse . . . one similar to the mare that is often ridden
by your daughter, Miss Jane."

Clara could wait not a minute longer. Clutching her
stomach in an effort to ward off the queasiness rising
into her throat, she ran frantically toward the house. She
needed to get her cloak. She needed to find Jane . . . to
warn her of what the dragoons already knew about her.
If they had unmasked her, that meant they already knew
her identity. They would be coming after her . . .
here . . . possibly tonight!

She couldn't let this happen to Jane. Seeing a gar-
dener on the path, she brushed away the tears and ordered him to go to ask Paul to ready a *good* horse for
her. She had to find her sister . . . somehow.

Conor's blood was already on her hands. She could
not bear to go through life with her sister's blood on
them, too.

Jenny's cottage consisted of three rooms. In size and
in its furnishings, it was far more comfortable than many
a tenant's hovel. But still, for someone of Lady Spencer's
quality, it would normally be considered hardly suitable
for entertaining.

Jane, however, was relieved to see that the visitor was
so comfortable in the cottage. She made no hint of finding anything offensive in Jenny's home. In fact, as Jane
watched the two women chatting amiably before the
small peat fire, she was extremely pleased with Alexandra's affability and natural charm in her manner toward
Conor's aunt.

Jane waited, impatient to learn the reason for this un-

expected visit. Nothing could have been wrong with Nicholas, or Lady Spencer would not be so calm, she decided. But there had to be a good reason. Fey and Paul would not, under normal circumstances, reveal Jane's whereabouts to anyone. Nonetheless, Alexandra had been brought here by their direction.

Jenny soon excused herself and left the two of them alone. Lady Spencer turned her sparkling eyes on Jane.

"I have seen your paintings."

"You have?" she replied, surprised.

"Yes. Jane, you have tremendous talent. I cannot tell you how impressed I was in seeing them. Your work is . . . inspiring!"

"I don't know if—"

"But I have a favor to ask of you," Alexandra said, going on to explain her elaborate plan of displaying some of Jane's paintings during the ball for the purpose of regaining the local English gentry's respect. Jane tried patiently to listen to everything the good lady said.

"But none of this I care one whit about," she interrupted finally, not wishing to give Lady Spencer any false hope by her continued silence.

"It is an artist's natural inclination to fear sharing her work with others. We all fear the rejection of an audience. None of us wishes to be embarrassed by criticism or even by some offhand remark. I believe it is quite normal to want to keep our work and ourselves safely in seclusion. Most of us claim that we only like to paint for ourselves."

"I do not *claim* that, Alexandra. I *do* paint for myself. To me, taking a brush to the canvas or charcoal to paper is not for the sake of creating a piece of art. I do it to let out the emotions that are trapped inside of me." Jane spoke passionately. She followed the other woman's gaze to the drawing tablet on the windowsill beside her. Jane had been sketching when Lady Spencer had arrived. "I hope you will forgive my bluntness, m'lady, but even if I had the slightest desire to share my work with others, these people would be among the last I would choose. Gaining the respect of my father's friends is not high on my list of what I wish to do with my life."

Jane wished she could get up and walk about the

room. She was feeling frustrated, crowded. But her bruised ankle stopped her.

"But, my dear, people need something to talk about. Rather than prattling on about the past over and over again, would it not be far more pleasant if they had something as thrillingly powerful as your art to discuss?"

"I care nothing for their pleasantries." Jane shook her head in disagreement. "I have never cared about what they think of me, but I refuse to put myself in a position of having to endure their criticism in any public arena. I do not need them, and they have no use for me. I am quite resigned to things as they are."

"I understand your bitterness." Alexandra leaned forward in her chair, lowered her voice, and touched Jane gently on the knee. "But can you not see that what I am trying to do has a purpose far grander than allowing you to make peace with a few provincial snobs who cling to the outdated prejudices of yesterday?"

Jane's heart started beating faster in her chest. She had feared that Lady Spencer's true purpose today had nothing to do with the paintings.

"My purpose is far more selfish. I am trying to do this for Nicholas . . . and for you," the older woman continued. "I have watched what your absence over the past few days has done to my son. For the first time in his life, Nicholas appears . . . well . . . lost. His spirit, his joie de vivre . . . it all seems to have lessened dramatically since you have been away from Woodfield House. And now, here I am . . . and I find the same kind of melancholy afflicting you."

Jane blinked back the tears suddenly burning her eyes.

"You two simply *must* resolve your differences." She clutched Jane's hand. "And though I know that nothing of your past matters at all to Nick, I also know that *you* would be far better resolved to a future together if you were able to walk away from some of the darkness of your past."

Jane had made love to Nicholas. She had given her body and her heart to him. But looking down now at her own black apparel, she knew she still had far to go to leave her past behind.

"My dear, I am here to help you in whatever way I

can. I have connections in England, you know, and there is always a way to improve on matters of the past." The intense blue eyes were pleading when they met Jane's. "Please allow me to make a difference."

The young woman looked down at her own fingers clutching at Alexandra's hand like a sailor gripping a lifeline. A desperateness was wracking her body and soul. By all the saints in heaven, she needed help in more ways than she could name. Jane believed her only chance of ever finding happiness again lay with Nicholas . . . and her love for him. Despite the endless tears she'd shed since arriving at Jenny's cottage, though, she didn't need to remind herself that she was still there because of her sister's request. She could not ruin Clara's chances when her own future was so uncertain.

"No one can make a difference." Jane shook her head, avoiding the older woman's gaze. "And I truly appreciate your belief in me. But there is just too much scandal in my past . . . in my life now . . ."

She let go of Alexandra's hand and stared at the fire.

"Nicholas and I have no chance of happiness. I should have stopped it before anything began. It is my fault. I am to blame for his situation. I am sorry."

Despite the pain in her ankle, Jane pushed herself to her feet and stood by the window. The view before her was a blur, but she held back her tears, refusing to allow herself to fall apart before this woman. Not after everything that she'd just said.

Lady Spencer said not a word more, but Jane heard her rise from her chair and walk out of the room. Only after the door had closed behind the visitor did Jane allow the tears to come. They were bitter tears, helpless tears, angry tears . . . for she knew there would never be another chance for her. She was now a captive to her own past and family for life. There could never be an escape for her.

Jane quickly wiped the tears from her face when she heard Jenny enter shortly after.

"I . . . I am sorry, Jenny, that you were forced to entertain this afternoon. I never thought . . . I never imagined anyone would be coming here . . . like this."

"Never ye mind, lass. I don't mind that one. In fact,

I should say I liked yer Lady Spencer a great deal. In many a way, she reminded me of ye, my joy. Aye, she's the kind of woman I'd like to be seeing ye become when ye reach her age."

Jane looked over her shoulder at the older woman and tried to smile. But the small boulder lodged in her throat would not allow it.

"Why are ye doing this to yerself, child?" Jenny scolded. Seeing Jane's stricken face, she hurried to her side and wrapped her arms around her. "When are ye going to stop punishing yerself?"

"I don't know what you mean."

"Stop the mourning. Let him go, my dove. Nine years is far more than enough. Conor is dead, and ye must be living. Do ye hear me? Ye must be living!" Jenny's voice was becoming increasingly urgent, impatient. She drew back and looked into Jane's face. " 'Twas not yer fault that he was hanged. The lad knew what he was doing. He understood the dangers and the risks, both with the Shanavests . . . and with wanting ye. He lived every day of his life as he pleased. I was his kin. I raised him as my own. And I tell ye now that my Conor would not be having anything to do with ye if he saw how ye're fading away with him gone."

"I am not fading away." Jane stepped to the hearth. The peat threw very little heat, but she could feel her face burning. "I picked up where he left off. I have kept our band of Shanavests to the course . . ."

"Nay, my joy. You have lost the spirit of Egan. I think ye are no longer Conor's 'wee fire.' " Jenny moved beside her. "Egan would know how to let that boy's memory rest. Ye talk about guilt. How would ye feel if yer situations were changed about? What if, after these many years, ye were looking down from St. Brigid's right hand, only to see such sadness afflicting *him*? Do ye think 'twould make him happy to see ye throwing away a chance like the one ye just sent packing with Lady Spencer? Do ye truly believe our Conor would be one to hold a grudge if ye were to settle with this woman's son and finally begin living?"

Of course, she thought, considering the size of the

cottage, it would only be natural for Jenny to hear everything that had been said. "I . . . Sir Nicholas . . ."

"I have ears, child." Jenny placed a gentle hand on Jane's shoulder again. "With Ronan's big mouth yapping, everyone from Cork to Limerick knows the baronet is sweet on ye. And everyone knows that ye have feelings for him, too."

Before Jane could say a word, Jenny continued. "And that's the way it should be. Finally, someone has come to call who is deserving of my Egan." The older woman smiled. "Just knowing that he didn't give you away that first day! And later, hearing what he did for Kathleen— old fool that I am—sure ye can't blame me for hoping something might happen between the two of ye. And today, after meeting himself's own mother . . . well, darling, I can only ask what ye could possibly be waiting for?"

"I cannot." Jane shook her head adamantly. "There is more dividing us than Conor and the Shanavests and . . ." She drew a deep breath. "It is no use, Jenny. He and I . . . we just cannot."

The older woman frowned at her for a long moment before speaking.

"This has something to do with yer sister, does it not?" she asked, her disapproval evident in her tone. "Everything, no doubt."

"Leave Clara out of this." Jane ran her hands up and down her arms. "Please just accept what I say and let me be."

A lengthy silence fell over the room while Jane once again found herself struggling in her own thoughts. Jenny's tone was much softer when she spoke again.

"Ye still must go back for the doings at Woodfield House tonight."

Jane looked with surprise into the woman's face. "But I—"

"Liam sent me a message. Finn wants you to go back—ye must make yerself visible, he says. Ye must attend yer mother's ball. Ye must pretend that there is nothing wrong and that ye know nothing of what happened last night."

After her years with the Shanavests, Jane had mastered

the ability to block the dangers of raids and their aftermath from her mind. With the exception of tending her swollen ankle, she hadn't given much thought this morning to the trap and to her unmasking last night. It had been dark, though, and she had never really come face-to-face with anyone after the mask had been torn off.

She frowned. Queen Mab, though, had been seen close up by a number of soldiers. And it was possible that someone might have guessed that Egan was a woman. "Has there been any significant news? I am certain no one saw me."

"All I know is the message that he sent."

Finn had said the same thing to her last night—about resuming her other life.

"But the complications of going back . . . I cannot just walk in with that ball tonight . . ." Not to mention that she would need to face Nicholas again. Perhaps it had been a cowardly path, but she hadn't thought she could face him. She knew she could not explain things to him after her meeting with Clara.

"This is not for ye that I am speaking, now. You must do this for the rest," Jenny insisted. "Even the smallest of suspicion falling upon ye, and more than a few of us would be tied to the band through you. That includes those at Woodfield House. Jane, ye have no choice."

Jane sat down in the nearest chair. The pounding in her head was now a hundred times worse than the ache in her ankle. She couldn't argue against what Jenny was saying. With Musgrave's sharp claws poised over her, it was very well possible that he would make the connections. "I . . . I wish I had thought of this . . . while Lady Spencer was still here."

"She *is* still here." Jenny shrugged at Jane's immediately suspicious glare. "I asked her to wait in her carriage and give me a chance to talk to ye. I knew ye had to go. And as I listened, I thought, 'What better ruse than this . . .'"

The older woman continued to explain, but Jane had an uncomfortable feeling that she had been duped.

# Chapter 25

There was no time to be wasted.

Jane was not at the parsonage at Ballyclough, and Mrs. Brown said she had not seen her sister in the past few days. Clara asked about the whereabouts of Parson Adams, but then refused the housekeeper's offer that she wait for him there. Setting off on foot and in the direction she was pointed, she walked as fast as her legs could take her toward the lower village until she saw him coming along the knoll, beyond the Mallow road.

Her customary reaction to seeing him—the inability to breathe, the hammering of her heart in her chest, the images of them together in her mind—all of this quickly came and went as the pressing nature of her search washed them away. Clara ran toward him for a few steps, slowed to a fast walk, and then ran again until she reached him breathlessly.

"Henry! You must help me. I am looking for Jane, but . . . but . . . I have no idea . . . idea . . . where else . . . to look . . . It is so urgent!"

Placing a hand on her chest to calm her breath and find her voice, she looked into his face for the first time and was surprised by the sadness she saw there. Her heart sank. She placed a desperate hand on his arm.

"No! Please do not tell me something has happened. Please . . . no!" The tears fell fast and furious, and denial twisted her throat into a knot. "Not Jane . . ."

Clara felt him take her by the arm and lead her away from the road and the curious eyes of the villagers. She was vaguely conscious of moving down a path across the stony brook and then up through green fields. The tears, though, continued to fall.

"It is all . . . my fault," she hiccuped. "If I had not . . ."

"Nothing has happened to Jane," he assured her calmly.

Clara stared unbelievingly into his red-rimmed eyes. "But . . . you . . . you look like . . . you have been . . . that you are upset!"

"I have just left a funeral." The gray eyes looked back at the lower end of the village. "The tanner Darby O'Connell's wife, may she rest in peace. God knows she never knew any until now."

"Oh. I am so sorry," she whispered, wiping away at her face. "Was she young?"

"Very."

"And she left children?"

"One died during the childbirth that killed her. There are three more young ones left behind."

Clara wiped away more tears. "And . . . the . . . husband?"

"Nearly mad with grief, poor devil."

Her tears would not stop, and she dashed at them incessantly. She couldn't seem to get hold of her emotions. In a moment, Henry placed an arm gently around her shoulders. It only made things worse as she melted against him.

"I am . . . so sorry," she sobbed. "Here, I did not even know the woman. But it is so sad and I am so worried about Jane. But I cannot . . . find her . . . and I know she is angry with me. She might not even believe what I have to tell . . . her. But I overheard . . . Captain Wallis talking to Father . . . and . . . I have to find Jane . . . to warn her."

Clara hadn't even realized that she was babbling until Henry turned her around in his arms. She stopped abruptly. Her face flushed with heat when his hand lifted her chin until she was looking into his intense gray eyes.

"Start from the beginning. What was it exactly that you overheard?"

Clara took a deep breath and blurted out word for word everything she'd heard by the paddock.

"Captain Wallis did not say that they think Jane is

the rebel Egan, but if they are looking for a horse like Jane's . . . and if they come tonight and arrest her, I . . ." Clara broke down under the weight of her own misery. She could not even try to control the sobbing that was robbing her of her breath. The tears continued to fall even when Henry pulled her against him. His strong hands caressed her back. Her head nestled beneath his chin.

"You cannot allow yourself to fall apart like this. We cannot give them confirmation of something they may only suspect."

"Please, Henry! I have to find her." She clutched at the lapel of his coat and looked up into his stern face again. "We cannot let them catch her. Please . . . !"

"We shan't let them take her away," the parson assured her solemnly. "I want you to get back and prepare for the ball as if everything is as it should be. Pretend nothing has happened."

"But I cannot. I must find her . . ."

"This is all nothing more than an opening gambit. Musgrave is beating the drums of rumor, and then waiting to see who runs. If he had proof that Jane is the rebel, he would have already had Captain Wallis and his dragoons turning Woodfield House inside out."

"But you do not know that for certain. Henry, I cannot chance that she might . . ."

"You must trust me, Clara." He took hold of her shoulders. The gray eyes bore into her. "I shall be there tonight . . . and I will try until then to find Jane. She must be present as well. Musgrave is a coward, and he must be faced down."

Twinges of doubt still raked at Clara's insides. "But what do we do if he decides to arrest her tonight?"

"Out of respect for your father, Sir Robert would not risk making a scene during the ball. But I give you my word, I shall come up with a way to thwart him if he is so foolish as to act. Nothing will happen to your sister, Clara. Nothing."

Henry's assurances worked to calm Clara's worries. But the growing awareness of the touch of his hands and the gaze on his face revived another deeper ache. It might have been entirely the fault of her hopeful imagination. Or the pressure of his fingers still on her arm. The closeness of their bodies. The feel of his warm breath so close. And then she saw his gaze fall on her lips.

She prayed to God that he would kiss her.

"Go," Henry whispered hoarsely. His hands dropped from her shoulders. "We must be at our best tonight."

Clara didn't give a rush about the appropriateness of any of it. She wrapped her arms around his neck and planted her lips firmly on his for an endless moment . . . before turning and walking away. He hadn't responded to the kiss, she thought, glancing back as she reached the edge of the village. He was still standing where she left him, staring off into the green fields.

But he hadn't pushed her away, either.

"She *is* here, Nicholas. Really she is." Frances nodded emphatically at him from her horse. "I saw Jane with my very own eyes. She came back with Mother not half an hour ago."

Nicholas dismounted, handed the reins of his steed to a groom, and started quickly toward the manor house.

"But you cannot go to her," the young woman warned, urging her mare up the path alongside the garden. "The guests will begin arriving in less than three hours. Mother and Jane are in the middle of some little scheme having to do with some of her paintings. And just before I came down from the house, I heard Fey ordering a bath brought up for Jane. And after that, she still needs to dress and do her hair and all the other things to get ready. And you have a lot to do to get ready yourself, as well, Nick!" Frances glanced from the tip of his muddy boots to the stained shirt and unshaven face. "You look absolutely hideous. By the way, your valet is already waiting in your room and . . ."

He started toward the archway. Frances reined her horse to a halt.

"And Mother told me to warn you not to scare her off again," she called after him.

He stopped at the door and turned to frown fiercely at her. "Do you mean to say that Jane was staying away because of me?"

Frances carefully weighed her words before speaking

again. "No. I do not know that exactly. But I did hear Jane tell Fey that if you asked to see her . . . well, to say that she was not available."

Without another word, Nicholas turned on his heel and yanked open the door.

Every member of the gentry within fifteen miles appeared to have ridden over for the ball. The noise of the throng, mixed with the harmonic rhythms of the music, drifted up the stairs and into her bedchamber.

The invited guests had arrived. The rest of the Purefoy family was already down playing their parts as hosts. But Jane continued to sit rigidly on the edge of her bed, dubious and fretful as she returned the gaze of the stranger reflected in her mirror.

She had thwarted the hairdressers' insistence on using plumes of feathers and whole gardens' worth of flowers in her hair. She'd then refused to wear the tall, powdered wig that Lady Spencer had brought in. As a compromise to everyone, though, she'd allowed them to gather and arrange her own dark hair, without powder, so that a few ringlets framed her pale face while the rest was piled up safely behind.

The hair she could live with, but the elegant dress that appeared was an ordeal that she hadn't been prepared for.

At the same time, she had not been able to fight wearing it. She could not bring herself to hurt Lady Spencer's feelings . . . not after everything she had already done for her. From the embroidery on the soft yellow and white silk to the fitted bodice with its lace and ruching, to the quilted petticoats with their lace and fringe hem, this was perhaps the most graceful and beautiful dress Jane had seen, never mind worn. But this high style hardly helped to ease the tension that coiled inside of her.

There were people down in the Hall and in the parlors whom she had loathed for all of her life. There were others whom she had hoped might once again respect her, but who had never been able to overlook her transgressions. And her family? As far as any of them knew, Jane wasn't attending the ball tonight.

And then there was Nicholas. Her hand unconsciously traveled to her exposed throat. As she sat and looked at the ample skin showing above her breasts, Jane realized what she feared most was his reaction.

There was a soft knock on the door and Jane rose immediately to her feet. She cast a final glance at the mirror. She only wished she could feel some of the reflected woman's apparent confidence. It was amazing what some clothes and powder could hide.

Alexandra's encouraging smile helped a little.

"Lovely," the older woman whispered confidentially. "It is late, my dear. I do not want you to miss a moment more of the admiration pouring forth in the Blue Parlor. Almost everyone has come through at least once already. And some of the guests have decided not to move an inch until I reveal the artist's name. It is most exciting."

*Until they find out it is me.* Jane didn't voice her concern and instead quietly accompanied Alexandra downstairs. Her ankle still hurt dreadfully whenever she put weight on it, so she tried to take her time. Without asking any questions about the nature of the injury, Lady Spencer had been very considerate earlier in the afternoon and she continued to be so now.

The stairs were agonizing, but as Jane descended—and as the curious gazes of a few guests who were mingling in the entrance hall fell on her—she found herself growing totally numb. When she and Alexandra finally reached the bottom, Jane was certain that no one had even recognized her, for the faces continued to be friendly, even admiring.

"The worst is over," Lady Spencer whispered softly, touching her on the elbow and nodding toward the parlor and where a small crowd of people were blocking the doorway, waiting to enter. "Shall we go in there and stir the pot a little?"

As the two women started past the front door, though, Jane cringed as a late-arriving guest entered and stepped into their path. Sir Robert Musgrave had no difficulty recognizing her.

"Miss Jane, I cannot believe my eyes."

The hush that fell over the bystanders was immediately followed by urgent whispers. She could almost feel the news rippling through the parlors and the Hall.

"Sir Robert." She nodded politely, trying to mask all traces of hostility in her voice and hide, as well, the unnerving sense that every eye was now on her.

"Miss Jane, I must say you look absolutely stunning." He stepped so near her that his presence encroached upon the very air she needed to breathe. He lifted her hand to his lips, but his smile was cold. "I truly approve of your choice of hairstyle . . . and this dress! You are a marvel, I must say. The style is elegant and the fit is fashionably provocative . . . within the bounds of propriety, of course." He lowered his voice. "So very much like yourself."

Jane tried to show nothing under his predatory gaze.

"I have to admit, though, I find myself speechless at seeing you attired in something other than that dreaded black."

"I find you are not *completely* speechless, sir," Jane replied matter-of-factly. "Now if you will forgive us, Lady Spencer and I need to speak with her daughter."

"But I cannot let you simply disappear, Miss Jane. Not until you promise me the pleasure of a dance."

"I fear, sir, that I cannot promise any such thing." She looked impatiently past him. "Please forgive us, but I believe I just saw Miss Spencer pass by the parlor door."

Stepping around him, Jane nodded politely to her companion, and the two made their way toward the parlor.

"You have wonderful poise," Alexandra whispered a moment later, as Jane sailed past the open stares of the guests with her head held high. "I am very proud to know you."

These last words almost pierced Jane's emotional armor, but she fought it off. The throng of people by the door to the parlor parted, and she followed Alexandra into the crowded but now silent room.

The canvases she and Lady Spencer had chosen earlier had been arranged on temporary wooden easels in various places around the room. Now, however, all gazes were fixed on her and not on the paintings that had drawn them into the parlor initially. Jane searched the expressions of the strangers and those she knew. She saw Henry standing beside Clara by the window. Her sister's gaze fell to the carpeted floor, but the minister sent Jane an encouraging nod. She couldn't worry about Clara's reaction to her arrival now. Frances beamed at her enthusiastically from across the parlor. Next to her, Jane found the one she'd been looking for all along. Her heart pounded, and her stomach danced at the sight of him.

"I cannot be more pleased with this warm reception . . ." Lady Spencer began, speaking in a clear voice to everyone in the room. Jane found she had some difficulty focusing on her friend's words, for only Nicholas existed now.

He was impeccably dressed, but Jane thought he looked tired. He held a glass of port in one hand while he casually leaned a shoulder against the mantel of the hearth. Even from this distance, Jane could see the way his eyes studied every inch of her body from the tip of her shoes to her hair. His attention was the warmth she'd lacked. She waited until his eyes finally met hers, but she started at the hurt she saw in them. Hurt she knew she herself had caused.

" . . . and so the treasure lies among you." Lady Spencer took Jane's hand. "Miss Purefoy . . . yes, indeed . . . Miss Jane Purefoy is the artist of these splendid works which we have all been viewing so appreciatively."

There was a very brief moment of silence, and then someone started clapping from somewhere to her left. That one person's applause quickly spread, and Jane watched with utter astonishment as every person in the room and around the door joined in. As she turned to look at Alexandra, a loud conversational buzz erupted around her.

Jane had no idea what to say or how to act. This positive reception of her work was totally unexpected. But what was even more astounding was the way the guests immediately approached her with congratulatory comments and questions about her style and her subject matter.

Trying to answer whatever she could to the best of her abilities, Jane searched for Alexandra at her side and found the older woman wearing a proud smile and standing away from her by a series of paintings she particularly liked. She glanced again in Nicholas's direction and found him raising his glass in a toast to her.

"And what is this all about?" Lady Purefoy's cheerfully complaining tone rang out from the hallway. "What kind of a ball is this where everyone deserts the dance floor and crowds into parlors? Is there card playing going on in here? Come now . . . ."

A few guests shifted around and others followed the hostess in.

"Oh yes," she said. "Lady Spencer's special arrangement. I'd almost forgotten. What have we here?"

Catherine waved the fan she was holding and peered about in surprise.

"Oh, my! Lady Spencer, are you in here?"

"I'm here."

The crowd around Jane parted and Catherine Purefoy became slightly paler when she saw her older daughter standing at the center of the crowd.

"Why, Jane! Whatever are you . . . ?" She quickly tried to recover her composure and looked at her houseguest. "Lady Spencer . . . I thought when you said you wanted to use this room . . . I never imagined that you meant . . ."

The hostess waved her hand vaguely at the paintings and failed miserably at hiding her confusion. She shook her head and tried to begin again.

"Ah, but Jane . . . dear . . . I did not know you had returned!" she finally managed to get out.

Jane took a step toward her mother to explain, but the magistrate's voice by the door raised the hair on her neck.

"Were you away, Miss Jane?"

There was no reason for this loud and public question, and she so wished to tell Musgrave exactly that, but her mother's answer cut off the opportunity.

"Indeed, Sir Robert. Jane has been away for three days." Catherine smiled in embarrassment at the group. "This was the reason for my surprise . . . my *delight* in seeing her. I had no idea she was planning to return in time for the ball. I mean, it is always a joy for a mother to see her children, but since I did not know where she'd gone, and I received no message about her time of return . . ."

A murmur of disapproval rolled through the room, though Jane had no clear idea whom it was aimed at. She reached for her mother's hand and looked beseechingly at Clara, hoping for her sister's assistance with taking control of this situation. But Clara's flushed face was turned toward Henry Adams, and she was whispering something into his ear.

"And I notice that you have sustained an injury, Miss Jane." Musgrave was cutting through people and coming closer. "Tell us, is it your knee or your ankle?"

"You were not unwell when you left, Jane," Lady Purefoy asserted pointedly.

"And you are such a fine rider that I doubt you would have fallen from your horse. Now, you wouldn't have sustained such an injury jumping from the roof of a building, would you?"

He was now standing before her. His gray eyes watched her every move.

"I have been long accustomed to taking the stairs, sir," she put in acidly, hoping to cut short this very public inquiry.

"And the cause and nature of the injury?"

"That is none of your concern, sir," she answered curtly. "I should think someone with your responsibilities would hardly have the time to concern himself in such an ongoing fashion with my foolish mishaps."

The magistrate opened his mouth to respond, but Jane saw his eyes narrow and focus on someone behind her.

"If you will forgive us, Sir Robert, Lady Purefoy mentioned that this is, after all, a ball. And I have been waiting too long already for this dance that Miss Jane promised me earlier."

The heat that rushed through her when she heard Nicholas's voice buoyed her immediately. Her cheeks burned and her eyes misted over with affection when she turned and met his intense blue gaze. The tongues were wagging again, but Jane didn't care as she slipped her hand through his proffered arm.

"Are you ready?" he whispered softly as they started toward the door.

"More than you know. More than I ever was." He cupped her hand on his arm, and she moved closer. He was trying to give her support for her ankle, but she wanted to melt against him, kiss him, explain to him everything that had happened, and tell him what a lost soul she was without him.

Jane was surprised to see her father standing just inside the doorway as they approached. She immediately bristled, expecting to see his disapproval. But his look was reflective, mysterious.

"If you have just a few moments, Miss Jane, there are a few questions that I still need to ask."

From the steely frown on Nicholas's face, she could tell that Musgrave's persistence angered him as much as it did her. He pressed her hand reassuringly, though, and turned without letting her go.

"Really, Musgrave. Can this not wait?" Nicholas asked impatiently.

"I am afraid not, Sir Nicholas. My duty as magistrate, acting on behalf of the Cr—"

"Are you here as a guest or as a government official?" Nicholas's sharp tone and question silenced the crowd and a path opened between the two men.

"I fear my duty must always supercede—"

"That is too bad for you, sir. However, the rest of us are not afflicted with the same burden. Would you mind allowing us to enjoy our host's amusements and hospitality?"

"I would if I could, sir." The magistrate stepped toward them. "I assure you that there is no need for a private conversation . . . unless you need the opportunity to think of an excuse for this good lady's injury."

The baronet's words were cold and measured. "This is not the time, sir. But I assure you, you and I will have a private discussion in the *very* near future."

"What was it the last time?" Musgrave asked, ignoring Nicholas's threat. "You struck her face with the stable door, was it not?" He laughed without mirth. "Perhaps this time we should just say you pushed her from her horse, thereby causing the pronounced limp she suffers from tonight."

"Sir Robert," Lady Purefoy gasped. "What are you saying?"

Nicholas's hands dropped to his side, his tone icy. "Be clear, sir. Are you accusing me?"

"No, of course not!" He laughed again, though no one else seemed amused by the confrontation. "Surrounded by all this magnificent art, I am simply trying to be creative."

Jane could not take any more of this. She understood the threat in Musgrave's words, and she had no wish for Nicholas to fall victim to it. She pressed a hand on his arm and faced her foe.

"I believe this unpleasantness is entirely unnecessary." She looked around at the room full of people. "If you have *official* questions to ask me, sir, why not proceed in private. Surely there is no reason to deprive my parents' guests of their evening of enjoyment."

"But is this not as much entertainment as any promenade or dinner or bottle of port, for that matter?"

"For you, perhaps," she replied. "But not for anyone else."

"Have you been drinking heavily, Sir Robert?" Lady Purefoy asked hopefully.

"No, madam." He turned his back on the hostess. "And I happen to disagree, Miss Jane. How often will these good people have an opportunity to witness the King's magistrate acting to solve a crime?"

"Very well, sir," she responded coldly. "Ask your questions and be done with it."

"As you wish." He bowed with a mocking flourish. "Would you enlighten us as to where you have been for the past three days?"

"I was visiting a friend."

"Did you take a carriage or ride your fine horse?"

"As is my custom, I rode my horse."

"And does this friend live anywhere near the village of Banteer?"

She paused, considering her answer. "I believe it would be safe to say my friend lives in that general direction."

"What did you do while you were staying there?"

She shrugged. "Nothing unusual. We visited."

"And what were you doing last night?"

"This is becoming quite tedious, Sir Robert."

"Did you go to Banteer last night?" He walked toward her.

"I cannot think of any reason why I would be in Banteer, sir . . ."

"But you were seen there, last night, Miss Jane."

"Was I?" She met the man's accusatory gaze at the same time that she felt the brush of Nicholas's arm against her own. His strength flowed into her, and she found comfort in his presence beside her. "I am certain whoever *imagined* seeing me must be mistaken."

"Do you have anyone who could confirm your claim?"

She hesitated, unwilling to use Jenny's name. As far as the magistrate was concerned, there could be no connection between the two women. Even if Jane were to escape this time, Conor's aunt would know no peace for as long as the magistrate held power.

"Yes."

Henry Adams's voice drew everyone's attention to him. A murmur again rippled though the crowd.

"I was with Miss Jane last evening."

Jane felt Nicholas stiffen beside her.

"Parson," Musgrave started, surprise evident in his voice. "Are you saying you visited Miss Jane at her unnamed friend's house last evening?"

"No." The minister moved to Jane's side, and she felt suddenly dwarfed between Nicholas and Henry. "No. What I am saying is that Miss Jane has been a guest at the parsonage in Ballyclough for the past three days. This unnamed friend she speaks of is I, Henry Adams."

# Chapter 26

"I do not know what all this secrecy is about. But I know she wasn't there, Nicholas. I went after her," Lady Spencer whispered anxiously. "I know she wasn't staying with Parson Adams."

Nicholas had managed to stand by Jane as notes of scandal mingled with those of Purcell and Handel. He'd stayed beside her as Adams had responded to Musgrave's question about the whereabouts of Jane's horse last night, and listened with appreciation as the parson had verbally attacked the magistrate about the lack of order in the district . . . evidenced by the fact that horses routinely disappear from stables at night, with only some of them reappearing a few days later. If the horse that was seen was indeed Jane's—though it was doubtful, he asserted—this was obviously what had occurred.

Musgrave had clearly been thrown off stride by the parson's shocking claim, and his complaint—seconded by several landowners looking on—further disoriented the man.

Nicholas continued to stand with Jane and Adams until the magistrate had said something about the ineptness of the dragoons assigned to him and grudgingly mumbled an apology for creating such an inopportune disturbance. Once Musgrave had withdrawn, Nicholas had also taken his leave.

He could not remain beside her and pretend he was unaffected by the parson's announcement. He knew that Jane was not at Ballyclough. He himself had gone there looking for her. What bothered him greatly, though, was that Adams seemed to know more than he did.

Nicholas had left the house and was standing in the field beneath the paddock wall, staring out into the blackness covering the valley, when his mother had caught up to him. Behind him, the stables were bustling with activity as carriages continued to be sent up for guests who'd had their fill of food, drink, dancing . . . with a bit of scandal thrown in.

"Well, this is a party no one will soon forget," she said. "Everyone is gobbling down the supper our hostess prepared and is heading for the hills. And to think that in London one would have no chance of *pushing* anyone out the door. The wolves would be waiting around, hoping for a bloody finish!"

"There may be blood, yet."

"I shouldn't think so," she replied. "Parson Adams and Sir Thomas have locked themselves away in our host's study. But I am quite uneasy about any solution that those two might come up with."

Nicholas said nothing, and Alexandra waited a moment or two before pressing him.

"Jane needs you, Nick. She is trying to be as brave as she can, but I know she will fall apart if you do not go back to her soon."

"Henry Adams has been doing an excellent job helping her. I would hate to interfere."

"You cannot mean what you are saying." She touched him on the arm. "Nothing that Musgrave said to her, no look of severity from anyone in attendance, upset her as much as when you walked out of that room. It is as plain as those stars in this sky. She needs *you*, Nicholas. You."

"And tell me. Did she say that? Did she send you after me?"

"Jane would have if she thought it at all possible. But how could she?" Alexandra stepped in front of him. "Every movement she makes, every word she says, is being carefully scrutinized by a dozen people at any given moment. Those who have not left yet are watching her closely, waiting for something noteworthy to carry to the club, or the card party, or whatever it is they do out here to socialize. She is bearing it well, for the moment, but I do not know for how long."

Surely, it would be easier just to ride away and forget he'd ever met this woman, he thought. But he couldn't. The old Nicholas could have done just that and never looked back. But the new Nicholas Spencer—the one already far too consumed with Miss Jane Purefoy— could not.

"Where is she now?"

"In the library. The musicians have packed their instruments and trotted off for their supper in the servants' hall. I should think the house will be empty in another hour. Lady Purefoy is still bustling about, of course, trying to put a good face on everything and looking foolish for her efforts. But the girls and Jane are waiting in the library for Sir Thomas and the parson to end their discussion."

Clara was consumed by the darkness outside the window. Frances was pretending that she was deeply involved in a book she had open on her lap, though she hadn't turned the page for quite some time. Lady Purefoy barked more orders at the servants and returned to sit heavily on the sofa. Her agitated fingers opened and closed the delicate fan she was holding.

Jane immediately stood up when she saw Nicholas enter with Lady Spencer. Without any regard for her mother's disapproving glare, she had managed to get halfway to him when Henry Adams and Sir Thomas appeared in the doorway.

Everyone stared at the two men.

Henry's expression was guarded as he cast a brief glance at Jane before focusing his gaze on Clara. Sir Thomas headed directly to a side cabinet holding a bottle of port and glasses. He poured himself a full glass and gestured an offer to the other men. Both declined. He downed the wine and poured himself another before turning to Jane and addressing the group.

"The Reverend Henry Adams has asked for Jane's hand in marriage."

The very breath was caught in Jane's chest at the announcement. She turned in confusion toward Nicholas, still standing by the door, and saw the flash of anger, hurt, betrayal even as he returned her gaze. Tears pooled in Jane's eyes, and she shook her head helplessly. Henry was still staring at Clara. The younger sister's face had fully turned toward the window.

"What *wonderful* news!" Lady Purefoy piped up, breaking the heavy silence. "Reverend Adams and Jane . . . who would have thought it? But considering what was said tonight . . . and Parson Adams's excellent reputation . . . it makes perfect sense." The fan opened with a snap of her fingers, and she waved it before her face. "Actually, it will be seen as a most loyal and generous act. Absolutely the thing to do . . . saving our Jane from her shocking past."

"From the warm reception your daughter received tonight—before the good parson *saved* her—I would have hoped that you'd realize that Jane is a prize in her own right."

Alexandra's sharp retort in her defense made the tears fall for the first time onto Jane's cheeks. Nicholas was glaring at Henry fiercely enough to cut him to pieces.

"Oh, we knew all along Jane had some talent." Catherine waved her fan dismissively in the air. "But a good brushstroke does not arrange a good marriage or hide the scandal of one's past."

"Naturally, we disagree there, too, Lady Purefoy," Alexandra persisted. "It is generally the support of one's family toward its members—or the lack of it—that sets the limits to how others in their set behave openly in most situations."

"Not that this concerns you, given your son's lack of interest in Clara, but *I* did not push Jane into the arms of any papist cur. She did the damage. She can bear its consequences."

"None of us, I am sure, is completely without some youthful indiscretion in our personal history," Lady Spencer said mockingly. "And I wonder what would have happened to *us* if we all were blessed with such righteous and unforgiving parents as she."

"There is no point in this." Catherine closed her fan with a snap. "The announcements will be sent to the papers tomorrow. We shall set a date for no later than a month, though if we could arrange it sooner, so much the better. If you have no objections, Parson, we shall simply send notices of the wedding to our family from England and your older brother and . . ."

"What do *you* think of this, Jane?"

Sir Thomas's gruff question was so abrupt and out of character for him that Catherine continued to speak a few more words before realizing her husband had asked the question. Jane was fairly astonished, too. She could not remember the last time her father had directly addressed her.

"I . . . I believe we all are jumping at shadows." Jane quickly found her voice. She turned to Henry first. "I am honored and touched by your offer. But I am greatly distressed, as you and I both know there has never been anything that might be construed as improper between us. *Ever*. You spoke before the magistrate tonight to protect me from certain accusations. However, there is no reason for us to act rashly . . . and thereby encourage any wrongheaded notions by those who were here tonight."

Jane turned to her mother. "Henry and I have spent many days together since childhood. In the recent years—and since his installation at the parsonage—I have spent many nights, as well, at Ballyclough as a guest of his and Mrs. Brown's. As we speak, these good people are assisting a widowed friend and her children. There are justifiable reasons for me to be staying at the parsonage. If you were to take the time and explain the situation that way, there should be no reason for Henry's reputation to be tainted or linked in any way with mine."

"But Jane, that is an excellent offer! No matter *how* everything might be explained."

"An excellent offer for *whom*?" Jane lashed out at her mother. "Shall we punish Henry for being noble and wanting to do the honorable thing for me? Shall I marry him against my will and, in so doing, rob him of any chance of future happiness with a woman who could be deserving of him? I believe the only one who will benefit from this *excellent* offer of marriage is *you*, Mother . . . for you shall finally be rid of me."

"Sir Thomas." Catherine turned pleading eyes on her husband. "Tell her she must marry."

The ex-magistrate did not say a word, but his dark gaze locked on his daughter's face. Jane was surprised to find herself capable of looking into the man's eyes without the hostility of a lifetime clouding her vision. She found him different from the man she knew him to be. Something unexplainable had penetrated the layers of harshness and arrogance. She answered his unspoken question.

"I should like to wait and let the rumors fade." Jane turned to Henry and smiled gratefully at him. "You understand."

He nodded.

Before anyone could move or say anything more, Alexandra spoke out. "Perhaps distance, as well as time, can be of assistance in this situation."

She paused and then turned her attention to Catherine. "What would you say, Lady Purefoy, if I were to take your two daughters with me to England on a holiday for a few weeks or so. Perhaps, during their absence, explanations can be circulated and rumor will die a natural death. More importantly, however, they will get a chance to become better acquainted with my family."

"Oh . . . !" The suggestion clearly startled the hostess. "Do you mean Sir Nicholas would be accompanying you back to England, as well?"

Alexandra received a nod from her son. "Of course. Nicholas and Frances will both come back with us. And I shall even arrange that we all escort them back to Ireland in a month or so."

The suggestion brought immediate life to Lady Purefoy's demeanor. Jane and everyone else could plainly see that the woman's delight centered on the prospect of Clara and Nicholas spending time together. But Jane was too drained to worry about any of this now. She had avoided one disaster with Henry; now she had a short holiday left to convince Nicholas that—even though she loved him—he had to accept that there could never be a chance of a future between them.

"Sir Thomas," Catherine called jubilantly to her husband. "What do you think of Lady Spencer's brilliant idea?"

The ex-magistrate gave a curt nod. "I agree. Jane needs to be away from this blasted Ireland."

# Chapter 27

Seated in the spacious library of his Berkeley Square townhouse, the Earl of Stanmore watched with a great deal of interest and curiosity as his best friend paced back and forth across the room. He had never seen Nicholas as enraged as this.

Very interesting, indeed, he thought, hiding a smile.

Stanmore had already pieced together that his friend had sailed from Cork City on Sunday, arrived in Broad Quay in Bristol the same night, and had ridden all day yesterday to arrive in London late last night. And already this morning, Nicholas had tracked down the Lord Lieutenant of Ireland, who happened to be in London en route to a shooting party in Yorkshire.

Stanmore glanced at his pocket watch. It was barely ten o'clock in the morning, and Nicholas seemed to have the rest of the day filled with meetings with Crown officials and who knew what else! By the devil, he'd never known Nicholas to rise before noon, unless it was for some sporting reason.

"Stanmore, you know I have never been in the habit of asking favors of my friends. But this time I am making an exception." Nicholas came to an abrupt stop before the earl's desk. "Meet with him at noon. Stress everything I have told you. It is essential that something be done about Musgrave before he does some irrevocable damage."

"But you have already told me that the man was very sympathetic to your concerns and promised to look into it."

"Perhaps he will, but I cannot afford the matter to be put off. It is crucial for him to act immediately. In hearing it from you, one of the distinguished members of the House of Lords, in addition to hearing it from the Surveyor of the Navy . . ."

"Blast, Nicholas! Have you already been to Nathaniel Yorke's house, as well, this morning?"

"Of course not! I went there last night." He planted his hands on the earl's desk. "This is very important to me, Stanmore. More so than you can ever imagine!"

The chiseled features of the earl reflected his genuine interest as he leaned back in the chair.

"Who is she?"

Clara had not weathered the rough journey from Ireland very well, and as a result of staying beside her sister, Jane had seen very little of Nicholas during their trip. Even those few glimpses, however, had been better than his disappearance soon after their ship tied up in Bristol. Nonetheless, she could not bring herself to ask his mother or sister about his whereabouts or his expected return.

Curiously, after spending the night in an inn at quayside in the port town, Lady Spencer had developed a keen interest in visiting an "ancient" friend in Bath. As they breakfasted, she'd mentioned that a visit to the nearby resort city would also have its advantages for Clara, who could spend a couple of days recovering there before they hired a carriage for London.

And then, for some inexplicable reason or other, Frances was extremely impatient to get back to London. So after a short discussion, it was agreed that Jane would accompany the younger woman to London and Lady Spencer would follow in a few days with Clara.

During the trip, which had been broken up into comfortable stages over two days, Frances had spoken ceaselessly, telling Jane everything about the school she had been attending in Brussels to her excitement over settling into a girls school in England. She'd also made certain to drop Nicholas's name in at least every other sentence, singing his praises in a way that Jane knew only a sister trying her hand at matchmaking for her brother could do. Jane had been touched by the attempt, knowing all the while that there was not a thing she could say or do to make Frances understand how unlikely such a union could be.

That would be a conversation for Jane and Nicholas alone, and until then, she would keep her sorrows to herself.

In the afternoon of the second day, Frances stirred from the nap she'd been taking as the escalating city noises announced the arrival of her coach in London. She gave Jane a sleepy-eyed smile and stretched. Once again, Jane was overwhelmed by the young woman's beauty and innocence . . . and her strong resemblance to Nicholas. She had been trying so hard not to dwell on the talk that the two of them *had* to have. There had not been an opportunity to explain anything to him since the day she'd fled Woodfield House in the early hours of morning. Their last moments alone together had been spent making love on the small cot in her work area.

Not a bad memory, Jane thought, quickly blinking back tears and lifting the shade to look out onto the busy streets.

"I cannot believe what good time we made," Frances said excitedly, moving to the seat facing Jane and looking out, as well. "Perhaps after dinner, if you don't mind, I can invite my friend Elizabeth to come over for a little while. Her family has a house on Leicester Square— quite near Nicholas's—and although she is younger than I by a year, we really enjoy each other's company. She is quite lovely."

"No, I don't mind at all."

Frances placed her hand on top of Janc's. "And thank you for staying with me . . . with us. I remember, from Clara's last visit to London, that you have some family here. But I am so glad that you have decided to stay with us instead."

Jane smiled warmly. "I would have never left Ireland if I had to spend my time here with my parents' family. I am afraid my father's sisters have never recovered from the scandal of my youth. And on my mother's side . . . well, perhaps we should just not mention them."

"When was the last time you were here?"

Jane thought back. "Three years ago. I was here when one of my aunts, the youngest sister to my mother, was marrying. We arrived a week before the wedding, and I left for Ireland two days later."

"They asked you to leave before the wedding?"

Jane smiled gently at Frances's shocked expression. "It was a mutual decision. I was not going to wear anything but black to the ceremony, and this did not agree with the flower bouquet the bride was carrying."

Frances blinked once and then burst into laughter. Jane couldn't stop herself from joining her.

"I must say, Jane, you have become my ideal," the young woman said a moment later, her beaming smile lighting up the carriage. "I so admire your courage . . . your intelligence . . . your independence . . . your forthrightness. I strive to become like you someday."

"Oh, Fanny." Jane grasped the younger woman's hand tightly in her own. "Contrary to what you think . . . I am someone to avoid. Nothing good will come out of becoming as ill tempered as I have become."

"I beg to disagree with that." She leaned forward and smiled meaningfully. "You have not only managed to capture Nicholas's interest, you have redirected his life entirely. I should say—remembering the impossible bachelor rogue that he was before—you have accomplished a most astonishing feat."

"There are much easier ways of capturing a man's interest than the route I have taken."

"But I doubt there are many that are more exciting."

Before Jane could argue further, Frances pointed to an approaching street. "And here we are! That is Elizabeth's house. And right there . . . on that side of the square . . . is Nicholas's."

Jane looked out the window at the line of fashionable houses surrounding a large fenced area of greensward and walks with a garden and statue in the center.

"The gilded statue of the man on the horse—" Frances pointed again. "That is the first King George."

Jane's attention was still on the house. She did not know if Nicholas was in London or elsewhere.

The carriage rounded the square and came to a stop in front of the house. Instantly, footmen and servants were lining up before the steps as Jane followed Frances out onto the street. They had obviously been expected, for more servants rushed out to carry up the baggage.

It was the smell of London that struck a chord in her memory. So different from the clear farm air and the smell of peat, here the crisp autumn air carried with it the not unpleasant scent of coal fires.

Inside, she was introduced to the house steward, a rather formidable-looking rough named Charles, who appeared to be blind in his left eye from some horrible injuries he'd sustained on that side of his face. The housekeeper, Mrs. Hannagan, was a surprise to Jane, for the woman was from Dublin and as cheerful as she was apparently efficient. Their reception was warm, and, to her delight, the housekeeper answered the question that had been burning on Jane's tongue since yesterday.

"Sir Nicholas has been out all day, miss. But he did send a message around noon that if you were to arrive early enough, that you should rest and be ready for a late dinner at the home of the Earl of Stanmore's house tonight. Lady Stanmore insisted, miss."

Jane remembered Nicholas mentioning the name and referring to them as his best friends.

"Oh, they are in London?" Frances asked in obvious delight.

"Only for a few more days, Miss Fanny. They'll soon be leaving for Solgrave—that is their estate in Hertfordshire, Miss Purefoy—but Lady Stanmore has insisted on meeting Miss Purefoy and visiting with you both."

As they were ushered upstairs to their rooms, Jane spoke up. "I think it would be best if I were to stay behind. I am a stranger and . . ."

"Do not even think it!" Frances gave her a bright smile. "Knowing my brother's friends, the main purpose of this dinner tonight is to meet *you*." She shook her head before Jane could speak. "You heard what Mrs. Hannagan said. They want to meet *Miss Purefoy*."

"But that is surely Clara and not I."

"They met Clara last spring." Frances patted Jane's hand. "Accept it! You will have to spend another evening under the lens. But this time I believe you will not mind it."

"And why is that?" Jane asked suspiciously as Mrs. Hannagan directed a serving maid to open the door to a spacious and beautifully appointed bedchamber.

"Because Stanmore is dashingly handsome. Because Rebecca is about your age and is as untraditional as any countess in England. And because they are the happiest married couple I have ever encountered in my life. Is that not so, Mrs. Hannagan?"

The housekeeper smiled in agreement.

"Trust me, you shall love them." Frances nodded with all the conviction of a true woman of the world. "And *they* shall love you."

No stone had been left unturned. Of that he was certain.

As a result, Nicholas was late in arriving at his friends' Berkeley Square town house for dinner. Philip, Stanmore's ancient steward, greeted him with uncharacteristic warmth, however, just inside the front door.

"And how was your day today, Sir Nicholas?"

Nicholas studied him with suspicion as he handed his hat and gloves to a doorman. In light of the rigidly unresponsive manner with which the steward customarily addressed anyone, the simple query constituted a fortnight's allowance of pleasantries. Perhaps a month's worth.

"Very well, thank you. And how was yours, Philip?"

"Despite it being a little cold for September, I was able to accompany Lady Stanmore and the young masters to St. James's Park this afternoon. Master James is starting his session at Eton this fall a month late, you see, on account of the excitement of having a new brother. Of course, Daniel . . . you remember my brother Daniel, sir? The steward at Solgrave? Of course, sir. Well, Daniel has already arranged for the lad's tutor, Mr. Clarke, to meet with us at Solgrave. As was the case last year, we already know that Master James will be far ahead of the other pupils when he arrives at school next month."

Very well, Nicholas thought. That constituted roughly a year's measure of chitchat for Philip. He bit back his smile at the change in the steward. Rebecca's positive

influence during the past year on Stanmore and on everyone else around them had been the most amazing
thing to observe. But this drastic change in Philip since
Nicholas's last visit was inexplicable. He was a hard old
nut, but something had managed to soften his shell.

"And where is everyone, Philip?"

"His lordship and your sister and Master James are
in the East Room, sir. Her ladyship and Miss Purefoy,
however, went upstairs to put Master Samuel to bed, as
he was becoming quite . . . assertive, sir."

Nicholas paused by the upward sweep of stairs in the
hope of catching a glimpse of Jane. All of the arrangements he'd made with his mother to send Jane and Frances ahead while she took Clara to Bath had worked out
perfectly. Now he had to capitalize on his efforts.

He was certain that Jane's change of heart and disappearance from Woodfield House had been the result of
some discussion with Clara. Whatever words had been
exchanged between the sisters had once again planted
in Jane's mind the idea that Nicholas was destined to be
married to the younger sister.

The ship out of Cork City had not even passed Knock-
adoon Head before he realized his only opportunity lay
in separating the two. That way he would at least have
a chance to talk some sense into Jane.

"May I be bold enough to congratulate you, sir?"

Nicholas turned in surprise and found Philip standing
beside him. There was no reason for denial. The man's
meaning was very clear.

"She hasn't agreed to marry me yet."

"Fear not, sir. I believe you are second only to his
lordship himself in persuasiveness. If he was happy
enough to succeed, then I shall place my wager on you."

Nicholas smiled and fell in with the steward as he
started toward the East Room. "I know it has taken me
a long time to admit this, Philip, but I am actually starting to like you."

"Your secret is safe with me, sir."

Everything Fanny had said about this family was true.
In spite of the fact that Jane was quite prepared to

dislike the Earl of Stanmore, a well-regarded member
of the House of Lords, after only a few hours in his
company she could not stop herself from liking and re-
specting him. Quiet and direct in speech, Stanmore was
a dashingly handsome man as well as quite obviously
intelligent and surprisingly broad-minded.

And the countess was a rare gem. Unpretentious in a
manner unlike any of the aristocracy Jane knew, Lady
Stanmore had a beauty that radiated from within.
Rebecca, as she insisted on being called, had welcomed
her as if the two of them had been lifelong friends. By
the end of the evening, Jane had fallen under her charm
so much that she found herself wishing that a long-term
friendship between them could be possible.

Why, even these couple's children were exceptional.
Their older boy, James, who had turned eleven this past
summer, appeared slightly hard of hearing in one ear
and only had two fingers in his deformed right hand. But
neither of the problems affected either the lad's spirit or
his attachment to his infant brother.

The young Samuel Fredrick Wakefield, only two
months old, demonstrated his strong personality at regular intervals. Holding the round-faced baby had made
Jane's heart swell with unexpected emotion. And later
on, when she'd watched Rebecca nurse the child herself
and put him in his crib, Jane had found a startling maternal yearning clutching at her breast.

The only thing that had exceeded those feelings had
been the fluttering heat that had erupted within her
upon coming downstairs and finding Nicholas standing
in the East Room. His eyes smiled warmly when he saw
her enter.

Other than some cordial and public pleasantries, not
much more had been said between them. But he rarely
ever took his eyes off her for the remainder of the
evening.

As the farewells were said and they prepared to leave,
Rebecca pulled Jane aside for a private word.

"Jane, I have already done my best to impress it on
Nicholas, but now I am petitioning you. Do please come
and stay a few days with us at Solgrave. Our short visit

tonight has only managed to whet my appetite for getting to know you better, and I am so eager to have a longer visit with you."

Jane was pleased with the invitation and said so. "My sister and Lady Spencer should be arriving in London tomorrow or the next day, I should think. I should tell you I am very much under their direction for the length of our short stay in England."

"Very well." Rebecca smiled and looped her arm through Jane's. Together, they walked toward the open front door. "Then I shall send a letter to Lady Spencer about it and make sure you all come to Solgrave."

"I, for one, would be delighted." She returned the warm smile of the countess and said goodbye to Stanmore before following Frances out into the pleasantly cool night. A carriage and a groom were waiting for them on the street, as well as several of the Stanmores' footmen.

"I had the best of times." Frances's happy smile turned into a yawn that she hardly tried to hide. "But I believe I should spend most of the day tomorrow in bed."

She was handed into the carriage first, but just as Jane started to climb in after her, Nicholas's firm grip on her elbow held her back. "You go on to the house, Fanny. Jane and I will walk the few blocks home."

Jane's stomach leaped pleasantly and her heart began pounding hard in her chest, but she was not so blinded not to notice the glint of Fanny's mischievous smile as the young woman sank back into the carriage seat. "I hope you won't think me impolite, Jane, but I am not waiting up."

After the carriage had pulled away, Nicholas's hand tightened on her arm. "I hope you have no fear of walking with me."

She shook her head, but couldn't bring herself to look into his face. His touch, his voice, the promise of the two of them alone together again set the tingling feelings racing along her skin. He dropped his hand, but they fell in step as they strolled down the street.

"How careless of me not to ask! How is your ankle?"

"Perfectly well, thank you." She looked about contentedly. "They are a lovely family."

"It is hard to believe that they have already been married over a year." He cast a parting glance back toward the house. "Time passes by so quickly."

"Lady Stanmore told me how she and James had been living in the American colonies for nearly ten years before coming back to England and meeting the earl."

"She does not share the story of her life with many people. She obviously likes you."

"The feeling is mutual. I believe I am quite fortunate to have had the opportunity of meeting them. Thank you."

"Well, after the relentless questioning that Stanmore subjected me to this morning—during which time he forced me to talk about nothing but the mysterious and beautiful Miss Jane whom I was so absorbed in—there was no getting away with it."

Surprised, she glanced up at him, only to be staggered by the look of tenderness in his blue gaze.

"I have missed you, Jane."

The force of the simply spoken words caused her heart to lodge immediately in her throat. She couldn't say the words, but her hand moved on its own accord and slipped through his arm. The streets on the next block were darker, with only a single lamp hanging from a house near either end. He tightened her hold against his side.

"Though I knew the horrible chaos of war in my army years and even sought out the pleasures of confusion later in my unpredictable, unprincipled rogue's life, I had never truly understood the painful joy of turmoil until I fell in love with you." They halted in the darkness. "No one could have described it to me. No matter what my past experiences were with women, I was unprepared for the ups and downs of what we have gone through."

"I am sorry, Nicholas," she whispered guiltily. "I know I've done a great deal that needs explaining, but nothing about me has ever been simple. I should have done a better job of protecting you . . ."

"No." Nicholas's hand pressed hers on his arm. "Perhaps it sounds foolish, but I am trying to become a better

man—a more worthy human being—because of you. And
finally I find I am able to feel . . . to love . . . to plan . . .
to want a future for us. And all because of you. I have no
regret for any of this. My only problem is I am impatient
to begin having you beside me for the rest of my life."

She turned her head away abruptly to hide sudden
tears. A carriage rolled by them on the street, the driver
eying them suspiciously as he passed. They continued
along the sidewalk in measured steps, but Jane was too
numb to feel the ground.

"I had promised myself that I would not rush you again.
And here we are, our first moments alone together in days,
and I am doing just that." He pulled her closer to his side
until their arms and hips brushed and their bodies moved
in unison. They turned onto Leicester Square. "I shall try
to be better. Can you forgive me?"

She laughed through the tears and brushed away the
wetness with her free hand. "Yes, I think so."

"Then it is settled," he said more cheerfully. "Being
the paragon of courtesy that I am and knowing that you
must be quite tired from the day of traveling, I shall
allow you to get a good night's sleep tonight."

"That is *very* generous of you, sir."

"But tomorrow is a different matter," he warned.

"And how is that?"

His voice dropped, his tone low and confidential. "Because tomorrow I need you to arise early. I plan to take
you around London and show you some of the unsavory
elements of Sir Nicholas Spencer's life."

"Are you telling me you are not *perfect*?"

"Far from it, my love." He walked her up the stairs
to the front door of his town house. After a rather
weary-looking doorman opened the door and greeted
them, Nicholas walked her as far as the bottom of the
stairs. "Now you go up and latch your door before another unsavory part of me comes out."

Jane smiled, but before she could turn away he brushed
his lips across hers. It was a chaste kiss. Curiously enough,
it was entirely different from everything they had previously shared. But it was also a reminder of the passion
that flared between them whenever they touched, and of
the love that lurked just beyond the mist.

# Chapter 28

Jane stood over the trunk, staring at the layers of clothing separated by delicate papers. How Fey had managed it, Jane wasn't quite sure, but there was not a single black dress in the thing.

She smiled. How could she be angry? Fey had just known intuitively that Jane's few days in London should be unrelated to anything in her past. This was a time for color and silk and lace.

Frances had not yet stirred when Jane came down around seven, but to her delight Nicholas was already up and ready to start the day. His weariness had disappeared, and he looked refreshed and buoyant.

"I am very happy that you awakened so early. I have much to show you."

"How about your sister?"

"I would suppose she shall be sleeping for most of the morning. After that, she will want to visit some of the slew of friends that Charles tells me have been beating a daily path to my door since we left for Ireland."

She couldn't think of any reason to object, considering she was so looking forward to spending this day in his company.

Once they had breakfasted, her host escorted her to his waiting phaeton and helped her in.

"For two night owls like us," he remarked with a smile as he took up his whip, "to set out so early in the day is rather an accomplishment."

"Where are you taking me this morning?"

"You ask too many questions. Patience, my love." He

touched her affectionately on the knee. "You shall find out soon enough."

With a groom mounted behind them, Jane found herself rolling through narrow side streets. Skirting Covent Garden, they were very soon cutting into the heavy traffic of the Strand and heading for the Temple Bar and the City of London. Carriages and carts vied for space and pedestrians risked their lives on the crowded thoroughfare, and very shortly Nicholas turned off onto a lane so narrow she wondered how he even saw it. It was soon obvious that he knew it well, as he drove on with confidence through a rabbit warren of twisting alleys and lanes.

As her host maneuvered around carts and an overturned sedan chair that had been stripped of its essentials, Jane realized that this was not the fashionable London that she remembered. The neighborhoods quickly grew poorer. The light and air here became dark and heavy with dampness and the smells of poverty. Many of the houses—mere skeletons lacking windows and doors—seemed to lean upon one another for support. Some had simply collapsed into themselves from neglect.

And everywhere she looked, it seemed, Jane saw people who equaled the houses in obvious need.

"You are still not telling me where we are going!"

"You shall see in just a few moments."

True to his word, at the shadowy twist in the alley, they came upon a squalid river or canal. Jane was unsure what it was, for it was filled with slow-moving liquid of some unnatural color, and Nicholas reined in his team. The waterway, lined with dilapidated houses that hung out over it at rakish angles, contained the moss-covered remains of indeterminate objects and reeked of sewage. A rickety bridge led across, and dozens of the neighborhood's inhabitants stopped to look with surprise at the carriage . . . until they recognized the driver.

Cries of "Halloo, Sir Nicholas!" or "If it ain't our own Sir Nicholas!" or "Oy, Nick, we've not seen ye much o' late," rang out, and he waved back as he carefully urged his team across the bridge.

"These people know you," she whispered with amazement. More people waved at them as he arrived on the other end.

"I have a bad habit of getting around." He brought the phaeton to a stop beside a deserted warehouse of crumbling brick, and climbed down. Ragged folk passed going in either direction, but only the legions of street urchins stopped to cast more than a curious glance at them. Along the buildings lining the thoroughfare, men and women stood or crouched in the idleness that poverty breeds.

Even as he turned to smile encouragingly at her, it occurred to Jane that she didn't know of anyone in his class who would dare to set foot in neighborhoods like this, but Nicholas showed no hint of either fear or disgust. When he reached for Jane and motioned for her to climb down, she didn't hesitate.

"Despite its rather unpleasant appearance," he said, seeming to read her thoughts, "so long as you are in my company, you can walk in this quarter in complete safety."

"I am not worried." She gave him a confident smile.

"I know . . . I know. Nothing is too threatening for the celebrated Egan. Nonetheless, hold on tightly to your handkerchief and purse." He grinned, clutching her hand in his all the same as he turned her down the narrow lane. "Now I can get to the purpose of why I brought you here."

They may as well have been strolling in St. James's Park. He seemed as much part of this world as that one.

"You probably already know this, but in England— in the view of most of my well-to-do contemporaries— poverty is a regrettable but necessary state of affairs. The poor must labor to fuel the machinery of society."

"It is no different anywhere."

"Indeed. And while the working poor are essential to a country, their work and their lives are not considered honorable. Even from the pulpits we hear it declaimed that there is some flaw in their characters that has made and kept them poor. Their sins drive them to poverty and poverty requires them to perform the drudgery that supports the rest of us."

Jane held back her own opinion, for she doubted these were Nicholas's views.

"There are many distinguished members of our society who still believe that the classes into which we are born were established by God. It is a system established for the purpose of order. To have superiors, then, you must have inferiors. Some exist to serve and obey, while others are born to command."

"This is the thinking that allows such brutal repression in Ireland."

"And other places, as well." His blue eyes met hers. "And that is why I brought you here. I wanted you to see that the suffering is not limited just to Ireland. Right here in London"—he made a sweeping motion of the people around him—"one finds the poor and hungry. There is suffering right beneath our almighty noses, but our response is the same."

"Society *chooses* to not see them," Jane offered. "Those above consider these people only good for cleaning their houses and sweeping their streets, for plowing their lands, for digging out their quarries, and serving in their armies and in their ships."

"And that is only the honest work."

"And they wonder why those in slums like this riot. And they wonder why people like those in Ireland and in the colonies in America chafe under the heavy yoke."

"Yes." Nicholas's grasp tightened. "But not everyone is so ruthless. Not all of us are blind."

He returned the greeting of a crippled old man leaning against the bare planks of a house before turning his attention back to her. "I brought you here because I wanted to show you my cause, Jane. Doing something for these people, especially those who are young and homeless, has been my own way of alleviating my personal guilt. And though this is not as heroic as anything you have done in Ireland, it is a starting point for me."

She shook her head. "You can make a difference here. The mere immenseness of the poverty of cities makes any contribution much more heroic than anything I have done."

"But there is so much to do."

He looked into an alley so tangled that no light reached the ground. Jane could see movement at the end of the alley, but whether it was human or animal, she could not tell.

"I brought you here so you would know that no matter where you go or live or decide to spend the rest of your life, there are people who will need you. Everyone in this country is not a Musgrave. There is bad and good. There are those who want to dominate, and some who want to share the bounty. And then there is one who wants you at his side in life and in love . . . for eternity."

She was so affected by his last words that the noise and people around them had become a blur. All she could see was Nicholas. A tug on her skirt, though, drew her attention to a little girl who was looking up with huge brown eyes at the two of them.

"Beggin' yer pardon, Sir Nicholas, sir."

She dropped her hand from Jane's skirt when their attention turned to her. She was dressed in a filthy and torn print frock and a broken black chip bonnet. Jane saw the child was wearing no shoes. "Ye dunno me, sir, but I'm Bessie's sister."

"Bessie, you say?"

"Oy, sir. A whiles back I used to share a room—'twas jist a hole, sir, really. But Bessie an' me was livin' with my brother . . . off Drury Lane. And then the Irishman and his slut come an' tossed us, sir."

"This is quite a history for one so little, Miss . . . Miss . . ." Nicholas crouched down until he was more at eye level with the child. "Since you know me, then perhaps we should be properly introduced."

A soft blush crept up the dirty cheeks. "My name is Sally, sir." She gave a shy curtsy and pushed her long rusty hair under the bonnet as she looked up at Jane.

"Nice to meet you, Miss Sally. And this is Miss Purefoy."

"Good to meet you, Sally." At Jane's smile, the girl blushed deeper and rubbed the palm of her hand on her thin dress.

"Do I know your brother?" Nicholas asked.

She shook her head. "But ye might be knowing Bessie . . . or maybe not. She's two years older than I, an' last winter—after we got tossed by the mick—ye found 'er an' took 'er to one o' yer houses . . . the one by the market."

"Why did you not come with her?"

She blushed again. "I was afraid, sir . . . I ran an' hid. But I ain't afraid now. D'ye remember her?"

"I am sure I will remember her as soon as I see her."

"Last summer, Bessie an' me used to go about the streets sellin' watercreases."

"Did you?" Jane asked encouragingly.

"Aye, miss. We'd go, 'Four bunches a penny . . . watercreases!' Our mum learned us to needlework and knit when we was little. I used to go to school, too. But I wasn't there long. I've forgot all about it now. 'Twas such a time ago." The girl's fingers twisted nervously before her. "But my mum died a few winters back, an' my brother took off last month, an' I had to move out o' the place here . . ." She pointed vaguely toward a nearby alley.

"Where do you live now, Sally?" Nicholas asked gently.

She looked down at her bare feet. "I've been on the streets for a whiles, sir. But I've not been goin' hungry. I work . . . I goes to a woman's house till eleven o'clock on Saturday nights. All I have to do is to snuff the candles and poke the fire. They is Jews, sir, and have their Sunday on Saturday, an' they won't touch anything; so they gives me my vittals an' a penny besides." The child's feet shuffled on the dirt. "But winter's coming, I know . . . an' I miss Bessie."

"Then you shall move into the same house with Bessie."

Nicholas continued to talk to the young girl, but Jane found herself concentrating on him while fighting her own emotions. She had loved him before, but now—as she watched his gentle and caring dealings with Sally— her affection for him grew even greater.

When they worked their way back to the carriage and climbed in, they took Sally with them. Whatever else Nicholas had intended to show her, though, was put aside. Bessie, it turned out, was not at the house "by the market," and as a result Jane received a tour of several of a group of houses that Nicholas, she learned, had created to shelter street children. It was almost noon before they found the sister and settled Sally in with people who would care for her.

When they finally returned to Nicholas's house on Leicester Square, it was early in the afternoon, and they were told that Frances was visiting her friend Elizabeth and should not be expected for dinner.

"Thank you for today," Jane said under the watchful gaze of the fierce-looking steward. There were messages waiting for Nicholas when they'd arrived.

"I have to see to a couple of correspondences in the library," Nicholas told her. "Why not try to rest and come down and meet me there later . . . whenever you are ready."

She nodded and went to her room. Once inside, though, resting was the last thing on her mind. This side of Nicholas—the philanthropic part of him—had opened her eyes to the rest of his character. For the first time, she thought, she could really see him. Understand him. Much the same as she did, Nicholas presented only one side of himself to society. His was an attitude of a confirmed rake—sporting, independent, careless, and self-centered. He was outspoken, arrogant, and openly disdainful of the system that mandated how he should live his life. But in private, he could pursue his own valuable interests without the pressure of society's constraints. His generosity was for the sake of people in need and not contingent on the fashionably fickle philanthropies of the *ton*.

She learned today, from the people she had met in their tour, that Nicholas had established so far nearly a dozen safe houses for children across London.

Standing before the window, she knew that she admired him and loved him for the man that he was and couldn't wait to tell him so.

An hour was all that she was able to stay away. Dressing in a soft yellow dress that she once again wondered how Fey had managed to have made for her, Jane cast a final look at herself in the mirror before going down. Of everything in the trunk, this was the least conservative of the garments, and as she descended the steps, Jane's stomach was already dancing with the memories of their lovemaking in Ireland.

There was no denying it. She loved him. She respected him. She desired him.

The visits yesterday seemed to have paid off. The letters he'd received this morning were very encouraging. Nicholas sealed the last of his responses and handed them to his waiting steward.

"Have them delivered this afternoon, Charles."

"I shall have it done, sir," the burly middle-aged man assured him. "And how was your ride with Miss Purefoy this morning?"

"It was fine," Nicholas answered, straightening the papers on his desk.

"I hope you ain't tired her too much."

"I did not."

"Jack tells me you missed more than a few of the famous visiting places in our fair city."

Nicholas lifted his gaze at the jocular tone of his steward. "Miss Purefoy had already seen all that rubbish before. And before you ask . . . yes, she appeared to have enjoyed our little excursion. And yes, you may report all of this to Mrs. Hannagan."

"She'll be pleased . . . though I'm guessing she already knows." The man grinned crookedly, showing a missing front tooth and managing to look only slightly less ferocious. "We're all thinking Miss Purefoy's a keeper, sir. We just thought you might need to be told."

"Thank you, Charles. Now did I mention that I wanted those letters to be delivered today?"

"Aye, sir." With a polite bow the steward left the room only to knock a moment later to announce Jane's wish to see him.

Nicholas immediately rose to his feet. He felt almost foolish, the way his heart swelled in his chest when he saw her face.

"Am I intruding?" she asked shyly when Charles closed the door on his way out.

"No. I am quite finished." He came around his desk. "How was your hour's respite? Recovered from our jaunt?"

"I was too restless to lie down." She glanced back toward the door and smiled. "I made the mistake of saying the same thing to Mrs. Hannagan, and the sweet woman was ready to call in a doctor to have me bled. I have to thank Charles for coming in and putting her mind at ease."

"They are quite the pair, those two. They have been with me for years and can be quite entertaining." He let his gaze wander appreciatively over the dress she was wearing. "Mrs. Hannagan is easily rattled, but Charles took far too many blows to his head in his youth to let anything affect him."

"Blows to the head?"

"He was a boxer. A very good one, too, until a sly fox blinded him in his left eye at Wetherby's on Drury Lane. After that, the poor devil took quite a beating on that side for several years."

"So you took him into your service."

"Had to. He would have been killed if he'd continued to fight."

She continued to stand by the door, so he approached her.

"But I don't want to talk about Charles right now."

Her dark gaze flashed with awareness. "What do you want to do, sir?"

He took both of her hands in his and placed kisses on the soft palms. "Where did we leave off our conversation this morning?"

Instead of answering, she freed her hands and slipped them around his neck. "I do not feel much like talking right now."

Desire surged in his loins. "Then what . . . what exactly do you want to do, miss?"

She raised herself on her toes and brushed her lips against his.

"This." She repeated the kiss—this time with much more heat.

Nicholas lost himself in the seductive play of their mouths as soon as she pressed her body against his. She was all woman and fire, and he couldn't get enough of her. His mouth slanted deeply over hers and his hands were possessive when they caressed her back, her breasts, cupping her bottom, and pressing her hard against him.

"I want you, Jane. By 'sblood, I have missed you."

"I have missed you, too."

Her hands moved beneath his jacket as he tasted the skin of her neck. His hands began to loosen the laces on the dress.

"We should go upstairs."

"No. Here." She pulled him toward the nearest chair.

He was too focused on the moment to object to anything. His jacket was tossed to the floor. The front of his breeches were opened as he sat back on the chair. Jane lifted her skirts, and he drew her onto his lap, impaling her with a single thrust as she straddled him.

Nicholas echoed her groan as her muscles closed around his member in the tightest of fits.

"You are so exquisitely perfect," he murmured. He pulled down on the neckline of her dress, freeing her ivory breasts. He sensed her holding her breath as his tongue started running in circles around one of her nipples. With her moan of pleasure, he greedily took her fully into his mouth.

Jane dug her fingers into his hair and guided his mouth to her other breast as her hips rose and moved around him.

He struggled for a moment to keep her steady and try to salvage some of his restraint. But when Jane's head fell backward, she looked like a goddess riding him, and he lost all control.

Their release was fast and joyous, and each clasped the other in their arms as the fulfillment of their desires bonded their bodies and their souls.

For a few moments each of them fought to catch their breaths. Their bodies were still joined at the most intimate of places. Her dress was a shambles—half on, half off her body. His own shirt was partially unbuttoned and her cheek was pressed against his shoulder.

"Well, this was certainly a most pleasant surprise," he whispered against her hair some time later, once he'd found his voice. The soft laugh he heard made him smile.

"I cannot believe I seduced you," she whispered, sighing contentedly.

"So . . . trying to take all the credit, I see," he teased, sliding his hands beneath her skirts and along the smooth skin of her thigh. "Do you mean you refuse to recognize how strategically I planned all of this?"

Before she could respond, a soft knock on the door jerked Jane off his chest. She looked frantically at him before trying to back off his lap.

"One moment, Charles," he said, grinning in spite of himself. He pulled up his breeches while trying to help her adjust her dress. "The poor devil will be terribly shocked."

A second knock came, but before Nicholas could call out again, the door opened slightly, and Clara's face appeared.

# Chapter 29

Shock had made her stare for a moment longer than she should have. Shame then made her stumble backward as she turned and ran frantically upstairs.

Clara needed a place to hide, but upon arriving at the top of the stairs, she looked wildly about her, not knowing where to go or which room was safe.

They had not officially arrived yet. Lady Spencer was still outside, chatting with some lady who had been passing in an open carriage on the street. Servants were running about, either outside seeing to the luggage or inside preparing to receive the guests. One of them had told her that Miss Purefoy was in that room—the library—so Clara had knocked. Hearing no answer, she had simply peeked in.

She brought a hand to her mouth. It was only obvious what they had been doing. Too . . . too obvious. Crazy thoughts of pretending the whole thing hadn't happened ran through her head. She would just go back outside with Lady Spencer, she thought, and wait to enter the house officially with her. Whirling to run back down the stairs, Clara didn't make it a step, for Jane was facing her on the top stair.

"We . . . it was raining endlessly . . . in Bath," Clara stuttered. "So we decided . . . to come back to London . . . sooner than expected."

"Come with me, Clara." There were tears in Jane's eyes when she took hold of Clara's arm and dragged her up another flight of stairs.

The young woman went along without a struggle. At

the top they entered a bedchamber that she realized was Jane's.

"A lovely room," Clara whispered. "Bright sun comes in through those . . ."

"Please do not do this to me."

Clara turned and watched her sister leaning against the closed door.

"Do not pretend that nothing has happened, or that you failed to see us downstairs." Jane pushed herself away from the door and took a step toward her. "Be honest with me, Clara. Let me bear the guilt and the blame. Release your anger, somehow, instead of holding it in."

"Jane, you are a grown woman. What you do with your life . . ."

"What I have done with *your* life is what we are discussing now," the older sister said brokenly. Her cheeks were flushed. "Clara, I know you asked me, pleaded with me to leave Nicholas alone. You said that you were interested in him. That you were somehow planning to convince him . . . to marry you."

"But you could not do it."

"No, I couldn't. The fact is . . . I . . . we . . . love each other. And though I know that there is no chance of us ever having . . . a future together . . . at the same time . . . if you really wanted him . . . if you loved him even close to how much I love him . . . if you knew the man that he is . . . then I would . . . I would stay away." Jane batted at the tears coursing down her face. "But he deserves more than a mere contract. He deserves someone who will truly care. And *you* deserve to find a man who can love you as well."

Clara sat on the edge of the bed and battled her own raw emotions in response to Jane's fierce sadness.

"It is the most astonishing thing to be in love, Clara. As desperate as my life might appear to you—despite the fact that I may never have a settled future—loving Nicholas and being loved by him has given me something I have never had before. He has given me something I never felt with Conor."

Henry's face was so clearly etched in her mind's eye that Clara had no difficulty conjuring his image now. She did indeed know what it was to love . . . and to feel its pain. "But we are not all born to be strong. We cannot all simply go after what we want and succeed in getting it."

"But you were born strong." Jane crouched before her. "You and I are sisters—we are made of the same stock. While I have led my life as a rebel, you have striven to conform and to obey, to be the perfect daughter to our parents. In the process, though, you have caged up your own spirit." Jane's hands cupped Clara's. "You cannot continue to shoulder blame for me, to be the ever-compliant peacemaker in our parents' home. You cannot go on forever saying and doing what pleases everyone else and forgetting about yourself."

A memory long buried forced tears to Clara's eyes. She looked down at their joined hands.

"Blame belongs to those who have sinned, Clara. My past is my own doing. The life I have led has been led by my own choosing. Our parents' differences are as old as time, and there might never be a way to resolve it. But that is their life, not yours." Jane's voice dropped low, her tone filled with conviction. "Break the shell, Clara. Let me see my own sister. I thought I was seeing a glimpse of it that morning when you asked me to leave Woodfield House and Nicholas's life. But I know now that wasn't really you. Your reaction to what you witnessed a few moments ago confirmed it. You do not care for him enough even to fight."

"It is true. I don't love Nicholas. I told you that. I don't think I ever shall," Clara whispered. "And I am not angry with you for any of it."

"But I am angry with myself," Jane answered. "And it is not because of any regret over what Nicholas and I have shared, but for the years that I have allowed you to hide within your shell."

She reached out and lifted Clara's chin until their tearful gazes locked. "Tell me how you feel. Help *me*, and let me help *you*. Clara, it is time you pushed aside this facade of indifference."

"Sometimes I fear there is nothing inside of that shell." A choked cry escaped the younger sister's throat and she looked away. "It hurts too much to change."

"Why? As I see it now, it is hurting you more to stay the same." Jane again drew her sister's face around. "You are so sad, Clara. And I am not talking about today. You have been so sad for so long . . . and I cannot remember when it was that you changed."

"I know when it was that I changed." The words bubbled up inside of her. She had reached her limit, and there was no stopping the long-hidden truth. "My life changed forever when I walked into that village nine years ago and saw my sister keening over the corpse of her lover. I changed the day I saw you curse everyone who was responsible for Conor's death . . . even though you didn't know enough to curse me. I chose to keep a secret and hide my own sin."

Jane's face was bloodless when Clara looked up.

"It was my fault that Conor was arrested that week. It was my failure to do what you asked me. If I had delivered your message to him, he would not have come that morning. He would not have been captured . . . or killed." Clara sobbed wretchedly. "I was too afraid of doing anything against Father's wishes even then, so I lied to you and said that I had delivered your message. And then I saw what my lie did. It cost Conor his life. And with it, I destroyed your very future."

Clara buried her face in her hands and wept. "I am so sorry, Jane. I never knew . . . never thought how horrible the consequences could be. And for all these years . . . this thing has been sitting in my heart . . . and . . . and then I was so ruthless to you again . . . asking you to leave Nicholas when I really didn't want to marry him. I was so confused after Henry had proposed to me . . . before I ran away and ruined everything again. I just . . . I am the most hateful person . . . and you never see it. I have been ruined from the inside, as if some horrible worm has eaten through my soul . . . leaving me hollow. Yes, hollow . . . with only the shell for the world to see. Instead of trying to help me, you should hate me."

The mattress shifted. A moment later, Clara felt Jane's hands gather her tightly against her.

"I will *never* hate you. Do you hear me? Never. You were a mere child when I made you take that message.

Father had me locked away, but it was very wrong of me to put that weight on you." Her words were soothing. "And knowing Conor, he would never have changed his plans, no matter what message I sent or what danger awaited him. He was resolved for us to go through with it. His decision had been made."

Jane gently caressed Clara's hair as she spoke. "You see . . . the fault was with me for getting you involved at all . . . and with our father . . . and with this country . . . and also with Conor and me for being so unprepared and so blind." She brushed the wetness from Clara's cheek. "But one thing I have recently learned . . . the time comes when we all must part with the past. No matter who is to blame, I have finally decided to live what is left of my life. It is time to give over the pain of what went wrong. And Clara, you need to try to do the same. Life is too precious. *You* are too important to me. We must change the way things are." She placed a kiss on the younger sister's brow.

"But for so long . . . I have just been the same miserable pretender. I don't know how to change."

"Oh, yes. You do." Jane smiled gently. "And with some intensive tutoring from me, you can still earn the title of the second wicked Purefoy girl."

Clara felt a sense of giddiness rising inside of her. She hugged Jane fiercely and let the sadness ease its way out of her body.

"Thank you. Thank you for always being there for me. And thank you . . . for your offer of making me wicked." She pulled back and wiped the tears off her face. "I truly need it."

"Very well." Jane clutched her hand. "But before we start our first lesson, what was it that you said about Henry Adams proposing? I didn't think it was my imagination that there was something peculiar about you two."

"What on earth did you tell her? She didn't look at me crossly once during the dinner. In fact, I should say Clara seemed unusually cheerful this evening."

No sooner had everyone retired for the night than

Nicholas had been at her door. He had been genuinely concerned over what had happened this afternoon, and he and Jane hadn't been able to share a private word all night.

But simply talking had proven too difficult for them both.

"Do you really expect me to reveal a confidential conversation between two sisters?" she teased, rolling Nicholas on his back and stretching her body on top of his. She kissed his neck—tasted the hollow of his throat. "Do you know this was the first time we made love in a real bed?"

"You are changing the subject." His muscular arms wrapped around Jane, impeding her movements. "What did you tell Clara about us, Jane?"

"I told her that I love you."

The change in his face was stunning. The intensity of his blue eyes scorched her. She realized that this was the first time she had actually declared her own feelings.

"And did you speak them only for her sake?"

She shook her head. "I love you, Nicholas."

Jane heard the short breath that escaped his lungs, and she thrilled to his kiss. His manhood was hard once again, and she felt the molten pools forming within her, as well. But before their bodies could join again, he gently cupped her face and pulled back.

"What else did you tell her?"

"I told her you love me, too."

"What else?"

She shook her head in confusion. He rolled them on the bed again until he was covering her.

"Didn't you tell her that I have asked you to be my wife?"

She hadn't, but there was no need for an answer as he seemed to read her silence.

"Jane, I know I am undeserving of you, but . . ."

"It is the exact opposite . . . and you know it." She wrapped her arms around him and met his gaze. "I love you, Nicholas, and I am willing to spend the rest of my life with you . . . but not in marriage."

"Why not?" His temper flared.

"I have said it before, but you don't seem to want to hear any of it." She sighed. "There is scandal in my past. I never wish to taint your family name with . . ."

"Bloody hell." He pushed himself up, looming over her. "To be sure, you are the most stubborn woman ever born. Why can you not get it in your head that nothing of your past will have the slightest effect on our marriage—or in the way people treat you in the future?"

"And you are the most stubborn man," she retorted. "What is wrong with the two of us continuing on as we are? I might even consider leaving Ireland and coming to live in London. I could become your paramour . . . or concubine . . . or whatever it is they call those women these days. Mistress . . . that's it."

"I cannot believe you can offend me so casually!" He lifted his weight off of her and sat up. He ran a weary hand through his long loose hair.

Jane touched his back, sat up, and placed a kiss on his shoulder. "I was not trying to offend you. On the contrary, I am being helpful."

"Then don't be," he snapped, glaring at her.

A pang of vulnerability pierced her heart. Her face must have shown it, for he reached out gently and touched her face.

"I love you, Jane. Do you understand? I love you. I want to spend the rest of my life with you as husband and wife." His hand moved down and rested on her flat stomach. "Do you realize, after what we've shared, you might already be carrying our child?" He didn't wait for an answer. "But whether we have our own, or care for all the waifs who wander the streets without home or family, would it not be wonderful to work together to make a difference in the world?"

"I do." She drew her knees against her chest and set her chin on them. "But it is so complicated. I must do the right thing for you . . ."

"But how about us?" he prodded, wrapping an arm around her shoulder and pulling her against him. "Like it or not, it is already us, Jane, and we can do the right thing together."

He kissed her again, and she felt all of his passion and frustration in it. She could easily lose herself in the warmth of his mouth, in the caress of his hands. But he pulled away. Stretching her out on the bed, he pulled the bedclothes up and tucked them around her body.

"You are not staying?"

He shook his head.

"You need time to think . . . to sort things out in your mind. And I need time to cool my blood." His fingers twirled a strand of her hair. "I want you too much, Jane, and I am afraid I might be scaring you with so much pressure."

She opened her mouth in denial, but he placed a finger on her lips.

"Please . . . tonight . . . just think of us."

# Chapter 30

Jane was pleasantly surprised when Mrs. Hannagan announced Lady Stanmore's arrival the next afternoon. She was even more delighted by the warmth of the greeting she received from Rebecca.

"I am so sorry that no one else is here this afternoon but me." Jane accompanied the other woman back to the drawing room and where she had been brooding and sketching for most of the afternoon. "Lady Spencer took my sister and Miss Frances out to visit some friends, and I haven't seen Sir Nicholas all day."

"Well, there is no need for an apology, for I came over just to see you." Rebecca glanced at the unfinished sketch on the end table before taking a seat. "I see Nicholas is not boasting about you without grounds. You are *very* good."

Jane was embarrassed about leaving her work out in the open. The exposed drawing was an attempt at capturing Nicholas's face, but no matter how many times she'd worked the sketch, she still couldn't take the expression of hurt out of his eyes.

"I . . . I have had very little formal training, and I fear it shows dreadfully."

She took a seat next to Rebecca as Mrs. Hannagan arrived, ushering a servant carrying a tray of tea and biscuits into the room. While the tea was being poured, Jane watched the two women chat pleasantly about the trials of new motherhood. A moment later, the housekeeper and serving girl left the two of them alone, closing the door on their way out.

"Do you know, this is the first time I've been separated from Samuel since he was born?" Rebecca turned
her attention back to Jane. "Stanmore likes to tease me
endlessly about my attachment to our sons."

"They seem like such happy boys."

"That is true so long as they have my undivided attention. Of course, there is no one to blame for that but
myself." She smiled. "I suppose this is one of the trials
of late motherhood. You have more experience in life,
but at the same time you are less willing to take a
chance."

Jane sipped her tea. Nicholas had told her that
Rebecca was only three years older than she was.

"But I am sure you are wondering what I am doing
here."

"Perhaps a little. But whatever the reason, I am glad
for it."

"I am, too," Rebecca answered heartily, picking up
her own cup. "It has been over a year since Stanmore
and I were married. But despite all of the socializing
that goes with my husband serving in Lords, there are
very few women in London whom I would consider
good friends."

She declined the offer of biscuits.

"Not that I have any great problem with that. My life
is so full, and—this may strike you as odd—my husband
and I have become best friends to each other. But still,
when fate directs me to someone special like you—
someone caring and intelligent and independent, someone who does not quite match society's expectations for
women—I cannot help but want to pursue that
friendship."

If those words had come from anyone else, if they had
been spoken in any other way than the way Rebecca
said them, Jane might have taken umbrage. As it was,
though, she found herself completely at ease with the
mixture of frankness and gentleness in the woman.

"You have a gift of making people feel quite special."
Jane smiled. "Your happiness is enviable."

"I must admit to you that I wasn't always as happy."
Rebecca took a sip of her tea and put the cup and saucer
on the table. "I did my best with James for the ten years

we lived in Philadelphia together, but there were as many hard times as there were good times. For those ten years, fears of my past, mixed with the uncertainties of the future, always preyed on my mind."

From the first moment they'd met, Jane had realized there was much more to this woman than met the eye.

"And even when I returned to England," Rebecca started again, "and after Stanmore and I became . . . intimate . . . I still had strong doubts of ever finding lasting happiness. You see . . . Stanmore wanted permanency . . . marriage . . . stability, but I thought myself unworthy of his attention . . . of his name."

"But Nicholas told me you are a half-sister to Lord North."

"Neither Stanmore nor I knew that then, and even if I did, it wouldn't have made any difference to me." She glanced in the direction of the closed door before turning to Jane again. "I had fled from London ten years earlier because I was certain I'd killed a man—in defense of my virtue—but I had killed all the same. But despite my refusal, Stanmore was not willing to give up our future. He threatened to abandon his life in England and return with me to the colonies. And since I refused to let him, I was sure he would go to the King if he must, to secure a pardon and have me stay."

"What happened?"

"Stanmore's lawyer *and* Nicholas discovered the truth about the alleged murdered man. As I was told later by them, I had only managed to wound the monster. A few years later he was killed by an angry husband."

Jane tried to stop the trembling of her hand as she placed the cup and saucer on the table. Though their backgrounds were very different, the similarity in how they felt—of not wanting to injure the man they loved—was so startling.

"Despite the connection to Lord North, the announcement of Stanmore's and my marriage was not without gossip and insinuation. But we managed to survive it very well, I think." She smiled proudly. "Knowing what I do now, having faced the elite in the course of dozens and dozens of social occasions, I can tell you that what they say means nothing when a marriage is strong."

Rebecca touched Jane gently on the knee. "I know you may think it is easy for me to say these things, since all of this is behind me. But if I could offer you a little advice . . . just listen to your heart and fear nothing about what others might think."

"Did Nicholas ask you to come and speak with me today?"

"No, he didn't. But seeing you at our home two nights ago brought to my mind memories of myself." Her gaze was direct yet tender. "Anyone watching you two can see that he is so helplessly in love with you . . . and that you are so deathly afraid."

Jane closed her eyes for an instant and then let out a long breath. "My fear is not of him. I love him more than I can ever put into words."

"And that is why you are trying to do what is right for him." She completed her thoughts.

Jane's head swam with all the difficulties ahead of them, but she also dared herself to imagine all the possibilities. The second far surpassed the first. It was a while before she turned her attention back to Rebecca.

"I appreciate what you are trying to do for me . . . for us."

She squeezed Jane's hand gently. "I did not come here for any answers, only as a woman paying a visit to a new friend." Rebecca smiled, rising to her feet. "But I had better get back before testing the patience of little Samuel's nurse."

"When are you going down to Solgrave?" Jane asked as she followed the other woman to the door.

"Tomorrow morning. And the invitation stands. Please come and see us."

"I shall try." Jane returned Rebecca's affectionate hug. "And thank you."

Mrs. Hannagan joined them by the open front entrance and wished Lady Stanmore good-bye, as well. When the countess's carriage had pulled away, Jane walked back inside with the housekeeper.

"I do not intend to be intrusive, Mrs. Hannagan, but do you know by any chance when Sir Nicholas is expected back today?"

Mrs. Hannagan gave Jane a warm smile. "Of course

I do, miss. He returned only a few minutes ago, but I told him that you and Lady Stanmore were having a private talk, so he went up to change for dinner rather than break in on you ladies."

Nicholas had just taken off his jacket and his cravat and was ready to take off his shirt when there was a knock on the door. Assuming it was his tardy valet, he called for the man to enter. He was surprised and delighted to see Jane's face peer around his door.

"May I come in?"

"Please do." He took a step toward her, but then stopped. It had been a struggle last night to walk away from her and to leave this morning before she woke up. It was far too easy for both of them to give in to their passions every time they came together. But that was not the way he wanted to share his life with her. There was so much more between them than just the physical fulfillment of their bodily desires. He was resolved to keep his distance and give her time to make a decision.

Jane entered the room and closed the door, leaning her back against it. He was still powerless when it came to resisting her, so he moved to the far side of the room to pick up a clean shirt. "I heard that you and Rebecca were visiting downstairs."

"We were."

He quickly shed his shirt and began pulling on the new one. "And how was your visit?"

"Yes."

His fingers paused. Nicholas struggled to keep his voice steady. "What did you say?"

Jane pushed herself away from the door and started toward him with measured steps. "I said 'yes.' "

"Yes . . . meaning . . . you had a pleasant visit?"

She shook her head, and then smiled and nodded. "We did have a very pleasant visit."

She came to a stop right before him. Her hands were clasped behind her back. Her chin lifted, her dark gaze charged with emotion.

"But I am really saying 'yes' to your proposal . . . 'yes' to spending the rest of my life with you."

Nicholas didn't give her a chance to take another

breath before he lifted her into his arms and whirled her around in a burst of excitement. "My God, I love you, Jane. You have made me the happiest man alive."

"And you have made me the happiest of women." They both came to a stop. She cupped his face in her hands and stared into his eyes. "There is still a great deal that we have to work out."

"We will . . . together."

"And it might take some time before I can sort everything out in Ireland."

"Then we shall sort everything out together, for I am not letting you too far out of my reach."

"There will be many who will be shocked by the news of our marriage."

"But there are others who will be delighted." He kissed her lips. "But none of them matters, anyway."

Jane hugged him tightly, feeling on her cheek the strong beat of his heart. She wouldn't let the doubts cloud her mind. She was through guessing how it was possible for everything to resolve itself.

For the first time in her life, she was daring to live beyond her dreams.

# Chapter 31

When Jane arrived back in Ireland a week or so earlier than they'd planned, she found that nothing had changed and yet everything had changed.

Only Frances, already registered in a girls school in London, had stayed behind while Nicholas and Lady Spencer had traveled with her and Clara back to Woodfield House.

Although Jane felt no connection with her father—and certainly didn't care to seek his approval for this marriage—she had decided to abide for once by the etiquette of polite society. She had even encouraged Nicholas to withhold any announcement of their upcoming union until they'd had a chance to inform her parents. Of course, Nicholas's lawyers had carried a letter to the Purefoys ahead of time with directions to draw up the necessary papers, and the Spencers were told, as were the Stanmores, and a small but select number of Nicholas's closest friends. By the time the official announcement was published in the papers, Jane hoped, all of it would be nothing but very old news.

Despite the excitement of Nicholas's immediate circle of family and friends in England, Jane was completely unprepared for the warmth of the welcome that they received upon their return to Woodfield House. Everyone behaved as if there were nothing unusual about the baronet proposing to Jane. It was almost as if there had never been scandal associated with her name at all. Her mother was utterly jubilant, and her father more cordial than at any time Jane had seen him in her life.

"The proper announcements shall be sent out no later

than tomorrow morning," Lady Purefoy announced joyfully to the women who had left Sir Thomas and Nicholas in the dining room the night they arrived. Jane had never seen Nicholas more enthusiastic about talking to her father alone than tonight. "If you can help me, Lady Spencer, with the names and addresses of those you wish to notify, we can have them all go out tomorrow."

"I shall be delighted to be of any help that I can," the other woman offered.

"And I'd say this wedding absolutely demands two elaborate receptions—one here following the wedding service, and one in London." Catherine beamed at the prospect. "Perhaps we can arrange them so they will be only a month apart."

"Indeed, and the sooner the better," Alexandra agreed. "Before leaving London, I warned Mrs. Hannagan—she is Nicholas's housekeeper—to start . . ."

The two women continued to chat like the best of friends planning the most important event of their lives. Jane quietly moved away from the conversation and joined Clara by the window.

"I thought he would be coming here tonight," Clara whispered to her sister. Her gaze never left the road winding up through the valley toward Woodfield House's stables.

"I thought so, too." Jane stared in the same direction. "I sent a message to him, myself, as soon as we arrived. Mother does not seem very much concerned about the gossip that will surround Henry concerning what he said on my behalf the night of the ball. But it is important that he hear about my engagement to Nicholas from us, rather than being caught off his guard by someone else."

"The lawyers have been here nearly a week already." Clara's gaze seemed troubled when she turned to meet Jane's. "Perhaps he already knows . . . and he is upset . . . even jealous . . . and . . ."

"There is little chance of that jealousy business, little sister. Before I accepted Nicholas's proposal, I had to let go of my uncertainties and fears. You must do the same." Jane placed a comforting hand on her sister's arm. "Knowing Henry, he is probably busy right now with some act of charity, or some emergency."

"Then we may not see him tonight at all." Clara hugged her middle and looked longingly out the window again. "By heaven, I have missed him. And there is so much that I want to tell him. You . . . you have let out a monster in me. Now that I know what I want . . . and I have decided how to go about getting it . . . waiting patiently has become torture."

Jane smiled at the love and enthusiasm that had transformed her sister. Once they'd talked and Clara had explained about Henry's first proposal and her refusal, everything made sense. Thinking back, she could clearly recall all the signs that should have given her sister away.

"If I could escape, I would walk all the way to Ballyclough . . . barefooted, if I had to," Clara whispered impatiently. "This wait may kill me, Jane."

"You do not need to go on foot." She gave her sister a knowing look.

Clara cast a quick look at their mother. Lady Purefoy was still deep in conversation with Alexandra about the wedding arrangements. "Will you help me?"

"Of course, but only if you promise to ask Paul to arrange for a carriage and a couple of strong and trustworthy grooms."

"I will." Clara excitedly squeezed Jane's hand. "Thank you."

Clara slipped quietly toward the door, but Lady Purefoy's sharp eyes immediately noticed her daughter's movement. "Where are you going, Clara?"

"We are going for a walk in the garden." Jane immediately joined her sister. "You are doing such a fine job with your planning that we thought—if you don't mind—we would go outside and enjoy a little of this beautiful autumn night."

"Of course, we don't mind." Catherine smiled pleasantly. "But wear a wrap or something, you two. I do not want either of you catching a cold before the coming celebrations. And have Fey send out a servant with a torch for you. And . . ."

Side by side, the two young women left the room. Once outside, a fit of giggling took hold of Clara. "I cannot believe how much fun it is . . . to sneak out like this."

Jane was *certain* she had created a monster. "I think I will walk down to the stables with you, just to make sure that you do not do what you threatened just now— walk to Ballyclough, I mean."

At that precise moment, a distraught-looking Fey appeared from the servants' hall. Taking hold of Jane's arm, she begged for a moment's time with her . . . alone. Too excited to wait, Clara whispered her promise again to Jane and ran for the stables.

Jane turned to the housekeeper, who was obviously wracking her brain for the right words. But no choice of words could lessen the impact of the news she needed to share.

Egan was one of the last to arrive at the Shanavests' urgent gathering.

The number of men and women who had turned out was surprisingly large. But as Jenny told her the moment she crouched beside her, the purpose of the meeting had nothing to do with the terrible news Fey had conveyed. She shook her head at Egan's questioning look and motioned for her to join Liam, who was standing at one end of the dilapidated barn.

From Fey, Egan already knew that the magistrate had arrested the families—wives and children—of both Patrick and Liam early that morning, only a few short hours before the two men's return from Kildare.

The news was devastating, and as Egan made her way through the group, her mind cast about for different solutions. None, however, was comforting.

Liam was speaking to someone standing in the shadow of a rough-hewn post, while Patrick was crouched before a small peat fire not far away. His face showed the depths of his torment, and he did not look up when she touched his stooped shoulder as she passed.

At Egan's approach, Liam ceased his conversation with the stranger beyond.

"I am so sorry." She placed a hand on Liam's arm. Too many regrets were running through her. It was because of her that Patrick had been forced to go. If she had stayed behind instead of going to England . . .

Shaking herself, she forced back the guilt and tried to

focus on the present and how she could be of any use. "I came as soon as I heard the news."

The leader's expression showed how grateful he was to see her. "We'd better get started."

She nodded and took a step to the side. Glancing at the man standing beside her in the shadows, she realized it was Finn. She wasn't surprised that he was here or that he was wearing a mask and staying to the shadows. He was more of an outsider than she was . . . and she could hardly begrudge a man for trying to protect himself. After all, someone had identified Liam and Patrick.

The gathering hushed as Liam spoke a few words in greeting and then began explaining what had occurred at the meeting in Kildare.

"Every part of Ireland was represented. Indeed, not all of them go by the name of Shanavest, and there was some grumbling about that, to begin. But the grievances are all the same. Evictions, ill treatment of tenants by landlords and their dogfaced agents, land grabbing, the increasing brutality of the king's troops . . ."

Egan couldn't help but be impressed that, in spite of the distress of his own family, Liam was able to relay so clearly what he'd seen and heard.

"Although it was enlightening to see such a fine show of Irish fighting this tyranny in every part of this country for the same cause—'twas distressing to me and to Patrick that—"

"What of Ronan?" someone interrupted. "Ye seem to have lost him along the way."

"Good job getting rid of him." A few laughed.

"I didn't know that Ronan was going with them," Egan said quietly to Finn.

"Once you left for England, he couldn't keep his drinking or his tongue under control. The bloody fool was just too much trouble to keep around. It was my suggestion that Liam take him along. Sure enough, after meeting some of the groups from the north, he decided to take his leave and head north where the fight is more to his liking." The words, spoken in English rather than Gaelic, turned Egan's head sharply toward the man standing beside her.

"Henry?" she murmured.

"Finn, if you please." He squeezed her hand affectionately. "You are not the only person in Ireland who happens to be someone else as well."

"I . . . for so long now . . . you didn't tell me! Why now?"

"Listen to what Liam has to say. Not much matters after tomorrow night."

Confused, Egan turned her attention back to the meeting.

". . . far north and around Dublin itself, violence is becoming part of their everyday life. Killings, house burning, maiming of livestock has replaced filling in ditches and tearing down hedges and walls." Liam spoke with conviction. " 'Tis a vicious circle that is being created. They believe it works. But for us . . . the simple peace-loving people that we are . . . working together for the . . . the peace that we want for our . . . families . . ."

Her heart ached as Liam's voice faltered. He had to take a moment to gather himself before he could speak again.

"What Liam is trying to say"—Patrick rose to his feet—"is that 'twas clear to us that the Shanavests are going a different way from what we have always wanted. They seek blood . . . we have only shed it when we thought it necessary. We say that this group . . . our group . . . of Shanavests should disband . . . at least, for now. Despite everything that these people to the north and east are doing, there is no proof that any of it is working."

"If anything," Liam started again, "there is more retaliation against the tenants and cottagers in those areas."

"If we *were* to disband," Jenny called out from her corner, "and if we were to spread the word that we are doing it as a peace offering, do ye think the magistrate will let go of yer families?"

The question set a rumble of other questions and comments going in the assembled throng. Everyone knew about the two men's families.

"I don't know," Liam said softly. "But Patrick and I decided to tell you this long before we heard about our . . . our . . ."

" 'Tis worth trying," someone called, his comment seconded by others.

"I'm too old to be doing any more fighting," an older man announced to the cheers of some others.

"I've not lost the stomach for it," a young woman said.

"Nor I," added several others.

"We have nothing to lose," Jenny announced after realizing Liam was not confident enough to give an answer. "And we can always form our ranks again."

Silence fell over the barn until Patrick's brother-in-law spoke up. "But what of the deadline? Are we just going to stand by and watch our women and children hang?"

"Aye! The deadline is in two days."

Patrick's words sharpened Egan's attention. She knew nothing of this deadline or what the conditions were.

Jenny faced the crowd. "We'll spread word of our intentions. Send a message to the magistrate even. We shall talk as tough as that bloodless bastard Musgrave. We shall tell them that we want those women and children freed. He cannot hang innocents under such conditions."

Many voiced their agreement.

Egan turned to Finn. "What is this about a deadline?"

"The magistrate is looking to repeat the show of strength his predecessor employed nine years ago," he replied. "If certain leaders of the Whiteboys fail to turn themselves over to the dragoons at Buttevant by a certain time, he will hang their families."

Jane felt her blood run cold. "He wants Liam, Patrick, and me."

"He also wants Finn," the masked rebel responded. "All of us are to hand ourselves over to Captain Wallis before dawn, the day after tomorrow, or those women and children will die."

"He cannot."

"You know he can . . . and he will."

Egan let out an unsteady breath. "Jenny's recommendation will not work. Besides, Musgrave knows that he has us. We *will* hand ourselves over to save these families."

Finn nodded solemnly. "Yes, I know. That was why I said before . . . not much matters after tomorrow night."

One last meeting. One last midnight ride. One last night to be with him.

How quickly things change, she thought. Finally, violently, irrevocably. Shadowed by a cloud of doom, Jane took her time riding back to Woodfield House.

After everyone else had gone, the four rebel leaders had remained behind and talked. Finn had already tried to find out where exactly the two families had been taken, but he'd had no luck. Liam and Patrick, both distraught over the news, had not been any more successful. The only thing they had been able to discover was that during their absence, the dragoons seemed to have been doing an extensive search for any who were missing from the area. As luck would have it, somehow attention had been drawn to them.

Egan had had nothing to offer tonight. Suddenly the reason for her happiness had dissipated. Indeed, everything she and Nicholas had planned *was* as insubstantial as air.

The four had agreed tonight that there would be no substitutes. They all had been willing to meet again tomorrow night after midnight and go through with the exchange.

The only complications lay with arranging for a safe place for Liam's and Patrick's families to be taken to once they were released. With the two men as good as dead once they were in Musgrave's hands, Liam and Patrick wanted to know their loved ones would be safe.

Jane guessed it was already well past midnight when she returned Mab to her stall. The house on the hill was dark and quiet, but she knew that Nicholas would be awake and waiting for her. Moving in the darkness of the stable, she made her way toward the hidden passage leading from the tack room. She'd had no chance to tell him where she was going tonight, or when she'd be back. And now that she knew the truth, Jane also knew that she could not say a word to him about what was to come.

"Clear moon. Good night for riding."

Jane's heart leaped in her chest. Her hand was on the dagger at her waist before she recognized the voice as that of Sir Thomas. Shocked by the realization, she turned to find her father stepping out of the shadows of the tack room.

"Indeed," she answered simply. The fact that he was seeing her dressed in breeches, instead of a skirt—that she was out riding alone long after everyone else had been settled for the night—or that he might guess at some of her secret activities—no longer bothered her. She had nothing left to lose.

"It was very quiet around here without you going out and coming back in all hours of the night."

She bit back her surprise.

"But it was also very rewarding to know that for as many days as you were away in London, you were safe." He clasped his hands behind his back and glanced out a small window toward the house. "Nicholas and I had an extensive talk. Actually, 'battle' might be a better way of describing it."

With every sentence, he was managing to confuse her more, and Jane had difficulty keeping up her pretense of indifference.

"He wants none of your fortune."

She didn't know she had any.

"He insists on taking no land, no money, no dowry settlement of any kind. And he *is* pig-headed, by thunder."

Emotions rose up in Jane, even though she already knew how unselfish Nicholas's love for her was. It was the loss of it that made a tear slip down her face.

"But I can be as pig-headed as he is, devil take him. You are my oldest daughter. Rightfully, most of what your mother and I have should go to you and your future children." He actually chuckled. "But have no fear. We successfully settled our differences, but not before I forced him to become more flexible. This old soldier is not so easily beaten."

Jane cleared her throat, making sure she had a voice.

"I cannot understand the trouble you are putting yourself through. He already knows how my family perceives me. Nothing you say or do will make a difference in his opinion."

"Do not mistake me. I like him. But I don't give a damn about his opinion. It is you that . . ."

"Why?" The question wrenched itself from her breast. "What is all this about? Suddenly you act as if you care!"

"I have *always* cared about you, Jane." He took a step toward her.

"That's a lie."

"Do not speak to me in . . ." Sir Thomas forced himself to stop, and he ran a weary hand down his face. "Jane . . . I admit . . . I know I made a horrible mistake nine years ago. I knew you . . . I should have known that my action . . . in ordering that boy to hang . . . would not return my daughter to me. Ah, Jane! From the time you were a wee child you were different. You loved, you cared . . . you became a part of the people around you. Your mother and I came to Ireland when you were barely four years old, and not a year later you were running barefoot in those hills looking no different than the hungry Irish tenant brats."

She told herself she had no time to hear any of this. But her feet had become permanently rooted to the floor.

"When you were eight years old, you became deathly sick. Do you remember? All because one of the tenants had sold off his youngest daughter to the tinkers to pay a physician's fee when fever struck down the rest of the family." He came still closer. "Catherine and I thought we were going to lose you."

Jane looked down at her boots, fighting back tears.

"You brought her back," she said. Her father had a heart then.

"It was unfortunate that the girl died the year after when the fever came back to the valley. You mourned her as if you had lost your own sister." His voice was gentle, understanding. "I know you have been involved for years with these Whiteboys. You might think . . . that boy . . . Conor was the reason . . . or perhaps it was me and your will to go against anything I do or say. But even without us, you were . . . you are a person that had to be involved. You see injustice and you need to react."

"If you knew hanging those men was an injustice, then why didn't *you* do anything about it? Why don't you do something for the Irish now?"

"By the time my eyes were opened, a great deal of damage had already been done. I did the only thing that I could. I resigned my post."

"How convenient." She didn't bother to hide any of her hostility when their gazes locked. "But I have no time left to set blame or to try to reform . . . or educate you on how much there is left that can be corrected."

"Who would be better than Egan to offer vision to a blind man?"

His words stopped her from walking away.

"I knew about your activities with your blasted Shanavests, but I never knew you were Egan, the fearless leader of these people, until the morning of the ball." His gaze was actually admiring. "I should have known that you could not go down any road halfway. It has always been everything or nothing with you."

He was confusing her more than he had any right to do.

"Sir Nicholas tells me that you two plan to divide your time between England and Ireland. I am not asking any questions about what is to become of Egan, but I do ask you to make time to show me . . . to educate me . . . to make me understand where a change might still make a difference."

*Why now?* she thought. *Why must he be so late?*

"Believe me when I tell you that my motivation is not to set a trap for the others . . . or . . ."

Her gaze narrowed. "But the trap has already been set," she blurted out bitterly. "Even on the eve of the Shanavests' disbanding."

"What trap?"

She shook her head, walking away.

"You are too late, Sir Thomas. You are far, far too late."

# Chapter 32

Finn had just closed the stall gate in the parsonage's stable when a woman carrying a small lamp approached the doorway. Thinking quickly, he tucked the hat and the mask under an old saddle blanket lying on the ground.

"Is that you, Henry?"

"Clara?" He straightened up, surprised. It took him a long minute, though, before he found the rest of his words. Like a beggar starved for sustenance, his eyes hungrily took in all of her. "What are you doing here at this late hour?"

"Waiting for you." She put the lamp down outside the stable and entered. "I arrived just as Mrs. Brown was going to bed. We had a cup of tea before I sent her up, and then I waited in your parlor for a while. After that I spent some time in your study . . . then back to the parlor . . . then I came out and waited in your garden."

She stopped a breath away from him. Her gaze took in his rough, homespun woolen clothing, his high boots.

"You still haven't told me why you are here."

Her white teeth flashed prettily as she smiled in the darkness. "Mr. Adams, you look more like a highwayman than a respectable minister."

"I do not know what you are about tonight, but I clearly need to find a way to get you home." He took her by the arm and started to lead her out of the stables, but she planted her feet.

"I have been away for more than a fortnight."

"I know."

"Then you should also know this is no way to greet someone whom you have been missing terribly."

He met her challenging and playful glare. "When did I say . . ."

She silenced his question by sliding easily into his arms and capturing his mouth in a kiss.

A throaty groan escaped Henry and before he could stop himself, he had deepened the kiss. His hands were greedily pressing every curve of her body against his. She moaned softly into his mouth when his palm cupped her breast through the dress.

He abruptly ended the kiss, pulling his hands away from her as if burned.

"No! This is wrong." He tried to take a step back, but Clara followed him, her hands reaching out to him.

"Do not dare to deny that you feel nothing for me, Henry Adams. And do not lie about not wanting me. False denials and lies are wrong, too. More wrong!"

She clutched at the lapels of his jacket, and as he backed against the gate of the stall, her body trapped him.

"I was young . . . stupid . . . impressionable in the most naïve way, but I loved you even then. I made a horrible mistake in believing that my parents knew what was best for me. But I was wrong!" She raised herself on her toes and looked into his eyes. "I told you before, and I am repeating it again. I love *you*. I want to marry *you*. No one else. And I don't give a rush if I must wear the same dress for the next twenty years . . . or if we have to live in a one-room hovel for the rest of our lives. So long as I am near you, then I shall be happy. And I shall make you happy, too."

She brushed another kiss across his lips and then let her hands drop. "And I am not giving up. I shall stay after you, Henry. I shall pester you, remain a thorn in your side, until you are ready to face the truth." She walked away then, but turned by the door to the stables. "Now, you of all people, a man who constantly preaches forgiveness, might consider practicing a little of that yourself."

"Clara . . . I . . ."

"I'll be back."

\*    \*    \*

The sharp knock on the magistrate's door brought the man's head up.

"Bloody hell. What now?" Musgrave muttered before calling irritably, "Come in."

As the door opened, Sir Robert hastily covered the correspondence he'd been reading again and again for the past three days. He was not surprised at all to find Sir Thomas Purefoy accompanying Captain Wallis.

"How delightful to find you here at such an early hour of the morning, sir," Musgrave said, rising to his feet. "I was planning to stop at Woodfield House later today to give my regards to Miss Jane. I hear she is back from England."

"She is." Sir Thomas refused the offer of a chair.

"And did she have a pleasant stay?"

"Very. Thank you."

"You can leave us now, Captain," Musgrave said, dismissing the man.

"I hope you have no objections, Sir Robert, but I asked Wallis here to stay. This is not a social visit."

Musgrave nodded curtly and sat back in his chair behind his ornate desk. "What can we help you with today, Sir Thomas?"

The ex-magistrate took a folded quarto sheet of cheap, unmarked broadside from his pocket. Opening it, he flung it on Sir Robert's desk.

"These are circulating all over Munster. This one was found on the desk of the director of the new Butter Exchange in Cork City. Are you aware of it?"

"Yes, I am." Musgrave disdainfully brushed the paper aside. "I find nothing of value in it. None of the printers in Cork admit to having printed it. I think it is not worth the paper it is printed on."

Sir Thomas snatched up the paper, summarizing its contents as if Musgrave were not capable of comprehending it by himself. "It is a call for peace by the Whiteboys. By thunder, these notices say that the Shanavests are disbanding."

"I know what it says, Sir Thomas." He leaned back in his chair. "But as I said before, I find no value in it at all."

"And why is that, sir?"

"Because I shall accomplish the same thing without any noble peace offerings from them."

"And how is that?"

"By arresting and hanging them one by one . . . starting with their leaders." Musgrave smiled proudly. "This trash you hold shows that they are beaten. And now I shall crush them. With no leaders, there will be no band of ruffians. No band of ruffians, and there is no resistance. The lessons you have taught me have been invaluable, Sir Thomas. I am finally learning."

"You tried to take them before, but had no success."

"This time is different. I have bait, you see, and they shall come to me."

"What are you using as bait? Or should I ask . . . whom?"

"I am afraid I must refrain from answering."

"You do not trust me, Sir Robert?"

"It is not a matter of trust, sir, but the sensitiveness of the subject." Tired of the other man looming over him, Musgrave rose to his feet and faced the older man across the desk. "When you hanged those five Whiteboys nine years ago, you all but crushed the resistance in this area for years. Before dawn tomorrow, I shall hang four of the most active of the rebel leaders and start my campaign to eradicate the Whiteboys entirely."

"But there was no offer of peace back then. I would not have ordered the killing if there had been an option."

"You say that now, but I think not." Musgrave shrugged. "We all want to leave a legacy behind. I should like to be remembered as the one who hanged the cursed Liam . . . and Patrick . . . and Finn . . . and Egan. Yes, I should like it much better than being remembered as the foolish magistrate who agreed to let them disperse . . . for as long as it suited them."

Sir Thomas leaned menacingly over the desk. "We are discussing human lives. You kill those people now, and you stir up rebellion in others. Vengeance drives people to do mad things, Musgrave. The course you are choosing will bring unnecessary dangers to our own people's lives."

"How different a tune I hear now, Sir Thomas, from the one you were whistling scarcely a month ago."

"Speak plainly, Musgrave."

"Excuse me, Sir Thomas, but we are all entitled to make our own mistakes before we learn from them." He motioned to Wallis to open the door. "Now if you will excuse me, I have a great deal of work left to do before the arrests and the executions tomorrow morning."

Purefoy's face was fiery with rage when he stormed from the room ahead of Captain Wallis, but Musgrave didn't care a whit. He dug out the familiar letter from beneath the other sheets of paper.

The official correspondence in his hand had come from the Lord Lieutenant of Ireland three days ago. Musgrave had been called back to England. He was relieved of his duties . . . immediately.

He was no fool. He knew Nicholas Spencer was responsible for this. The insolent dog had been the only one who had ever threatened his authority, and Spencer had been completely charmed by the beautiful slut, Jane Purefoy. He must have acted quickly when he'd gotten to England.

The magistrate threw the correspondence back on his desk. Well, the Lord Lieutenant would have to wait, for he was going nowhere until he had finished with his plans. Indeed, Sir Nicholas's interest in the Purefoys would make her hanging all that much more satisfying.

Yes, some had to die—most especially Egan—before Musgrave obeyed any order inveigled by some cocky London rogue.

And yes, despite the former magistrate's illustrious past, Sir Robert didn't trust Sir Thomas Purefoy further than the length of his own sword.

Nicholas's arms tightened instinctively around Jane as she tried to slide from the bed. She turned and found him sound asleep. A tighter knot grew in her throat, strangling her, but she again fought back the tears. She forced herself to lift his hand slowly off her stomach as she slipped from under it.

Jane knew she was on the verge of falling apart, so she hastily pulled on her clothes. At the door, she looked one last time at his muscular arm spread over the side of the bed where she'd been pretending to sleep only minutes ago.

She had refused to get involved with announcements and wedding plans today. This day had belonged to only the two of them. Their lovemaking tonight had been hungry. She had touched him and kissed him and given herself to him as if there were no tomorrow.

And indeed, there would be no tomorrow.

He had wanted to talk of the future, but she could not bear it. She had wanted only rapture, the pure and simple joy of drowning in the moment, in the night, in each other.

She gave him one last look and a smile. Then she slipped out of his chamber, finally letting the tears fall, marking their final farewell.

Jane had to stop at her room and change into the clothing that signified that she was Egan. Although by dawn there would be no question that the two were one and the same, she refused to give Musgrave the satisfaction of arresting Jane Purefoy. No, it would be Egan that he hanged . . . Jane Purefoy would remain in the heart of the man she'd just left.

The ritual of carefully putting her hat on and pulling it low over her eyes, of sliding the dagger into its sheath, of tucking her pistol into her belt, was performed slowly, thoughtfully. Each movement brought back to her fully the purpose behind the cause she'd been fighting for. Each movement, completed one last time, fortified her spirit that she was dying that others would live.

She used the secret passageway to make her way to the stables. It was already past midnight, and the familiar sounds and smells of the old dark structure struck her fully tonight. These were things she wanted embedded in her memory, as well. She moved silently toward Mab's stall.

Aside from losing a life with Nicholas, she had one

great regret. Musgrave. The man would probably be li-
onized in the Houses of Parliament for his attention to
duty, cheered in the offices of the Lord Lieutenant,
toasted in the homes of English landowners.

But he had no empathy for the Irish. He would never
feel remorse for his brutality. Egan had a hard time believing he would go through with his promise to free the
families of Liam and Patrick in an exchange. She had
said so last night. But the other three men had been
willing to trust in Musgrave's honor.

She had the sickening feeling that *everyone* was to
suffer tonight.

Egan frowned when she looked into Mab's empty
stall. Confused, she looked for her saddle and found that
missing, too. Hoping that Paul had been alerted to when
she would need the mare, she walked out to the paddock, where the stable master might possibly be waiting
with her horse.

It was all quiet there, too. No horse, no Paul, no
anyone.

Beginning to feel a little rattled—for time was running
short—she moved hurriedly into another stall and saddled one of her father's horses instead. In all these years
nothing like this had ever happened. Paul knew that
Mab was not to be moved or ridden by anyone else.
Everyone knew.

A few minutes later, she left Woodfield House behind
and galloped through the night. The more she thought
of it as she rode, though, Egan was actually relieved that
Queen Mab, at least, would not fall into Musgrave's
hands.

The sharp knock on the door brought the startled
magistrate straight up in his bed. His mind and his eyes
needed a moment to adjust to the suddenness of the
disturbance. A soldier's urgent call outside his door
made him push the covers aside and rush to the door.
His unhappy manservant stood holding a candle behind
a young dragoon.

"What?" he screamed at the young man, who stood
ready to knock again on the door.

"'Tis Captain Wallis, sir." The soldier took a step backward. "He . . . he has . . . left the barracks. I rode here directly to let you know."

"Left to go where?" Musgrave snapped.

"To Cuchulainn's Seat."

The confusion and question must have shown in Musgrave's face as the young man quickly explained again.

"The captain and two dozen of his personal guard took all the prisoners for the exchange with the rebels. The captain told Corporal Evans that the meeting place and time had changed, and . . . and that you were already aware of it."

*"What?"* Musgrave's roar sent both soldier and servant back another step.

"We . . . had . . . no way . . . of knowing . . . sir . . . until . . . Sergeant Powers came back on duty . . . and he said . . . if you didn't go with them . . . then you didn't know. Begging your par—"

*"When did they leave?"* Musgrave shouted as he rushed about his room, dressing in haste.

"Just over an hour ago, sir . . ."

"Wake up whoever is left in the barracks." As the man leaped to go and do as he was told, a forbidding thought occurred to the magistrate. *"Wait!"*

Thinking a moment, he then gave the dragoon specific instructions of whom he should fetch . . . including his own man Sergeant Powers.

Captain Wallis had far more influence with these soldiers than he'd been able to achieve himself. And if the treacherous dragoon officer had decided to garner a few laurels for himself, then Musgrave doubted he would be able to get all of Wallis's men to fight against him.

But there were always a select few who stayed loyal to a cause.

Yes, this select few would be all that Musgrave needed to snuff out this untimely show of independence.

# Chapter 33

The light from the torches on the ruined walls of the castle could be seen easily from the distance. As Musgrave and his men drew near, two dragoons appeared, riding toward them. The magistrate didn't order his own troop to stop until the oncoming riders had reached them.

"Where is Captain Wallis? What is the meaning of this?"

"He is waiting for you at Cuchulainn's Seat, sir," one of the men replied. "The exchange has been made."

Musgrave stifled his angry outburst. "He has the rebels?"

"Aye, sir," the second soldier responded.

Cursing openly, the magistrate spurred his horse ahead of the others. Halfway up the hill, another half-dozen dragoons were guarding a number of horses. He paused by the group momentarily. Jane's high-spirited mare pranced among the rest.

"Whose horse was that?" he asked brusquely.

"The rebel Egan's. She is in shackles up there with the other three."

His temper somewhat controlled, Musgrave ordered his own men to take positions along the road up the hill with the rest of the dragoons. Now that he had the rebels, there would be no taking them away. This might be a salvageable situation, after all.

Captain Wallis saluted smartly but was obviously avoiding looking at him directly as the magistrate remained atop his horse.

"There was no waiting, Sir Robert. The blackguards sent the message that they did not trust us to release their women and children in Buttevant. They wanted to make the exchange here. That was easily accomplished. We sent their women and children down that hill, one by one, as the leaders came up the same road." Wallis motioned for a soldier to take the bridle of the magistrate's horse as he finally dismounted. "This is the kind of action you have been encouraging for some time, sir. I know how much the arrest of these people means to you. I did not want to lose the—"

"Take me to them," Musgrave snapped at the man.

Of course, the Irish bastards were right. He had no plans of freeing those families. How much more dramatic the final execution would be with the wives and children watching and weeping. How much fiercer his reputation would be when he then marched the families directly to the docks and onto a ship bound for Australia!

He fell in step with Wallis. Of course, one of the disgraced families would remain. What a stir that would make in the Lord Lieutenant's office! They could do nothing to him, the hero who had ferreted out the very daughter of the great Sir Thomas Purefoy.

"There they are, sir." The captain gestured toward what must have been at one time the keep's great hall. A gaping hole showed that the floor was only slightly above the castle courtyard.

Looking through the crumbled stone walls, he could see the four people crouched down with their hands behind their backs, tied to each other in a circle. Musgrave pushed Wallis aside and climbed the half-dozen steps to the entryway.

They all were wearing black. No white shirts for them today, he noted. A woolen hood had been pulled over each prisoner's head. Musgrave roughly yanked the hood off the first. The man's head jerked back, and Sir Robert studied the rebel's calm expression. He showed no fear, in spite of the noose that was awaiting him.

"This one calls himself Patrick," Wallis quickly offered from the doorway.

Musgrave kicked the second man before pulling the hood off his head. This one's face showed his hatred, and he growled something in Gaelic.

"Liam," the captain said.

Musgrave gave the rebel another solid kick and moved on. He was about to pull the hood off the next one when something occurred to him. Of the two that were left, one had to be Egan. Wallis had met and seen Jane Purefoy on a number of occasions over the past few years. Why, he wondered, hadn't the captain mentioned the taking of the former magistrate's daughter?

From the long legs and size of the boots, Musgrave could tell the next rebel was a man. He stepped past him and stood over the last hooded figure.

From beneath the shapeless woolen sack, he could see tendrils of dark hair showing.

"Am I correct to assume this one is Egan?"

"She is, sir. You cannot imagine our surprise in finding that we knew her."

His elation returned, and he yanked the bag off her head. As the woman's dark eyes snapped up to his, Musgrave stared for only an instant before drawing the dagger from his boot.

"There shall be no hanging for this one."

Stepping beside her, he quickly put the knife to her throat.

"Drop it now . . . or you shall die." With the point of the knife pressed against the woman's throat, Musgrave looked up in surprise at the pistol pointed at him. Rage boiled up inside him when he met Sir Thomas's cold gaze.

"What do you care if she dies?"

"If one drop of her blood is drawn, you are a dead man."

"Very clever of you to hide your daughter and switch this one in her place." Musgrave's hand didn't waver. "But regardless of whatever you think you are doing, as magistrate I can do as I please."

"You were formally relieved of the duties and authority of magistrate nearly a week ago."

"That's a lie." Musgrave cast a quick look at the number of dragoons who had gathered behind Wallis. "Arrest this man. He is interfering with—"

"Both Captain Wallis and I received copies of the letter sent to you by the Lord Lieutenant. We had our own additional orders attached to it."

"This is a trick." He looked angrily at the watching soldiers. "You just want to execute these four yourself. You then can keep your slut of a daughter and still add to your glory!"

"As I tried to make you understand yesterday, with the Whiteboys offering to disband, our best course is to let them. Our own landowners and the tradesmen in Cork City are tired of the injustices Parliament is afflicting us all with. Our own people are crying out for change."

"You mean your daughter."

Sir Thomas ignored the comment and spoke clearly and methodically. "Killing these people will only stir the cauldron of violence. Hang them and it could be another dozen years before we have a chance of bringing any real peace to this region. Now drop that knife."

Musgrave's attention shifted to the man entering the hall from a side chamber with one of Wallis's dragoons behind him. Spencer.

"You . . . !"

The former magistrate saw the look in Musgrave's face change. As the man yanked back the woman's head to make the lethal cut, Sir Thomas fired his pistol. Musgrave's body jerked with the bullet's impact, and as his dagger fell harmlessly in the woman's lap, he dropped like a stone to the ground.

Pandemonium immediately erupted in the castle and down the hill. Shouts and orders rang out from Captain Wallis.

Nicholas tucked his own pistol back into his belt, hardly glancing at Musgrave as he stepped over the dead body. Sir Thomas was checking the neck of the woman as Nicholas pulled the hood off the last rebel's head. Paul's grinning face was the one that looked up at him.

"That bullet came a wee bit close, I'm thinking?" he said with a chuckle.

"Closer than you know," Nicholas replied with a nod toward Sir Thomas. Quickly Nicholas freed the man's hands and cut the ropes holding the others.

Acting on Sir Thomas's and Captain Wallis's orders, the stable master had arranged for himself and the other three servants to substitute themselves for the rebels. The Lord Lieutenant's directions were clear. The two were to assess Musgrave's response to being relieved before acting to forcibly remove him. No one knew, though, how far he would go.

"You need to catch up to them," Sir Thomas ordered Nicholas. "Before they walk through those barrack gates in Buttevant."

"Are you coming along? You were the one who made this work. I think they should know it."

Sir Thomas shook his head. "Until the Lord Lieutenant sends another magistrate I must act for the Crown." He lowered his voice. "The devil take me, I have no wish to be in a position of identifying any of these rebels if this madman's replacement should ask me."

Nicholas knew that Sir Thomas might retain the position of acting magistrate for years . . . if the Crown's bureaucracy functioned with its usual lack of efficiency. But the man was correct; it would be better for him not to see the faces of the rebels. And one rebel, in particular.

As Nicholas turned to leave, Sir Thomas stopped him.

"But . . ." The old warrior's face softened slightly. "But tell Jane I'm trying."

There were still two hours left till dawn when the four rebels approached the last hill. Beyond it, they knew, lay the River Awbeg and the village of Buttevant.

The moon, still high in the sky, illuminated the solitary rider waiting for them on the crest of the hill. Jane immediately recognized him. She would know him anywhere.

"I did not tell him," she said quickly, seeing Henry's sharp look. "I told no one."

Not waiting for a response from the others, she spurred her horse toward Nicholas. He, too, having recognized them, rode in her direction. She couldn't be angry with him for being here. But seeing him this last time only added to the piercing pain of losing him.

The tears were already dancing on her face when she reached him. "What are you doing here?"

"Tell them to go back," he urged, nodding toward the three men who had reined in their horses. "There is no longer any need for an exchange."

"Nicholas, we *must* go or innocent people will die."

"Their families were freed tonight. But these men must turn back before one of Musgrave's men sees them and decides to finish something that his leader could not."

"I do not understand."

"Then come with me so I can explain it to them, as well."

Feeling somewhat stunned, Jane watched Nicholas nudge his horse toward the other riders. Pausing for a second to make sure she was indeed awake and that this wasn't a dream, she started after him.

None of them had bothered with masks tonight, and Nicholas simply stared for a moment when he came face-to-face with Henry Adams.

Jane addressed Liam and Patrick. "Sir Nicholas says that your wives and children have been freed."

Nicholas went on to explain that Musgrave had been killed tonight and the new, temporary magistrate strongly believed that he should reciprocate the offer of peace by the Shanavests.

Patrick and Liam looked at each other in disbelief.

"But as I was telling Jane, for the next few hours and until the change of command is completed, we do not want you anywhere near Buttevant."

Clearly neither Patrick nor Liam seemed to be able to fathom what he was hearing, and they looked at Henry in confusion.

"Sir Nicholas is not one to lie," the parson assured them quietly and confidently.

The burst of excitement from the two men was instantaneous. Patrick leaned over his horse and took Jane in an affectionate hug.

"Well, Egan . . . er, Miss Jane. Why not bring this

one around, sometime? Some o' these English can grow on ye."

"I thought you were disbanding," Nicholas said, apprehension creasing his brow.

"Patrick is talking about raising a cup or two, if I'm not mistaken," Liam said.

"Aye. Come around anytime. My wife brews the best ale from here to Limerick."

"I am not doing anything right now."

"Oh, yes, you are." Jane put a hand out and took hold of the bridle of Nicholas's horse, eliciting teasing comments and catcalls from the two men.

With a few parting words, Patrick and Liam rode off in the same direction they had all come. Henry, though, stayed and faced Nicholas's open amusement.

"Then you must be . . ."

"Finn," Henry said quietly.

"But why?" Nicholas questioned, his face growing serious. "What did Sir Thomas say? 'What would a respectable English churchman be doing fighting for a handful of discontented papist peasants?' "

"The answer is not so easy. I may have begun fighting for them because I witnessed great injustice . . . or because I believe compassion belongs to no single religion." Henry gave a short laugh. "Or maybe because, as the second son of an English naval hero, I have too much fight in my blood."

"I didn't even know that Henry was Finn until two nights ago," Jane admitted.

"Even though Liam and Jenny have known it for some time, I would have continued to keep that little secret if circumstances had allowed it."

With their horses standing side by side, Nicholas and Jane had at some point clasped hands. Henry's gaze now fell on their entwined fingers. "Mrs. Brown tells me there are marriage plans in the works."

Jane turned and smiled at Nicholas. "Now there are."

"Would you do us the honor of wedding us in your chapel?" Nicholas asked Henry.

"The honor will be mine," the parson replied pleasantly. "Of course, that is if I fail to convince Clara that she should marry me on the same day." He rubbed his chin thoughtfully and met Nicholas's astonished gaze. "You see, I am nothing more than a poor parish minister and it only makes sense for you to pay for the two sisters' wedding feast."

"I will be happy to pay for a honeymoon on the Continent for you and your bride, Parson Adams, so long as this wedding takes place in less than a month."

The two men grinned and shook hands on it, and Jane couldn't remember a happier moment in her life.

Henry rode away, leaving Jane misty-eyed and overwhelmed by this sudden turn of events. She looked into Nicholas's eyes. "You knew I was going away last night. Thank you for not trying to stop me."

He brought her hand to his lips. "You were Egan long before I met you. Your dedication and honor were on the line tonight. I knew you would not have me until you felt your duty had been done."

"You helped me . . . helped us. You saved our lives."

"But I cannot take credit for the events of tonight."

"I recall Stanmore mentioning some correspondence regarding Musgrave when we were in London."

"That was just a preliminary step," he admitted, smiling crookedly. "Through some people I know, I was able to persuade the Lord Lieutenant of Ireland that Musgrave was teetering on madness. Sir Robert was issued an order and called back to England, but when we arrived here, I found out that the cur was ignoring the order."

They nudged their horses down the hill and away from Buttevant.

"Someone else was far more influential in what happened tonight."

Her mind raced, trying to think of whom he could mean, to no avail.

"Sir Thomas," he said.

As the name sank in, a hundred feelings washed through Jane. Shame mixed with pride. Relief mixed with disbelief. Gratitude mixed with hope. She looked blankly ahead and they rode along in silence.

"He saved my life," she finally blurted out. "He saved

the lives of these men and their families. And yet, I . . . I cannot bring myself to face him . . . to thank him."

"I think he knew as much. He asked me only to tell you that he is trying."

She stabbed away at a runaway tear. "It was so much easier to hate him—to ignore the possibility that he had some compassion left in him."

"I do not believe he expects you to forgive and to forget overnight. At the same time, I believe that he is trying to be a different man. Perhaps you should simply let it rest at that." Nicholas's hand reached for hers again. He pressed her fingers again to his lips. "I believe the sun is about to rise for us."

Jane looked up to the sky lightening in the east. A new day beginning. She let out a ragged breath and tried to cleanse her mind and heart of everything that was past. She met Nicholas's loving gaze and thought of their own new beginning—of their marriage.

"Us! I love that word," he teased.

"Us," she repeated, and then smiled. "I must say you were pretty easily gulled into paying for my sister's honeymoon."

He laughed. "I would pay for a honeymoon for everyone from Cork City to—where did Patrick say?"

"Limerick."

"I would pay that and more for that smile on your face."

She leaned toward him. "I should have asked for more."

"Anything, my love," he said, pressing his lips to hers.

She drew away, but for only a moment.

"Well . . ." she whispered, smiling happily. "This is all I shall ever want. Just 'us.' "

# Epilogue

## London, Christmas Eve

She could have been murdered on the Cheapside. She could have been drowned in the Thames. She could have been kidnapped in Westminster.

Nicholas stormed in the front door, stomping the snow off his boots. He'd been to Stanmore's . . . and to his mother's new house. No one had seen any sign of her.

He threw off his cloak and hat as Charles appeared. "We've been scouring the neighborhoods, Sir Nicholas. Nothing. Mrs. Hannagan's about to have a stroke for worry, sir, and the guests are arriving in an hour."

"Damn the guests." He turned to one of the grooms. "Did you check again with Mrs. Cawardine?"

"Aye, sir. The painter lady was certain that her ladyship had promised to come by for luncheon with Sir Joshua Reynolds himself, sir, but she never arrived."

Nicholas glanced at his pocket watch. It was already past six. Queasiness had gripped his stomach an hour ago when she should have been home, and it still had him. She hadn't looked very well this morning. He should have been more forceful in asking her to stay at home.

If anything had happened to her, he'd just . . .

"The carriage, Sir Nicholas!" the footman shouted in the front door. "Just coming up the Square, sir!"

Nicholas strode out the door, pushing past the man and frowning up at the worried-looking driver reining in the team before the house. As the carriage lurched to a stop, Nicholas yanked open the door, only to see his beautiful wife's smiling face greeting him. She was shivering in her gray wool dress. No cloak. No hat and gloves, and God knew what else was missing. At least she had a blanket around her.

"You gave them away again to some poor beggar on the street, didn't you? By 'sblood, Jane, how many times must I tell you that if you catch your death in this cold . . ."

"Now, Nicholas . . . there is no need to frighten these two friends of mine." She pulled down the blanket covering her lap and the filthy faces of two street urchins peered out from either side of her.

He immediately climbed into the carriage and closed the door to keep out some of the cold. "Who are these two? And where did you find them?"

"They haven't told me their names, yet." She hugged each of them to her side. "But I think proper introductions can only be made after they get a warm meal in their bellies and a warmer bath."

Nicholas sighed in resignation. "And would you like Mrs. Hannagan and Charles to entertain the guests while we take these two to Angel Court?"

"No! It is Christmas Eve, Nicholas." She gave him a pleading look. "Can't they stay with us . . . for a while, anyway?"

It was impossible for Nicholas to refuse his wife anything. He wrapped his coat around her and motioned through the window of the carriage for Charles to approach.

The children were wrapped in the blanket and hurried into the house, but Jane put a hand on his knee, holding him for a moment.

"Nick, it is all right, isn't it?"

He put his arms around her, grateful that she was home and safe.

"The poor, dear creatures were so lost . . . and alone . . . and hungry. Everyone I asked on the street said they'd just been sleeping in an alley and begging there for weeks." Her eyes shone with her tears. "You don't mind me bringing them here, do you?"

He shook his head and pulled her tightly against his chest. "I don't mind at all, my love."

She held tightly to his hand. "But you've already told me it is generally better for these children to move into one of the houses . . . since there may be other children there that they know . . . and . . ."

"It is very well to bring them here, too," he assured her, kissing the wetness off her cheeks.

"And we can raise the three of them together. We can take—"

"Three?" he asked, looking around the carriage.

When she took his hand and guided it to her belly, his words caught in his throat. He stared at his own fingers spreading possessively over the life that was growing inside her.

"Jane . . ."

She nodded once. "One more wee one won't be too much trouble?"

There was no fighting his emotions.

"Not at all, my love." He drew her tightly against him again and let his own joyful tear fall. "Not at all."

# Author's Note

⸻

Since the twelfth century, England's heavy hand has gripped Ireland's heart.

Peaceful settlers. Conquerors. Colonizers. The English have been a part of Irish history for nearly a millennium. Since almost the beginning, they have tried to dominate and plunder this land of artists, scholars, and saints.

In the early eighteenth century, the governments under the first Hanover kings began instituting "Penal Laws" that were intended to strip the Irish of all land and all civil rights. The brutal and repressive policies imposed on the Irish at the time have been described as no less than cultural genocide. By the mid to late 1700s, however, the English landowners and merchants who had been long settled in Ireland were also chafing under the repressive colonial policies. Many saw the essential unfairness of the situation for the Irish, too, and petitioned for changes. They were, however, largely without a voice in Parliament. The situation for the Irish was truly desperate, and they began to organize themselves into resistance movements from Tipperary to Ulster.

The Whiteboys that you have just read about were a real part of that resistance. All over Ireland, these groups sprang up. The Ribbonmen. The Defenders. The Oakboys. The Rightboys. Every part of Ireland had its own bone of contention, and every resistance movement had an organized response to it.

When we introduced Sir Nicholas Spencer in *The Promise,* we knew—long before we ever finished Rebecca and Stanmore's story—that he was a man who needed a very special heroine. Jane Purefoy and her volatile and dangerous world in Ireland seemed to offer us just that. We hope you enjoyed the story.

Finally, we'd like to thank Timothy O'Sullivan for his help with Gaelic. We'd also like to thank Miriam O'Sullivan—friend, expert on Ireland, and travel agent extraordinaire—and her husband, Greg O'Sullivan, who not only helped us with our research but also helped to keep us safe from "bears" taking up residence in our garage! Thank you.

As always, we love to hear from our readers. Email us at mcgoldmay@aol.com. Or visit us at www.May McGoldrick.com.

# Forest
of
## Shadows

*For all who are brave*
*enough to be afraid.*

Copyright © 2019 Disney Enterprises, Inc. All rights reserved.
Illustrations by Grace Lee © Disney Enterprises, Inc.
Design by Winnie Ho
Composition and layout by Susan Gerber

Published by Disney Press, an imprint of Disney Book Group. No
part of this book may be reproduced or transmitted in any form or
by any means, electronic or mechanical, including photocopying,
recording, or by any information storage and retrieval system, without
written permission from the publisher. For information address
Disney Press, 1200 Grand Central Avenue, Glendale, California 91201.

First Hardcover Edition, October 2019
1 3 5 7 9 10 8 6 4 2
FAC-020093-19231
Printed in the United States of America

This book is set in Yana Regular.

Library of Congress Control Number: 2019937392
ISBN 978 1-368-04363-2

Reinforced binding

Visit disneybooks.com

# DISNEP
# FROZEN II

# Forest
## of
# Shadows

An Original Tale by

# Kamilla Benko

# DISNEP PRESS
Los Angeles · New York

# Fear

will be your

*enemy.*

—Grand Pabbie

# Prologue

THE SKY WAS AWAKE, and so was the forest.

Anna of Arendelle hugged her cloak tight as the bare branches clacked like teeth above her and the wind tugged at her braids. She peered into a bush. As far as she knew, bushes weren't supposed to have eyes. But then again, five-year-old princesses weren't *supposed* to be alone outside the castle at night, either. And yet here she was . . . although Anna hadn't started off the night alone. Her sister, Elsa, was somewhere out here in the snowy woods, too. Possibly hiding in the very bush that Anna tiptoed closer to at this moment.

Three years older than Anna, with wide blue eyes and a shy smile, Elsa was the kind of girl who could sit for hours without swinging her legs and whose tidy white-blond plait always hung straight down her back.

Grown-ups often remarked how well-behaved Anna's big sister was . . . but they didn't know Elsa the way Anna did. Underneath the polite and poised exterior was a mischievous sense of fun. All Elsa needed was an excuse, and Anna was happy to be just that: Elsa's excuse to slip into her cloak and sneak out of the castle to build a snowman and play hide-and-find under the northern lights. Which was exactly what they were doing now. Elsa had already found Anna in a tree's hollow, but Anna had been looking for Elsa for what seemed like forever . . . or at least five minutes.

The leaves rustled again, and Anna clapped her hands over her mouth to stop a giggle from escaping. Yes, there was *definitely* someone watching her from the snow-covered thicket. Holding her breath, she stepped closer. She was pretty sure it was Elsa, but there was always a chance it could be a Huldrefólk, one of the rumored hidden people who dwelled in the streams, under the rocks, and in the bedtime stories told by their mother, Queen Iduna. Anna's heart beat faster. If it *was* a Huldrefólk, she just *had* to see their tail. She'd always wondered if their tails were flowing like a horse's, or bushy like a fox's, or long and skinny like a mouse's.

But Anna had a feeling she knew who the figure

hiding behind the bush was. Anna parted the leaves, and in the colorful glow of the dancing sky, she caught a glimpse of blond hair. So, not a Huldrefólk. Just a sister.

Laughing, Anna shook the bush. "I found you! Your turn to be the Crusty Troll!"

Elsa didn't respond.

"I said, I *found* you." Anna peered through the foliage. "It's my turn to hide—that's the rule. Come on out!"

Anna's sister turned her head, and that's when Anna realized her mistake. It wasn't blond hair she had spotted in the shifting light.

It was white *fur*.

Anna's scream stuck in her throat as a giant white wolf prowled out from the thicket with unusual grace, its long limbs uncurling like smoke. Its fierce yellow gaze fixed on her, and Anna's eyes ran down its huge, horse-sized body . . . to see four fearsome paws, each the size of one of the large shields of her father, King Agnarr. But that wasn't the worst of it.

No, the *worst* was the red-stained fur around its claws and jaw.

Red. The color of blood.

*What had happened to her sister?*

"Elsa!" Anna screamed. "Where are you?"

The wolf leapt.

Anna ran.

Her heart slammed in her chest, each breath a sharp knife as she tried to run faster, and faster—but she knew she couldn't outrun a wolf. Spotting a fallen log, she dove behind it, her knees tucked to her chest as she tried to make herself as small as possible. Though her lungs ached for air, Anna held her breath, not wanting to give herself away with even the tiniest exhale. One second passed, then another, and another. Had she lost the wolf?

Snow fell thick and silent. Anna shivered, wishing she'd listened to Elsa when she'd told her not to wear her most beautiful green cloak but to put on her everyday thick woolly brown one instead.

*Elsa.* Where was Elsa?

As quiet as a shadow, Anna peered around the log, half expecting to come nose-to-snout with the wolf. Instead, all she saw was an army of trees casting ghastly shadows onto the snow-covered ground. And as the wind picked up, so did Anna's ice-cold fear. If she walked through the fresh snow, the wolf would be able to see exactly which direction she'd gone. And if she didn't walk through the snow . . . she might never find her sister.

*Red on white.*

*Blood on fur.*

Anna couldn't stay behind the log forever. Peeling off her cloak, she arranged it on the ground, bunching it into the shape of a five-year-old girl taking a nap. Then she moved into a crouching position. So far, so good. She took a slow, steady step backward. And then another, and another, carefully weaving her way in reverse between the trees, the same way the Huldrefólk in her mother's bedtime stories were said to travel so they could keep their tails hidden. But Anna didn't have a tail to hide. Instead, she was leaving a fresh trail of footprints in the snow— footprints that would always lead *away* from where she actually was.

"Elsa," she whispered, "you've won hide-and-find. Please come out."

But still there was no reply. The snow fell faster, so Anna moved faster, darting between trees, diving behind boulders, and all the while scanning the snowy woods for a sign of her sister—any sign. But there was not a footprint to be seen. It was as though her sister had been erased. As though . . . but the thought was too horrible for Anna to finish.

From somewhere nearby, the wolf howled.

Anna froze. She knew that sound. It was the same sound her father's hunting dogs made when they'd picked up the scent of a fox. The wolf howled again, but this time it was a little farther away. Anna's decoy had worked! She spun around and ran. The snow fell faster, the thick flakes clumping on her eyelashes and making it hard to see.

"Elsa!" The name ripped from her throat. "Elsaaaa! El—" She choked on the word.

There, standing in front of her, wasn't her sister, but the wolf.

Once more, its fierce yellow eyes were fixed right on her.

How had it gotten ahead of her? There was no time to think—only to run.

Anna pumped her legs, sending snow flying up around her. She couldn't stop. Her entire world was snow and fear and cold, and then suddenly—endless sky! Anna stumbled to a halt. She was at the edge of a cliff. An inky expanse of nothingness lay before her, but she knew whatever she found lurking behind her would be far worse.

*Hot breath.*

*Sharp claws.*

*Sharper teeth.*

"ELSA!" she yelled again.

But Elsa did not appear. If her sister wasn't here by now, something horrible *must* have happened. Pain seared itself across Anna's shoulder blades. She had hesitated for too long. The wolf's claws had connected with her back. Anna stumbled forward.

She plunged over the edge—

And woke up.

A cool, comforting hand was on her forehead, and as she blinked, Anna saw her mother's face sharpen into focus. The queen's blue-gray eyes shone with concern, and her chestnut brown hair cascaded down one shoulder, loose from its usual upsweep of braids and bangs. A large burgundy scarf, stitched with a multitude of snowflakes and complete with purple fringe, had been thrown over her shoulders and was covering up a lavender nightgown.

Anna shot up. "Where's Elsa? Did the wolf get her?"

"Anna, it's all right." Her mother sat and wrapped an arm around her. "All is well."

"There was snow," Anna said, her heart still pounding. "And trees! I was running, and then . . . I slipped!" She struggled to sit up against her pillows. "Elsa was there, and then she wasn't. I was so worried!"

Her father strode forward with a tray bearing mugs of hot chocolate. "You had a bad dream," he said. His ruddy blond hair, usually brushed back neatly, was tousled, as if he'd just come in from a midnight ride. For some reason, he was wearing his navy-blue uniform resplendent with badges and golden epaulets instead of a nightshirt. Bending, he placed the tray on the bedside table. "Elsa is in her room, asleep, as we all should be at this hour."

But that didn't seem quite right. The last thing Anna remembered was being awake in this same bed, watching the dancing sky through her window, wanting to wake Elsa up to . . . do something. But what? Anna squinted her eyes, trying to remember through the pounding in her head. Odd. That's all she *could* remember. The only thing after that was the outline of her nightmare: a mountain, a wolf, and bitter cold.

Her father settled next to her mother and handed

a warm mug to Anna. "Drink up," he said. The steam uncurled from the mug, moving with the same effortless grace as the wolf.

Anna shivered, still a bit shaken, but she had never said no to hot chocolate. She took a sip, and as the liquid slipped down to her belly, it warmed her stomach.

Her mother patted her knee. "You know, when I have a bad dream, I always imagine crumpling up the nightmare and tossing it out the window so that Frigg has something else to fish for besides the moon and the sun. You remember the old story I used to tell you about Frigg the Fisherman, right?"

Anna did, but she shook her head. She wanted her mother to keep talking. She leaned back as her mother began the tale of the boastful fisherman who kept casting his nets for bigger prizes and accidentally found himself stuck in a nighttime ocean of stars. Anna soaked in the comforting presence of her mother, who always smelled like calming lavender.

The memory of the nightmare faded, replaced by what was real: her cozy bedroom decorated with pink wallpaper, thick ornate rugs, an oval painting of Arendelle Castle that she loved to admire, a tapestry of queens, and flickering candles in the sconces on the walls. Though no flames burned in the fireplace, a few embers still glowed like dropped jewels. And her parents there beside her were the coziest details of all. Anna's eyes grew heavy.

"Feeling better?" her father whispered when her mother finished her tale.

Anna nodded, and he smiled.

"Everything is always better with hot chocolate," he said.

"We should wake Elsa up." Anna's eyes fluttered as she held up her empty mug. "She'd like this."

She almost missed her mother and father exchange a fleeting glance at her words. There was a shift in the room, as if a cloud had drifted past the window.

"Elsa needs her sleep," her mother said. "And you should try to get some rest, too. Agnarr, can you please hand me that extra pillow?"

Anna's father stood and walked over to the white-painted chair that had been dragged from its place by the wall and now stood between Anna and the fireplace. Another pillow and a crumpled pile of blankets lay on the floor around it, as if it were a makeshift bed.

Anna looked from the floor to her parents. They only stayed in her room if she was really ill. . . . "Were you sleeping in here?" Anna asked. "Am I sick?"

"You're just fine," her father said with a soft smile. Picking up the pillow, he placed it under Anna's head while her mother tucked the blankets tight. Anna wiggled her toes to loosen the covers just a bit as her parents extinguished the lights and headed for the door.

"Sweet dreams, Anna," her mother whispered from the doorway, the light from the hallway outlining her and Anna's father.

"Sweet dreams . . ." Anna murmured back, sinking deeper into her pillow.

The patch of light grew smaller and smaller, until, at last, it vanished as the door clicked shut. Anna listened to the sound of her parents' footsteps recede before she turned her cheek to stare out her window.

The sky was asleep now, the ribbons of color from the northern lights tucked beneath a patchwork quilt of clouds. But the moon stayed bright. It glared down at her like one of the wolf's yellow eyes. Watching. And waiting. But for what?

Cold again, Anna pulled the covers over her head, but sleep never came.

*Sixteen Years Later . . .*

# Chapter One

ANNA FLEW DOWN the carpeted castle stairs of the second great hall, taking them two at a time.

She nearly tripped on the landing, but she didn't bother to slow down. The clock tower had already tolled ten in the morning, and she'd *promised* Elsa she wouldn't be late. For a second, she thought about sliding down the banister. It really was the fastest way to get around, but at twenty-one she was too old for such things . . . right? Right. But . . .

Anna's feet slowed. The white wood of the banister gleamed with a recent polish and the promise of speed. And her new riding boots with heels—a gift from a dignitary from Zaria—hadn't been broken in yet and weren't exactly the best for running. She glanced over her shoulder. No one was around. Decision made, she hauled the skirt of her dress into her arms, slung a leg over the banister, and slid the rest of the way down, landing with ease as she reached the first-floor landing. She flew through the castle doors and raced outside, toward the stables.

"Elsa! I'm here!" Anna whisper-called as she moved through the barn doors and entered the quiet world of sweet hay and softly munching horses. She smoothed down the back of her black dress and checked to make sure that her long chestnut brown hair was still pinned in place by a double braid. "I'm not late! Well," she amended, "not *that* late. But I was having the most fascinating dream where . . ." She trailed off, and looked around.

Her only audience was the alert ears of the castle horses and the litter of barn kittens that came stumbling toward the stables' entrance whenever someone entered. But there was no sign of Elsa. Anna brushed her bangs off her forehead, confused. Somehow, even though she'd overslept, she had managed to beat Elsa. Which was odd. Very, very odd. Elsa was *always* on time; it was one of the many reasons she was such a great queen, beloved by all of Arendelle.

Picking up a purring gray kitten that had begun to bat at her bootlaces, Anna took a step toward the livery. Maybe Elsa had gotten here *so* early that she'd decided to inspect the recent delivery of apples. Careful to keep her voice low so as not to startle the horses, Anna called out again. "Elsa?"

"You're looking in the wrong place," a friendly voice called from the far end of the stables, and a second later, Kristoff Bjorgman's head popped over a stall door, a pitchfork in his hand and a bit of straw in his hair.

Anna grinned. She always did whenever she was around Kristoff—she couldn't help it. When Kristoff had first started to visit the castle frequently three years before, Gerda, one of the people who had known the girls since they were young, and who also helped them schedule their time, had remarked to the sisters that he resembled the mountains from which he harvested ice: broad and solid. Elsa had whispered back that he seemed "nice." When Anna had pushed her for a little bit more, Elsa had added "blond." All of which was true, but to Anna, Kristoff wasn't just a mountain man or "nice" or "blond," he was her best friend—and definitely something *more*, even if he did sometimes smell like a reindeer. Which was completely understandable, given his other best friend, Sven, *was* a reindeer.

Sven's head popped over the stall door to look at Anna, and he twitched his ears in a friendly hello. Though Anna had invited both Sven and Kristoff multiple times to take up residence in one of the many spare rooms of the castle, they both preferred to stay in the stables. Anna suspected they enjoyed the less confined living space of the barn after spending the summer months in the mountains harvesting ice for the kingdom.

"She's not here?" Anna asked, bending to set the kitten down gently. It scampered away to join the others.

Kristoff moved his hand under Sven's lower lip and began to wiggle it as he said in Sven's voice, "Someone's not *listening.*"

Anna smiled at Kristoff's "Sven Talk"—he was always dialoguing for his reindeer friend. It was silly, but she loved it, and so she took "Sven's" advice and listened to her surroundings. At first, all she could make out was the occasional swish of a horse's tail flicking flies away and the mewling of the kittens tumbling around one of the water troughs, but eventually, beneath the usual sounds, she heard an odd buzz that sounded like . . .

"Oh!" Anna's eyes widened and she hurried to the far end of the stables, where there was a little window. Peering through it, she saw just what she had suspected: a small crowd of villagers gathered in the courtyard. And though Anna couldn't see exactly *what* they were surrounding, she knew exactly *who* it would be: Elsa.

Wherever Elsa went, people seemed to follow. They were there in the morning, asking her questions about what should be done in the afternoon, asking what they should be doing in the evening, asking what they should do tomorrow. Elsa's table in the council chambers was always heaped with papers, and more often than not, Anna only caught a glimpse of her sister as Gerda ushered her from one appointment to another, always tapping the comically large calendar like a metronome to keep Elsa on the day's beat.

And Elsa's frantic schedule had only gotten busier over the last month, because at the end of this week, she would at last follow the tradition started by their grandfather King Runeard: setting off on a grand tour of the world. In five days, Elsa would leave from the Arenfjord, the body of water on which Arendelle was built, sailing past Weselton and the Southern Isles before heading east to explore lands like Zaria, Royaume, Chatho, Tikaani, Eldora, Torres, and Corona, to name a few. Elsa would meet *everyone*: dignitaries and dancers, scientists, painters, and prized mountain goats. And she would be going without Anna.

When Kai, the castle's old steward, had first mentioned it was time for Elsa to start planning for her grand tour, Anna had assumed she would be going with her older sister. But as the months dwindled down to weeks and then to days, Elsa still hadn't invited her. And it wasn't as though Anna hadn't given Elsa plenty of chances to ask her. Only last week, Anna had oh-so-casually mentioned that it had always been a dream of hers to see the Chathoan ballet—and she'd said so in Chathoanese. She'd spent days perfecting her accent. Before that, she'd performed Tikaani's national anthem for everyone at the castle, with an accompaniment by Olaf, the snowman whom Elsa had created three years ago with her magical ice powers, on a carrot-nose flute.

So far, though, none of Anna's efforts had worked.

But that was going to change today.

Or so she had planned.

Still peering through the window, Anna frowned as even more villagers in brightly colored shawls and jackets entered through the castle gates and hurried to join the crowd around Elsa.

Anna had been racking her mind all week and had finally decided that the perfect time would be *this* morning, during their last scheduled sisterly ride through the woods before Elsa's departure. Anna knew that Elsa found the quiet of the forest peaceful, and she hoped that it would lead to the perfect moment to ask Elsa if she could go on the grand tour with her. A ride was also a good opportunity to prove that Anna could be a useful traveling companion. That she was helpful and wouldn't get in the way. But that was part of the trouble. Elsa didn't seem to need any help.

Though Elsa had only been crowned queen three years before, Anna already knew her older sister would be remembered as one of the great rulers of Arendelle, like the ones who appeared on the tapestry that hung across from Anna's bed. Her sister appeared to always have everything under control—even her magical powers—with a regal presence that all respected. Whenever Elsa listened to Anna, she made Anna feel special and important, and at twenty-four years old, Elsa carried herself the same way she seemed to do everything: effortlessly.

"It's been like that since she got here," Kristoff said, coming to stand next to Anna and look out the stables' window. "Which," he said, giving her a teasing look, "was half an hour ago."

Anna made a face. "I know, I know—I overslept . . . again." She needed to find some way to pull Elsa out of the crowd for their horseback ride. Before Elsa left her.

Something tugged on Anna's foot, and she looked down to see that the tiny gray kitten had returned, determined, it seemed, to catch those devious laces.

"Hey, Kristoff?" Anna said slowly, still watching the persistent kitten, only the size her palm, take on her large boot. "I think I have an idea. Do you have a minute?"

"For you?" Kristoff winked. "Always."

Anna grinned as she wrenched the kitten off her laces and placed it into Kristoff's arms. "Perfect! So, here's the plan. . . ."

A few minutes later, Anna left the stables and hurried out to the friendly crowd in the courtyard. As she got closer, she could hear their questions piling up all around Elsa.

"Your Majesty, the chimney in our forge has cracks, and I'm worried it won't be mended in time for the winter," called Ada Diaz, a woman with curly brown hair standing next to her wife, Tuva Diaz, who had even curlier brown hair. They were the best blacksmiths on the continent and were known for making the luckiest horseshoes, though it seemed even an abundance of lucky horseshoes weren't as helpful as their queen's collected wisdom.

"I was here first," another familiar-looking villager sniped at Ada before turning in Elsa's direction and bowing. "Your Majesty, you promised that the rocks in my garden would be removed by the beginning of autumn, and look—" He held up a red oak leaf. "It's autumn!"

"Ah-hem," yet another said. "The *Village Crown* is waiting for you to announce who the judges will be for the harvest festival this year, Your Majesty. Do you have the names?" Though Anna couldn't see this particular person in the crowd, she knew, just by hearing his voice and grating, know-it-all cough, that it was Wael, the self-proclaimed reporter for the village, whose slick black hair always matched his ink-stained hands.

Sidling toward Elsa, Anna counted down silently. *Three . . . two . . . one . . .* Then she signaled for Kristoff.

"Oh, my goodness, Sven!" Kristoff proclaimed loudly from the stables' entrance. "Look at these adorable kittens!"

"They're cuter than you!" he said in Sven's voice.

And during the brief second that everyone in the crowd turned to look at the kittens frolicking in the far corner of the courtyard, Anna darted into the throng, grabbed Elsa's hand, and pulled her around the back of the stables and inside.

"Anna!" Elsa gasped as they ducked around a corner, where the fully saddled Havski and Fjøra, the swiftest horses in the stables, stood waiting for them. "What are you doing?"

Anna grinned. "Breaking you free!"

"But . . ." Elsa protested, sweeping a loose tendril of ice-blond hair off her forehead, "the villagers, they need my help—"

"I know!" Anna nodded. "But Kai and Gerda can

handle their requests, and it's important for you to ride out one last time before you set sail—just to make sure everything is in order. Don't you agree? Besides," she added, beaming even wider, "don't you *want* to spend some time with me?"

Even though she'd been handling complaints all morning, Elsa still seemed regal and calm. The wind blew though an open door and buffeted her diaphanous blue split cape and coat, and tugged at the fishtail braid hanging over her left shoulder. For a moment, she looked like a timeless, valiant queen from one of Anna's history books. But the next second, she flashed a grin at Anna, and it was like it had been before—when they were just two children sneaking out of their bedrooms for a nighttime adventure.

"I suppose I could let Kai and Gerda take care of things—just this once," Elsa said.

Anna let out a whoop of joy. She swung up onto Havski's back while Elsa took a moment to clamber on top of Fjøra, a beautiful horse with a black-and-white striped tail. Finally, after a few attempts, Elsa mounted. Together, they trotted out of the stables and left the courtyard, with Anna waving to Kristoff, who smiled from under a pile of kittens batting at his face.

The sisters crossed the Bridge of Arches and took in the wild, fresh autumn air. Behind them, nestled in the shadow of soaring mountains, the castle sparkled and shone with the decorative touches of Elsa's ice magic. Anna kicked her horse into a canter, and Elsa did the same.

Arendelle was a kingdom of wilderness, of rugged coasts, deep blue waters, and towering ships. Lots and lots of ships. They came from everywhere, bringing people from all over the world who were happy to settle down in the picturesque kingdom—people who were happy to answer Anna's invitation to share memories of their own countries so she could learn about their customs. Memories that could help Anna prepare Elsa for the grand tour . . . if only Elsa would let her. Because while ships brought people to the kingdom, they also left with people. The royal ship currently sat in the harbor, loaded with goods and waiting for Elsa to board.

As they rode past the expanding village and people waving excitedly at them, a delighted fizziness filled Anna's body. This was the *best* part of opening the kingdom gates three years ago—all the new people and new ideas that had trickled in. Although the village was more populous than ever before, with more and more people having moved there, Arendelle would always be Anna's heart and home. That was one thing that would never change.

As they moved beyond the houses and shops, the forest of Arendelle flourished around them, showing off in bright yellows, deep reds, and burnt oranges that reminded Anna of bonfires and melted caramels. A happy sigh slipped from Anna. The autumn leaves had just begun to turn and change, and the living things of the forest seemed to be settling into themselves, the same way Elsa had settled into being queen. Anna didn't particularly like change. She always wanted things to stay the same. These days, Anna barely got to see Elsa, who was constantly cooped up in the council chambers poring over paperwork, or else leading important meetings that Anna also attended. But she was happy watching Elsa come into her own, even if it meant their relationship was evolving as a side effect of it.

The horses slowed, picking up an easy trot side by side. Wondering if *now* was the moment, Anna glanced over at Elsa. Her sister wore a far-off and pensive look on her face.

"What are you thinking about?" Anna asked.

"Oh." Elsa looked up from her reins. "Nothing . . . just, you know, work."

"Want to tell me?" Anna said, trying to keep her eagerness down to about a level eight, instead of her usual level ten. "You remember what Father always said, right?"

Elsa tilted her head. "What, that 'burdens should be shared'?"

Something scraped in Anna, like a rough crumb caught in her throat. Because . . . well, her family's burdens and secrets *hadn't* been for everyone. Or at least, they hadn't been for Anna. Her father had let a mountain troll bundle away Anna's memories of Elsa's ice magic, and he, her mother, and Elsa had all worked together to keep it a secret from Anna.

And it had stayed a very, *very* big secret, until Elsa's coronation day, when Anna had pushed the new queen a little too far and Elsa had lost control of her temper—and her ice powers. Which, at the time, had seemed as terrible as the vast and eternal winter that had taken root in the kingdom, but in hindsight had been the best thing to ever happen to Anna. Not only had it marked the beginning of a new era with her sister, but Anna had also narrowly managed to avoid a very . . . *hasty* . . . marriage with a prince who had deceived her.

"Nope! Not that one!" Anna shook her head, wishing she could shake away the uncomfortable feeling. "The *other* saying—the one about 'many hands make light work.'"

"Oh." Elsa laughed. "He had a lot of sayings, didn't he?"

Anna waited for Elsa to keep talking, but she seemed to have forgotten Anna was there again even though she was trotting alongside her.

"Hey, Elsa?" she tried again.

"Hmm?"

"Bet I can beat you to the clearing!"

"What?"

But Anna had already kicked Havski back into a gallop. Havski surged forward, setting Anna's heart free. Riding the gray horse was like riding an avalanche: fast, thrilling, and powerful. Adrenaline rushed through her, and without thinking, she let go of the reins.

"What are you doing?" Elsa shouted from behind her.

"Flying!" Anna shouted back. She flung out her arms. Cool wind flowed over her face, and it seemed to blow away that tight feeling that had settled on her chest since Elsa had announced she was leaving. Elsa yelled something, but the wind swept her words away.

"What?" Anna glanced over her shoulder.

"BRANCH!" Elsa yelled again.

Anna swung forward just in time to duck beneath a birch tree's low-hanging branch. Giggling, she hugged Havski's neck and the horse snorted in response, never missing a stride. And why should he? They'd grown up together, and for a long time, he'd been the closest thing Anna had had to a best friend. They'd dodged thicker branches and jumped across wider rivers together. Picking up the reins again, she kept them loose and let Havski settle into a breathless canter.

Gradually, his strides shortened and he transitioned into an easy trot before reaching a mossy clearing. There was a crunch and the sound of twigs snapping, and Anna twisted in her saddle just in time to see Elsa and Fjøra blunder into the clearing. A single scarlet leaf had snagged on Elsa's hair, and it looked almost as though the forest had crowned her its autumn queen.

Anna grinned. "Isn't this fun?"

Sweeping away loose strands of her blond hair, Elsa plucked the leaf off her head, looked at it, and began to laugh. "It is," she agreed.

Anna felt like a miniature sun had ignited in her chest.

Eventually, they neared the tamed, bountiful farmlands, and Anna, sneaking glances at Elsa, saw that her sister had finally settled into her saddle and was looking around the landscape with curious eyes. She seemed at ease. She seemed relaxed. Maybe it was time for Anna to finally ask her burning question. As they turned left, they passed a beautiful orchard with bright red apples and autumn leaves so orange that the world looked like it had been set aflame. *Apples. Perfect.*

Anna pointed at them. "Did you know that there's an apple on the royal flag of Zaria?" she said oh-so-casually. "And that's because it's always customary for a guest to present an apple to the host." A worry pricked Anna's thoughts. "Your ship *does* have apples on board, right?"

Elsa shook her head. "Yes, Anna—you've made sure of it! If I have any more barrels of gifts you've suggested for everyone, my ship will be too heavy to leave the harbor!"

Anna swept her bangs out of her eyes and laughed. "What would you do without me?" She tugged on the reins, gently pulling Havski to a halt. "Elsa, I wanted to ask you something. I was wondering if I could join—" But before she could finish, Havski's ears flattened as a rustling came from nearby.

A villager burst from the underbrush, panting heavily as she lifted her green skirts high so she could run.

It took Anna a moment to place her—there were so many new villagers in Arendelle these days—but then she recognized SoYun Lim, a girl Anna's own age who'd recently started to herd cattle on a farm not far from there. Anna had talked to her over the summer, during one of the castle's hosted bonfire nights, and had asked her about her native country of Chatho. Research, of course, for the grand tour. In fact, SoYun had been the one to help Anna perfect her Chathoanese accent.

But that girl always seemed as calm as a lake on a windless morning, her quiet nature soothing the animals she tended. The girl standing in front of her now was disheveled. Her jet-black braid, which usually hung as straight and tidy as a clothesline, was a series of escaping loops, and she had on two different boots—the left foot was clad in a tall black boot, while the right foot wore a soft brown leather one. But it wasn't the strange state of her clothes or hair that sent warning bells tolling through Anna. It was the girl's expression—wide-eyed, as though she'd seen a ghost—and the frantic way in which she flailed her arms to catch their attention.

"Your Majesty!" SoYun bobbed her head toward Elsa in a slight bow. "Thank goodness I caught up with you—something *terrible* has happened!"

# Chapter Two

"SOYUN! WHAT'S WRONG?" Anna swung off Havski, landing in a pile of leaves before hurrying toward her.

"It's my cattle," SoYun said, looking from Elsa, who was cautiously dismounting from Fjøra, to Anna. "They're—oh!" SoYun shook her head. "I don't even know where to begin!" Tears formed in her eyes.

Anna opened her mouth to respond, but stopped herself to give Elsa a chance.

Elsa stepped a little closer. "How about if you take us to your cattle, and you can tell us all about it on the way? Say whatever comes first, and we'll piece it together, all right?"

SoYun blew her nose, then nodded. "I'm just up that way," she said, and broke into such a fast walk that it almost could have been a jog. Holding on to the horses' reins, the sisters followed, trying to catch SoYun's story as she told it.

"It started a few days ago," SoYun said, her voice ragged, "when I tried to call the cattle in—you know how it usually works like a charm."

Anna did. Calling cattle was an old Arendellian custom of singing high notes to summon the animals home. Much practice and control was required in order to do it properly, as it was so much more than a simple call. It was a fairy-like sound. A sound that raised the hair on the back of Anna's neck and let her know—really, truly, deeply *know*—for one single instant that any difference between her and the earth and wind and sky was only an illusion. SoYun was now one of the best cattle callers in the village. She never had any trouble. In fact, when the cows wouldn't come home, people always went to SoYun for help.

"And so, I went out into the fields," SoYun continued, "and tried to sing them home. But . . ." Her shoulders slumped. "They never came. Not even when I pulled out my bukkehorn. I went out looking, and when I finally found them . . ." SoYun's voice broke off.

"What happened?" Elsa pressed as they cleared a copse of maple trees and entered into a meadow nestled at the foothill of a blue mountain, where Anna could just make out a neat farmhouse among even neater rows of golden fields, and a herd of cattle circled around a large white boulder.

"*This* is what happened." SoYun led them forward. As they got closer to the herd, Anna realized the cows weren't ringing a white boulder after all, but a sleeping bull.

"That's Hebert," SoYun said. "The leader of my herd."

*Hebert.* The name struck a familiar chord in Anna, and she remembered that a year before, during the harvest festival best-in-show competition, a large energetic bull with that name had won first place. But that bull's hide had been as black as a raven's wing, while this one was entirely white.

SoYun took a shuddery breath. "A few days ago, I noticed he had a sprinkle of white hairs, which wasn't too strange. He's getting up there in age. But then, the next morning, the white increased pretty dramatically, until he was as you see him now."

Elsa raised her eyebrows, as if to say, *That's it? Some white hair?*

But Anna remembered when a lock of her own hair had turned white as a result of an accidental strike from Elsa's ice magic when they were children.

SoYun tugged on the end of her long braid and bit her bottom lip. "But I wouldn't have bothered you just because of that, Your Majesty. There's . . . there's more."

"Like . . . ?" Anna didn't take her eyes off the figure of the sleeping bull, his great horns curved up to the sky in twin points.

"He'd been acting funny for a few days, too—at first it seemed like he was scared of something he couldn't see, like a draug," SoYun said, referencing a terrifying mythological zombie Anna had heard spoken of around castle bonfires. "And then," SoYun continued, "he ran around the field until he broke into a panicked sweat, which seemed to turn his fur white. And finally, his pupils grew wide, *huge*, until his eyes were completely swallowed by inky black." SoYun made her eyes wide as she looked at them. "And then he started groaning like he was in horrible pain, and fell down, until, at last, he slept."

Anna exchanged a confused look with Elsa. Anna didn't usually think of sleep as a *bad* thing. In fact, the more sleep she got, the better.

Elsa's eyebrow quirked again. "Slept?" she asked.

"Yes," SoYun nodded vigorously. "But not a *usual* sleep. A *deep* sleep. No matter what we do—yell, shake him, splash water on him—he won't wake up. It's been days. Which means he also hasn't been eating."

Now that SoYun had mentioned it, Anna could see the bull's ribs jutting from its sides, the white fur making it far too easy to imagine him as a pile of bones bleached by the sun. Anna wrapped her fingers in Havski's long silky mane—she didn't know what she would do if something like that happened to him. At the same time, any thoughts Anna had about a connection between her once-white streak of hair and the blanched bull fell away. After all, when Elsa had turned her hair white, Anna had been in danger of turning to ice, not falling asleep.

SoYun looked from the bull to the girls, and a tear rolled down her cheek. "He's fading away right in front of us—and the other cattle are showing similar symptoms, too!" SoYun gestured to a sweet-looking cow with long lashes, and eyes that moved back and forth like the pendulum in a grandfather clock. It was as if the cow was tracking something that wasn't there. Or rather, tracking something invisible that only the cow could see.

"What if," SoYun continued, "they *all* fall into the deep sleep, and then . . ." The fear in the girl's voice was tangible and sharp.

Anna reached out and hugged her close. "They'll be okay," Anna said. "Don't worry. We'll find a way to help, won't we, Elsa?"

Elsa reached out and patted SoYun's shoulder a few times. "Yes. You did exactly right by coming to tell me."

*Me.* That small word echoed through Anna's whole body. There had been a time, she was sure, when Elsa would have said *us.*

Anna spun to Elsa. "I have an idea," she whispered. "We should visit the trolls." Though only as tall as Anna's waist and covered in moss, the tiny mountain trolls were the most powerful creatures Anna knew. Grand Pabbie, the oldest and arguably the wisest troll, would sometimes use the aurora's glow to show glimpses of what might be or, occasionally, to deal with all matters that could involve magic. If anyone could help SoYun and her cattle, Anna knew it was the trolls. Because as she had learned, when mysterious happenings occurred that raised questions, it was best to visit mystical creatures for answers.

Elsa smiled. "That's a great idea, but I think we may only have time to look in the castle library. Why don't we try that first? Remember what Father used to say."

Anna scrunched up her face, trying to remember which of Father's many sayings Elsa could be referring to. "'Anna and Elsa, always lean on each other for help'?" she guessed.

A slight smile appeared on Elsa's lips, though it was tinged with sadness. "He did say that. But he also said, 'The past has a way of returning.' We should find out if this has happened before, and at the very least, gather information that might be of use for the trolls."

Elsa made an excellent point, and Anna was suddenly excited to check the library together. Both sisters enjoyed curling up with a good storybook there, but the library also held books about the histories of the kingdom, the royal family, and the townspeople. If any place in the castle had answers, it would be there.

"Does anything help with the symptoms?" Elsa asked SoYun.

SoYun, who'd knelt down to stroke Hebert's nose, glanced up. "Mint seems to help them stay alert. The smell is sharp for their noses, but it doesn't last for long."

"Mint," Elsa repeated. "I'll make sure to write that down in the report. Remind me, Anna, won't you?" After making sure they had taken in all there was to know regarding the symptoms, they bade their farewells to SoYun, Hebert, and the rest of the cattle.

As Anna hauled herself onto Havski, she called back, "Don't worry, SoYun! We'll fix this. I promise."

Anna and Elsa spent the rest of the afternoon in the castle library. So far, absolutely nothing mentioned sick cattle ever falling into seemingly endless sleeps in all of Arendelle's history. Which meant that there were no suggestions for a cure for the Blight, as Elsa had decided to call the sleeping sickness.

Elsa sat in the window seat, flipping through a book, while Anna sprawled out on the couch in front of the fire, lifting a book overhead to read. A sharp knock resounded throughout the library, followed by

Kai's urgent voice. "Your Majesty, are you in there?"

"I'm here, Kai!" Elsa called.

The ornate door slammed open, and the usually calm man entered looking flustered, his scarf undone instead of knotted neatly at his neck and his ruddy eyebrows knitted together. Anna's heart sped up. As steward of the castle, Kai was a man of decorum and protocol. He *always* bowed when he greeted them, no matter how many times the sisters had begged him to stop. But not now.

"What's wrong, Kai?" Elsa stood up from the window alcove and hurried toward him as Anna set down her book and bolted up from the couch.

"Grave news," Kai gasped out, sounding as though he'd run to get there. "The Westens' entire herd of goats have seemingly dropped down in the middle of the field, and they simply won't wake up. The family is asking for you to come quickly, Your Majesty."

Dread crept over Anna, and she turned to Elsa. "Do you think . . . ?"

Elsa nodded. "It's certainly possible. But we still haven't found an answer." She looked from the tall piles of books to the high, full bookcases, then back at Kai, clearly torn about what she should do next.

"You should go," Anna urged her. "Just to make sure it's the same thing."

Elsa tugged at her fingers, a habit Anna knew was left over from the days when Elsa always wore silk gloves to repress her powers. Anna reached out to rest a hand on Elsa's forearm. Startled, Elsa looked down and, realizing what she had been doing, gave Anna a small smile as if to thank her. She folded her hands neatly in front of her.

"If you're worried," Anna said, "we should divide and conquer. Send Kristoff and Sven to the trolls, since we haven't found anything useful, and I'll stay here to keep looking for answers. I can handle it."

Still, Elsa hesitated, and Anna wondered why. Did Elsa not like her recommendation? Or did Elsa not trust her to handle this job? But at last, Elsa nodded, and relief settled over Anna as her sister said, "That's a good idea. I'll let Kristoff know before I go, but I promise I'll come right back." And with that, Elsa hurried out after Kai, leaving Anna to search for solutions on her own.

Hours passed, and the wax from the candles cascaded onto the table in little pools, but Anna hardly noticed—she kept bouncing from book to book, trying to find answers . . . and failing. A gentle breeze twirled in from the open window, sending many of the open books' pages fluttering, as well as scattering a sprinkle of goosebumps across Anna's arm and stirring up the ash in the fireplace. Soon, that very same breeze would be filling Elsa's sails to take her far, far away.

Travel by ship made Anna nervous. Seven years had passed since their parents had set out on a voyage to the Southern Sea that had been meant to last only two weeks, but had turned into forever. The days following the news had been the darkest of Anna's life, and the nights had been worse. Sleep had been impossible. The insides of her eyelids were the color of the fathomless waves that she imagined took her parents. Sometimes, even now, her parents' absence would startle her all over again, fresh and sudden as a bee sting. But as the years went by, the pain had become less immediate, old childhood nightmares faded, and she could remember her parents—her mother's loving lullabies, her father's teasing humor and tall tales—with joy.

Her reunion with Elsa had helped. When Elsa had shut herself away as a little girl, Anna was left with only her own memories of their parents. But since Elsa's bedroom door had opened, Anna's collection of stories about their parents had multiplied. And while the stories didn't fill the hole in her heart, they did help smooth out the jagged edges.

She may not have her parents anymore, but she had her sister, and that was enough. Enough to make her wish Elsa wasn't leaving her behind. She would be leaving her . . . *unless* Anna could prove her worth. Unless she could prove she was more than just the silly little girl who had talked to the portraits in the gallery and said yes to an offer of marriage to the evil (and thankfully now exiled) Prince Hans after less than twenty-four hours of knowing him. Anna knew Elsa valued her despite those things, but she still felt lingering insecurity.

Anna glanced at the stone statue of the horse that stood in the corner of the library as if it would have the answers they needed. But all it had were delicate stone seashells and starfish carved into its mane, and an angry expression on its face. It was an old statue, and Anna had been afraid of its bared teeth, its two front hooves furiously out in the air, and its blank eyes. Once, when she was four, she'd used up all of her mother's cosmetics trying to make the horse look happier before her mother had discovered her and carried her out of the room, warning her not to touch the statue again. Young Anna was always being told not to touch things, like guitar strings, and oil paintings, and her father's swords, and . . .

"Wow, what happened in here?"

Anna startled at the sound of the voice. Dragging her eyes away from the statue, she looked up to see the round shape of Olaf standing in the doorway.

As children, Elsa and Anna had made up stories about a snowman named Olaf with branches for arms and a carrot for a nose. Years later, on the day of Elsa's coronation, Elsa had accidentally lost control of her ice powers and brought Olaf to life. Since then, he'd become the castle's resident snowman and a member of the sisters' family. He used to have a snow flurry hovering over his head that prevented him from melting, but since Elsa's powers had grown and changed, she was able to do away with it and instead enchant him with a permafrost that served the same purpose. Now, Olaf's eyes widened as he took in the library. Or rather, the *mess* in the library.

"It's easier for me if I sort things into piles," Anna explained, following his gaze to the towers of books scattered across the floor. She hadn't realized how . . .

*enthusiastic* she'd been when she'd pulled titles. There might actually have been more books on the floor than there were left on the shelves. It certainly wasn't Elsa's neat and methodical system, judging by the volumes Elsa had left standing in perfect stacks in the window alcove.

Olaf nodded. "That makes sense. When you build a snowman, you always have to start with piles. Unless you're Elsa, of course." He pointed. "Which ones are those?"

"Books about sicknesses," Anna said. "The pile next to that is about animal anatomy, and the one next to that is about sleep." Each title was bursting with possibilities.

Olaf moved to the last pile, his twiggy hair just visible over the stack. "And this massive one?"

"That's my 'to be read' pile."

"Oooh, it's so much bigger than all the rest," he observed.

Anna shrugged. She had set aside these books as not currently useful but interesting enough that she wanted to check them out later. Poems were great because of their beautiful imagery and brevity, but she also loved the thick tomes of artists through the ages. And, of course, there were novels where people found true love, or undertook a dangerous quest, or were reunited with loved ones lost.

Anna rubbed her eyes and adjusted the skirt of her dress, which had begun to bunch around her uncomfortably. "Where have you been?" she asked.

Olaf wandered from pile to pile. "The village library, listening to a lecture on *Dante's Inferno*—the hotter the tale, the better."

Anna smiled. After her first birthday party following Elsa's eternal winter, Anna had taught Olaf how to read, and ever since, the snowman had become obsessed. He liked books of all sizes, but his favorites were the thick tomes on philosophy—and beach reads, which he so often insisted were just as important as the classics. Anna didn't disagree.

"So, why are you rearranging the library, anyway?" Olaf asked.

Taking a deep breath, Anna quickly explained about SoYun and her cattle and how Elsa was out now, checking on the Westens' goats.

"It seems that you could use some help," Olaf said, straightening a coal button. "And in the wise words of many a philosopher, four eyeballs are better than three."

"Is that what they say?" Anna asked, resting her head on her palm.

Olaf whipped out his favorite pair of ice spectacles, specially made for him by Elsa. "Indeed," he said. "They also say to 'start at the beginning.' So, we'll start with the letter B, for *beginning*." He pointed, and Anna followed his scraggly finger to the middle shelf of the nearest bookshelf behind the horse statue.

"Sure," Anna said. "You look at that while I finish this one."

Olaf clambered onto a table beneath a portrait of King Agnarr's coronation, then jumped onto the stone horse's back. Carefully, he shimmied onto one of the rearing legs and pulled himself up, wobbling precariously from side to side. "Almost . . ." he said, reaching out.

Anna could see he was struggling, so she leapt up and hurried over to him.

"Just a little bit further—whoops!" There was a click followed by a great grinding, like the sound of gears turning on each other, as the horse's rearing leg that Olaf stood on sank down like a lever. Dust swirled into the air, and Anna squeezed her eyes shut, turning her head away to avoid swallowing any more of the grime. And then . . . everything was still.

Everything was silent.

"Wow," Olaf breathed. "Now that's something you don't see every day."

Anna's eyes flew open, and she gasped.

The bookcase behind the statue had swung inward like a door. No, not *like* a door. It was an *actual* door, opening to reveal an arched entryway and, beyond it, darkness. And maybe—just maybe—something that would hold answers and help Elsa figure out how to cure the Blight.

Squealing, Anna plunged into the secret room—and immediately crashed her shins against something. She winced. Whatever she'd hit was definitely going to leave a bruise. Why hadn't she thought to grab a candle? Turning to head back, she saw Olaf waddling toward her, a candle in his hand. He stopped in front of her, the flame casting a creamy orange glow across his concerned face.

He raised a skeptical eyebrow. "I thought you couldn't see in the dark."

"I can't," Anna said. "Do you mind sharing the light?"

"Nope!" Olaf handed it to her. "You'll need it to see that person standing right behind you."

# Chapter Three

ANNA WHIRLED AROUND, stifling a shout.

But as she held up the candle, she realized it wasn't a person at all, but a metal helmet expertly forged to create the illusion of a fearsome grimace and sharp teeth. It had thrown her off at first, out of sheer surprise and because it was different from the helmets that Arendellian soldiers wore. In fact, the more she looked at it, the more Anna was certain that this helmet came from the same era as Aren of Arendelle, from that long-ago age of heroes that was now more legend than history.

As she raised the candle higher, the sphere of light widened to reveal the rest of what they had found: a windowless room filled from flagstone floor to vaulted ceiling with sparkling shelves.

The shelves had been carved into the stone walls, and unlike the rest of the castle, these walls hadn't been papered or painted over or decorated with rosemaling. They were left bare, and the tiny crystals embedded in the rock seemed to wink a friendly greeting as the candle's light passed over them. It wasn't just the rock that glittered underneath a layer of dust, but also the many strange and wondrous objects that sat on the shelves: a gleaming pair of silver scales, schematics of what looked like a dam, glass beakers and bottles filled with fascinating specimens of flora and fauna suspended in brackish water.

And there were books. They spiraled upward into the rafters of the ceiling, the only surface that had been painted and resembled a sky alive with the northern lights along with familiar constellations: Ulf the Wolf, Frigg the Fisherman, and many others. There were wide books with thick leather spines, tall books with thin spines, books with yellow pages, books with ragged pages, squat books, medium-sized books, and tiny books no bigger than a thumb. Anna's mouth dropped open. No matter how different they looked, each book had the possibility of containing the answers that she so desperately needed.

Olaf teetered forward into the room. "Oooh, more books! *Secret* books!"

"Secret books . . ." Anna mused, and her initial excitement dimmed. She knew she should have been more excited at the discovery of the secret room, but something about the *secretness* of it all pinched, leaving her feeling slightly bruised. She slowly made her way to the shelves. She wondered who had used this room. Arendelle's royal family had lived in the castle for decades—ever since her grandfather King Runeard had overseen its construction when her father was just a boy. Perhaps this room had been a place of solace for a long-ago aunt or uncle.

Anna skimmed the titles. Some were written in languages that she didn't know but recognized from her research for the grand tour. Others were in indecipherable symbols. But the ones that she could read made her heart backflip: *Hulda's Hideout; Scrolls of Trolls; Of Nightmares and Nixies; Quests of Yore; Sorcerer's Craft and Games; Legends of Magic; Deciphering Magic . . .*

Magic. Anna's thoughts pulsed with the thump of her heart. Magic. Magic. *Magic!*

Magic was not *unknown* in Arendelle. After all, Elsa had magical abilities that no one in the kingdom had ever seen before. Or at least, no one alive had ever seen. In some of the old stories that were favorites of Queen Iduna's, magic abounded. She'd told tales about tablecloths that could produce banquet-sized feasts in the blink of an eye, and boots that could travel seven leagues in a single step—of shape-shifters who lived in an enchanted forest, and stones that could turn lead into gold . . . but those were made up. Make believe. Pretend.

However, in the last three years, Anna had seen incredible things, *impossible* things, come to be. A sister who could be one with the earth and sky and build ice palaces with a few breaths and some nimble flicks of her wrist. A queen who could harness the cold. If Elsa could exist, as Anna very much knew she did, then why couldn't other impossibilities exist as well?

Why couldn't there be a spell of sorts, or an enchantment, that could fix whatever was happening with the Blight? Sure, Anna was hoping to find something in this room to help with the problem at hand, but *after* that, who knew? Maybe there was knowledge somewhere in there that could stop horse-shoes from ever rusting, bread from ever going stale, or candles from ever melting down to stubs and going out. She'd be a hero.

"Aha." Anna pulled a thick volume from a shelf and plopped it down onto a bare worktable in the center of the room alongside the candle. "This one might have something helpful." She tapped at the title and read it out loud to Olaf. "'*The Alchemist's Almanac: A Guide to the Care and Keeping of Fields, Accurate Accounting of the Weather, and Wheat.*'"

Olaf looked down his pair of ice spectacles at Anna. "Not exactly my genre."

Anna smiled.

"Ooh, this one seems cryptic and dense!" Olaf said, tugging out another thick book. "Here! You might like it, too!" He held it up for Anna to see. Its cover was a beautiful brown with black lettering. The title wasn't written in an alphabet Anna recognized, but as she squinted at the book, a forgotten memory—more of an impression of sound and color, really—coalesced: The soft fabric of her mother's dress beneath her cheek as Anna snuggled into her lap. A warm pressure at her side—Elsa, who'd climbed up to join. Words, low and gentle and hazy as her mother read out loud from a book, its cover the color of Anna's new riding boots. Lullabies about secret white rivers and Earth Giants and lost legends of yore . . . Could it be?

Setting the almanac back on the shelf, Anna cracked open the new book and saw the title again written in runes. Someone had written next to them, in pencil, the words *Secrets of the Magic Makers.*

Anna's breath caught.

It was her mother's handwriting.

Anna would know it anywhere.

This book. This *room*: her mother had known about it; she had been here. These books and objects about magic were *hers.* Suddenly, Anna's chest felt too small for her heart. Or maybe her heart was too big for her chest. *Secrets.* This castle was full of secrets she had not known—was not *allowed* to know. Questions rattled through her: Why was Anna always shut out? Why had her mother collected all these books about magic? And . . . did Elsa already know about this room? Like when they were children, was Anna the last to know again?

"Anna?" She felt a gentle pat on her shoulder. "Don't judge a book by its cover."

At Olaf's words, Anna felt her ribcage loosen, just a tad, but it was enough that she could breathe again. Olaf had been the friend of both sisters; he was a little bit of Elsa and a little bit of Anna, created by them together. And looking around, Anna didn't think Elsa knew about this secret room. After all, Elsa had been so good about filling Anna in on everything she had missed during the time when her head had been under the troll's persuasion, when she'd been made to forget Elsa's magic even existed. Elsa didn't keep things from Anna, not anymore.

"I'm not, Olaf." Anna flung back a braid. "This book . . . it was my mother's."

"Oh." Olaf peered down through his spectacles. "Her reading selection appears to have been very *specific*. I'd rather check out this book." He waved a slender black volume in his hand. "It's about dangerous shape-shifters living in a cursed forest."

"Why don't you give it a read?" Anna asked. "Who knows—maybe it'll mention cursed animals, too."

"Holler if you need me!" Olaf plopped down at the worktable to page through it.

Meanwhile, Anna's eyes prickled. Her mother's

book. She flipped through the rest of the thick pages. The runes looked like meaningless constellations, but the translations next to them had been made by her mother, and she would follow her mother's footprints, or fingerprints, as they were, anywhere.

*Secrets of the Magic Makers* seemed to be a book of old tales, brief histories, and maps showing the way to the Valley of the Living Rock, but also a glossary of sorts, naming all kinds of creatures that only existed in lore. Spirits of wind, water, and fire. Earth Giants. Nattmara. Huldrefólk. They all sounded so familiar, but it was like Anna was trying to stare through a bedsheet hung out to dry. At some point in her life, she'd known what these bedtime-story words had meant in crystal-clear detail, but now she could not make out any more than the slightest shape. Sadness crept over her.

Mother would have known. Anna hadn't just lost her mother when the ship sank beneath the Southern Sea's waves. The world had lost Queen Iduna's stories and lullabies, and there was no way to recover them. Or was there? Anna kept turning the pages. There were too many emotions at war within her to settle on any one page, on any one definition. Faster and faster she flipped through the book until fragile pages slipped out and flitted to the floor.

Anna froze. As carefully as she could, she picked up the papers to realize with relief that they weren't pages from *Secrets of the Magic Makers* at all, but scraps of research that had not yet been bound in. One page displayed some familiar-looking blueprints: it was Arendelle Castle. Anna squinted at the page. She, like Gerda, already knew all the secret passages and places that were marked, except for one that drew her attention now and the one she was currently *in*.

Below the castle, something called the Earth Giant's Passage seemed to run from somewhere beneath the ice room next to the kitchen and then turn south, under the waters of Arenfjord, to . . . to somewhere. Anna couldn't tell. The black ink ran off the page, unfinished. But instructions had been printed in the margins. *Three flagstones in, two across.*

"*Fascinating,*" Anna whispered and set aside the blueprints. As soon as she found something to help the animals, she would *definitely* be taking a trip to the ice room. She shuffled to the next piece of paper. It was a map of Arendelle and the land that surrounded it. Markings circled a black sandy beach and a place called the Dark Sea, and scrawled across it in that same clean flourish that distinguished her mother's handwriting was one of her father's many sayings.

*The past has a way of returning.*

It was underlined twice, as if it meant something important. Anna squinted at the words, trying to make sense of them. But she was confused. The past *was* the past, so how could it ever come back? And why would her mother have written it on a map . . . a map that was stored in this particular book in this secret room? Was it supposed to mean something?

Anna yawned. Maybe the words didn't mean anything special at all. Most likely, she was only looking for meaning because she so badly wanted meaning to exist. And because she dearly missed her mother and, for a moment, had felt close to her again as she read her book. Or maybe it was because she was tired. So very, very tired.

Anna had no idea how much time had passed since she and Olaf had entered the secret room, and with no window, it was impossible to tell. Tucking the map back inside the tome, she looked up to find Olaf balancing on a dusty wooden chair as he pulled a snow globe from a shelf.

"Hey, look what I found!" Olaf called. "Snow that can exist in summer—just like me!" He plopped a kiss on the globe. "Hello, little pocket flurry." Giving it a shake, he sent the glittering snow swirling around a miniature of Arendelle Castle carved from a seashell. It was pretty, and Anna had definitely seen that snow globe before: not the actual snow globe, but a sketch of it in her father's sketchbook she still kept in a place of honor on her dressing table.

"I think my father also knew about this secret room," Anna said, "which means that there's only one family member who might not know about it yet." She snapped *Secrets of the Magic Makers* shut. "We have to go tell Elsa!"

"Tell me what?"

# Chapter Four

ELSA HAD RETURNED.

And though Anna knew her sister had been up since way before her, had held a meeting for the villagers, visited a farm, scoured the library, then visited another farm, she was still crisp and clean, her blond braid a streak of sunshine against the burgundy of their mother's cozy scarf, which was now wrapped around her shoulders. Elsa stood still, her mouth open, staring in what could only be called astonishment at Anna and Olaf inside the secret room.

"H-how? I mean, did you . . ." Elsa sputtered. "What *is* this place?"

Happiness and relief washed over Anna. From the expression on Elsa's face and the way her voice shook, Anna knew—the same way she knew that ice was cold and fire was hot—that Elsa had not known about this particular secret. For once, Anna had not been the last to know.

"We found a clandestine room," Olaf said. "*Clandestine* means secret. But I guess now it's not so clandestine. Unless you can keep a . . . what's the noun form of *clandestine*? Keep a *clandestiny*?" He still held the snow globe in his hands. "Do you mind if I show this to Sven?" And before the sisters could reply, he skipped out of the room.

"I don't know, exactly," Anna said in reply to Elsa's question. "But isn't it *wonderful*?" She gestured to the secret room's shelves and fought the urge to giggle as Elsa took a few steps into the room and looked around, her eyes wide, taking in the dried herbs, the gleaming copper spyglass, and the creamy swirl of what appeared to be a narwhal tusk. Elsa moved closer to the shelves.

"How did you *find* this place?" Elsa asked.

"Olaf," Anna said. She filled Elsa in on the items, the map, the notes, and the book she felt could hold the answers to their problems. At the mention of their parents having been in this room, Elsa gasped.

"And so," Anna concluded, "I bet we can find something in here about the Blight."

"I don't know about that," Elsa said. "But whatever is affecting SoYun's cows is also affecting the Westens' goats. I couldn't wake them up. I tried everything."

"I mean, look at this title!" Anna plucked the *Alchemist's Almanac* from the shelf and turned back to Elsa, but Elsa's attention seemed to have snagged elsewhere, onto an old golden frame that had been carefully leaning against a wall. The painting inside of it was muddied by grime, but Anna thought she could just make out a pair of eyes and a strong jaw: a portrait.

Picking it up, Elsa blew, and a puff of dust ballooned into the air, settling on Anna's face. Anna sneezed while Elsa held out the painting at arm's length and squinted. "I *think* this is supposed to be Aren of Arendelle. The painting is so dirty, though, it's hard to tell."

Anna placed the almanac back on the shelf and peered over Elsa's shoulder. "What makes you think it's Aren?"

Aren was a legendary leader from times of old—the

very, *very* old, before the last ice age, even. So old, in fact, that it was most likely the famous warrior had never even existed.

"See that?" Elsa pointed at a dark smudge. "I think that's supposed to be Revolute, his sword with a 'yellow diamond, bright as an eye.'"

Anna stared at her sister. "Are you . . . quoting something?"

"Yeah," Elsa admitted. "That's a line from the *Saga of Aren*, written by an unknown poet whom some claimed was actually Aren's true love."

It sounded kind of familiar to Anna. While she knew everything that there was to know about Arendelle, there were still *some* things, like these fine details, that she knew she'd *once* known but had forgotten. The things that she'd forgotten were usually stories her parents had shared. Embarrassment crept through her. She hated when she forgot things!

She tried to remember everything she could about Aren. There were endless stories and epic poems about his brave deeds—from helping the Huldrefólk hide their tails to journeying under the sea to sing with mermaids or questing to mountaintops to meet the sun. According to that particular story, Anna recalled, the sun had been so impressed with Aren that she'd given him a sword called the Revolute Blade. With the sun's sword in his hand, Aren had carved the fjord between the mountains. And not just any fjord, but *this* fjord: Arenfjord, the backbone of the kingdom of Arendelle.

"Is that the one that goes, 'Revolving moon and spinning sun, forged a crescent blade,' and . . . something, something, something, 'May the flags of Arendelle ever wave'?" Anna asked.

Elsa nodded. "Exactly." Anna's embarrassment subsided as Elsa pointed a little above the smudge to a blur. "I think that might be the yellow diamond in the pommel, and then there"—she moved her hand—"see how the blade curves? According to myth, the curve is where the sword first struck the earth. That's how the sword got its name. 'Revolute' means 'curved.'"

"Magic swords are nice and all," Anna said, tilting her head and fanning herself with her hand. It was getting hot in the windowless room. "But I don't really see why it would be helpful to be able to make cuts into the earth."

Elsa fiddled with her braid as she looked at the painting. "Apparently, the sun bestowed Revolute with great powers, and with the sword in his hand, Aren became known as the protector of the people, unifying them against a dark fright. He was a great leader." A strange expression settled on Elsa's face. "History seems to be *full* of great leaders."

Anna glanced at her sister. For some reason she did not quite understand, Elsa seemed to have left the room, even though she hadn't physically gone anywhere. She no longer looked at Anna. Instead, her gaze was fixed on a shelf full of books, bottles, and jars.

"Why were they studying magic? And why did they seal off the room and never tell us about it?" Elsa asked, her voice so soft that Anna wondered if she'd meant to say anything at all. Elsa stood there, with her back impossibly straight, standing the way a queen should. But at that exact moment, Anna didn't see Elsa, queen of Arendelle. She saw Elsa the lonely child, who'd spent her days alone in her room with only patterns of frost to keep her company.

Anna reached out to touch Elsa's arm. Her sister was stiff, as if she didn't just wield cold and snow, but were made of it. "I have the same question," Anna admitted, glad they were in this together. "But think about it: why do people study art?" she asked. "Why does Baker Blodget spend her entire life in pursuit of baking the best butter biscuits in the world? Why does Kristoff keep trying to sing?"

Elsa remained silent, so Anna answered for her, reaching down to pick up *Secrets of the Magic Makers.* "Because talents are worth exploring. Because butter biscuits are delicious, singing is fun, and your magic is beautiful, Elsa. Maybe they wanted to know more about it."

She slipped a hand in Elsa's, and waited. A few seconds later, Elsa squeezed her fingers, and Anna squeezed back. Without meeting Anna's eye, Elsa moved away from her and toward the exit.

"I need to go." Elsa's voice was quiet. "This place creeps me out."

"What do you mean?" Anna didn't think she had ever been in a more beautiful room with still so much to explore. The possibilities were endless!

"It's all these things in jars." Elsa waved her hands. "Contained and locked away."

"Well," Anna said, tucking *Secrets of the Magic Makers* under her arm, "maybe that just means it's time for them all to be brought to the light of day."

Excitement again rose within her. "The answers to how to stop the Blight could be in here! Maybe there's even more magic out there, magic that can actually help us!"

Elsa flinched.

"I—I didn't mean it like that," Anna said. "Your magic is really helpful. Just not in *this* situation."

Elsa took a step back. "I need to help the livestock before we can start really delving into this room, okay?" Elsa said. "There's no time to waste. I . . . I have to go."

"Of course. But—but *we* . . . I can stay here and keep looking for clues," Anna suggested. "We may be able to find the answers to what's happening to—"

Elsa shook her head. "I really think we should leave this place alone for now."

"Hold on," Anna said, desperate to keep her plan in place, desperate to help. "There's so much we haven't uncovered! The books might have the answers!"

"I have to go now." Elsa's voice was sharp as an icicle.

"But we—"

"*We* should leave this room in the past. There has to be a reason Mother and Father wanted to keep it secret. Besides," she said as she gestured toward the door, "the answers to our problems are out there."

*No,* Anna thought, her fear big and full and pressing against her chest. It was happening again. Her plan to prove herself to Elsa was falling apart! Who cared about being able to go on some silly grand tour? Anna wanted to do what was best for everyone, but she seemed to have a knack for doing the complete opposite these days.

"Stay away from this room, Anna," Elsa continued, turning away from her and stepping toward the library. "It was left hidden for a reason. Let's keep it that way."

"*Elsa—*"

"Leave it alone." And when Elsa spoke in *that* tone, more like a queen than a sister, Anna knew there was no point in arguing.

Silently, Anna nodded. As she placed *Secrets of the Magic Makers* back onto a shelf, Elsa returned to the library and strode to her next scheduled appointment. But Anna couldn't bring herself to leave—not just yet. She let herself look one last time at this secret room, imagining how her mother might have sat at that worktable, translating symbols into words, while her father studied the objects on the shelves and cracked a clever joke.

Without really thinking about it, Anna reached her fingers back toward *Secrets of the Magic Makers*, but they stopped just short of touching the soft leather. Elsa might be really upset with her if she found out what Anna was thinking, but Elsa would be even *more* upset if the animals kept getting sick. It would be worth it, Anna told herself firmly, when everything had been fixed—when *Anna* had fixed things. Besides, Elsa had only said that Anna needed to stay out of this room, but she hadn't said—or at least, hadn't said *specifically*—that Anna couldn't take some of the room *with* her.

And with that, Anna tugged her mother's book free and hurried away.

# Chapter Five

IT WAS VERY LATE NOW, and Anna was hungry.

Stopping to grab a plate of cheese, crackers, and apple slices from the kitchen, she chatted with the castle cooks, catching up on local gossip: who was most likely to grow the biggest pumpkin in the village patch this year, how many people would attend the annual harvest feast, and the very exciting rumor that an engagement ring had been purchased at the jeweler's shop, but by whom?

Usually, Anna would have loved to stay and muse, but she knew the more time she spent down there, the less time she'd have to research. And so, excusing herself with her cheese plate, Anna rushed into her warm bedroom, clambered into her most comfortable pajamas, and began to read.

*Secrets of the Magic Makers* was more than just a collection of stories. It almost seemed like a field guide, as if someone had traipsed through the wilderness collecting information on various mythological creatures while also gathering ingredients for turning flowers into frogs. There were histories of enchanted forests, and things that looked like recipes. And while several of the text passages had not been translated by her mother, many had.

Anna followed her mother's handwriting like a hungry bird trailing crumbs. Crunching on her crackers, she read of shape-shifters who lived with herds of reindeer; talking trees; draugs; and boys who were no larger than a thumb. There were pages and pages of the unknown language, and every so often an illustration accompanied the symbols. Anna wondered if Kristoff would know anything about the runes, or if he had ever come across anything in the Valley of the Living Rock that might help. Were they runes of the mountain trolls? Or something else?

Her mother seemed to have skipped translating the pages with the more creepy-looking sketches. Anna flipped past a sketch of a man seemingly screaming in agony, then one of another man lying on a stone table as blue smoke curled from his head and a troll stood over him with its arms held high. Finally, she landed on a page that, based on its illustrations, seemed to detail the *Saga of Aren*.

The physical features of the legendary hero were much easier to see in this book than they had been in the portrait Elsa had uncovered. Aren had a shaggy head of yellow hair and a bright blond beard with a few skinny braids tucked into it. His face was more square than it was round, and his hooked nose put Anna in mind of an eagle. Though there were only runes on the page—no translation—Anna recognized some of his more famous exploits. In the corner was a sketch of the waterfall whom Aren had tricked into helping him breathe underwater. And just to the right of that, a sketch of the sun, each ray a delicate sword with a yellow diamond in its pommel, just like Aren's famed Revolute Blade. And in the last corner, far right and down, lounged a scrawled dragon. Anna turned the page, and cringed.

A sketch of a wolf, so realistic that Anna half thought she could feel its hot breath blasting from the pages, snarled up at her. Her mother seemed to have only gotten to the very beginning of the page, and had translated only a single word: *Nattmara*. Anna frowned. Yet another one of those once-known-now-forgotten words from her childhood. In frustration, she flipped the page. She'd had enough of not knowing—and enough, as a five-year-old, of that scary recurring nightmare, thank you very much.

The next installment that made her pause her was a recipe. It was a loose page, simply tucked into the binding, but it had been neatly titled in her mother's handwriting: *MAKE DREAMS COME TRUE*. There was another word scrawled in the margins in the same handwriting: *SPELL?* Anna's fingers traced the word *spell*. Not a recipe—*magic*.

She had never known anyone other than Elsa to be able to use magic before, and Elsa certainly didn't incant words or spells when she created and manipulated snow and ice. The magic was part of Elsa. It ran within her. Shortly after their reunion, Anna had asked Elsa what it felt like when she twirled her hands. Elsa had described it as an overwhelming emotion, a *feeling* that would eventually grow so big it had to find release in some way.

"Like when you want to cry but you hold on to

it because you don't want others to see?" Anna had asked.

"Yes," Elsa had said, "but not just crying. Sometimes, it's the feeling of clamping in a giant laugh in a time you're supposed to be quiet, like in the chapel. It seems that if I listen to the feeling, to the magic, and release it, I can manage it."

A poem in a book didn't seem like the kind of magic Elsa possessed, but that didn't necessarily mean these words would *not* hold any power. These words. This *spell*. Excitement trilled through Anna.

The more she looked at the words, the more certain she felt that everything they needed was right here, in their parents' research. She just wished she knew what knowledge lay behind the untranslated sections. Anna squinted at the symbols, as though by simply staring at them she would come to understand. But no knowledge came, only heavy eyelids.

She wondered if Kristoff had found out anything helpful on his trek to the valley. She wondered if SoYun was still out in the field, trying to keep her cattle awake through the night. But most of all, she wondered what her parents would have done in this situation.

"Anna and Elsa, always lean on each other for help,"

Father had said. He'd have wanted her to tell Elsa about this spell, but first, she just needed to rest her eyes. Anna's thoughts slipped over and past each other like darting fish as her eyelids drooped lower, and lower, and lower. . . . She needed to fix the Blight. . . .

*The court of Royaume was just as beautiful as Anna had always dreamed, and she knew she was dreaming—not only because she'd never been to Royaume, but also because everything felt too perfect and fragile to be real. Besides, Elsa would never be caught dancing in real life, and there she was, spinning on the dance floor, arms flung wide as if she were trying to embrace the chandeliered ceiling above them.*

*Anna grinned. "You look like a tree caught in a gale!" she shouted over the high song of violins and flutes.*

*"And you look like you're dizzy," Elsa said.*

*Anna shook her head. "Dizzy? Why—oh!"*

*Before she could finish her question, Elsa grabbed her hand and began to twirl her, her diaphanous white skirts fanning around her like a skein of sparkling snow.*

*Anna threw back her head and laughed, imagining what a sight they must make on the dance floor. Elsa, dressed all in white spangled with pearl seeds, was the very embodiment of winter, while Anna's headdress and gold skirts helped her masquerade as summer.*

*The grand ballroom blurred around her, seeming to turn into streaks of paint. Her head began to pound, but it was so rare to see Elsa silly and carefree that she didn't want to tell her to stop. Instead, Anna closed her eyes, trying to hold on to this moment, even if it was only pretend . . . but was it?*

*She was feeling really dizzy now. No matter how much fun Elsa was having, it was time to stop.*

*"Hey, Elsa? That's enough!" Anna opened her eyes and gasped.*

*Her sister was no longer twirling her.*

*Instead, a tall stranger in coattails and a silver wolf mask stood where Elsa had been.*

*Anna stumbled to a halt. "Pardon me." She removed her hand. "I need to find my sister."*

*The dancer bowed, the silver wolf mask nearly tipping off his nose. "As you wish, Princess Anna."*

*The blood in her veins turned to ice. Anna knew that voice. It was a voice she didn't want to hear again. She peered uncertainly through the dark eyeholes of the mask. "Prince— Prince Hans?"*

*"The very same." A diamond ring suddenly materialized in his hand. "Your sister said I should give this to you when I ask for your hand."*

*"My—my hand?"*

Hans grabbed her wrist and jammed the ring onto her finger. "Your hand in marriage, of course. Your sister has given her blessing. She has no use for you."

Anna yanked her hand away. "I don't believe that," she said, craning her neck to see if she could spot her sister in the glittering hall. But no one was there. The decorations, the musicians, the dancers . . . all had vanished, leaving her completely alone with the prince of the Southern Isles—her villainous almost-husband, who had tricked her and the rest of the kingdom before Anna uncovered his awful plans to kill Elsa and take over Arendelle.

Hans laughed, an awful sound, made worse by the way it turned up into a howl at the end. As Anna watched, the silver hair of his wolf mask rippled in the draft as if it were real fur, and his nose elongated, becoming more and more snoutlike.

More and more wolflike.

Until suddenly, there was no Hans, just a great white wolf with amber eyes and teeth the size of dinner knives. It was the same wolf that had stalked her childhood dreams. But while most things from childhood seem to become smaller as one grows, the wolf had, in fact, only grown with Anna. He was fiercer now. Hungrier.

The wolf licked his maw and advanced.

Wake up, Anna, she thought frantically, tripping on her

*skirts as she tried to scramble backward.* Wake up! Wake up! *Wake up—*

"Wake up!" Anna sat straight up. The sound of her own voice shattered her nightmare. Relief, warm and sweet as fresh honey, coursed through her. It had been so long since she'd had this particular dream, this particular nightmare, and the fear it spawned was unfortunately as familiar as the ache of missing her parents. And this time, there was no Mother to tell her a distracting story or Father to bring her hot chocolate.

*Always rely on each other for help.*

Leaning forward, Anna grabbed *Secrets of the Magic Makers*, which had slid to the foot of her bed. She tucked it close to her chest and raced into her parents' old bedroom. Not because she thought they would be there, but because Elsa had moved into it after her coronation, abandoning her childhood bedroom. But looking around the room and at the dying fire, Anna wondered why Elsa had not yet returned. She reassured herself that sometimes queenly duties could last all night.

She walked back to her room. Before clambering into bed, she stopped by her dressing table and took hold of her father's sketchbook. King Agnarr had been a talented artist, wielding both his pencil and sword with ease. On the bad days, when Anna felt most alone, she liked to open his sketchbook up and see the world as he once had. There were images of Arendelle Castle, as well as the far-off lands he'd seen on his grand tour.

Elsa would leave on her own grand tour in just four—no, now *three* days—and if Anna could heal the animals before then, there was still a chance she'd be able to sail away with Elsa.

Returning to her bed, Anna decided that she'd wake up extra early to show Elsa the spell first thing. And so, with her father's sketchbook on one side of her pillow and her mother's book on the other, she at last dared to close her eyes.

The wolf did not return.

# Chapter Six

ANNA HEARD THE SOUND of chimes and footsteps from somewhere in the castle.

Dawn had broken, spilling warm autumn sunlight across her face. Keeping her eyes closed, Anna stretched, enjoying the coziness of her quilt and the softness of her pillow. Just a few more minutes. She could afford to wait before she found Elsa, asked more about the Westens' goats, and told her about what she'd found last night in their mother's book. After all, she was so comfortable that it would be a *crime* to untuck herself, and—

Her thoughts screeched to a halt.

*Secrets of the Magic Makers.* The book with spells in it. The book with a potential cure for the animals.

Anna lurched up, eyes flying open—only to be blinded not by the light of dawn, but by golden mid-morning sun. She'd overslept again!

Faster than Sven could chomp a carrot, Anna tumbled out of bed before she could even untwist herself from her quilt. She grabbed *Secrets of the Magic Makers*, and with her blanket flapping behind her, she sprinted through the dressing room and downstairs. Not bothering to knock, she flung open the door to her parents' old bedroom. The bed was neatly made, the ashes cold in their hearth.

Of course—her sister would have been up for hours at this point. Elsa, for some strange reason, enjoyed mornings. She said they made her feel fresh as new snow, while they made Anna feel as fresh as chicken droppings. A headache pounded at her temples. Even though she'd overslept by hours, it had been a restless sleep, as it had taken her long hours to relax after the return of the childhood nightmare.

*Think.* Where would Elsa be at this time of day? Whirling from the bedchamber, Anna ran down the hallway to peer through open doors. Elsa wasn't in the library or council chambers. Maybe the portrait gallery? Anna flew downstairs and made a sharp turn on the landing—and barreled into something warm and solid.

Anna flew backward, sprawling onto the ground. A dull pain rattled through her backside, but thankfully, the majority of her fall had been cushioned by the carpet. *Ow.*

"Hey!" the warm wall grumbled from above. "Watch where you're going!"

"You watch where *you're* going!" Anna replied, and instantly regretted it. That's not what someone hoping to be a royal ambassador on a grand tour should say. "I'm sorry," she added, looking up to see the old, wrinkled face of Madam Eniola staring down at her.

"Anna!" Madam Eniola bobbed a curtsy, her long brown skirt contrasting with the bundle of white ribbons she held in her arms. "My apologies, I didn't recognize you in your . . ." Her eyes swept up and down. "Quilt?"

Anna winced. Royal ambassadors should also probably remember to put on proper clothes before carrying out their important missions—and to comb their hair, too. Her hair didn't look so much like hair as it resembled a bird's nest. "That's all right." Anna clambered to her feet. "I should have been paying attention." *Like always.* She pulled her quilt tighter around her and hoped it looked more dignified than her ruffled pale green nightgown and bare feet.

Anna knew Eniola as one of the new villagers who'd moved to Arendelle from Tikaani, and specifically as the one who had taught Tikaani's national anthem to Anna. Eniola lived in a cozy cottage on the outskirts of the farmlands. Holding her chin up, Anna asked, "What brings you to the castle, Madam Eniola?"

Eniola sighed, and the creases on her face, which already held more lines than King Agnarr's old sailing charts, seemed to increase tenfold as she frowned. "I'm here to speak to the queen." She pursed her lips. "We *all* are."

Anna arched an eyebrow. *"We?"*

Eniola stepped back to reveal more villagers lined up outside the Great Hall, staring at Anna. She recognized many of her friends—the candymaker, the farmer, the gas lamp lighter, the miller, the two blacksmiths, and many more. Many, *many* more.

Anna's eyes widened as she saw that the line of villagers extended from the double doors that led into the Great Hall all the way through the second great hall and into the portrait gallery. Anna's mouth went dry, and she cleared her throat. "Why do you need to see Elsa? Erm, *Queen* Elsa?" she asked.

Eniola held out her bundle of ribbons, which Anna saw now were not actually ribbons at all. They were strands of wheat, but instead of the long golden straws Anna was used to seeing from the tower window, *these* strands were short and mottled white—moldy and rotten all the way through and recognizable only by the heads of grains at the tops. Even as Anna stared, a few seeds crumbled off into white dust. First the animals, then the crops. What was going on?

"We woke this morning," Eniola said, "and it's all like this—everything!"

The villagers grumbled in agreement behind her.

Anna needed to tell Elsa about all these villagers—*now*.

"Excuse me." Anna tore her eyes away from the pitiful bundle in Madam Eniola's arms and hurried downstairs in the direction of the Great Hall. "Pardon me, coming through!" The line shifted to allow Anna to wiggle by, and as she did, she saw that each and every person held white bundles similar to the one that Madam Eniola held: the pumpkins, usually the color of the sunset, had large unsightly splotches splashed across them, while the apples, usually red, round, and crisp, seemed to have the same consistency as raw dough. Up and down the line, Anna saw dried corn husks, white-mottled potatoes, and carrots as pale as cream. Every crop, every vegetable, every grain Anna could think of, was destroyed. Rotten.

*The Blight.*

Anna picked up the pace. Squeezing past a harried-looking woman, she at last made it through the doors and into the Great Hall.

The Great Hall, as its name suggested, was exactly that: *great.* It was the largest room in the castle, with tall windows and a gleaming chandelier, capable of fitting a hundred dashing lords and twirling ladies, Elsa's throne, and a massive chocolate fountain all at the same time. Once, it had even hosted an entire ice skating rink when a late winter storm had threatened the annual ice dance competition.

But now, for the first time Anna could remember, the Great Hall felt small. The single file line cutting through the portrait gallery hadn't prepared her for the absolute crush of people that filled the Great

Hall. Even on the busiest market day on record—shortly after Elsa's coronation, when everyone had come to see their new magical sovereign—there had not been *this* many people. Or maybe there had been, but joy didn't take up nearly as much room as fear. Fear filled the hall, as large and present as one of the Earth Giants in her mother's tales. The voices all around Anna were pulled tight, sounding as if they would break at any moment.

"Everything is gone! It's been ruined!"

"My cattle! They won't wake up!"

"Never in all my days! It's as if the very earth has gone awry!"

"Do you think this has to do with the Northuldra?"

"No," someone grunted. "King Runeard, may he rest in greatest peace, made sure they would never trouble Arendelle again."

"And the animals . . ."

Anna heard a strange noise from outside. It sounded like a mix of children learning how to play the violin crossed with the sounds of a zoo. Peering through the window, Anna gasped. The courtyard was just as full as the Great Hall, filled to the brim with farmers and animals. Sheep had broken loose from their shepherds, and the herding dogs, usually so careful, seemed distracted, following something in the air that no one else could see. All the animals looked like walking ghosts, their fur and hides the same sickly yellow-white. And even as Anna watched, a cow and two horses knelt to the ground, their eyes as large and black as lumps of coal, their mouths open and tongues lolling out until, suddenly, they fell asleep.

Anna's stomach turned. "Excuse me," she said over and over again as she tried to wade her way to the front of the hall, toward the throne where Elsa must be. Grumbling people followed in her wake as she wove in and out of the crowd, and more than once, she had to tug her quilt from beneath someone's boot.

But with one last push, she made it to the throne, relief washing over her as she found Elsa standing there, just as Wael, the local journalist, yelled out, "That's not going to help us!"

"Wael," Elsa said, "if you would please only just—"

"*Ah-hem!* Winter is fast approaching." Wael's ink-stained fingers gestured wildly. "We will have nothing to eat! We deserve answers—and it's *your* responsibility as queen to give us answers and take care of your people! We don't have enough food to last the week!"

A hush fell over the Great Hall at his words.

Elsa stood tall, not backing down, but Anna knew her sister. She could see the overbright sheen of her eyes. It wasn't just ice that could sparkle in chandelier light. Tears could, too.

Anger, bright and hot, swept through Anna. "Don't speak to my sister that way!" she burst out as she reached Elsa's side.

"Anna," Elsa said, her voice low, "I've got this, it's fine—"

Anna glared at Wael. "No, it's not!"

The man glared right back.

"Elsa is doing her best," Anna plowed on, her words coming fast and furious. "She has a plan! She'll fix everything before she leaves on the grand tour!"

Next to her, she heard Elsa's breath catch. "Anna—"

"That's in just three days," a tired-looking villager said, her arms full of what Anna thought was supposed to be emerald zucchini but now looked more like great white slugs. "Can the queen really—"

"Anna—" Elsa tried again.

But Anna didn't listen. She was going to stick up for her sister. Elsa might be able to stand there and listen to people doubt her, but Anna wasn't going to have any of it.

"Of *course* Elsa can!" Anna said, holding on to their glowing secret, the promise of the mysterious book.

"ANNA." Elsa flung out her hand. There was a time when icy spears would have sprouted from the floor, but Elsa had control of her magical powers now. Instead of a dangerously pointed ice spear, it was now just a gesture—to remind her sister to watch what she said. "I apologize for my sister," Elsa said to the Great Hall at large. Her chin had lifted in the exact same way Anna remembered her father lifting his during special ceremonies, when he was trying to be his most regal.

Anna opened her mouth to protest, but one glance at Elsa's expression squashed any words she had left. Her cheeks flushed. Burning anger transformed into burning embarrassment. What had she done?

"I understand your concern," Elsa continued, her voice steady and cool. "And I share it. What I've been trying to say is, to show my commitment to solving the problem of the ruined crops and sick animals, I'm postponing my grand tour until I can sort out this troubling matter at hand."

"What?" Anna gasped before she could stop herself, shocked her sister would cancel her grand tour. She didn't understand what Elsa was thinking—what if postponement convinced the dignitaries and people from other lands that Arendelle wasn't, in fact, opening its gates, but closing them once again? And from the shocked look on Wael's face and the murmur of the crowd, Anna knew she wasn't the only one surprised by this announcement.

If they hadn't been standing in front of a large crowd of stressed villagers, Anna imagined Elsa would be rubbing her temples and sighing right about now. But they *were* standing in front of stressed villagers, and her sister never failed to live up to what was expected of her: she was queen, regal and unflappable.

"Because," Elsa said, speaking loud enough for all to hear, "the royal ship is loaded with rations of food, apples, wheat, dried vegetables, cheeses, cans of pickled herring, and sausages. We need to share our surplus, or else the villagers with Blight-stricken farms will suffer further." Once again, Elsa had come up with the perfect solution—one so obvious Anna wondered why she hadn't thought of it herself. Elsa was *so good* at seeing the larger tapestry, while Anna let herself get distracted by whatever thread was dangling in front of her at that very moment.

"That amount of food will only last us all three days at the *most*," Wael protested. "And what makes you think the food on your ship hasn't soured, *Your Majesty?*" There was something about his all-knowing attitude that made Anna want to release Marshmallow, Elsa's dangerous giant snowman—and Olaf's little brother—on him. But seeing as that wasn't an option, since Marshmallow was currently the housekeeper for the ice palace on top of the North Mountain, she'd settle for glaring at Wael instead.

"I'll scour our kitchen here," Elsa offered.

Beside her, Kai scribbled a note onto a ream of parchment, while brown-haired and kind Olina, in charge of overseeing the kitchen staff, clasped her gloved hands together in deep thought. Nothing ever missed Olina's careful eye, and Anna knew that she was probably already running through a mental list of food the castle kitchen could provide.

"What if *that* food's gone bad, too?" cried a voice from the crowd.

Anna held her breath while everyone stared at Elsa.

Elsa, however, looked at only one person: Olina. The woman gave a slight shake of her head: the kitchen was still fine. Anna exhaled, thankful that at least this one piece of news wasn't terrible.

"As your queen," Elsa said loudly, her voice strong, "I will see to it that you have food."

The crowd murmured, but Anna could hear the shift in tone. The conversation around her no longer vibrated with the intensity of a string pulled too tight. Instead, the words loosened and the conversation relaxed as the villagers considered Elsa's proposal.

"I think it's a good idea," Tuva called out. "My wife and I accept." And the two blacksmiths nodded in agreement.

"I accept, too," Eniola called out, and soon other villagers voiced their agreement as well. All except for Wael, who only reluctantly nodded, but not before adding, "Fine—but the *Village Crown* will make sure that you keep Anna's promise that the solution will be found before three days are up."

Pride filled Anna as Kai led the disgruntled villagers back out of the castle and toward the harbor to collect the supplies from the royal ship. She felt like cheering, but instead she settled on a quiet squeal, and whispered to Elsa, "That was *brilliant*."

But Elsa didn't smile back. Instead, she walked to one of the more secretive side entrances to the Great Hall, hidden from view by a tapestry. "Anna," she said without turning around, "can we talk for a minute, please?"

Anna's smile slipped away as she followed her older sister. She might not know why the farm animals were sleeping or why their fur was turning white, or why the kingdom's food seemed to be turning to dust and ash, but she did know one thing: she was absolutely, completely, 100 percent in trouble.

"*Three days?!*" Elsa whirled on Anna as soon as the tapestry fell back in place, obscuring them from view. "Anna of Arendelle, how on earth can I fix this mess, and so soon?" Even though Elsa didn't raise her voice, Anna could hear her frustration boiling underneath. "Between this and Kristoff—"

"*Kristoff?*" Anna interrupted, furrowing her eyebrows. "What about Kristoff?"

Elsa closed her eyes and rubbed her temples, just

as Anna had suspected Elsa had wanted to do earlier. "He's not here. I thought he'd be back by now, but . . ."

Worry zipped through Anna, but she forced herself to shrug. "I'm sure he's fine," she said. "You know how happy Bulda is whenever he visits." She smiled, thinking of the mountain troll who'd raised Kristoff as her own. "I bet you he's delayed because he's so full of mushroom stew that he's too heavy for Sven to carry, and they have to walk."

But it seemed Elsa couldn't be distracted from her worry, not even with the funny image. Elsa shook her head. "It's so much pressure. I don't know what I can do."

"You mean, what *we* can do . . . with a secret book full of magic!" Anna said.

Elsa groaned. "*Oh,* Anna!" She shook her head. "I know you want it to be, but I don't think magic is the answer to all of our problems."

"Okay, I hear you, but *look.*" Anna held out *Secrets of the Magic Makers.* "There is so much information in here." She flipped through the pages until she found the one she was looking for. "See? This one grants your *dreams.*"

Elsa sighed. "Anna, I told you not to go back in the secret room."

"I didn't go *back* into it. I grabbed this book before I left the first time. Look at it!"

Reluctantly, Elsa glanced down at the page that had been pushed under her nose, but before she had a chance to skim, Gerda pulled back the tapestry, wearing her signature green skirt, jacket, and cap, and holding Elsa's great big calendar.

"Your Majesty, I'm sorry," the woman said, and Anna could hear the sympathy in her voice, "but even with the grand tour postponed, this fiasco with the sickness has put us behind schedule. And now you must write explanations to all the different dignitaries and heads of countries to explain why you can't make it."

Elsa took a deep breath. "Yes, of course, Gerda, you're right. The work of a queen is never complete." She glanced over at Anna, who held her breath. "Here. Let me have that book. Maybe you're right. I promise I'll look at it as soon as I have a spare minute."

"Of—of course," Anna said, happy to share. But she would have been even *happier* if Elsa had told Gerda that Anna had found something important. That they were working on discovering a solution *together*.

"I'd like to meet with an animal expert now to get their opinion," Elsa said, and Anna noticed again that she was tugging on her fingers. "And a botanist. I'm not sure what should be done first. . . ."

"If you need someone to write letters, I can help with that," Anna offered. "I've read up on all the different etiquettes of each country."

"That should be just fine, dear," Gerda said, her pencil already flying over the calendar to adjust it. "Just make sure Elsa signs them before you mail them."

"I will!" Anna promised, happy to help Elsa and happy to have something to do while she waited for Kristoff to return to the castle. She had so many things she wanted to ask him, starting with, *How do the trolls say we can cure the Blight?* and leading to, *Do you know how to read the mysterious ancient runes in my mother's book?*

"Thanks, Anna," Elsa said as Gerda hurried away to arrange everything. "If that's all taken care of, then I need to get going. I'll make sure I visit you before I go to bed, okay?"

But she turned before Anna could even nod.

And though Anna stood in the middle of a crowded castle still bursting to the brim with villagers, the sight of Elsa walking away from her had never made Anna feel more alone.

# Chapter Seven

THROUGH HER BEDROOM WINDOW, Anna
watched the exodus of the castle staff trailing over
the Bridge of Arches and into the darkening village.

That afternoon, Elsa had given the staff the option
of taking off from work with pay so that they could
go help their nearby relatives whose animals and
crops were suffering from the Blight. After she had
written the letters, Anna had changed into her travel
cloak and spent the rest of the day helping unload
food from the royal ship and handing it out to the
villagers amidst the groaning of sick animals.

She'd wanted to cover her ears, but then she
thought that would be the cowardly thing to do.
She couldn't just ignore the ugly things in the world
around her. If people did that, no one would ever

help at all, and nothing would become well again. And so Anna had gone to help the farmers dab white fur with wet washcloths to try to keep their livestock alert. She'd stroked a sad little foal's fuzzy ears as it curled up next to the sleeping form of its mother, who did not so much as stir at the foal's pitiful nickers.

Anna turned away from the window and paced, still in her travel cloak from earlier. Just as she'd thought, Elsa hadn't come to see her. She knew her sister was busy, but ... Anna glanced out the window again, and made up her mind. Lighting an oil lamp, she quickly made her way through the now empty halls of the castle to Elsa's council chambers.

As Anna approached the doors, she was surprised to see no yellow light trickling out from beneath. Her breath quickened. Maybe something else had gone wrong in the village, something so bad that it had pulled Elsa away from the signing of the dignitaries' letters.

Anna knocked, and when there was no answer, she let herself in.

Elsa was nowhere to be found.

But—Anna felt her mouth tighten.

There, lying unopened on the desk, was *Secrets of*

*the Magic Makers.* It was clear Elsa hadn't touched it. But she *needed* to! Anna knew people said she was too optimistic, naïve about the way the world worked, and maybe that was true, but she had faith in stories. And she had faith that there was a solution to any problem, just as long as one kept looking. She just needed to get Elsa to listen to her.

Anna hurried back through the castle, gripping *Secrets of the Magic Makers.* She looked everywhere for her sister, until her eyes grew heavy with sleep as the sky continued to darken outside the castle. Maybe Elsa wasn't in the castle at all. Reluctantly, Anna trudged back to her room.

And then . . .

Voices.

Voices coming from Elsa's bedroom. Anna pressed her ear to the bedroom door, and though she couldn't make out the words, she recognized the low timbre of Kai's voice as well as Gerda's northern cadence.

Anna staggered from the door. Elsa was having a meeting without her! There was a time when Anna knew Elsa would have invited her to each and every single meeting, would have sought out her advice, but now . . . now it seemed Elsa no longer had any need for her little sister at all. Elsa had chosen to shut her out once more.

With all the dignity she could muster, Anna walked slowly away from the door, but as soon as she was out of sight from Elsa's bedroom, she broke into a run, trying to escape the emotion that threatened to overwhelm her. Rushing into the sanctuary of her own bedroom, Anna slammed the door shut and sat cross-legged on her shaggy pink rug, *Secrets of the Magic Makers* spread open in front of her. She studied the book, which blurred slightly in her gaze from unshed tears. Anna flipped through it again, and a loose page fell out, one that looked like it was ripped from another book.

Reaching for it, Anna was reminded of the same loose page that had given her so much hope the previous night. The page with a spell to make your dreams come true. Her tears dried up, and Anna felt her sadness replaced by another rising emotion, one growing so fast and so big that it seemed to take on a life of its own. For a moment, she thought she understood what Elsa experienced when she used her magic. Anna *had* to let this wild, untamed hope free— even if Elsa didn't think it would work, there could be no downside to trying. And if it worked, maybe the doors to council meetings would reopen to Anna. Maybe the strained tension between Anna and Elsa would disappear. Because that was her dearest dream: Anna hoped she could help the people of Arendelle, working together with Elsa to find a solution that would make everything right again. And in the process, Anna hoped Elsa would realize she needed her sister, just the same way that Anna needed Elsa.

Tugging out the loose page, Anna whispered the words out loud:

> *"Wild, awake!*
> *Wind and snow!*
> *Plant the seed*
> *And watch it grow!*
> *Say this spell,*
> *And you shall see*
> *All your dreams*
> *Come to be!"*

A beat of silence. Anna felt foolish. What had she thought would happen after she read the spell? That her sister would materialize in front of her? Come racing in with open arms and lead her back to the secret room? Without her wild hope tugging her forward, Anna deflated. She crumpled up the dream spell page and put it in her cloak pocket, not wanting to look at it anymore.

From the dressing room, Anna suddenly heard footsteps followed by voices.

"Poor thing, there is so much on her mind," a voice floated through the door. Anna recognized it as Gerda's.

"She bears so much," Kai agreed, his voice loud and clear as they passed right by her door.

The council meeting must be over by now. Which meant that at any second, there would be a knock on her door, and Elsa would ask to come in. Any second now, she'd tell Anna how sorry she was that it took her so long to listen to Anna's suggestion and that Anna was right, they needed to look at the books in the secret room. Then Anna would show her *Secrets of the Magic Makers* and the loose page with the spell, and they would fix everything. They would do it together. After all, they were sisters.

Anna sat up straighter on her rug and waited . . . and waited. The knock never came.

————

Anna's dreams were nightmare-tossed yet again. She dreamed of dark shadows in treetops, Earth Giants destroying the village, and a shipwreck on a stormy sea. And then—ice. Anna had told Elsa she did not remember the moments during which she'd turned to ice. But that was a lie. She would never forget the horror of warm flesh turning cold, then all sensation fleeing as her warm blood frosted into stone-cold crystal. She would never forget the last bit of heat escaping through her final breath, would never forget seeing her sister sob, and the unique pain of not being able to do absolutely anything at all. Tonight, Anna's nightmares would not *let* her forget. And so Anna's dream morphed. . . .

*She was a girl of ice, standing outside the castle, only able to peer into the window and never enter through the doors. Inside, she could see Elsa reading aloud to a girl, whose glossy white hair was pulled back in two braids. Anna didn't recognize the girl—her back was to the window—but she did recognize the girl's dress, a soft green one with sunflowers embroidered on the hem. Anna's birthday dress. She could see Kristoff entering the room, strumming his guitar and smiling at the girl.*

Who are you? *Anna wanted to yell at the ivory-haired*

*girl.* Turn around! *But her frozen lips could not speak, and Anna had to wait, impatiently and horribly, until, at last, the girl turned around to reveal . . . Anna's eyes. Anna's nose. Anna's smile. The white-haired girl was Anna—but she wasn't. Anna had been replaced. By this other person. And no one in the room, not Kristoff, Olaf, Kai, Gerda—not even her own sister—realized it. Or maybe they did and they simply did not care. A high howl pierced the air, and the ice shattered. It broke away from Anna like a suit of armor, revealing her true self beneath. Suddenly, she could run, but the castle had shifted into a wide white tundra, and there was no place to hide before the wolf appeared. Because it was already there.*

*Without turning around, Anna felt the yellow eyes of the wolf fixed on her back. She ran. Yet, no matter how hard she pumped her legs or how fast her heart beat, nothing seemed to change. There was just a flat expanse of gray snow below her and even grayer sky above. The world was colorless and bleak and without hope, and then—*

*An explosion of red pain burst through her vision as the wolf's claws raked and sank into her back.*

*Anna expected to wake up—she always woke up.*

*But this time, she didn't.*

*Instead, the wolf flipped her over onto her back, opened its huge jaws, and swallowed her whole.*

Anna's eyes flew open. Sweat sheened her skin and she felt hollow, as if her insides had been scooped out, like a gutted pumpkin. Something prodded her back.

"Troll's toes!" Anna exclaimed to nobody as she pulled the book out from beneath her. Sometime in the night, she must have dozed off on the floor and rolled onto the book, its thick spine digging into her own, explaining the sharp pain of the wolf's claws in her nightmare. Anna let her head sink back onto the floor and flung her hand over her eyes.

"This is getting ridiculous," she muttered, hoping the sound of her voice would chase away the lingering fear. "You're too old for this kind of stuff." Though, she didn't *feel* old. In fact, that was kind of the problem. These last two days, she had felt *oh so very young* indeed. And that ache that always lurked just beneath the sea of her thoughts surfaced, sending a ripple of sadness through her.

How she missed her parents. Her mother would have fixed everything with a story or two about silly and magical things, like shaggy goats outwitting trolls, or an empress who forgot her clothes. And her father, he would have chased away any lingering fear with a candle that crackled and emitted a sweet, soothing scent, or a warm mug of hot chocolate.

*Mmmm . . . hot chocolate . . . with marshmallows.*

"Come on, Anna." She spoke out loud again, trying to shake the loneliness. "They're not here, but you can definitely get your own mug of hot chocolate. It's not like the wolf is hiding beneath the bed or something." She let out a soft little "Ha!" for good measure. The sound wasn't very convincing, but there was no one she had to convince but herself. And so, she got off the floor, and the terrible, awful nightmare that had ended differently than it ever had before—with the wolf finally winning—slipped from her tired mind.

Anna realized she was still in her travel cloak, but she didn't care. She could change into her pajamas once she got back. Taking a flickering candle from her bedside table, Anna was her own source of light in a castle of darkness. The flame was weak, yet just bright enough for her to make her way through the familiar halls and down to the kitchen. And—wait. What was that?

Lifting the candle up a little higher, Anna paused on the stairs. She thought she'd seen a bit of movement, a skim of white. But as she strained her eyes to peer beyond the candle's light, Anna didn't see anything unusual or out of place or snarling with fangs. . . .

"You're being silly," she chided herself. "Keep going. Remember: marshmallows!" Still, the memory of the nightmare resurfaced and trailed her through the corridors, down the stairs, and into the kitchen.

The kitchen was the beating heart of the castle, the cheery red-glow of its stoves producing delicious banquets and even more delicious heat that cut through the autumn's creeping damp.

Tonight, though, the kitchen felt oddly empty and quiet. The pots and pans, instead of being clanged around by busy cooks, were hanging quietly on their hooks in neat lines next to colorful garlands of garlic, dried peppers, and herbs that draped from the ceiling, dropping down to tickle the lids of jams, beets, and pickled herring. Usually, at least one cook remained to keep an eye on the fire stoves, but Elsa had dismissed the cook staff, too, including Olina—which meant only Anna, Elsa, Olaf, Gerda, and Kai were sleeping in the castle that night. Which explained why it felt particularly quiet, dark, and empty.

That—and the fact that Sven and Kristoff still weren't back yet. At least, Anna didn't think they were back yet—she didn't know for sure. Usually, outings to the Valley of the Living Rock didn't last this long, and since he knew things weren't going too well with the villagers, he'd know not to linger. He was a mountain man; he could take care of himself. But still, Anna began to worry and hoped they had made it back. Despite her optimism, she always worried for those she loved. It was what made Anna . . . Anna.

She sighed, heart heavy, and shuffled over to the stove. Making hot chocolate was simple, and while she wasn't great with cooking that required twenty different detailed steps and ingredients and lots of fine chopping, she was adept at mixing delicious chocolate powder with milk and setting it on the stovetop. But as Anna stirred the pot of warming milk to stop a skin from forming, she heard a soft clatter.

She stopped stirring. "Hello?" she called hopefully. "Kristoff, is that you?"

No response.

She thought she heard the sound of footsteps fading away, but from the other side of the kitchen leading toward the stairs. Maybe Kristoff was wearing his earmuffs and hadn't been able to hear her through the fluff. Typical Kristoff. Or maybe it was Olaf. Perhaps he was up for a night of reading a gripping passage about existentialism or a book on another -ism.

Quickly, Anna turned off the stove and removed the milk. The hot chocolate would have to wait. The footsteps were too intriguing. If it was Olaf, she'd leave it alone. But if it *was* Kristoff, she had to know what the trolls had said about the Blight. Still . . . it wasn't really cold enough yet for Kristoff to be wearing his earmuffs. Like Elsa, the cold didn't seem to bother him as much as it did the non-mountain folk. After all, he'd grown up in the cold. Taking the candle, Anna followed the footsteps up the stairs to the rest of the castle.

"Kristoff? Is that you?" she asked.

It sounded like the person was walking through the portrait gallery, then the second great hall, and finally, the Great Hall. She stood in the doorway, lifting her candle as high as she could. It only shed light on the polished wooden floor. She hadn't heard the footsteps *leave* the Great Hall, which meant Kristoff, if it *was* him, was still there in the dark room with Anna. She stepped inside, peering behind each column that lined the wall of the cavernous room. She yanked at curtains and moved from one to the next.

"Kristoff?" Anna called. Her candle's flame danced this way and that. Nothing, nothing, nothing, two yellow eyes, nothing, nothing—Anna stopped breathing.

*Two yellow eyes.*

She brought the candle back around and saw the form of a wolf.

White and massive, exactly like the one in her nightmare.

Except this time, it was different.

Because Anna was awake.

# Chapter Eight

ANNA HAD ONCE HEARD that when someone faced death, their life flashed before them.

But as she stood there in the gloom of the Great Hall, with the yellow eyes of the wolf fixed on her, it wasn't her life that flashed through her mind—it was the details of the Great Hall. The quivering red curtains that outlined each pillar. The gleam of the curtain's rod in the glow of the candle. The heat of the candle wax as it dripped onto her skin. She noticed all of this in the breath it took for the wolf to growl. Then it leapt at her.

Anna jumped out of the way, the knife-sharp claws missing her by mere inches. The wolf growled in frustration, and the sound seemed to reach into Anna and scrape against her insides, but she managed to drop her candle, grab the curtain, and tug—hard, sending the curtain's rod clattering onto the floor. Snatching it up, Anna half ran, half stumbled toward the great double doors that seemed as far away as the moon.

One stride, then another, and then—she was through!

Slamming the doors shut, she pushed the curtain rod through the two handles, locking the doors in place just as the wolf threw its bulk against the other side with all its might.

*THUMP!*

The doors rattled, but stayed shut.

*THUMP! THUMP! THUMP!*

How long would the curtain rod hold? Anna had never seen a wolf so large. Or rather, she had, but only in . . . Something stirred inside of her, something she knew she needed to examine closer, but the little feeling about what could have brought the wolf from her dreams into the castle would have to wait for when she wasn't running for her life.

"HELP!" Anna yelled as she sprinted away. "WOLF! BIG, MASSIVE WOLF! IN THE CASTLE!" The only thing that beat faster than her heart was the single insistent question pounding through her brain: *What to do? What to do? What to do?* She'd faced a pack of wolves before, when she and Kristoff had journeyed to the North Mountain to try to find Elsa—but Kristoff and Sven weren't here right now. She needed to find Elsa, and quickly. She flew up the stairs in the second great hall. She needed to find help. But as she sprinted down the hall that led to Elsa's bedroom, she saw a flash of white up ahead. The wolf—it had somehow escaped the Great Hall!

She groaned. It was just like in her dreams; the large-as-a-bull wolf seemed to outwit and outrun her at every turn. But *how?* She knew wolves were fast, but they couldn't possibly be *this* fast. Gasping for breath, Anna pivoted and sprinted down another hallway. She turned left, right, and then left again. She didn't know exactly where her feet were taking her, but she realized she would be near Kai's room if she made a final left. Maybe she could hide in there!

As the castle's steward, Kai had protocol for everything, from the right way to hold a teacup to the exacting ritual of snuffing out the candles and oil lamps one wick at a time. There was a chance that maybe he already *had* a plan for a wolf breaking into the castle. *A wolf! A wolf! A wolf!* Her breath came short and fast. From somewhere behind her, she thought she heard a howl. Only twenty more feet until she reached Kai's room . . . five feet . . . one foot . . .

"KAI!" Anna catapulted into the steward's room and bolted the lock behind her. She noticed his form lying in his bed. "Kai, wake up! There's a wolf in the castle! What do we do?"

But the man remained completely still.

Unease trickled through Anna. It wasn't as if she were being quiet. In fact, she was being very loud. Why wasn't Kai waking up? She lit a candle from his bedside to see.

Kai twisted and turned under his blanket, and as the light hit his eyelids, he muttered, "No, please . . . don't!"

He was in the middle of a nightmare.

Anna knew from personal experience that no one should be woken in the middle of a bad dream.

But there was a wolf now pawing outside the room.

Usual rules did not apply.

"Kai, wake *up!*" Anna shook the steward's arm. "Please, please, *please* wake up."

Kai's eyes snapped open, and Anna staggered back. The steward's eyes were usually the same brown-green color as changing autumn leaves or muddied creeks. But instead of looking into warm hazel eyes, she was staring into two inky pits. His pupils had swallowed his irises, turning his eyes completely black. *Just like the cattle.*

Suddenly, Kai sat upright, and screamed.

And screamed.

And screamed.

And screamed.

He screamed as though long claws were tearing out his heart. As though sharp teeth were sinking into his skin. As though he were being eaten alive from the inside out.

Anna placed a hand on his shoulder to try to comfort him, but he didn't react to her touch. It was as though she were invisible. Kai couldn't see her—couldn't sense her. He was lost.

The pawing outside the door grew faster. Hungrier. More desperate. And as the scratching grew in intensity, Kai's black eyes suddenly shifted again. One moment, they were black, and the next, they were yellow . . . and glowing.

Anna's heart seemed to fly up into her throat and she almost choked as she staggered backward.

What was *happening*?

The scratching stopped. Or had it? Anna couldn't be sure, as Kai's scream continued to fill the room, making her clutch her ears. She needed to get out of there. She needed to find Elsa, Olaf, Kristoff, and Sven, to warn the others. The people of Arendelle were in danger. All of this was Anna's worst fear, worse than her wolf-filled nightmare. Because it was real. It was happening. How and why, she would still have to think on later.

She took a step toward the door. Kai's yellow eyes stayed transfixed somewhere beyond her, as though witnessing unseen horrors. She crept by him and pressed her ear to the door. Nothing. Not so much as a yip. But what if the wolf was out there, waiting for her in silence? And worse: what if it *wasn't* out there, and was headed for others instead?

"ELSA!" Her sister's name ripped from her throat as she undid the lock and ran out of Kai's room, leaving him screaming and writhing. "ELSA! ELSA! ELSA!" she yelled.

Minutes before, Anna had felt the quiet of her home. But it wasn't quiet anymore. Now she could hear more screams echoing throughout the castle. Screams she recognized as Gerda's. Anna had the sinking feeling that if she went to her, she would be too late, that Gerda would have the glowing yellow eyes like Kai. She practically sobbed. *"ELSA!"*

The door to their parents' bedroom slammed open, and a moment later, Elsa appeared in the hallway, still in her work dress but wrapped in their mother's scarf, and with heavy bags under her eyes. Olaf waddled behind her, in a fuzzy yellow robe and with a matching sleep mask pushed up on his forehead. He also held the snow globe from earlier.

"What's wrong?" Elsa asked.

At the sound of her sister's voice, Anna almost collapsed with relief that Elsa wasn't asleep and screaming. And Elsa's eyes were blue—blue as the sky, and blue as a song.

"A-a wolf!" Anna sputtered, wrapping Elsa and Olaf in a fierce embrace. "Wolf! Kai! Gerda!" she gasped and then choked out, "Eyes! Glowing yellow eyes!"

"Elsa," Olaf whispered, "she's not making any sense."

The next second, Anna felt a cool hand on her forehead as her sister checked her temperature. At Elsa's touch, Anna felt her frenzy subside, just a little.

She wasn't sure if it was Elsa's magic, or if it was just because the gesture was so familiar and comforting, but it made her want to cry. Their mother had done the same thing whenever Anna had woken up in a sweat from the fearsome nightmare that had plagued her childhood.

Anna managed to take a deep, shuddering breath. "That's because nothing makes sense!" After they bolted upstairs into the council chambers and locked the doors, Anna told them what had happened. The story came out jumbled, details piling up all out of order. Elsa didn't interrupt. She listened, and when Anna at last came to the end of it, she gave her a firm and understanding nod.

"Are you sure you didn't just have a bad dream?" Elsa said.

"It sounds like it," said Olaf, pushing his sleep mask up a little higher.

Anna stared at Elsa. "What? No! There is a *wolf* in the castle!"

Elsa rubbed her temples. "It's late. We should get back to bed."

"*What?*" Anna pulled away from her sister. "You don't believe me?"

"Question." Olaf had unbolted the lock and peeked through the doors. "Wolves usually have four paws, two eyes, and long, sharp teeth, right?" When the sisters nodded, he pressed a hand to his mouth and tilted his head. "Then I'm preeeetty sure we should believe Anna."

The door flew open, blowing off Olaf's robe and mask, and sending the snow globe falling to the floor with a *crack*. The wolf had found them. Its sharp shoulder blades jutted up and down as it moved, like some sort of terrifying carousel creature. Its long legs brought it closer and closer, following Anna, Elsa, and Olaf as they backed up and skirted around the long table.

Before Anna could scream, a wall of ice erupted from the wooden floor. Jagged crystals raced up to the ceiling in the center of the room, knitting themselves together to form a thick protective barrier, with Anna, Elsa, and Olaf by the doors and the wolf walled off on the fireplace end. Anna's gasp of surprise turned white in the cold of Elsa's magic.

"*Now* do you believe me?" Anna asked her sister.

Elsa ignored her. Her eyes swept the room. "We need to go find—"

But Elsa's words were cut off.

*THUMP. THUMP. SCREEEECH!*

Cobweb-thin lines scattered across the ice wall as the wolf pawed at it, its claws screeching. It was a terrible sound, even worse than the sound of teeth scraping against a fork, which until then Anna had thought to be the most awful sound imaginable. The ice wall wasn't holding. It was shattering.

"*Run!*" Elsa shouted, raising both her arms.

Anna didn't need to be told twice—and Olaf was already right by her side. Sprinting out the doors of the council chambers, they made their way for the stairs, down toward the great front doors that would take them to the castle bridge. But as Anna and Olaf neared the landing to the first floor, two pairs of yellow eyes shone at them from the shadows, blocking their path to the front entrance. Kai. Gerda.

Anna's stomach twisted. She'd been right, but oh! How she wished she'd been wrong. Gerda's friendly face was now an oval of agony—her eyes and mouth were all wide and round as she screamed and lurched toward them, something glistening in her hand: a pair of sewing scissors. And next to her, Kai clutched a red-hot poker.

"Put out the flames. The house is burning," Kai croaked, jabbing the iron at them as though *they* were the phantom flames attacking him. "It's burning!" he cried.

"Well, this can't be good," Olaf whispered as Gerda stepped forward with the blades of the scissors snapping open and shut, open and shut.

The look in their yellow eyes was not human, but something else.

Predatory.

*Wolf*like.

*It's a wolf pack,* Anna realized with horror.

Suddenly, a great shattering sound erupted above them, as if a thousand crystal goblets had been smashed . . . or one gigantic wolf had managed to break through a magical ice wall. A second later, Anna heard her sister's footsteps on the stairs behind her and Olaf.

"KEEP GOING!" Elsa shouted down to them.

"But Kai and Gerda want to prevent us from imminent escape and possibly cause us harm!" Olaf called back, darting behind Anna's travel cloak and away from the hot poker.

"Don't stop!" Elsa called.

Anna didn't know what to do—Kai and Gerda were blocking the only path to escape the castle, and a massive wolf was barreling down the stairs toward them. The only direction left was *down*—but there was no castle exit in the below-ground kitchen, and they would end up trapped there, or worse, in the ice room.

*Wait.* The ice room. There was something important about the ice room. Something Anna had wanted to check out . . . the blueprints! The blueprints that had shown a secret passageway that led out from underneath the castle.

"Elsa!" Anna yelled at the top of her lungs. "Meet us in the ice room!"

Anna and Olaf practically flew down the rest of the stairs with Elsa bringing up the rear as she blasted the stair landing with mirror-smooth ice, making it difficult for the pack to follow them down the stairs. Anna didn't turn around, not even when she heard two *thuds* and a *whoosh* that she assumed were Kai and Gerda slipping on the ice, unable to chase any farther.

But that didn't mean the wolf, with its large hooked claws, couldn't navigate a bit of ice.

Anna, Olaf, and Elsa continued racing downstairs. They burst into the kitchen, only to discover they weren't alone.

Kristoff sat in the middle of the room at the long table, scarfing down a sandwich, and by the number of crumbs scattered in front of him, it wasn't his first sandwich of the night.

Relief washed over Anna: Kristoff was back, and he was okay! Anna took stock of the details. Kristoff's blond hair was tangled, as if he'd spent the night in the woods or the mountains. His patched traveler's pack, lantern, and pickax were slung across his shoulders, as if he'd been too hungry to wait even a second more. Sven made happy munching noises as he buried his nose in a bag of carrots. They must have only just returned from the Valley of the Living Rock. Horror collided with her relief. Horror, because she'd thought—she'd *hoped beyond hope*—that Kristoff and Sven were far, far away from the castle and somewhere safe in the woods. Relief, because she wouldn't have to face this terror without him. Kristoff looked up, a crumb dropping from his chin.

"Hi, Kristoff!" Olaf darted into the kitchen and sprinted past the table. "Bye, Kristoff!"

"RUN!" Anna yelled, barreling toward him. With one hand, she grabbed Kristoff's elbow and pulled him after her.

"*Mwaf?*" he asked, his mouth full of sandwich.

But Anna didn't have time to explain, because the wolf was there, there in the kitchen. And though it was impossible—all of this was *impossible!*—the wolf seemed to have grown three feet since they had left it in the second great hall. Its shoulders brushed the sides of the door as it swaggered into the room, eyes glowing, jowls drooling a thick slime.

Kristoff dropped his sandwich onto the floor. "*MWAFFFF!*" he yelled.

Now all five of them—Sven, Elsa, Olaf, and Kristoff, with Anna in the lead—sprinted toward the back of the kitchen, to the door that led into the ice room. Anna pushed open the heavy door and held it as Kristoff, Olaf, and Elsa ran through. But where was Sven? Peering back, Anna's heart stopped.

Fear seemed to have frozen Sven in his tracks. He

remained still, a carrot in his mouth, as the wolf loped closer to him. It knocked aside the long wooden table with an ear-bleeding screech of its legs against stone.

"Sven!" Anna shouted. *"Run!"*

But it was as if Sven couldn't hear her. Instead, his eyes remained fixed on the wolf's glowing ones. He lifted a hoof, and took a step . . . *toward* the wolf.

"SVEN!" Kristoff yelled from over Anna's shoulder.

At the sound of his best friend's voice, the wolf's strange hypnosis over Sven seemed to shatter. Sven staggered backward, tripping over his hooves as he twisted on his haunches and stumbled through the door, leaving Anna just enough time to slam it shut on the wolf's slick snout. Sven wobbled beside her, shaky but safe, and Kristoff threw his arms around him. Elsa blasted the door with ice to hold it, and with a wave of her hand, thirty or so blocks of ice scraped across the rough stone floor to settle in front of the door, for good measure. But would it be enough?

Elsa panted and tucked a loose strand of hair behind her ear. "It might be a strange wolf with glowing yellow eyes, but it has to have a hard time clawing through stone and ice!"

The sounds of the wolf clawing and pawing

against the door made it sound like perhaps, just maybe, it was making impossible progress.

"Now what?" Elsa called, taking in the room. "Why did you want us in here?"

"One second!" Anna said, squeezing her eyes shut, not just to try to keep out the mental image of the wolf hunting them, but to try to remember what the blueprints had said about the entrance to the Earth Giant's Passage. Something about *three flagstones* . . .

She counted three flagstones in, and two across, and hurried to one in the center of the room. As she knelt down and placed her fingers around the edge of the stone, she hoped with all her might that the blueprints had been complete, that they weren't just a fanciful wish of her heroic grandfather King Runeard, who had built the castle.

Holding her breath, Anna pulled, and the flagstone lifted away, revealing carved stone steps leading down into darkness. "Yes!" Grinning, she gestured to the entrance. "Olaf, you first!"

"Oh, I can't wait to go somewhere new!" he said with an excited wave of his arms.

*Aroooooooooooooooooo!* The sound of the wolf's howl seemed to burrow its way toward them, twisting and tumbling around Anna, surrounding her, becoming both up and down and around.

"Me first!" Olaf hopped down the steps.

Covering her ears to drown out the howling, Anna followed him, along with Elsa and Sven. Kristoff was last, and as he clambered down, he pulled the flagstone securely back over them, plunging them into utter darkness. For a moment, Anna was aware of everyone's breathing, and she wondered if they could all hear the pounding of her heart.

"What *was* that thing?" Kristoff finally whispered.

No one responded, but Anna knew.

It was not just a wolf.

It was a nightmare.

*Her* nightmare.

And it was coming for them.

# Chapter Nine

ANNA'S HEAD POUNDED, her stomach twisted, and her heart hurt.

She wasn't sick, and yet, in a weird way, she wished she were, because colds came and went of their own accord, but this—this aching feeling—*she'd* brought that upon herself. Just as she *must* have brought the wolf upon the castle. She wanted to believe it was a coincidence that the wolf had appeared after she'd read aloud the "Make Dreams Come True" spell, but she couldn't.

Anna had dreamed of the wolf her entire childhood. Now, Kai and Gerda—people who had loved and raised her—had yellow eyes and were trapped in their own nightmarish realities. Why hadn't she listened? Elsa had *told* her to leave the secret room alone, that their parents had probably left it a secret for a reason. And now, Anna had unleashed her nightmare on Arendelle.

"It's a good thing it's so dark," Olaf said from somewhere to Anna's left. "If there are flesh-eating monsters down here, at least we can't see them!"

"Always looking on the bright side," Kristoff's voice called back. "Anna, what is happening? What is a wolf doing in the castle? And where are we now?"

"Elsa," Anna said, fumbling in her cloak pocket for the scrap of spell with one hand, and reaching blindly out into the darkness for her sister's shoulder. "I need to tell you something—"

"One second, Anna," Elsa's voice said from a little further away. "Kristoff, can we get some light?"

There was a rustling, followed by a *scritch* as Kristoff struck a match and lit the lantern clipped to the outside of his traveler's pack. Usually, Anna felt better when there was light, but the wavering lantern flame cast huge shadows across the rough rock walls and across her friends' faces, distorting their familiar features and turning them into strangers.

And—Anna's breath lodged beneath her ribcage—was that a glint of yellow she'd spotted in Kristoff's eyes?

"Seriously," Kristoff said, his face twisting with frustration as he ran expert hands up and down Sven's withers, and then peered into Sven's ear. The poor reindeer was trembling from his close encounter with the wolf, and was standing so close to Kristoff he was almost on the mountain man's toes. "Would someone *please* tell me what is going on?"

As he patted down Sven's quivering legs, he turned his head, and the yellow speck Anna had thought she'd seen disappeared. It had only been the lantern reflected in eyes. Her panic dissolved, just a little, and she took in where she had led them. They were at the start of a tall, wide tunnel, hewn directly from the rough rock of the castle's tiny island. The path led away from them, disappearing into more darkness.

"Where are we?" Elsa tilted her head back and looked up, wide-eyed.

"It's called the Earth Giant's Passage," Anna said. "It was on the blueprints in the . . . the secret room."

Elsa looked at her for a long moment. "You and that secret room."

"What?" Anna said. "It *was*! And *that secret room's blueprints* got us away from the wolf!"

"So," Elsa said, clasping her hands together, "do you know where this passage goes?"

"Not . . . *exactly*," Anna admitted. "I think it goes under the fjord, but it wasn't clear on the blueprints."

"So, you're telling me it could lead to anywhere, including a dead end?"

Anna's stomach twisted. "I . . . I didn't think of that."

Elsa sighed and shook her head. "It's fine. I'll think of a solution."

The words stung Anna, as though Elsa had physically thrown them at her. Anna had let her down. If Elsa was *this* upset about just the blueprints, what would she say if Anna told her she had recited the spell? When exactly was a good time to admit to your sister you'd messed up big-time?

Suddenly, Sven bellowed. His eyes rolled back, and Anna could see white ringing them. In that same instant, from high above, Anna could hear knives being sharpened. No, not knives. *Claws*, scraping against a flagstone floor. The wolf was digging for them.

"We have to go. Now!" Elsa whirled away from

Anna, transforming from annoyed sister to commanding queen. "I'll go first, in case . . . in case there's anything up ahead. Olaf, do you think you could . . . ?"

"Put my eyes on the back of my head?" Olaf swiveled his entire head 180 degrees. "Already done."

Elsa nodded. "Thanks. And if things happen, I want you all to run without stopping. Got that?" Without waiting for a reply, Elsa took the lantern from Kristoff and strode forward through the tunnel, the lantern scattering pale shadows across the rough stone walls.

Kristoff offered his shoulder to Sven, who rested his head on it. "What kind of *things* do you think Elsa meant?" he whispered to Anna.

"I think she means if anything goes wrong, we're supposed to leave her to handle it," Anna explained.

"Like, if there's a cave-in," Olaf added helpfully. "Or an avalanche, or if there's a monster, or if you lose a nose, or if the wolf or Gerda or Kai attack us again, or if Kristoff's eyes turn yellow—?"

Anna threw a hand over Olaf's mouth, stopping the plethora of awful possibilities. "We'll be fine if we just stick together." She wished and hoped that was true. She withdrew her hand from Olaf, and smiled. "Besides, we have something the wolf doesn't have."

Kristoff raised an eyebrow. "What's that?"

Sven's ear perked also, waiting for an answer.

Anna nodded toward the light, and felt her own frustration fade. Even though her sister's outfit was simple enough—a sensible heather-blue split dress perfect for long days at a desk or afternoons visiting a farm—it still glimmered where the lantern's light kissed it, just the way that everything Elsa touched seemed to sparkle afterward.

Anna smiled. "We have Elsa." And with that, she hurried to catch up.

They ran as fast as they could through the passage, which is to say not very fast at all. In part because the passage was so roughly hewn that it proved tedious to navigate, and in part because Sven still seemed shaken and terrified of the wolf, which was presumably still scrabbling at the flagstone somewhere far above them. Sympathy flitted through Anna. As terrified as she had been, it must have been a thousand times worse for a reindeer, whose greatest natural threat was the wolf. Anna noticed that Kristoff kept a hand on his best friend's neck, and now and then, she caught an occasional note as Kristoff sang to him.

Meanwhile, Olaf, his eyes facing backward, kept treading on the hem of Anna's travel cloak. The third time it happened, Anna stopped, recalling how Elsa used to carry her long ago, and crouched in front of him. "Olaf, how about a piggyback ride?"

"Don't mind if I do!" Olaf said. But without his eyes facing forward, it took him more than a couple of attempts, one of which knocked Anna flat onto her belly. "Ta-da!" Olaf climbed onto her back. "I did it!"

"You did," Anna grunted. "Just stay put while I try to get up."

"Anna?" Olaf asked, sitting on her back. "Are you okay?"

Anna replied, somewhat breathlessly as she pushed down with her palms, "I'm fine."

And that's when Elsa screamed.

"ELSA!" Anna cried as a new strength flooded through her. She launched to her feet. Pulse in her throat, she flew down the passage, Olaf clinging to her neck. The tunnel was dark but for the slightest halo of light.

"Elsa! Kristoff! Sven!" Anna cried. "What's wrong?!"

Horrible thoughts stampeded through her mind,

but Anna was able to slam them all out except for one: an image of the wolf, silent as the moon, stalking Elsa, while Elsa's blue eyes drained of their color and shifted to a glowing yellow.

The tunnel bent slightly, and then there they were: Elsa, Kristoff, and Sven. Anna scanned them for any signs of injury, but nothing seemed amiss. No one was bleeding. In fact, there was no sign of anything wrong. And, the more she thought about it, there was no way the wolf could have possibly passed her in the passage to have reached them up ahead.

"What's happening?" Anna panted. "Why did you scream?"

"Sorry," Elsa said, her cheeks flushed pink. "I guess I'm a little on edge, and then when I saw it, I, well . . ." She gestured behind her.

The tunnel had widened into a chamber, though Anna could see that it narrowed again on the far side of the hall. It looked like a python that had swallowed a whole egg, the egg visible in its gullet. And in the farthest shadows of the chamber, Anna saw—

"A dragon!" Anna exclaimed, stepping backward only to tread on the hem of her cloak.

Olaf spun his head around to face forward again,

prodding Anna's ear with his carrot nose. "Silly Anna. It's not a dragon, it's a boat *shaped* like a dragon."

Kristoff rested a hand on Anna's shoulder. "Don't worry. Elsa thought it was a dragon, too," he said with a kind smile.

Anna squinted in the dimness. It was a boat. Or a longboat, actually. Unlike the tall, multi-decked and multi-masted ships with butterfly-wing sails in the harbor above them, *this* boat was sleek, and laid long and low to the ground like a canoe. It had one simple mast, and its only height came at the front and back, where its wooden planks were swept up into the graceful point of a dragon's tail at one end, and the dragon's fearsome teeth at the other. It took her breath away—though part of that was due to jogging with a snowman on her back.

"This isn't just a tunnel," said Elsa. "I think it's . . . a tumulus."

"Oooh. A tummy *what*?" Olaf asked.

Elsa smiled, but it seemed tinged with sadness. "It's a burial mound," she explained. "In the long-ago days, people used to build large dirt mounds called tumuli and lay their fallen leaders in their boats, along with everything they would need to take with them into the afterlife, favorite things like bronze shields, drinking goblets, and gold coins."

"It's beautiful," Anna said, wanting to explore this unexpected treasure. She loved nothing more than answers, and a broken bit of pottery or a single glass bead from a long-ago age could tell a lot about the cultures and tales that had been lost to time.

*Later,* she told herself. *One more reason you have to fix what you've done.*

"I wish it were a real dragon," Olaf said, interrupting Anna's thoughts and pulling her back to the present.

"I think a wolf is more than enough to deal with right now," Elsa said, already holding up the lantern again and taking a few steps away.

Kristoff nodded. "If we don't move, this place may become a *new* grave site."

Olaf shook his head. "Poor Fredrick. I don't think he'd like this place very much."

"Who's Fredrick?" Anna asked.

"The wolf," Olaf said, as though it were obvious. "He looked like a Fredrick, don't you think?"

"I wasn't talking about the wolf," Kristoff said, and shrugged his traveler's pack higher onto his shoulder. "I was talking about *us.*"

They continued to move, faster now and silent. They needed to save their breath to navigate the dark and twisting shadows of the passageway. After a few minutes, Anna thought she felt the ground begin to slope upwards, but she couldn't be sure, and she didn't want to get her hopes up.

"Do you hear that?" Elsa asked suddenly.

Anna listened. She did hear something—a low rumbling. A sound that was almost like thunder, or what she imagined a sleeping Earth Giant's snore would sound like, or—

"A waterfall," Kristoff said. "I think we've gone under the waters of the Arenfjord and ended up on the other side."

New energy quickened their steps. A few minutes later, they turned a corner to see a frothy curtain of water cascading down rock and a weak, gray not-quite-light trickling through into the tunnel. It was that time of night that wasn't night at all, but the earliest moments of morning, the few minutes before the sun would break the line of the horizon.

Night would soon be officially over, but . . . what other nightmares had Anna dreamed that could come true? Would her teeth start to fall out? Would she look down to see she was standing in only her underwear? Or maybe it would be a brand-new nightmare, one where Elsa exiled her from the kingdom once she learned about Anna's wayward spell.

*The spell.* Her stomach twisted. Anna didn't like when secrets were kept from her, but holding her own secret made her feel like she'd eaten some of the Blight-stricken food. Now that they were leaving the tunnel, away from the wolf for at least a moment, she needed to tell Elsa. Maybe together, they could figure out a counter spell. Anna took a deep breath.

"Elsa? I have something to tell you—"

Elsa held up her hand. "You don't have to say it."

Tilting her head, Anna squinted at her sister. "Say *what*?"

"'*I told you so*,'" Elsa said with a small, tired grin. "I get it. You found the passage, and it was helpful. I'm not going to say otherwise. Can we please make a truce?"

Anna gaped at her sister, not knowing what to do. On the one hand, she was pleased that her sister seemed happy with her. But on the other . . . Elsa didn't know that all of this was Anna's fault. And while Anna wasn't exactly *lying*, the more seconds that ticked by, the more uncomfortable the omission made her feel, as though she were more of a scribble of Anna than an Anna who fully filled in all her lines. She hated to keep a secret—but she was more afraid of losing her sister. Oh, *now* what should she do?

But she was spared making a decision when Olaf emitted a squeal of glee directly into Anna's ear. He jumped down from Anna's back, and she stumbled slightly from the sudden lack of weight.

"Hooray!" Olaf cheered. "We're not going to die in a tummy lice!" And then he sprinted down the path. Anna's breath caught. He wasn't really going to run straight through a waterfall, was he? Turns out he was, because in the next second, the water pounded on Olaf's shoulders as he waded into it.

"Oooh! A somewhat *unpleasant* massage!" he said, and then the snowman was through to the other side.

Anna heaved a sigh of relief. Sometimes when Olaf tried something new, he'd fall apart, and they'd have to take time to go looking for his arms or nose or other body parts. And there was no time to spare, not when the wolf could show up at any moment.

Even though she didn't *think* it could dig through solid rock, she couldn't be sure of anything anymore.

She glanced over her shoulder for the billionth time, just to check again.

Kristoff reached out a finger to test the temperature of the waterfall. "Yikes!" He yanked his hand away, and the tip of his finger was bright pink. "That's ice-cold, even by my standards!"

"Hardly," Elsa said, examining it. "Or else it would be frozen." She smirked.

Kristoff made a face. "Touché."

"I've got this." With a flourish of Elsa's lantern-free hand, an arch of ice appeared in the middle of the falls, sending water flying into the breaking dawn and scattering rainbows everywhere.

And as Anna walked under the arch, leaving behind the shadows of the passageway, she felt her headache lift slightly. Her stomach untwisted just a bit, too.

Wolves did exist, yes, but so did rainbows and sisters. There *had* to be a way for Anna to fix her mistake. And there had to be a way she could fix it herself, without adding to Elsa's pile of work. She just needed time—*space*—to think it through.

The Earth Giant's Passage had deposited them on a small ledge that overlooked the village, and the group paused to take count. They were all there, though Anna noted in the dim light of dawn that Olaf's twiggy hair seemed a bit bent out of shape, and new purple crescents had appeared under Elsa's eyes. Kristoff, too, looked bedraggled, even by his usual standards. The cold, crisp air tugged at the fabric of Anna's attire, giving her goosebumps. She pulled her travel cloak closer around her and was thankful she hadn't changed into pajamas.

"I think we should warn the village," Kristoff said, shifting his weight as Sven moved his head onto his shoulder.

Anna's headache returned with renewed vigor, but she tried to focus. Because Kristoff was right. "Yes! We warn the village! Tell them to stay inside!"

Elsa shook her head. "You saw that wolf. I don't think hiding is going to help."

"Then we need to tell them to get far away!" Anna said as she tried to push her loose hair out of her eyes. She wished she'd thought to grab a spare hair ribbon so that she could wrangle her hair into manageable braids, instead of letting it hang loose and tangled around her shoulders.

"But then again, what if the wolf is there now,

prowling the village?" Kristoff asked, and then switched to Sven Talk. "What if he's already full?"

It was almost *too* horrible of a thought, and Sven's ears, which usually pricked forward, seemed to droop like a pair of discarded socks as he swayed on his hooves, looking as though a sneeze from Kristoff would be enough to knock him over.

Anna glanced at her sister, waiting for her to decide what to do. But Elsa didn't say anything. Instead, she stared out across the Arenfjord toward the castle. And even though the castle looked the same, it didn't feel the same. Anna knew all too well that things didn't have to *look* different in order to *be* different. One morning, she'd gone to bed having two parents. The next morning, she'd woken up an orphan.

As she squinted at the castle, Anna caught a speck of white in the window of the guard tower. Beside her, Olaf had put his ice spectacles back on, and was staring at the castle windows as well.

"Fredrick's looking for us," he said, adjusting the lenses so they sat better on his nose. "It doesn't seem like he knows we're gone . . ." Olaf lifted a hand to shield his eyes. "Oh, no, never mind. He does."

"How do you know?" Anna asked.

Olaf pulled his gaze away. "Well, I think he misinterpreted why I raised my hand."

"What does *that* mean?" Elsa asked.

"He definitely took it as a friendly wave to come and join us. Which I think is what he's going to do."

"Elsa?" Anna's voice squeaked.

Elsa's brow furrowed the way it always did when she was looking for something she'd misplaced, or, more likely, that Anna had removed and forgotten to put back. She seemed to be sinking deep within herself. Then, taking a deep breath, Elsa gave the lantern back to Kristoff and raised her hands, like a conductor about to direct a symphony.

At first, Anna didn't see any change, but then she noticed the waterfall's roar had grown quiet. Looking behind her, Anna gasped.

The water was no longer in the waterfall.

Instead of trickling down the sides of the fjord and into the sea, the water was rushing upward, climbing the air as if it had been shot up from a geyser. It arced over the colored rooftops of the village below, its glittering tail reminding Anna of a comet. Her gaze followed its path to the castle, where it dipped and played around it, circling once, twice, three times, again and again until a dome of ice—seamless as an eggshell—covered the entire castle. Elsa had isolated their home inside of its own gigantic snow globe, preventing anyone from getting into the castle—but more importantly, keeping what was already there inside.

She lowered her hands. Her pink cheeks flushed, but her eyes sparkled. Anna had always thought creating ice with magic seemed like it should be exhausting, like trying to run up a mountain in ten seconds, but Elsa always seemed the most *Elsa* after she'd wielded her magic. And she was only getting better at it with each passing day.

"That was beautiful," Kristoff said, awe making his voice sound more solemn than usual, and Anna understood exactly how he felt.

"Thanks." Elsa bit her lip. "I just hope it holds the wolf. Now, we need to go warn the villagers, and get them to safety—just in case."

Anna nodded her head in agreement, tearing her eyes away from the ice-domed castle. Elsa was right. They would go to the village, and then maybe she could—

But Anna's thoughts jumbled up like crooked teeth as she looked away from the dome and back at her friends. The first true ray of morning sun had not just illuminated the beauty of Elsa's creation; it had also brought to light something else: an unmistakable smattering of white in Sven's dun coat.

The Blight had struck again.

# Chapter Ten

"SVEN!" KRISTOFF CRIED, holding up his friend, whose head lolled so low to the ground that his antlers skimmed the frost-covered grass.

Sven let out a rumbling groan, and the sound squeezed the breath out of Anna's lungs. No—not Sven. He'd been fine only an hour ago!

"Mint," Elsa said faintly, and when Anna turned to look at her sister, she saw that Elsa looked as shaken as she herself felt. "SoYun said that mint helped Hebert, and it was effective with the goats I saw the other day, too."

"The botanist's shop!" Anna said, tearing her eyes away from Kristoff's devastated expression and looking out at the village below them. "Gabriella always has mint in her shop! And if *that* doesn't work, Baker Blodget—"

"It'll work," Elsa said, cutting in firmly. "I was there earlier to ask about herbal remedies, but no one was home," she added. "She must be back by now."

With that, they ran down the path to the village, Kristoff keeping a hand on Sven the entire time while Anna's eyes remained fixed on the homes and shops ahead. The sooner they could evacuate the villagers, the sooner they could come up with a plan for how to defeat both the Blight *and* the wolf.

How much bad luck could a single kingdom have at once?

But it could be far worse. Anna knew that. Sven was still in the early stages of the Blight, after all. He could be doubling over in pain, he could be falling over, plunging into that unshakable sleep that would leave him unable to run from the wolf's teeth.

*The wolf.* Did *it* have anything to do with the Blight? Anna remembered the way Sven had stood still in the kitchen as the wolf stalked toward him, as if those yellow eyes had pinned him in place. But that didn't make sense. The Blight came *before* the wolf, but maybe the wolf had so terrified Sven—had so rattled him to his reindeer core—that his body's defenses had been jostled enough for the Blight to settle in and begin to creep through Sven like a thorny, resilient weed.

But at least Sven was moving. He was still strong enough to trot, and he carried Olaf on his back, the snowman holding his own carrot nose in front of the reindeer's muzzle on a string to keep Sven awake and motivated. Anna wished that she had something as simple as a carrot to cheer up Kristoff.

When she'd first met Kristoff, she'd thought he was just a perpetual grump, but as she spent more time with him, she realized that he was someone who loved to laugh and wore a smile easily. Now, though, she could see the solitary mountain man slowly returning. Worry carved lines into his face and his mouth tugged down.

Anna slowed to a walk and slipped her hand into his. "Hey. It'll be okay. I promised we'd fix this mess in three days, and we will. Wolf and all."

Kristoff shook his head, brown eyes troubled. "I just don't understand what's happening. First the Blight, and then I couldn't find the trolls, and then—"

"Wait, what?" Anna gasped. "What do you mean, you couldn't find the trolls?"

"They weren't in the Valley of the Living Rock, and they didn't leave behind any message," Kristoff explained. He shrugged carelessly, but Anna could see the tension in his broad shoulders. "They're mysterious creatures, I get it, but they usually at least leave me snail mail." Snail mail, as Anna knew from experience, was notes written on the bottom of leaves with the help of friendly forest snails. They tended to be a bit difficult to read, and very, very sticky.

"Have they ever done that before?" Anna asked, but before Kristoff could answer, Sven's head jerked up, his ears swiveling forward.

Kristoff dropped Anna's hand. "What is it, boy?"

But Anna thought she knew, as a soft, far-off wailing met their ears. It almost sounded like the wind, mournful and ghostly, but the pitch of it sent a rush of goosebumps cascading across Anna's arms. Because it was *not* the wind. *This* was an utterly human sound—and it was coming from the village.

"*No*," Elsa breathed, and Anna felt sick again. They sprinted the rest of the way.

The village of Arendelle curved around the harbor, balancing along the bay like a flock of birds ringing the edge of a birdbath. Anna had always taken pride in the village's vibrant homes, painted with bright splashes of color and trimmed with exquisite detail. Many villagers liked to add personal touches that matched the personality of those living inside—and Anna knew and loved each and every one of them. There hadn't been one week in the last three years that she hadn't made a trip into the village, even on the days when Elsa wasn't able to join her.

On a usual morning, the villagers woke early, gathering fresh loaves of bread for breakfast and exchanging news from the previous day. Anna much preferred the village to the castle, and she loved having friends. Friends like Baker Blodget, who always had a spare basket of fresh butter biscuits to share with the children—and, occasionally, Anna. Or Akim, the seamster who was deft with the knitting needles and had made Anna her very own hat with cat ears. And then there were the three sisters, Supriya, Deepa, and Jaya, who couldn't wait to see Anna every week to discuss the latest books they'd read and turned into a play.

That was how a usual morning looked. But this was not a usual morning. Not at all. The cobble-stoned streets were empty of people, but full of their screams. Before the wolf had entered the castle, it must have attacked the village.

"NO—" Anna began to yell, but Elsa put a hand over her mouth, stifling her cry.

"Shhh." Elsa pointed to a window. Peering inside, Anna saw Madam Eniola fast asleep, her nightcap askew on her gray hair. Her eyes were closed, but her mouth was open in a bloodcurdling scream. And Anna knew deep in her bones that if Madam Eniola's eyes were to flutter open, they would be as bright yellow as the wolf's. Like what happened to Kai and Gerda.

"If we provoke them," Elsa whispered, "I think they'll attack us."

Anna nodded, sensing that her sister was right. "We just need to get some mint leaves for Sven," she whispered. "Then we can go."

"We don't split up," Elsa said, looking each of them in the eye and taking Olaf's hand. "We stay together, we stay silent, and we keep moving." Spoken like a true leader.

They moved through the cobblestoned paths toward the market. Anna shuddered as they rounded every corner. Though there was no one in the streets, she had the constant feeling that someone was watching—as if all the windows were eyes staring at them.

Or as though a wolf were in the shadows, just waiting to pounce.

But, Anna assured herself, Elsa had sealed off the castle. The wolf, *her* nightmare wolf, was trapped inside, contained until Anna could figure out a better plan. Once they got help for the exhausted Sven—who now lifted each hoof as though it were heavy as a boulder—Anna would figure out a way to sneak back into the castle and read through each and every book in the hidden room, page by page, searching for a counter spell. There had to be one, even if she couldn't remember having seen one. And if the counter spell's runes hadn't yet been translated . . . well, then she would just have to figure out how to decode the language, even if it took her twenty years.

Worry gnawed at her stomach. She knew she did not have twenty years. She might not even have a day. Who else would the wolf enchant with its nightmare bewitchment? What would happen to all of them in the end?

They reached the forest-green doors of the

botanist's shop, and Elsa turned toward her companions. "Stay with Anna," she instructed Kristoff, and before Anna could stop her sister, or join her, Elsa was inside Gabriella's shop. Anna made to follow her.

Kristoff stepped in front of her with a gentle smile. "Elsa said to stay," he said.

"I can't let her go in there alone!"

"I think she's got it covered," Kristoff said, even as he unhooked his pickax from across his shoulder. "She *is* queen."

"She's my sister first." Anna looked at Olaf. "Please stay with Sven and make sure he doesn't fall asleep." Olaf saluted her as she went through the doorway, Kristoff just behind her. Inside the shop, a wailing scream reverberated, a sound so loud and clear and *sad* that Anna wished she could stick one of the many bunches of dried herbs in her ears to drown it out. Then—the screaming stopped. A moment later, Elsa came flying down the staircase.

"Go!" Elsa said, her voice wild with fear. "We need to leave now!"

They hurried out and slammed the door, and then Elsa sealed its seams with ice, for good measure. "I accidentally woke the botanist," Elsa said, panting.

And indeed, Anna could hear footsteps as Gabriella moved inside.

"Did you get the mint?" Kristoff asked.

Elsa held out her hand, flashing a bit of green leaf under Sven's nose.

Sven's head jerked up, and Anna noticed with relief that his pupils contracted, ever so slightly as he inhaled the sharp scent.

"Then what are we waiting for?" Anna said. "Let's *go.*" But before she could turn around, there was a flash of movement out of the corner of her eye.

Kristoff had raised his pickax over his head. "Quiet," he whispered, not taking his eyes from the road. "Something's coming."

A shadow moved toward them across the cobble-stones. Anna held her breath. A figure came into view. Tall, and quick. Elsa raised her hands, and then . . .

"Hoo-hoo," a voice whispered. "Girls, is that you?"

*"Oaken,"* Anna whispered.

Sure enough, there stood Oaken, a large, power-fully built man with shoulders as wide as a rowboat and legs as thick as tree trunks. But despite his rather formidable height, Oaken's round cheeks were as rosy as a porcelain doll's, and his auburn beard and the

frizz poking out from under his cap clashed glori-
ously with the green wool knit sweater that Anna
knew his nan had made for him.

Oaken lifted a finger to his lips. Then he clasped
his fingers together. He looked as though he'd aged
ten years since Anna had seen him just the other
week during a visit to his trading post. Exhaustion
sullied his face, and the cap on his head was askew.
His ruddy muttonchops twitched as he blinked wide
blue eyes. He beckoned.

Together, they walked quietly but quickly through
the empty streets, following the dirt path that Anna
knew would take them down into a grassy valley
surrounded by silver birch trees. But even though
Anna knew the path well, everything seemed different. Trees that should have felt as familiar as old
friends became just another potential place for a wolf
to hide. Had it escaped the hold of the castle? As
soon as they stepped out of the village, Elsa turned
around, and again waved her hands, directing a rush
of cold and a flurry of ice over the village.

A minute later, the village, too, was encased in an
ice dome, the screaming sobs muffled. Elsa didn't say
anything as she hurried to catch up with the group,

but Anna could read the expression on her sister's face clear enough: *I had to. For their own good. And for ours.* And Anna knew her sister was right. What if the wolf got out of the castle, and was feeling hungry? What if the sleepwalkers accidentally wandered out of the village toward the castle and freed the wolf? What Elsa had done was the right thing to do.

Finally, it was safe for them to speak.

"Thank the glaciers you're all right," Oaken said. "We hoped you were okay when we saw the ice encase the castle."

Anna's hope, which had been slipping away from her since Gabriella's shop, caught on his word.

"*We?*" Elsa repeated excitedly, clearly thinking along similar lines. "So, not everyone is asleep?"

Oaken nodded. "A handful of us managed to flee to my Wandering Oaken's Trading Post—"

"And Sauna!" Olaf inserted. "Oh, I'd like to go into your sauna!"

"And Sauna, yes." Oaken nodded. "That's where we're going now." Oaken was a shopkeeper who sold a little bit of this and a little bit of that, from carrots to snow shovels to healing draughts and more. But most famous of all was his sauna, a room of cedarwood and steam that could make even the coldest winter nights feel like a balmy evening in the jungle.

His shop sat in a small pocket in the forest, a little way off from a small creek that fed into a larger river and on the path that led to the North Mountain and the sparkling ice palace Elsa had crafted when she'd first experimented with her powers three years before. The little wooden cabin had been built with loving attention to detail, with geometric patterns carved into its logs, and tall windows fitted with diamond-paned glass.

Oaken took great pride in his shop. He'd once admitted to Anna that he used to think about becoming a designer before figuring out his real joy in life came from taking care of people and making sure they could get whatever they needed from him—for a fair price. Kristoff would disagree with that last part.

Oaken's trading post was open around the clock, and weary travelers could always find the sauna and a pile of fluffy towels ready and waiting to warm them. But as they neared the shop, Anna saw that for the first time in three years, the curtains were drawn, and a little painted sign hung in the window: CLOSED.

"This way," Oaken whispered, leading them

around to a back entrance that Anna had only seen but never entered. He knocked on the door: one long tap, followed by three quick ones. Nothing happened, and then Anna spotted a tiny quiver behind the curtains.

"Password, please?" came a man's voice.

*"Surplus,"* Oaken whispered.

There was the sound of footsteps, then several clicks and a jangle of metal before the door creaked open.

"Hurry, hurry," Oaken whispered. He swept Anna, Elsa, Kristoff, Sven, and Olaf inside, then stepped into the cabin himself, twisting the doorknob to make sure it was locked. Satisfied with his work, he turned to face them, looking concerned. "Four-footed animals aren't usually allowed inside Wandering Oaken's Trading Post and Sauna. This is an exception, *ja?*"

"He's very well-behaved," Anna said of Sven. "I promise he won't be a problem."

Oaken's expression shifted, and he nodded. At last, they were all safe.

Metal screeched again as Oaken slid several bolts shut and clicked no less than seven padlocks. The shopkeeper wasn't taking any chances of letting a wolf enter his cabin and mess up his tidy shop. Anna looked around. Well, what *used* to be his tidy shop.

"Oh, dear," Elsa murmured.

Oaken's shelves, stuffed with an odd assortment of goods—flowerpots sitting on top of books, next to a corner of rakes and barrels of candied nuts—usually marched in straight lines throughout the shop. But now, the shelves and all their wares had been pushed to the edges. Reinforcements for the windows, Anna guessed. In case someone—or some*wolf*—tried to break in. It looked as though the cabin itself were preparing for a great war, and it wasn't just the cabin that was ready for a fight. Looking around, she spotted two villagers in the storeroom. Tuva the blacksmith, her hammer dangling from a tool belt, stood guard at the front door, and at the counter, scribbling across old receipts, was Wael.

At the sight of him, Anna felt a twinge of embarrassment and an even stronger pinch of annoyance. If the journalist hadn't goaded her yesterday, maybe she wouldn't have promised everyone that Elsa could fix everything in three days, and then maybe Elsa wouldn't have had a council meeting without her. And then maybe Anna wouldn't have accidentally spelled the wolf out of her nightmare.

"Where is everyone else?" Olaf asked as he hopped off Sven, made his way into the center of the room, and peered behind overturned bookshelves. "Are they all in the sauna?"

Tuva shook her head. "This is all of us. We're the only ones left."

Anna froze. Earlier, she had assumed she'd find at least thirty or forty other villagers crammed inside. Not just *two*. She looked over at Elsa, but if her older sister had been expecting to find more villagers in there, her expression didn't show it.

Elsa nodded. "Okay. If this is what we have, this is what we have." And though her voice was calm, Anna saw that she played with the tassels of their mother's scarf. "Can someone please tell me exactly what happened?"

"I can." Wael held up a piece of paper. "I'm writing everything down."

Elsa, Oaken, and Tuva moved toward the countertop, but Anna made her way to the corner, where

Oaken had dropped off a pile of thick wool blankets that Kristoff was now crunching into a soft nest around Sven.

"I don't understand." Kristoff shook his head. "He was fine when we were looking for the trolls, and even when we got back to the castle, he seemed good. I mean, hungry, but good." He shook his head. "I *know* it sounds ridiculous, but it's like he got the Blight by just *looking* at the wolf. He's been out of sorts ever since!"

"True." Anna leaned close to Sven and waved the mint leaves under his nose. "Come on, don't fall asleep!" she said.

But the reindeer's eyes drooped. It was exactly as SoYun had described. The Blight was coming on quickly and horribly. Kristoff gently shook his muzzle again and again. There was nothing they could do.

"At this point, we need a mystic," Anna said, thinking of the magically inclined wise-folk who existed in legends.

"Anna? Kristoff? Can you come here?" Elsa called.

Anna and Kristoff hurried over. As they neared, Wael held out mugs to them. "No one wants to fall asleep, just in case."

"Just in case *what?*" Anna took a sip. She almost choked. It was the strongest cup of coffee she'd ever tasted, and she could practically feel the tips of her hair twist up as the coffee coursed through her. Based on Kristoff's now red cheeks and the tremor of Elsa's hand, Anna suspected that they, too, had not been ready for the jolt.

"Everyone who was asleep when the wolf ran through town has stayed asleep," Tuva said, her usually cheerful face somber. "Only the people who were up late at night avoided falling under its sleeping curse," she continued. "That's why we made the coffee so strong. Who knows what will happen if we fall asleep?" It was a terrible thought, made all the more terrible by the sudden exhaustion that washed over Anna. All she wanted to do was curl up and sleep.

"I was awake, but Gerda and Kai, well, they must have been asleep, because, I mean, they would never . . ." Elsa trailed off, at a loss.

"Didn't they attack us?" Olaf asked.

"Well, they didn't know it was us!" Anna rushed to clear her friends' names. "And they weren't exactly themselves. . . . I think they thought we were part of their nightmares." Speaking about them, Anna hoped Kai and Gerda were okay, and that the wolf hadn't hurt them any more than it already had.

Tuva nodded. "Exactly the same with my wife. Ada attacked me, all the while screaming for me to come help her. And there was absolutely nothing I could do." The expression on Tuva's face broke Anna's heart. She knew only too well what it was like to feel helpless. Tuva collected herself and continued. "I left her at home. She just kept screaming and screaming. . . ."

"Anna, you said we need a mystic, *ja*?" asked Oaken, tapping the tips of his fingers together. "Maybe Sorenson can help!"

"Sore-what?" Olaf asked.

"Sorenson," said Oaken. "He's what you'd call an expert in myths and lore. He's the mystic of Miner's Mountain."

"No one lives on that mountain but bears and lynx," Kristoff said.

The coffee was way too strong. Anna could have sworn she'd just heard Oaken say that an expert in myths and lore—a *mystic*—lived on Miner's Mountain.

Elsa tilted her head. "What?"

Oaken started to say something else, but Anna was too distracted to pay attention. Mystics didn't exist. They were just characters in stories Anna and Elsa's mother would tell them before bed as young girls. Mystics were rumored to dabble in potions, enchantments, and powerful spells—but such people simply didn't exist, or so Anna had thought.

But if anyone would know how to reverse an accidental spell, it would be a mystic. Suddenly, finding Sorenson seemed more promising than returning to the secret room. Anna shook her head. If anyone had told her a week ago that she would be seriously considering seeking out a mystic, she would have laughed. But then again, she never would have believed that a nightmare wolf would be stalking the kingdom.

"Why haven't we heard about Sorenson before?" Elsa demanded.

"He keeps to himself in a tall tower," Oaken explained. "But if this is a curse, he could help!"

"Is he . . ." Elsa waved her fingers, sending a dance of snowflakes twirling through the room. "Like me?"

"Why, no." Oaken shook his head. "No one is like you."

"We need to get to him!" Anna said, turning to her sister, who looked less than convinced. Anna whirled to Kristoff and, seeking backup, asked him, "Don't you agree?"

But Kristoff didn't seem to have heard her. He was looking in Sven's direction, and mumbled, "Why is this happening?" His coffee splashed out of his mug as his hands shook—from worry or from the coffee, Anna could not tell. "Where did it come from?"

"Magic," Oaken said. "It has to be." His words seemed to suck the air out of the room as Anna cast a glance at Elsa, only to see that her sister seemed to have, at the same time, both curled into herself and become rigid, like a nautilus's shell.

"Did *you* do this?" Wael asked Elsa.

Anna's headache returned with furious force. "Elsa would *never*—"

"Of course she wouldn't!" Tuva said. "And no one is saying she would. But between the rotten crops, the sleeping animals and people, and now the wolf—what else could it be but a curse or a spell of some sort?"

At the blacksmith's words, guilt surged through Anna. Now was the time for her to come clean. "Elsa?" she said tentatively. The entire room looked at her, and she winced. Her voice had gone *very* squeaky. "Er . . . could I . . . *talk* to you for a moment? In private?"

"It's not like this is a very big place," Elsa said.

"Excuse me?" Oaken interrupted. "What did you say?"

Elsa gaped. "I mean, I didn't—it's lovely, but it's not, you know, the biggest—"

Taking advantage of Elsa's fluster, Anna pulled her sister away from the others and ducked behind the store counter. "We have to go see Sorenson," Anna whispered, fumbling in her travel cloak pocket for the loose page from *Secrets of the Magic Makers*.

Elsa looked up at the ceiling and sighed. "Anna, I've told you, magic isn't—"

"I know, I know." Anna nodded. "It's not the solution. But it might be the reason."

"What?" Elsa asked. "Anna, what are you trying to say?"

"Now, don't get mad," Anna said. "It's just—you see, I heard you having a council meeting without me, which is fine, but for some reason it upset me. I took back *Secrets of the Magic Makers* for some light reading, you know, because Mother always used to tell us stories at night. So, I found this song, more of a poem really, well, maybe it was a spell, only it turns out that maybe, possibly, it just might have—"

"Anna." Elsa sighed, burying her face in her hands.

"The point is . . ." Anna took a deep breath and held out the loose page from the book. "Arendelle is cursed . . . and . . . I may be the one who cursed it."

## Chapter Eleven

ANNA HELD HER BREATH as Elsa took the page, her eyes wide, scanning it line by line.

"Anna—did you see the small note at the bottom?"

"No," Anna said, turning red. "Why? What's it say?"

Elsa moved the paper in front of her, along with a magnifying glass made of ice that she'd crafted.

Peering through the ice, Anna read:

*SPELL NOT GUARANTEED TO BE EXACTLY WHAT YOU WISHED FOR.
**IF NOT REVERSED, SPELL SHALL TAKE ROOT PERMANENTLY ON
ITS THIRD SUNRISE.*

"Oh," Anna said. "Yeah, I . . . definitely didn't see that."

Elsa bit her lip, and her eyes shimmered.

"I'm sorry." Anna shook her head, all the while hoping she could shake away the words. "I was only trying to help."

Elsa sighed. "I know. I can't be upset at you for that."

There was something about Elsa's words that made Anna want to curl up and cry. She almost would rather have had Elsa yell at her than sigh like she had. If Elsa *had* yelled at her, it would have meant that she thought of Anna as someone who had the ability to shape the kingdom's future, but that sigh . . . it was the same sound her parents had made when a five-year-old Anna accidentally broke a clay figurine of a salamander over the mantel. "I thought it was a dragon," a sorry Anna had told them. "I thought that it could fly!"

*It's okay*, they had said. *You didn't know any better.*

"Anna!"

Kristoff's yell cut through Anna's thought spiral. She shot to her feet. Kristoff never yelled like that. Not even the time Anna had set fire to his sleigh to save them from a pack of *normal* wolves, of the animal—not magical—variety.

"What's wrong?" she called. Because something *had* to be wrong for him to sound like that.

"Sven." Kristoff's eyes and hair were wild. "He fell asleep. He won't wake up."

Anna ran out from behind the counter, aware of Elsa following close behind. Sure enough, Sven's eyes were shut and his sides heaved with ragged, labored breath.

Kristoff rubbed Sven's cheek with the back of his hand.

*What to do, what to do, what to do!*

But there was nothing Anna *could* do, except . . . "Elsa!" She whirled around to see her sister. "We *have* to meet this Sorenson person—he may be Sven's only chance!"

"But—"

"We can ask him about, you know." Anna bumped a little against the word *spell*, not wanting to admit to everyone just yet who exactly was responsible for the wolf. "And we can see if he knows how to cure the Blight!"

At least the Blight wasn't *her* fault. It had happened before Anna had said her spell, but still . . . it was rather curious that both the Blight and wolf shared similar symptoms: a strange kind of sleep and color-changing eyes. Anna felt like she was looking at a puzzle with a shifting picture. They could be related, but Anna wasn't sure *how.*

"Oaken, where exactly in the mountain does Sorenson live?" Elsa asked as Anna hurried back over to the counter.

Oaken pulled out a map and spread it smooth in front of the register, then traced a path east, to Miner's Mountain. He tapped his finger at the base of the mountain. "Follow the Roaring River past the Black Mountains until you see the signs for the abandoned mines. Beware. They're dangerous."

Kristoff leaned forward to get a closer look. "Dangerous *how?*"

"They're known for awful cave-ins and terrible landslides," Oaken said.

"And the Huldrefólk who live in the heart of the mountain," Tuva added. "They're tricky. Sometimes, they help. Other times, they lure humans off the safest paths."

Wael rolled his eyes. "The Huldrefólk aren't *real,* you know. They're just bedtime stories, an excuse for people who can't follow directions and a scapegoat for when things go missing."

"The Huldrefólk are dangerous," Tuva continued, ignoring Wael. "*You* know the stories. They like to hide in the shadows. They're thieves—they steal things." The blacksmith dragged her eyes back to Elsa. "I think it would be wiser if you fled, Your Majesty. Maybe another country will have the answer, and they can bring help."

Anna was too stunned to speak. She couldn't believe Tuva was suggesting they leave their home when it needed them most. And from the look on Elsa's face, she knew her sister felt the same way.

"Thank you for your advice." Elsa stood up to pick up her cloak. "I appreciate it. But it's my job to remain in Arendelle with everybody, and to find a solution, Huldrefólk or no. I'll leave now."

Anna shot up. "Don't you mean *we'll* leave now?"

With a flourish, Elsa swirled her cloak onto her shoulders. "No, Anna. You heard them. It's too dangerous. I think it would be best if you all left on the royal ship, at least until things are back to normal. I can protect myself."

Anna could hardly believe her ears. She couldn't leave Arendelle in such a state of danger. "It's not about protection," she said, her thoughts flying fast, trying to come up with a winning argument that could convince Elsa. "It's about . . . about . . ." She looked down at the mug in her hand. "It's about keeping you awake!" she finished. "You need at least one person with you who can keep you awake—"

"And another who knows the way of the mountains," Kristoff added. Anna noted with gratitude that he'd already shouldered his traveler's pack and added a coil of rope to his belt, even though he did cast a worried look at his sleeping reindeer friend. Anna knew how it must feel to volunteer to be separated from a sick and sleeping Sven, but she also knew that it would be even harder for Kristoff to not at least try to help. It was the way she felt, too, and part of the reason why she loved him so much.

Olaf popped up from Sven's blanket nest. "And a snowman who likes warm hugs!"

For a moment, Elsa stood still, as though she'd been carved from ice. Anna had already started planning how she would sneak away from the royal ship if her sister ordered her aboard, but finally, Elsa raised her hands in surrender. "All right. Anna and Kristoff will come with me. Oaken," she said, turning to him, "would you please lead the others to the royal ship? Set sail south as fast as you can, and stay there until you hear word from me."

"And if we don't hear back?" Wael asked.

Anna stuck her chin up. "I promise you—you will."

Oaken lifted a thick finger and pointed out the window. "Then I suggest you leave now. The morning is almost over, and you'll want to reach Sorenson's before nightfall. And remember: beware the Huldrefólk!"

As Elsa and Kristoff did a final check of their supplies, Anna fidgeted with the crumpled spell in her cloak pocket. It might have caused trouble, but it was something her mother had touched, and the thought comforted her. Fastening her cloak, Anna went over to Olaf, who was shoveling a few more carrots into his own traveler's pack.

"I'm coming, too. I'm a snowman adventurer! A snoventurer!"

Anna smiled and placed a hand on Olaf's back. At

least bravery existed in her snow friend, even if it was lacking in others. "I know you are, but Olaf . . . I need to ask you to stay here."

Olaf's grin slid off his face. "You—you don't want me to come?"

"I do," Anna said, and it was the truth. Olaf might be silly, and he could occasionally lose his head, but he was wise in ways of the heart and he knew how to bring warmth to cold places. And Anna had a feeling that, soon, they would be in need of hugs more than ever. In fact, she could use one herself now. But the people standing before her could use him even more. She picked up his carrot nose and set it back in place. "Kristoff needs you here to keep an eye on Sven, and Elsa and I need you here to help the villagers stay awake as they carry Sven and head to the ship." Anna ruffled his twiggy hair.

"Oh, I already have tons of ideas to keep them awake!" Olaf assured her, brightening. "The question is: How will I choose *which* idea?" He began to tick off his repertoire on his fingers. "I could sing soothing lullabies, do an interpretive dance of falling autumn leaves, recite the names of all the best beaches in the world in alphabetical order—"

"Remember," Kristoff interrupted as he came over, his traveler's pack heaped with the added supplies from Oaken, "you're trying to *stop* them from sleeping. Not *put* them to sleep."

Anna nudged Kristoff's boot with her toe. "Hush," she whispered.

"I'll start a rousing game of charades. Or, no. What about jokes?" Olaf said. "Everybody loves jokes. They'll be laughing too hard to sleep. Ahem." He straightened his top coal button. "What do snowmen eat for lunch?"

"What?" Oaken asked.

"I'm not really sure. Snowmen really don't eat anything, which is a bit perplexing. There was the time I tried eating fruitcake, but it kind of went right through me."

Kristoff cocked an eyebrow while Anna giggled.

"Perfect. See, Olaf? You'll be great!" Anna said. But as she followed Elsa and Kristoff to the door, the laughter within her faded. Dangerous things lurked outside these doors, and in the mountains. Dangerous things lurked within books, too. Dangerous power, it seemed, also lurked somewhere within Anna.

But here was her chance to fix things. Here was

her chance to prove herself to Arendelle. To prove herself to Elsa. And if she didn't, if she *couldn't*, the nightmare would be complete.

The wolf would swallow the world, starting with everyone she loved.

# Chapter Twelve

THE SUN SHONE with intensity in the sky, a bright flat disk that sparked the colorful splendor of autumn leaves.

Usually, Anna loved nothing more than sunny fall days, those afternoons when the sky was as blue as could be and everything around her was golden. Usually. Today, though, the sun was *too* bright. It showed too many things: their footprints on the path, their shadows creeping across the ground, the bright gleam of Elsa's hair. All were as visible as could possibly be. Beacons for the wolf that might as well have screamed *DELICIOUS MEALS WENT THAT WAY.*

Even though they had all guessed that the wolf would not move during the day, and that it was still trapped in the castle, there was no real way to be sure. So they stayed away from the cleared wagon path that followed the Roaring River, and instead stuck to the interior of the forest, picking their way over fallen logs and stumbling against rocks hidden by piles of leaves. Anna tripped more than a few times over wayward roots. Sneaking through the woods while imagining a wolf chasing her was all too familiar to Anna.

After a little while, an embarrassed Anna admitted to Kristoff what she had done. And instead of being upset at her, he hugged her. He understood that all she had wanted to do was help, and he was optimistic about their plan to save Sven.

"I don't get it," Anna said, trying to keep her voice quiet enough not to attract attention, but loud enough for Kristoff and Elsa to hear her over the crunching of leaves. "I have good dreams all the time. I've dreamed about flying, and living in a castle made of chocolate, and unicorn quests, and—"

"And me, obviously," Kristoff suggested with a cheeky grin.

Anna nudged his arm. "Focus," she said, trying

to sound stern, though she knew her cheeks were turning pink.

"I'm just glad you didn't dream of something *really* scary—like a land-walking shark," he said.

Anna smiled. "Is that *your* most terrifying nightmare?"

"No." Kristoff shook his head. "When I was little, I used to have nightmares about Bulda trying to spoonfeed me mushroom soup."

Anna paused to unhook her cloak from a thorny bush. "That's not scary at all."

Kristoff adjusted his traveler's pack. "Have *you* ever had a troll try to spoon-feed you?"

Anna giggled and turned to Elsa, trying to invite her to the conversation, but Elsa didn't so much as crack a smile. She'd been practically silent since they'd left Oaken's trading post, and Anna had the sinking suspicion her sister was upset with her.

"H-how about you, Elsa?" Anna tried to keep her tone light and airy. "What's your worst nightmare?"

Elsa pushed back a branch. "I don't have nightmares."

From out of the corner of her eye, Anna saw

Kristoff pick up the pace. He always liked to avoid spats whenever he could. And he, like Anna, could detect one brewing.

"Come on, Elsa." Anna took a quick side step to avoid the branch whipping back toward her as Elsa released it. "*Everyone* has nightmares. I'm your sister. You can tell me. You all know my nightmare now—a massive, girl-stalking wolf."

Elsa flung their mother's scarf over her shoulder. "I don't know what to tell you, Anna, except that *I* don't have nightmares."

Anna's sinking suspicion was no longer sinking. It had hit rock bottom, and anchored in the pit of her stomach. Elsa was definitely upset with her, and the worst part—the absolute *worst* part—was that Anna didn't blame her. Anna was a little furious at herself.

Snowflakes drifted in the shafts of sunlight that trickled down through the trees. Anna looked up. The sky remained as blue as ever, which meant there could only be one other source of snow.

"Elsa, why are you making flurries?" Anna held out a finger to capture a miniscule ice crystal. "We can't have snow. We'll leave footprints. More than the ones we're already leaving in the mud."

Elsa stopped and looked at her. "It's not me."

"Then what do you call this?" Anna held out her finger.

Elsa inspected the flake, and her pale cheeks grew even paler. "That's not snow."

"Anna! Elsa!" Kristoff yelled from ahead. He stood on top of a wooded knoll, looking down at something on the other side. "Come quick!"

They stopped caring who—or what—might hear them, and ran, coming to a halt beside Kristoff. Anna gasped. The forest ended on top of the knoll, and a red farmhouse sat before them, cradled by fields of wheat; wheat that was all white, translucent even, in the sun's sharp light. As Anna looked, a breeze rippled through the field, dislodging the grains and sending up billows of what looked like ash.

The Blight was spreading.

"We can't keep tiptoeing around," Kristoff said, and Anna could tell he was thinking of Sven's white coat that matched the terrible white powder. "All this darting and dodging is taking way too long. We have to move way faster!" He was right. But Anna didn't know what to do.

Even from this distance, she could spot little

white huddles among the fields. Cows that had fallen asleep. Horses that had dropped in their tracks. Any animal that could take them farther or faster had fallen sick. The only thing that looked normal in the bleached autumn landscape was the navy thread of the Roaring River that wound its way to the base of Miner's Mountain in the distance.

"Can you freeze the river?" Anna asked Elsa. "Then maybe we could cross it."

"Huh." Elsa tilted her head. "*That's* an idea! Maybe these will help, too."

Elsa waved her hands, and Anna felt like she'd grown three inches. Looking down at her feet, she realized why: Elsa had transformed Anna's walking boots into a pair of ice skates. Anna wobbled, but Kristoff grabbed her elbow, keeping her upright.

Elsa nodded at the rushing river. "We can ice-skate."

That was *not* what Anna had had in mind. She gulped. It was a good idea, but Elsa was the skater, not Anna. And when Anna did skate, she preferred to skate on smooth, solid ground. On a river, there was always the chance the ice could break, pitching her into icy water. "We'll be exposed on the open river," Anna said slowly. "We won't be able to hide."

"Luckily," Elsa said as she made her way down the knoll and to the river's edge, "you're traveling with an expert in ice. I can make the ice just thin enough that it'll support our weight, but anything heavier—like a giant wolf—will crash right through it." And with that, she stepped out onto the water.

As the toe of Elsa's skate touched the surface, a bloom of ice crystals appeared on the river. The crystal blossoms doubled, then quadrupled, then further multiplied, until the entire surface of the river had transformed into a sheet of wild ice blossoms refracting over and over and over again in the blinding midday sun.

It was, Anna admitted to herself, another one of Elsa's great ideas and magical creations. But just not one she really cared for all that much. She trusted her sister, though, and so she moved to the river's edge. The ice was so thin she could see straight through it, as though it were the delicate pane of her bedroom window.

"Come on, Anna," Kristoff said, "we're losing time!" He jumped out onto the river with his own ice skates. The sheet of ice jounced like a trampoline beneath him, but it held, just as Elsa promised it would.

"I won't let anything happen to you, Anna," Elsa said, reading her sister's worried expression. "This is our best chance, and we don't have much time to fix this nightmare."

Elsa was right. Anna had gotten them into this mess. And now she needed to fix it. Taking a breath, she stepped out onto the ice. Elsa led in front, each stroke of her feet scattering ice crystals across the surface.

Lined on either side by trees in their autumn splendor, the river looked like a diamond necklace set against a cushion of red. And as Anna got her feet under her, she felt her heart lighten, just a bit. The rattling, windswept leaves sounded like applause. She took courage in the sound. It was as though Arendelle were cheering for her, wanting her to succeed. And she would. She wouldn't stop until Arendelle was safe.

Hours passed. Wind snarled Anna's hair, and the constant rush of cold wind meant her nose had started to drip. Her feet were beginning to ache. Elsa's magical skates usually fit just right, but today they squeezed a bit too tight, as though Elsa had forgotten Anna had grown up. Disheartened by the thought, she tried to shake away her melancholy. Anna hit a divot—and tripped. Before she could smash her nose into the ice, a hand caught her arm.

"You okay there, Twinkle Toes?" Kristoff asked.

"Totally," Anna said. "I meant to do that." Even though her ice-skating had much improved since her first lesson with Elsa, she wasn't winning a competition anytime soon.

"Sorry," Kristoff said. "I didn't mean to ruin the Anna Axel."

Putting her nose in the air, Anna sniffed. "I guess I can forgive you."

Kristoff grinned, his hand slipping into hers. "Are you sure?" And then he was off, skating backward as fast as he could, pulling Anna after him. The world around them blurred as he whirled her around, as confident on the ice as he was on solid ground. Faster and faster they skated, balancing on a thin edge between control and out-of-control. Ahead of them, Elsa cruised with ease, not noticing them tilting, slipping, flying, until—

"Look out!" Anna shouted as the river took an unexpected bend. But the warning came too late. Kristoff didn't have time to pull them to a new course, and they skidded off the river and into a tall pile of maple leaves. Lying back, Anna watched as a swirl of golden leaves fell around them.

"I meant to do that," Kristoff said.

"Mm-hmm. The same way I meant to do the Anna Axel?" she asked.

He nodded. "Exactly."

"ANNA!" Elsa's voice tore through the air.

"I'm here!" Anna stood up and shook out her travel cloak to send leaves skittering to the ground. "We had a bit of a misstep. Er, mis-*skate*."

Elsa's blade sent a spray of powder over them as she came to an abrupt stop in front of them. "This isn't a time for game-playing!"

The world as Anna knew it slowed, then froze. And though Elsa hadn't done any magic—there had been no twirl of her hand, no blast of her ice, no ice shard burrowing its way into Anna's heart—Elsa's words froze something deep within Anna. Her *hope*. And things that are frozen . . . shatter. Anna could feel the splinters of her broken hope tumbling through her like smashed glass, making every breath, every blink, painful as she looked at her sister, queen of

Arendelle, who no longer had any place for her sister's silly antics.

"I *know* it's not a game," Anna retorted.

"I don't think you do," Elsa said, her voice carefully controlled. Anna wanted to shake her perfect sister, to see some sort of crack, to show her that she saw her as an equal. But that tone—that disappointed tone—revealed all too well exactly what Elsa thought of Anna. And then Anna was no longer hurt, no longer numb, no longer frozen. She *boiled.*

"I'm *not* a child," Anna said. She was grateful that the ice skates' blades made her taller than she usually was. "Do you think I don't know?" With each word, her voice got louder and louder until she practically shouted. "Do you think I haven't been *trying?*"

And before she could hear Elsa's reply, Anna flung herself out onto the ice.

Digging the blades in deep, she pushed and pushed, going faster and faster. Anna felt too much. She *was* too much. That was the trouble. She was too distracted. Too carefree. Too ridiculous for anyone—even for her sister—to see how she could be helpful to the kingdom.

The wind whipped her cloak behind her, but she leaned into it, wanting to feel the fresh iciness against her hot, angry skin. For a moment, she thought she heard Elsa calling out to her, but she didn't stop. She wanted to skate away from it all. Away from that disappointed note in Elsa's voice, away from Kristoff's undeserved gentle kindness, and away from her own messy, tangled emotions.

Away from her giant, cursed mistake.

The ice groaned beneath her weight, her blades scratching out a mournful note that Anna couldn't escape. *Faster, faster, faster!* If only she could skate as quick as the wind, maybe she'd melt into it and be swept away from all that she'd done.

And that's when the ice cracked.

# Chapter Thirteen

ONE SECOND, everything was cold and dry.

The next second, everything was cold and wet.

The water dragged at Anna like it had fingers.

She gasped once—a single great breath of air—before it pulled her under.

The world below the ice was dark and quiet, peaceful even, except for the wild scream that worked through Anna.

She was *cold* again! She would *freeze* again! And if she died . . . would the wolf win? Anna kicked. She couldn't let everyone down! But no matter how much she willed her feet to propel her back up to the surface, the heavy blades of her skates dragged her down . . .

down . . .

down into the dark.

Or was it *up*? *Sideways*? The dark, ice-cold quiet was disorienting, and her thoughts began to slow. And then, a beam of light shot past her as someone chopped through the ice from somewhere above. Anna felt the water underneath her move like a giant horse, a black wave of water that surged beneath her, and she was flying up through the water and toward the surface with all the strength of a geyser. The water didn't have the temperature of a hot spring, though, but of an icy slush. *Elsa*. Moments later, after much spluttering and coughing, Anna was in the arms of Kristoff and Elsa.

"Thank you for saving me," Anna whispered, shivering.

But Elsa didn't acknowledge her words. Instead, her sister said, "Kristoff, you need take her back to Oaken's."

"What?! No," Anna croaked. "I'm fine. I'll be fine."

"But Anna," Elsa said, throwing her hands up in protest, "you almost drowned."

"Almost," Anna protested. "I've *almost* done a lot of things. I have to help with this!"

Elsa shook her head. "I'm just not sure."

"Why are you always trying to push me away?" Anna asked.

Elsa looked stung. "What? Anna, what are you talking about? *When* do I push you away?"

Anna grew quiet. "I'm sorry. I . . . Please, I *need* to accompany you." For a second, Anna thought Elsa would say no, but then something seemed to melt in Elsa.

She wrapped Anna in a hug. "I'm sorry, too. I didn't mean to yell—I just . . . I'm upset, I guess."

"I didn't mean to cast a spell," Anna said, needing to get the words out now. "I had no way of knowing it would bring my nightmare about the wolf to life."

Elsa shook her head. "It just . . . When did you start having the nightmares?"

"When I was a little girl, and then, this week the nightmare came back." *Ever since I realized that you were going to leave me behind for the grand tour.* But Anna didn't say that last bit out loud.

There was the *scritch* of a match as Kristoff lit a small pile of branches he'd gathered. He gestured the sisters over to the fire.

"When did you *first* have the nightmare?" Elsa prodded as they huddled close to the flames. Steam rose from Anna's clothes as they slowly dried.

Anna thought back. "I think it was the night

you . . . you know." She touched the spot in her hair where the white streak had once been, recalling once more when Elsa had accidentally struck her there with magic as a young girl. "I can't believe you've never had bad dreams."

Elsa shrugged. "The last time I had a bad dream, I must have been eight years old. I woke up and my entire room had turned into a winter landscape." She shook her head. "I felt so bad! Everything got wet and they had to bring in new furniture and carpets for me."

"And you never had the nightmare again?"

"No." Elsa leaned her head back and looked up. "Father taught me a bunch of tricks to try to control my emotions, my magic. I remember he came into my room once with a mug of hot chocolate—"

"He used to do that for me, too!" Anna said.

Elsa smiled, and Anna smiled back, enjoying the surprise bridge that linked them.

"And Mother joined him and told me to imagine bunching up all the nightmares and throwing them out the window," Elsa said. "I used to think that when I balled them up, I would throw them and pretend to feed them to the constellations in the sky."

"I used to do that, too!" Anna said, feeling closer to her sister than ever. "I'd pretend to give them to Frigg the Fisherman so he could fish for them. But the trick didn't stop me from having nightmares."

Elsa shrugged. "Mother's trick worked for me. I haven't had a nightmare since."

"I'm sorry to interrupt," Kristoff said, "but speaking of stars . . . it's getting late."

The sisters smiled, and Anna felt a little bit better, if not completely. Her clothes were still damp, but no longer dripping.

After putting out the fire, Kristoff stepped back on the ice, and Anna followed after him. But the bright hope that had been so certain before now seemed to have been left behind in the maple leaf pile at the riverbank.

Soon enough, the sun began to set, casting long shadows on the ice as they continued to skate up the rest of the Roaring River. Anna couldn't help thinking that their shadows looked like drowning figures trapped beneath the ice.

They were quiet as they skated. Anna didn't want to accidentally step on the tenuous peace between her and Elsa, while Kristoff seemed to be lost again in his own worries. Kristoff's birth parents had died long ago, and for the early part of his life, Sven had been his only family—until they'd both been adopted by the mountain trolls. The farther they glided away from Sven, the quieter Kristoff became, until, at last, it became unbearable for Anna. She needed a distraction—for all of them.

"Kristoff, have you ever met the Huldrefólk?" she asked, blurting out the first thing she could think of. "Did they ever visit the trolls?"

He shook his head. "Not that I know of," he said. "The trolls like to hide, but the Huldrefólk—well, they *really* like to hide, right? I don't think anyone's ever seen one."

"They're known for finding lost things, too," Elsa said, slowing down so the other two could catch up with her. No one in Arendelle, or probably in the whole world, for that matter, was as comfortable on the ice as Elsa. While Elsa always moved with grace, when she skated, she was *more* than grace. She became someone with wind in her veins and wings on her feet. "It's said that Aren of Arendelle once went to visit them."

"But his adventures led him to many make-believe creatures," Anna said as his tales gradually came back to her. "Like mermaids and dragons."

"Right," Elsa said with a nod. "So maybe the Huldrefólk are like dragons and don't exist at all. Maybe Aren never even existed."

Kristoff made a face. "So why do you two know so much about this guy if he may or may not have existed? He's just a legend, right? A myth?"

"Possibly. It's said he did a lot of great things for the land," Anna said. "He carved Arenfjord himself, you know. Or so the old myths go."

Kristoff snorted. "Yeah, right. That's the most ridiculous thing I've ever heard."

"You've never heard the story?" Anna asked in surprise. "I thought everyone knew it."

Kristoff jabbed a thumb at his chest. "Raised by trolls, remember? Some of us didn't have fancy lessons growing up." There was something strange lurking in his voice, as though Anna had hit a nerve. It must have had to do with his worry for Sven. She turned to Elsa and asked, "You know the saga verbatim, right?"

Elsa nodded. "It helped pass the time when I was

growing up." She paused a moment, seeming to collect herself, and then spoke the familiar lines that signified the beginning of a story: "'A long time ago, in the time before time, a great darkness swept over the land . . .'"

Anna held her breath as Elsa recited the ancient tale and described how an everlasting night had set over the mountains, and how humankind had fled to their boats for safety. Humans then lived on the waters for hundreds of years, until the day a strange sickness smote them. Scared, the people had asked the most ancient of water spirits for help, and the Water Spirit had told them that they were withering away without a place to plant their roots—they needed to return home. But all were too scared, except for a young boy.

"'Young as the morning, as fierce as a twig, Aren stepped out onto the land . . .'" Elsa recited.

They skated in rhythm to Elsa's voice, a stroke of one leg, then the other, a beat that flowed through Anna, and calmed her. Impossible things had happened in the past. So why couldn't they happen in the future?

She took heart as Elsa described how Aren had climbed up the highest mountain to bargain with night and bring back the sun, and how when he'd finally freed the sun, the sun had gifted him the Revolute Blade and told him how to bring his people home: by carving a new path for them, right between the protective mountains.

Elsa's voice picked up speed as she reached the crescendo of Aren's very first quest, and Anna couldn't help mouthing along with the words as she suddenly remembered.

"'Revolving moon and spinning sun, forged a crescent blade. From light and dark within the heart, the burnished sword was made. The curving arc of Revolute shimmered in his hand. He raised it high above his head, and smote the edge of land.'"

Without missing a beat, Elsa reached out a hand for Anna, gesturing for her to join her on the final stanza of Aren's first adventure, which Anna found herself happily able to recall. Together, the sisters finished telling the tale: "'The sea rushed in as hidden power flowed from the gleaming sword, and shaped the rock and forest crown of the first majestic fjord!'"

Their voices rang out as one, the words triumphantly echoing across the ice.

"Not too shabby," Kristoff said. "It kind of reminds me of the troll ballad about Dagfinn the Dusty, a troll who was allergic to mountains and would accidentally cause avalanches wherever he went by sneezing boulders out of his nose."

"Wait, what?" Anna giggled. "That's what trolls say boulders are? Troll boogers?"

Kristoff shrugged. "Well, yeah. I can sing it for you, if you'd like."

"Maybe later," Elsa cut in, stopping with a spray of ice. "We're here." She pointed up at a sign:

MINER'S MOUNTAIN

WARNING: KEEP OUT

NO TRESPASSERS OR GOATS

HULDREFÓLK ARE WATCHING!

Anna looked up at the sparkling summit of Miner's Mountain. If she squinted her eyes just so, she thought she could make out the mystic's tower. But it was so high up and so far away that from where she stood it looked more like a chimney that had been stuck on top of a roof rather than a tower on a mountain. It would take *days* to climb all that distance.

For people who didn't have a magical sister, that is.

Elsa waited for Kristoff and Anna to step off the frozen river before she did so herself. As soon as Elsa was on the bank, the ice cracked, and blue water began to flow once more. With a twirl of Elsa's hand, Anna's ice skates melted away to reveal her boots beneath, but Anna hardly realized it because of the great whirlwind that kicked up around her, snow climbing into the air higher and higher, until solidifying into a grand icy staircase.

Elsa had done it again. While the staircase of ice was long and ever so high, with nothing but a curving, slender handrail, it would be much easier to navigate than a treacherous and tedious rocky trail. There must have been at least a thousand steps in the ice staircase—Anna couldn't be bothered to count. Either way, they were going to climb it, because, at the very top, answers were waiting for them.

"Classic," Kristoff said to Elsa.

"Thanks," she replied.

One step, then another, they ascended.

At first, Anna didn't bother holding on to the fragile railing, but about two-thirds of the way to the top, she looked down and gripped it tight. The staircase was clear as glass, and Anna—though brave—wasn't entirely comfortable with the sight of her feet seemingly dangling above thin air. From this height, the pines seemed to shrink, smaller and smaller and smaller. As they moved up, the sun moved down.

At long last, in the blazing sunset, they reached the top. From there, the tower was much taller than Anna had realized—and much more jumbled. The rocks that made up the tower seemed to be haphazardly arranged, and certain stones seemed to be on the verge of slipping out of place. In fact, the tower did not look unlike the staggered piles of books Anna had left in the library. Elsa reached the door to the tower first, and paused. Her hand remained still, raised out in front of her, as if she couldn't decide whether she should knock.

Anna pulled her cloak to her chest as the wind sang around them. "What's wrong?"

"What do I say?" Elsa asked.

"You knock and say hi, and we'll go from there," Kristoff called. *"Hurry."*

"What Kristoff said," Anna said, watching the sun sink over the horizon.

Elsa threw back her shoulders and knocked.

Then the three of them stared at the door and waited, but nothing happened. Was no one home? The thought filled Anna with a heavy dread. They had come all this way, and Sorenson was not there.

Elsa knocked again. Nothing.

"Stand back," Kristoff said. He moved in front of Elsa and put his shoulder to the door. But it was sturdier than it looked. He lifted his pickax high.

"Why don't you try the handle?" Elsa asked.

Kristoff raised an eyebrow and did just that. The door swung easily open.

"Huh," he said as he put his pickax away. Without saying another word, he went inside.

Anna exchanged an amused glance with her sister, and they followed him through the doorway and into the tower. From the outside, the tower had looked about to topple, but the inside seemed solid enough, made up of rock and wood and books.

Anna had always imagined a mystic to be exacting, the kind of person who might label the spices in their kitchen cabinet, but everything seemed to be randomly placed. Plants sprawled on top of books, and books on top of statues. On the far side of the circular room was a spiral staircase. There was practically everything under the sun in the tower room.

Except for a mystic.

# Chapter Fourteen

KRISTOFF GROANED, letting his traveler's pack thump to the floor. "He's not here. Now what?"

"I'm sure he'll come back," Anna said, unclasping her cloak. The tower felt especially stuffy after being in the wind all day long. "In the meantime, we wait."

*Arooooooooooooooooo!*

A long, low howl wrapped around the tower, carving a pit in Anna's stomach—was it the wolf? Had it escaped Elsa's ice dome?

Kristoff, however, remained calm. "It's just the wind. Trust me." He picked up a small guitar that leaned next to a potted plant. "Growing up with trolls, you know what's the wind, and what's a wolf." He strummed the guitar. The tinkling sound filtered through the air, pretty, if a bit off-key.

Anna's fear receded a little, and she hoped he was right. "I'd rather the wolf be stalking us here and leaving the villagers alone," she admitted.

"Very noble of you," Elsa said. "We'll stay, but just until we figure out a plan in case Sorenson doesn't come back soon."

"Maybe there's a book or something here that can undo the curse," Anna said. "One that's already been translated."

"That's a good idea," Kristoff said. "I'll take the upstairs. You two search down here." And with a nod at the girls, he lit his lantern and disappeared into the swirl of dark steps above them. Anna thought she knew why he wanted to search a floor by himself. When Anna was upset, she always sought company, but when Kristoff was upset, he liked to be by himself or with Sven. And with Sven in trouble, she knew Kristoff was having a hard time, too.

Elsa sighed. "Ugh. I knew coming here was a bad idea."

Anna felt herself bristle like the gray barn cat, but she didn't want to fight, not again, not so soon. They had come a long way, and they had more of a way to go. So she kept her voice light. "We don't know that yet. Let's just give this room a chance. Please?"

Elsa crossed her arms, but after a second, Anna knew she'd won. This round, anyway. They divided up the circular room. In the light of a dying fire, she could see the walls were plastered with detailed star charts and strange silver instruments that hummed, and a delicate gold miniature of the solar system that was so beautifully done, Anna thought it was a shame that she couldn't study it for hours and tell the children of the village all about it. She also found a calendar with all the phases of the moon laid out, three miniature telescopes, powder-filled glass vials, and an old sundial, its copper face green from the years it must have spent out in the harsh elements. And last but not least, a hunk of blue-black rock that was labeled METEORITE.

"This mystic seems to really like the night sky," Anna called to Elsa.

"I noticed," Elsa said as she straightened a frame. "Did you see the ceiling?"

Anna tilted her head back and gasped. A star map had been painted above them in deep blues and indigos. Delicate lines of silver paint connected some of the stars, tracing the outlines of fantastical beasts, crowns, and heroes. They were familiar images, and Anna recognized them as constellations. But there was something else about the illustrations that seemed familiar to her, though she couldn't quite place her finger on it. . . .

"It's so pretty," Anna said. "It's the prettiest ceiling I've ever seen."

Elsa nodded. "I like it, too. It even has my favorite constellation—Ulf." She looked over at Anna and smiled. "Ulf the Wolf was always my favorite. I made Mother tell me all his stories."

The sisters kept searching.

Sorenson's thinking seemed random, and his shelves didn't appear to be organized in any particular order that Anna could tell. Though, when she peeled back the first book's cover, she wondered if maybe he had ranked them by stench. Many of the books had dark stains on their pages, and a couple of them even had their own furry patch of mold. But for someone who was known to be an expert in myths and lore, Sorenson didn't appear to have many books on those topics. The closest thing was a small slate covered with strange symbols in chalk, but upon examining it, Anna saw it wasn't magic, but physics.

Wandering over to the last bookshelf, Anna skimmed the titles: *Book of Later Han* by Zhang Heng, *Almanack* by Richard Saunders, and *Book of Optics* by Hasan Ibn al-Haytham. Picking up the first title, Anna flipped through the pages to see sketches of instruments that looked quite similar to those sitting on the mystic's shelves, along with annotations of water clocks and wind flows. No mention of curses, or of dream spells gone awry.

"It's funny," Anna called out to Elsa as she tapped the book back onto the shelf. "I wouldn't think that a mystic would have so many books on science. I thought he would have more spell books and stuff. You know?" She paused, waiting for her sister's response. But when Elsa didn't say anything, Anna called again. "Hey, Elsa?"

"Anna, can you come here?" Elsa asked.

Anna followed her sister's voice to where she stood in a back room, more of an alcove really, that contained a tiny kitchen. Anna hurried over to her sister to find her gaping open-mouthed at a table. It looked ordinary enough, but then Anna saw it: on the center of the table was a pot of soup.

A *steaming* pot of soup.

Anna's stomach flipped. For that twist of steam to exist, someone had to have been there recently.

"Where's Kristoff?" Anna whispered. She'd planned on checking on him, but had become distracted by the many books and treasures. The mystic's mind seemed just as distracted as her own. And now Kristoff had been gone upstairs for at least ten minutes, and he'd not come back down.

"Anna," Elsa whispered, "I don't think we're alone here."

"Exactly so," said a low, raspy voice.

Anna spun around as a man stepped off the staircase landing and into the tower room. He was short, barely up to Anna's shoulders, and he wore his long silver beard down to the floor. Anna had the fleeting thought that he looked a bit like the nisse from her mother's tales, those tiny gnomelike creatures that would adopt a family to both hinder and help. The only thing he was missing was a nisse's traditional pointy red hat, but he did have a sharp, glinting spear—and it was aimed directly at her heart.

Anna stopped breathing. In the corner, she saw Elsa raise her hands. They were trembling. But there was Elsa, once again ready to step in. Anna knew better than anyone how much Elsa never again wanted to use her powers to harm another—not after the disastrous consequences that had occurred the last time, when she had turned Anna to ice by accident. But Anna also knew that Elsa *would* use her powers to protect Anna—and Anna could not allow that. Not when Anna could do something about it herself.

"Hi! I'm Anna! This is Elsa!" Anna smiled, trying to inject as much cheer and goodwill into her voice as possible. "We're sorry to intrude. We promise we weren't going to eat your soup—it smells a bit funny—er, that's so rude of me. I'm sorry. I mean, it doesn't smell bad, but I'm not really sure I recognize that spice? But we're not here for spices. Please don't hurt us!"

*"Hurt you?"* The man looked dizzy from trying to follow Anna's words. "Why would you think I would want to hurt you?" His voice was deep and grating like gravel.

"Umm." Anna's eyes flew to his hand. "Because of the spear you're holding?"

"What sp—? Oh!" The man lowered the point of his spear. "This isn't a spear, it's part of a weather vane. That *mountain man* upstairs broke it when he barged onto my peaceful observation deck unannounced! He's *exceedingly* lucky I finished my Highly Flammable and Very Dangerous Combustion Powder last night, or he might not have ten fingers. Hmph."

Anna blinked as the man shoved the pointed weather vane under her nose, and she took in the large golden *N* that twinkled in front of her. *N* for north. "Ha ha," she said, and pushed the golden point away from her. "What a silly mistake. Is the, er, mountain man . . . all right?"

"He *will* be, once he cleans up the mess he made," the short man said, shooting her a glare. "He's *also* lucky he didn't come next month and disturb my view of the meteor shower. But that's what *I'm* doing here. I live here. Always have. My question is: what are *you* doing here?"

"We're looking for the *great* mystic Sorenson," Anna said, trying to sweep a curtsy, but her knees were still shaky from misinterpreting the weather vane, and she almost knocked over a nearby bust of a man in round reading glasses. "We're assuming that's you?"

The old man snorted. "I'm Sorenson, but I'm no mystic."

Elsa stepped forward, her hands no longer raised, but now clenched in the folds of her cloak. "But the villagers say you *are* a mystic."

"I'm a *scientist*," the man said, using the weather vane to reach through his thick beard and scratch the underside of his chin. "Though I suppose the villagers might not see that much of a difference between me and the old mystics of legendary tales."

*A scientist.* Anna tried not to let her disappointment show. It was great to be a scientist, but not when one needed a mystic to save a kingdom from a vicious magical wolf. How would a scientist be able to help with a terrible curse? "We're sorry to have bothered you." Anna stepped aside as Sorenson shuffled past her to check on his soup. "Oaken had told us that you're an expert in myths and lore."

"Oh, but I am." Sorenson gave his pot a stir. "Mythology and science are familiar friends—both seek for the *why* behind things. Both look to provide an explanation for the natural phenomena of the world around us. And all myths contain a kernel of hard truth." He took a sip of his soup and winced before tossing in a pinch of salt. Only after he took another sip and nodded his head in satisfaction did he look back at the sisters. "Though I *am* curious as to why the queen and princess of Arendelle are here seeking an expert in myths and lore. Something must be truly wrong."

"Because," Elsa said, her voice low but steady, "Arendelle has been cursed."

"And we need your help to figure out how to undo it," Anna added, attempting to gloss over the fact that *she'd* been the one who'd cursed it. She tried not to look at anyone, but Elsa caught her eye and nodded. For a moment, it felt like an ember from the fireplace had broken away from the logs and settled somewhere in Anna's heart. Even though snow and ice flowed through Elsa, she always made Anna feel the warmest. Maybe everything wasn't lost, after all.

Except, Sorenson's reaction wasn't exactly encouraging. His bushy eyebrows shot up so fast that they almost skidded off his face, and Anna wondered for a minute if he would laugh. Instead, he opened an old trunk and began pulling out empty bowls.

"In that case," Sorenson said, "someone please fetch the mountain man from the observation deck and have him rebuild my fire. It seems as though you have a story to tell, and I'd rather be warm while I listen."

A few minutes and a roaring fire later, Anna, Elsa, and Kristoff gathered around Sorenson's table, each taking turns sharing all they knew. Anna heard Elsa describe the unnatural quiet that had befallen SoYun's farm and the way the trees in the kingdom's orchards were not only producing mushy gray apples, but had also become gnarled, as though they were twisting away from something—the wolf, Anna guessed—as it had passed by. But did that mean the wolf had been present before she read the spell? And if so, how?

Then it was Kristoff's turn, and he described how the forest, too, had been quiet, though he did not mention the trolls or their surprising absence. Arendelle's mountain trolls were private creatures, and for the most part, they liked to keep themselves hidden from humans, with a few special exceptions. Kristoff wouldn't mention them to just any person, and though Sorenson was now feeding them warm soup that tasted of mushrooms and roots, Kristoff was still protective of the concealed trolls who had raised him as part of their family, and, after all, Sorenson *had* forced Kristoff to clean up his mess out on a chilly observation deck.

Finally, it was Anna's turn. She began with the

crumpled piece of paper with the "Make Dreams Come True" spell on it, and how she'd had a nightmare, and gone to the kitchen to make some hot chocolate. She told him how she'd seen something out of the corner of her eye and followed it to the Great Hall, where she'd seen a wolf—the same wolf from her nightmare. And how her friends' eyes had turned inky black and then glowing yellow while they seemed to have lost themselves in the strong hold of a nightmare sleep. As she completed her tale, Sorenson stood and went to his shelves. Pulling out two books, he returned to the table, the wooden floorboards beneath his boots creaking slightly as he walked.

"I think," Sorenson said, placing the books on the table and slipping back into his stool, "that the answer can be found in one of these."

Anna looked at the books. One was a tome called *Psychologia*. The other was a slim leather volume with block letters stamped across its cover:

NATTMARA

"*Nattmara*,'" Elsa read out loud. "I know that word."
Anna knew the word, too. She'd heard the word

before, long, long ago, but she had *seen* that word recently as well, as a non-translated entry in *Secrets of the Magic Makers*. A vision sprang to her mind: a sketch of a man screaming in agony, and the drawing of the wolf . . .

"Yes." Sorenson nodded. "You probably do. Nattmara often show up in the sagas of old, and those stories are often told to children as warning tales." Flipping open the ancient book, he pointed to an illustration of a child sleeping in bed. "Another name for a Nattmara is 'Nightmare,' because that's what it is—the embodiment of our deepest fear."

"Embody-*what*?" Kristoff asked.

"It means that nightmares can take on a physical shape and exist outside of your mind," Elsa said.

"Precisely." Sorenson held up his pointer finger. "The act of burying fear is what manifests the Nattmara. And eventually, the fear is too big to keep inside. They can take the shape of anything, and this particular one seems to have taken the form of a wolf. Nattmara tend to roam the world, leaching energy from all living things. Their very presence can cause trees to twist away from them. They feed on fear, and so they seek to *create* fear."

Anna's eyes widened as she listened, trying to grasp onto the strange ideas.

Sorenson flipped the page to another illustration, this one of a swirling storm of black sand. "A Nattmara is also able to turn itself into black sand in order to slip through cracks—cracks in doors, and cracks within the heart. There is no escaping them, unless you're brave enough that there is no weakness for the Nattmara to enter through."

He looked up, his brown eyes locking on Anna. "And if a Nattmara is allowed to run loose for too long, then a kingdom and everyone in it can fall into an eternal nightmare sleep. And as it grows more powerful, more people can become afraid, and it can gorge itself on fear, becoming bigger and bigger." He tapped the page. "Or so the age-old myth goes."

Anna blinked, breaking away from Sorenson's deep gaze. "You don't sound like you believe in this myth," she said, puzzled. "But doesn't what's happening in Arendelle now *prove* that the myth is real?"

"Not at all," Sorenson said, shaking his head and sending his long beard swaying. "What do they teach in schools these days? The Nattmara is a creature of myth, and like all myths, it's an explanation to a greater mystery. In this instance: where do night-mares come from?"

"Pardon me," Elsa said, while Anna and Kristoff exchanged puzzled glances, "but I don't understand your question."

Sighing, Sorenson shook his head. "Let's look at it a different way. Did you see the signs for the mines that warn to be wary of Huldrefólk?" He paused, and when they nodded, he continued. "The mines were abandoned nearly twenty years ago, because of strange and mysterious things that kept going wrong. Cave-ins started to occur with increased frequency, and miners that had worked their entire lives in these tunnels began to get lost. Now, what was the explanation?" Sorenson looked from Anna to Elsa to Kristoff.

"Huldrefólk," Anna said, thinking back to the sign they had passed and Oaken's warning. "The myste-rious, elf-like people known as the Huldrefólk are rumored to live throughout Arendelle in mounds and under rock. They are a mischievous bunch, not necessarily bad, but they enjoy pranks above all else. They have a bit of a reputation for being thieves, but some stories insist they are simply collectors, borrow-ers of lost things. But unlike the mountain trolls, they are just a story that parents tell their young ones to go to sleep."

"Exactly," Sorenson nodded. "The miners believed the Huldrefólk were angry that they were impeding on their territory. They thought the Huldrefólk were creating the cave-ins to scare the humans away."

"It seemed to have worked," Kristoff remarked. "I noticed some boards over the mines' entrance."

"It did work," Sorenson agreed. "And a good thing, too, because the mines had been overworked. The miners weren't in danger from territorial Huldrefólk. The human miners were in the middle of a danger of their own making. It was *their* pickaxes that had made the rock walls too thin to hold the weight of a mountain. Nothing mythical about it; just old-fashioned greed."

"So," Elsa said slowly, "you're saying the Nattmara probably has a simple explanation, too?"

"A *scientific* one," Sorenson clarified. "Most likely, our answer is in this." He tapped the book labeled *Psychologia* with a grimy fingernail.

Anna turned this information over. What Sorenson had said seemed simple enough, but she had seen the wolf. She had seen Kai's and Gerda's eyes.

The "myth" had seemed very real as it had chased her and her friends through the rooms and halls of the castle.

"But say it *is* a Nattmara that is doing all of this," Anna argued, not wanting to leave empty-handed, not wanting to leave without at least *one* answer. "How can we defeat it?"

"That's easy enough," Sorenson said, pulling out another book, this one titled *Mythica Explainia*. "You can only defeat a myth *with* a thing of myth. But it's not like Revolute exists. None of it really truly does."

"Revolute?" Kristoff asked. "That was Aren's sword, right?"

"The very one." Sorenson nodded. "Aren was said to have defeated many a mythical beast with his sword. The very sword, some say, that the sun herself gifted to him for ripping holes in the night sky so that she could watch her children during the day. Those rips, of course, are what we call stars." He smiled up in the direction of his painted ceiling. "See? Another myth seeking to answer how things came to be."

"Great!" Anna felt hope lift within her for the first time since they'd arrived at the tower. "So we need Revolute! Where is it?"

Sorenson burst into laughter, but as he did, he took in the serious expression on her face, and shook his head. "I'm sorry, but it's unlikely that Aren *himself* ever existed—*or* his mighty sword of myth. It's likely that there was a strong warrior from way back when, but he probably never met the sun or faced a great dragon, or carved out the Arenfjord. That's just legend—like the Huldrefólk or the mountain trolls."

"But the trolls exist," Kristoff said with a shrug. "They raised me."

Sorenson stared hard at Kristoff. Then he cupped his hand around his mouth and whispered in Elsa's ear, *"Is the mountain man okay?"*

*"Kristoff,"* Anna corrected, "is amazing. And the trolls *do* exist. And the Nattmara exists. And the Huldrefólk, well, they probably exist, too!"

Sorenson sat back, snapping his book shut. "Magic and myth don't exist," he said.

Elsa smirked and flicked her wrist. A second later, Anna felt a cold kiss on her cheek. She looked up to see a delicate snow flurry hovering above their heads.

There was a loud clatter as Sorenson tumbled from his stool. "In all my days! The rumors are true!"

Elsa smiled. "You haven't come down your mountain in a very long time, have you, Sorenson?" And so, Elsa began to tell Sorenson all that had happened in the last three years. And with each new thing he learned, Sorenson had another question.

Kristoff drummed his fingers on the table impatiently, and only when Anna laid her hand over his did he stop. "Sorry," he whispered, "but while we're talking, Sven is still sick!"

Anna knew that Kristoff was right. "Let's keep looking," she said quietly.

Kristoff crept over to the bookshelves while Anna cracked open the volume on the table. She skipped past passages about talking trees and a playful wind spirit until, finally, she found what she had been looking for: NATTMARA.

Sure enough, all that Sorenson had said was written there, including a few additional pieces of information:

*The Nattmara is created when a child's fear grows too big to be contained and the child's fearful heart calls out to them.*

And then, a little below that:

*Trolls tremble at the Nattmara's howl
while the Nattmara flees from the sun like a shadow.*

Nothing in the section said anything about a spell that was able to manifest a Nattmara, or banish it. But it was useful to know that the Nattmara didn't like sunlight. And it explained why the trolls had most likely gone missing. Frowning, Anna thumbed through the pages and reread an entry about the Huldrefólk. She stopped upon a line:

*Huldrefólk always find that which is lost.*

*That which is lost* . . . Anna's heart quickened. Maybe, she thought with rising excitement, that also meant the Huldrefólk could find a mythical sword that was lost to history. It was a slim hope, but a hope she clung to nevertheless. Maybe they needed to go to the mines to find the Huldrefólk—*despite* the warnings.

But they didn't have much time.

They only had two more sunrises left before the spell became permanent—and the night was no longer young.

"You know," Sorenson said to Elsa, "your mother came here once, seeking answers. In fact, she was the one who painted my ceiling."

Anna froze. Their *mother* had been here? It couldn't be. Why on earth would their mother come to visit Sorenson? Answers to *what*? And suddenly, she realized why the painted ceiling looked familiar. It reminded her of the painting of the northern lights and constellations that decorated the ceiling of the secret room.

Slipping the book into Kristoff's traveler's pack, Anna opened her mouth to ask Sorenson more, and to tell the others her idea about going to the mines. But as Anna looked up, she noticed something strange across the tower room: an army of black ants pouring in from under the door. She shut her mouth.

No. Not ants.

*Black sand.*

The Nattmara had found them at last.

# Chapter Fifteen

AS THE BLACK SAND trickled into the tower room from beneath the door, thoughts, dark and sticky, clung to Anna like oil.

Thoughts like bugs crawling into ears, teeth rotting and falling out, waves black and drowning, and a door. A large white door with purple flowers repeating over and over again, each one telling her that she was not good enough, that she was not wanted, that she was shut out. And as the thoughts hit her, pounding as relentlessly as a stormy sea, Anna felt it hard to breathe. Her heart tightened as if something was pressing on her chest. The weight made it hard to speak, but she must—she had to warn her friends.

"Y-you guys," Anna whispered, trying to get her mouth to work. But in those few precious seconds, the sand had spilled into the room, forming a dark puddle. The grains lifted and swirled into the air, as if each grain had its own pair of miniature wings, its own brain, and then they swarmed, creating the outline of a shadow. A wolf's shadow.

Fear gave her strength. "Nattmara!" Anna yelled.

The sand solidified into the great white wolf. Now the creature was as big as the length of wall. Its head practically scraped the painted ceiling.

As if in slow motion, Anna saw the others turn. Kristoff's mouth dropped open, while Elsa's eyes widened in horror. But it was Sorenson—the old scientist who believed in the entanglement of science and myth, myth and science—who reacted first.

"Close your eyes!" He bolted up and grabbed for one of the many glass vials near him.

Anna shut her eyes. A second later, there was a bright flash even through her closed eyelids, followed by the yelp of the wolf. *No. Not a wolf,* Anna corrected herself. *Nattmara.*

"Upstairs!" Sorenson yelled. "Run!"

And even though she had closed her eyes to the flash, black dots still spotted her vision as she stood and ran with Kristoff toward the steps. Taking them two at a time, she was aware of screaming and a noise that sounded like sharpening knives. Glancing backward, she saw Sorenson at the bottom of the stairs, and beside him, Elsa, shooting ice javelins at the wolf again and again and again.

But the ice javelins, sharp and lethal, seemed to do as much harm as a toothpick plunged into water. Each time Elsa let loose an ice javelin, it soared through the air toward its target—but it never *hit* its target.

The Nattmara didn't seem to be made of fur or bone or muscle. Or anything solid, really. Because as ice javelins were about to pin its paws down in place, the wolf's paws dissolved at their touch, shifting and morphing its shape like—*like sand*, Anna realized.

It was as Sorenson had said. The Nattmara could take any form. Seep through the cracks in any door. Slip into the fragile spots of a person's heart. It fed on fear, but how could they not be afraid of it? It *was* fear. A bit of black sand floated toward Anna, and her breath caught again. The sticky thoughts rushed back into her mind: *She'd* done this. She couldn't do anything right. She never could. She'd failed Elsa.

"ANNA!" Kristoff, his traveler's pack dangling from his shoulder, pulled her arm. "KEEP GOING!"

The sound of his voice—full of worry and care—snapped Anna back into herself. She ran with him, and didn't stop racing up the dizzying, tight spiral of steps until she exploded out into the cold, open air of Sorenson's observation deck.

Any other time, she knew she would have loved to stay up there. The mountain air was so clear that the stars above pulsed bright. The moon overhead was round and ripe, just begging to be plucked from the sky and put into her pocket as a sweet treat for later. And in the center of the circular deck, standing like a newborn colt on spindly legs, gleamed a copper telescope. It pointed to the heavens, an instrument that helped seek answers in the celestial dance. It was all strange, fascinating, and beautiful. And a dead end.

Just like in Anna's nightmare, there was no place to run.

The wolf, still behind them on the tower stairs, had cornered her, this time on a wooden deck, hundreds of feet in the air, and the only means of escape—jumping—definitely didn't bode well for any of them. They were trapped!

Sorenson's shoulder collided with hers as he shot past her to the edge of the deck. Leaning over the simple wooden railing, he grasped at the night air and then pulled back. In the light of the full moon, Anna could make out the silver glint of something in his palm: a wire cable—one so thin it seemed to vanish only a foot away from the tower.

"Grab the tablecloth!" He gestured to the long wooden workbench that stood next to the telescope. It was covered in beakers, thermometers and barometers, pencils and quills, abacuses, rulers, flasks, and pages of calculations. And seemingly all of Sorenson's life's work sat on a little lavender tablecloth neatly embroidered with a crocus. If the tablecloth were pulled, all of that work—years and years of it—would smash onto the deck, lost forever. Anna hesitated.

"Do it!" Sorenson roared at her.

But Anna couldn't, she just couldn't. It was a table of answers, the work of a lifetime of gathering information. So Kristoff reached behind her and tugged the tablecloth free. With a tremendous clash, the beautiful and strange devices fell to the floor, the sound something similar to the breaking of a heart.

"Now tear the cloth!" Sorenson commanded.

The sound of the wolf's vicious barks and the scrape of ice filled the air. Elsa had made it to the observation deck and stood at the entrance, flinging her hand out again and again and again. With each flick of her wrist, the doorway filled to the brim with ice—fresh ice, new ice, ice without cracks.

For a moment, anyway.

Because then the Nattmara would slam itself against it, sending cracks scattering across the surface, and a little more black sand wisped through the cracks each time.

Smooth ice.

Shattered ice.

Smooth. Shattered. Elsa was holding the Nattmara and its sandy paws at bay, but even Elsa—brave, strong, wise, magical Elsa—couldn't keep at it forever. Already, Anna could see the weariness in the slope of her shoulders. The snap of her wrist grew looser with each deft gesture.

*Riiiiiiip!* Anna turned to see Kristoff obeying Sorenson's orders and tearing the tablecloth into thick strips, but Anna didn't offer to help. Instead, her mind had become preoccupied by something else. Each time Elsa flung out her wrist and filled the doorway with ice, Anna thought the Nattmara grew a little bigger. Smooth ice. Shattered ice. Smooth ice.

Yes, Anna was sure of it now. Whenever Elsa shot a magical blast of ice at the creature of myth, its paws expanded, its teeth sharpened, and its strength doubled.

"Elsa!" Anna cried. "Elsa, stop! Your magic! It's making it stronger!" But between the snarling of the Nattmara, the tearing of the cloth, and the sound of ice cracking again and again and again, Elsa couldn't hear her. Their only way of surviving in this moment would be if they escaped.

"Hurry!" Sorenson cried. "Take some!"

Anna took a bit of tablecloth from Kristoff and stumbled toward the scientist. Grabbing the strip, Sorenson looped the cloth over the thin wire, making a *U* with the fabric.

"Hands," he grunted.

Anna obliged, holding out her wrists as he tied the dangling ends of the cloth strip under Anna's armpits to create a makeshift harness.

Sorenson patted the rickety wooden railing. "Climb up."

Anna did as she was told. Only when she was balanced on the topmost rail, facing the mountain slope far beneath her, did Sorenson's plan truly sink in. "Wait a second," Anna said, twisting to face him. "You can't be serious."

"Hang on tight!" Sorenson pushed her—hard.

With a squeal, Anna slipped off the observation deck in a rush of wind and stars. She screamed. Careening down the mountain nearly felt like flying, but *definitely* felt like falling. The cable jounced and jiggled as she sped down the mountainside.

Wrapping her wrists in the tablecloth, she held on for dear life as her legs swung beneath her. From somewhere above, she could hear Elsa and Kristoff and Sorenson shouting as they zipped down behind her. Thank goodness they were safe!

Anna almost laughed—but the ground was rushing toward her, and coming up way too fast. Straining her eyes against the dark night, Anna followed the path of the rippling cable; it disappeared into the branches of a tree at the foot of the mountain, near the entrance to the mines. That much was good.

But what wasn't good was how fast she was approaching the very solid trunk. If she hit the tree at this pace, she would definitely break a few ribs, and that was *if* she was lucky. She needed to slow down.

"SNOW!" she yelled back at Elsa. "SNOW! SNOW SNOW SNOW!" She thought she heard Elsa shout back, but Anna couldn't tell. The wind stole whatever words left her sister's lips. She just had to hope and trust that her sister would know what to do, the way she always did.

Ten feet away from the tree. Now five. Now two. Anna released the tablecloth and set herself free. She tumbled through the dark air for what felt like a year but was likely only a moment, and then—

*WOMP!*

A cold tingle enveloped Anna, as refreshing and comforting as one of the bubbly drinks Oaken sold at his lodge. Soft, pillowy snowflakes had cushioned her fall. Elsa had done it again. But there was no time to catch her breath. Instead, Anna rolled out of the way as Elsa, Kristoff, and Sorenson plopped into the snow pile like ripe apples falling from a tree.

Anna shot up. "Everyone okay? Where is it?"

Everyone nodded, then Kristoff pointed.

Anna turned. It was hard to see in the dark, but she could just make out a patch of shadow barreling down the mountain like an avalanche of black snow: the Nattmara. Still on the hunt.

"The mines!" Anna said. "Hurry!"

"They're not safe!" Sorenson said. "Cave-ins and toxic air—"

"And Huldrefólk!" Anna said. "Elsa, remember the myth!"

Elsa gasped. "'*Huldrefólk always find that which is lost.*' Aren's sword!"

"It may be our only chance!" Anna said. "We have to find them and ask where the Revolute Blade is!"

"But—" Sorenson's protest was cut off by a long howl, a howl that rose in pitch until the very air of the kingdom became a scream, and Anna staggered under its weight.

Clasping her hands over her ears, Anna ran past the warning posts, ripped back the wooden boards that had been nailed up over the entrance, and dove into the gaping mouth of the mines. Her friends followed her. The howl reached them even there, and Kristoff struggled with his traveler's pack to light his lantern, but at last they could see.

All around, there were passages: thin ones, wide ones, narrow ones, up and down and around. But which led to a dead end? And which led to chambers of poisonous gases or pits with sharp sticks or sleeping bears? Most importantly, which would take them to the Huldrefólk?

"Which one, Sorenson?" Anna asked.

But the old scientist looked perplexed. His long silver beard tufted in all directions, as if it, too, were confused.

Standing beside Anna, Kristoff swung his lantern, sending arcs of light rippling across the walls and floor.

Something glinted in the rock, and Anna looked down. She was standing on something long and metal: the tracks for mine carts!

"This way!" Anna said, taking off in a sprint as she followed the tracks.

A second later, they arrived in a large chamber where, at the far end, sitting comfortably as if it had been waiting for them all along, was a wooden mine cart.

Kristoff gestured to it theatrically. "Ta-da! Your chariot awaits, m'lady."

"Why, thank you, kind sir!" Anna clambered in, with Elsa and Sorenson climbing in behind her.

Kristoff pushed the cart, trying to get the rusty wheels to move forward. They rolled a bit then stopped, and Anna saw why. A rope had been tied around one end of the cart, anchoring it to a jutting boulder.

"May I?" she asked him, reaching for his lantern.

He handed it to her. "You may."

Anna held the lantern's flame to the rope.

The Nattmara's howl was even louder now, impossibly so, and the tunnel shook.

It had arrived.

Each step of its giant paws sent a tremor through the earth.

And Anna could see that her guess had been right—each time Elsa used her magic, the Nattmara seemed to have grown more fearsome and more horrible. It stood in the mouth of the cave, eclipsing the light of the moon, black sand sweeping around it as its eyes shone yellow.

In Anna's hands, the rope charred—blackening, thinning. Finally, it snapped. But the cart stayed put.

"Why aren't we moving?" Elsa cried out.

"We're too heavy for it," Anna said, desperation whirling through her. "Maybe if we rock a bit—"

"No need," Sorenson interrupted.

"What do you mean?" Anna demanded.

But the scientist only smiled—and then launched himself out of the cart. He sprinted toward the mouth of the mines . . . toward the Nattmara.

"Noooooo!" Anna yelled, though she couldn't hear herself in the ocean of the Nattmara's howl.

But Sorenson had done the trick. With his weight gone, the cart rose and the wheels rolled forward, slow at first, then faster and faster—and then the cart plunged, forcing Anna to drop Kristoff's lantern. It crashed to the floor of the cart, but the light didn't snuff out. Rough wood cut into her hands as she clung to the sides of the cart for dear life.

It barreled down the tracks, screeching through jolting turns and sharp twists, threatening to buck them out at every turn.

"We're going too fast!" Elsa shouted. "Slow down!"

"The brakes aren't working!" Kristoff yelled back as he retrieved his lantern and held it out in front of them. "And the steering stick is stuck!"

Anna felt her mouth open in horror as she frantically tried to think of a solution.

"Lean right!" Kristoff bellowed.

Anna and Elsa flung their weight to the right, and the cart shifted on the track, following the curve of the rail. Kristoff continued to yell instructions. In this way—with Kristoff calling out and Anna and

Elsa leaning this way and that—they were able to direct the cart, zigzagging down into the mountain's core instead of dropping vertically. They would roll to a stop at some point. *Wouldn't they?*

And then, suddenly, there was light up ahead. An exit!

"What *is* that?" Elsa shouted. "We're nowhere near morning!" She was right, and as Anna's eyes drank in the light, she realized it held a strange aqua glow. Before she could wonder too much where it came from, Kristoff yelled, "LAKE!"

*SPLASH!*

In an explosion of lukewarm water, they careened into an underground lake. The cart rolled forward in the rippling water, then stopped, the surprisingly shallow body of water bringing their wild ride to an end. Kristoff's lantern went out, smoke snaking off into the air.

Anna allowed herself to be still. To feel the air in her lungs and hear the quiet of the subterranean world. But it wasn't utter silence. Far from it.

All around them was a soft splish-splash as stalactites dripped water into the reflective lake that was illuminated by the strange light. Anna looked down at the water and then up in wonder. She finally knew the source of the light. Dangling from the cave ceiling were a million tiny glowworms, each one giving off a gentle light the color of the bluest ice. They reflected onto the surface of the lake so that it looked they were in a bathtub under a galaxy of stars. It was a secret world of sound and water and light, both comforting and glorious.

"Is everyone okay?" Anna asked.

Kristoff winced slightly, but said, more or less cheerfully, "Yep!"

"Yes," Elsa said. "I hope Sorenson is okay."

Anna hoped so, too, but she didn't want her sister to worry. "I'm sure he's fine," Anna said, mustering as much enthusiasm as she could. "That scientist has more tricks up his sleeves than appointments in your schedule." She stood up slowly. "And *everyone* will be okay once we have the sword to break the Nattmara's curse." Careful to keep her balance, she rose to her tiptoes and examined a glowworm. "Wow," she breathed out. Each glowworm looked like a beaded necklace and hung like an icicle, beautiful and perfect.

There the sound of swirling water. Anna looked over to see that Elsa had clambered out of the mine cart and stepped into the lake. It was shallow, only coming up to her sister's waist. She didn't bother to lift her cloak out of the water, but instead let it float up around her, so that it almost looked like she'd grown a twinkling mermaid's fin. Now *mermaids* were something Anna wished were real. And maybe, just maybe, they were. Elsa waded to the rocky banks.

"Where are you going?" Anna asked.

Elsa stopped to look up at the steep track they had careened down only moments before. "I can't hear anything," Elsa whispered, as though they were little girls again playing hide-and-find in the chapel and waiting for their parents to discover them.

"That's good, right?" Kristoff's voice was hushed. "The Nattmara couldn't have followed us. We were going impossibly fast, and there were too many tracks for it to know which ones we chose."

"Look up," Elsa said grimly.

Anna followed her sister's gaze. In the glowworms' light, she could make out a dozen different passages above them, each one leading to somewhere. To *many* somewheres. Anna tensed. They had lost the Nattmara. They had lost Sorenson.

And now they were lost, too.

# Chapter Sixteen

ANNA, ELSA, AND KRISTOFF couldn't stay in the cave of crystal-clear water and glowworm light forever.

Because now, even the quiet was dangerous.

It had been nearly twenty-four hours since Anna had last slept, and judging from the dark bags under Elsa's eyes, it had even been even longer for her. But it was Kristoff who was suffering from exhaustion the most. Looking for his troll family, he'd already done a hard day's ride before arriving back at the castle, only to flee. He had been awake for too long. He needed sleep. They all did.

But if they slept, it might make it easier for the Nattmara to track them—and Anna knew it wouldn't give up. That was the nature of a nightmare—one second, they were forgotten, and the next, they exploded into sharp memory. Anna, Elsa, and Kristoff had to keep moving through the mines. They had to keep their feet shuffling forward, their eyes open. If one of them slept, it could be the end of them all. They had so many people to save.

And so, after gathering strands of glowworms to hang around their necks and wrists, they decided on a tunnel—not because it was familiar, but because it seemed to go more *up* than the others. Using the skills he'd learned on the mountain, Kristoff had been able to help them all scale the wall with his rope to reach the highest passageway.

As they trudged forward, Anna tried to think about energizing things: sunrises, sledding, playing with the children in town, Olaf. But instead of making her feel excited and awake, they only made her feel sad and even more tired. She wondered if she would ever feel awake again. Kristoff stumbled beside her. Instead of catching himself as he normally would, he dropped to his knees and sank back onto his heels.

Anna stooped beside him and rested a hand on his back. "Are you okay, Kristoff? You have to get up!" She nudged him.

Kristoff mumbled in reply and laid his head on the ground. "This rock is so soft."

Anna pulled on his arm, but instead of yanking him to his feet, she only succeeded in making herself more tired, and she, too, sank to the ground.

Kristoff was right. The rock was soft and still and it *wanted* her to lay her head down on it. It was warm, and from the depths of her sleep-addled mind, Anna remembered a lesson Gerda had taught her, about how the earth was a crust of dirt floating on top of hot magma, and that sometimes, little pockets of heat would spring warm water from the rocks underneath. Even though these carved tunnels within the mines had never seen the sun, they felt like a touch of summer—of lying on rocky beaches kissed by the sun. All Anna wanted to do was to stretch out her tired muscles and sleep there. *Anna!* From a long way away, she heard someone calling her name. *Anna, get up!*

"Just a few more minutes," Anna mumbled.

A slap of cold air hit her. Anna jolted upright. "Hey!" She wiped away what seemed to be the remnants of a snowball from her cheek.

"What was *that* for?" Kristoff protested, snow also flecking his face.

"I'm saving your lives," Elsa said. She conjured another snowball, which she juggled. "On your feet, or it's more ice in your face. We have a deal?"

"Blargh!" Kristoff sputtered. "Just let us sleep!"

"Sorry, but I can't do that." Elsa shook head. "Anna! Oh, for goodness' sake."

Anna felt another slap of cold snow and jerked her head up. "Sorry, sorry," she mumbled, her tongue feeling too thick for her mouth. Snow glistened at Elsa's fingertips, and something niggled at Anna's mind. It was something important. It had something to do with Elsa and her magic. But what was it?

As Elsa wound her arm, ready to pitch another snowball at either one of them, Anna remembered. She shot up tall and nearly jumped.

"Elsa, stop!"

Her sister dropped her snowball to the ground, where it landed with a small *puff.* "You promise to stay awake now? Because there's more snow where that came from."

But Anna was no longer sleepy. Far from it. "You can't keep using your magic," she said. "On the observation deck, I noticed that every time you did, the Nattmara grew."

"Oh." Elsa folded her arms across her chest. "Great."

Anna rooted around in Kristoff's pack and pulled out the book, flipping open its pages to confirm her theory. But they were soaked through from the lake, the ink indecipherable. She sighed.

*SNORFFF!*

The sisters looked down to see Kristoff's eyes had closed again, a strangled snore escaping from him as his head drifted toward his chest.

"What are we going to do about him?" Elsa asked.

"Umm." Anna cast about for an idea—*any* idea. Usually, they came sharp and sure, but lack of sleep was making her feel fuzzy. All she could really focus on were their shadows thrown by the glowworms onto the cave wall opposite them. Shadows. Shadows similar to the famous shadow puppets of Zaria. She'd read how the puppeteers were often as famous as singers, and could fill whole theaters with their performances. If they could ever defeat the Nattmara and make everything right again, maybe she would invite some of the puppeteers to come give a performance in Arendelle. Everyone had liked it so much last year when Kristoff had performed his musical. . . .

"That's it!" Anna shouted. *That's it, it, it.* Her words

echoed down the rocky corridor. Crouching down to be at the same level as Kristoff's fluttering eyelashes, she began to sing: *"Goblin toes are ugly, and Hulder tails are sweet—but you would never catch me, sweep one off his'* . . . paw!"

It was a silly song that Kristoff had made up for the last spring festival. The children in the village had loved it, and had performed it for the kingdom under Kristoff's encouraging eye. When Anna had first met the mountain man, he'd been snow-crusted and only grunted a few words to her. She never would have thought that underneath the rough exterior, and a dirt patch or two, his real language was song.

Kristoff had a gift for melody, and though he didn't mind the odd soup stain on his shirt and didn't care about the difference between a salad fork and a dessert fork, he was sensitive about song lyrics. Particularly to songs he had written.

"Huh?" Kristoff's eyes flew open. "It's supposed to be 'sweep one off his *feet!*'"

Eyes sparkling, Elsa sang the next verse. *"Goblins like to eat a lot, and Hulder like to sing—but you will never find one with a feathered'* . . . nose!"

"No!" Kristoff surged to his feet. "That doesn't

rhyme! And what does a *feathered nose* even mean?"

"Now we got him," Anna whispered to her sister, and she grabbed his hand. "Come on, Kristoff, sing it for us?"

And Kristoff—poor, tired, sorrowful Kristoff—sang.

Together, the three of them moved forward through the darkness, their voices echoing so that they sounded like an entire choir rather than just three fatigued friends hoping to survive, hoping to save the kingdom that Anna loved more than anything. She gave herself over to the sound, letting it sweep her along.

They sang about the Huldrefólk. They sang about Aren and his gallant sword. And then they sang a silly ballad about a goose who fell in love with a duck.

As they reached the end of the song, Anna thought about how beautiful Elsa's voice sounded. She hadn't known her sister could hit quite such high notes, or even sing harmonies. Anna stopped singing, wanting to listen closer. And that's when she realized that Kristoff had stopped singing . . . and so had Elsa.

In fact, all three of them had fallen silent, and yet the song continued. It climbed around them, higher and higher.

It was as though the rocks themselves were singing. But that couldn't be—could it?

Elsa pointed down a passage to their left. "It's coming from there."

Anna turned toward it.

"Hold on!" Elsa grabbed her. "What makes you think we're going that way?"

"Why wouldn't we?" Anna said. "We're lost, and we need help. Besides, something so beautiful can't possibly be dangerous!"

Elsa stared at her. "Did you learn *nothing* from your engagement with Prince—"

"Shh," Kristoff interrupted. "The singing's stopped."

And so it had.

Anna whirled on Elsa. "We missed out on someone who could have helped us!"

"Or maybe we missed out on whatever could have *eaten* us," Elsa said.

Kristoff gulped. "Or maybe they're right behind you."

"Very funny, Kristoff," Anna told him.

"No," he protested. "I'm . . . serious. Look."

While Anna had been talking with Elsa, they had walked into a new portion of the mines.

Unlike the other passageways, this one had never seen the tip of a pickax. Because all around were crystals—and not just any crystals. Each one was taller than Kristoff and as wide as a tree trunk. They jutted from the walls and the ceiling, angled every which way to form a forest of sparkling rock. Each crystal was a shifting white, as though when the crystals had formed, they'd been filled with smoke.

But it wasn't the crystals' unusual size or color that made Anna gasp or caused Elsa to grip her so hard that Anna could feel Elsa's fingernails digging into her shoulder. Sitting astride a crystal as large as a pony was a little child.

At least, Anna *thought* it might be a child, as the figure was definitely child-sized, about as big as a three-year-old human. In the dim light of the glowworm bracelet she'd put on, Anna could just make out the gleam of an eye, and soft-looking gray leggings that glimmered slightly as the child kicked out their legs.

The child began to sing again, though the melody had no words. Just clear, round notes.

With a gasp, Anna began to run toward the child, stubbing her toes and just missing occasional low-hanging rocks. But she didn't care. All that mattered was that there was a child under the mountain who had been left alone. And Anna never wanted *anyone* to feel alone or left out—not ever. Not if she could help it.

Worry pulsed through her, followed by guilt. She hadn't even *heard* of a child missing from the village. She knew she'd been distracted with Elsa's impending grand tour, but she couldn't have been so busy as to not have heard about a missing child. She wondered how long the child had been down there, where the guardians were, or—she realized with a lurch—maybe the question should be, what had happened to *them*? Did the Nattmara get them?

But before she could get more than a few feet from the child, she felt someone tug on the back of her cloak, yanking her.

"Anna," Elsa whispered, voice as low as could be, "do you see the ears?"

Anna squinted, trying to see what Elsa saw. At first, she couldn't, as the child's curls bumped over where she expected the ears to be, except . . .

Anna squinted so hard now that she could see her own eyelashes.

And then, she saw them: the child's ears rose to slender points, like the tips of a dragonfly's wings.

Suddenly, Anna remembered a bedtime story from a long, long time ago, back when she and Elsa had shared a room. *They are tall and strong, with sharp ears. And they're sensitive. Which is why, little Elsa,* Mother had said with a tug on the hem of Elsa's pajama bottoms, *if you ever see one, you must not mention their tail! It's rude.*

*And if you do*—a young Anna had popped up from behind her pillow fort, making a scary face and shaping her hands into claws—*they might eat you!*

Elsa had burst into giggles, which had only made Anna wrinkle her face more and add an extra growl.

*All right, enough,* Mother had said, scooping Anna up in one arm to plop her beside Elsa before she sat next to them on the bed. *Cuddle close. Scooch in.*

Anna had let her face fall back to normal, but she'd kept her fingers curled into claws as she cozied up next to her mother and sister and asked, *Momma, what do their tails look like?*

*No one knows,* Mother had said, and fixed a ribbon in Anna's ponytail. *They keep them hidden under skirts or keep their backs to the wall at all times.*

*But I wanna knoooow,* Anna had whined, and her mother had kissed the top of her head and laughed.

*Everyone is entitled to their secrets,* she'd said. *Especially the hidden people.*

The hidden people.

Or, as the Arendellians called them . . .

"Huldrefólk," Anna breathed. And as she spoke the name aloud, Oaken's words came back to her, sharp as a stalactite.

*Beware the Huldrefólk.*

# Chapter Seventeen

THE CHILD'S—*Hulder's*—melody flew off on invisible wings and faded again into silence.

Anna burst into applause; she couldn't help it. After all, the little Hulder didn't *seem* dangerous.

"That was *incredible!*" she exclaimed. "What's your name?"

For a moment, the Hulder seemed to stare at Anna in the glow-light, luminescent eyes boring into hers, and then the Hulder tumbled backward off the crystal.

"No!" Anna said as she rushed behind the crystal to check on the child, hoping the tiny Hulder hadn't hurt themselves.

But as she rounded the tree-trunk-sized crystal, she saw that the Hulder was no longer behind it.

The child had disappeared, except for the sound of footsteps pattering down the dark passage up ahead. Without a second thought, Anna took off.

"Anna!" Elsa called from behind. "Wait! Slow down! You're going too fast!"

"Anna!" Kristoff shouted. Their warnings echoed off the rocks around them, but Anna disagreed with them both: she was going too *slow*.

The Hulder was quick—Anna wasn't sure if it was footsteps she was following now, or just the quiet drip of stalactites in the distance. Still, they had come to look for the Huldrefólk, the only ones who might be able to help them find the Revolute Blade, the only ones of myth who might be able to save them all from Anna's terrible mistake. And so Anna ran on, only just missing the occasional low-hanging rocks. Suddenly, the Hulder screeched. It sounded frightened, and Anna hoped the Hulder wasn't in trouble.

"Hang on!" Anna shouted. She ran faster and faster, and then her foot caught—on a rock, a divot, or a root, it was too dark to tell—and she toppled to the ground, her hands out to cushion her fall.

Pain cracked through Anna's ribs as she slammed into the solid rock. She was going to have one giant bruise in an hour. Everything hurt. Everything but her right arm, which she'd flung out far in front of herself to try to break her fall. And as Anna looked at the glowworm bracelet dangling from her wrist, she saw why: her right arm had not hit any rock at all. All that hand had hit was thin air. Anna was glad she was already lying on the ground, because she thought she might faint if she were still standing. She'd followed the Hulder—and had almost run off a cliff and into an abyss.

She could still hear the Hulder's cry. Tuva's warning from the trading post came back to her. *They're tricky. Sometimes, they help. Other times, they lure humans off the safest paths.* And maybe, Anna thought, lure them into an abyss. There was always a chance that the Hulder child had done this on purpose, had perhaps meant to distract Anna and Elsa and Kristoff away from the Huldrefólk's home.

But even as these dark thoughts gathered into a cloud, Anna scooted forward on her belly, toward the sound of the Hulder's cry. It didn't matter what the Hulder's intentions had been—but it did matter that the Hulder was stuck and scared. Once she wiggled to the edge, Anna leaned her chin out and peered down. The Hulder had tumbled over the edge, but by some luck or miracle, the child had caught themselves on a small ledge five feet down. It would be easy for Kristoff to lean over and reach the Hulder, but even as Anna watched, the rocky ledge was crumbling away under the child's weight.

"Elsa! Kristoff! Help!" Anna shouted as she inched forward even more, letting herself dangle over the edge, her hand outstretched. "Grab my hand!" she called down.

The Hulder raised a hand, but Anna was still too far away. She had to get *closer*. Wiggling forward, Anna lowered herself down inch by fraction of an inch. Just a little bit farther now . . . She strained her fingers forward, willing them to lengthen—and that's when she felt the crumbling of the earth beneath her own weight. What was once solid ground turned to gravel, and Anna skidded forward, headfirst into the dark abyss. She screamed.

But before she could shoot past the Hulder and plummet into the vast void, two pairs of hands grabbed her ankles from above. *Kristoff! Elsa!*

She lurched to a stop, face to face with the little cat-eyed Hulder, who was still mostly in shadow, and who, if Anna had to wager a guess, looked terrified of her.

"Hi," Anna said, trying hard to iron out the quiver in her voice. "My name is Anna, and I'm not going to hurt you." She offered out her hand. "Come with me!"

The Hulder hesitated a moment, then gripped Anna's palm. The child's skin was smooth and dry, like one of the little lizards Anna had read about that populated the Chatho deserts. But even with the Hulder so close to her, it was hard to see them properly. It was almost as though the child had been made of shadow or carved from a mirror. Trying to make out the details was a little like trying to hold tight to a bar of soap: the harder one squeezed, the quicker the soap slid away; the harder one looked, the quicker the Hulder seemed to vanish.

Gripping the child with all her strength, Anna called, "Pull us up!"

There was a grunt, and then Anna and the Hulder rose to safety, just as the little ledge deteriorated into nothingness. She and the child were dragged back onto solid rock. Before Anna had a chance to release the Hulder, Elsa and Kristoff wrapped Anna into a tight hug, and she leaned into their warmth.

"Anna," Elsa said, voice tight. "I couldn't . . . I mean, you almost—"

"Key word: *almost*," Kristoff cut in with a wink.

Anna smiled at him. He always seemed to understand her, to know that if she thought too much about what had just *almost* happened, she would sit there forever and turn into a fossil.

"I'm here," Anna said. She could have stayed there forever in their arms, but for the wiggling Hulder she held.

The child pushed out of the group and plopped onto the floor—still far enough away that all Anna could really make out was a pointy elbow, but in more detail than before. Now Anna could see that the Hulder's skin was the exact color of the bluish rock that filled the mines. Anna frowned. When she'd first spotted the Hulder, she'd thought the child's skin was a smoky white, similar to the crystal the Hulder had been sitting on. A funny, tickling idea crawled into Anna's mind: she'd been right both times. The Hulder had been smoky white *and then* a bluish gray. The Hulder's body had first looked smooth, then as rough as the stone wall. Maybe the Huldrefólk were like octopuses in the deeps of the Southern Sea, able to change not only their color but also their texture.

"Wow," Anna said, trying to collect herself even as a stream of rapid thoughts dashed through her mind. First thought: *This is so cool!* She was thrilled to learn about this wonderful trait of the Huldrefólk. The second thought came fast on the heels of the first: if Anna could change color and texture, she'd head to the portrait gallery, stand in front of all her favorite paintings, and feel what it was like to be Lieutenant Mattias, her father's old official Arendellian guard, for an afternoon. And finally, her third thought: the last time she'd been in the castle, she'd seen the wolf, and everything had changed. A shudder ran down her spine.

Elsa knelt before the child. "Hi there, little one. I'm Elsa. What's your name?"

The little Hulder burst into tears that sparkled like gems.

"Oh, no." Elsa jerked back. "Here!" She conjured a snowflake and presented it.

"Elsa," Anna hissed. "No magic, remember?"

The snowflake burst into water droplets. Elsa's cheeks turned pink and her hands clenched at her sides. "I'm sorry," she whispered. "I forgot." It was sad that Elsa had spent most of her life trying to suppress her magic. It truly seemed a part of her, as natural as breathing and blinking. Having to refrain from using it again was probably taking some getting used to.

Anna felt sorry about it. She took a deep breath. They had to get out of there. They had to find Revolute and defeat the Nattmara, not only for Arendelle, but for her sister. She couldn't let Elsa shut herself away again.

"Ow!" Elsa yelped.

Looking down, Anna saw her sister's thick braid held tight in a chubby fist.

"Ow-ow!" the little Hulder repeated, and gave another pull, as if Elsa's braid were a rope.

"Owowowow!" Elsa unwound her hair from the child's fists. "I'm not a horse."

"Horse!" the little Hulder said. "Horse! Horse! Horse!"

Elsa sighed while Anna covered her mouth to hide a giggle. She understood the Hulder's fascination with Elsa's braid. When she'd been little, she, too, had pretended Elsa was a racehorse and had ordered her sister to charge up and down the castle hallways. Once, she'd even gotten Elsa to neigh.

The little Hulder let go of Elsa's hair and toddled over to Kristoff. "Horse!" the child proclaimed.

"Hey," Kristoff protested as the Hulder ran around him. "You're one to talk."

"Hey! Hey! Hey!" the little Hulder said. "Talk, talk, talk!" Though the Hulder was running in circles around Kristoff, the child ran sideways, long gallops, keeping their back to the wall at all times.

*To hide the tail!* Anna realized with delight. Maybe she would finally be able to find out the answer to her childhood question about whether they all had tails.

"They're a bit . . . hyper?" Elsa tugged her cloak so that it would hang neatly again.

"No more than any other child," Anna said, thinking of the children she'd often run into in the village. "But most children wouldn't know how to get around a cave, while this little one might be able to lead us to the older Huldrefólk who can help us."

Tucking strands of hair back into her braid, Elsa looked doubtful. "Maybe?"

Taking note of what had happened to Elsa, Anna pushed her own hair back to make sure it wasn't easily accessible before getting on her hands and knees. "Hi," she said. "Do you remember my name?"

"Anna! Anna! Anna!" the Hulder screeched.

Anna blinked. She hadn't been expecting *quite* so much enthusiasm. "Yes, that's right. What's your name?"

"What's your name?" the Hulder repeated.

"Anna," Anna said.

"Anna," the Hulder repeated.

"Wait." Anna rubbed her forehead. "Your name is Anna, too?"

"Wait." The Hulder mimicked her again. "Your name is Anna, too!"

"Like I said," Elsa said, her lips twitching, *"hyper."*

"I might be wrong," Kristoff observed, "but I *think* they're just repeating everything you say."

"Hyper! Everything you say!" the Hulder echoed back.

Taking a deep breath, Anna spoke as quickly as she could, giving the Hulder no chance to repeat her words until she was done. "Hi, I'm Anna! My home is Arendelle, like you, but above the ground."

The Hulder looked at her in complete astonishment. "Home?"

Anna nodded. "Yes, *home*. Where do you live? We'd like to meet your family."

The Hulder looked at Anna, then nodded. "Home!" And then the Hulder was off—running backward as easily as if they had eyes in the back of their head. And maybe they did. After all, as Anna knew from old bedtime stories, no one had ever seen a Hulder's back.

"Come on!" Anna shot to her feet. "We have to follow!"

The Hulder ran impossibly fast—and unlike Anna and the others, the Hulder was short enough to avoid low-hanging rocks, while Kristoff had to run at a crouch. Up, down, and down again, they sprinted through seemingly endless corridors of crystals and sparkling rocks. Anna couldn't understand how the Hulder—Dash, as she mentally nicknamed them, taking a page from Olaf's book—was able to tell the difference between the tunnels. Maybe it was some special Huldrefólk trick. After all, Huldrefólk could always find lost things. Maybe it meant they could never become lost themselves.

A strange thought crossed her mind, and she

wondered if that meant the Huldrefólk *always* knew what they should do next. How fantastic would *that* be? Maybe that's how Dash had found them so quickly. Or maybe Dash had found them because Anna, Elsa, and Kristoff *were* the lost things.

Anna shook her head. She had so many questions, and there was so little time to attend to them all.

But there was one thing she could do. "Kristoff? Elsa?" Anna waited until they both looked at her, and then said, "I think I know what happened to the missing trolls. I read in Sorenson's tower that they always flee the land when a Nattmara appears."

Anna heard Kristoff let out a great sigh of relief. "Good," he said. "Then that means they're safe."

Soon enough, another sound began to play under the staccato of their footsteps. A strange, shuffling, creaking sound.

"Do you hear that?" Anna called back between breaths.

"Yeah," Kristoff said. "Do you think—?"

"Maybe," Anna replied, slowing to a walk. She didn't need him to finish his sentence to know what he was thinking: *Nattmara.*

"We should stop," Elsa said. "Take a moment

to scout out what's happening. Huldrefólk can be mischievous . . . especially if they think we're here to take something that doesn't belong to us."

"But if we stop," Anna said, "we'll lose Dash!"

The corners of Elsa's eyes crinkled in confusion as she navigated around a large boulder that Anna had simply scrambled over. *Dash?* she asked.

"The Hulder," Anna explained. She turned back to see if Kristoff needed any help with the boulder, but he'd simply shoved it to the side, clearing the way.

"It's too late," he said. "We already lost them."

In the two seconds Anna had taken her eyes off Dash, the child had sped out of sight. "No," Anna breathed. "We have to keep up!" She broke into a run again, fresh fear giving her newfound speed. "Dash doesn't know about the Nattmara!"

But as Anna rounded the final bend, she saw where the sound had been coming from: an underground city carved out of the rock itself.

The secret home of the Huldrefólk.

Just as the world above, so was the world below. Cozy homes were carved into the blue-gray stone, and orange light spilled out from them, as welcoming as a smile. The pebble-lined streets were alight with glowworms, so it was easy to see what various mine carts pulled: one held a pile of stalactites bundled like firewood, another was filled to the brim with glowing mushrooms the size of sun hats, and another was heaped with water-clear rocks that Anna thought might be large diamonds.

And the Huldrefólk. The adults appeared to be tall, built more like sapling trees than people, with long limbs and long necks. And similar to Dash, they were hard to see in the light of the underneath realm.

The glow-light wasn't the same as sunlight, bright and revealing, but the kind of soft glow that Anna associated with romantic candlelit dinners. It illuminated at the same time as it concealed, casting shadows that again helped to obscure the Huldrefólk. Still, even in the dimness, Anna could tell that they camouflaged into whatever it was that they were standing near, from onyx black to marble white and every shade in between. Some of the Huldrefólk looked as though they could be purple, others orange and green with sparkling, black-veined skin. The Huldrefólk—the hidden folk—could blend into any surrounding.

Which was great, Anna thought, but most

important, they were *real.* Real creatures who would have real answers to where they could find the real lost sword of Aren. The thing of myth they needed to save the day.

"Wow," Elsa whispered. "How beautiful. And peaceful."

"If Sven were here," Kristoff said, "I bet he'd eat all those mushrooms, and then his teeth would probably glow for a week."

*Sven.* Anna wished the reindeer were with them. The way down to the village looked steep, and Sven was always good about finding the surest path down a craggy mountain. She scanned the side of the rock, looking for a pathway to the dwellings. Somewhere below, she was sure they would find the answers to how to set things right and heal Sven, and the rest of Arendelle, from the Nattmara's influence.

As she leaned forward to see better, Anna felt a sharp *something* prod her back.

"Kristoff," she said, swiping a hand behind her, "stop that. I'm just trying to see."

"I'm not doing anything," Kristoff said, standing to her left, a few feet away from easy poking distance.

The back of Anna's neck prickled.

Elsa stood to her right, her face pensive as she took in the city below them.

Suddenly, Anna became very aware of the feeling that someone was watching her.

Maybe even *a few* someones.

*"Oh,"* she heard Elsa squeak.

Anna turned, only to come nose-to-nose with a spear. And not just one spear.

*Many* spears.

# Chapter Eighteen

WHILE ANNA, ELSA, AND KRISTOFF had been taking in the sights of the village below, it seemed as though a storm cloud had gathered around them.

Though, of course, storm clouds didn't exist in the belly of the mines, nor were they capable of holding a spear to one's throat. No. The roiling, shifting dark shapes gathering around them were none other than Huldrefólk warriors.

Like the littler Dash, these ones, too, stuck to the shadows. In the glow, Anna could only make out the glint of an eye here, and the back of a hand there. But she didn't need to be able to see their faces to sense how they felt about three human trespassers in their secret city: they were not very happy at all.

"H-h-hi," Anna stuttered to the spear tips, trying

to remember the etiquette of meeting a new group of people. It wasn't the exact same as meeting the prime minister of Torres, but she knew that dignitaries were sensitive, so polite manners seemed the safest bet.

*Step one: Introduce yourself, and announce you are a friend.*

She dipped into a curtsy. "My name is Anna of Arendelle, and this is my sis—"

A spearpoint jabbed closer to her, and Anna went silent.

"Stop," a Hulder hissed. "Say no more, thief."

"I-I think there's been a mistake," Anna said, forcing a cheerful smile on her face. "We've come to ask for help. We're not here to take anything—"

"Take," the same Hulder spoke again, repeating Anna. "Take, take, take!"

"No," Kristoff said, his back against Anna's. "We're *not* here to take anything. We followed a little one—"

"Take little one," the Hulder repeated, and Anna could hear fury swell in the Hulder's voice. "Take little one!" The cry was repeated by another Hulder, and then another, until the entire shifting mass of spear-wielding warriors took up the chant.

Anna had a bad feeling. A *very* bad feeling.

"I think that they're accusing us of trying to steal Dash," she whispered.

"Ah," Kristoff said in a low voice, "well, *that's* not accurate."

"Wait!" Anna told the Huldrefólk, holding up her hand. "We weren't trying to kidnap anyone!"

The Huldrefólk's chant changed. "Liar, liar, every word!"

Anna shook her head, trying to make sense of them.

"We're not," Elsa spoke up, her voice smooth as ice, though Anna could hear the friction beneath the surface. "The little one found us. We were singing, and then my sister rescued the child from falling into a dark abyss—"

"The abyss!" another Hulder with a higher voice interrupted. "The abyss! Take to abyss! Take to abyss! Liar, liar, every word!"

*Uh-oh.*

"Um," Anna said with a gulp. "I think they want to—"

"Drop us off in the abyss?" Kristoff finished. "Yeah. I got that, too."

"Wait!" Anna tried again. "There's a giant wolf out there that'll be here before you know—" Anna's sentence was cut short as a warrior rushed forward and tied what felt like a handkerchief around Anna's mouth, making it impossible for her to shout.

But even if she could, would it help? They were so far underground, and the villagers who were still awake were far away, likely and hopefully already onboard Elsa's royal ship. Sorenson was gone, having been left to face the Nattmara. And next to her, Elsa and Kristoff were also being gagged. Hard roots pressed into the soft skin of Anna's wrists as her hands were pulled behind her back and bound.

After checking to make sure the knot was tight, the Hulder who had bound her nodded. "March."

Single file, they walked in front of the Huldrefólk. Anna kept her eye on Elsa's braid as it swung, and was grateful when Kristoff accidentally stepped on her heel. It made her feel better knowing they were both there. At least they were all in this mess together.

Anna thought the Huldrefólk would take them away from their hidden city, back to the abyss from which they'd saved Dash, but instead, the warriors marched them down a narrow path, away from the abyss and the swarm of glowworms and fluorescent gardens. Anna's bad feeling only grew more insistent the longer they walked away from the city. Sweat beaded on her forehead, and her ribcage felt too tight as she breathed in the stale and stuffy air.

How far underground *were* they? Then the smell of rotten eggs punched her nose, and her eyes watered. It was the smell of sulfur, or else the Huldrefólk had some major issues with their plumbing. The air grew hotter still until it almost seemed to take on a rosy glow. A red light danced along the walls ahead of them, an unusual color that typically could only be found in the most spectacular summer sunsets, or in Tuva and Ada's forge, or . . . no. Anna's heart flipped.

Or in the center of an active volcano. *Liar, liar, every word* plus *abyss* apparently equaled throwing the group of human trespassers from Arendelle into molten rock.

The red glow grew brighter, and while the Huldrefólk seemed as cool as ice cream in the middle of an eternal winter, sweat now drenched Anna. She imagined that if it got any hotter, her eyebrows would slide right off her face. Even if Elsa could use her magic here—even if it wouldn't draw the Nattmara straight to them—what chance did winter's cold have against the melting powers of red-hot magma?

Now it was in front of them, a round circle of red that pulsed like a beating heart. Anna stumbled to a stop, but the Huldrefólk shoved her forward, and though she could not believe it was possible, she grew even hotter.

"Stop," Anna garbled through her gag, her mind racing as she skipped over steps two through ten of diplomacy. "We'll give you chocolate!" The words came out muffled.

It wasn't actually a step of etiquette—truly, bribery didn't belong on the list at all—and nothing in all her reading had prepared Anna for the possibility of being thrown into a river of lava by a hosting nation.

But it didn't work. They pushed her forward. Even though it was hotter than Oaken's sauna, Anna went numb as she saw Elsa's boot hang over the edge, the toe turning red in the glow. Anna struggled harder. If they disappeared on their mission, no one would ever know how the Nattmara came to be or how it could be stopped. No one would survive it. Being thrown into lava wouldn't just mean the end of Kristoff, Elsa, and Anna—it would mean the end of Arendelle. They would have failed. *She* would have failed. Emptiness yawned in Anna, threatening to swallow her whole.

All she had wanted—*ever* wanted—was to always do more and, out of true love for her sister, help her.

Although the whole kingdom had seen Anna save her sister three years ago, she had since wondered who *wouldn't* save their sister. And still, Anna couldn't get past that she was the one who had provoked Elsa into casting an eternal winter then, and now she was the one who had called a Nattmara to the land. She would never feed Sven a carrot again. She would never hear more about Olaf's warm philosophy on life. She would never get a chance to learn about the natural and celestial worlds from Sorenson. And it was all her fault.

From the corner of her eye, she saw Elsa whip her head so fast that her braid slapped her Hulder captor's nose, taking them by surprise, while Kristoff flung himself backward, slamming his captor into the wall. The two managed to wrestle out of their binds in the process.

*Come on!* Anna told herself. *They're still fighting. You can, too!* She wanted to cheer them on, but she needed to save her breath. And besides, there was still a gag in her mouth. Her guard dragged her forward, closer to the edge of the molten lake, while Anna freed her hands.

"HALT!" A deep voice reverberated around the rock, sending tremors through the earth.

But there was no way Anna was going to stop fighting. She lunged to the side, free of the Hulder's stony grip, and tore off her gag. She took a few running steps away from them before realizing she wasn't being chased. Instead, the Huldrefólk knelt to the ground as a fourth Hulder appeared in the red haze. This Hulder seemed to be the tallest of them all, their hair a wild black mane surrounding their face, and on their head they wore a circlet of something shiny. It took Anna a minute to realize it was gold.

*The leader of the Huldrefólk.*

And on the Hulder leader's shoulders sat a small, familiar figure.

"Horse!" Dash yanked on the Hulder leader's hair.

Anna sank into a curtsy, and after she coughed pointedly in Kristoff's direction, he bowed. Elsa, however, stayed as upright as an icicle, befitting her rank.

*"Psst! Rule number one,"* Anna murmured loud enough so that Elsa could hear.

Elsa nodded and spoke. "Greetings. I am Queen Elsa of Arendelle, and this is my sister, Princess Anna, and her . . . er, our guard, Kristoff Bjorgman of Nowhere in Particular. We greet you in friendship."

Anna held her breath, wondering if the leader would accept.

"Friendship," the Hulder leader repeated. And then, to Anna's utter astonishment, the Hulder continued in full sentences. "I apologize for my family. They can be a bit overprotective." In the dim light, Anna saw the Hulder pat Dash's dangling knee. "Young Echo, however, has cleared up the misunderstanding, and she and I welcome you to our domain. I am the king of the Huldrefólk."

"You're not repeating everything," Elsa said, clearly too surprised to worry about manners.

The imposing Hulder king inclined his head. "We like to use other people's words so that we can wrap ourselves up and hide within them. It's very rare for Huldrefólk to actually have to compose something new. That's part of the reason why Echo found you—she wanted to collect your song. Songs are easy to remember. Easy to echo back."

"Echo!" Dash—now Echo, Anna realized—repeated the word from her perch.

Anna knew she should probably let Elsa do all the talking, but her curiosity was too much. "Why do *you* talk in your own words?" she asked.

"Because I am not only the king, but also the librarian," said the Hulder leader. "I've spent years visiting the world above, collecting items as well as stories, and I have enough words at my disposal. And so, I would like to apologize again for your initial greeting." The Librarian King reached for Echo and set the child on the ground.

"That's it?" Kristoff burst out. "We're almost thrown into a lake of lava, and all you can say is 'I'm sorry'?"

"I'm sorry!" Echo squealed, moving toward Kristoff.

"Does 'We're *very* sorry' make it any better?" the Librarian King asked. "Usually, the only humans who make it down this far want to take precious stones and gems from our mountain, or to capture a member of our domain to make them find iron ore deposits for their weapons and the like."

"We're not looking for stones, gems, or iron," Elsa said. "We're looking for a sword of myth, the Revolute Blade. Can you please help us find it?"

The Librarian King's eyes flashed. "'Revolving moon and spinning sun, forged a crescent blade. From light and dark within the heart, the burnished sword was made.'" He looked down at them. "That's the one, yes?"

Anna nodded, feeling this was a good sign.

"And," he continued, "I suppose this has something to do with the Nattmara that has come to Arendelle?"

Anna gaped. "How did you know about the Nattmara?"

"Just because you can't see us doesn't mean we're not always there." The Librarian King studied them a second more. It was impossible to make out any expression on the leader's face. The Hulder's textured skin had taken on the appearance of the cracked rivulets of lava, and was hard to see against the molten backdrop. But then, he must have made a secret signal, because the guards bowed before each of them and then hurried away, keeping their backs to Anna and her friends. It only took the hidden people a couple of steps until they seemed to have disappeared entirely, though Anna knew they must still be there, great masters of camouflage that they were.

The Librarian King turned. "Now, all of you, come with me."

Anna's heart leapt. At last—she had *not* led them astray!

"We don't always know the answer—but we do know where to *find* it," the Librarian King continued.

Allowing the humans to walk in front of them, the Librarian King and Echo escorted Anna, Elsa, and Kristoff away from the lake of molten rock and toward a tranquil tributary of water where rafts bumped and prodded against each other.

Anna looked at Elsa and Kristoff in the gloom, and a smile spread across her face. "This could be it!" she whispered. "We may finally find the sword!"

"Let's wait and see," said Elsa, ever the one to freeze the excited mood.

Echo tugged at Kristoff's tunic, and they began to toss stones into the water.

"My assistant will help. She will take you to the Library of Lost Things," the Librarian King told them. "If my people ever came across the legendary sword, it will be there—that is, if the sword truly exists."

Elsa shot Anna a look, and Anna bit her lip. She hoped against hope that it did.

"We are sorry for bringing the Nattmara to your door," Elsa said. It wasn't lost on Anna that her sister had used the word *we*.

The Librarian King shook his head. "The Nattmara is one of the many natural enemies of the Huldrefólk—we both seek to reign the dark. But while the Huldrefólk love the night for its quiet privacy, the Nattmara prefers to use the dark as a weapon. Fear not: the Nattmara cannot pass into the borders of our domain. As long as you're within the Huldrefólk realm, the Nattmara cannot touch you. We are the hidden people. We keep ourselves hidden, and now that you're with us, we'll keep you hidden as well."

Relief filled Anna, and then a thought stirred. "Umm, I have a question for you," she said. "We lost a member of our group. Is it possible for the Huldrefólk to find him? He's kind of short and stocky, with a long silver beard that touches the floor, and he's grumpy." Anna paused, then added, "He's nice!"

The Librarian King inclined his head. "As you know, Huldrefólk are seekers of lost things. Collectors.

If your friend is still free of the Nattmara, then I'm sure we can locate him."

"Land ahoy!"

Anna looked to the water, where a gray raft glided in front of them and bumped against the bank. A cheery-looking Hulder (as Anna thought she could make out a smile in the dim glowworms' light) waved at them and leaned against the long pole she'd been using to steer the vessel.

"Ahoy! Ahoy! Ahoy!" Echo cried out, and left the game of skipping rocks with Kristoff to fling herself onto the raft and into the new Hulder's arms.

"This is my assistant, Obscuren," the Librarian King proclaimed. "She will help you find what you are looking for and will be your guide in my domain."

Anna scrambled onto the raft, settling herself next to Kristoff. It was only then that she noticed the unusual material it was made of. While rafts were almost always constructed of wood, this one seemed to be made of floating stone. As she peered closer, she saw tiny holes perforating the surface, making the texture of the raft seem more like bread than rock.

"I think this is a pumice raft," Anna said to Kristoff, who nodded.

"It is," he said. "Rock from the volcano."

Anna felt a tug on her hair as Echo crawled into her lap, quietly chanting, "Row, row, row your raft!"

"Say your goodbye," the Librarian King instructed Echo. "It's time for dinner."

The little Hulder's eyes swam with tears. "Stay!"

"I wish you could," Anna said, and was surprised when she realized she meant it.

Miner's Mountain was beautiful, full of unexpected surprises and even more unexpected friendships. She liked the little Hulder and her penchant for flying ahead as fast as possible. Anna bet Echo could show her many things—glowing crystals, ice caves, maybe even a sleeping bat or two—but she needed to fix her mistake before she could explore the wonders of the mountain further.

"Besides, you'd be bored if you joined us," Anna said. "We won't be singing anymore, and being on a raft makes it hard for you to dash anywhere."

Head tilted, the little Hulder considered this bleak reality, then clambered out of the raft to join one of the Huldrefólk guards who'd seemingly materialized out of nowhere.

"Bye!" Echo proclaimed from the riverbank, waving. "Bye-bye-bye!"

Anna's heart squeezed. "See you later. Stay out of dark abysses, okay?"

Elsa was the last to step onto the raft. When she'd settled her cloak around her, she looked back at the Librarian King. "Thank you," she said. "For all your help. I promise we'll keep your secret, and we will keep the mines closed. Your city will remain hidden."

The Librarian King bowed in thanks, and then Obscuren pushed them across the glassy surface of the river.

The raft rocked as they navigated the underground waterway, the air refreshingly cooler now.

Obscuren took in their drooping eyelids. "You can sleep," she said. "I know my way around the river. And as the Librarian King said, you are hidden here with me, even from the Nattmara."

"Are you absolutely . . ." Whatever Kristoff had been going to say was lost in a yawn.

"The Nattmara cannot find our domain," Obscuren

reminded them. "We are cloaked from it. You can rest here, safely, without any fear of losing yourself over to its influence. Sleep. Rest. I'll wake you when we reach our destination."

Obscuren had barely finished before a snore ripped out of Kristoff, and in the next second, Elsa, too, was asleep. Anna, however, stayed awake. Though she had been daydreaming about sleeping, she found she couldn't close her eyes. Every time she did, her stomach hurt too much. Because each moment asleep was a moment she wasn't fixing her biggest mistake: the Nattmara she'd accidentally welcomed into Arendelle with a spell. Obscuren's voice interrupted her thoughts, and Anna pulled herself out of them.

"Sorry, what was that?" Anna asked.

"I said," the Hulder repeated, "that you should sleep, too." Obscuren pushed on the pole, and the water sighed as the raft sliced through it. The river flowed through winding tunnels with low ceilings, though here and there little beaches seemed to jut into the waterway, and Anna thought she could make out the distant shape of a Hulder or two watching them. This close to a Hulder who was *not* trying to kill her, she could finally make out a more definite shape.

Obscuren looked almost human but for an overall spindly appearance, pointed ears, and changing skin. At the moment, the Hulder's eyes were a beautiful shade of orange, a color that made Anna think of the end of autumn or the start of spring. They seemed to take in everything around them, and as Obscuren looked at Anna, Anna wondered if the seeker of things could find Anna's deepest secret in her eyes.

"Obscuren," Anna said, "do you know how the Nattmara came to Arendelle? I think I know, but I'm not entirely sure. The Blight started before the Nattmara arrived. I'm a bit murky on the details." She held her breath, waiting for Obscuren to somehow say the words that were blaring through her mind as loudly as a goatherd playing the tungehorn: the *spell*. It must have been the spell, as much as it didn't make sense that the animals and crops had grown sick before she'd read it. But after she read the spell, the wolf appeared. Of that much Anna was certain— just as she was certain it was her fault.

Obscuren was silent, but it wasn't the kind of sharp silence of being ignored. This quiet had a thoughtful quality to it, as though she were weighing each word before speaking.

"A Nattmara doesn't appear out of thin air," the Hulder said. "They are made, formed from an event in a person's life that grows so big they can't keep it inside anymore, and the fear becomes so large that it takes on a life of its own."

Anna nodded. Yes, that was what Sorenson had said. *The fear is too big to keep inside.* "Sooo," Anna said, "you don't think that someone could have, I don't know"—she tucked a strand of ruddy hair behind her ear—"said a spell, or something, and brought the Nattmara to Arendelle?"

Obscuren gave a shake of her head. "I don't believe the poems that humans call spells are really anything other than just that: poems. They may be able to conjure a beautiful image or a moment of time, but that is a different kind of magic entirely."

Anna wasn't sure what to say, but she was comforted. Because Anna *had* read a spell . . . but it sounded like even if she had never said it out loud, the Nattmara still would have come to the kingdom.

Anna still would have accidentally called it, with or without a poem. Because the night that it had materialized from her dreams was the same night she'd heard Elsa holding a council meeting without her, and she had felt her heart break a little. It was the moment she had realized her greatest fear had come true: that Elsa really and truly had no need for her at all. And because of that, her nightmare—her *fear*— had manifested in the form of the Nattmara that was now stalking them all.

"And I guess," she said, trying to keep her voice light, "if there's no spell to call a Nattmara, then there's probably no spell to banish one, right?"

Obscuren shook her head. "I wouldn't think so. I've only ever heard of one warrior willing to face the Nattmara, and that was Aren, with his mythical Revolute Blade that contained a strange power."

*Revolute.*

With Kristoff and Elsa asleep and nestled against her back, and Obscuren in the front, keeping an eye on Anna and her friends, the mythical curved sword shone like a lighthouse in the dark river of Anna's worry, and, at last, she let her eyes drift shut to sleep.

# Chapter Nineteen

WHEN OBSCUREN WOKE ANNA, she felt better rested than she had in a long, long time.

Next to her, Kristoff stretched, half his hair smooshed against his cheek where he'd lain on it. "Up, up, and away," Kristoff said with a yawn.

Elsa, however, still managed to look regal, even though Anna could see the pattern of pumice pores on her face. Anna giggled, motioning to her sister's cheek.

"You should take a look at yourself," Elsa grumbled with half a smile.

Anna peered into the river. Sure enough, she looked the same as she always did when she woke up: a bit like a woodland creature with a slobber problem. Anna patted down her stray hairs with river water, and she found comfort in the way that some things stayed the same. Elsa smiled at her, and Anna guessed she was thinking the same thing, too.

"We're here," Obscuren said as they glided up to a post.

While they waited for Obscuren to secure the raft, Anna looked around, but even holding out her wrist with the glowworm bracelet, she couldn't see any sign of a library . . . or where one could possibly be. The banks of the underground river were narrow, no wider than a foot or two, and as far as she could tell, nothing had been carved into the rock's surface except for a few crumbly-looking steps.

"Where is it?" Anna asked. It had been nice to sleep and all, but being awake again meant she was more aware than ever of the time that was slipping away. They had only one more day of sun and a single night left before the third sunrise made the Nattmara's reality permanent—assuming that the spell really had been what brought the Nattmara to Arendelle in the first place. Obscuren hadn't though so, but Anna couldn't shake Sorenson's words. *All myths contain a kernel of hard truth.* The spell might not have been real magic, but that didn't mean the warning wasn't true. At any rate, Anna was not willing to risk it.

"Up, up, up and away," Obscuren said, seeming to settle into another's words comfortably, as if the conversation of the previous night had been a bit of a strain for her.

Elsa wobbled out of the raft first, followed by Kristoff. When he turned to offer his hand to help Anna step out, she ignored it and leapt over the side. Obscuren indicated with a nod that they should take off their glowworm bracelets and leave the little creatures on the post. With a wistful sigh, Anna unwrapped the glowworm and gave it a little pat in thanks.

"Will it be okay here?" she asked.

"Home is where the heart is," Obscuren said, and when Anna looked for clarification, the Librarian King's assistant explained, "I'll take them back with me. They're not needed where we're going."

And with that, Obscuren left the raft behind and stepped off into the darkness, silent as the moon sailing through the night sky.

Anna, Elsa, and Kristoff followed her, not nearly as gracefully, but they managed to reach the beginning of the steps and started to feel their way up the side of the rock, following the carved path that wound its way to the cave ceiling.

"Stop a moment," Obscuren said, and there were a few quick taps, and then a *creak* as the Hulder pushed open a square hatch in the ceiling. Light streamed through.

Squinting her eyes against the unexpected brightness, Anna emerged from the dirt floor of a round room with stone walls carved with runes and windows blocked by grassy tussocks. She caught a glimpse of blue in the window. Her heart leapt. "Wait, is that *sky*?" she asked.

"We're in a turf house," Elsa said as she shrugged off her cloak and her mother's scarf before stepping aside from the trapdoor to make space for Kristoff to climb up beside them.

Of course! Turf houses dotted Arendelle's wilderness of scraggly birches and spruces. They were made by digging a dwelling-sized hole deep into the ground, which was then covered by a roof made of grass. Turf houses came in all shapes and sizes, but Anna's favorites were the ones that looked like Earth Giants sunk into the soil, the green grass of the roofs resembling troll hair. Anna looked around, hoping to see a neat row of books. "Um, Obscuren, are you *sure* this is your library?" she said.

It didn't look so much like a library as it did a too-crammed gift shop. Sure, there were a few books scattered here and there, with bleached covers that looked like they'd been forgotten long ago and left out to wither in the sun. But mostly there were *items*.

There were sideways chairs lying on top of rolled-up rugs next to a careful stack of mirrors. There was a pile of gardening tools, broken clay figurines, and more than one pile of rusted old keys. And there were socks—lots and lots of mismatched socks.

"Welcome to the Library of Lost Things," Obscuren said. Above the ground and in the warm light of the turf house, the Hulder seemed to look less like rock and more like a tree, softly sprouting leaves where before there had been the rough texture of a pebble.

"Before you say anything, we did not steal any of these things. We simply find things that are lost and give them homes. That includes everything from missing spectacles, to hair bands, to legendary swords. Please," the Hulder continued, stepping aside, "feel free to roam."

"Thank you!" Anna cheered.

"Can the Nattmara find us up *here*? Or are we still hidden and all that?" Kristoff asked, peering out a window.

"With me, you are still hidden from the Nattmara," Obscuren said.

"Phew!" Kristoff said.

"That's a relief," said Elsa, peering through the mess of objects.

"We should split up," Anna said, then looked at Elsa. "Right?"

Elsa nodded, and so the three of them began their search.

Some of the lost objects were beautiful—bronze vases from another age and even a necklace of heavy sapphires that Anna thought would complement Gerda's eyes—if Anna were able to turn them back from yellow, that is. She set the necklace down and hurried to the next pile. She picked up a round mirror. It was little, meant to slip into a pocket, and clasped cleverly to look like a clamshell. She opened it, then set it to the side. It was pretty, but not what she was looking for.

Scanning the room, Anna searched for a glint of metal, trying to find anything that could possibly be the sword of myth. She moved aside a rickety chair and a mountain of missing socks and tried to push down her disappointment, but it kept rising, like a hot-air balloon, not wanting to be weighed down. There had to be *something* in this library. Anna's thoughts skidded to a halt. Her eye had caught on a statue in the center of the room. It was a figure of a human girl in a sky-blue dress with a glittering train, and a platinum blond braid. It looked to be about as tall as Elsa's knee, and it also happened to look *a lot* like Elsa.

Anna gasped as she stepped closer. It *was* a statue of Elsa. Specifically, the one the sisters had installed in the town cuckoo clock a few years before. Last spring, the Elsa figure had disappeared in a sudden storm, blown away by unusually strong winds. Anna peered at the statue.

A little green wreath with candles had been perched on top of statue Elsa's head, and Anna had the briefest thought that the statue looked more comfortable here, surrounded by other wondrous things, than it had looming above the masses, day in and day out. She was glad the Huldrefólk had found a new home for it, and so she kept searching.

But no matter how hard or long they looked, they did not find the coveted sword in the turf house.

The closest things to a mythical sword they'd managed to unearth were a few shields and helmets from the time of King Runeard, but nothing older than that. Anna's shoulders slumped. If the Huldrefólk didn't have Revolute, and if Sorenson was lost, and if the trolls had fled the Nattmara . . . what were they going to do? They were running out of places to find answers.

"There's not a single sword in this library!" Elsa said to Obscuren an hour later as the gang flopped in front of a large fireplace to eat from Kristoff's traveler's pack.

Obscuren sighed. "So it appears." The Hulder's skin had taken on the runes of the turf house walls, and speaking to Obscuren now almost felt like talking to alphabet soup. She seemed to droop slightly, and it was clear to Anna that Obscuren wasn't used to having to converse so much.

"Why not?" Kristoff asked. "Arendelle's history seems to be full of swords, as far as I can tell. Why didn't the Huldrefólk ever find one? Maybe it's at another location?"

"Sometimes," Obscuren said, settling down onto the dirt floor to rest, "great swords are buried with their heroes."

"*ARRGH!*"

Anna's heart began to pound furiously as a cry that sounded a bit like a seagull reverberated through the turf house. Wide-eyed, Anna turned to see what had made such a terrifying sound—expecting to see the Nattmara or a mob of yellow-eyed villagers coming for them—but all she saw was Elsa, who'd leapt to her feet.

"Well, that's just great!" Elsa's blue eyes flashed and her cheeks reddened. For the first time in a long time, Anna thought that her sister looked visibly upset.

"What's wrong?" Anna scrambled to her feet, too. "We just need to find out where Aren was buried—"

Elsa snorted, and it was such an un-Elsa-like sound that Anna grew quiet.

"We *can't* find where he was buried." Elsa paced the floor. "Don't you remember the story? Aren was swallowed by a dragon!"

Anna blinked. "He *was*?" She'd forgotten that. She glanced over at Kristoff, who was looking at Elsa with something like awe, as though he couldn't quite believe that calm and collected Elsa was panicking.

"Yes," Elsa said, exasperated. "A dragon came to the fjord, and it threatened to eat everyone! And so Aren, our greatest leader besides King Runeard, who loved his home and people more than anything, decided to go face the dragon . . . who"—Elsa paused, then changed to her most dramatic voice—"'lives where the sea is a sky,' and never came back." Elsa took a deep breath. "Because the dragon swallowed him. And dragons don't exist, and neither does this sword, and Anna, oh, I've tried listening, but there's nothing we can do!"

"Curious," Obscuren called out. During Elsa's tirade, the Hulder had gone to a stone wall. "That's not what *all* stories say." She waved a delicate arm at the walls around them. "In that long-ago time when Huldrefólk and humans were more comfortable with each other, we would meet here, in a place of compromise between earth and sky. Each community carved their stories into these walls. This is one of the oldest turf houses. And here, the myth of Aren changes, slightly.

"This"—the Hulder pointed at a carved rune that looked like a sideways S-shape—"according to *our* legend, says that a great danger came from the waters, and in order to save his home and people that he loved, Aren set out in a boat and was never seen again."

"How is *that* any better?" Elsa asked, and Anna was shocked to see her sister's foot twitch, as though she had just resisted the urge to stomp her feet. "That just means Revolute is probably somewhere at the bottom of the ocean, and even if it *were* possible to scour all the waters, we just don't have time." Elsa turned sharply, sending her braid whipping out behind her and almost smacking a shocked Kristoff across the nose. "So you see," she addressed Anna, "we're never going to find Revolute!"

But actually . . . Anna *did* see.

Anna opened her mouth. "Elsa—"

"The Nattmara is still out there, the Blight chokes the land, and all of our friends are probably stuck in a nightmare by now!"

Kristoff flinched at her words.

"You wanted to visit the Huldrefólk because they were supposed to be able to tell us something," Elsa continued, "to show us the way to a made-up sword. Is there anything else, any other clue—"

"Elsa—"

Her sister threw her hands in the air. "The people are all counting on me!"

*"ELSA!"*

Elsa's furor stumbled to a halt, and, panting, she looked over at Anna, who pushed away a smile.

"How can you be so *calm* at a time like this?" Elsa demanded, and Anna had to stop from giggling.

"I'm calm because I learned from the best," Anna said, and she could feel a fiery hope burning bright in her chest. "And because I know where Revolute is."

# Chapter Twenty

"WAIT, WHAT?" ELSA SAID.

Anna couldn't help smiling now at hearing her signature line coming from Elsa's mouth.

"What do you mean, *you know where Revolute is?*"

Somewhere along the way, it had clicked as Anna stared at the carvings on the walls and listened to Obscuren's tale. The Arendellians' story and the Huldrefólk's story were different, but the same. Like Anna and Elsa. And just like the royal sisters, the stories made the most sense when they were together.

"Why can't *both* things be true?" Anna suggested. "Why can't he have been eaten by a dragon, as our story says, *and* be sent out on a boat? It's all in the stories—Aren was swallowed by a dragon who lived in a place where the sea is a sky."

"But for the sea to be a sky, you have to be under the . . ." Elsa's voice trailed off and her eyes lit up. "The Earth Giant's Passage! It goes under the fjord, which means the sea is the sky. And that's where the *dragon* boat is!" Elsa's hand flew to her mouth in wonder. "The tumulus," she said softly. "It's Aren's tumulus, which means . . ."

"That's where Revolute is buried," Anna finished with a nod. "Exactly."

"Way to go, Anna!" Kristoff said. "You solved it!"

"Thanks!" She flashed him a smile. "This means we have to go back to the castle," Anna said, looking up at the Hulder, who stood there tall and impassive as they spoke. "And we need to get there as soon as possible! Elsa, can you . . ." Anna twirled her finger.

"*Magic?* But it'll draw the Nattmara right to us," Elsa said.

Obscuren chimed in. "If you wanted to use your magic without the Nattmara sensing it, I think it would need to be now."

Elsa nodded. In the safety of the turf house, she crafted a sleigh of ice—ice so clear that Anna could see right through it. It was practically invisible. And then Anna felt a whoosh of cold air blow by her, and she shivered as snowflakes danced in the air, shaping themselves into a massive snow bear, who loomed much too large in the tiny turf house.

"Elsa," Anna said, taking in the snow bear with wonder, "he's beautiful."

The bear growled.

"He says his name is Bjorn," Obscuren translated.

"I can hear my reindeer, Sven, talk, too," Kristoff said to the Hulder. His voice sounded glum, and Anna knew he was still worried about his best friend. She hoped Sven was all right, and, at the very least, safe on the royal ship.

Obscuren rested a hand on Kristoff's arm and flashed a sad smile. "The Huldrefólk are known for finding things that are lost, because we know how to listen," she said. "But we're not the only beings who listen. Animals can, too. They can tell a kind heart from one filled with cruelty. And I suspect, Kristoff, that you're someone who knows exactly what Sven is saying to you."

Kristoff shook his head. "I just hope he's okay."

"If we leave right now, he will be," Anna said,

trying to say it with so much confidence that it would just *have* to be true.

As quickly as they could, they buckled the snow bear up to the sleigh, and then said their farewells to Obscuren.

"In my family," the Hulder said, "we don't say goodbye."

"What do you say, then?" Anna asked.

"We say, 'Till we see you again.'"

Anna smiled. "Till we see you again."

"Maybe," Obscuren said, already disappearing behind a stack of lost and broken plates. "But I'll probably see you first. Unless you look very, very closely."

Obscuren reached out an arm and cracked open the door. There was a second while the Hulder took in the land, and then she flung the door open wide for the bear and the sled. "Remember," the Hulder called as they slipped from the safety of the turf house and slid out under the sky. "Home is where the heart is. Good luck, friends of Arendelle."

"Goodbye, friend," Anna said.

But Obscuren was gone.

As Bjorn loped away from the turf house, home

did not look like home anymore. Anna saw a haze had settled over Arendelle as color drained from the world. It was as though the earth itself were afraid, turning pale with fear. Anna held out her hand, studying it in the sunlight. It still looked pink in the cold. Glancing at Elsa, Anna was comforted by the fact that her mother's scarf, wrapped around Elsa's shoulders, was still burgundy, while Kristoff's hair was still the color of wheat. The color that wheat was *supposed* to be, Anna corrected herself. But there was still time before sunset. There was still time to remedy this all.

"It looks like the forest after a fire," Kristoff said, glancing at the terrain as he guided the snow bear around a bend with a careful tug of the reins.

"What do you mean?" Elsa asked.

"The way the ash drifts," Kristoff explained. "It floats on the air instead of falling."

"Maybe," Anna said, trying to force cheer into her words, "that's a *good* thing. I read in the library that forest fires are necessary to clear the bramble and make way for new life."

Kristoff shook his head. "Tell that to the people who've lost their homes." He jounced the reins, and the sleigh went faster.

Anna held a spyglass of ice from Elsa up to her eye, scanning the horizon for any sign of the Nattmara. So far, so good. There was no sign of the wolf. Well, no signs other than this pale shadow of their home and the fearful thump of Anna's own heart.

Except, what was that? A dark smudge seemed to move from the washed-out green of the spruces.

"Elsa," Anna whispered, and slipped the spyglass back to her sister. "Something's moving. Over there."

Elsa peered over her shoulder, then looked ahead again. "You're right," she said. "I think it's following us."

Kristoff snapped the reins harder and Bjorn veered right, sending a swirl of pale white leaves into the air. Anna looked back. The smudge also veered right. Yes. Whatever it was, it was definitely following them. Bjorn's ears swiveled, and then Anna heard it.

A cry: *Ahhhhhhhh!* It seemed to come from the direction of the smudge. And it wasn't the bone-cold howl of the Nattmara. This noise sounded almost human, as though someone were trying to call out a name. In fact . . . *Ahhhhhh! Naaaaaaaa!*

"Stop!" Anna lurched upright. "It's Sorenson!"

Elsa gasped. "What?"

Kristoff pulled the reins, flinging Anna into Elsa as they sped back to the scientist. As they got closer, the cry became clearer. "Annaaaa! Elsaaaaa!"

"Sorenson!" Anna shouted, relieved he was okay.

Or was he? The scientist looked the worse for wear. His coat was torn, shredded by the Nattmara's claws, and he limped, his ankle swollen. But he was alive, and not only that, his eyes didn't appear to be either pitch black or yellow.

"Stop the sleigh!" Anna said, and Kristoff pulled Bjorn to a walk.

The snow bear snorted, protesting the change in pace.

"Sorenson!" Anna called as she swung out of the sleigh and hurried toward him. "We're so glad to see you! How did you escape?"

"Hello to you, Anna, and to you, Your Majesty," Sorenson said. He spoke in a strange cadence, as if he had somehow managed to twist his tongue as well as his ankle. "I'll tell you all about it in a minute. Just let me catch my breath."

"We don't really have time," Elsa said, looking to the sky. The sun was definitely low now, approaching dinnertime. "How about you tell us in the sleigh?"

He nodded. "That's a good idea, but we can't take a sleigh where we need to go."

"And where do we need to go?" Anna asked. She stepped over to Kristoff's traveler's pack and sifted around for a spare splint. Aha! There it was. She knew Kristoff rarely left home without it. The splint was for ice mountain emergencies, but Kristoff liked to tease her that he needed to make sure he had one on hand at the castle for the amount of times she'd managed to trip or stumble over something.

Anna sat down and offered the scientist the splint. "How did you escape the Nattmara?"

Sorenson said, "I found a thing of myth."

Anna's eyebrows shot upward. "You found Revolute?"

Sorenson tilted his head, and with his long silver beard, he looked a little bit like a confused dog. "Did you figure out where it was hidden?"

Anna grinned. "Yes! Well, we know where to look. It's in—"

"What did *you* find, Sorenson?" Elsa asked, stepping in between them. She'd arranged their mother's scarf around her shoulders like a cape.

"Ah, I found a cure," Sorenson said, and he tapped his fingertips excitedly together. "But it's hard to explain. I'd rather show it to you first. It won't defeat the Nattmara, but I believe it will clear up the Blight from the animals and the crops."

"What?" Kristoff, who'd been waiting in the sleigh, jumped out. "There's a cure? We can help Sven?"

"Allegedly, yes," Sorenson said. "And the Huldrefólk have it."

"I don't know about that," Elsa said, tugging on the fringe of her scarf. "They're our friends, I think, and they didn't say anything about having a cure."

"Yes." Anna nodded. "And they are *definitely* our friends."

Sorenson's face crinkled and he shook his head while he sighed. "Whatever they told you is wrong," he said. "The Huldrefólk are thieves. You should not have trusted them."

"No," Anna said, standing up for Echo, the Librarian King, and Obscuren. "They find lost, unwanted things and give them homes. They find 'that which is lost,' like your book says, sir."

But Sorenson kept shaking his head, his long beard waving like one of the windswept pennants on the castle wall. In the lengthening light, his beard looked more white than silver. "Then my book must be wrong, because the Huldrefólk have a thing of myth hidden in their hot springs, not more than a mile away. I discovered that if a Nattmara-touched animal drinks the water, they will be cured, even if you *don't* defeat the Nattmara by sunrise of the third day."

"Let's go!" Kristoff said, the hope so bright on his face that it hurt Anna to see. "If it's only a mile, we could get a cup of the water from the hot springs, just in case, and still make it back without losing that much time!"

Bjorn's snuffle was louder now. The bear wanted to move. He wanted to *go*. Yet Anna was torn . . . until she saw the expression on Kristoff's face.

Kristoff's best friend was sick. And he had no way to know what had happened to Sven in the time they'd been gone, but he'd risked his life over and over again just for the chance that he could help make Sven feel better. How could Anna say no to that?

"Elsa," she said, turning from Sorenson, who still nursed his ankle on the splint, and from Kristoff, who looked like he was about to go sprinting in any direction as soon as he heard where these curing springs were. "I think we should get the water, as a precaution."

Again, Elsa looked at the sky and bit her lip. As Anna saw her sister take a deep breath, she knew she wasn't going to like whatever she was about to hear.

"We can't risk it," Elsa said, still keeping her gaze on the sky, and on the floating bits of ash that looked like snow but weren't. "I'm so sorry, Kristoff, but we can't. Even if the spring water *does* work, there's no way we can bring back enough for everyone in all the kingdom . . . and what about the sword?"

The look on Kristoff's face was unbearable. "So *now* you think the sword is real?"

"Elsa!" Anna said, looking between her sister and the man she loved.

"I understand your responsibility to the kingdom," Kristoff told Elsa, "but Sven is family to me."

"Kristoff," Elsa cut in, and her eyes were wide with hurt, though Anna didn't know why her sister would be upset. "I'm saying *no* because it endangers too many people!"

Anna took a deep breath, ready to argue more, when Bjorn let out a great bellow.

Whirling around, she turned to see that Sorenson

had taken Kristoff's pickax from the sleigh and was trying to yank the bear out of his harness.

"Sorenson?" Anna said, forgetting her frustration with Elsa as she took in the man's peculiar actions. "What are you doing?"

"Nothing, nothing," Sorenson said, reaching down to fiddle with a buckle. But as he bent down, Anna noticed something falling from his pocket.

If the world had been its normal color—dark emerald hues mixed with the rich blue of the mountains and the oncoming colors of fall—she would never have noticed it. But the world had turned ashy white, so what tumbled from Sorenson's pocket stood out like a stain. It was sand.

*Black* sand.

# Chapter Twenty-One

"NATT–NATT," ANNA SPUTTERED, trying to get the warning out.

But it was too late.

Already, as she watched, sand swirled from out of Sorenson's eyes to reveal not dark brown irises as Anna had thought, but eyes the color of a hornet's jacket. And then the sand swirled into Sorenson's heart. A place for the Nattmara to roost until the sunset. *Trolls tremble at the Nattmara's howl while the Nattmara flees from the sun like a shadow.* But nightmares could still hurt, even in the day.

"Nattmara!" Anna finally bellowed, and it was as if her shout had broken some strange enchantment. A moment ago, she'd felt utterly suspended outside of herself, and now she was moving faster than she could think. "Run!"

But Kristoff and Elsa had already seen what Anna had not been able to say. Kristoff took a running leap for the driver's seat of the sleigh while Elsa grabbed Anna's hand and pulled her safely inside.

"Mush!" Kristoff shouted, and Bjorn, already deeply unhappy about the break from the run and nervous around the man who did not smell quite right to him, shot off.

"Go! Go! Go!" Anna yelled when she was able to make her mouth move again. She twisted around just in time to see Sorenson bare his teeth, and then he reached into his coat pocket and pulled out a glittering vial of violet powder—the Highly Flammable and Very Dangerous Combustion Powder. The scientist, now the Nattmara's puppet, raised the vial high into the air.

"FASTER!" Anna cried, just as an explosion fell short of them, barely missing the sleigh.

They careened out of control, the ride far from smooth as it was still early fall, and the ground was only just hard enough for the sleigh's runners to work. Any other sleigh would not have been able to make it across the rough terrain of scrub, brush, and rock, but an Elsa-made sleigh was as slippery as could be, and twice as fast.

Another vial of powder whistled by Anna's ear, and she turned her head just before violet fire could engulf her. From the corner of her eye, she saw Elsa raise her hands.

"No!" Anna yelled. "You can't! The Nattmara will only get bigger and more powerful!"

Elsa lowered her hands, and Anna faced forward.

"What's that?" Anna asked, pointing at a dark line in the earth that loomed ahead.

"That," Kristoff said with a gulp, "is a canyon. A very, very, very *wide* canyon."

Another whistle hit the air. Another blast.

"We have to lose it!" Anna yelled. "Faster! Faster! We'll be able to clear the canyon!"

"No, we won't!" Elsa shouted. "We're too heavy!"

The dark line was thicker now, the chasm closer and wider. Just a few more seconds until they would be able to try to clear it, to try to soar over the deep trench.

"Elsa, here!" Kristoff thrust the reins into Elsa's hands before turning to Anna. "I think I can hold Sorenson off until sunset," he said, looking straight into her eyes. "Tell Sven I said he should listen to you." His words came too fast, and the meaning came too slow.

Anna shook her head. "Wait, what?"

But then Kristoff was kissing her. His lips pressed to hers, warm and light and as strong as a promise . . . but a promise for what? Before Anna could gather up her thoughts and piece together what he was telling her, her lips were suddenly cold again. The kiss, over.

And Kristoff was turning away from her, balancing on the edge of the sleigh . . .

"No!" Anna gasped as his words became clear.

But she was too late. Kristoff leapt from the sleigh, and Anna screamed.

"What's happening?" Elsa yelled, tearing her eyes from the chasm and looking back just as Kristoff landed hard on the ground, both knees bending to absorb the impact, somehow managing to stay on his feet. And then he was off, running toward Sorenson.

"KRISTOFF!" Anna shouted. But without his added weight, the sleigh slipped faster.

The bear's heavy paws sent mud flying as he barreled his way toward the chasm, taking Anna farther and farther from Kristoff.

"KRISTOFF!" Anna shouted again. "KRISTOFF, COME BACK!"

But Sorenson had seen him now. The old man raised Kristoff's pickax, its two hooked ends gleaming like wolf fangs as he moved toward Kristoff, who was now armed with only a fallen tree branch.

In any other circumstance, the victor of the fight would have been unquestionable. Kristoff was young, strong as an ox, and fresh from a summer of hauling blocks of ice up and down the mountain and from doing handiwork around the castle, while Sorenson was wizened with age, his face a crinkled map, his short limbs thin from years of sedentary study.

But the Nattmara had lent Sorenson its predatory grace and ruthless instinct. Sorenson moved like hot oil, fast and crackling, guaranteed to cause pain, sliding so fast it was hard to tell if Sorenson was now man or wolf or both. His swollen ankle did nothing to slow him.

Sorenson chopped down with the stolen pickax, Kristoff only just whirling away from being sliced in two. He barely had time to look up before Sorenson was on him once more. The pickax swung down again and again with the deftness of a sewing needle.

Still, Anna could see Kristoff's shaggy yellow hair dipping and dodging, tucking and rolling, just as the trolls had trained him to do. Anna wanted to leap off the sleigh and run to his side more than anything.

"Do we go back?" Elsa called, the older sister asking the little sister what to do. And of all times, Anna thought.

Elsa's cloak snapped in the wind, and though she looked shaken, she still gripped the sparkling reins with the same steadiness as when she'd held her coronation scepter. They were almost upon the chasm. "You need to tell me, now!"

*Yes.* With the whole of her heart, Anna wanted to grab the reins from Elsa's hands and tug the bear back toward Kristoff and the Nattmara-possessed Sorenson. But she couldn't. She wouldn't.

The shadows were already long. Night would soon be here—and then there would be dawn. The *third* dawn, the last dawn if Anna couldn't get Revolute first. Kristoff had given her a gift—a chance to undo what she had done. And she couldn't let it go to waste.

"Keep going," Anna croaked, even as her heart cracked. Hot tears flew down her cheeks, mingling

with the ash from the sky as Elsa tightened the reins
and Bjorn jumped.

Anna's heart dropped into her stomach as they
soared over the chasm.

For a long moment, they seemed to dangle in the
air, suspended by nothing thicker than spider's silk
over the gaping mouth of the earth. If they didn't
make it across, the sharp rocks hundreds of feet
below were ready to rip and chew them apart.

Anna tried to cling to the sleigh's sides, but Elsa's
creation was flawless. There was no rough patch of
ice she could grab hold of. No uneven knot she could
clutch. And so Anna clung to the only thing she
could: her sister.

Seconds seemed to pass, and still the other side
felt as far away as forever. And then, with a bone-
rattling thump, the bear's paws touched back down
on the ground, and the sleigh and the sisters slammed
down behind him—hard. They had made it.

"Anna, I can't breathe!" Elsa squeaked out.

Anna let go of her sister, whirling around to see
what had happened to Kristoff. She could just make
out two figures beyond the chasm, but she could no
longer tell which blur was the pickax and which was

the branch. They grew smaller and smaller as the bear lengthened his strides and the ground flew by, but she kept her eyes on the battling figures.

Anna knew this dance could only last so long. In just a few hours, the sun would drop behind the horizon, and then the Nattmara would stop hiding in Sorenson's body and resume its full power as the fearsome wolf.

Or would it possess Kristoff before then? Would Kristoff be smothered by a nightmare reality? He'd live in his own horror-scape, where there were no trolls or reindeer, or quiet mountain solaces, or Anna. A nightmare world that might last forever, unless she and Elsa could stop it first.

"Can we go any faster?" Anna's throat was so tight that her question was barely more than a whisper. In fact, she wasn't actually sure she'd said anything at all. She felt about as substantial as a shadow and just as useful. She wasn't sure Elsa had heard her until she felt her sister's hand squeezing hers.

"We'll go as fast as the wind," Elsa promised, both hands back on the reins.

They slid through the rocky terrain of the mountains, hurtling at a breakneck pace until

Bjorn's wild run ended at a cliffside. A river rushed nearby, gaining speed and sound as it hurried to the mountain's edge. They had reached the waterfalls— and the entrance to the Earth Giant's Passage, to Aren's tumulus.

"We're here." Elsa stumbled out of the sleigh. "Hurry!"

Looking down, Anna could make out the distinct shape of Arendelle Castle. The ice bubble Elsa had so carefully and beautifully made had fractured, leaving sharp shards of ice around it, a terrain as dangerous as broken glass. Next to it, Anna could see the village, the color of its homes still cheery despite the terror that Anna knew it now housed. But at least, she saw with relief, the ice dome Elsa had made for the village still held.

She looked toward the port. The royal ship, too, was gone, and Anna hoped that Sven, Olaf, and the villagers were far away by now, and safe. She couldn't handle it if one single soul more was hurt because of her. Because Kristoff . . . No. She couldn't think about Kristoff. Not now.

Slipping out of the sleigh, she helped Elsa free the snow bear from his harness. Without it, Bjorn looked ten times fiercer and ten times wilder, and Anna was aware that with just a single paw, he could crush her as easily as she could crush a crocus. But then, the bear shook himself, his fur rippling like seaweed, and pushed his cold nose into Anna's hand. He snuffled, and Anna flung her arms around his snowy ruff.

"Thank you," she said, squeezing Bjorn and allowing herself a moment of wonder. She was hugging a bear. *She was hugging a bear!*

Elsa nodded. "Yes, thank you, Bjorn."

Bjorn waited for Anna's one last squeeze, and looked at Elsa. He seemed to nod his head in her direction. But then he pulled away—and ran in the direction of the Nattmara, and Anna understood.

He'd helped them as best he could, and now he would try to lure the Nattmara away from them while they searched for Revolute.

"Come on," Anna said, excitement rising in her chest as she headed toward the waterfall. "If we're right, we're about to fix everything!"

Elsa wrapped her scarf tighter around her shoulders. "But if we're wrong, then . . ."

Anna was glad Elsa didn't finish her thought, because she couldn't bear to hear it.

# Chapter Twenty-Two

THEY WERE WRONG.

*Anna* was wrong.

In the light of a torch that Elsa had found and ignited, Anna looked again at the dragon boat's empty hull, a lump filling her throat.

Once, there might have been mounds of gold, pottery, lush cloaks, and jars of rare spices to help send Aren the warrior on his valiant voyage.

Once, this might have been a splendid place of sleek polished wood, a fitting resting place for Aren and his mighty sword.

But now the rotten boards were barely strong enough to hold a dusty footprint, let alone a thing of myth. Elsa stood in the hull with Anna, turning over a small clump of dirt with the toe of her boot. A cloud of dust trailed into the air, and Anna sneezed.

"We're too late," Elsa said as she stepped over the remains of what might have once been an oar, "by a thousand years, give or take. Maybe Revolute was here once—maybe this had even been Aren's final resting place, but . . ." She trailed off, her eyes lingering on the holes in the porous old wood. "I think this boat has been empty for a long, *long* time."

*No.* They had come too far, risked too much.

"Revolute is around here," Anna said, kicking another clot of dirt with her boot only to reveal . . . more dirt. She knew many boats had secret watertight compartments in the floor, but she had searched and found none. "It just has to be here!"

But even as she said it, Anna knew that wasn't necessarily true. In fact, nothing *just had to be* anywhere. If *just had to be* counted for anything, then a great storm would have never met Mother and Father's ship. It would mean that King Runeard's life wouldn't have been taken by dangerous northerners, and that young Elsa and Anna would have known their grandfather. It would mean that Sven would have never gotten the Blight, and that Anna would have never called a Nattmara to the kingdom by manifesting it from her fears and nightmares.

Suddenly, it was *just all too much*. Anna felt the weight of all the earth and sea and castle fall onto her shoulders and crush her, snuffing out her last bit of hope. She had not found the Revolute Blade, and she never would. She would never be able to defeat the Nattmara. She would never see Kristoff or Olaf or Sven ever again. She stepped out of the boat and lowered her head into her hands, and tears began to fall.

"Oh, Anna," Elsa said, following her.

Anna felt pressure on her shoulder as her sister crouched down next to her in the flickering torchlight.

"Please, please, please don't cry," Elsa said. "It's not your fault. If I had been doing a better job, I would have recognized the signs, and we could have stopped the Nattmara before you called it into the kingdom."

Anna knew Elsa was trying to be comforting, but her words only made Anna feel a hundred times worse. They were just more proof that Elsa didn't need Anna anymore—that, in fact, Elsa might even be better off without Anna.

Anna dragged her face away from her hands, and

leaning against the rough-hewn wall, she put her head back and looked up at the dragon figurehead, its mouth opened in an eternal snarl, unable to ever really stop thieves from stealing its treasures. Anna closed her eyes, shutting out its accusing wooden eyes.

Maybe it would be best for Elsa and all of Arendelle if the wooden dragon could just come to life and swallow Anna and her great disappointments whole, like how the wolf had swallowed her in her nightmare. She wasn't exactly sure *what* that would do, but . . . Anna's runaway thoughts lurched to a halt as an idea grabbed on to them. She looked back up at the wooden dragon, its mouth gaping open.

"Elsa!" Anna rose to her feet.

Elsa lifted the torch as she stood, too. "What is it, Anna?"

"I think I know where the sword is!" And without waiting for her sister to interrupt, Anna continued to barrel ahead. "We were just looking in the hull of the boat, because that's where one would end up if you were eaten—in the belly of a dragon, or in the boat. But the myth doesn't say that the dragon *ate* Aren, it says—"

"He was swallowed," Elsa said, eyes growing wide. "Revolute could be hidden in the dragon's mouth!"

Anna nodded. "Exactly!"

The dragon's snarling mouth reared several feet above their heads. Usually, Elsa would be able to wave her hands and make a staircase out of ice. But they weren't under the Huldrefólk's protection anymore. If Elsa used as much as a lick of her magic, the Nattmara would be upon them in seconds.

Crawling out onto the dragon's neck also wasn't an option. The boat was a thousand, maybe even *thousands* of years old, and the peeling, splintering wood had as many holes as a sponge. The whole thing looked like it might collapse if Anna so much as breathed on it.

Elsa planted the torch in the ground and crouched down. "All right, get on."

"What?" Anna looked at her sister, confused.

"We need to get someone up there. I think you can reach it if you get on my back."

"A piggyback ride? Really?" said Anna, a grin breaking across her face. "You haven't offered me one of those since before the gates closed."

"Well," Elsa said with a smile, "I guess I owe you at least one more."

Kicking off her boots, Anna scrambled up onto her sister's back. Then, balancing herself against the wooden hull, she placed her feet on Elsa's shoulders and pulled herself into a standing position so she was eye to eye with the dragon.

Even though centuries had scrubbed it clear of most of its details, up close, Anna could still see the hatch marks that hinted at scales, and the expression of the dragon. From below, the expression had seemed to be of a snarling angry beast, but now, Anna thought maybe it wasn't angry, just protective. Nerves bubbled throughout Anna's body.

This was it. Their one shot. Their last chance.

The Revolute Blade, the very thing that had carved out Arenfjord and made a home for a wandering people. A sword forged from a curved sunbeam with an unusual power, a gift from the sun herself. They would defeat the Nattmara. They would cure the crops and animals and people of the Blight, and free everyone she loved from their own terrifying nightmares.

"Do you have it?" Elsa asked from underfoot.

# CHAPTER TWENTY-TWO

*Whoops.* Anna's mind was running away again.

"No, not yet!" Anna said, reining in her galloping thoughts.

"Well, hurry up! You don't exactly weigh the same as you did when you were five."

No, Anna wasn't five years old. She was capable of making serious mistakes, but she was also just as capable of fixing them. And so, she reached her hand into the dragon's mouth.

At first, there was nothing there. Frowning, Anna leaned farther into the dragon's gaping maw, her elbow disappearing, followed by the rest of her arm, until the wood hit her armpit. Worry crept through her. If the dragon's head was hollow, would she need to crawl all the way in? She wasn't sure if she would fit. If only Olaf were there, he'd be able to send his hand down inside. Or even Sven would have been helpful, with his sensitive nose. But they weren't, so Anna would have to do it herself.

"Anna," Elsa said, "your foot is starting to dig into my shoulder."

"Sorry," Anna said. "Just one more second." Taking a breath to balance herself, she rose to her tiptoes, stretching, reaching until her fingers brushed something cold and metal-smooth. Something that fit comfortably in her palm as she wrapped her hand around it. Something that sent a note of anticipation through her. Anna pulled.

At first, there was resistance, and then a whisper of metal, a noise that almost sounded like a dragon's sigh as its secret came loose. And then Anna's hand was back in the rippling orange light of the torch.

*Could it truly be?*

The hilt was wrought from gold, and in the center of the pommel, like a miniature sun, sat a yellow diamond. The gold of the handguard had been worked to look like little rays of the sun, leading down to the blade.

And the blade . . . it was made of a blue-black metal—the same color as the meteorite in Sorenson's observation tower. It curved, the slight *S*-shape mirroring the inlet of Arenfjord, where myth said Aren had made the legendary cut.

But Anna hardly dared to believe that what she held was what she needed it to be. Not until she'd carefully slipped down from Elsa's back. Not until Elsa tore a scrap of cloth from her split dress and began to polish the top of the blade, right below where it met the hilt. Not until she could read the letters that had been etched into the sword itself did Anna believe:

R-E-V-O-L-U-T-E

They'd found it. The carver of the first fjord.
The myth and the solution.
The Revolute Blade.

# Chapter Twenty-Three

"WE DID IT!" Anna shouted, forgetting the need to be quiet and embracing Elsa.

"Careful!" Elsa twisted the sword away. "You don't want to accidentally stick us."

Though Elsa's warning wasn't really all that funny, for some reason, it planted a seed of humor in Anna. A giggle slipped out, and then, a bloom of laughter. And instead of trying to trap it down, Anna let it rush through her, throwing back her head and laughing long and loud. Elsa looked confused, which only made Anna laugh harder.

Then, ever so slowly, Elsa's lips began to turn upward, and she giggled; then she, too, laughed, loud and free. Their laughter echoed around the Earth Giant's Passage, bounding and rebounding, patching the tiny rip in Anna's heart caused by constant worrying.

Because Anna had done it. She'd proven to Elsa that she still needed her little sister who made mistakes. She'd proven that she could actually accomplish exactly what she had planned to do.

Suddenly, Elsa stopped laughing, and it was only Anna's laughter that bounced around the walls, sounding alone and by itself.

"Hey," Anna said, somewhat breathless. "What's wrong?"

Elsa held her finger to her lips, and Anna listened. Without the protective barrier of laughter, she could now hear another sound coming from beyond the waterfall and the passage. A long, low angry howl.

The Nattmara was nearing.

"We need to get out here," Anna said, slipping her boots back on. "Or else it'll trap us in the tunnel."

"Agreed." Elsa nodded. Already, she was tightening the band around her braid. "But Anna, I think—"

"That we need a plan," Anna said, finishing her sister's sentence, as they so often did. "Yes, you're right! The plan—the-plan-the-plan-the-plan . . . You use your magic to distract the Nattmara—only for a second or two!—and then I'll surprise it with Revolute. That's a *brilliant* idea, Elsa!"

"But I—" Elsa began, and that was all Anna could really make out, because she'd already tugged Revolute from Elsa's hand and begun to sprint down the passageway for the exit and the Nattmara. Fear thrummed through her veins, and yet, she had Revolute.

She had hope.

Anna squeezed the hilt tight, the yellow diamond pressing into her hand. It almost hurt, but still she kept running, trusting in the power of the myth and trusting her sister to follow behind her with an icy blast or whirl of hard wind.

The still-frozen waterfall sparkled up ahead, and Anna squeezed herself out onto the narrow ledge and exited the passageway only to stop in her tracks. Because the land sprawled before her was not the home she knew.

Her home had a cheery village with painted houses, a fjord full of rich blue waters, and a vibrant display of autumnal colors that would have made her paint set jealous. But the land before her was bleached white, as though this reality were being erased to make way for the nightmare that was settling in for eternity. Like storm clouds rolling in, the Nattmara prowled the village edge.

When Anna had first spotted the wolf in the Great Hall, it'd been bigger than any wolf she'd ever seen, but not abnormally so. Then it'd become twice the size of a normal wolf, then the size of a bull, then the size of a knoll. But now, its eyes were level with the second-floor windows of the village townhouses.

It was exactly as Sorenson had foretold. Each hour that the Nattmara had not been banished, it'd grown in strength and size as it gorged on the fear that had swept over the land. Each stride of its paw seemed to cover a mile, and wherever it passed, the trees twisted away from it, as if they, too, could sleep and dream and wanted none of the Nattmara's offerings. As if poplars and aspens and spruces, too, wanted to run away.

Anna had thought that the Nattmara would come directly for her, its accidental summoner, but instead of tearing up the path that would take it to the waterfall and to Revolute, the Nattmara turned . . . and loped back toward the village.

In the time that it took Anna to blink, the giant

wolf had arrived at the edge of the protective ice dome over the village. Rearing back on its hind legs, it struck the dome with a heavy paw.

*THUMP!*

The ice stayed whole and smooth. The dome was working—but for how long? The Nattmara swung again.

*THUMP!*

Anna frowned. Had that thump been followed by a cracking sound? The Nattmara only needed to make a fissure as thin as a hair for it to be able to trickle though Elsa's barrier in its black sand form.

"Anna!" Elsa said, flying out from behind the waterfall to join Anna on the ledge overlooking the village. "I need you to—"

"We have to go help them!" Anna yelled, desperation making her voice shrill. The villagers—they had no idea of the danger they were in. They were all asleep! She took a step forward to run—but her foot stayed put, rooted to the ground as though it had been locked in place.

*What?* Anna looked down to see a lacy frost pattern rising up from the ground, snapping together like links on a chain and wrapping around her foot.

While Anna gaped, something tugged on Revolute, and without thinking, Anna let go. Too late, she realized what she'd done. Looking back up, she saw Elsa standing in front of her, holding Aren's sword with both hands. She no longer looked like Anna's older sister, or even a queen. She looked like a soldier.

"Elsa." Her words sounded small even to her own ears. "What are you doing?"

"I'm sorry," Elsa said, and Anna could hear the truth in her sister's words, but still, Elsa made no move to stop the advancing frost. It circled around Anna, shuttling back and forth on itself like yarn on a loom to form a white tapestry, rising higher and higher. "I failed to protect the kingdom," Elsa said, "but I'm not going to fail you, too!"

*Failed?* Anna didn't know what Elsa was talking about. Elsa never failed at *anything*.

"Elsa," Anna said as the frost crystals scattered up over her head, dancing into a domed roof. "I don't *need* to be protected!"

It felt like Anna's whole being had contracted and collapsed in on itself, like a black hole or a dark abyss. She felt as though she'd become no bigger than the head of a pin. The last frost link clicked into place, finishing not a tapestry, but a bubble-like tent. Anna found she could move her feet again, the frost chain that had held her to the ground slithering away to weave itself into the structure. It didn't matter, though, if Anna could move her feet or not, because Elsa hadn't bothered to make a door.

"I love you," Elsa said, sounding for a moment like she was younger than Anna or even Echo. And then she was running, sprinting down the dirt path to the village below, Revolute a curved gleam in her hand.

"Come back!" Anna yelled. *"Elsa!"* She pounded her fists against the frost, but the walls were so strong, so solid, and so cold, that each pummel felt like a bite. The frost links held fast, keeping Anna locked away.

Anna was useless as she watched Elsa reach the end of the path and run toward the Nattmara. Useless as the Nattmara caught Elsa's scent and turned toward her sister, its fearsome claws extended. And useless as Elsa strode forward, ready to become the great ruler that Arendelle needed . . . just as Aren had done. But it would be okay. *It would be okay it would be okay it would be okay.*

Elsa wielded the myth that could defeat the myth. She held in her hand the crescent blade that had carved their home on Arenfjord. If Revolute could do that, *surely* it could defeat a Nattmara summoned by a scared little sister. Still, Anna held her breath as she watched, too far away to help, yet at the same time too close, because she could see it all.

A howl of wind clashed with the howl of the wolf as Elsa intercepted the Nattmara at the base of the Bridge of Arches. Elsa looked like a doll in front of the monstrous wolf, which had grown so tall that its ears were at the height of the castle's waving flags. Even from a distance, Anna could see the slip of saliva that hung from the Nattmara's fangs as it began to circle her sister, its great yellow eyes locked on Elsa.

This was a thousand times worse than any of Anna's nightmares. In all her nightmares but the last, she'd been in some sort of control. She'd always been able to puzzle her way out somehow, or distract the creature long enough that she could wake up. But even if Anna *could* break free from the frost bubble, she would not be able to wake up.

The wolf and her sister circled each other.

Elsa's cloak and scarf flapped in great gusts of wind as she twirled one hand and clutched Revolute with the other. But something was wrong. Even though Elsa was controlling the gusts of ice, no matter which direction she commanded the snow and ice to go, the wolf would force her to turn her back into the magic so that her hair and billows of icy magicked air constantly whipped into her eyes. There was no way for Elsa to clearly see.

And then, the Nattmara attacked.

Elsa and Revolute whirled away, the Nattmara's teeth snapping on thin air. It retreated for a moment, then struck again. This time, a terrible screech filled the air as a fang scraped across the blade. Or maybe the screech was Anna's own scream. Because Elsa now lay between the Nattmara's giant paws, sprawled like a spider, her limbs askew, and her hand empty.

Revolute flew through the air, a blue-black streak, and landed several feet behind Elsa. Anna saw Elsa's hand sweep out, trying to feel for the sword without taking her eyes away from the Nattmara.

"REVOLUTE!" Anna shouted, though she knew Elsa wouldn't be able to hear her. "TO YOUR LEFT!"

The Nattmara licked its maw, its fangs poised above Elsa.

For a moment, Anna saw in startling detail the gleam of the Nattmara's claws and rise in her sister's chest as Elsa took a deep breath.

Then, the Nattmara lunged down.

But in the space that it took for Anna to blink, Elsa had lunged, too. She grabbed for Revolute's hilt. In one fluid movement, she held it up in front of her—the ancient blade flashing in the light of the setting sun—and thrust it into the roof of the Nattmara's mouth.

Anna waited for the Nattmara to fall and disintegrate into dust, defeated at last by a thing of myth, just as Sorenson had said that it could be.

Instead, the world slowed and stilled as the Nattmara bit down. And Revolute—the great, mythic sword of Aren's oldest hero, the sword that had carved the Arenfjord from the mountains, slain beasts, and conquered nightmares—shattered like glass. Bits of the meteorite blade sparkled as they sprayed uselessly to the ground, raining down on Elsa, who now lay completely defenseless in front of the Nattmara.

"ELSA!" Anna roared, pounding at her prison of frost. "ELSA! Use your magic!"

Maybe it was a trick of the wind, but Elsa appeared

to turn her head in the waterfall's direction. For one second, it almost seemed that Elsa looked at her. Glancing down, Anna saw that the frost bubble had started to dissolve into thin air—not good! If Elsa's magic was dissolving, that must mean that Elsa was weakening, too.

But Anna was now free!

She began to run down the path even though she knew that she would not make it in time, but still, she had to try. Elsa would have—no, Elsa *had*—done the same for her.

The Nattmara threw back its leviathan head and howled its victory. And as it rose once more above her sister, its white fur shifted into a glittering black as the Nattmara morphed into a cloud of sand that stood out starkly against the faded landscape. The bits and pieces swirled together, forming a spinning column.

And then the sand slammed down into Elsa's chest . . . and disappeared.

"Elsa!" Anna sobbed, stumbling into range. "Elsa!"

Her sister sprawled on the ground, her eyes closed and her blond hair coming loose from its braid and spilling onto fallen leaves. Scattered around her like a broken halo were the blue-black shards of what had once been the great sword Revolute.

And though Anna knew what would happen next, she still wasn't prepared for when Elsa's eyelids fluttered open to reveal glowing yellow eyes.

Anna's stomach heaved at the sight of the wolf's eyes in her sister's familiar face. Her stride slowed. "Elsa?" she called out hesitantly.

Elsa opened her mouth . . . and screamed.

And then she raised her hands, blasting Arendelle with her powers, her usually white snow and white ice now replaced by *black* snow and *black* ice.

No, not black snow *or* black ice. Black *sand.*

As Elsa continued to scream, the sound swept through Anna, hollowing her out like the wolf's howl had, until there was nothing left except for Elsa's scream within her, reverberating against her ribcage, echoing again and again in her complete emptiness. In her utter aloneness.

Revolute had shattered, and Elsa's eyes were yellow.

"Elsa," Anna sobbed, not knowing what do. "Elsa . . . Elsa . . . Elsa!"

But the figure who had been her sister did not even turn to face her.

With great heaving gasps, Anna gathered the shards of the sword into her cloak pocket—a futile hope. Because Revolute, the famed sword of myth, had not been enough to defeat a beast of myth. The myth was no longer a myth. It had not saved her sister. And the sound of Elsa's scream—or was it the wolf's howl?—pulled her into the black dots gathering at the edge of her vision. Anna didn't know which was which, but the nightmares stormed in and dragged her down.

"Elsa," she managed to croak out one last time. No longer knowing what was real and what was a nightmare, or if they were now truly one and the same, Anna saw Elsa at last turn to her.

Elsa raised her hands, and black sand erupted from her palms toward Anna.

Darkness swirled around Anna, and then, at last, there was nothing at all.

# Chapter Twenty-Four

ANNA WOKE TO HER MOTHER singing a lullaby.

She knew it was just a dream, and so she kept her eyes shut, letting herself drift in the familiar and comforting melody. Though she couldn't make out the lyrics, she had a sense of the story behind it. A story from long ago, in that time before time, when the world was sprightly green and the rivers bubbled with enchantment. That time when the sun would step down from the sky and walk along the earth, just to feel the grass tickle her feet and to discuss philosophy with the wind. It was an olden song, a song of strength and meekness, revenge and love. The sound was sweet, but it was not real. Anna knew that.

Mother was gone. Father, too. And now Elsa . . .

*Yellow eyes and a haunted kingdom.* Tears dripped from

beneath her eyelashes, but Anna still didn't open them. She wanted to stay suspended in the dark, cocooned away until someone had cleaned up her mess.

Something cold patted her cheek. "Anna, quit joking around. Wake up."

This voice was familiar, too.

Anna opened her eyes to find herself nose to carrot with Olaf.

"You're leaking," he informed her, referring to the tears she was shedding.

"Olaf, what are you doing here?" Anna swiped at her eyes and looked away from Olaf's nose to see branchless trees swaying above her. No, not trees—masts. Three tall ones, each strung with the ropes and nets of a working ship and boasting wide billow-ing sails.

Above the slap of the waves, Anna could hear singing—but it wasn't her mother, it was Tuva the blacksmith, who stared out at the dark night over the royal ship's rail, her lilting voice filling the salt-sprayed air.

"Anna's awake!" Olaf shouted.

"How did you get here?" Anna asked Olaf. "How did *I* get here?" She looked around and beside her, and saw Sven wrapped in a large blanket, still fast asleep, though his legs twitched and sweat sheened his almost now completely white coat. Only a little patch of brown fur remained on his flaring nose.

"Hoo-hoo!" Oaken said, stomping into view, his cheeks a bit redder than usual from the cold sea air. "We watched everything from the harbor! When Scary Elsa vanished inside the castle, we crept ashore and carried you back. We thought both you and Sven would rest better next to one another."

"I thought you had already sailed away!" Anna said, perplexed. She also wondered why she hadn't fallen under the nightmare sleep. She studied her hands, not sure what she expected to see.

"We were going to," Tuva called from the ship's stern, her hands on the helm. In the yellow lantern light, the blacksmith looked ragged and her curly hair had been tugged into a cloud of frizz by the wind. Her brown eyes, however, remained warm as she looked at Anna. "But then we had a change of heart. And a good thing, too—or else we wouldn't have been able to pick up SoYun."

"Since I live on the outskirts of the village," SoYun said softly as she appeared from behind the post, a coil of thick rope in her arms, "the wolf ran straight by—and at that very moment, the rest of my herd fell asleep. I realized I had to go seek a solution myself. So I rowed out onto the sea, hoping to find someone awake on the water, and that's how they"— she gestured to Tuva and Oaken—"found me."

"I'm so glad," Anna said, and she was pleased to note that while SoYun's long black braid wasn't yet in its usual tidiness, she looked less terrified than when she'd come upon Anna and Elsa in the woods. In fact, SoYun looked determined.

"But," Anna said, looking back at Tuva, "what kind of change convinced you to return?"

"You," Tuva said simply.

Anna blinked. "What do you mean?"

Tuva turned the wheel, and the sails above rippled in the night breeze. "I mean," she said, "that if a young woman like you could stick around, even though all was falling apart, and you don't have powers of snow and ice, and I doubt you can lift a blacksmith's hammer above your head for even a minute—then why couldn't we? After all, Arendelle is just as much our home as it is yours.

"We'd only sailed out a little ways when we

realized that we *needed* to return. And so, we agreed to turn around in case you were still out there. And you were. So we scooped you up just in time and carried you to the ship, and now we've set sail again."

"We're keeping an eye on the castle," SoYun added. "Elsa . . . she's . . ."

"Still in there," Tuva finished darkly.

"Thank you. H-how long have I been asleep?" Anna said. Her thoughts reeled with the vision of Elsa falling victim to the Nattmara.

"Only a few hours!" Olaf called from the prow. "Which is actually a short amount of time when you take in the eons of our galaxy."

Anna's heart sped up. It was still the same night. "And when's sunrise?"

"In just an hour," Oaken said.

An hour. Arendelle had a single hour before this terror became permanent. Uneasy, Anna rose to her feet and headed to the railing. She stared down at the black waters of the Arenfjord. They slapped relentlessly against the ship's hull, giving rhythm to the terrible thoughts that swarmed through Anna's mind: Elsa, failure, Elsa. A tear coursed down her cheek. Anna's greatest fear wasn't a wolf. It never had been.

It had been losing her sister.

Olaf took Anna's hand in his. "You're melting," he said. "I wish I could share my permafrost with you."

Anna smiled as she wiped her face with the back of her hand. "I'm okay, Olaf." She paused. "Actually," she admitted, "I'm not okay. All along I wanted to go on the grand tour with Elsa on this very ship, but now . . . It was supposed to be a journey that Elsa and I did together."

And though Anna didn't say it, she thought: *Just like taking care of the castle is something we're supposed to do together, too.* But even after the trip to the Huldrefólk, Elsa still hadn't trusted her to get rid of the Nattmara, and now, their one and only chance of defeating the nightmare—Revolute—lay in tiny jagged pieces in her cloak pocket.

Sven suddenly bellowed, and Anna looked just in time to see him thrash wildly, his legs moving as though he were running for his life, even as he slumbered.

Anna ran over and sank down beside him, her skirt billowing around her. Careful to avoid his hooves, she reached out and tenderly began to pat his nose. Slowly, Sven stopped kicking, but his ears continued to twitch.

"I ruined it all," she said, continuing to pet Sven gently on the head. "I thought I finally had the answer. But"—she drew a long, shuddering breath—"I thought wrong. And Elsa—she was right not to trust me to come along on her grand tour, or to defeat the Nattmara, or to do anything at all."

"Ah-hem," came a familiar throat-clearing. She turned to see Wael climbing up out of the ship's hull.

Quickly, she looked away and kept her head bent toward the water, using her hair as a curtain. She didn't think she could stomach the nosy journalist's judgment. She barely felt like she could handle anything at all.

"Ah-*hem.*" The throat clearing became more insistent. "I couldn't help overhearing, but, well . . . have you been belowdecks yet? To Elsa's study?"

Anna shook her head. She'd been to the royal ship to help unload rations, but she had made it a point to avoid Elsa's cabin, unwilling to see it piled high with the luggage that would accompany Elsa far from home.

"Then I suggest you check it out."

"I don't know," Anna said, thinking of the wild hair that now fanned around Elsa's face and the yellow eyes of the Nattmara set into her sockets. That image would haunt her forever, she was certain of it. "It—it would hurt too much to see right now," Anna said.

Olaf slid his hand into hers. "Sometimes, you walk into a cave thinking you'll find wolves inside, but they turn out to be puppies."

With a heavy sigh, Anna shuffled after Olaf, following him and Wael downstairs to Elsa's study. As she walked, she kept sneaking glances at Wael. She was surprised that he'd been willing to come back and help her.

Wael caught one of her glances and exhaled. "I know what you're thinking," he said as he stepped onto a groaning stair.

"You do?" Anna said, her cheeks warming slightly.

Wael nodded. "You think that because I ask you and your sister hard questions about the kingdom, that I must not like you or Arendelle very much." He opened the door to Elsa's floating quarters and paused a moment to look at Anna. "But the truth is, I ask hard questions because I *love* Arendelle so much, and because I believe in you and Elsa. You know, asking questions is often the first step to accomplishing something."

And Anna was surprised to realize that yes, she *exactly* knew. She smiled at Wael and said, "Thank you so much for your questions, and for coming back to help us." And she meant it with the whole of her being.

Wael returned the smile and stepped back so that she could enter.

Anna gasped. Everywhere, there were sunflowers. Painted sunflowers danced across wooden beams and were carved into the handles of the cupboards. A plush sunflower rug, cheery yellow and spring green, lay at the base of the stairs.

Sunflowers weren't Elsa's favorite flowers. They were *Anna's*. Elsa must have asked that the entire study be decorated to remind her of her sister. To remind her of home. And in the center of the room hung a newly commissioned portrait of two little girls, one with white-blond hair and the other chestnut brown, skating across a frozen pond. The entire room felt like a hug.

Wael went to the desk and pulled out a page from the stacks that had already accumulated in anticipation of Elsa's grand tour. "This is the one that I thought you might like to see," Wael said, handing it to her before slipping out, leaving Anna alone with Olaf.

Anna peered down at the paper, then did a double take. It was a proclamation written in Elsa's elegant handwriting:

> I, Elsa, Queen of Arendelle, do hereby proclaim my sister, Anna of Arendelle, Keeper of the Kingdom while I sail on the grand tour. She is kind, thoughtful, and loves Arendelle with the whole of her heart. There is none better than her to watch over the kingdom while I am away.

At last, Anna had an answer. The reason Elsa had not invited her on the grand tour—it wasn't because Elsa thought Anna was incompetent. It was because she *knew* Anna was helpful, and she needed Anna at home to keep an eye on things. Of course Elsa didn't want Anna leaving Arendelle. Arendelle needed Anna just as much as Anna needed it.

"Now that's true love!" said Olaf, who had angled his head to read it.

"It is," said Anna with a sad smile. All this time, Anna had thought that Elsa believed she was useless, but maybe that wasn't the case at all. Maybe the only person who hadn't believed that Anna was helpful... was Anna *herself.*

She remembered the ice bubble that Elsa had enclosed her in. She'd thought it had been Elsa doing one more protective big sister act, but what if it was meant to be more than that? What if she wasn't trying to be protective of Anna, but she was instead *arming* Anna, forcing her to wait and watch, because she trusted her to figure out the solution if the worst should happen?

"Olaf," Anna said, "would you mind getting Tuva down here, please? We don't have much time."

Half an hour later, though, Anna's fragile hope had once again unraveled. She'd laid out the collected pieces of Revolute across Elsa's desk to see if Tuva could piece them together, but the blacksmith shook her head. "The pieces are too small, and the metal—I've never seen anything like it before. Maybe I could do it if Ada"—her breath caught on her wife's name—"were around and I had access to our forge, but there's no way it can be fixed in time, and definitely not on this ship without the proper tools."

"Why would you fix it?" Wael called from the doorway. "The sword didn't work the first time—what makes you think it would work *this* time?"

"Because," Anna said, keeping her eye on the porthole. *Was the night sky beginning to brighten?* "You can only defeat a myth with a thing of myth, and Revolute is definitely a thing of myth. Besides"—she turned her head to look at the map of Arendelle pinned to the wall. It reminded her of the map she had uncovered in the secret room, the one where her mother had written one of their father's many sayings—"my father used to say the past has a way of returning."

"And what goes around comes around again, like a sneeze in the wind," Olaf added. He sat at the desk, examining the pieces of the shattered sword. "Maybe you should look at Revolute and Aren's past."

Anna sighed. "I would, but I don't exactly have a copy of the *Saga of Aren* on me at the moment, and Elsa's not here to declaim."

"Ah-hem," Wael coughed. "Elsa is not the only one who studied the classics."

"Apologies, Wael," Anna said. "Please perform, but quickly." Unease filled her, but she tamped it down. "We're running out of time."

"'Revolving moon and spinning sun, forged a crescent blade . . .'" Wael began, and Anna half listened as she tried to skim the other documents that might be helpful.

"Hey, Anna," Olaf said, "don't you think it's funny how you can find love in the most curious places?"

Anna tried not to sigh. She loved when Olaf discussed philosophy—*usually*—but now, mere minutes before sunrise, was not the time. "Yeah, sure I do. Why are you asking?"

"Because," Olaf said, "it's sitting here on the desk."

Anna looked over, trying to see what he was talking about. She had not realized that Olaf had been rearranging the broken pieces of Revolute, specifically the top part of the blade that had held the inscription of the sword's name, which now spelled out:

L-O-V-E R-E-T-U

"'The sea rushed in as hidden power flowed from the gleaming sword,'" Wael continued to proclaim—and Anna's heart skipped a beat.

*A hidden power.*

Anna's heart began beating again, but twice as fast, as thoughts tumbled through her mind and she took in the other letters. A grin spread across her face.

"Oaken!" she yelled up to the deck. "Turn this ship around again! We have a kingdom to save."

# Chapter Twenty-Five

ANNA KNEW WHERE TO FIND HER SISTER.

The nearer the night drew to sunrise, the more foreign Anna's home had seemed to become. Knobby branches twisted every which way, as if a forest of shadows had taken root in the land. And overhead, a great sandstorm spun, its center positioned directly over Arendelle Castle. Its great winds raised up high waves, and Anna and the rest of the crew covered their noses and mouths with the silk scarves that were originally meant to be gifts to the court of Corona, but now acted as shields so that they could breathe without inhaling sand as the royal ship glided closer.

Oaken steered the ship while Tuva barked commands at Wael, and SoYun and Anna helped with a complicated system of ropes and pulleys. Wael looked a little green around the gills, and Anna was grateful that she herself had a strong stomach.

But it was Olaf, a snowman who was used to falling apart and rolling in several directions at once, who was the biggest help. He made sure that the items on deck didn't slam into anybody and that the still-sleeping Sven stayed safely out of harm's way.

"Sharp turn!" Oaken warned, and the next second, he'd turned the royal ship to be parallel to the castle gates. But there was still a sizable distance between the ship's deck and land.

"This is as close as we can get without smashing the ship!" Oaken called.

Anna stared down at the choppy gray water. Black sand sullied its usually white foam. She'd have to jump! But then she saw SoYun's rope. Remembering how she'd escaped the Nattmara from Sorenson's tower, she called to SoYun to throw the rope and latch it securely to a streetlamp.

When it was done, Anna clambered up onto the top rail. "Wish me luck!" She took the free end of the rope from SoYun—and jumped! Three long seconds passed as she soared into the air and over the water, and then, let go. With a thump, she landed on the castle grounds.

Anna winced, not because of the pain, but because she should have made a quieter entrance. Two pairs of glowing yellow eyes suddenly appeared at the front entrance to Arendelle Castle: Kai and Gerda. And their hair, too, had turned snow-white.

They still opened their mouths in a scream, but only a rasp came out. Anna shook her head in sorrow. Kai and Gerda had been trapped in a screaming nightmare reality for almost three whole days. It was a wonder they had any voice left at all. Unfortunately, they still seemed able—and eager—to wield their household weapons. The glint of Kai's fire poker and Gerda's sharp scissors still cut through the black sand.

*What to do what to do what to do!*

"Hoo-hoo, yellow-eyed wolf helpers!" Oaken called as he swung over the water and landed with surprising ease next to Anna. "It's not polite to attack guests!"

"Oaken! Get back on the ship!" Anna instructed. "It's not safe!"

"Don't worry, Anna," Oaken said with a nod to the ship where Wael, SoYun, Tuva, and Olaf were calling out to Kai and Gerda from the deck, distracting them from Anna. "We've got this, *ja*? We'll lure them away and make sure they don't come to any harm—or cause any. Now, go help Elsa!" He turned to Kai and Gerda, and waved his arms. "Over here!"

Anna nodded her thanks and rushed inside to find her sister . . . if there was anything left of her. She didn't have a solid plan, but she was brave, and she had hope. And that would have to be enough.

The sand seemed thickest near the entry of the Great Hall, so Anna ran there as fast as she could on the strange combination of sand and hardwood. It slowed her progress, but still Anna pushed forward toward the double doors. Sure enough, as she drew closer, she could hear sobs. Shoving the doors open, Anna raced in.

Her sister sat on her throne, her yellow eyes staring unblinking into a dream that Anna could not see. As Elsa wept, strange flurries of black ice circled above her head. Anna's heart squeezed.

"Elsa?" she whispered. "Elsa?"

But her sister's expression didn't change. Not wanting to startle Elsa, Anna slowly moved toward her. Suddenly, from the corner of the room, she heard a long, low growl. It was happening again! Her night-mare! It prowled out from behind the pillar—and attacked.

But Anna was prepared. She'd left her cloak unclasped for this very reason. And as the wolf leapt at her again, Anna flung her cloak off her shoulders and for the first time, instead of running away from the wolf, she ran *toward* it. She held her cloak above her head like a banner as she sprinted between its two front paws, each one as large as a boulder. The wolf realized a moment too late its prey's route. Its teeth snapped down around the cloak, catching only fabric as Anna let go of it and raced under the protection of the wolf's belly.

Holding her breath, she paused just long enough to hear the shred of cloth as the Nattmara's teeth ripped the cloak, not quite yet realizing it was only a decoy. The charade would not last long, but it had bought her precious seconds.

Scurrying out from under the wolf's tail, Anna hurled herself toward the throne.

Twelve feet left. Six. Three. She was almost there!

*Arooooooooooooo!*

The Nattmara had realized she had tricked it!

Anna's blood turned cold as she glanced back. She shouldn't have.

Because the wolf was upon her.

Claws the length of butcher's knives raked across her back. She squeezed her eyes shut, waiting for the pain . . . but it never came.

In fact, Anna didn't feel a *thing*.

Her eyes flew open just in time to see the Nattmara attack her again, but instead of colliding with her, it sailed right through Anna as though *she* were the one made of sand instead of the wolf. Her heart slammed into her chest. She hadn't felt any pain. Had she become a ghost?

The Nattmara snarled, clearly as confused as she was. It lunged again, this time teeth first, but Anna felt nothing more than a light breeze as its fangs grazed her throat, leaving not a scratch. Like wind grasping at her. And for the first time, Anna didn't feel the suffocating pull of the Nattmara on her thoughts, making her think terrifying and helpless things. Again, and again, the Nattmara attacked her, but nothing it did could hurt her.

Anna's mind whirled at a frantic pace. Whenever she had been around the Nattmara before, thoughts of not being good enough had filled her and held her down. But now—now Anna knew, recalling the proclamation in Elsa's traveling study, that she *was* good enough, and that she had always been.

The truth in those inked words seemed to have mended the cracks in her heart.

She was no longer afraid. The Nattmara could no longer harm her . . . so why was Anna's nightmare still there?

Anna couldn't concentrate! Elsa's scream dug at her, and though the Nattmara's fearsome claws could not hurt her anymore, each time Elsa wailed, Anna felt as though she'd been physically punched.

"Elsa!" Anna cried, staggering toward the throne. "Whatever you're seeing, it isn't real! It's just a nightmare!" Her thoughts dashed frantically, and she grabbed onto one before it slid by. "Remember Mother and Father!" she said. "Hot chocolate! Cozy stories—" Anna broke off.

*Wait a second.*

Pretending to give her nightmares to Frigg the Fisherman had never helped Anna. But now she recalled Elsa's words from two days earlier. *Mother's trick worked for me. I haven't had a nightmare since.*

Another thought darted by, this time, a memory of Sorenson's voice, and his confusing words suddenly had meaning: *The act of burying fear is what manifests the Nattmara,* he'd said.

And now Anna understood. Fear only grew the longer it was ignored. Avoiding a nightmare only made it more powerful, more terrifying when it finally erupted again. And if Elsa had ignored her fears for years—if she had banished her nightmares away, then maybe they had taken on their own life, taken on their own shape. . . .

*Ulf the Wolf was always my favorite,* Elsa had said in Sorenson's tower. What if, instead of handing her nightmares over to a friendly fisherman as Anna had tried, Elsa had imagined feeding her fears to a hungry wolf?

Anna's ideas came to her even quicker. Elsa's rejected nightmares and fears, unable to latch onto Elsa but more powerful than most people's fears, had weaseled their way into another scared, lonely child's dreams—a child whose loneliness had gaped wide within her, leaving room for black sand and dark dreams to creep into her heart. A heart that had cracked when the child had been separated from her sister. *Anna's* heart.

Realization thundered through her: Anna had not created the Nattmara—not with a spell or her own great worries. The wolf that had first appeared to her on that night sixteen years ago was not a manifestation of Anna's fear. There had been another scared and lonely child in the castle beside her then, one who had also feared being separated from her sister: *Elsa.*

The Nattmara was Elsa's nightmare! It was *Elsa's* fear that they needed to conquer!

But . . . Anna had no idea what her sister was afraid of. Elsa was the strongest person she knew, a great queen, brave in the face of danger, determined, and regal.

*What to do what to do what to do!*

The Nattmara, frustrated by its futile attempts to inflict harm to Anna, let out an earsplitting howl. The sandstorm whipped up faster. While Anna might be safe from the beast's attacks, Arendelle was not.

Anna ran toward Elsa, and though her stomach hurt as she looked at Elsa's yellow eyes, she didn't look away. The Nattmara had only come when they'd been separated—either by their parents when they were young, or by Elsa's queenly responsibilities. So it would only be defeated, Anna guessed wildly, when they were together.

All Anna needed to figure out was what scared Elsa—but she truly had no idea what that could be.

"Elsa!" she cried as she approached the throne. "Elsa, I'm here! What's wrong? What are you so scared of that you can't tell me?"

Elsa just screamed harder, and the rush of black sand still spilling from her palms came quicker. It began to pile into a barrier between them, filling up the Great Hall. Eventually, it would reach the rafters, and then the ceiling, burying Elsa on her throne. Wait a minute—the throne!

They were in the Great Hall; the Nattmara had chosen it, so it must be Elsa's least favorite room in the castle. And as Anna looked at the flurry of sand circling Elsa's throne, spiraling up above her head to form a glittering crown of darkness, the answer came to her: Elsa was scared of being a bad queen.

"The people are all counting on me!" Elsa sobbed in her nightmare-scape. "Please! I'll be better!"

Anna, no longer afraid of the Nattmara—but much more afraid of losing her sister forever—sprinted up the dais and grabbed Elsa's hand. Elsa yanked it away from her, but Anna held tight.

Suddenly, Anna could see into Elsa's nightmare: the endless meetings that Elsa felt awkward leading, not knowing what to say to people after having had very little social interaction for most of her life. Anna had always just thought Elsa was a good listener. Everyone seemed to think she was so wonderfully collected, but in truth, her quietness wasn't composed thinking, but a deer-in-the-path-of-an-arrow kind of fright.

And the Nattmara had made her a bad queen— with the Blight. It all made sense to Anna now. Before the Nattmara had the strength to take on the physical shape of a wolf, it had seeped into the kingdom as a sickness, stalking the kingdom the same way it had stalked Elsa's mind. And with the Blight came the people's constant worry and questions, and Elsa had become more overwhelmed and even more fearful that she could not protect them. She had begun to crack at the seams while trying to keep it all inside. She had not been able to sleep . . . and so, Elsa's suppressed nightmares had found another sleeping, worried sister to haunt until, at last, the fear in Arendelle—Elsa's fear—had grown so great and powerful that the Nattmara could at last be seen by everyone. Because above all, Elsa feared hurting the kingdom—again. Of hurting Anna, again.

"Oh, Elsa," Anna whispered, her heart aching. "Why didn't you just tell me?" Anna held on to her sister's hands, even as black sand pelted them from all around. "You're perfect just the way you are! You're a *great* leader! You pay attention to details, and your quietness gives you space to listen. I'm so proud of you, Elsa. You're a wonderful sister, and you're a role model for me. You're someone I look up to!"

Was it just Anna's imagination, or was her sister now squeezing her hand back? Ignoring the thrum of the Nattmara's anger around them in the form of black sand spraying Anna's face from all sides, Anna continued to talk, focusing all of herself on her sister—letting her know how she felt about her, just in the same way Elsa's proclamation had shown Anna the truth.

"You know that I am better than who I think I am!" she yelled over the wind and battering sand. "I was so scared that you didn't need me anymore since I wasn't invited on the grand tour. But then I saw that the tour had nothing to do with me, and I realized that you are right—I am helpful, and I am always here for you and for our people, no matter what! Just as I know you are here for me!" Anna wasn't sure if she was getting through to Elsa, but still she hung on, despite the growing swarm of assaulting black sand.

Elsa's eyes shut tight. And then . . . "Anna?"

"Elsa!" Anna cried. "I'm here! I'm always here!"

Elsa turned her head, and Anna saw that her eyes were no longer yellow, but back to their usual beautiful shade of light blue. "Anna," Elsa said, voice raspy from all the nightmare-induced screaming. "Of *course* I need you."

The Nattmara threw back its head and howled in rage, the sound echoing endlessly around the hall.

Elsa clutched tight to Anna's hand. "Why is it still here?" Elsa whirled her other hand up, ready to blast it with ice.

"No!" Anna shouted. "You can't fight your fear—it only makes it stronger! Just as you can't ignore your fear, because out of sight, it grows in strange ways and mutates."

"Then what should I do?" Elsa asked, her voice cracking. "Dawn is almost here!"

"Accept it," Anna breathed, praying she was right. "It's okay to be afraid, Elsa. You just can't let the fear take control of you! Fear is the shadow of love. You only fear because you care so much about Arendelle and about me, and that's what makes you a great queen and a great leader. And a great sister. That's why we *love* you, Elsa."

It was the riddle that Olaf had helped her solve when he had rearranged the letters of the sword. Not *R-E-V-O-L-U-T-E* or *L-O-V-E R-E-T-U*, but *T-R-U-E L-O-V-E* was the way to defeat the Nattmara. And *that* was a thing of myth.

Elsa didn't say anything, but then she held out her hand again. The giant wolf paused, the winds calmed down, and with each step the wolf took toward the sisters, it grew smaller. By the time it reached Elsa's outstretched hand, the wolf was the size of a little wolf-puppy. It still had sharp teeth and claws, but it was manageable and could be contained.

"My fear," Elsa said in awe. "I was so afraid of being a bad queen, but I don't need to worry about that anymore. Because I've got you, Anna."

Anna smiled and stayed put as the white wolf pup approached. She wasn't scared of Elsa's fear—it was a part of her sister, and she could never be afraid of her. The Nattmara's power was truly done at last.

The puppy touched its nose to Elsa's hand and turned into a cloud of sand, shimmering in the air, and then . . . just a single grain of black sand lay before the sisters. With a flick of her wrist, Elsa captured it in an ice crystal and caught it in her hand. Then she held it up to the dawn's first ray of light.

"How?" she breathed. "How did we defeat the Nattmara without a thing of myth?"

"Because," Anna said, peering at the crystal, "we *do* have a thing of myth—we've had it all along. Aren didn't become a myth because he just so happened to own a fancy sword. Swords and crowns don't change who we are."

Elsa slipped the single grain of sand into her pocket. "Then what does?"

"True love," Anna said, referencing the hidden power that the *Saga of Aren* spoke of. "The power that carved out Arenfjord. The same power that gave Aren the strength to go out in his boat to face an unknown danger, or up a mountain to face a dragon. It doesn't matter which really happened—what matters is the choice he made."

Suddenly, it hit her how sleepy she was, and her thoughts came to her like a lap of quiet ocean waves.

"It's like how Sorenson said all myths contain a kernel of hard truth. It wasn't a magical sword that carved out a home on the fjord. The myth wasn't about the creation of the *actual* fjord—it was a myth about how, through love, Aren and the others in his generation believed in each other and trusted each other and loved each other enough to settle here and carve out a home for themselves, and for their future children, families, and friends. For us. A place where Arendelle's flags could always fly strong."

"True love," Elsa mused. "The thing that can move mountains and defeat nightmares."

"Exactly," Anna said. She led Elsa over to the window, to the curtain she'd first spotted the wolf hiding behind. "Our love is worthy of the great myths. Us. The royal sisters of Arendelle." Anna pulled back the curtain.

Sunlight rushed in. Dawn had fully broken, and the sun streaked across the horizon, brilliant gold in a gray-satin sky, shining down on a land full of vibrant color. No trace of the angry black sand or deathly pale rot remained.

And as she squinted in the direction of the rising sun, Anna noticed a figure walking toward the castle. There was something about the clothes and the shaggy hair that looked familiar. . . .

"Kristoff!" Anna shouted.

Elsa rested a hand on Anna's shoulder. "Go get him," she said.

Anna grinned at her sister, then took off, flying into the second great hall and outside the castle, and then Kristoff was in her arms, kissing her again and again. She kissed him until the memories of the past few days faded away, and for the first time in a long time, she felt like everything was going to be good again.

With tears of joy streaming down her face, she took Kristoff's face in her hands. "I'm so glad you're okay," she said.

"You know I will always come back to you," Kristoff said, giving her a playful wink.

"Me too!" a new voice commented.

Anna looked up to see Olaf sitting on Sven's antlers. Sven's fur was still mottled white, but his eyes were bright and shiny once again. The smell of the sea lingered on his coat.

"*Sven!*" Kristoff cried with delight. Planting one last kiss on Anna's cheek, he hurried over to the reindeer and hugged him tight, while Sven nuzzled him back. "You're finally awake!"

He wiggled the reindeer's lower lip and added in Sven Talk, "And you look like you're half asleep."

"Group hug," Elsa said as she approached, and she enveloped everyone in her arms.

And with a happy yawn, Anna leaned her head against Elsa's shoulder as the village bells began to toll across the fjord, calling all to rise and wake.

*One Month Later . . .*

# Chapter Twenty-Six

AUTUMN LEAVES BLAZED in a golden glory.

The sky was a blue so clear that when Anna looked up, she thought she could practically see the domed palace of the sun where Aren had supposedly retrieved Revolute. She smiled to herself as she made her way through town back to Arendelle Castle, greeting everyone she saw.

"Nice to see you, Baker Blodget! Good day to you, Gabriella! Hello, Ada!"

"Hello, Anna!" Tuva's wife called from behind a cart of beautiful golden wheat. Her hazel eyes sparkled. Not a hint of yellow lupine eyes to be seen.

"I'm glad to see you!" Anna said with a grin and a wave. She was practically skipping in her skirts. "We'll have the best harvest festival ever tomorrow."

"I hope so," SoYun said as she herded a healthy Hebert along the road.

Madam Eniola curtsied, her arms laden with green zucchini. "I'm just glad the aphid outbreak that affected all my crops has cleared up."

Anna arranged her face into what she hoped was an understanding—and not in any way knowing— expression. It had been one month since the events of the Nattmara. She wasn't used to keeping secrets, and she didn't particularly like it, but the villagers who'd fallen under the Nattmara's enchantment had no memory about the danger they had all come so close to. In fact, all it seemed anyone could remember— apart from SoYun, Wael, Tuva, Olaf, and Elsa—was a light aphid breakout on some of the crops that had coated the harvest in white scales.

Even Kristoff and the others who hadn't been under the Nattmara's spell for all that long seemed to remember events differently. He recollected some of what had happened, but wasn't able to parse out which memories had been real and which had been simply figments of his nightmare.

"Extra, extra, read all about it! Get your copy of the *Village Crown!*"

Anna looked over to see Wael selling his newspaper. Already, he had a crowd of villagers gathered. Many didn't bother to wait before spreading open the paper and reading the day's events right then and there. She caught a glimpse of the current headline: "More Than Royal: Sisters Are True Friends of the Kingdom." Anna grinned.

Entering the castle, she took the steps three at a time, the letter she had picked up clutched in her fingers. She went to Elsa's council chambers and knocked. Six staccato raps followed by two spaced-out ones. *Do you want to build a snowman?*

"Come in!" Elsa's voice floated through the door.

So much had changed in the past month—at least, that's how it felt to Anna, whose heart was much lighter than it had been in a long time. But she knew things hadn't really changed for Elsa. After all, she still had to face the stress of leading the kingdom, and somehow, the stacks of papers seemed higher than ever before. As Anna entered the council chambers, she saw that Elsa, as always, was leaning over her table, her long quill scratching away at the reams of parchment.

Elsa remembered the whole thing, as did Anna.

Anna suspected it was because her sister had been the reason the Nattmara came to Arendelle in the first place. It had been with both of them for much, much longer than a few nightmarish days. It had been with them for practically their entire lives, and was not easily forgotten.

Anna knew, too, that if Gerda or one of the royal handlers reached into the secret pocket sewn into the left sleeve of Elsa's dress, they would find an ice crystal, perfect in its clarity except for the single grain of black sand at its center. Elsa would keep it with her always, close to her heart, acknowledging it, allowing her fear to motivate her, but not letting it take control.

"Elsa," Anna said, flapping the letter under Elsa's nose until her sister looked up from her paperwork. "Guess what I got!"

Elsa propped her chin on her hand and smiled. "A letter. I can see it in your hand."

Anna rolled her eyes. "Yes, okay, but guess from *whom* I got it!" But she didn't bother to wait for Elsa's guess and plopped it down onto the table.

"Ugh, stop adding to my piles! Wait a second," she said as she read the address. "It's from Sorenson?"

Anna smiled. "It is! He wants to come visit. He says that he had a dream about us, and that he thought Mother would have liked for us to meet."

Anna liked the grumpy old man and was pleased he hadn't come to any lasting damage after the Nattmara attack, though she still felt bad that his life's work had been ruined on the observation deck of his tower. She was looking forward to showing him the library in the castle, as well as the even bigger one down in the village. And she was eager to find out what he would have to teach her about the stars and about seeking answers in the world around them—and about the secret room. If being Elsa's sister weren't a full-time job, Anna thought she might want to become a scientist herself one day.

Elsa smiled. It was a true smile, if also a tired one.

"Are you feeling better?" Anna asked.

"Yes—actually, no," Elsa said, catching herself. She was trying to be more honest with Anna—and herself—about what she was feeling. "I've been distracted of late."

"Perfect," Anna said.

Elsa's eyebrows rose in surprise. "Perfect? What do you mean?"

"Because I know exactly how to help. Come with me." She led Elsa out of the room and into the library.

There, Anna waltzed over to the horse statue and gave the hoof a tug. The bookcase swung open to reveal the secret room, but this time, no dust flew into the air.

She beckoned Elsa inside, and smiled when she heard Elsa's gasp of delight.

When Elsa had been busy in the council chambers, Anna had been busy herself, prettying up the secret room and making it a fully cozy Elsa hideaway. She'd brought in more lanterns and settled comfy pillows around the floor, and even had the portrait of Aren restored. It now hung prominently on the wall, Revolute shining at its center as a symbol of hope and a reminder of what actually shaped the world.

"I know you're tired and people keep interrupting you," Anna said. "You give so much to the kingdom, but you need to take care of yourself, too. This can be a place for you to get away and just be you. Where you can rest and take a quiet moment to yourself, where no one will know where to find you. The past is in here, Elsa, but so is the future. I want you to remember that I will always believe in you."

"Thank you, Anna." Elsa turned to give her younger sister a hug. "This is magnificent."

"And," Anna said with a cheeky smile, "I'm reinstituting family game night."

Elsa twisted her lips into a wry smile. "I would like that, but I always have so much work . . ."

"Sure." Anna shrugged. "And it's not going anywhere."

"Game night . . ." Elsa said, looking around at the notes, books, and records their parents had collected. Anna had carefully placed *Secrets of the Magic Makers* in the center of the worktable alongside their father's sketchbook. Even though it didn't contain any actual spells, Anna sensed that it was important. After all, every story held some truth.

"Remember how we used play charades with Mother and Father?" Elsa asked.

Anna nodded. "You know," she said, not sure how exactly to put her feelings into words, "I like this room because I can see a glimpse of who they were. I feel like here maybe they're not so lost to us after all. Though I still wonder why they never told us about this room. And I wonder what they were looking for. And why Mother visited Sorenson."

"Maybe we can ask him when he comes to visit," Elsa said. "But maybe," she added, fiddling with her sleeve cuff, "they were looking at magic. What must they have thought of my having magic, when no one else does? I mean, I can create these magical, wonderful things. . . ."

"Could be," Anna said. "Speaking of your creations, I haven't seen Olaf all day. Do you know where he is?"

Elsa smiled. "I do. And this time, *I* have a surprise for *you.*"

"But it's not my birthday," Anna said, all the while running through a catalogue of things she could possibly be getting.

"You're not the only one who can plan a surprise," Elsa said with a smile. They dashed up to Anna's favorite turret, and Elsa led her out onto the little balcony.

"How did you find the time to plan a surprise?" Anna asked.

"There," Elsa said, pointing in the direction of the open sea. "What do you see?"

Anna squinted. She couldn't be certain at first, but then . . . "Elsa!" She gasped. "Those are ships! And they're flying the royal flags of . . . Is that Zaria? And that one has the royal flag of Corona! And the third one—that's the flag of Eldora!"

Elsa nodded. "Exactly right. The grand tour was cancelled, but the dignitaries understood. So much so, that they accepted my invitation to visit Arendelle now that the gates are open. This way, neither one of us has to leave home, where we are *both* needed."

Anna's grin felt so big that her cheeks couldn't contain it. And as she looked down, watching the villagers meet the arriving visitors, Anna thought she saw a shiver in the shadows, and maybe, just maybe, a flick of a tail. Anna waved down, and she could have sworn that she saw a small Hulder waving at her from the shoulders of a taller one before slipping away again.

There was a slam of the door, and then Anna heard a thumping on the stairs before Kristoff burst onto the balcony, Sven with Olaf on his back following in his wake.

"Sorry!" Kristoff said. "I didn't mean to be late. I was having an argument with Sven about something I just brought back from the trolls! He's been funny lately. I keep thinking that he's trying to tell me something—maybe about a ship?" He shrugged his shoulders. "But as far as I know, Sven's never been on a ship."

Sven nudged Kristoff with his antlers while Anna and Elsa exchanged a look of surprise. Other than their small group, the others didn't seem to remember the Nattmara—but maybe the animals did.

Sven looked better than ever, Anna noticed. His curly reindeer hair was back to a rich brown without any unusual sprinkling of white. The Nattmara hadn't caused any lasting damage.

In fact, it had taught Anna that Elsa didn't have to be perfect, just as Anna didn't have to be perfect. She could make mistakes—and to be honest, she *would* make mistakes. And that was okay. She had Elsa and Kristoff and Olaf to help her. And the gates were open. And yes, there were still secrets, there was still so much she didn't know, but finding the answers to those questions would be an adventure . . . and she would not have to go on the journey alone.

There was nothing to fear.

"Look!" Olaf said, pointing toward a streak of light in the sky. "A chunk of space rock is falling through the atmosphere and burning up!"

# CHAPTER TWENTY-SIX

"Or," Elsa said with a smile, "you could just say it's a falling star."

"A shooting star," Kristoff offered as he leaned against the rail and took Anna's hand in his.

She squeezed it back. "A wishing star," she said.

But at that moment, standing with her friends, looking up at the brilliant light of the meteor shower arcing over Arendelle, Anna had nothing to wish for at all—because everything she could have wished for was right there beside her.

*One Week Later...*

# Epilogue

ANNA DREAMED.

*In the darkness, a single ember drifted. It tumbled endlessly through a void until, at last, it tangled in black branches. It pulsed, once, twice, and then, the spark began to lengthen. Like a salamander, the fire spread wide and flames began to crawl, creeping, illuminating an entire wood. First a twig, then a branch, then a tree. A tree, then a forest, then a world. Smoke and white-hot heat wrapped around the trees, twin ribbons that tightened and obscured. That tightened and choked. Screams rose, and the whole forest vanished in a plume of thick smoke, and then . . . A shift.*

Anna dreamed.

*Back into the void, and this time, the darkness moved. It slipped and slid, a rough whisper scraping against her ear. The darkness was not dark at all, but a never-ending desert of black sand. Sand filled her ears, her eyes, her nose, her mouth. She waded through, unable to see, unable to breathe, unable to know, and then . . . A shift.*

Anna dreamed.

*No longer rough, the sand melted, turning to liquid, growing heavy, and falling in a soft black rain to a great crater, until it brimmed, overflowing. The dark was an ocean now. Each slap of a wave left a swirling froth of white, brilliant against black water. Brilliant against the dripping mane of a midnight horse. The stallion reared from the Dark Sea's deepest depths, screaming its freedom as it shrugged off the ocean's weight and galloped across the waves toward her. Its heavy hooves drummed a rhythm that took over her heart, and then it bucked, and it was not Anna whom the horse chased, but Elsa. Its eyes glowed white as it bore down on her sister . . .*

Anna woke up.

Her heart slammed against her chest as though she'd been running, and the questions scrolled through her mind: Was it happening again? Was the nightmare back? Anna felt a bit disoriented. It took her a moment to register that she wasn't in her own room. She was in their parents' room. That was right. She and Elsa had fallen asleep together after Anna sang one of their mother's old lullabies, a favorite about a secret river.

Elsa had seemed distracted and pensive during the night's game of charades, so Anna had sung to bring a bit of lightness back into Elsa's heart.

Anna stared up at the frothy canopy of the bed, and then glanced away. It looked too much like the white sea-foam that the rippling stallion had spat out as it galloped toward her. A water horse, she realized, reminding her of the statue outside the secret room.

Relief sighed though her. These were just normal nightmares, then. No wolf. The Nattmara was gone. She had nothing to fear. They were just a collection of images from the week's events, from things around her home. There was no need to be afraid of her dreams, not anymore. And with that thought, Anna's eyes slowly began to close . . .

And then they flew open. They had fallen asleep together. *But Elsa was not there.* Elsa wasn't leaving Anna behind. . . . She wouldn't do that again. Right? Anna tried to keep calm. Elsa had probably gotten up extra early to tackle the stacks of papers waiting for her.

A breeze curled through the room, and Anna shivered. At least she knew why she was cold: the balcony door had somehow blown open while they had been asleep. Slipping out of Elsa's bed, Anna grabbed their mother's scarf from where Elsa had draped it across an armchair. Wrapping it around her shoulders, Anna stepped toward the balcony doors.

She expected to see what she always saw: the village ensconced in deep blue shadows, only punctured here and there by the orange flames of lanterns in the courtyard directly below. But as she drew closer to the balcony, a strange feeling flitted through her. An unease. A sense. Or, as Olaf might say nowadays, a "gut-wrenching trepidation." She knew, in the way that maybe only a sister could know, that something was about to change forever. And when Anna stepped out onto the balcony, she saw that it already had.

The night glittered—the air glittered—the world glittered—as a million ice crystals of what looked like frozen rain hung suspended, like diamonds or glass shards that had forgotten gravity existed. Beautiful and sparkling. Fierce and deadly. Each crystal was razor-sharp, and each pointed in the same direction, toward a figure who stood far away, alone in the night.

"Elsa?"

Her sister stood in the twilight, the waves of the Arenfjord behind her. And though it should have been impossible for Elsa to see Anna from such a great distance, Anna saw her sister shift—and lock eyes with her.

A brilliant white light in the distance shattered the darkness, illuminating for a single breath the look of awe on Elsa's face.

And then the ice crystals began to fall.

Anna flung herself away from the balcony, dashing through the halls and down the stairs. Her feet thudded against the flagstones. Reaching the bottom floor, Anna threw open the castle doors.

She stared at the ice crystals still suspended in front of her. "What?" she asked herself. The ice crystals filled the night with an eerie whistle as they tore through the air, only to end with a shout as they splintered across the cobblestones at her feet, making Anna's path to Elsa slippery and dangerous. But when was it not? And when had it ever mattered?

Securing their mother's scarf, she raced out into the streets to find Elsa. The wind tugged at Anna, it howled, and then—the lanterns blew out. Something was wrong. Anna passed villagers peering out of their suddenly dark homes. In the place where Arendelle's flags always flew strong, they had gone deathly still.

Darkness, once again.

# Acknowledgments

MAGIC EXISTS IN MANY FORMS: in words, in art, and in story. Any magic in this book is thanks to the incredible hard work of many people.

Thank you to my editor, Eric Geron, dream-maker, door-opener, and Arendelle's ultimate guide. This novel would not exist without his boundless creativity and enthusiasm, careful eye, and willingness to discuss all things Anna and Elsa at any time of the day. Spells might not exist in our world or in Arendelle, but if anyone could speak a spell to make dreams come true, it would definitely be him.

Much gratitude to the directors and producers—the magic makers!—of *Frozen* and *Frozen II*, in particular, Jennifer Lee, Peter Del Vecho, and Heather Blodget, whose creativity and insight were instrumental in this tale. Thank you for telling and promoting stories not only about strong girls, but about caring girls, who seek to change the world around them for the better—and do.

A warmest thank-you to the incredible artistic talents of Mike Giamo, Grace Lee, Winnie Ho, Al Giuliani, and Susan Gerber for the stunning cover and inspirational beauty of Arendelle. Thank you, too, to Heather Knowles for knowing the sisters inside and out, and to Alison Giordano for her help.

Crafting three-dimensional characters is always a challenge, but this challenge was made a thousand times easier by Kristen Bell, Idina Menzel, Jonathan Groff, and Josh Gad, who have each breathed life into their characters with their incredible nuance and heart.

Thank you to my agent, Stephen Barbara, whose support and guidance is practically mythic. To my parents, Marguerite and Zoltan Benko, and my siblings, Gabriella and Matthias, thank you for putting up with princess obsessions for many years and for believing in my wildest dreams. In particular, thank you to my husband, Andrej Ficnar, who has not complained about *Frozen* playing on repeat throughout the home and who was always patient while I lost myself in a fantastical winter wonderland.

And finally, thank you to the kids and grown-ups around the world who love Anna and Elsa. Because of you, there are more opportunities than ever before to tell tales about princesses saving the day. Thank you for making room for complex heroines in your life and for coming on this journey with them.

*Keep Dreaming!*

Dark Sea